Pterippus

The Awakening

Kristl Thompson

ShutterBug Studios
Odessa, Missouri

Copyright © 2009 by Kristl Thompson
Cover art © Stephanie Habelitz
Internal Art © Stephanie Habelitz

This is a work of fiction. All events and characters, with the exception of a few well-known historical figures, are products of the author's imagination and are not to be construed as real. Any resemblance to real persons living or dead is purely coincidental and not intended by the author. Where real-life historical figures appear, the situations, events and dialogue concerning those persons are completely fictional and are not intended to depict actual events or to change the entirely fictional nature of the work.

ISBN: 978-0-9829170-0-8

Printed and bound in the United States of America

This book is dedicated...

...to my children, for bringing with their newborn cries
my tears of joy...

...to my husband, for igniting the flame in my heart
and for keeping it burning still...

...to my mother, for giving me the roots for a firm foundation
and for being my rock during the trials of life...

...to Deb, Jessica and Bridget, for always
being there to listen to my windy ramblings...

...to Adrian, just for being who you are...

...and to everyone out there who still believes in magick...

...never stop looking for it.

CONTENTS

CONTENTS

CONTENTS

Awakening - noun: an act or moment of becoming suddenly aware of something; adjective: coming into existence or awareness

Prologue: Fifteen Years Ago

Rohan strained to hear what was being said behind the thick oak door, but his struggle went without reward. His mother had magickally sealed the room. Neither light nor sound could pass through the barrier.

Can you hear what they say, Verasant?

He waited through the silence, and then the answer came…*I cannot.* Rohan frowned at his obstacle, then raised his hand to it, moving it slowly back and forth until the door dissolved beneath the translucent tendrils of light flowing from his fingers.

Verasant, he said, in awe that he was able to break through his mother's magickal seal even this much, *can you get through that?*

It is not an opening within the wood, said the voice, *but a projection upon it. The shield is intact. Still, a solid attempt.*

"I need to know what they say about me," he muttered aloud, though he knew Verasant could hear him. Verasant was unlike any other creature Rohan had met, though Verasant had yet to reveal himself to him. As far as Rohan knew, he was the only one to whom Verasant ever spoke.

I told you of what they speak, said Verasant. *The doorway has opened this day. They will choose to send you through it.*

"Mother will defend me."

Yes, and she will fail. The Council is decided. They have only to discuss the proper way to send you and with whom you will stay upon your arrival.

I don't want to go to Earth. Isn't there another way?

There is always another way, but there is only one right way.

Rohan sighed and wandered from the protected door of his mother's enchantment room toward his own. He knew Verasant was right, but the thought of going to Earth depressed him; it had since the first time Verasant revealed his own destiny to him just over a year ago. It was Verasant who taught him how to delve into his past lives, to take vision quests to learn things that would help him on his path in this life. He'd rejected the idea at first, and a part of him still held to his denial, but he knew the outcome.

He paced around his bedroom, awaiting the inevitable as doubt tested his patience. Every second that passed swelled his anger and strengthened his resolve. He was leaving, alright, but he wasn't going to Earth. He would go somewhere else, anywhere else but there. Perhaps it was time for him to start looking for the place in his dreams, the place far beyond the largest mountain range, where nothing bad ever happened, where fathers didn't die and mothers didn't send their sons away.

Your mother comes, said Verasant, and Rohan froze, staring at the door from across the room as he uttered the words that would seal her out. She was strong, yes, but so was he.

"Rohan," whispered his mother through the door.

"I'm not going," he said.

"It must be done," she said, and continued her explanation, but Verasant's voice in his head drowned out her words.

We've discussed this, Rohan. It is your destiny to do this.

Only if I choose it.

You must choose it. You are the only one who will succeed.

I haven't yet! Every past life, every time, I failed.

The road to success is paved with failure. I taught you to see those things so you may learn from them. The time is now, Rohan. If it wasn't, I would not be here to guide you through it.

Are you coming with me?

Rohan waited through Verasant's silence. His mother was trying to open the door, and a surge of satisfaction shot through him that she could not get through his magick.

That is the wrong kind of pride, Rohan, said Verasant, disapproval tainting his words. Rohan deflated a little, and Verasant continued. *I will attempt to come with you, but I do not know the outcome. This is not a doorway like those of the trolls. It is a portal designed only for certain souls to take them where they must go. It may not allow me to pass. Even if it does, things might be...different.*

Will it take me to her?

I believe it will, but it may take me elsewhere. It could take me beyond both worlds.

To the ephemeral?

Perhaps my time in this world comes to an end. If that be the case, it is meant to be. The risk is worth the reward. Your mother awaits an answer, Rohan. Open the door.

Rohan released the magick sealing the door and it swung open as he contemplated Verasant's conclusion. Ashya stood before him, her eyes glistening with tears, and the rest of his anger evaporated. She had fought the Council to keep him with her and she had failed.

"Don't be angry, Rohan," she said, trying to be stern though it sounded like a plea.

"I'm not angry, Mother," he said. "I know you tried. I just don't understand. What about free will? Isn't that why the Council rebels against tyranny, so that we may always have a choice?"

"You have no choice in this matter; son. No one does, not even the Council. It is bigger than any one person, than any group of people. This affects the course of the entire world."

He struggled for an argument, but the knowledge that he would no longer be able to fly whenever he wanted struck him, and the weight of that revelation sparked his desire to do just that.

"Can we run?" he asked. "I want to stretch my wings, just one more time."

"Of course we can. I will meet you outside in a few moments."

She left him alone, and he knew it was to allow him time to say goodbye to everything his life was built upon. He gazed at the midnight blue walls he had painted himself only this past winter and the huge stardust violets of the same color hanging in each corner like miniature galaxies. He'd built special planters for them so they would stay alive, and as he left the sanctity of his room, he knew they would grow there still, awaiting his return.

His mother stood in the open space of their yard, staring at the sky. The moon was full, enhancing the power of the night as it enhanced the shimmer of her features; her billowing robes of white, her pale skin, her golden hair...each sparkled in the moonlight's embrace. He watched her transform from her human appearance, amazed at the way her robes became her hide and her hair became mane and tail of spun gold. Her blue eyes turned dark as her golden horn spiraled out of her forehead. He often wondered if it looked the same when he transformed, but the pain of it always kept him from watching it in a mirror. He exhaled, then called forth the magick.

He cringed as the first of his bones cracked, his collarbone separating to follow his shoulders as they twisted forward, his arms and legs contorting to the same length, his fingers and toes becoming hooves. He never focused on the change after that, for the pain was nearly unbearable as the rest of his body took shape, but never so much to prevent him from it, for he loved to be in his magickal form. When the huge black wings sprouted from his back and the golden horn from his forehead, the pain followed them outward for only a moment, and then it was over.

Rohan watched as Ashya raced into the forest, then he darted into the sky above her. From that angle, he noticed for the first time that the sky was brighter than it should be, even with a full moon. Far in the distance was a single star hovering close to the ground among a grove of trees, shining so bright that no other could be seen in the sky.

Can you see it, Rohan? asked Ashya. *It is the portal that will take you to the other world.*

It see it, he answered. It was captivating, a magnet, and he was the metal drawn to it. He shifted his thoughts, hiding them from her telepathic abilities so he could contact Verasant. *Do you feel it, Verasant? It's calling me.*

I feel it through you, Rohan. You are excited.

I'm excited every time I fly.

This is different.

Yes, agreed Rohan, *this is different.*

Rohan touched the ground at the edge of the grove, the star so close he could almost touch it, and beneath it, a huge spiraling vortex of translucent silver whirled into oblivion. The nearby trees were shrouded with an incandescent glow, rejoicing in the return of something long awaited for. They spoke their praises to Rohan as he walked past them, their whispers soothing him through the pain of becoming human again. Ashya was waiting at the edge of the doorway, her human eyes shining with tears.

"How will I know where to find the Chosen One?" he asked, reaching for her hand without looking at her. He couldn't tear his eyes from the sight in the grove.

"She will come to you. You will know when she does and when the time is right, you must convince her to return with you."

"And if she doesn't want to come?"

"You will find a way to convince her. She must come, for it is her destiny."

Ashya and Rohan stared at the doorway in silence, watching the mysterious spiral swirl of its own volition, like the air had caught a silver cloud and forced it to its will, spinning it into a shimmering whirlpool of light and dark. He took a deep breath, preparing himself to step through it, but his mother held tight to his hand.

"Rohan," she said, "I have a gift for you." He stepped back from the door and faced his mother, exhaling the breath he realized he had been holding. Ashya removed from a fold in her cloak five crystals suspended from a black metal chain and spaced evenly around the circle it made. Each crystal was a different color, representing its elemental quality with pride. The colors were so vibrant, they reflected in Rohan's eyes as he stared at the necklace in awe.

"The Elemental Children," she whispered, showing her great respect for the gift, "have blessed each crystal with the nature of their elements. The green crystal, blessed by the faeries, is to aid in your Earth magick and keep you solid and strong like the ground beneath your feet. The dragons blessed the red crystal, to assist with your Fire Magick and to keep your heart passionate and your soul raging, unstoppable like a fire until you accomplish your task. Promise me, son, that you control it, for fire can easily spread and rage out of control."

"I promise," said Rohan, a shiver of fear chilling his spine.

"The blue crystal was blessed by the merpeople, to strengthen your growing Water Magick. It will keep you steady and constant as the stream, and just as unyielding. The yellow crystal was blessed by all the unicorns, including myself. It will aid in all matters and magick related to the element of Air. It will give you energy and swiftness in your endeavors. The white crystal is from the drove of trolls, who scoured the beyond to find it. It will bind the balance between the other crystals and it will allow you to communicate with the trolls, who control the doorways between our world and Earth. They will allow you unlimited passage."

"Okay," he whispered, his voice so faint that could she not read his thoughts, Ashya would not have heard him.

"The chain that holds them together was forged in the deepest fires of the underworld by the dwarves to complete the elemental circle. Together, these crystals will keep you connected to all of us, so you will know what happens here while you are completing your mission."

Rohan stared at the necklace during his mother's description of it. The chain was quite delicate. Each of the five crystals was vibrant in color, as full of life as the magick they carried. Even the white crystal was brilliant white, more like a pearl, really, but for its crystalline shape. He held his breath as Ashya placed it around his neck and he could feel its power coursing through his blood the moment all five crystals touched his skin. He felt stronger at once, ready to take on any challenge that lay before him.

"Thank you," he said, his heart suddenly happy, so happy in fact that he felt it might burst. Ashya, her heart heavy from sorrow, yet full of pride for her son, enfolded him in her embrace one last time and planted a kiss on top of Rohan's chestnut mop.

"Go now, before the doorway closes."

Rohan took a step closer to the doorway. *I can do this*, he thought, and took another step. He could see nothing through the doorway and had no idea what lay just on the other side. Intrigue held him in place, challenging him to defy his destiny, but he felt all of life's mysteries calling to him and he was sure they would be solved by the end of his adventure.

He looked back at his mother and blew her a kiss. *I love you*, he thought and a moment later, he heard her thoughts reach him. *I love you, my precious son.* He was watching her as he took his final step into the doorway. The last thing he remembered seeing of his world was a golden tear on the face of his unicorn mother's cheek.

It may have been only moments, or perhaps an eternity, that Rohan floated through the weightless void. Time did not exist, nothing existed except for himself and a dark figure, shrouded in mist.

Verasant?

It is I.

Where are we?

We are nowhere.

Where are we going?

I know not.

What manner of creature are you, Verasant?

The shroud of mist dissolved, and Rohan smiled as the figure before him cleared to reveal Verasant's magickal form...the body of a horse, the tail of a lion, the wings of a thunderbird, jet black dusted with gold. Verasant was a pterippus, just like him.

Happy Birthday, Lilly

Lilly stood on unfamiliar ground, though she knew where she was. The deep violet mountains were impossible to mistake. They were farther away than in the past, and settled on the east horizon instead of the west, but it was the same mountain range, and there was nowhere on Earth with mountains that color.

A cloud of smoke rose between the large circle formed by mountain after mountain, and the smoke formed a circle of black clouds. She could see something flying above the smoke, but what it was, she did not know. It was bright red, the color of fresh blood. *Is it a bird?* she thought. *Surely not. Birds have feathered wings.* This creature seemed to have wings like a giant bat, only the wings were as red as rest of it.

Lilly closed her eyes, wishing she was closer to the events in the distance. When she opened her eyes again, fear gripped her. She found herself in the midst of a duel. The red creature she had seen was a dragon and it was now circling directly above her. Another dragon was before her on the ground, and seemed even bigger than the other. It was a green color, but purple as well, depending on the way the light touched it. It turned its green-yellow eyes toward her for a moment, then braced itself, aiming its mouth at the dragon above. It gnashed its long, razor-sharp teeth together as it let out a sound Lilly could only describe as something between a growl and a belch.

A stream of fire spewed from the dragon's mouth higher than any of the mountains surrounding them, continuing for an eternity. It blazed so long, in fact, that the red dragon dove suddenly toward the ground. The dragon on the ground, which Lilly just realized had no wings, closed its mouth, stopping its rain of fire, and turned toward her. *Run*, it said, though its mouth did not move. *He needs you now. Go to him.*

The groundling dragon ran, drawing the flying enemy away from Lilly. She looked around, unsure of what to do now. *Who needs me?* she thought. She closed her eyes again and a moment later, she was standing in the middle of a great battle. Hideous creatures unlike any she had seen were charging each other. Some were driving stakes into another. Some were shrinking for no apparent reason. Others were dropping at her feet, instantly paralyzed. A bolt of lightning struck the ground beside her, yet there was not a single cloud in the sky to make the lightning.

Other creatures were in the sky, participating in the same battle. Some carried passengers, like the half-horse, half-bird that screeched as its front talons gripped the first of three necks of the enemy it was after. A reptilian head dropped to the ground, clawed off by that strange creature. It reached for another head, one that looked like a lion, but was struck by the huge creature's lion paws. It momentarily lost its balance, but recovered, screaming its displeasure, as did the evil-looking woman riding it.

Some of the creatures in the air looked like humans with wings, some horses with wings, some were dragons and some seemed to be flying with no wings at all. The ground was covered with the bodies of dying beasts; blood saturated the ground beneath them. Lilly stood in shock at the commotion around her. *What is going on?*

Lilly was knocked over by what she first thought was a rider on a horse, until she took a closer look and realized that it was a horse with the head, arms and torso of a man where its horse head should have been. *A centaur,* she thought as memory graced her. Being hit made her remember that she was actually in the middle of this battle. She ran as fast as she could away from the war being waged before her eyes. Fear and confusion flowed through her, giving her unfound strength as she fled the carnage. Her flight came to a halt when a body fell from the sky and landed at her feet.

The man that had fallen had a spear in his chest, close to his heart, if not in it. He groaned, and seeing that he was alive, she pulled him to safety. Away from the battle, Lilly was able to see the bigger picture. It was devastating. Creatures of all kinds and all sizes were dying or dead and those alive were fighting to the death. They fought with torn flesh, blood flowing from their terrible gashes. Some had bones protruding through their skin, and yet they fought, only stopping when the final blow was delivered.

Lilly held the fallen man's head in her lap as she sat, stroking his chestnut hair. He groaned again, and then whispered her name. When she looked at his face, she felt the color drain from her own.

"Adrian?"

"LILLY!"

Lilly opened her eyes and looked around. Her sister, Beth, was sitting beside her, smiling. She sat up, taking in the lavender walls and smoky-gray carpet. This was her room. She had been dreaming.

"Sorry I woke you," said Beth, not sounding the least bit sorry. "I wanted to be the first to wish you a happy birthday."

"Thanks," Lilly replied. Dream or not, she was unsettled by the images still clear in her mind.

"Are you okay?" Beth noticed Lilly's condition and stopped smiling.

"Yeah, I'm fine." She threw the covers off of herself and got out of bed. "Another dream."

"One of those bad ones?"

Lilly nodded, still trying to sort out all that she had seen. She opened her closet door and grabbed a worn pair of blue jeans and a tee shirt that read *You may think I'm nuts, but the voices in my head tell me I'm fine.* After looking at it for a moment, she shook her head and threw it at Beth.

"You can have that shirt. I've always hated it." She searched through her closet again and finally decided on a rainbow tie-dyed tee shirt she had bought a few months before.

"How bad was the dream?"

"It was bad, Beth." Lilly was always honest with her sister. In fact, Beth was the only person who truly knew everything about her. She knew she could tell her big sister anything and no matter what it was, Beth would understand.

"Do you need to see Dr. Hoffman again?"

"No." Lilly's answer was quick, perhaps too quick from the skeptical look Beth gave her. "The last thing I need," she added before Beth could interrupt, "is to talk to a shrink whose own son ran away."

"Lilly!" exclaimed Beth. "That's an awful thing to say."

"Well, he should have stayed here. He should have stayed with me." She sat on her bed, still holding her clothes. Beth scooted closer to Lilly and put her arms around her.

"Can I ask why you care so much about him? I mean, Adrian was always kind of different." Lilly glared at Beth, shaking off her embrace. "Sorry, but it's true."

"I don't know why," said Lilly. "I just know that when he was around, I stopped hearing the voice, and the dreams weren't bad. They were beautiful."

"Well, have you been hearing the voice again?" Leave it to Beth to ask a question that presents the answer.

"No," admitted Lilly.

"Then stop worrying so much. Hurry and get dressed. I want the details of this dream before school." With that, Beth left the room, closing the door behind her.

No, you don't, thought Lilly, but she knew she would tell her sister anyway. After all, what were sisters for, if not to share your deepest secrets with?

Lilly stared at the changing scenery as Beth drove home. Her day had been a long one. She'd tried to stay focused, but the terrible images of her dreams kept forcing their way into her thoughts, making it impossible to concentrate on anything else. She had told Beth all about the dream at breakfast and her practical sister's reply was, "It was only a dream, Lilly. It was your overactive imagination getting carried away. Dragons aren't real, you know. This isn't either." Beth's reassurance, however, wasn't enough to put her at ease. Something was wrong; she could feel it. Maybe he didn't fall from the sky with a spear in his heart, but he could still be hurt. Her dreams meant something. That much, she knew. Her concern was what they meant.

As the minutes passed, so did the houses, spreading out further and further the closer they approached their own. The trees surrounding them became more concentrated as the number of houses dwindled, thick and foreboding to anyone who did not know the secrets of their splendor. Beth chatted away, oblivious to Lilly's silence, still going on about a boy who had asked her to go with him to tomorrow's football game and the party afterward.

"Kara is going to be so jealous when she sees me show up with Brett Sheridan," she babbled as she turned onto the gravel road that came to a dead end at their driveway. "She's been after him for months, and he asked *me* out! Brett Sheridan! Can you believe it?" Lilly smiled and rolled her eyes. At least someone was happy on her birthday.

When the car rolled to a stop in the driveway, Beth sprinted into the house, leaving Lilly to gather her things. She took her time, knowing Beth was in the house already, calling her best friend, Kara, to find out how jealous she was.

As she closed the car door, her father pulled his ancient car into the driveway. He called it *classic*, but Lilly didn't see the beauty of it like he did. She knew when he looked at that car, he saw it the way it was when he first bought it, before seventeen years and two children had ravaged it. The sleek cobalt exterior had once been perfect in appearance; not a single scratch could be found. Now it was littered with dings, dents and rusted areas, its shine faded to a dingy, murky blue.

Andrew Barrett was tall and thin. Over six feet tall, his arms and legs were long and lean, yet he was stronger than he looked, for it was all muscle. He wore wire-framed glasses over his vibrant green eyes, which Lilly thought made him look distinguished, though somewhat older than his forty-one years. Traces of gray had begun to find their way into his nearly-black hair and clean-cut goatee, giving him a salt and pepper flair, and his long face was slowly showing signs of age. What were once considered laugh-lines were now prominent wrinkles.

He was once as young as his car, thought Lilly. The years had taken their toll on both of them. Lilly waited while her father gathered his briefcase and laptop from his car and walked toward the house. As he passed her, she fell into his pace and they entered to house together. She didn't know why, but looking at her father made her feel sad, and no matter what happy thought crossed her mind, the sadness remained.

"Have a good day at school, honey?" he asked her once they were inside. He relinquished his portable office in his favorite recliner and gave Lilly a hug.

"It was okay, I guess."

"You guess? You mean to tell me that you didn't get carried around on the shoulders of all your friends for your birthday?" She threw him a pained look and started up the stairs to her room.

"What friends, Dad?"

"Your friends do not matter in numbers, my dear," he said. She stopped on the third stair, waiting for him to finish. "Most people who come into your life won't stay long, but there are relationships we build with a few special souls that last a lifetime. A single relationship with a great friend is better than many relationships with mediocre friends. Remember...quality, not quantity."

"Yeah," she muttered. "Too bad all the quality friends leave."

"One left, Lilly," he said, eyeing her over the top of his glasses. "Just one."

"The only one." She could feel her mood darkening, but she had too much respect for her father to remind him that her mother had left, too. Instead, she walked down the two steps before he could say anything else, retreating to her piano, her only consolation.

It was actually her father's piano, a gorgeous black Steinway grand that he'd bought when he and her mother got married. She could never remember him playing, but she assumed he didn't have the heart, nor the time, since he became a single father. He'd been delighted when, at a young age, Lilly had shown interest in the instrument, and he encouraged her to play. She'd never been one to watch television, and though she loved to read, she hadn't picked up a new author in three years unless it had been assigned by her teachers. Playing the piano was her only source of comfort, the only way she knew to get her mind off of her loneliness.

Her fingers found the keys to reverberate her mood, a mournful melody composed mainly of black keys, the sharps and the flats. It was a musical description of herself, her mind too sharp for potential friends not to be intimidated, her heart too flat to care. Except for playing, she didn't care about much of anything anymore, not since Adrian abandoned her. Her birthday was just another reminder of his absence. Now the dream flowed through her fingers, violence, anguish. She pounded the keys, her frustration echoing through the room.

It wasn't all bad, she told herself. *If it wasn't for all the fighting, it is really a beautiful place...* She concentrated on the melody, which became less sullen as she forced her mood to do the same. By the time she finished the song, another of her many creations, she had herself convinced to at least try to have a good birthday.

Abandoning her only pleasure, Lilly went to her room where she pulled out her books and flopped on her bed, spreading them out and opening a notebook. She wanted to get as much homework out of the way as possible. She couldn't just sit here all weekend and wait for nothing to happen, *again.* Maybe she would go to the game tomorrow, too.

The next thing she knew, she was on the battlefield, the chaos escalating around her. Adrian was in her arms, barely clinging to life. Lilly reached for the spear protruding from his chest, but in his last bit of strength, he grabbed her wrist and stopped her.

"Leave it," he gasped. "I'll only die faster if you take it out."

"Die faster?" she asked, horrified. "I can help you. Let me try."

"Lilly, you must keep fighting. It is your destiny to finish this." His voice was weak and a deep gurgle rose in his throat, then a sudden rush of blood trickled from his mouth. She held his head and cried, rocking him back and forth as he died in her arms. The chaos that surrounded her didn't matter. She didn't care if she was killed right there. At least then she could stay with him forever.

A loud thundering roared closer as a herd of centaurs came trotting toward her. They stopped beside her and the nearest one offered her his hand.

"We must go," he said, his voice both soft and urgent. Lilly turned away from the creature and buried her face in Adrian's still-warm neck. She could see nothing, hear nothing. The world had suddenly gone silent.

When she lifted her head, she realized she was clutching her pillow. Wet circles had formed on it and she realized that she had once again been dreaming. In her sleep, she had knocked her books onto the floor, her homework untouched. She sat up and ran her hands over her face, then fled the room.

Her father prepared her favorite meal for her birthday, meatballs and mashed potatoes with a tomato-based gravy. He bought a cake and snuck it into the house while she dozed. She took a seat at the table next to her father and they waited for Beth to get off of the phone. Finally, she entered and plopped down in her chair.

"I was right," she exclaimed, a silly grin plastered on her face. "Kara's eyes probably turned green she is so jealous."

"Jealous of what?" asked Andrew, scooping piping hot meatballs from the small feast before him and filling his plate. He handed the spoon to Lilly next, who did the same.

"That Brett Sheridan asked me out. She's been pining after him for years."

"Yeah," stated Lilly, "her and every other high school girl."

"So," Andrew said, then popped a meatball in his mouth and chewed thoughtfully while both of his daughters stared at him, waiting for him to continue. He swallowed and smiled at them, then looked at Beth. "Who is this Brett Sheridan?"

"Only the most popular boy in school, Daddy," Beth answered, as thought her father should have known the answer already.

"Oh," he replied, raising his eyebrows.

"And the quarterback," piped Lilly, "and a straight A student. I'm telling you, she should marry him before he gets away." She smiled playfully, happy the attention was focused on her sister's news instead of her birthday. Her father caught her eye and joined the fun.

"In that case, I'll schedule some time off work," he mused, chasing a meatball across his plate. "I know a good band that could play in May. Is a spring wedding alright with you, honey?"

"Very funny, Dad," Beth muttered. Andrew chuckled and finished clearing his plate. Lilly smiled and forced her thoughts on her meal, though she was not the least bit hungry. She knew how hurt her father would be if she passed up the meal, knowing the trouble he had gone through to make it just for her birthday, so she forced it down. After the meal, cake and probably ice cream would follow. Andrew always made sure they had a traditional birthday, even if it was only the three of them.

Lilly waited for him to say something about it. She had hated her birthday since she could remember. It was a depressing day for her, and she assumed for her father as well. The day she was born was the day her mother had left them. She never understood why, but because it happened on her birthday, she had always blamed herself. Her one fear was that her father did, too, but he never acted like it mattered to him.

Beth started chattering away about the big game the next night and Andrew listened, attentive. He glanced at Lilly and flashed her a smile. She returned a weak smile and excused herself from the table.

"I'm going for a walk. Can the cake wait a little while?"

Andrew kissed her forehead. "Sure, honey." He stood and gathered the dirty dishes, carrying them to the sink. A pang of sadness swept through Lilly as she watched him and she fled the house, hoping to leave behind the melancholy she felt.

Outside, the sky was clear. The sun was setting and tomorrow, the days would be shorter than the nights. Today, her birthday, was the Autumnal Equinox, only one of two days in the whole year when day and night are equal.

Perfect, she thought. *Longer nights to come. More time to dream about things that scare me to death.* She sighed and leaned against a thick elm tree, staring off into the darkness. A sudden movement in the trees caught her eye, but as she stared, only darkness stared back. She closed her eyes and thought about Adrian. Why he would not leave her thoughts, she didn't know. She wished with all her might that something would happen to ease her mind about him and the terrible dreams she'd been having.

Lilly, whispered a voice, drawing out her name like a snake hissing in the grass. Her eyes snapped open at the sound.

"Hello?" she said aloud, looking again at the place she had seen the movement. "Is anyone there?"

For a moment, she heard nothing in the silence of the forest. When she finally heard the voice again, she raced toward her house and went straight to her room, slamming the door hard. Whoever the voice belonged to knew what today was. The deep, drawn out voice still lingered in her mind.

Happy birthday, Lilly, it had said.

A Matter of Trust

Lilly frowned as she stared around the huge room. She would rather be anywhere else but back in Dr. Hoffman's office, waiting for him to join her. Although it was Saturday morning, he had made an exception to see her. She had been his patient off and on since she was a small child, ever since she started hearing voices, or rather, one voice. She'd been having the terrible dreams since she could remember, though she remembered none more terrifying than the most recent.

She studied the room, noticing the changes since her last visit over three years ago, right after Adrian disappeared. The walls, once papered in beige and burgundy wallpaper, were now blue and ivory. The blue chairs were now burgundy, and the chaise lounge had been reupholstered in an ivory velvet material, its oak arm the only giveaway that it was the same refurbished piece. Only his shelves and desk were unchanged.

Lilly couldn't help the smile playing at her lips. The color combination was the same, just relocated to different areas of the room. It suited him. He was a man who liked change, but he kept enough familiarity in the room for his patients. The only real change was an assortment of books lined neatly on his bookshelf, and it looked to Lilly like his collection had grown considerably in the past three years. Books stretched from end to end. The figurines that once filled the gaps in the bookshelf were gone. Lilly was trying to remember the details of those figurines when the door opened and Dr. Hoffman walked in, carrying two Styrofoam cups. He handed one to Lilly.

"Hot chocolate," he stated, and sat behind his desk. Lilly was silent as he retrieved a legal pad and a pen from his desk. He looked at her expectantly, but she was suddenly at a loss to speak. She always felt so silly telling him about her dreams and even more so about the voice that had been afflicting her for so long. He sat silent, sipping his coffee, and waited for her to open up to him. She wondered how long he would wait in silence before he finally said something.

Nearly ten minutes later, the silence was still unbroken. Dr. Hoffman shifted in his chair, leaning back slightly to stretch his back. Lilly chose that moment to speak up.

"Have you heard from Adrian?" she asked.

Dr. Hoffman didn't seem to notice the edge to her voice. If he did, he overlooked it. His bushy eyebrows danced above his brown eyes, which seemed to sparkle with laughter despite his serious demeanor.

"I haven't spoken with Adrian," he said, choosing his words carefully, "since the day he left." He leaned forward and studied her expression. His soft eyes bored into hers, slowly coaxing her out of her shell. "Is this what you really wanted to talk about?"

Lilly lowered her eyes, reluctant to tell him why she was there. She had always held a grudge against him for allowing Adrian to leave, for not finding a way to keep him here. Now, she was expected to tell him everything. It all came down to a matter of trust: Could she trust him and still remain angry at him? He waited patiently until she lifted her eyes to him, then raised his eyebrows in such a way that compelled her to speak.

"I had a dream about him," she blurted, and before she knew it, the words flowed from her like a flood pouring over a barricade. He listened without interruption to the smallest details of the dream and to the many questions that plagued her mind. *Where did he go? Is he alright? Why hasn't he tried to contact any of them? Why did he leave in the first place? What does this dream mean and why doesn't it ever change?* "And then I heard the voice again," she exhaled, ending her rant.

Lilly sank into her chair, a sense of relief washing over her now that everything was out in the open. Dr. Hoffman removed his eyeglasses and ran his hands over his face and up through his sandy blonde hair. He leaned back in his chair and exhaled deeply. They both sat silent and the good doctor allowed everything to sink in. He sat for awhile, staring at nothing in particular, before clearing his throat.

"Well," he said after the eternal silence, "it seems we are back where we started eleven years ago. Bad dreams and voices only you can hear."

"One voice," Lilly corrected him. "Always the same one."

"Rowan?"

"What?" She didn't remember ever knowing the voice had a name.

"When you first came to me, you called him Rowan. In the beginning, I thought perhaps he was just an imaginary friend, but the things you knew...for a four-year-old, it was astounding. Every question I asked you that first day, you answered, and you told me that Rowan was the one who knew all the answers."

"I don't remember that," Lilly told him, struggling to think back to the first day she entered Dr. Hoffman's office. Her memories were all jumbled together, one long stream of visits to his office and later, his house, where she met Adrian. *That* day, she could remember clearly, as though only days separated her from it rather than years.

Dr. Hoffman, whom she called Eric when they went to his home, was an old friend of her father's. He had been Andrew's best man at his wedding and had been the first to the hospital the day Beth was born, a box of cigars in his hands as he circled the waiting room, passing them out to anyone who had an urge to celebrate. Lilly knew that was why, when she started having the bad dreams and hearing the voice, her father had brought her to him.

The day Lilly met Adrian, her father had taken her and Beth to Eric Hoffman's house for a backyard barbecue. Lilly had worn a blue sundress adorned with bright yellow sunflowers, coaxed into it by her father, complete with the frilly socks. She'd hated the dress, but conceded to her father and wore it anyway, under the stipulation that she could wear any shoes she wanted. He'd agreed and she'd chosen to wear her raggedy blue and white tennis shoes, nearly worn out from the time she'd spent playing in them.

Adrian had walked up to her as soon as they entered the back yard. He was a skinny kid with auburn hair and pale blue eyes, and was wearing denim shorts and a blue tee shirt with a faerie on it that read: *Do you believe in magic? I do.* He wore no shoes and his feet were darkened from the dirt. Lilly stood clutching her father's hand, staring at the unusual boy before her. They remained there for a moment, sizing each other up.

Eric walked toward them, grinning from ear to ear. "Andrew," he said, sticking out his hand, "it's good to see you again."

"It's been a long time," Andrew replied, taking Eric's hand and shaking it. Eric released his hand and looked from Lilly to Adrian to Beth, then knelt down beside Adrian.

"Adrian, this is Lilly," he said to his son. "She's going to be in your class at school next month. And this is Beth. She'll be in first grade this year." Adrian looked at Beth, then back to Lilly, still trying to decide if he should talk first or wait for her to say something. He opened his mouth to speak, but Lilly beat him to it.

"That's a girl's shirt," she told him in a matter-of-fact tone. He looked down at his shirt, then back at her again.

"So?" he said. "Those are boy's shoes." She looked down at her shoes and back at him. A broad grin painted his face. "Come on," he said, grabbing her hand. They ran to the swing set, laughing, and from that day on, they were best friends.

Lilly was still lost in reliving the memory when Dr. Hoffman snapped her back to the present by clearing his throat. She met his eyes and caught him smiling.

"What were you just thinking about?" he asked her. "You looked so peaceful, I hated to interrupt."

"The day I met Adrian."

"You really miss him, don't you?"

"Don't you?" Her tone was incredulous. How could he ask her such an ignorant question?

He sighed. "Of course I do, but leaving was the best thing for him."

"He was twelve!" She felt her anger returning to her and crossed her arms, hoping that would be enough to restrain her feelings until she could leave. This was getting her nowhere.

"That he was," said Dr. Hoffman, stealing a glance at the photograph of Adrian smiling back at him. He stood and began pacing the room. "Adrian has always been special, Lilly," he began as he returned to his chair. "He came to me and told me that he was meant to do something great, that he knew what he had to do and that it meant he would have to leave me behind for a while. I tried to talk him out of it, I really did, but no matter what I said, he had an answer for it.

"I didn't understand why he wanted to leave. I told him that I wouldn't let him go, that I would find a way to stop him from running away from here. Do you know what he said to that? He said that he wasn't running away from anything; he was running *toward* something: his destiny. He was so passionate about following his destiny, about finding his path. He told me that he was going whether I agreed with him or not, but it would be easier for him if I gave him my blessing and told him that I loved him. So that's what I did."

Lilly stared at him in shock, her mouth agape. "You just let him go?"

"I had to. He told me when he left that I would see him again, though it would be many years before that happened. I gave my boy a kiss and then shook the hand of the young man he'd become. I told him that I loved him and to take care of himself and I would wait until I saw him again." Dr. Hoffman wiped a tear that had gathered in his eye.

"Why didn't you try harder?" Lilly exclaimed. "How could you just let a twelve-year-old walk out to be on his own like that?"

"Because deep down, I knew he was right. I don't know how I knew, but after I grieved for my loss, I felt better knowing that he was doing what he wanted and that he would be happy. That's all parents really want for their children, to know they are on the right path and that it will lead them to happiness."

Lilly pouted in her chair, her questions not only unanswered, but rapidly growing. She frowned, shaking her head, and then looked at Dr. Hoffman, her eyes piercing his. He averted his eyes, then reached for the eyeglasses on his desk and put them back on.

"As far as your dreams go, I've told you before, they are just dreams. You are worried about Adrian and you are not being honest with yourself about how you feel. Because of that, your subconscious is doing it for you. Go back to your journal and let it out, everything you told me today and everything I told you. Maybe that will help you sort those feelings out.

"As far as the voice is concerned, perhaps it is nothing more than your subconscious trying to reach you during your waking hours. I suggest talking with it. See if it answers you. See what it has to say. It may very well have answers to your questions."

Lilly pondered this as Dr. Hoffman stood up and pulled his wallet from his pocket. He removed a business card and handed it to her.

"That has my cell number on it. If anything comes up and you need to talk, call anytime." She took the card, defeated.

"Anytime?"

"Yes," he said, taking her hand and squeezing it in his, "anytime."

It was early afternoon when Lilly returned home. Beth had driven her into town, but rather than bother her, Lilly walked the five miles home, giving herself plenty of time to mull over her issues. Her father was in his recliner, his laptop resting on his lap as his fingers flew over the keys. She'd entered so quietly, he had yet to notice she was home. She stood there, staring at him. He was a handsome man, but since her mother had abandoned them, he had never even tried to find a new wife. The thought had never really occurred to her before; now she wished it had.

Andrew stopped typing and leaned back, stretching his long arms high in the air. He noticed Lilly and smiled, getting up from his chair.

"How was Dr. Hoffman?" he asked, just as he always had whenever she returned from a session. She just shrugged and started toward the stairs, then stopped and whirled around.

"Did he ever tell you about Adrian leaving?" she asked him, her eyes pleading for an answer. He shook his head.

"No, he didn't. I would have listened if he ever had, but he never brought it up and I never asked."

Lilly nodded and hugged her father. "You should, soon," she told him, not really knowing the reason she said it, and then disappeared to her room.

Once she was in her room, Lilly looked around, feeling lost in everything familiar. She walked to the full-length mirror beside her closet and studied her reflection. Her shoulder-length copper hair framed her face, which was thin like her father's, though not as long. She had his eyes, too. Adrian had once said they reminded him of emeralds, the perfect shade of green. She had no freckles like most other redheads she knew of; the only flaw that marked her face was a teardrop-shaped birthmark below her left eye, barely darker than the rest of her fair skin. She scrutinized her appearance as a whole and decided that she didn't look any older.

On her bed were two gifts. The larger one was wrapped in colorful wrapping paper with the words *Happy Birthday* scrawled all over it in elegant black print. The other, a box no bigger than a softball, was wrapped with the comic section of the newspaper. She picked up the larger of the two and opened it. Inside was a book bound in hard black leather and a package of black pens. She took the book out and opened it. It was full of blank pages. Only the first was written on. It read: *Fill me with your most precious thoughts.* Underneath the note, Beth had written: *Happy 15th, Sis.*

Lilly smiled and put the gift to the side, then reached for the other. It was very light and she knew immediately that her father had bought her some type of jewelry. She opened it and despite her suspicions of its contents, she was shocked when she saw what was inside. A thin silver chain held a charm of exquisite beauty. The charm, which Lilly knew was called a pentacle, was a star surrounded by a circle, the whole thing barely larger than a dime. The symmetry was perfect, but what truly caught her eye was the color. It seemed to be silver, but as it turned in the light, flecks of green, blue, yellow and red emanated across it.

Lilly put it around her neck and went to the mirror again. The necklace was long enough to fall beneath the collar of her shirt, so she pulled it over the top and turned before the mirror, watching as the light played across the magnificent trinket.

It's beautiful, said a voice, and Lilly knew immediately that it was *the* voice.   She looked around and saw no one.   She wondered if Dr. Hoffman's advice would work and decided to talk back to it.   *What could it hurt,* she thought, *if it's just my subconscious?*

"Who are you?" she asked, sinking onto her bed.

You know who I am, the voice replied.   *Search your memory.   I am there.*

Her memory?   Lilly tried for the second time that day to remember her childhood and the mysterious voice that belonged to someone named Rowan, but nothing triggered the memory she was looking for.

"Rowan?" she asked, hoping she was right, yet praying that she wasn't.   How would she explain to her father that she was talking to her imaginary friend again?

That's what you called me when you were very small.   You never did learn how to pronounce it right, I take it.   I am Rohan.

Okay, thought Lilly, *now we are getting somewhere.   The voice has a name.*   She mentally ran down her list of unanswered questions, trying to decide which one to ask first, and settled on the most basic.

"What do you want?"

It is necessary that I talk to you, said Rohan, urgency flooding his voice.   Once again, questions filled Lilly's mind, answers to them left void.   The newest question floated across her mind slowly: *Why is some voice from my subconscious so intent on speaking to me?*

I'm not *your subconscious,* Rohan interrupted her thoughts and she could feel his annoyance.   *I am quite real.*

"Then why can't I see you?" she asked.   "And why am I the only one who can hear you?"

Come to the clearing in the forest, his voice echoed in her mind.   *I am there and I have the answers you seek.*   And then he was gone.   Lilly called out to him, his strange name rolling easily off her tongue.   She knew, however, that he would not answer.   It was as if he were a guest in her mind, uninvited though he was, and she could feel that he was no longer there.   The only trace of his visit was an echo in her thoughts: *I have the answers you seek...*

Getting to the forest was more of a challenge than Lilly expected. Beth cornered her in the hallway, demanding her opinion of which shirt she should wear to the game later that night: a thin, long sleeved white blouse that buttoned up the front or a short sleeved red turtleneck sweater cut off just above her navel.

After Beth had argued the advantages and disadvantages of each shirt, Lilly, with little effort, convinced her to wear the white shirt over the red, and then escaped downstairs before Beth had the chance to ask for her opinion of how she should do her hair. Lilly smiled. Little Miss Practical was a nervous wreck for her date.

Downstairs, Andrew was on the phone, pacing in frustration. As Lilly sprinted past him, he snapped his fingers at her and motioned for her to wait. She sighed and leaned against the wall, glancing toward the door in anticipation. She thought she would burst before he finished his conversation.

"I have to go back to the lab," he blurted as he returned the cordless phone to its receiver. He grabbed his laptop from his chair and shoved it into his briefcase, snapping it shut hard. His thick eyebrows were furrowed, his mouth pinched together into a tight frown.

"Forty samples contaminated," he muttered to himself, rushing around to gather his glasses, keys and coat from their various resting placed. He looked at Lilly and his face softened.

"I'll be gone all night," he told her with a sigh. "Beth's going to the game. Her curfew is midnight. Will you be alright by yourself until then?"

"Of course," she reassured him, thrilled at the idea of having an evening alone. "Go fix the lab."

"Yeah," he muttered in distaste, scanning the room to make sure he wasn't forgetting anything. His eyes rested on Lilly and her new necklace caught his eye. He reached out to touch it, running his index finger over its minute form, then put his arm around his daughter and held her for a moment.

"Do you like it?" he asked her, his demeanor the complete opposite from moments ago.

"I love it, Daddy."

"It's been in my family for a long time," he told her, eyeing it again, as if it held some strange power that captivated him in its wake. "Longer than even I could tell you, longer than anyone in the family can even remember. Promise me that you will keep it safe."

"I promise," Lilly whispered, wrapping her fingers around it. Fear gripped her as she tried to comprehend why her father was suddenly so calm, yet so somber at the same time. Andrew kissed her forehead and hugged her again. A strange chill ran through her and she felt like it was the last time she would get to hug her father. For some strange reason, she suddenly didn't want to let go.

"I love you," he said as he released her, a sadness in his voice Lilly couldn't quite put her finger on. "Happy birthday, baby." With that, he took his things and walked out the door.

Lilly stood in the kitchen where her father had left her, still clutching the charm around her neck. A chill ran through her again and she released it. For a brief moment she had forgotten that the owner of that mysterious voice in her head was outside right now, waiting for her just beyond the edge of the forest. She flew out the door and across the back yard as fast as her feet could carry her. The fear she felt in her father's goodbye melted away as a rush of excitement replaced its void.

She was out of breath by the time she reached the clearing at the forest's edge. It couldn't be seen from outside the forest, but if a person knew which trees to walk through, they would be led straight to it. It had always been Lilly favorite place to spend her free time, even as a child, because it was like walking through a doorway to another world. She stopped to catch her breath beside a large rock, the same one she and Adrian had climbed on as children. He was the only other person in the world who knew of her secret place.

The clearing itself wasn't very large. In fact, it seemed quite small in comparison to the enormous trees that created its perimeter. Their foliage formed a canopy high above the clearing that sheltered it from the rain during even the harshest storm, and it created a cool shade during the hot summer months.

Lush grass covered the ground beneath her feet and was littered with an assortment of wildflowers, ranging in color from deep red and violet to bright yellow, pink, lavender and white. Stones were scattered haphazardly across the ground. Dark green moss covered them like a blanket, camouflaging their granite exterior, and crept along the bottom edge of a fallen log in its path. Birds twittered in the trees, ruffling their feathers against the cool breeze that floated in the air. Before long, they would be seeking warmer weather. Winter was already creeping toward them.

Lilly inhaled, breathing in the calming peace this place had always provided her. She disappeared to this clearing many times over the years, a secret for her and no one else. Since Adrian left, she returned more often, always seeking a solace, but never fully able to grasp it. She had decided long ago that if she ever ran away, she would come here to live, alone in her serenity. Her energy restored, she stood up and looked around for Rohan, but saw no one.

"Are you here?" she asked, feeling foolish that she was talking out loud to no one, but as the final word left her lips, she heard his reply: *I am here.*

She held her breath in suspense, expecting to see someone emerge from the trees, but no one came. She waited in eager silence for something to happen. When nothing did, she spoke again.

"If you are here," she said, "then come out so I can see you. You told me to come here, remember?"

Silence. Lilly waited again, but the only sounds to reach her ears were the songs of the katydids, lulling the sun to sleep as evening crept over them. She shook her head and turned toward the direction of her house.

You had more patience when you were four years old than you do now. Lilly stopped at the sound of Rohan's voice and whirled around, expecting to see him somewhere in her clearing, but she was once again disappointed.

I will come out, he said, *when I think you are ready to accept the truth. You asked if I remembered asking you here. I remember so much more than that. I maintain my silence because finding the right words is difficult. I have much to say and you have much to hear, from me and from yourself. I just want to get things right this time.*

"What do you mean 'Get things right this time'?" Lilly made her way to the large rock and climbed onto it, getting comfortable. She had no idea why, but she felt compelled to stay and listen, even if she couldn't see him yet.

The answer to that question, he replied after a moment's hesitation, *will come with time. For now, I want you to sit and relax. You have a memory locked inside your head that you must remember before I will show myself. You have many questions about me and what all of this means. The answers to those questions lie within that single memory.*

"Look," said Lilly, exasperated, "I've tried to remember things from my childhood. I can't do it."

Just close your eyes, he whispered, *and let me do the rest.* She closed her eyes as silence enveloped her again, wondering how she could have such a hard time remembering him, yet she could remember what she was wearing the day she met Adrian, which was very near the same time. She tried to focus on that memory, hoping it would rekindle the ones she couldn't reach, when she felt a hand on her shoulder.

The world suddenly slipped away from her. She could no longer hear the katydids singing or feel the cool breeze that found its way into the clearing. She tried to open her eyes, but found it impossible. As panic built inside her, unfamiliar images flashed through her mind. She saw things from her dreams; mystical, beautiful things that didn't seem real. The last image she saw before she was able to open her eyes was a large, translucent vortex swirling before her and a flash of brilliant white light.

When she opened her eyes, she was on the ground. The air was much warmer and the flora was the most spectacular green she had ever seen. The birds were no longer in the trees, but at her feet, plucking their breakfast from the ground. She looked around and realized that things were much more different than she first realized. The moss that had covered the stones was barely there, and the fallen log was gone.

"What happened?" she asked, staring in awe at her altered surroundings.

Just pay attention, was Rohan's reply. She wanted to ask him more, but before another sound could escape her lips, a young girl walked into the clearing and climbed onto the rock, *her* rock. She started to object, but caught her breath as she noticed the girl's features. The girl, who was no more than five, was wearing denim shorts, raggedy blue and white tennis shoes and a blue tee shirt with a faerie on it that read: *Do you believe in magic? I do.* Her copper hair was pulled into two long pigtails and a teardrop-shaped birthmark decorated her cheek just below her left eye.

It's me, she thought, then watched in silence as the little girl stood on the rock and quietly said, "Rowan?"

If awe is what she felt when she saw her five-year-old self standing before her, complete disbelief could only describe what she felt next. Emerging from the trees was a huge horse-like creature, larger than the largest horse Lilly had ever seen. His entire body was ebony, his mane like spun gold, as was the hair surrounding his jet black hooves. His black tail had the same golden hair on its end, though it was more like a lion's tail than a horse's. A horn, the same golden color as his hair, protruded from his forehead and spiraled to a point at its tip. Folded at his sides were large wings, just as black as the rest of his body.

Under the sun, his golden features sparkled with wild abandon, while his muscles rippled with amazing clarity as he walked toward the rock and the small child sitting upon it. Flecks of gold danced their way over his feathered wings as the sunlight struck them. It seemed as though he had been sprinkled with gold dust. Even his black eyes retained a golden hue.

How are you, Lilias? the massive creature said in Rohan's voice. Lilias shuffled her feet a bit, then squatted on the rock and wrapped her arms around her knees. The horse approached the child until his head was inches from hers and looked into her eyes. *What troubles you?*

"How come nobody believes you are real?" Lilias's voice trembled as she spoke. Lilly could feel the child's emotions, *her* emotions, flooding back to her as the memory played out before her eyes.

They do, in my world, but in my world, they haven't forgotten magick. It is an easy thing to forget when you do not see it every day. The people in your world stopped looking for it generations ago. Now they teach their children not to believe it. When they stopped looking for it, they didn't notice it disappear.

"Tell me about your world again," said the child, climbing onto the massive horse's back. He pranced around and spread his enormous wings, which nearly filled the width of the clearing, then folded them again, surrounding the child like a makeshift saddle.

In my world, his gentle voice murmured, *faeries dance around the plants, bringing strength to the trees, bringing blooms to the flowers and bringing life to new seeds. Mermaids sing to passers-by and unicorns wander through the forests, sharing their magick with all whom they encounter. Children younger than you are now already learn and practice magick every day. By the time I was seven, I was embarking on my destiny to find you.*

"But I won't get to go when I am seven, will I?" Lilias's interruption gave him pause.

No, he finally said, *not when you are seven. We must wait until you are old enough to be there without being noticed. Besides, your father needs you now. He's not ready yet to accept that you must follow your destiny. And you must, my darling child, for the fates of both our worlds depend on it.*

"Why?"

Because, Lilias, you are the Chosen One. There is no other who can complete the journey that you are meant to take.

"When will we go?"

When the time is right, we will go.

"But not for a long time, right?"

Yes, not for a long time. Why?

"Well," said the small child, the same worried look from before on her face, the same fear in her heart, "everyone thinks that I don't need to talk to you. I want to, but I can't keep it a secret anymore. I have a new friend now and I don't want to keep secrets from him." Tears streamed down her face as she spoke.

Rohan was silent for a long while. When he spoke, Lilly could feel the sadness it carried. *I understand.*

"Are you mad at me?" the child's voice quivered.

Of course not. Half the point of waiting to go is so you can live your life. They're right. You're right. I don't belong in it anymore, at least not for a while. But I want you to make me one promise.

"Anything."

Don't forget about me. As his voice echoed in her mind, Lilly felt the warmth dissipate. She closed her eyes as she felt herself disconnecting from the magick. When she opened them, Rohan stood before her, just as magnificent as he was in her memory. The sun had nearly disappeared by that time, so Lilly could not see the flecks of gold that had played across his feathers and his other golden attributes did not sparkle as they had in her memory, but he was still the most glorious thing she had ever seen.

Do you remember now? he asked her, shaking his head and giving life to his magnificent mane. Lilly tried to speak, but no words came to her lips. A cool breeze swept past her and she realized her face was wet. The emotional trip through her mind had released a deluge of tears. She approached Rohan slowly, without fear, without question. The previous trepidation she had felt about the events in her life vanished as the voids of her past overflowed with recollection. New tears sprung to her eyes as she touched his face.

"You came back," she whispered, allowing more tears to fall.

I was always here, he replied, bowing his head toward the ground. Lilly noticed a golden tear on his face and caught it in her hand. Her hand sparkled where it had landed, as though it, too, were made of gold dust.

"You must have been so lonely. I am so sorry I didn't keep my promise to you."

Do not dwell on it. It was a sacrifice I made willingly, for the sake of destiny. He pranced in a circle, shaking his head, flipping his tail and ruffling his feathers, displaying his delight in their reunion. She smiled, truly happy for the first time since Adrian had left. She laughed as he continued his spectacle. When he finally regained his composure, his eyes took on a serious glint and Lilly realized why he had chosen now to come back to her. The time had come to leave this world behind her and embark on the journey that would lead her to her destiny.

Are you ready? he asked her, as though he knew what she was thinking. She shrugged her shoulders. She felt deep in her heart that she was ready to face whatever lay before her, but again, it came down to trust. Could she trust that feeling? Could she trust herself? She gazed at the creature before her, the one friend who had stayed, and knew she could trust him.

"How do I explain to my family why I'm leaving?"

You don't.

A violet haze had settled over the forest in evening's wake. Lilly walked as quickly as her feet would carry her back to her house. She had very little time before Beth would arrive home and more to do than she realized. Rohan had explained to her the importance of appearances and how they would deter the evil rapidly approaching her.

Your family must believe that you have run away, he told her. *That is the only way they will be safe when she comes for you.* When she had asked him who was coming for her, his reply was, *I will answer all your questions later. Right now you must take advantage of your family's absence. Be quick.*

She was out of breath when she got back to her room. As she gazed around it, she was struck by the reality that this would be the last time she would ever be here. Her possessions would be left behind, waiting forever for her unlikely return. Rohan had told her to pack as though she was running away and she laughed aloud as the irony of the situation took hold of her. She really was running away to her clearing.

She snatched a black duffel bag from her closet and then paused, wondering what kind of clothing they wore in Rohan's world. Jeans and solid colors would have to do, since she had nothing else to speak of. She folded the three pairs of jeans and seven shirts so they would fit inside the bag, then shoved some sweats, socks and undergarments in after them. She looked at the different items scattered over her dresser and desk and decided that there were certain things she would take with her if she "ran away". She packed the blank book Beth had given her, a few pens and pencils, a smooth black stone Adrian had once given to her which he had called a worry stone, a hairbrush, toothpaste and her toothbrush from the bathroom and a few ponytail bands, which she shoved in her pocket. She took her favorite picture of her family from the wall in the hallway and removed it from the frame, placing the photo carefully in the book she had packed and hanging the empty frame back on the wall. She scanned the crowded bag, trying to think of anything she may have forgotten, then closed it up and started for the door.

Halfway down the stairs, she stopped and raced back up them, then dove into the bottom drawer of her desk and retrieved the small, faded tee shirt she had been wearing during her last meeting with Rohan. She folded it carefully and placed it in the bag, then closed it up again and headed outside, grabbing her leather jacket from its hook by the door on her way out. She did not look back as she made her way to the clearing. If she did, she would change her mind about leaving.

When she arrived in the clearing, the huge creature she had left there was gone. Instead, a young man paced before the large rock. Long, dark chestnut hair framed his chiseled face. His eyes were a vivid shade of gray-blue. The moonlight that managed to seep through the thick canopy above them enhanced his handsome features and Lilly thought she caught a glimpse of golden undertones in the man's hair and skin, though she couldn't be sure. He wore plain clothes: dark brown pants were tucked into boots of the same color and a beige shirt was tucked into the pants. A sheathed blade hung at his hip.

Lilly stopped at the sight of him and stared for a moment. He seemed familiar to her, yet she knew she had never seen him before. She would have remembered meeting someone like him. The man halted his pacing when he noticed her.

"Finally," he said, sounding very relieved. "What kept you?"

"Nothing kept me," she answered. "I packed as fast as I could. Where's Rohan?"

The man did not answer her. Instead, he turned away from her and let out a low whistle, which rang out over the clearing like a melodic foghorn. Lilly watched in disbelief as a tall, hairy creature appeared out of thin air and walked toward the man, his furry hand extended in welcome. This creature stood at least ten feet tall and it was covered in shaggy brown fur from head to toe. It had a friendly face and dark, gentle eyes. Its huge feet did not escape Lilly's attention, and she suddenly realized what the creature was.

The young man talked to the Sasquach in a low voice while Lilly tried to wrap her mind around the fact that Bigfoot was real, and then they both turned their attention to her. She waited as they finished speaking to each other, and when the creature motioned her toward them, she approached with caution.

"She knows the rules?" the Sasquach asked the man, who nodded.

"She knows enough," he replied, "and what she doesn't know, she will learn."

"Give her your instruction while I prepare for your passage." The Sasquach walked away from them to a deeper part of the forest. The young man returned to Lilly's side and looked her in the eyes, his expression serious.

"There are some things you must know before we go. Pay attention, for these things cannot be forgotten. First..."

"Wait," she interrupted. "I want you to answer my question first. Where is Rohan?"

The young man smiled and Lilly stared in wonder as his dark hair turned a sparkling silver color and his eyes turned hazel green. Wrinkles began to form on his smooth skin, which faded from bronze to frail white. Where the young man stood only moments before, an old man remained. "I *am* Rohan."

"What...how did you do that?"

"One of my magickal gifts," he said nonchalantly, his voice reflecting the same age his appearance did. "Now, listen carefully. We are about to pass through a doorway to my world. Things are very different there, but you needn't worry about that which you do not know. This identity was given to me by a powerful wizard named Gustave, so that I may use it to fulfill my destiny and continue his legacy. Many in my world know him well and he is renowned for scouring your world in search of special people and bringing them to our world to become apprentices. Since no one must know of your whereabouts, here or in my world, we will travel together...I, as Gustave, and you as Gustave's new apprentice.

"When we arrive, we will travel by foot to my former home. Before we arrive there, I will teach you some basic magickal protection, how to guard your mind from others and how to deflect unfriendly magick. But, that will come later. For now, you must think of a name for yourself, a name that will not give any indication of your true identity."

Silence ruled the clearing as they waited for their departure. The air that had merely been cool a few hours before was now bitterly cold. Lilly watched the clouds her breath produced as she tried to think of a new name for herself. Just two days ago she had been a normal fourteen-year-old girl. Now she was fifteen, pledged to a destiny she knew nothing about and headed into an uncertain future led by a magickal creature that gave the term "hiding in plain sight" a whole new meaning.

She was still lost in her thoughts when the Sasquach returned to the clearing. She picked up her bag and flung it over her shoulder. The Sasquach paused when it noticed Rohan, still disguised as Gustave, and smiled, causing the moustache-like hair around its mouth to lift, framing its teeth like hair frames a face. Lilly concealed her own smile, hoping it couldn't read her thoughts. The last thing she wanted to do was offend this creature.

"It is time," said the Sasquach.

It once again disappeared into the trees, leaving Lilly and Rohan to follow. At the edge of the clearing, Lilly couldn't help but look at it one last time. Although it was dark, she could see the faint hints of moonlight gleaming off the large rock that had become her private salvation. A smile tugged at her lips, though she did not know why. She thought she would feel sad leaving her family behind, and although she did feel a sense of heartache at the thought of leaving them without an explanation to her disappearance, a calming sensation washed over her, dulling the heartache before it started.

She fixed the image of her clearing firmly in her mind and turned away from it to face the destiny that awaited her. Her mind raced as she trekked through the thickening forest toward the others, thoughts of her father and sister coming home to find her gone. She wished she could explain where she was going, *why* she was going, but she knew she never could. Without warning, a single thought of Adrian entered her mind. She wondered if he felt the same mixture of happiness and grief that she felt now, leaving behind all others to begin a new journey, *her* journey. *Maybe*, she thought, *I'll find the answer to that question, too.*

Rohan and the Sasquach were waiting patiently for her to catch up to them. When she did, the Sasquach raised its arms above its head, pushing its palms together, and brought them down as though it were praying. As Lilly observed the strange creature's actions, she noticed that a white glow was radiating from its clasped hands. Without a word, the beast opened its hands, cupping a small ball of white light. The orb grew in its hands until it was the size of a basketball, and it glowed brighter as it increased in size.

Suddenly, the glowing ball jumped from the creature's hands as though it had a life of its own. It spun wildly, rotating so fast Lilly thought it would spin into oblivion. It continued to grow as it changed the direction of its spin from constant revolutions to a swirling pattern. It started to flatten and in a matter of seconds, there was a vortex of translucent silver swirling before them. The trees around them were illuminated by the remarkable display, bathing in the brilliant light.

The Sasquach moved to the side and Rohan stepped forward. The silver hair that decorated his head glowed bright white as he stood before the doorway. He held his hand out to Lilly, who was rooted where she stood. Her mouth was agape with wonder, her eyes as large as saucers.

"Come," said Rohan, his voice soft in the presence of the passageway. "It's time to go."

Lilly stepped toward him and took his hand. She glanced back at the Sasquach, who smiled again and nodded at her. She smiled in return, and then faced the swirling wall of light. Her fate lay just beyond it. Rohan squeezed her hand gently.

"Once we step through the doorway, there is no turning back. Are you certain of this?"

"Do I have a choice?"

"You always have a choice. Sometimes it is the only thing you have."

Lilly pondered his words. This was it. If she walked through that doorway, she would be leaving this life behind her. If she didn't, she would continue to live as she had up to this moment. The thought of leaving frightened her a little, with so much uncertainty in her path, but the thought of staying frightened her even more. If she stayed, she was certain that she would continue to feel lost, like she didn't belong. Somehow she knew she belonged on the other side of that doorway. She turned to Rohan and grinned.

"Let's go."

Rohan stepped forward into the swirling mass and disappeared from her sight. She turned one last time to look at the Sasquach. It smiled again, its eyes shining with hope.

"This is the life you have chosen," it said to her, its deep voice rumbling with pride. "Live well, choose wisely, and take care to keep that which you love close to your heart. Only then will the outcome of your life, and the lives of countless others, be bright. Go now. He waits for you on the other side."

The Sasquach placed a hairy hand on her shoulder and pushed her gently toward the doorway. As she walked into the vortex, she felt uplifted, like everything wrong with the world was being washed away. She closed her eyes as the brilliant light surrounded her. Confidence replaced the grief she felt at leaving behind her family and a great feeling of adventure inoculated her senses, filling her with the promise that finally, she would feel like she was truly meant for something significant.

The Mysteries of Magick

Lilly awoke the next morning feeling more refreshed and more vibrant than she ever felt before. She had never had such an amazing dream. She stretched in a long, drawn-out movement, yawning as she opened her eyes, and it was then that she realized she had not been dreaming at all. Her amazing journey into a new and fantastic world had actually happened. She smiled and snuggled deeper into the blanket she had cocooned herself in before falling asleep.

When they arrived the night before, she and Rohan had trekked a good mile in complete darkness and complete silence. He'd said nothing until it was time to stop for the night. As he set up camp, complete with a tent furnished with pillows and blankets, and then started a fire by which they ate a quick meal of fruit and biscuits, he informed Lilly of the next day's plans.

They were going to walk, stop for lunch, and walk again until it was time to stop for the night. Along the way, he said he would start teaching her the basics her future training would be built around. This intrigued Lilly. She couldn't wait to have some of her many questions answered. She wanted those answers immediately, but she knew Rohan was tired. Disguised as an old man, his fatigue was apparent in everything from his eyes to the way he hunched as he sat. She wondered if being disguised as an old man inflicted the same physical ailments of someone who was actually that age. She added that question to her ever-growing list.

They had gone to bed shortly thereafter, and while Rohan fell asleep immediately, Lilly lay awake, her excitement building a wall to prohibit sleep from entering. She did sleep eventually, and although she had only slept a mere four hours, she now lay fully awake and ready to start the day, no matter how much walking was involved.

She listened to Rohan's even breathing for a while, just happy to feel so awake and alive. When he started snoring, she decided to leave the tent and explore the new world around them. She scrambled out of her blankets, ran her hairbrush quickly through her hair and grabbed her coat before crawling through the heavy cloth door.

The shock of the cool air stole her breath and she slipped her jacket over her bare arms. She was still wearing the same clothes she'd had on the day before, shoes and all. It surprised her that it was so chilly. The tent had been so warm, she was sure it would be a warm day. In spite of the chill, however, the day still proved to be beautiful. Keeping the tent in her sight, Lilly began her exploration, taking in the smallest details of the forest that surrounded them.

They were in a clearing; not a large one, though larger than the one she had left behind. The trees that circled the clearing were colossal. She examined the intricate grooves winding their way through the bark, the brilliance of the leaves' green hue, the way the limbs reached far out over the clearing, each one an arm waving at the rising suns. She studied a trail of black ants marching in formation down the trees, carrying their treasures triumphantly toward home.

She closed her eyes and let the sounds of the forest surround her. The leaves rustled ever so slightly in the breeze. Birds sang their morning praises, chirping happily as they danced across the clearing floor and found breakfast. In the distance, Lilly could hear the murmur of a stream trickling its way along its path. She inhaled deeply. Although the chill in the air and the tint of changing colors on some trees disagreed, Lilly thought it smelled like spring.

When Rohan exited the tent, the first thing he saw was Lilly standing at the edge of the clearing with her eyes closed and a silly grin on her face. He smiled, relieved that she had already discovered the beauty of his world. He knew before long she would be fighting to save it and he knew that it would be such a daunting undertaking, she would have to be reminded of what she was fighting for. Though he had not misled her about the future, he knew she had no clue what she had committed herself to. For the moment, he was content that she seemed happy with her decision.

He raised his right hand and held it in front of his face, his palm facing outward toward the tent, and made a single wiping motion. His hand glowed as tendrils of swirling metallic green extended toward the tent. As he closed his fingers into a ball, their camp disappeared with the tendrils, leaving only Lilly's travel bag and a pack of his own. Lilly opened her eyes in time to see the tent and the fading strands of magick disappear as Rohan stood before it.

She had not asked him the night before where their tent and bedding had come from; she had been grateful just to have it. Now she knew. Magick had made it happen. They sat around the remnants of their fire as they ate bread and apples. Rohan stood as he finished and made the evidence of their stay vanish.

"Come on," he said, heaving his bag over his shoulder, "we have a lot of ground to cover today." Lilly tossed the remains of her apple into the forest and grabbed her own pack, then followed him into the deeper areas of the forest.

They had been walking for about an hour when he spoke again. Lilly had been as patient as possible, waiting for him to say something, anything. She had been looking forward to their walk that day, but in the deep parts of the forest, the scenery was always the same. Trees, flowers, grass, moss; all the typical forest ornaments. Beautiful thought it was, she bored quickly as the pack she carried grew heavier with each passing minute. A conversation, at least, would take her mind from the boredom. When he spoke, Lilly thought that finally, her training would begin. He had said that he was going to teach her the basics, whatever *those* were, to give her a foundation to build upon, but his words were sporadic, obscure, even pointless, or at least she thought so at the time.

"You are no longer Lilias," he told her. "You are, and always will be, the person you have become, but your name does not determine who you are. It does not rule you. Only your true name does that, and Lilias is not your true name. Neither will be the name you choose to be known as here. You must think hard on it, for from the time you decide what it will be, that will be who everyone here believes you are, and for them to believe it, you must also believe it. Think on it." And that was all he said to her.

She waited for him to say something else, but he seemed to withdraw into the melancholy state he'd maintained since they had arrived. She'd noticed that he seemed disquieted before, but his behavior was nothing like it had been before they crossed through the doorway. *I couldn't get him to leave me alone there,* she thought disparagingly. *Now I can't get him to talk to me at all.* She frowned at the mystery of his attitude. Rohan, it seemed, had his own set of issues to sort out.

"What is my true name?" she dared to ask him.

"That is one of the countless things you must discover for yourself."

"I thought you were going to teach me the basics," she muttered, perturbed by his lack of interest in her future training, the training he was so keen on only yesterday.

"I am," he replied, "but you must have patience. You have a great deal to learn and a very short time in which to learn it."

"So teach me something!" Her patience was at odds with her curiosity, and her curiosity was winning. "What does it matter about my name? A name is nothing important. You said you were going to teach me about magick."

"And I will," he sighed, feeling the age of the old man he pretended to be. "Before I can, however, you must learn to be patient and you must learn to make wise decisions." He stopped walking and found a fallen log, then lowered himself onto it and motioned her to sit beside him. She complied, frustration blaring from her eyes. "A name is nothing important, you say? Have you considered that every name in the world, in any world, has a meaning behind it, not only to the one who gives the name, but also the one who accepts it? The name Regina, for instance, was once a word for queen. Honoring your daughter with a name like that, knowing the meaning behind it and teaching her the meaning behind it sets her on her path of which two outcomes are possible. The first path ends in greatness; the second, insignificance."

"Why insignificance?" Lilly was intrigued with the depth of this seemingly simplistic thing.

"A person does one of two things with the meaning of his or her name. He either honors it and reflects in himself the person his name identifies him as, or he dishonors it and reflects the opposite. And when your name means something *you* think may be evil, or wrong, dishonor is not such a bad thing."

Gustave's wisdom shone bright through Rohan's disguised eyes. Lilly met his eyes with her own as understanding crept into her mind. Struck by the realization that this was indeed an important lesson, she began to think about her own name. Other than life, it was the only thing her mother had ever given her and she found herself resisting the change.

"What does Rohan mean?" she asked, trying to clear her mind of her mother.

"It means *ascending*." A smile played at the corners of his mouth as he remembered his mother's sense of humor. She had named him Rohan Athanase; together, his full name meant *eternally ascending*. Of course, being a unicorn, she could see the future of her unborn child. She claims she had chosen Athanase before she ever had her first vision, but the sight of her toddling son flying throughout the house, going as high as he could, provoked the name Rohan in her mind. She'd seen that vision of him the same day his father had died, just days before he was born. He shook the thought from his head.

"Think on it as we walk," he told Lilly, regaining his stature. "We have much ground to cover. If we make haste, we could be there tonight."

They continued their trek deeper into the forest. Both of them were ready to stop, but the incentive of a real bed and a hot meal drove them to take another step. Lilly felt her load growing heavy again; her legs screamed their opposition as she forced them forward, one step, then another, then another. She tried to focus on possible names for herself, something different than what her name was now, something that would shield her from being discovered by the enemy, whoever *that* was. Despite her effort, she felt she could not forsake the only legacy her mother had left her.

She tried to focus on other names, but the letters of her name floated around in her head, colliding with other possibilities and shoving them from her consciousness. *Lilias Hope.* She knew that her middle name meant hope, or trust, but her first name, she was unsure.

The feeling she was having over her name changing was playing at her mood. She'd wanted to start learning magick; now she was stuck on this problem. *How can I be the Chosen One,* she thought, *if I don't have enough strength to give up my name?* But she knew why she was having so much trouble and she didn't know how to do what was expected of her without making a deeply emotional sacrifice.

Her thoughts drifted from her name to her mother. She wished she had even a single memory of her. Her mother had disappeared from the hospital right after she was born. From the stories her father had told her, she was born early, and because of her size, she was immediately rushed from the room to the newborn intensive care unit. Her father had gone as well, wanting, in his words, to ensure that the doctors were doing their jobs. According to him, when she started showing improvement, he returned to her mother's room to find only a note: *Take care of our daughter, Lilias Hope.* That was all it said. There was no explanation, no reason why she left. Lilly felt a pang of sadness wash over her as the world in front of her dissolved into the surroundings of a hospital.

The walls were a beige tone that covered everything from floor to ceiling. Lilly stared, amazed, and began to walk down the long corridor. Most of the wooden doors were shut, though a few were open. Ahead of her, a team of doctors rushed through a door and flew down the hallway, leading a small incubator with a tiny baby inside. Right behind them, her young father followed, fear on his face. Lilly approached cautiously, unsure of what she was about to see, but entered the room anyway.

A young woman Lilly knew was her mother sat on the bed while a nurse busied herself with her care. She laid back, exhausted after the labors of childbirth, and then sprung up again, nearly knocking the nurse off her stool.

"Go," said her mother. The nurse gave her a puzzled look, but did not leave until she yelled, "Get out!" Scurrying from the room, the petrified nurse closed the door behind her. Her mother sighed and relaxed for a moment before standing and slipping her coat over her hospital gown. She winced and clutched her stomach, then let out a low moan and breathed through the pain. After another moment, she found a pen and some paper and wrote her rushed note, placing it on the pillow before fleeing the room.

Lilly read the note and whirled around to follow her mother, but as she went through the door, the scenery around her faded into a thick forest where a confused old man stared at her.

"Are you alright?" he asked her, eyeing her with suspicion. He had a feeling that she had just experienced what was called a memory quest, and if she had, then time was of more importance than he thought. Her powers were already beyond her control. If this were true, he had to get her to their destination as soon as possible.

Lilly didn't answer his question. The vision she had just witnessed played in her mind again. She had seen things that her father had not told her, but more than that, the note her mother had written in her vision did not read *Lilias Hope*. It read *Sophia Elli*.

Why is it different? she wondered, trying to produce the vision again. She knew the real note her mother had written had said *Lilias Hope*. She'd seen it many times in the baby book her father had started for her; the penmanship beautiful despite the shaky hand that had written it. So what was the connection? Why, in this vision, was this one fact altered? And why couldn't she follow her mother through the door? Why did it bring her back so soon? She wanted to see more. She had to find out the truth about her mother's disappearance. She tried again, but for all her effort, she could not get the vision back.

She knew Rohan was speaking to her, but his words made no sense. Her head began to feel as though someone had emptied it of all it contained and filled it with helium. The dizziness spread to her vision, which began to blur. She watched the figure of the old man before her fade in and out. *He's playing a trick*, she thought, but his image began to sway. Nausea rooted itself in her stomach and she felt herself falling. She tried to stop herself, but her arms had abandoned her. She had no strength left.

It seemed she would fall for an eternity; the ground beneath her feet was so far away. The last thing she remembered seeing before the world went dark was the white hair of the man called Gustave flying violently around his head as he rushed toward her.

Rohan sat on the packed dirt that made the forest floor. Lilly was lying on the ground beside him, still unconscious. It had been over two hours since she had passed out, and now, endless thoughts collided in his mind as he tried to decide the best course of action. If they continued walking, it could be up to two more days before they arrived. Her strength, or lack thereof, would hinder them to the highest degree. If he decided to fly them there, he would risk giving away the anonymity he knew was vital to her safety, but they would arrive by nightfall.

She began twitching in her comatose state, a sign that strength was returning to her body. He sighed in relief, knowing that she would awaken within the hour. The suns were high in the sky, casting vibrant rays through the canopy above them. While time was of the essence, Rohan knew what he had to do. The risk involved bombarded his senses, but he fought his intuition and stood.

He closed his eyes, trying to sense if there was any danger near, any indication that he would be seen. Deciding it was safe, he opened his eyes and felt the power flow through him, surging through his blood as he pushed off the ground with his feet. His body hovered over their resting spot as a blinding white light emanated from him. The old man, complete with his staff, disappeared in the glow and was replaced with the body of a young man.

The young man who lowered himself to the ground was a sight that would stop any passerby in his tracks. He was tall and thin, yet very strong. The sunlight that managed to find him struck his golden skin and danced its way across his muscular chest. His blonde hair fell to his shoulders in soft curls and gave him the appearance of a Greek god. His eyes were brown, deep and intense, and he wore only pants and boots, the reason for his apparel obvious. No shirt would cover the huge black wings that protruded from his equally toned back.

He resumed his position on the ground beside Lilly and waited, mustering his patience from the depths of his core. It was hard to stay calm when things went so unexpectedly wrong. Her twitching was becoming more frequent, and more violent, but she was still not awake.

She had a memory quest, Rohan thought, amazed that she could even call upon one. *She's more powerful than I thought*. It was this realization that soothed the fears he'd stewed over all day, and since he began implementing his plan to bring her here, he finally felt he'd made the right decision by bringing her early. He expelled a sigh of relief.. *She is ready.*

Lilly's head was pounding when she began coming around, throbbing incessantly to the rhythm of her heartbeat. When she opened her eyes, she was relieved to find herself protected from the bright suns, although the shaded area was still more than she could handle. She suddenly regretted leaving behind her sunglasses. She pulled herself into a sitting position and looked around. She was alone.

Before she could gather enough strength to call out to Gustave, an angel appeared from the forest carrying some odd-shaped fruit. He tossed her one of the orbs and she caught it, her lightning-quick reflexes surprising her. The fruit was perfectly round, much like an orange in shape and size, but its outer skin was more like an apple, and it was purple, as was the stem atop it. She studied the fruit, then the winged-man who had tossed it to her.

"Rohan?" she asked, her voice no more than a whisper.

"It's still me," Rohan replied, sitting on the ground beside her. "How are you feeling?"

Lilly felt like she'd been dropped from a very tall tree and hit every branch on the way to the ground. "Terrible," she muttered, still unsure of the food she was holding. "What happened?"

"You went on a memory quest," he told her, then added, "*alone.*" He bit into the fruit he was holding with great delight, allowing the excessive juice to dribble down his chin. Lilly took note of the soft pink flesh it contained and wondered what this strange new fruit tasted like. She's never been one of those people who liked to eat exotic food and she rarely tried new types of food at all. Her father had told her once that she was the most finicky eater he'd ever seen.

"Eat," Rohan commanded, sinking his teeth into his juicy treasure. "You need to regain your strength."

She cautiously took a small bite and was pleased to find that it was very similar to a plum. The juice trickled down her throat like sweet breath, awakening her senses instantly. She took another bite, savoring the sugary tissue. Many plums she had eaten were tangy, but this fruit was as sweet as if it had been formed from pure sugar cane. As she ate, the pounding in her head dissipated to a dull thump, still keeping time with her erratic heartbeat.

"What is this called?" she asked, devouring its remains.

"It's a kilpa. They are well-known for restoring strength, among other things." The smile on his face made her wonder what else the kilpa was known for. His mood had improved since her episode. *Maybe,* she thought, *his moods changes with his appearances.* She had no way of knowing that his earlier despondence centered around his own self-doubt.

"So what *exactly* is a memory quest?" she asked Rohan, who was finishing his second kilpa.

"A memory quest," he replied, "is a journey into your past, one in which you literally return to the memory as an omnipotent bystander. You can use them to view your past memories to discover things you don't recall. Any event you have ever witnessed or experienced is recorded in your mind, whether you consciously remember it or not. It is how I reminded you of our last day together."

Lilly was silent, letting the information sink in. She had been present for her own birth, obviously, but she had been removed from the room the moment she was born. Why, then, did she witness what her mother had gone through?

"What did you see?" Rohan asked her, curious about this girl he'd observed over the course of her life, but had never really gotten to know. He knew that everything happened for a reason and he wanted to know why this had happened with no warning to someone with no magickal training.

"I saw my mother running away from the hospital room after I was born. I tried to follow her out the door, but it brought me back here." Lilly felt uneasy telling him about her mother, but after this phenomenon had taken her, she felt she had no choice but to tell him anything he asked. She was on unfamiliar ground with both the magick and the world she had entered. Keeping things a secret would only cause him to distrust her and if he didn't trust her, he would never answer her multitude of questions. Besides, he might understand what she had seen better than she did.

Rohan's expression had changed dramatically. He was no longer smiling; instead, concern radiated from his eyes and his brows were lifted high into his hairline...shock. Thoughts flew through his head as he tried to sort out the events.

It's not possible, he thought. She couldn't have seen the memories of another person unless she'd called forth a vision quest, something that no human being in the history of magick had ever done for the first time alone. Those who had attempted it either went mad or died from the aftereffects. *How,* he wondered, *could she go on a vision quest, alone and with no magickal assistance, yet suffer so little from it?*

He threw the pit of his barren kilpa on the ground and stood, his body now rigid with urgency. This was too much for him. He had to get her hidden now. If she was discovered before she was trained, it would be the end of *both* of their destinies.

"We have to go," he told her, his voice sharp, "and we have to go *now*. Can you stand?"

Lilly struggled to stand and succeeded after two failed attempts. She was fully alert, but her lack of strength shocked her. Her whole body trembling, she took a step toward Rohan and fell into him. She was trying with everything she had in her, but he knew she needed more rest before they could go anywhere.

"Sit back down," he commanded, and she sat, the hard pounding returning to her sore head.

"Why am I so weak?" she asked Rohan, who was kneeling in front of her. He made himself comfortable and instructed her to eat another kilpa.

"There are three types of magick," he began. "The most common for humans is fundamental magick. It is based on using objects or tools to aid in the centering of the magickal energy. Tools like wands, athames, charms, brooms, staves and even chalices direct the magick being used. They are usually decorated with crystals and while you may think they are merely decorative, the crystals are used to contain added energy to make the magick stronger. Potions and spells also fall into this type. Anyone can attempt to practice this type of magick, but having natural talent makes it stronger.

"Elemental magick is based solely on the elements: earth, air, fire and water. Timing is essential for certain uses. This magick is always stronger during the turning of the seasons, celestial events and the positions of the suns, planets and stars, and phases of the moon. It's very strong during ritualistic holidays, as well, which are typically celebrated by magickal creatures and humans alike. The natural talents of magickal creatures, and humans with innate natural abilities, fall into this category. Elemental magick, as a whole, is the most common form of magick."

Lilly sat wide-eyed, listening to his words, absorbing everything he was saying. *What type of magick happened to me?* she wondered, but she dared not ask him a single question until he had finished. She didn't want to distract him from her very first lesson and if she waited, that question could soon be answered. Rohan sighed, out of frustration or exhaustion, Lilly didn't know. He remained silent, as if this next type of magick deserved a moment of quiet reflection.

"The third type of magick," he continued, "is true magick. This type of magick is unlike any other. It can do anything you desire, but the outcome always has a cost. Magick of any kind requires energy, but while the other two types use the energy of items or nature as well as your own, true magick draws only on your own inner strength. If you try to use it for something you aren't strong enough for, it could have irreversible effects. It could drain you of all your energy. If it takes too much, it could kill you. If you lose control of it, it could kill someone else. It's astonishing and perilous, and very few creatures use it. Humans shouldn't use it at all. It's too dangerous.

"You have more natural ability than I've ever known of in a human, and your strength is...unbelievable, but you have little control. It's a dangerous combination because you are using the magick subconsciously. We have to get you to a safe place where you can start your training as soon as possible, before it happens again and you end up killing yourself."

The overload of information held Lilly's tongue. She had questions, but she was unsure of how much more information she could handle at that moment. She never imagined that using magick could actually kill her, and knowing that she could use it without even trying frightened her. What was to stop her from doing it again? She looked at Rohan and knew without a doubt that he was right. She had to start getting trained immediately, before any more damage was done. She'd been there for one day and she had already almost killed herself.

Rohan stood and held his hands out to her for support. She took his hands and pulled herself up. After eating the second kilpa, she felt almost normal again. Her headache was nearly gone, although the pain was replaced with a mixture of wonder and fright. She let go of Rohan's hands and stood for a moment, testing her strength. Sure she wouldn't fall this time, she took a few tentative steps. Her knees were weak, but held her in place. Rohan smiled and picked up her bag.

"Come on," he prompted. "We'll walk for a while." He eyed her warily, then added, "Just keep your emotions in check. Until you learn to manage your power, they will control it."

So continued their trek. They were both silent, each lost in their own thoughts. Lilly went over the different types of magick in her head, trying to retain everything Rohan had told her. She had a feeling that her training would be more difficult than she had anticipated, but it was too late to change her mind about her decision to follow him through that doorway, not that she really wanted to. She didn't allow herself to think about her family at all, but despite her efforts, she couldn't help remembering the discrepancy in her own memories and the one she had witnessed hours before.

While she focused on the puzzling events, Rohan's own mind was reeling. He never imagined she was this powerful, though he knew he should have. After all, she *was* the Chosen One. He just hadn't expected her magickal abilities to take control over her so quickly. It was the one danger he hadn't anticipated. He knew that every magickal being, human or not, had a magickal signature and now that she had used magick, she could be easily sought by the enemy. He would never allow her to be taken; he'd fight to the death to save her from whatever happened. He could handle Kylenin, as his training was not yet complete, but he doubted he would be strong enough to equal Dagana's power, let alone defeat her.

As evening fell, his thoughts drifted to his mother and he felt his excitement building. He'd seen her a few years ago during one of his many trips between worlds, but he was in disguise and she had not noticed him, which was his goal at that time. Although he had originally wanted to keep his return a secret, he found himself pleased at the turn of events. Now, instead of hiding his return from his mother, he could walk through the doors of his childhood home and embrace the woman who gave him life.

They had been walking for quite some time, though they hadn't covered half as much ground as they could have. The loss of energy Lilly had suffered slowed their progress tremendously. She did not want to spend another night in a tent. She wanted a bed, a bath and a warm meal, and she dreaded the thought of having to walk even more tomorrow. Her mood sullen, her entire body fought her as she tried to keep moving. When Rohan stopped and dropped her bag on the ground, she didn't know whether to be happy for the rest or upset because they still had so far to go.

"Put this on your back," he told her, motioning to the bag he'd abandoned at his feet. "Make sure it is secure."

Lilly barely had the energy to lift the bag, but she managed to strap it to her back. *Surely he can't expect me to carry this* and *keep walking,* she thought, and voiced her concern to him.

"No," he told her, looking at the dark sky which was no longer obstructed from their view. The moon was nearly full, casting its glow upon them. Stars twinkled with delight in the ebony void, proving their brilliance to all who gazed upon them. "I'm going to carry you."

"No," Lilly objected. "You are tired. Let's just sleep and we'll get there tomorrow."

"At the pace we are keeping now, it will be days before we can walk there."

"Days!" Lilly felt objections rising in her and Rohan quickly calmed her.

"Don't get upset," he told her, worried that her surge of emotion would provoke another magickal onset. "We're going to fly, or rather, I'm going to fly us there."

Flying had never occurred to Lilly, and she felt foolish that it hadn't considering he did have wings now. He'd said before that flying would expose them, yet he had reconsidered. She realized how much her display of uncontrollable power concerned him. He wrapped his arms around her, and she put her arms around his neck, careful to avoid his large wings. She wondered if he would have enough strength to lift her and the added weight of her bag. Rohan looked into her eyes and smiled, sending shivers of excitement down her spine.

"Don't let go," he whispered as he spread his beautiful wings. Their span was incredible, nearly twenty feet, she guessed, and as he lifted himself into the air, she clutched him tighter, willing herself enough strength to follow his command. As they rose, she felt his strength. The muscles in his chest and shoulders flexed with every flap of his wings, the rush of wind they created flowing over her interlaced fingers and down his spine.

He flew over the trees, slowly at first, giving her the opportunity to get used to his movements, and then, with incredible speed, he shot forward in a burst of momentum. High above the glade they had been walking through, Lilly could see how far the vast forest really expanded. Everything below them was blanketed in trees. Far in the distance to her right, she saw a large clearing with a river running through it, a great lake formed at its end.

They flew swiftly, covering the distance with unimaginable speed. She felt herself relax and gripped her hands together, determined to hold on, but she felt safe nonetheless. Deep within her, she could feel that he would do anything to protect her from harm. For the first time since she could even remember, she felt free, and she didn't want to lose that feeling. The desire to fly like this forever was now ingrained within her.

The flight didn't last as long as she would have liked. Rohan landed in the forest and for a moment, she wondered if he was just stopping to rest. When they were safely on the ground, he released his grip on her and took the bag from her back. As she let her eyes readjust to the darkness of the covered forest, she noticed a house just beyond the trees.

The house was a stone cottage. Its granite exterior had been formed by a master, strong and sturdy despite the materials it was constructed from. A stone walkway led to a thick door at the front of the house. The facing windows, ablaze the light, cast a warm glow over the ground beneath them. Smoke rose from the chimney, masking the black lace of the trees against the moonlit sky. *It's like a greeting card,* thought Lilly, and she shivered, aware of how cold it really was. Flying had heightened her senses and her increased adrenaline had warmed her blood, but the chill in the air struck her exposed skin, causing gooseflesh to rise over it.

"Come on," said Rohan, his excitement threatening to burst him from the inside out. He took her hand and together they followed the walkway to the door. Rohan's hand was shaking as he lifted it to knock, but before his hand touched the door, it swung open.

A beautiful woman stood before them, a subtle glittering over her skin in the soft light, the same shimmer in the golden hair flowing down her back. Tears brimmed in her eyes as she stared at them. She embraced Rohan as the tears fell and whispered, "Welcome home, my son."

Things Have Changed Since You Left

Lilly relaxed in a large, high-backed chair covered in red velvet, a pillow behind her head. The room was as big as her school's library and contained as many books, if not more, which lined the shelves running the length of the walls. Among them were titles such as *Common Practices of Fundamental Magick, Curing Magickal Ailments and Mysterious Maladies,* and *The Creation of the World: as Told by the Creators,* along with a vast array of others. She let her eyes wander from title to title, taking in the ornate decoration of each book's binding.

Rohan, no longer "wearing" his wings, was sitting in a chair opposite hers, quietly taking in the differences of his home. The library had grown ten-fold since he had left fifteen years before. His mother, it seemed, had spent those years gathering its now overwhelming collection of books. The size of the room had increased tremendously to hold the new additions. Tables and chairs had been added, as well as a desk. He wondered what other changes had befallen his home in his absence.

Candles sat atop the tables nearest to them, their wax traveling lazily down the sticks and landing within the confines of the sconces that contained them. Haunting music echoed softly through the room, the chanting a welcome break in the silence of the new arrivals. The drumming alone was enough to sooth anyone, but the ethereal voice was hypnotic. Lilly was taken in by the intoxicating voice of the woman singing to the rhythm of the beats. Her eyelids were heavy and she felt she could drift off to sleep and stay so for years.

Ashya entered the room carrying two steaming mugs, her eyes still glimmering with tears of joy. Rohan observed that she had not aged a bit in the years he'd been gone. Her hair had grown, now reaching to the bend in her knees, but aside from that, not a single hint of time passing was apparent. In her human form, she looked to be in her thirties, and certainly not old enough to have a son of twenty-two. She handed Lilly one of the mugs and Rohan, the other. Then she gathered her robes from behind her waist and pulled them forward to sit in a third chair that completed a circle around a small, round end table.

"The last time I saw Rohan," she told Lilly, "he was only seven. I've been dreaming of his return ever since and now, here he is, home at last." Her jubilation shone through her radiant blue eyes. Rohan smiled at her, his face flushing with a hint of embarrassment at his mother's attention.

Lilly smiled as well, feeling a strange sense of calm in the unfamiliarity around her. This mother's love for her son was so apparent, so real, that for a moment, thoughts of her own mother flittered through her mind. Did her own mother feel this way about her, despite the fact she had left her behind without looking back? Thinking about her mother brought the same dizziness to her again, the same pounding to her head. The room before her was beginning to fade and she shut her eyes, willing herself to remain where she was, hoping that she had enough control to avoid getting swept up in this powerful force inside her. She remained still, afraid that if she opened her eyes, she would find herself caught up in another memory, something she knew she didn't want.

She felt the throbbing in her head subside and opened her eyes. Ashya and Rohan were watching her curiously, though she noticed that in Rohan's eyes, there was fear as well. Ashya just watched her, a calm look on her face, as though what Lilly was going through was perfectly natural.

"Are you alright?" Rohan asked her, trying to hide the worry in his voice.

"I think so," Lilly replied, exhaling a long sigh and sinking back into her chair. She picked up the mug of warm fluid she had abandoned on the table and took a sip. The warm liquid trickled down her throat, warming her insides. It was slightly sweet, but had an odd bitterness to it. *I wonder what this is…*

"It is amstrung root tea," Ashya interrupted her thoughts. The surprised look on Lilly's face caused an uproar of laughter from Rohan. Ashya rolled her eyes at him and said, "Don't worry, child. It's discerning for newcomers who don't know the ways of magickal gifts. I don't know if Rohan has informed you about me, but I am a unicorn, an Elemental Child bestowed with the gifts of telepathy, teleproropathy, and telekinesis per vicus." Noticing the confused look on her guest's face, she continued with an explanation. "It means that my natural-born gifts are the abilities to communicate with my mind, to search the minds of others, which is also known as mind prowling, and to move objects or people through time."

"She can also see the future," Rohan added.

"Really?" Lilly asked with wonder.

Why did you tell her that? Ashya asked Rohan with her mind. *That's not true.*

It is true, he insisted, *just not entirely true.*

Lilly watched them interact with great interest. She smiled as they argued in their minds, wondering if she should tell Ashya that she knew what they were saying.

"How is it partial truth?" she asked after Rohan's final remark. Ashya and Rohan both stared at her. This time, Rohan's laugh was directed at his mother. He found her surprise comforting and conceded the argument. She had definitely *not* foreseen how powerful this chosen child really was.

"You can hear us?" Ashya asked Lilly, her attention now undivided.

"Yes," Lilly replied. "So you can't see the future?"

"Well," Ashya sighed, "I can see possible future events, but the future has yet to be written. It is constantly changing. Foresight is never exact, for any decision that is made can alter the course of those same future events. Not to mention that knowledge of the future inevitably changes it. If one knows something bad is going to happen and takes steps to avoid it, every event thereafter is altered." Fascinated, Lilly listened to her explanation. Her fatigue waned as the collection of information inside her head grew with every new fragment of knowledge she gained. She hoped they would stay here for a while so she could have a chance to read some of the books in this amazing assortment.

"Come now," said Ashya, rising from her chair, "let's get you settled into a bed. I know you must both be very tired." Rohan started to protest, but Ashya stopped him before he could utter a single word. "I know we have many things to talk about and we will, but now is not the time. The child needs to be rested before I can determine the course of her training and you need to be rested before you continue on the rest of your journey." She walked from the room, leaving Lilly curious about what journey Rohan would be going on and Rohan wondering how much his mother knew about the next course of his plans.

At least one thing hasn't changed, thought Rohan as Ashya led them through the entryway of the house, the hat stand and ancient grandfather clock still the only furniture in the room. She led them to Rohan's room, which had remained untouched in his absence. He smiled as he noticed the stardust violets in the corners; they had grown nearly four times larger than they had been when he left, proudly glorifying their beauty as they sparkled like the night sky. Lilly thought the room suited him well; she could picture him as a child, playing with the collection of stones arranged neatly on the shelves, yet it was just as fitting for the young man he had become.

"Goodnight, my son," said Ashya as she kissed his forehead, and then she led Lilly to another room. This room was large. Centered against the longest wall was a huge bed, a canopy of sheer white material over the top. The room was almost the same lavender color her bedroom had been; the carpeting a smoky gray. Ashya went to the only other door in the room and opened it, removing a satin nightgown and handing it to Lilly.

"This should suffice, unless you brought nightclothes with you." Lilly had brought some, but the gown Ashya held out to her was much more appealing. She took it, muttering a "thank you" under her breath. Ashya smiled at her. "My son is mysterious. He is very gifted in magick, as you must know by now. Even now he maintains his disguise."

Lilly didn't quite know how to respond to Ashya, so she stayed quiet and let her speak. "He has much fear, but I am very relieved he has returned. Perhaps his time at home will comfort him enough to reveal his true self again." She moved toward Lilly and kissed her on the forehead as well, as though it were a custom, no matter the relation. "Goodnight, child," she whispered as she left Lilly alone in the room.

What does she mean, Lilly wondered, *reveal his true self?* Ashya had recognized him the moment she saw him. *Even now he maintains his disguise.* Her words and her actions didn't make sense to Lilly, but the bed was so inviting, she didn't linger over the mystery. She was beginning to understand exactly how different things were going to be. Ashya was stunned when Lilly had heard their inaudible discussion. She had never intended to hear the conversation, it just happened. If it hadn't happened on its own, she probably wouldn't have known they were having a conversation with their minds. Her magick was emerging, but her control was a major issue.

Lilly undressed and slipped the gown over her head. It fell to the floor around her feet, so close that only her toes could be seen. She crawled into the soft bed and pulled the covers tightly around her, cocooning herself in their protective warmth. She began to drift off, falling into the realm of dreams, the very place that harbored her subconscious. Images flashed through her mind at warp speed, disappearing as quickly as they appeared in continuous succession. They began to slow until at last, they became clear. She saw her father replacing the photo in the empty frame she'd returned to the wall in the hallway. She saw Adrian giving her the little blue tee shirt on the last day she had seen him before he disappeared from her life. The images faded into an empty darkness. It was in this darkness that she found Beth calling to her.

Rohan sat at the ashy gray terrabok table and gazed around the room. In the past fifteen years, his mother had expanded the size of the house to make room for the library downstairs, and upstairs, she had used the extra space to expand the atrium as well. Both had grown considerably, as had the variety and sizes of the plants housed in the atrium. It now looked like a small jungle. Ivy clung to the walls in the kitchen, having long since made its escape from the glass house. His mother's magickal ingredients were no longer sprouts; they had flourished and now bore even more magickal parts that could be used. A kilpa tree grew in a ceramic flower pot in the corner, building its strength to survive the cold seasons it would endure when it was planted outside.

Rohan frowned in distaste. He knew he shouldn't feel so disturbed by the changes, but he had not expected so much to be different. He wondered if the Enchantment Room had changed at all. He hadn't been able to see the changes in the dark when they had arrived, so he didn't know. He highly doubted, however, that his mother would ever change that room. It was already large enough to hold fifty people, including a giant or two, and it was built for one purpose: magick.

Rohan abandoned his survey of the room when his mother entered. He tried to hide his feelings from her, but he wasn't quick enough. She smiled and said nothing until she had finished pouring three glasses of juice, placing them on the table. When she sat, she took a sip of her juice and set it back on the table, smoothing her white robes over her lap.

"You don't approve," she stated.

"I'll get used to it," he told her. "It's just that so much has changed."

"More than you realize, my son," she said in a serious tone. "Dagana has cast darkness upon the magickal community. Even members of the Council are afraid to use powerful magick out of fear she will view them as a threat to whatever she has planned."

"Foolishness," he muttered. "Together they could easily overthrow her."

"Don't you think if Dagana could be overthrown it would have been done already?" Her unexpected outburst startled him. "Before you left, she was on the verge of a downfall. Since then, something has given her new motivation."

"Kylenin."

"Exactly. She wants to put him on the throne, and with her newfound motivation, she has found many ways over the years to gain power. She uses any means she can to obtain what she wants. She has found a way to track magickal signatures, something you already know, but she can see how powerful those signatures are and she views every powerful being as a potential ally or a threat. If you don't join her, you are a threat and she will destroy any threat in her path.

"We are in dark times, my son, darker than you realize." She frowned, her eyes sparkling with future knowledge she was not ready to share. "Dagana is already more powerful than most and very soon, she will rise again. She will form alliances with creatures of evil and she will start a war that will plague our world. It has already begun. You must take great care, Rohan. I fear for your safety."

"What about the humans?" asked Rohan. "How does she view them?"

"For now, she does not believe they are a threat. To her, humans are easily controlled, simple-minded creatures. She feels superior to them and sees them as nothing more than an annoyance."

"That's good."

"No," corrected Ashya. "When the war begins, if she cannot manipulate them, she will try to exterminate them."

"Are you sure?" Her face answered his question; she had glimpsed into the future and she had seen these unfortunate events as though they had already happened.

He drank his juice in silence, waiting for her to change the subject. She sipped her own, watching him in patient silence. When he realized she wasn't going to speak first, he sighed inwardly. As powerful as he was, he still paled his mother in comparison.

"When will you start training her?" he asked, steering the conversation to where he knew it would end up.

"When she is ready," was Ashya's short reply.

"She *is* ready, Mother," he spouted. "She is more powerful than even you have foreseen."

"That's quite obvious. She heard us talking last night. Did you know she was telepathic?"

Rohan shook his head. "She never showed any signs of magickal talent on Earth, and telepathy isn't the half of it." He recounted the events that had occurred since he and Lilly had passed through the doorway. She listened to his tale of the vision quest, his opinion about her control issues and his decision to get her here as quickly as possible.

"Have you even taken her on a vision quest before?" she asked when he finished. He shook his head.

"No, but I did take her on a memory quest right before we left, something she had forgotten that involved both of us."

"It's all the same magick, son." Ashya quietly reflected upon her son's story, trying to find a connection between the facts. The sound of Lilly's footsteps ascending the stairs floated to her ears and she stood as Lilly walked into the room.

"Good morning," she said, lowering herself into the empty chair. She was already dressed, her hair pulled into a sloppy ponytail. The necklace her father had given her was around her neck. She had decided that no matter what, she would not remove it. "Is this mine?" she asked, motioning to the third cup of juice on the table.

"Yes," said Rohan. He had hoped to have this conversation with his mother alone. She would figure it out and tell him, of course, but Lilly might not be ready for some of the facts. The last thing he wanted was for her to become frightened of the power she had and refuse to use it, or worse, decide to leave. He watched her drink her juice and noticed that despite everything so far, she was in good spirits.

"How are you feeling?" Ashya asked her.

"I feel fine. Great, in fact. Thank you."

"Good. We have many things to discuss and I want to get you started on your training as soon as possible, but first, we'll eat." She waved her hand and three plates of food appeared on the table. Hers contained a mixture of fruits and pancakes while Lilly's and Rohan's held eggs, sausage and pancakes. Lilly smiled, grateful to have food in front of her that she recognized. They ate in silence, each pondering their own thoughts. Lilly was excited to training, having feared her magickal mishap would make Ashya want to postpone it. Of course, she could always start in the library if that were to happen.

Rohan ate slowly, savoring the meal. His own worries played at his mind. He would be leaving in a matter of days to continue his path. No one else knew of his plans and his biggest fear was that his mother or Lilly would be able to read his thoughts, which would hinder any progress he hoped to obtain. Their ignorance of his plans was crucial to his long-term success, which was ultimately the common goal. He knew someday they would discover his deceptions; he just hoped they would understand that it was all for the good of their futures.

When the meal was over, Ashya led them to the Enchantment Room. Rohan noticed that there were indeed some subtle changes, but overall, it felt like home. Knowing he was leaving soon gave him a nauseating feeling of homesickness. While his mood grew sullen by his own right, Lilly's grew to elation. She had never in her life imagined such a wonderful room. Shelves lined the circular room in its entirety. On them were herbs, potions and ingredients for other useful concoctions. Stones and crystals were piled there as well, sorted by their different sizes and colors. Cauldrons, chalices and goblets of every shape and size were lined where they could be accessed easily. Athames, swords, wands and other, much more unique weapons, were either organized on the shelves or mounted on the walls in between, along with many other magickal tools and items which Lilly could think of no words to describe. The only decoration in the room was the floor, a symbol of elemental balance that made the floor itself, the same symbol around her neck. She absently reached for it.

Lilly stared in silent wonder, afraid to disturb the sanctity of the room. The vast array of tools and instruments intrigued her and she wondered when she would get to use them. It seemed Ashya had read her mind, for she walked to a shelf directly opposite the door and removed one of several wands, which she gave to Lilly.

The wand was wooden, made from the same dark gray wood in the kitchen. Grains swirled their way from the tip of the wand to its base, where it met its handle. The handle itself was white marble, with similar gray swirling through it. A pentacle was carved into the marble and was adorned with five small jewels. At the topmost part of the star was a white crystal, with a yellow, red, blue and green crystal located clockwise around the circle at each of the four remaining points. As Lilly held it in her hand, she felt the power it contained. She had no idea that this wand was not a source of power, but rather a conduit for her own.

"From what my son has informed me of already," began Ashya, "you will not require the use of a wand for your magick, but for now, it will help you to control your power. Until you gain control, you will use this to keep from hurting yourself."

"Or someone else," Rohan muttered under his breath. Ashya shot him a look that clearly indicated he should stay quiet. "I'll be outside when you are finished," he stated, and then left the room, leaving the women alone.

"What's wrong with him?" Lilly asked Ashya when he was gone. She'd noticed his moods fluctuating since they had first come, but she had yet to figure out why.

"He's worried we'll be angry with him when he leaves." Lilly felt her heart skip. *He's leaving?* She assumed he would be staying with her during the course of her training. *I wonder where he's going...*

"He has more work ahead of him," Ashya interrupted her thoughts. "There are many things that he knows must be done now that you have arrived, but do not worry. You will remain here for a while. I must determine the best way to train you, for everyone learns magick in their own way. Besides that, I have spent much time collecting the books you noticed last night. There is much for you to learn, and I have a feeling you can read them faster than I could teach them to you by mouth." She reached for a wooden box no larger than a shoebox and took out five black stones of equal symmetry, piling them on a round table in the center of the circular floor.

"Control," said Ashya, "is always an issue with young sorcerers and sorceresses, especially when natural power is prevalent." She walked around the table as she spoke. A single stone moved from the heap in the center of the table to the outermost edge, threatening to fall, but never doing so. "When dealing with natural ability, which you obviously have, mastering the art of magick is the easiest thing to learn. You simply call for something, and it is yours." She stopped walking and opened her hand in the same instant the stone on the table's edge flew into it. "And should you wish another..." A second stone shot into her left hand at the speed of sound.

"You can do more than just call things to you. If you no longer desire it, send it away." The stone from her left hand returned to its place on the table. She held the stone in her right hand out to Lilly. "This stone is nothing more than a stone. It is called many things in many languages, but it has a magickal name as well."

"What is its magickal name?" asked Lilly, taking the stone. A peculiar warmth emanated from it.

"Only it knows. You see, magickal names, which many refer to as *true* names, are given by magick itself and are told only to that which is being named. Knowing the true name of an object gives you complete control over it. Knowing the true names of people works in the same manner. The only way to learn the true name of something is for it to tell you. Stones cannot talk, therefore I do not know its true name, yet I do have control over it." She held out her empty palm and the stone Lilly was holding flew from her hand and landed in Ashya's open palm. It then lifted from her hand and hovered in the air before circling the room and landing next to the others on the table. "This is because I *know* the stone. It is the same inside and out and all the way through. It has no mind, no control over itself. It simply is, which is why I know I can control it. I have much more strength than a small stone. It also explains why stones and crystals can store and direct magickal energy, but that lesson is for later.

"I will teach you the basics of true magick, its rules and limitations, and what you'll need to know to have control over your power. Something you must remember is that true magick is only as limited as its user; the more powerful you are, the more you can do, but your power must be divided between what you are trying to do, the strength it takes to do it and the strength it takes to control it. If you put too much power into the magick you cast, you could lose control of it, or you could use too much of your strength and end up killing yourself. It takes as much strength to contain your power as it does to unleash it, and once it is unleashed, only the strongest being can retract it without dying as a result."

"What about the other types of magick?" asked Lilly, worried that she was getting in far too deep with this dangerous type. The others Rohan had described sounded far less perilous.

"Rohan told you humans shouldn't use true magick, didn't he?"

"Yes."

"He's right," Ashya told her, "but I think you need to learn what it entails so you'll know why it is so dangerous. You will study many things while we train, including some fundamental practices. When your training here is complete, you will train with others in the elementals. Don't worry, though. Once you master the basics, and after you gain control over your natural abilities, the rest will come to you with very little effort."

Lilly was skeptical. Despite her fears of not being strong enough to handle what faced her, Rohan hadn't mentioned once that she would be training with anyone else. Why hadn't he told her any of this?

Ashya gathered the five stones in her hands and positioned herself so she was facing Lilly. The table they had been resting on disappeared into thin air. "Take a stone," Ashya commanded. Lilly took the topmost stone and held it in her hand. This time, she felt no heat, just a cold stone. "Sit in the center of the circle and close your eyes. Focus only on that stone. Learn its symmetry, its weight, the way is feels in your hand. When you think you truly know it, set it on the floor in front of you and lift it without touching it."

Lilly sat in the center of the huge circle that was emblazoned on the floor. The stone in her hand was cool and smooth, a perfect circle. It wasn't heavy, but Lilly held it for a moment, getting used to the way it felt. She put the stone in front of her and focused on it, trying to lift it from the ground. Nothing happened. She tried again, but the stone remained motionless. She felt discouraged, but she refused to give up. On her third attempt, the stone moved an inch to her left.

"Clear your mind of everything but your desire to pick up the stone," Ashya instructed her. She walked the circle around Lilly, still holding the other stones, but never set foot inside it. Lilly closed her eyes and pictured the stone, letting everything else fade from her thoughts. She pushed aside her worries, her doubt, even her excitement about learning magick. She opened her palm and imagined the stone was in her hand. She felt its weight, its flawless shape. Lifting her empty palm, she felt the stone lift as well. She held it in place, contemplating what to do with it next.

Outside the circle, Ashya had stopped walking to observe Lilly's progress. The stone hovered in front of Lilly's face as if it had stopped believing in gravity. She was about to tell Lilly that was enough when the other stones suddenly escaped her grasp and flew toward Lilly's head. They all stopped within an inch of the stone Lilly had lifted and formed a circle around it. All five stones started spinning like a whirlwind, slowly at first, then faster, until they were nothing more than a black blur. Ashya prepared herself for the fact that Lilly might be losing control and lifted her hand to stop the incident, but what happened next ceased her action.

The stones stopped spinning and scattered throughout the circle on the floor, each stopping at a point on the star formed within it. Lilly stood and the stones rose in perfect unison to her movements. Ashya stared at her, astonished. No mortal in the history of magick had ever accomplished such a feat on their first attempt. Most couldn't even lift the stone. Yet this girl had figured out how to not only learn the object correctly, but how to use the knowledge to obtain complete control over it. A thought occurred to her and she decided to test her theory. If she was correct, then there was little time to teach the girl what she must, for the method of training she would require was unique, and could only be handled by Masters.

Lilly opened her eyes and saw the stones hovering over the five points of the star. Excitement flooded her senses, distracting her focus, and the stones fell toward the ground. She quickly recovered them, only seconds before they hit the floor, and then smiled at Ashya.

"I did it," she said in a surprised tone.

"Very well," Ashya admitted. "Do you think you can put them back into the box?" Lilly sent the stones toward the box, which was sitting open on the floor outside the circle, and let them drop safely inside. She tried to close the lid, but it didn't budge. She used the same technique she had with the stones to try again and the lid slammed shut, echoing throughout the room.

"You are a quick study, but I'd like to try one more thing before we finish for today. You'll need to use the wand." She retrieved the wand from the floor where it had been abandoned and handed it to Lilly, suddenly realizing that this girl had accomplished an amazing task without the tool she had provided her. *Amazing,* she thought, knowing that the next task would reveal many things, whether she accomplished it or not.

"I want you to think of an object that you greatly desire, something you know well. It can be anything, as long as it isn't in this room and it isn't alive. Clear your mind and focus only on that object. When you are ready, I want you to call it before you with your mind. Use the wand to direct where it is to appear and make it materialize." Ashya's words confused her. How was she supposed to make something materialize if she didn't know its true name? She closed her eyes, trying to think of something she knew well. Her sunglasses! She already regretted leaving them behind and they would be useful to her. She thought about them still sitting on the desk in her room, imagined she was holding them, felt them in her hand and then pointed the wand to a spot on the floor. Nothing happened. She tried again. Nothing. After her third failed attempt, Ashya interceded.

"It's okay," she told her. "I am amazed you could even lift a single stone, let alone all of them. This was more of a test than a task I expected you to accomplish. Yet I wonder..." She retrieved a chalice from the shelf nearest her and set it on the floor in front of Lilly. "Can you make this disappear?"

"I can try," Lilly told her, honest about her lack of experience. She focused on the chalice, taking in every glorious detail. It was silver, with five red gems spaced evenly around its base. *Five again,* Lilly noticed, then pushed the thought from her mind and focused on her assignment. She stared at the cup so long her vision blurred. She waved her hand in a single motion across her vision of the cup and it disappeared. Ashya nodded and stepped into the circle, making the cup materialize in her hand. She sent it back to its place on the shelf and looked at Lilly.

"Try to conjure your object again," she instructed and Lilly tried again. Though she was holding the wand in her right hand, when she succeeded at materializing her sunglasses, she had forgotten to use it and her glasses appeared in her left. The wand clattered to the floor, forsaken in Lilly's amazement. She studied the sunglasses in her hand. Every detail was perfectly matched to her memory of them, including the small scratch at the far right edge of the lens from the time she dropped them on the concrete. *Unbelievable,* she thought, putting them on. She turned to Ashya and gave her a grin that would put the Cheshire cat to shame.

"Why could I do it now," she asked, "and not before?"

"I don't know why, exactly, but I know how." Ashya's theory was confirmed, but to what extent, she did not know. "Rohan took you on a memory quest, and then you went on your own vision quest. I read your thoughts, and then you heard our conversation. I demonstrated the stones and you achieved the same result. You made the chalice disappear because you saw me do the same to the table. It was only after I made the chalice materialize that you could do it. It seems that if you are in the presence of magick being utilized, you subconsciously gain the knowledge required to do the same."

Lilly removed her sunglasses. "Is that a good thing?"

"I don't know yet. It depends on how well you learn to control the power within you." Ashya's voice had a peculiar tone to it. Lilly couldn't tell if it was fear, awe, or a combination of the two, but she was proud of herself nonetheless. She had accomplished great things today. "I do know one thing for certain," Ashya commented, "a sorceress you are, and a very powerful one."

Rohan's Departure

A gust of wind swept through the glade where the stone cottage stood, carrying with it the fresh scents of pine and ripening elderberries. The suns were warm and bright, exactly how Rohan remembered his last day there. He was seated on a patch of thick grass, occasionally plucking a blade to examine it. There was no purpose to his actions but to keep his mind occupied. He knew it would be a while before his mother and Lilly were finished with their lesson. Containing his impatience, he let his mind wander.

His magick had strengthened over the years despite the fact that it takes practice to maintain the skills. Of course, the family his mother had chosen for him to stay with on Earth had been extraordinarily supportive. As he grew, he developed a strong bond with his foster parent, who was kind, understanding and very open-minded to the possibility that there was more to the world than even he could explain. The first time he ever saw Rohan use magick, he simply asked him to be honest about the things he could do. He listened as Rohan told him as much as he dared and allowed Rohan the use of his powers, with the understanding that his magick would harm no one. For this reason, Rohan was able to keep his magickal skills attuned until it was time for him to return. And when the time did arrive, he received only supportive actions and loving words, with the confirmation that biologically or not, he was always a part of the family.

He had grown to accept the fact that things were bigger than he'd ever imagined, though it did not comfort the homesickness he felt for this place. His childhood here had always been happy, just his mother and him. Their bond remained close despite the distance between them, and yet, a haunting feeling refused to leave his soul. He couldn't share his plans with his mother, and he hated not being able to tell her the truth.

She has her own secrets, he thought with disdain. *She always has.* But that reality only made him feel worse. He knew the secrets were about his father and more than anything, he wanted to know the truth about his life, and his death. Tears formed in his eyes and he changed his train of thought, driving them away before they could fall. The last thing he needed was to be confronted by his mother with his emotions written all over his face. He could barely keep his secrets hidden as it was. She could already read his mind and he couldn't allow her knowledge of his plans. Not yet, at least. If she asked him outright what was wrong, he knew he wouldn't be able to lie to her, nor would he be able to answer her. The predicament of this alone was enough to deter his good humor. *I'm home,* he fumed, *and I can't be myself.*

Pondering his own quandary long enough, he decided to sneak a peek at the lesson within the Enchantment room. He turned his body toward the rounded corner of the house and waved his hand in front of his eyes. The magickal window was one skill he had practiced often on Earth, mostly to keep a close watch on Lilly, and now he had it down to an art. He watched the scene inside. Lilly was standing in the center of the room, a wand in her hand. Seconds later, a pair of sunglasses appeared in the other. Rohan jumped up in disbelief, the window disappearing as he rushed into the house.

What is she thinking? he wondered. *She's not ready to conjure. That's apprentice-level training.* He bolted through the front door as Ashya abruptly exited the room of magick.

"We have much to discuss," she told him, "now." She walked past him through the front door and he followed, bewildered.

"She's conjuring?!" He felt his emotions coming to a head. "Are you crazy? It takes months of training to do it right. You'll kill her."

"She did it right the first time," Ashya told her son, pacing the packed dirt beneath the library window. "She's strong, Rohan, stronger than either of us imagined. I'm at a loss. I have no idea how to continue her training. She can literally do anything she witnesses." Ashya explained her theory to Rohan, who was equally shocked with the news. This would alter his plans, something he could not afford to do. His mind worked quickly to figure the best way to handle the situation. His original plan was to have her train with four of Gustave's apprentices, one of each element, but he now knew she needed much more training than that. "I think we should call the Council," Ashya whispered.

"No," Rohan responded too quickly. She cast him a quizzical look and he rushed an explanation before she could attempt to read his mind. "I don't think that is wise. The fewer people who know the Chosen One has arrived early, the better. She's a huge threat to Dagana, and that puts her in great danger. If they know she has arrived and they are captured, the fear that keeps them in hiding is the very doorway Dagana will use to gain access to their mind. Imagine if she found Lilly before she was able to defend herself."

"I respect your decision, son, but..."

"Mother," he said in a sharp tone, "I did not spend the last fifteen years of my life following my destiny to deliver the Chosen One straight to Dagana. I know I'm not a Council member, but it is my job to protect her and I will do so at all costs."

"What do you suggest?"

"I cannot be with her at all times throughout her training. She needs powerful trainers. I think you should consult Gustave. He is trustworthy, and he has trained many strong, capable Masters." He fed his mother the bait, hoping she would bite. Keeping his plans as close as possible to their inception was vital. Ashya considered his suggestion and, after a lengthy moment of reflection, she agreed.

"When were you planning to depart?"

"A few days from now I am expected in Hydrabaene. Why?"

A sad look crossed her face. She hated to lose any more time with her son than she already had, but she knew she it was necessary. "You must leave tomorrow at first light. Find Gustave and send him to me immediately." She tried to read his feelings about her command, but found his magickal defenses were as strong as her own. She put her hands on his face, gazing directly into his face. "I know you just arrived, son. I am so sorry I must ask this of you."

"I'll do what I must," said Rohan with no emotion in his voice. "It is my destiny." He kissed his mother's forehead and hugged her, enjoying the embrace he'd been denied for so long. "Do not fear. No matter where I go, I feel your love with me."

Lilly joined Rohan outside shortly after his conversation with his mother. She inadvertently felt his frustration as he stared into the forest and, walking up behind him, she took his hand. He looked at her, a sad smile on his face.

"You're leaving tomorrow?" she asked, already knowing the answer. He smiled in spite of himself. He had to inform her of his plan, but first he had to make sure that she could hide enough of the truth to shield his plan from Ashya.

"In a sense," he responded. "She is sending for Gustave."

"But you're Gustave."

"She doesn't know that, and she mustn't know." He told Lilly the tale of how he became Gustave, how the old sorcerer had sought him out at the time of his expiration to pass his identity to a new soul who would continue his legacy. Rohan had returned often throughout the years, always in disguise, to gain as much knowledge and experience as he could. He had even trained with the real Gustave for a short time. The old man had known of his unique abilities, even for a pterippus, and had fostered his powers, helping him to grow both as a magician and as a soul. Because of his power, he knew Rohan could keep up appearances in his absence, and when his end drew near, he relinquished his identity to his young apprentice. From then on, Rohan had to not only be himself, but Gustave as well. His visits between worlds became more frequent, but he succeeded in making the entire world believe he was indeed Gustave. He had even visited his mother once as the old man, surprised that he had been able to keep his true identity hidden from her.

Lilly listened to him without interruption and when he was finished, she nodded, retaining her silence. Rohan decided that he had to teach her a bit of his own magick. If his mother was correct, it would be easy.

"I leave in the morning," he told her, "and Gustave will arrive tomorrow without meeting me. You must give no indication that you know the truth about his identity, for my mother will notice it, even in your mind."

"How will I keep it from her?" she asked. He was asking a great deal of her and she knew it.

"I'm going to teach you to hide your thoughts," he said. "It's a good lesson to learn. Many people will try to prowl your mind as they encounter you, so it is something you should practice often to be prepared for your future endeavors." He stood in front of her and willed a secret to the back of his mind, something he wanted her to know when she could break through his defenses, though he doubted she would be able to yet. "I'm hiding something from you in my mind. I want you to try to discover it. I'm going to defend it magickally. From this, you should be able to learn the magick it takes. Now, sorceress, what am I hiding?"

Lilly focused on Rohan's mind, blocking out the sounds of the leaves rustling in the treetops and the birds twittering in their limbs. She sorted through the thoughts that came to her easily, pausing only when she saw his last day with his mother. The memory flashed through her mind as it did in his and she stored it in her own memory for later inspection. She sifted through some emotions he allowed her to see, but no matter how hard she tried, she could not reach the secret he obstructed from her.

When Rohan realized she could go no further, he sighed in relief. For a moment, he was worried she would find the secret and disrupt his plans further. She had not, but she had now experienced the magick it would take to block her mind from others. He instructed her how to separate the thoughts she would allow others to see and the ones she needed to hide, how to build a defense around them and shelter them from everyone, even herself, if necessary. When he finished his lecture, he stood before her, preparing himself to invade her defenses.

"Put in your defended thoughts all recollection of my association with Gustave," he told her. "I'm going to enter your mind and try to find traces of them. Because I know what I am looking for, it will be harder to defend them against me, but if you succeed, then you will be able to defend your mind from anyone, including my mother, who is a Master." Lilly went rigid as Rohan jumped suddenly into her head. She could feel him moving through her mind, sorting through the things he already knew. She had decided for the time being to hide only what he told her to. As she practiced this magick, she would add other things to it, like her own identity, so the enemies he had warned her about would not discover she had arrived.

It was an odd sensation to have him enter her mind. *If I can feel him,* she deduced, *I should be able to feel others trying to invade my mind as well.* Rohan continued for some time and she began letting her mind wander to other things, like the dream she'd had the night before about her sister.

Beth had been waiting for her in the corner of her mind, furious at her for leaving without an explanation. Lilly explained that it was something she had to do and gave Beth just enough of the facts to make her believe Lilly had left to find Adrian. Even though it was a dream, Lilly found herself unwilling to tell her sister the truth. Beth informed her that their father missed her, but was not reacting to her disappearance like Beth thought he should.

"He should be looking for you or something," Beth said, an edge of frustration to her voice. "He's acting like it's no big deal, like he expected you to leave." After that revelation, Lilly changed the subject to Beth's date, bringing Beth out of the anger she felt and into a more pleasant conversation. They talked for some time in her mind, and then said their goodbyes. Lilly promised her that she would see her again, though she couldn't promise when. Beth, in all her practicality, instructed Lilly to take care of herself and come home safely, though

Lilly knew she would never see her home again. Beth had disappeared from her mind then and she had awoken in Ashya's bed. For a moment, she wondered if it had been a dream at all, or if she was communicating with her sister in her mind without realizing it, but she decided it had to be a dream, because Beth wasn't magickal and she doubted her own diminutive powers could span such a great distance.

She focused her attention on Rohan, who had given up on trying to find traces of Gustave anywhere in Lilly's memory. She had accomplished the task he'd given her on the first try simply by being near him using the same magick. His mother was right. Knowing she could do this both increased and decreased his worry. She was strong enough to defend herself against others, but would she be strong enough to protect herself from her own powers as she came into them?

"Well," asked Lilly, "how did I do?"

"Wonderful," he told her. "I couldn't even find the name Gustave in your mind. I suggest you hide your identity as well and when you are introduced, use the name you have chosen."

"No," Lilly replied. "I'll hide everything I must to prevent anyone from finding out who I am, but my name will not give away my true identity. You said so yourself: 'Your name does determine not who are.' No one knows that I am the Chosen One, so if I can keep that hidden from others, why should I change my name?" Lilly had made this decision without discussing it with Rohan first. She knew there was a reason she'd had that vision quest and she knew that the discrepancy was important, but everything within her told her to keep the name her mother had given her. Above all, she would trust her instincts over the advice of others, no matter who it was.

"Do you think that is wise?" Rohan asked her. She had expected him to protest, so his question caught her off guard.

"Wise or not, I've made my decision." She didn't know if it was wisdom or foolishness, but her decision was based on her intuition and she planned to follow it through, no matter the consequences.

"Very well," he told her, dropping the subject. He knew her well enough to know that once she made up her mind, no one could change it for her. It was a huge leap of faith, but she was smart and strong and he was willing to accept the risk. "I leave at first light, but I'm yours until then."

"Good." She gave him a smile despite the fact she knew he was leaving. His return as Gustave would be as another person. This was the only time she would have with him for a while. "Tell me what your favorite thing about home is." She sat on the ground, staring into the forest and he joined her, relaying the information she requested. They talked for hours, learning things about each other that they didn't know. Lilly shared her favorite aspects of Earth, and the things she despised. Rohan talked longer, describing in detail the world he had brought her to. As he spoke, she closed her eyes and listened, letting the images of his description fill her mind. She couldn't wait to see the beautiful things he told her about, like Lanoissef Ridge, which lay at the bottom edge of Griffon Cove, or Guttlimb Falls, a waterfall located in the Coremdey Mountains that stretched along the outer edge of Orthix Zanbar, the forest they were in now.

Their conversation lasted until the last light of the suns disappeared over the treetops. The birds had stopped singing and had settled into their nests, but the song of the forest continued. Crickets chirped in the twilight, luring nightfall to the forest, and the winds whistled through the reed grasses, setting the symphonic atmosphere. The two of them sat in silence, allowing the magick of the forest to overtake them.

Lilly's mind still revolved over the exciting new possibilities of this world, while Rohan's thoughts had taken an unexpected turn. His heart was stricken with the sudden agony of having to leave the girl whose life was so connected to his. Even during the ten years she'd spent forgetting about him, he'd always been there to watch over her, leaving only long enough to accomplish some quick task before returning to her side. It was different now. She didn't need him to protect her now that she was here, and he had so much to do, it would keep him away for a lengthy time. His chest tightened, and he took a deep breath, forcing himself to relax. Ashya found them in this trance-like state as evening gave way to night. The knowing smile on her face sparked Rohan's curiosity.

"What?" he asked, suddenly aware that darkness had fallen.

"Come along," said Ashya, ignoring his question. "It's time for dinner." She walked into the house, never losing the regal poise she always seemed to carry. Her skin shimmered in the faint glimpse of moonlight, the golden glitter trailing over the robes swirling around her feet as she moved. The pair followed her, each pondering the events of the day, each knowing that tomorrow would be a turning point in both of their lives.

Lilly awoke with a start. It took a moment for her eyes to adjust to the darkness that enveloped her. The suns had not yet risen, but she was certain she'd heard a noise. The antique clock announced the hour through the closed door of her room. Four o'clock. She sat motionless, listening again for the noise that had startled her awake to be greeted only by the silence of the early morning.

She settled into the coziness of her bed, wondering if she had imagined hearing something in the dream she'd been having. She couldn't remember the events of the dream, but the face of the young man involved was perfectly clear in her mind. He was close to her own age, with chiseled features despite his youth. His eyes were a piercing steel blue and his thick blonde hair stretched to his armpits, barely covering his pointed ears.

He must be an elf, she thought, though she had never seen one. She closed her eyes and pictured his face, trying to recall the rest of her dream. His face was surrounded in her mind by total darkness. Slowly, a group of people surrounded the young man. She remembered that she had been standing in front of him. *A gathering,* she thought. *No, a duel!* The images appeared as her memories flooded back. They were in a duel circle formed by several large stones in an intricate, yet familiar pattern. *Stonehenge,* she realized, *almost.* It was similar, but had slight differences in the placement and size of the stones. The circle was much smaller.

The young man bowed to her, and she bowed in return, then both unleashed their spells to thwart the other. They were evenly matched in skill, but Lilly's power was stronger. She knocked him to the ground on her third spell, sending him forcefully to the ground. He touched the tip of his ear, which had been cut during their battle. She lowered her wand and held her hand in front of her, healing the ear, and then offered her hand to help him from the ground. Whether he accepted or not remained a mystery, as she was jerked again from the dream by a sound, this time recognizable. A door was opening.

Lilly tossed her covers aside and stumbled through the darkness of the vast room, opening the bedroom door just as the front door closed. She made it across the entryway in no time and reached for the door.

Go back to bed, a voice said in her mind as her hand found the doorknob. *I've located Gustave and I am fetching him now. He will arrive at dawn.*

Play along, Lilly thought in the part of her mind Rohan had taught her to defend. *Will you return with him?* she asked, knowing that Ashya might very well be listening to their conversation.

No, came the reply she predicted. *I am expected in Hydrabaene shortly. I will journey there and return when my task is complete. Give Ashya my love.*

I will, Lilly promised. *Stay safe, Rohan.*

She stood in the entryway long after their conversation ended. Her head knew the logic of his plans and understood why he had to leave in this manner, but her heart ached as she felt the distance between them growing with every passing second. She returned to bed only after the clock announced the top of the next hour in its consistent monotony. Her eyes refused to cooperate with her heavy lids as thoughts clattered through her head. She fought sleep for another hour before she conceded, allowing it to overtake her at last.

The Future King

Hundreds of leagues away, Queen Dagana paced the cathedral-like hall of her castle. Her heels clicked on the black marble floor, resonating up the fifty foot stone walls to the intricately painted ceiling. The scene above depicted a great war. Every detail of the blood and carnage overtook anyone who viewed the work. It showed creatures of all kinds fighting to the gruesome death, stretching down the entire length of the hall. The hem of Dagana's crimson gown whipped around her ankles, exuding the same anger she was fighting to suppress. Something had gone terribly wrong. She had been misinformed, but who was responsible, she did not know...yet. When she did discover the culprit, it would cost him dearly. Nothing was as important to her as putting her blood on the throne.

Her grandson was that blood. His very name meant *lord over the strong war*. By the time the coming war ended, he would be a king no one could deny. He would rule all, and with the power he possessed, he would be unstoppable. She would make sure of it. She had fostered him since the day he had arrived on her doorstep. Her daughter, Laurel, had given him life as she died. Having never been of much use to her mother, Laurel had strived to marry well as a means to escape the evil woman's grasp. She had married the Elfin prince, who had hidden her away for over five years. Then, as suddenly as she vanished, she reappeared, in labor and near death.

Dagana had just stared at her ingrate of a daughter, taking no initiative to help. Her personal maid had followed her to the door when it was announced Laurel had arrived, and she had aided in the delivery of the child. As he took his first breath, his mother took her last, but before she died, she had managed two words: *Kylenin Wyatt*. The baby wailed his lament, wriggling in the woman's arms as he searched in vain for his first meal. The maid looked at the queen, her hazel eyes ablaze with fear. Combined with her curly brown tresses, which scattered from her head in all directions, she resembled a crazed animal in the presence of its impending doom.

"What should I do, Your Majesty?" the timid woman asked.

"Kill it," Dagana had commanded. Her own child had served her no purpose; she had no need for another burden.

"But, Your Majesty, he is your grandchild." Dagana turned toward the woman, and though more than ten feet separated them, Dagana's relentless grasp curled around the woman's neck. The woman stumbled forward as the magick severed her airway, losing her hold on the baby as she scrambled to release fingers from her neck that were not there..

Dagana released her magickal grip when the falling child stopped only inches from the floor. He hovered for a moment, and then sailed directly into her arms. The moment she touched him, she knew. She could feel the power coursing through him. Although she had heard the prediction of a chosen child who would come to rule their land, she had never dreamed the prophesized child would be delivered to her. The Chosen One was supposed to be born of Earth, yet here was her grandson, displaying his powers only minutes after his birth, and he was now in *her* care. Royal blood flowed through his veins, he was born with the sacred powers and he was in her charge. Her world, in that moment, had finally righted itself.

Over the years, she had provided him with everything he needed to cultivate his magick, along with anything he desired but could not yet obtain magickally. His powers amazed her at every turn, far outranking her own, though she had never allowed him that knowledge, nor the knowledge that he was the prophesized child the entire world waited for. The one time she had sought a fortune teller for her own personal reading, she discovered that her life would end at the hands of her grandchild. For this reason alone, she kept him reliant on her. If he remained so, she could live without worry.

Things tonight were far from desirable. The boy was nearing manhood, but over the past two days, he had lost control. His magick was erratic, matched only by his temper. Dagana knew he was distracted. She could read his emotions easily, no matter how well he hid his thoughts from her. Yet, whatever the cause of his distraction, his magick should not be so deterred. She had called upon fortune tellers, sorcerers and every other magickal creature in her dominion that was gifted with foresight, but none could explain the strange occurrences happening to him. She tried everything to get results, even threatening them with the prospect of death, but still got no answers.

A thundering crash brought her running toward the source of the sound. It had come from Kylenin's room. She flung open the door to find him shaking furiously. He was sitting on the floor among shards of stained glass that littered the room like confetti at a party.

"What happened?" asked Dagana, staring at the chaos of the room. She waved her hand and the shards of glass returned to the empty window, reforming the scene of a chimera rearing on its hind legs, defending itself from a fire-breathing dragon.

"Leave it!" Kylenin shouted. The venom in his voice blared over the shattering glass, shards flying once more through the room. Dagana held her hand up, forming a protective barrier as the pieces flew toward her. She rolled her eyes. Whatever was disrupting his magick was also causing this emotional outburst.

"Do you think," she said in a cool tone, "that this is the behavior of a king?"

"I'm not a king," he spat.

"Not yet, but you do have royal blood, and in a few short years you will reach manhood. You will be the proper age to rule and if anyone were to witness this unruly performance, they would view you not as the ruler of a great kingdom, but rather, an insubordinate child." She flung her hand forcefully toward the window and the glass was repaired for a second time. Kylenin glared at her, daggers shooting from his eyes. She sat on his bed and patted the space beside her. "Come, child, tell me what vexes you."

Kylenin rose from the floor and took his place beside her. She put her arm around his shoulder and pulled him close, displaying her false love as she always had. His brows furrowed in anger and his mouth pinched together like the drawstring on a purse. He wouldn't meet her eyes, a sign, she knew, that he was trying to hide something from her. She prompted him again. The anger built in him and he exploded with such force, she wondered how soon it would be before he discovered that while she had more experience in the ways of magick, he had greater power.

"I don't know," he growled in disgust. "I haven't felt right for days and I have no explanation for it. *You* were supposed to figure it out."

"Everyone I've consulted tells me the answer lies within your own soul. It's not magick's doing. It is your own."

"But I haven't done anything!" he snarled. He jumped from the bed and began to unleash his foul temper, flinging his hands violently as tapestries fell from the walls and statues burst into flames. Dagana remained where she was, but stopped his magickal tantrum, knocking him to the floor with the wave of her hand.

"That is quite enough," she hissed. "I haven't the patience for this and you have none at all. Until you figure out what is disrupting you, we will train no further." A wounded expression replaced his anger. Her words had as much force as if she had slapped him across the face. He sat on the bed beside her and leaned against her shoulder.

"I don't know what to do," he admitted. "My dreams make no sense, my powers are erroneous and it's driving me insane."

"I think," said Dagana, rising from the bed with regal poise, "that the time has come to seek out the other half." Kylenin's expression changed again, this time to unadulterated shock. She had told him years ago that the time would come *after* he was king for such actions. What had altered her decision? "I know I told you it would be years before this time would come," she continued, reading his mind, "but it is quite obvious that things are not as they once were. I thought you would grow to be stronger on your own, but I now believe it would be better to find her. Together, the two of you will match no other, not to mention the subjects of your kingdom will better serve you with a queen by your side."

"But you are the queen," he protested. Laughter poured from her, shocking his senses. She rarely smiled, let alone laughed, and it unnerved him to bear witness to it.

"I will not be around forever," she told him, caressing his face. "You are of royal blood. I am not. I *earned* this kingdom. I fought for it through years of hard work, but it is your birthright. You are entitled to the throne." She rose from the bed and let her eyes scan the room before resting on him. "Get some sleep, child. We have a great adventure waiting for us."

Kylenin watched her go, letting her words sink in. The prospect of being entitled to the kingdom gave him little comfort. The many years he had spent with her had always been affluent, but an unsettling change had taken place. Two nights before, he'd had a dream that shook him to his core. A girl with long, dark hair and sparkling green eyes had challenged him to a magickal duel. He accepted the contest and while she did not kill him, she had defeated him beyond contestation. Yet, when the duel had ended, she offered her hand to help him to his feet and healed the damage she'd caused to his face and torn ear. Subconsciously, he touched the tip of his pointed ear as though to make sure it was still whole.

Is this the girl I am looking for? he wondered. She was certainly powerful, something Dagana had assured him long ago would be an attribute of his future bride. The dream had rocked him to his core; his magick hadn't been the same since. Reflecting on it now, however, he considered it a sign. The girl was either his soul mate or his enemy. Either way, if he ever crossed her path, he doubted he would accept the duel, should it be proposed. How would it look if the future king lost a duel to a common mortal?

The thought kept sleep from him, and he imagined what it would be like to be out among the world again. It had been years since Dagana had taken him anywhere of importance, and he was sure, by now, the rest of the world had forgotten about him. How could they serve a king they forgot existed? It didn't matter. They were going to find his queen, a promise Dagana had been dangling over his head for years. The time had finally come.

He leaned back in his bed, allowing the comfort of the huge pillows to overtake him. The dream had unnerved him, but knowledge of their upcoming journey eased his anxiety. For the first time in two days, his mind felt clear, and sleep found him at last.

The Sorcerer's Directive

"Something's changed, Gustave." It was the sound of Ashya's voice that pulled Lilly from sleep late the next morning. The tone of her voice put Lilly on edge, and she stayed in bed for a moment to listen.

"How so?" rumbled Gustave's gravely voice.

"My visions, things that were so defined, things that have been constant for years, are now unclear. Something has spurred Dagana into action again, and I can't see what it is."

"The prophecy is true, Ashya. What more proof do you need?"

Ashya didn't respond, and since silence was all that remained, Lilly threw the covers back and jumped from the bed. She remade the bed with the flick of her wrist, watching the blankets right themselves with unexpected pride that it took so little effort, then found her clothes and dressed in record time. She hurried up the stairs to find Ashya and Gustave sitting at the kitchen table.

Though she knew he was really Rohan, she showed no signs of recognition as she approached the table. The old man rose and offered her his right hand, his left firmly attached to his staff. She took his hand, shaking it gently.

"I have heard much about you, young lady," Gustave muttered in a gruff voice. "You seem to have quite a bit of natural talent."

"So I've noticed," Lilly replied, taking a chair between him and Ashya, who wore an expression of calm acceptance. Lilly could tell she had heard her conversation with Rohan in the early morning hours.

"Ashya tells me that your present training is in her hands," said the old man. His eyes bore straight into Lilly's. "How do you feel about this arrangement?"

"I think it's a good idea" she answered.

"I agree. I want you to remain here for a while. Ashya can teach you a great many things. When she feels she has taught you all she can, you will move on to train with four of my apprentices, each a Master in their element. With your unusual method of learning, I believe spending time with each of them will benefit you greatly and, who knows, you may teach them a thing or two as well." Gustave rose from his chair, using his intricate staff as support. Ashya rose as well, while Lilly remained where she was, bewildered at this development. Lilly gaped at the old man, who gave her a wink as he linked arms with Ashya.

"I will leave my instructions with Ashya," he told Lilly. "When she feels you are ready, she will pass them on to you. Until then, enjoy the serenity of this place. Once you leave, things will be very different."

Lilly felt the resentment rising within her as she considered his commands. He had told her not to reveal his true identity, yet he treated her with little regard while deciding her fate. He hadn't even asked her how she felt about training with his apprentices, whom she knew were trained by the *real* Gustave. She'd read it from his mind. She wondered how well Rohan really knew these Masters of magick. Something about his command gave her an uneasy feeling, but she couldn't put her finger on it. All she could do was accept the instructions he left with her, and with Ashya, who assumed that it was indeed the great wizard giving them and not her young son. Lilly decided she would play along, for now, but she was beginning to question Rohan's true motives.

He left without saying goodbye. In fact, he had not said another word to Lilly, which bothered her to no end. She wondered if the real Gustave acted in this manner. Was he so indiscriminate in the selection of his apprentices, or did Rohan do exactly what the old man would have done upon meeting her? Because she knew the truth about his identity, she assumed the meeting would be different, but perhaps it played out exactly as it should have. He *had* spoken with Ashya a great deal.

He'd tossed about his commands like they deserved no question, as though everyone he encountered was at his beckoned call. Ashya had listened to his instructions without end and had agreed to follow his wishes. Lilly was to be trained in as much defensive magick as possible, as well as anything else Ashya deemed necessary before she went forth on her next path. He'd asked Ashya not to mention the details of that journey until it was time for Lilly to leave, but the moment he was gone, Ashya sat with the girl and told her everything.

Per Gustave's mandate, Lilly would spend as much time as she could doing one of two things: learning magick from Ashya or reading informative books from the library. Magick would become second nature to her, as she was to practice or train at least three hours a day. She would read certain books and be tested by Ashya on the important information. When Ashya felt she was prepared, Lilly would proceed to Arthidgen where a man named Dorwynn would be waiting for her arrival.

"It will be some time, though," Ashya assured her, "before you leave. You have much to learn."

They spent a quiet evening in good conversation, discussing anything they could think of other than her upcoming training. Lilly spent much of her time talking about her family, her close bond with her sister and father, and the experiences she could remember about Rohan. She told Ashya about the night they returned, though she knew Rohan already had. Ashya listened, taking in her point of view of the occurrences over the past few days. When her time came, she spoke of Rohan, filling in details that helped Lilly to understand his personality better.

"He was always a smart child, and very powerful," she said, her voice overflowing with tenderness. "He had an inherent knowledge of the world at a very young age, a virtue indeed, but also his curse. It was decided he would leave to set forth on his destiny while he was still a child. I allowed it, despite my better judgment, and I still wonder if I made the right decision."

"I think you did," Lilly told her.

"He resents me for letting him go. I can feel it in him." Her eyes brimmed with tears. "You do know that he was in disguise when you arrived, don't you? That was not his true form." Lilly didn't know that for sure, but she wasn't surprised. He was full of secrets.

They sat a while longer in comfortable silence, and then decided to get some rest for the training that would begin the next day. Lilly made her way to Rohan's room, where she would be staying now that he was no longer there. She fell asleep admiring the shimmering flowers in the darkness and awoke the following dawn well rested. After a quick bath and a quicker breakfast, she felt revitalized. She eagerly made her way to the Enchantment Room for her first real lesson.

Ashya was waiting when she opened the door, again wearing the sparkling white robes that were her second skin. Lilly entered slowly, still marveling over the wondrous things the room contained. She met

Ashya in the center of the circular floor and faced her. Ashya explained the first lesson, which was how to defend her mind from others. Lilly dared not tell her that she had already learned this from Rohan. Within the first hour, Ashya was convinced Lilly was ready to be tested.

"I want you to defend your mind against me," she said. "I'm going to attack you, so to speak, with everything I've got. Don't be afraid if you fail at first. It's a difficult task, but I think you are ready to try." Lilly prepared for Ashya's mental attack knowing full well that she was a Master. What frightened her was that she couldn't fail this test, or Rohan's secret would no longer be a secret.

I can do this, she thought, hoping that if she could convince herself she could, it would make it true. Ashya delved into her mind, giving her an instant migraine. She could feel Ashya moving through her thoughts, searching for the secrets she was hiding. For an eternity, Lilly fought to keep Ashya out of that part of her mind. Her strength began to dwindle, but she refused to allow her entry. Ashya swayed where she stood and finally released Lilly's mind, sinking to the floor. Lilly knelt beside her, the migraine a distant memory.

"You have no idea how powerful you are," Ashya said breathlessly. Her assault on Lilly's mind had drained her own strength and she sat for a moment, panting. "I can't believe it. I trained for weeks before I passed that test."

"I passed?" Lilly asked, beaming with pride. She'd always been a top student in school, but this was a far cry from memorizing facts.

"You passed," Ashya confirmed, picking herself up from the floor. Once upright, she wobbled slightly. "I haven't felt this weak since the days of my own training."

"I'm sorry," said Lilly, disconcerted by her affect on Ashya.

"Don't be sorry!" The forcefulness is Ashya's voice caught her off guard. Ashya put her hands on Lilly's shoulders, their faces only inches apart. "Never apologize for what your power can do. Never. Understand?"

Lilly nodded, afraid to speak. Was Ashya angry at her for being more powerful that she was?

"On the contrary," Ashya replied, as though Lilly had asked her what she'd been thinking, "I am pleased with your progress. I am only disappointed in myself for underestimating you, or overestimating my own power. In any case, we should continue the lesson."

"Are you strong enough?" Lilly feared she would lose control and end up hurting Ashya, or worse.

"You will find," Ashya stated, "that the stronger you are, the quicker your energy will replenish. Come now, let us continue." Lilly took her place in front of her mentor. Trepidation and excitement clashed in her mind, waging their own personal battle, and she anticipated another magickal attack. What she failed to realize, however, was that Ashya was about to make her the assailant.

"Entering someone's mind takes as much strength as defending your own. Obviously, you know a bit from communicating with Rohan and from listening to our conversation, but communicating with your mind takes place in the part of your mind that remains exposed, the same part that houses your senses and makes you aware of what surrounds you. It is also where the connection is made that allows the mind to be entered. The average human keeps this part open for all to see."

"Is there a way to block that part off completely, in case you want to have a private conversation?"

"It is possible, but extremely difficult. In time, I believe you will be able to master that feat, but do not attempt it before you *know* you are ready. One small mishap and you could encumber the rest of your senses. Having a private conversation in your mind isn't worth the risk of going deaf or blind."

Good to know, Lilly thought. *So there is no way to completely block someone from your mind?*

There is a way to completely *block your mind, which I will teach you very soon, but that skill will not allow someone to communicate with you at all. Your mind would be closed to everyone, even the person you want to communicate with.*

Lilly smiled at Ashya's humor in continuing their conversation silently.

Since you have already made the connection, I want you to try to find what I am hiding. Opening someone's mind is like defending your own, only in reverse. It's also very dangerous to enter someone's mind without their consent. Besides being disrespectful, you could find yourself becoming an easy target for the same injustice. Anyone with a hint of magickal ability could kick you out of their mind, or worse, take hold and not let go. The minds are connected, which means, for a moment, your mind is in someone else's. If they don't let go of you, it could drain your power and kill you.

It seems there are a lot of ways to kill yourself with magick.

There are, which is why, except for creatures that are born with certain gifts, most magickal human are only born with one or two natural abilities. Let's proceed.

Lilly entered further into Ashya's mind and found her defenses very strong. She sifted through her memories and found one she had been wondering about: Ashya's last day with Rohan before he left. She quickly stored that memory in her own, and then went deeper still, until she found she could go no further. She pushed harder as she realized this was the part of Ashya's mind hiding information. Ashya's barricade was persistent, but Lilly was determined to pass this test as well. She pushed with as much strength as she dared.

Pain shot through her head, bringing more than just remnants of her earlier migraine. She thought she had made it through when the throbbing began, distracting her from her cause. She managed to get only a single word before she broke the connection: *Mylhan.*

Both Lilly and Ashya were exhausted after the intense lesson. Ashya, tired though she was, smiled at Lilly as they sat on the floor, too tired to materialize chairs. Lilly waited in anticipation to find out how she did, but kept her patience until they had both gained back strength. Finally, Ashya stood and helped her to her feet.

"Not bad for your first time," she said. "You were very close."

"Who's Mylhan?" Lilly asked, curious about the name she'd gotten from Ashya's mind. Ashya's face paled upon hearing the name and her jovial expression turned instantly to shock. Her mouth agape and her eyes wide, she stared at Lilly so long that Lilly began to regret succeeding at her task. Finally, she lowered her eyes.

"You passed," she said to Lilly in a flat tone as she walked from the room, leaving Lilly to wonder what had just happened and who exactly Mylhan was.

Lilly dared not ask again about the name she had learned in Ashya's mind, and Ashya had not spoken of the event since. Despite the setback caused by her unexpected entry into Ashya's deepest secrets, which consisted of three endless days with few words spoken between them, the days began to pass quickly. Lilly began each day as she had the first, with her morning ritual of a bath and breakfast. She and Ashya trained for four hours a day, followed by lunch. During their training sessions, Lilly learned other types of magick of the mind, which included how to travel by thought instantly from one place to another. She found it came easily to her, despite the fact that she could not go very far because a person can only travel to a place he or she has been to before.

Some things, like trying to conjure a living creature, she found extremely difficult. Her first attempt to conjure a simple fly was a complete disaster. The poor creature, if you could call it that, had misshapen wings, transparent, oversized eyes and no antennae. Though Lilly was discouraged, Ashya reminded her that it required innate knowledge of the thing being created, not just adequate power, in order to conjure it correctly. After extensive studying, Lilly managed to correctly conjure a ladybug, which flew out the window shortly after arriving.

She moved easily through the defensive magick, learning how to completely block her mind from others and how to magickally inspect her food and drink for any potentially harmful poisons. Ashya kept her guard up on this practice, often slipping potions or ingredients into her morning juice. While the concoctions were not deadly, they still managed to hinder Lilly's magickal practices. After she'd drunk one that contained an ingredient which caused her to float on the ceiling for hours, Lilly never again forgot to search her meals.

Ashya also coached her on how to prowl someone's mind undetected by literally becoming one of that person's thoughts, something that frightened Lilly. She assumed she would always feel someone in her mind, as she did Rohan and Ashya when they entered, but knowing that they could enter without her knowledge plagued her. Ashya did not, however, test her on how to do it.

"It is a very rare gift," she warned during her lecture, "and it is very difficult to do without being caught. Not to mention, it is highly immoral. I recommend always trying to get consent before attempting to go into someone's mind, to play it safe." Lilly felt better knowing it was difficult to do, but only a bit.

Ashya spent days coaching her on memory and vision quests. Though she had already experienced them, Ashya wanted to ensure she had the knowledge behind the magick, something she stressed often to Lilly throughout their months of training. She explained to Lilly a third kind of quest, called a requiem quest, which was an internal journey of discovery and often led to foresight of future events, but warned her not to attempt it in solitude as it was very easy to get lost in yourself or lose yourself in the grief of any future events you may see. Having another person present ensured there was someone to help you out of it.

When she wasn't training in the morning hours, Lilly used the time to practice what she had already learned. She gained exceptional control over her powers, learning how to stop and start their intention instantly. Ashya often caught her by surprise with some magickal task, which taught Lilly to use her magick instinctively as well. She became very skilled with her aim, directing her abilities exactly where she wanted them to go. She was becoming the sorceress Ashya already believed she was.

Her afternoons were spent reading book after book, being tested between each one. Ashya let her choose from a list of over forty books about different aspects of magick and magickal creatures. Several books, which included titles like *An Introduction to the Elements, The Power of Plants, Common Practices of Fundamental Magick,* and *Curing Magickal Ailments and Mysterious Maladies,* informed her in more detail of the diversity in the different types of magick, the various tools useful to the less-talented magician, commonly used ingredients for spells and potions, as well as what could potentially go wrong and how to correct things that did. One in particular, *Extraordinary Uses for Unordinary Ingredients,* told about rare magickal ingredients, what they could do and how to obtain them. Ogre's blood captivated her. It had many healing properties and aided in restoring vitality, but it was extremely difficult to get because those same properties healed an ogre's wound before much blood was spilled. To get any useful amount, the ogre shedding the blood often had to magickally keep the wound open, which meant it had to be given by his own choice.

Some of the books she had to read she found very boring, like *The Old Language: Using it with Magick,* or the dozens of books that translated the languages of elves, dwarves and other magickal creatures. She read them nonetheless, cover to cover, knowing that while she wouldn't remember everything they contained, having read them, she would be able to conjure the books at any time, should the need arise.

The Creation of the World: as told by the Creators was a detailed explanation of how Buthania was formed and how life and magick came to be upon it, and brought to light the beauty of the great sacrifices made by the children of the elements who made it all possible. *Rules of the Universe: The Science of Tradition* broke down the calendar year, which consisted of thirteen, twenty-nine day months, since the planet took exactly 377 days to circle its two suns. There were still seven days of the week and twenty-four hours in a day, and the moon was constant in its twenty-eight day cycle. Seasons each contained three months and one week, which made it easy to keep track of things like the first days of the seasons and the equinoxes.

Paganism: Histories, Holidays and the Birth of Christianity contained information about the religious practices of humans, both here and on Earth, with a very brief history of the religions, but mostly how they were practiced today and how Christianity was born of Paganism, a very controversial topic Lilly found strangely intriguing. It was the very last page of the book that stuck out well in Lilly's mind:

There is an inherent desire in every person to want to believe in something greater than themselves. Whether worshipping a God, a Goddess, both, or simply celebrating Mother Nature in all her glory, having faith in something is greater than having no faith at all, for without faith, you lack the courage to believe in yourself, which is no way to live. Whatever religion you follow, whatever deity you worship, never stop believing in what feels right to you. That alone is divine.

The book had been well researched and contained quite a bit of fact, but quite a bit was also the opinions and perspectives of one person, something which, he pointed out in the course of his writing, was exactly what each chapter of the Christian Bible contained. He had not included his name in the book, but it was still one of the more interesting books Lilly was required to read. She didn't miss a single question when Ashya had tested her on it.

Then there were books about magickal creatures. A simple dictionary on the known species of creatures, their typical talents and powers, and their weakness, both physically and magickally, an encyclopedia on the genealogy of the different species, and a detailed anatomy book of the same creatures, in which Lilly learned that dragons had three stomachs and that they didn't actually *breathe* fire, but rather their complex series of stomachs digested the food they ate, divided it into nutrition or waste and stored the waste in the extra stomachs, where it turned into a liquid first, and then a methane-like gas. The gas could be released simply by belching, and by gnashing their teeth, a spark would ignite the gas to create a streaming flame, making it seem like the creature was actually breathing fire.

Lilly read many books that were not on her list, including titles such as *The Secret Language of Names, The Facts Behind the Fiction: A Vampire's Perspective*, and *Mushroom Enchantments: A Complete Guide to Identifying the Magick of Mushrooms,* which contained a list of over four hundred names of people who contributed to the facts in the book, who for whatever reason during their research were unable to complete their work. Many of them had discovered maladies of unknown species of mushrooms by testing them on themselves, often without knowing how to cure them. Ashya told her that the book was under constant revision, as more species were discovered every day. She also read dozens of literature books written by creatures of every kind. They contained stories, essays, notable pieces of historical news, quotes and, of course, poetry.

When she wasn't training or studying, she spent as much of her spare time as possible outside, taking in the sheer beauty of her surroundings. Autumn whisked through the forest, leaving in its wake a display of color that stretched the sunsets across the entire tree line, creating an illusion that each one blanketed the entire world from top to bottom.

Cold weather swooped in, bringing with it winds that ripped the colored leaves from the trees, turning them into an intricate black lace against the snow that winter escorted to the forest soon after.

Lilly and Ashya spent their evenings involved in conversation. As the months passed, both began sharing the more intimate details of their lives. One night when Lilly least expected it, Ashya mentioned the name Lilly had discovered during her first day of training. They were enjoying a cup of hot cider in the late months of winter, watching the snow fall through the window, when Ashya became very quiet. Her face took on an expression with which Lilly had become very familiar, a look of dismayed solitude. She was silent for a while, then sighed and began to speak.

"Mylhan was my husband," she began. "He was Rohan's father. I've never told another soul about the circumstances surrounding his absence before now. They are something I've kept to myself for a very long time. Rohan doesn't even know the truth about his father, and I am going to trust you not to tell him. When the time is right, he must hear it from me." Lilly nodded her silent promise and Ashya told her story. She explained her reasons for not telling Rohan, which Lilly fully agreed were justifiable when she heard the whole truth. She comforted Ashya as the tears fell and when it was finished, she confirmed her promise not to reveal those truths to Rohan. Ashya was right. The shock of this astonishing information about his father would alter Rohan's view on everything, including his own identity. This was something he would need to hear only from her.

Spending so much time with Ashya, Lilly finally got to feel what is was like to have a mother figure. She felt safe knowing that there was someone here who cared for her like a mother would. That thought placated her as the time drew nearer for her to leave. As spring approached, Lilly was shocked that nearly six months had passed since her arrival on Nostobirem, which was what the planet was called. Every book on her reading list had been read and tested, and her training was nearly complete. She only had one lesson left.

Ashya was waiting for her, as usual, in the Enchantment Room, standing in the center of the circle emblazoned on the floor. Lilly entered and took her accustomed position in front of her. Ashya held a double-edged dagger, which Lilly knew was called an athame, still in its sheath. They were both made from silver and steel, the sheath adorned with five jewels, each a different color. The pentacle etched into the handle of the blade rested beneath Ashya's thumb as she removed the blade from the sheath.

"Today," said Ashya as she ran the knife's sharp point over her left hand, cutting a deep gash into her flesh, "you will learn how to heal magickally. It is a very rare gift. In fact, it is so rare that I have never met another who could do it." She held her right hand over the wound and, with a flash of bright light that emanated from it, the wound slowly healed itself from the inside out. Lilly inspected the flawless skin where the wound had just been, impressed, but she wondered why Ashya thought she would be able to do it, if it were indeed such a rare gift.

Ashya cut her own hand again and held it out to Lilly. She held her hand over the wound as Ashya had and for a moment, nothing happened. Then Lilly's hand began to take on an eerie glow. Wispy strands of light radiated from the wound, swirling rapidly as they repaired the damaged tissue beneath the surface of the gash. Bursts of white light exploded between the cut and her hand as the final repairs to the skin were made. When the radiance ceased, Lilly studied her work, amazed.

"Congratulations," Ashya told her, beaming.

"How did you know I could do it?" Lilly couldn't help but ask.

"You are the Chosen One, my dear. You can do anything." Ashya held her hands out to Lilly, who took them, clasping them tight. "Your training is complete. I have taught you all I know." Lilly was both thrilled and dismayed. The time had come for her to leave. She had been looking forward to it for some time, but she found herself having a hard time with the prospect of saying goodbye to Ashya. There was no need to say it, however, for she could feel the same sadness in Ashya and knew that she could feel her own pain in return.

"I want you to know how proud I am of you. I will not say goodbye, only good journey. I know we will see each other again very soon." The woman put her arms around Lilly and hugged her tight. "When you see Rohan," she whispered in her ear, "please tell him how much I love him, and how much I miss him." She released her hold on Lilly and turned quickly from her to hide the tears in her eyes. Lilly felt tears on her own face as she followed Ashya from the room.

They spent their last night together as they had always spent their evenings, enjoying good company and good conversation before going to bed. Lilly lay awake in the darkness of Rohan's room that night contemplating her future. She held the sheathed athame under the moonlight cascading through the window, watching as it highlighted the red, blue, yellow, green and white gems wedged in the metal. Ashya had given it to her as a graduation gift of sorts, and explained the meaning of the stones. Each color represented an element; the white stone centered the magickal properties they contained. Lilly didn't want to accept such an extravagant gift, but Ashya persisted until she finally caved. She slid the blade under her pillow and held it while she slept, clinging to it as though her life depended on it.

Masters of the Elements

Lilly sat after four straight hours of walking, thankful she had taken those forest walks that had kept her so fit. She slung the pack she carried off her shoulder and let it fall to the ground with a thud. It was the same pack she had arrived with, only now, there was also a cylindrical tube jutting out the top, the protective flap wrapped haphazardly around one side. The tube contained three maps Ashya had decided to send with her at the last minute, each rolled around another to avoid creasing the parchment they were scrolled on. One was a geographical map, showing the expansive land mass that was Buthania. The forest stretched the east coastline, the Coremdey Mountains along its western edge, and all the way along the south coastline, then back north along the east side of the Raderheir Mountains. Rivers wound their way through the entire map, lakes dangling along them like beads on a string. The map included everything: the forest, mountains, deserts, volcanoes, marshes, rivers, lakes, islands and the huge ocean surrounding it all.

The second map was only an outline of the first. Small black dots marked the locations of every town in Buthania, the roads to get from one to another drawn neatly among them. The third map, also an outline, showed the territorial locations of many magickal creatures, like Griffon Cove, where Griffons and Hippogriffs nested, and the Catacombs of Arshner, where the dwarves dwelled. It even indicated suspected locations to the lairs of some less-desirable beasts.

The amazing thing about these maps was that when they were placed on top of one another, they formed one map containing the information of all three. *Magick is a wonderful thing,* Lilly thought as she unrolled the maps, leaving them stacked as she tried to figure out how far she had gone. Jesfinarea was her first destination, barely a centimeter from where Ashya had marked her home. She'd told Lilly it would take her most of a day to walk the distance. According to the map, she was almost halfway there.

She retrieved the water skein Ashya had prepared for her, savoring every drop as the cool liquid trickled down her throat. Digging further into her pack, she retrieved the turkey sandwich and banana, her final meal from Ashya. She ate slowly, taking in her surroundings. The road wasn't anything more than a severely worn path. Prints of every kind were strewn across the dirt, as well as ruts where wheels had roamed. The trees formed a cavern over the road and green buds had sprouted along every branch, each the foundation for a new leaf. Blossoms would not be far behind as spring continued its passage.

Lilly finished her meal and rolled the maps carefully, placing them safely into the tube container that sheltered them. She forced the tube into her pack and tightened the drawstring as tight as she dared, then slung it over her shoulder and continued the trail toward Jesfinarea. If she kept her pace, she would arrive by nightfall.

The further she walked, the less dense the forest became. The sunlight found an easier path through the treetops, which warmed Lilly enough that she removed her jacket, hanging it on the map tube so she had her hands free, should the need for magick arise. Throughout the day, she occasionally wondered when she would encounter a magickal creature. She caught sight of several different species of birds, a squirrel, a whole family of rabbits and something she could only describe as the offspring of a hedgehog and a skunk. She was grateful it didn't seem to have anything else in common with the skunk besides its appearance.

By the time dusk began settling in, she could see the edge of her first destination. It didn't seem to be very large, but that didn't matter to her. She didn't really expect any town in this world to be very big. She wandered down the cobblestone street, taking time to admire the window displays set up by the shop owners. Most of the shops were closed, but a handful remained open to accommodate later shoppers.

Sparks flew out the side door of a blacksmith shop, the smith diligently pounding away at his metal. Lilly observed quietly, until the man stopped pounding and doused the red hot material with water. Steam filled the area at once and escaped through the open door, causing Lilly to take a few steps backward to avoid a steam bath.

"Can I help you?" said the blacksmith without looking up from his work. He was a solid man, about six feet tall, Lilly guessed, with a bald head and a neatly trimmed beard.

"I'm looking for lodging for the night?" Her statement sounded more like a question.

"Follow the road to the other side of town," the man grunted as he removed the object from its bath. "There's an inn. Ask for Tilda." He buried the formed piece of metal into a bed of hot coals, and then abandoned it there to pump the huge billows providing the air to keep them so hot. When he extracted it and began his banging again, Lilly realized he was forming a horseshoe.

"Would you happen to know of anyone selling a horse?" *Please,* she hoped, *let him know someone who has a horse for sale.* From what her map indicated, it would take her another three or four days of walking on foot before she made it to Arthidgen, which was where she was supposed to find her first elemental trainer.

"I know one man who might," the man said after a moment. "He'll be here at dawn to have his horse shoed. You can come back then."

"Thanks. I will."

The man's directions led her to a small building only two stories high. It wasn't in the best shape, but it was better than sleeping on the ground. Lilly approached the rotund woman at the front desk. Her murky brown hair had flecks of gray near her hairline. Her eyes were the same color as her hair and dark circles dangled below them, telling the secrets of her weariness.

"How can I help you?" she asked Lilly in a pleasant voice, tired though it was.

"I need a place to sleep for the night," Lilly told her. She hoped her general need would be enough to appease the woman. She eyed Lilly warily, unsure about this stranger in her establishment, then sighed.

"Just for one night?" Lilly nodded. "I got one room. Small bed, smaller bathroom. S'only got one desk and one lamp."

"I don't need much," Lilly told her. "I'll take it."

"Five kerim," the woman demanded. "Includes breakfast in the morning." Lilly dug into her bag and found the small pouch Ashya had given her. It contained pieces of gold and silver, each made into two different sizes. Ashya had given her a quick lesson on the monetary system of the towns. Kerim were the small silver pieces. Lilly fished them out and handed them to the woman.

"Your room's up the stairs, third door on the right," she said, producing a small brass key and passing it to Lilly. "Breakfast is served for two hours after sunrise. There are fresh towels in your room. If you need anything else, just come find me. The name's Tilda." Lilly thanked her and started toward the worn staircase butted against the wall farthest from the front desk. She climbed them, taking note of their rickety condition.

The staircase led her to a long hallway. She counted the doors on the right, finding her room. When she opened the door, she realized that Tilda's words did the room every justice she'd described. It was barely large enough to hold the twin-sized bed and two-foot square table that sat beside it. On the table sat a single oil lamp and a small box full of matches. A doorway, absent the door, led to a five-foot square bathroom with a wash basin, a small pot and a large claw-foot bathtub that took up the majority of the space within the room.

Lilly put her pack on the floor in front of the table and sat on the bed. Despite the shabby appearance of the place, the bed was quite comfortable. She stretched out on the bed and fell asleep on top of the covers as her exhaustion caught up with her.

Her dreams that night were filled with strange and confusing images. The blonde man she'd dreamt of once before was there, surrounded by nasty creatures clawing their way through a severe fissure in the ground. The demons were small, with thin, skeleton-like bodies that were as black as the hole they emerged from. Their fangs were black as well, each one long and thin and very sharp. Their purple-gray tongues were long and forked and thrashed around violently. They seemed to have no eyes, but rather vacant holes where their eyes should be. The man looked very pleased with himself as the demons gathered before him. He gave a command and they scattered, an evil cackle in their throats.

She awoke in a cold sweat, the images of the terrifying creatures fresh in her mind. She wondered who this man was and why she kept dreaming about him. She tried to fall asleep again, but it was useless. She lit the table lamp and took out the journal Beth had given her, every page still as fresh as when she had first gotten it. She dug out a pen and began to write, letting her fears flow from her body through her hand and onto the paper. By the time the suns crested over the trees, she had written more than ten pages, including every dream she could remember since her birthday and the strange vision quest she'd had about her mother.

She took a quick bath and dressed in a rush, hoping she had not missed the man who had a horse for sale. She left her pack, taking only the pouch of money with her, and headed to the blacksmith's. She all but ran to the smithy and arrived out of breath. The blacksmith looked at her, his face void of expression.

"You're late," he told her. "Finerell left ten minutes ago." Lilly's face fell. The smith took pity on her and added, "He'll return with the horse he's willing to sell after his breakfast. I told him someone was in the market."

"Thank you so much," she said, and dug in the pouch for a kerim and handed it to him. "For your generosity." The man took the coin and shoved it into his pocket.

"S'very kind of you."

Lilly returned to the inn with the sole intent of getting her things and going back to the blacksmith's to wait for the man with the horse. Tilda, however, would have none of her attempts to leave without breakfast. After insisting that she was not hungry over and over, Lilly finally gave up the attempt and decided to have breakfast before she left. She sat at a long table in what Tilda considered the dining hall and waited for her food. The plate that arrived moments later was so full of food, the plate itself could not be seen. Eggs and sausages steamed with fragrant aroma. Butter melted over the piping hot pancakes, which were drizzled with thick syrup. Strawberries and blackberries took up the rest of the space. A glass of milk accompanied the meal and Lilly ate, happy she had decided to stay. The massive breakfast was a tribute to the rest of the drab place.

She returned to the blacksmith's shop an hour later, her belly round from the small feast she'd just consumed, her pack over her shoulder. The blacksmith was talking with a short, ragged looking man, his image worn from years of working in the sun. It was obvious by his stained shirt and craggy overalls that he was a farmer. In his hand was a set of reins that led to a beautiful chestnut mare, saddled and ready to ride.

"Is this the young lady?" the man asked the smith, who grunted and nodded before disappearing into his shop. The man sized Lilly up. "You need a horse?"

"Yes, sir," she replied.

"This here is Adair. She's the best horse that I can spare to sell."

"Will she get me to Arthidgen?" Lilly asked. That was all she really needed. She wasn't sure what her path beyond Arthidgen was, or if she would even need a horse by then. If she didn't, she figured she could always sell the horse later.

"She's strong," the worn man said. "She'll get you to anywhere you want to go, so long as you treat her with the respect she deserves."

"How much?"

"Forty shenti," the man replied in a firm voice. Forty large gold pieces. Lilly knew she had enough, but she wondered if the price included the saddle as well. She voiced her question to the man. "If'n you want the tack as well, I'll need another five laukti." Lilly rummaged in her money pouch and took out forty large gold pieces and five small gold pieces, handing them to the man without question. She didn't know if the man was being fair or not, but she wasn't going to waste time trying to haggle him. He looked like he desperately needed the money.

He pocketed the money, then offered his hand. She smiled and shook it. He seemed rather pleased that she hadn't tried to negotiate a lower price, which made her wonder if maybe she should have, but it was too late now.

"S'been a pleasure doin' business with you. May your journey stay safe."

"Thank you," Lilly replied, securing her pack to the saddle. She climbed onto the saddle, getting used to the feel of it. She'd ridden often when she was younger, though not in the past few years, but she remembered enough of the movements and commands to get the horse moving in a meandering trot.

She rode through the streets of the town, getting a feel for the horse, *her* horse. Many of the shops were open for business, their doors open wide, their wares arranged meticulously outside. A group of children huddled in front of a confection shop, their eyes dancing with desire for the treats within. Lilly dismounted her horse and entered the store. The sweet aroma struck her immediately and although she had just eaten, her stomach rumbled its longing nonetheless. She purchased two bags of treats; a small bag containing a variety of hard candies and a large bag full of taffy. When she exited the store, she put the small bag into her pack and gave the cluster of children the larger bag.

"A gift," she said to the bewildered children. "Make sure to share them."

"Thank you," whispered a little boy in rather tattered clothing. He held the bag, unsure whether or not to believe he was actually holding it. "But why, Miss?"

"Because everyone needs a little reminder that happiness is within reach, even if it is given by a stranger." Lilly mounted her horse and the children ran behind her as she rode away, shouting their praises to her. She smiled, a happiness surging through her that she hadn't felt in quite a while. She led her horse to the road leading out of town and rode hard, putting as much distance behind her as she could.

Evening snuck up on her as she realized she hadn't stopped for a rest or a meal since she'd left Jesfinarea. Her horse seemed to be faring well, but she decided it was time to stop for the night. She checked the maps, which indicated she was less than half a day's ride away from Arthidgen. She removed the pack from the saddle to relieve Adair of some weight, then led her to a stream for a cool drink before tying her to a tree where she would make camp.

Night passed with little consequence. She listened in silence to the forest, the sounds of nocturnal animals rising for another night. Crickets chirped their tune and somewhere deeper in the woods, a night bird sang to the starlit sky. Lilly had yet to see a single traveler on the road, leaving her to wonder how often people strayed from their homes. Surely they traveled often enough to warrant an inn in such a small town as Jesfinarea, so where were they? Why hadn't she seen anyone yet? Not bothering to take the time to conjure a tent, she lay awake on a single blanket and stared through the trees at the jeweled sky, breathing deep, then fell into a dreamless sleep.

She awoke the next morning to the suns peeking over the tree line. Her horse was grazing on a patch of grass, content in the still of morning. Lilly changed her shirt, but didn't worry about her jeans, as they were still pretty clean. She could bathe and change once she made it to Arthidgen. She noticed a kilpa tree close by and gathered a few fruits for her trip. She fed one of the large fruits to Adair, who accepted it gratefully, kept one out for herself and put three into her bag for later in the day.

She continued her trek down the empty road at a good pace, stopping once during the ride to allow her horse some fresh water and another kilpa for both of them. The forest had become less dense and she knew that Arthidgen was only hours away. She slowed her pace a bit, trying to respect the hard work Adair had given her the day before, but the horse gave more, as though she could feel the excitement building in her rider.

When they reached the edge of the forest, Lilly could see Arthidgen in the distance. It seemed small at first, but as she approached, she realized that it was indeed a very large town. The sunshine beat down on horse and rider in the absence of the trees' shelter, causing them both to become hot and tired, but their pace never faltered. With an hour of leaving the forest, they had finally reached their destination.

Lilly rode slowly through Arthidgen, taking in the elaborate structures lining the brick-paved streets. Unlike Jesfinarea, whose buildings were built mostly of wood and rock, the buildings here were either stone or brick, mortared together well into their erect beauty. The bricks themselves were larger than the ones Lilly was used to, and they ranged in color from beige to blue to black. Only a select few were actually red.

Lilly dismounted her mare and led the animal as she looked from shop to shop. The town seemed deserted. Every door was closed and every window had its drapes drawn. Further down the road, a dog trotted across an intersection and disappeared down the crossroad. When Lilly got to the intersection, she stopped, trying to decide which direction she should go. An uproar of applause erupted from her left. She followed the road in the direction of the noise, hoping someone there knew how she could find the man called Dorwynn.

The road curved to the right and ended at a huge arena, which at the moment seemed to hold the entire town. Bleachers lined the interior perimeter of the oval structure. One portion was covered with a huge awning. It was empty of people, but there was a line of six hand-carved chairs shaped much like thrones, obviously for any royalty attending the events. Those sitting in the bleachers were all well-dressed, well-groomed citizens. The men wore suits of black, gray or tan, with appropriately matching neckties. Many carried pipes, taking puffs here and there while chatting and cheering. The women were dressed in varying fashions of formal dresses that hung to their crossed ankles. High-heeled boots were laced or buttoned on their dainty feet. Every child amongst them wore a bonnet or hat, their clothing as fashionable as their parents'.

It's like the Middle Ages, Lilly thought. The bleachers were even separated from a second section, where nearly twice as many people stood crammed side by side in almost half the total space. Children were perched on the wooden fence, though one could barely call it that as it was formed from posts into no more than a boundary marker. A person could easily slip through the spaces within the posts. What struck Lilly as odd about this group was while the people didn't sport expensive clothing, they were by no means wearing rags as the poorer people of medieval times would have been. The men wore everything from slacks to denim jeans or overalls, while the women wore elegantly simple sundresses and flat shoes or boots. Several women wore pants as well, something that definitely wouldn't have been tolerated on Earth until the past hundred years or so. The children were wearing clothing similar to their parents, much more casual, and more comfortable looking than the children in the bleachers.

Within the arena itself were more than a dozen swordfighters, divided into pairs. Among them were two women, each paired with a man for sparring. A bell sounded and swords banged against swords and clanked against shields. Lilly watched in amazement at the precision of the fighters, their feet dancing in fluid movements with their swift bodies. The crowd roared in delight as the swordsman yielded to their superior opponents. Before long, the group of sixteen dwindled to eight. The fallen men exited the arena while the rest gathered at the center to select their next partner by drawing colored stones from a black satchel. When everyone had chosen, they were paired with whoever had the same color stone.

"The pairs have been chosen," said the man holding the black satchel. He removed two sets of the colored stones and shoved them into his pocket. "Three rounds remain. Contestants, begin at the bell." The man walked across the arena, approaching the fence that Lilly stood behind. As he got closer, his face took on a quizzical expression. Lilly realized suddenly how out of place she must have looked to him, staring into the arena while still clutching her horse's reins.

"Good day," said the man, finally reaching where she stood. "Just arrived, have you?"

"Yes," Lilly replied to his friendly tone. His bright eyes, hidden only slightly by the graying hair on his head, smiled as much as his mouth did.

"You've arrived just in time," he told her, jumping atop the fence to watch the next match. "Tie your horse on that post there and join me." Shocked at the invite, Lilly did as she was instructed. After securing her horse and ensuring her pack was safe, she carefully climbed up the fence, balancing precariously beside him.

"I'm Warrick," he said. "Have you ever seen this type of competition before?" Lilly shook her head. "I expected as much. You have a sense of awe about you that only a newcomer has. Well, you are in for a treat. Only thing more exciting than the sword fighting is the jousting. Sorry to say it ended yesterday. Would you like me to explain the rules?"

"Yes, please." Lilly was delighted Warrick was so friendly. Finding Dorwynn at the moment was a mute point considering the entire town was gathered in such close quarters.

"Each match is determined by points. A contestant receives one point for any strike that causes his opponent to drop his shield. If a sword falls to the ground, two points are awarded. Once a contestant reaches five points, he wins and moves on to the next level."

"And if nothing is dropped?"

"Ah," said Warrick with an odd smile, "if both competitors manage to keep hold of their weapon and armor, it comes down to mere strength. One must wear the other down enough for him to yield."

The crowd cheered loudly as one of the fighters managed to knock both sword and shield from his opponent's hands in one swift move. The winner, a beautiful man with chocolate skin and long raven-black hair, helped his fallen contender to his feet. The cheering increased as one of the women fighters achieved the same goal against the man she was fighting.

"And the women fight as well," Lilly said under her breath. It wasn't as much a question as a statement of her observation.

"Why not?" the man beside her asked incredulously. She just shrugged, not really knowing how to answer. He looked at her, scrutinizing her appearance, and said, "You're from Earth, aren't you?"

Panic began to rise within her as she realized her mistake. Ashya had told her to take care not to give away any more information to stand out than necessary, yet in a simple conversation, she'd managed to give away important information to a complete stranger. She searched her mind for an answer she could give him without relinquishing any more information, but he spoke again before she had the chance.

"If you are from Earth, you must be an apprentice in the magickal arts. Tell me, who is your master?"

"Gustave," she answered. Warrick let out a boisterous laugh, drawing the attention of nearby spectators.

"The old mage must have decided to make Arthidgen his base of operations."

A deafening roar from the audience distracted them both. Only one pair was still exchanging blows, a woman with extremely long, flaming red hair that whipped around her as she expertly spun away from the man opposite her. In one swift motion she charged him, rapidly delivering blow after blow until she had disarmed him.

"Yield!" shouted the unarmed man. The crowd burst into applause.

"I shall return," said Warrick as he hopped from the fence with his little black satchel. The four remaining challengers gathered around him to draw their stones, then returned them after being paired with their next rival. He stood among them, his head close to the others as he spoke to them. He pointed to Lilly and all four turned their heads in her direction. A wave of self-consciousness washed over her.

He returned to the fence as the group divided into two pairs. The bell sounded and swords flew. Warrick repositioned himself on the fence beside Lilly.

"What did you mean," asked Lilly after he was settled, "when you said that Gustave had made this place his base of operations?"

"He's sent former apprentices here already. Look." He motioned to the arena. Lilly smiled. One of the two men in the ring must be Dorwynn.

"Which one is Gustave's former apprentice?" she asked.

"All of them."

Lilly watched as the swordsmen, and swordswomen, battled in the arena. The red-haired woman was fighting the man with the black hair, her lean body weaving expertly away from every blow he attempted. Though they were moving at amazing speeds, she noticed the man was wearing a leather harness around his bare chest. His arms were free to move about, but the straps criss-crossed over his back to hold his huge white wings flat against his back.

The other pair, also a man and a woman, performed a complicated series of techniques that reminded Lilly of a performance art show Beth had dragged her to last year. The blonde woman was lithe and thin and Lilly wondered where her strength came from, as she had very little muscle tone. Her opponent's muscles rippled under the suns, his body a deep, sun-kissed bronze against his fair-skinned opponent. His hair also showed signs of sun exposure, blonde highlights scattered throughout his chestnut hair. Something about him seemed very familiar to her, but she couldn't place it.

All four of the remaining participants seemed equally matched as their combat continued, though Lilly noticed that the blonde woman was beginning to tire. She'd already dropped her sword and shield, which had sent the crowd into a frenzy, but she fought valiantly, refusing to yield. A failed attempt to disarm her opponent was her downfall. She picked up her sword from the dirt for the second time and shook her rival's hand before leaving the field.

She arrived beside Warrick and Lilly out of breath after her exhausting ordeal. Lilly couldn't believe how beautiful she was. Her pale skin was flawless in every aspect, as perfect as the face of a porcelain doll. Her hair, nearly as pale as her skin, cascaded down her back, its decent ending at her waist. Her eyes were the same emerald green as Lilly's, sparkling wildly in the bright suns.

"Hello, Warrick," she greeted the man perched beside Lilly. "Is this the new apprentice?" Lilly's heart fluttered. That must have been what he had told them before the match. Knowing they were all former apprentices of the great Gustave, the *real* Gustave, made her more self-conscious than ever.

The woman didn't wait for Warrick to respond. "I am Amparo," she said, offering her hand to Lilly, who accepted it with caution.

"I'm Lilly."

"Are you enjoying the swordsmanship challenge?" She smiled a radiant smile, her attitude lighthearted although she had just lost. Lilly decided at once that she liked this woman.

"It's wonderful," she replied. "I've never seen anything quite so…competitive."

"Yes," the woman said, chuckling, "some of us more so than others." As if she knew he was coming, she turned just in time to face the dark-skinned man sauntering toward them.

"I think," said the man distastefully, "that anyone with such vast experience aught not be allowed to participate." He glared at the woman he had just lost the match to. She was bowing to the raving crowd, taking great pleasure in their adoring cries.

"And where," asked Amparo, "would your displeasure lie if Zephra had not been your opponent?" It was obvious to Lilly that her earlier remark had been about this man.

"Nowhere," he replied, "for I would have defeated all others." Amparo rolled her eyes at his conceit.

Warrick jumped from the fence suddenly and sprinted toward the middle of the arena to announce the final match. In his haste, he knocked Lilly off balance and she fell, landing in the winged man's arms.

"Opyre," announced Amparo, "meet Lilly, Gustave's newest apprentice."

"Pleasure," he said, staring deep into her eyes. Lilly was spellbound by his gaze, unable to take her eyes from him. His eyes were a strange bluish-violet color, unlike anything she'd seen before and they seemed to hold her within their grasp. She finally looked away when the man released his grip on her and lowered her to the ground.

"Why do you bind them," she asked, referring to the leather harness encasing his restrained wings.

"Some unfair advantages are more obvious than others," he answered, his expression souring. "Besides, I'm not about to allow a less-experienced opponent disable my ability to fly."

"Stop your whining, Opyre," said Amparo, her eyes gleaming with mischievousness. "You have no room to complain about over-experience. With the exception of Zephra and myself, you have more experience than anyone else who set foot in the arena today."

"That's not the point," he argued as he removed the harness and spread his wings. Lilly gasped at their enormous size. They were half again as large as the wings Rohan had flown her home with and she wondered what his wingspan was. She guessed it had to be nearly thirty feet.

The bell sounded in the arena and they all turned to watch the final match. The woman Opyre had just lost to seemed as strong as ever, while the man pressed through his deteriorating strength. The arena was more silent than it had been since Lilly first arrived and in that silence, she inadvertently heard two people talking to each other in low voices.

She could tell it wasn't a conversation of the mind and tried to block it out to avoid hearing a private conversation, but found she couldn't. It was almost as if whoever was speaking wanted her to hear what was being said.

"We should get this over with," said a woman's voice. "You have a job to begin."

"I always have something to do," returned a man's voice. "My job will wait until this is over."

"And keep the new apprentice waiting? Shame on you." Lilly's eyes scanned the bleachers, looking for anyone whose mouth was moving. They were talking about her, which meant that the man involved in the conversation was Dorwynn. Perhaps there were more of Gustave's apprentices were in the stadium.

"Would you put off her training until after the celebration," the woman continued, "or shall training commence immediately?"

"I supposed that shall depend on what she would prefer."

"If she is as green as I expect, you should get started as soon as possible."

"Isn't it as equally important she should learn the customs of our holidays so she may understand what she is training for?"

The woman didn't answer him, or if she did, Lilly couldn't hear. A sudden burst of energy from the weary competitor disarmed his foe and he lashed out at her, his sword glancing repeatedly off her shield until she yielded. The crowd went wild, making it impossible for Lilly to hear any more of the mysterious conversation. People began flooding into the arena to congratulate their new champion. Amparo grinned at Opyre.

"See," she said pointedly," Zephra has more experience than everyone in the town put together and she didn't win." Opyre glared at her. The woman, who Amparo had called Zephra, made her way to the group surrounding Lilly, fighting her way through the swarming crowd. They were so loud that Warrick's announcement of the new champion could not be heard over the commotion. Zephra flashed them a huge grin as she approached.

Lilly could tell at once that she was a magickal creature, but not what kind she was. Her hair was a deep violet-red, with thin streaks of orange-blonde that gave it a fire-like quality as it blew in the breeze. Her skin was extremely pale, as if the suns' rays had no effect on it whatsoever. Her eyes, however, were what captivated Lilly. They were unlike any color she'd ever seen, even more so than Opyre's, a deep violet shade with tiny flecks of gold that glistened in the sunlight.

"You let him win," Opyre stated sourly. "Why does he deserve such considerations over the rest of us?"

"Because," replied Zephra, "his circumstances will remove him from the next several competitions." Her eyes twinkled flirtatiously. "When your circumstances change, I will happily bestow the same kindness on you."

"Well don't think for one moment that I will be so generous when your own circumstances change. I don't *let* anyone defeat me. It is something they must do for themselves."

"Have no fear, Opyre," she said, her eyes dancing, "no one assumes you to be generous." Opyre's jaw dropped. Amparo laughed, her voice sounding like chimes in the wind. A smile crossed Lilly's face as well, something that did not escape Zephra's notice. "At last you've arrived," she said, focusing her strange eyes on Lilly. "I must admit, you're nothing like I expected."

"What were you expecting?" Lilly asked, unsure about this woman's intentions. Something deep within her stirred, something she couldn't describe. It was an odd sensation she'd never felt before and she didn't know if she should trust it or fear it.

"The way Gustave raved about you," Zephra responded, "I assumed you to be older, more experienced. How old are you, anyway?"

"Fifteen," Lilly answered, regretting it the moment she did.

"Fifteen!" laughed Zephra. "What was he thinking?" Lilly felt instantly threatened by Zephra. Anger bubbled within her, an anger like she had never felt. Before she could respond, however, Amparo came to her defense.

"You know better than to question Gustave," she spat at Zephra. "His wisdom and patience are the only reasons we are all Masters. One might have asked what he was thinking when he chose us for apprenticeship. Wouldn't you agree?"

Zephra was speechless, which pleased Lilly to no end. She turned to Amparo, who she now considered an ally.

"If you are all Masters," she said, trying to change the subject, "perhaps you know the whereabouts of another, a man named Dorwynn." The three Masters were silent, smiles on each of their faces that denoted they knew a secret she didn't. She was about to ask again when someone tapped her on the shoulder. She whirled around and found herself face to face with the man who had just been declared the new champion swordsman. He smiled at her and offered his hand.

"I am Dorwynn."

The New Champion

"You're Dorwynn?" asked Lilly. The man couldn't have been much older than twenty. She focused her emerald eyes on Zephra and raised one eyebrow. "And you were giving me a hard time about *my* age?" Amparo laughed. Zephra glared at Lilly, the orange flecks in her eyes spreading their glow through the violet parts. Even the seemingly pessimistic Opyre snickered. Dorwynn smiled at Lilly, his hand still outstretched. She shook his hand and a wave of familiarity flooded her senses as she realized who he reminded her of.

She knew it couldn't be him. Adrian was only fifteen, too, but this man looked like a cross between her memory of Adrian at twelve, when she had last seen him, and the Adrian she had seen in her dreams. Dorwynn had the same piercing pale-blue eyes that sparkled in the same way. This man could very well have been his brother.

"She gave me a hard time about my age at first," he told Lilly, his eyes shining. "We humans pale in comparison until we prove ourselves in the eyes of the magickal folk."

"Well," observed Lilly, "no one here looks old enough to be a Master." They all smiled, except for Zephra, whose sour expression remained firmly planted on her face.

"Let's see," said Amparo thoughtfully, "I will be four and one hundred years this autumn."

"Seventy-two at the winter solstice," chimed Opyre. Lilly was shocked, for neither seemed to be much older than their mid-twenties. She looked at Zephra, waiting for her next rude remark. Zephra averted her eyes, which were now a blazing orange-red. Lilly decided not to push the issue. Warrick pushed his way through the crowd, breaking the uncomfortable tension, and threw his arm around Dorwynn's shoulder.

"Come, Champion," he boomed. "We celebrate at Tanner's Tavern!" He started walking away, dragging Dorwynn with him.

"I guess we're going to Tanner's," Dorwynn called, trying to fall into step with the energetic man clinging to him.

"Tanner's Tavern," Lilly muttered. "There's a tongue-twister for you."

"Just wait until you hear forty drunken men trying to say it," laughed Amparo. "Come, Lilly, we have much to celebrate." She grabbed Lilly's hand and followed Opyre, who was already several paces ahead of them. Zephra lagged behind, silenced by her anger.

Tanner's was a huge tavern, the building itself three times larger than any other building on the block, and was constructed of large, smoky-gray bricks with a huge sign above the wooden door that displayed the name of the tavern in bright blue letters. The area inside was spacious despite the dozens of round tables scattered throughout the rooms. The tables were made of cherry oak, as were the six chairs surrounding each one. The bar stretched the length of the back wall. It split in the middle to allow the employees entry to the area behind the bar, where Lilly guessed there were more than a hundred glass decanters lining the wall, each one filled with liquid of different colors. Two massive kegs of ale sat at each end of the bar.

To the left of the entrance was a gaming area, which included a dartboard, two pool tables and a game Lilly had never seen before, where a small ball about the size of a ping pong ball was rolled down a long, narrow board. The point was to get the ball into the hole furthest down the plank by using the wooden handles jutting out each side of the starting end of the plank to steer the ball without losing it in other holes along the way. A piano was positioned right next to the front door and the huge empty area near it was full of dancing couples. A very tall man was sitting at the piano, moving his large fingers effortlessly over the keys to produce a beautiful melody, and Lilly felt a sudden longing to approach him, missing the feel of the ivory beneath her fingers.

Colorful rugs announced the paths across the hardwood floors to the entrances into the rooms jutting off each end of the main hall, the beige-yellow walls covered with elaborate paintings of magickal scenery. Lilly stopped to admire one in particular, a painting of a woman levitating in the center of a stone circle. A white light radiated from her and she was encircled by four dark silhouettes, each surrounded by a different colored light. She stared at it for a moment, intrigued.

"Beautiful, isn't it?" asked Amparo behind her. "It was painted over two hundred years ago by a famous prophet and hung here as a reminder that this had yet to come true."

"What has yet to come true?"

"The prophecy. It is believed that there is a Chosen One who will come to be our salvation against the reign of evil. No one really knows what the painting itself means, but it is an event that must take place for it to happen."

"Do you think it will come true?" Lilly asked, wondering how much more information Amparo knew. Amparo shrugged.

"Prophets have been seeing this and many other events over the past several hundred years, but one has yet to occur." She looked through the doorway that led to an outdoor seating area, an odd look on her face. Lilly wondered what she was thinking about and was about to ask when her mood suddenly lifted. "Come on," she said lightheartedly. "Let's join the others."

Dorwynn was already seated at a table with Warrick and Opyre, enjoying their first round of drinks. Passersby were congratulating him of his new championship, slapping him on the back or shaking his hand, all of them laughing and joking with him as if they were old friends. His blue eyes twinkled, enjoying the glory he was receiving while retaining his courteous and generous nature. Amparo and Lilly took their seats at the table and the gentlemen cheered at their arrival. Lilly looked around for Zephra. She knew she had been lagging behind, but had lost sight of her when they arrived. She finally noticed her in a nearby corner, watching the new stranger who had ruffled her feathers so. She walked toward the table when she saw that Lilly had seen her and took the only empty chair, which was directly across from Lilly.

"So," boomed Warrick, his boisterous voice carrying over the din of the tavern, "do you plan on entering any of the other events this week?" Lilly was interested in his answer and waited patiently for him to respond. She realized now that the conversation she had heard earlier had been between Dorwynn and Zephra during their sparring match. His reply would answer her questions as well. Would they be staying to enjoy the festivities, or would her training begin immediately?

"Well," Dorwynn replied slowly, his eyes focused on Lilly, "I'm not sure. I suppose it depends on what this young lady would like to do." His eyes twinkled and reminded her again of Adrian. He got the same twinkle in his eye whenever he was about to say something profound, or just plain ornery. Lilly hadn't expected him to leave the decision up to her and she knew by that twinkle that he had done it on purpose. He was testing her.

"Well, little lady," Warrick said, looking at Lilly, "what will it be? Will you stay for the rest of the celebration?"

"How long will the celebration last?" she asked.

"Three more days. Tomorrow is the archery tournament and the obstacle course. The next day will be the dagger competition, followed by the magickal duels, and on the final day, we honor those we are celebrating with a huge feast and a ceremony that lasts until dawn." Warrick slurped down the rest of his ale, grinning broadly. "So, what do you say?"

"I suppose," she said, choosing her words carefully, "some rest would be a welcomed break. I've been training since I arrived, except for the few days I spent traveling. A few days of peace would be great." The table cheered, except for Zephra, who seemed ready to be rid of her. Lilly ignored her glare, but felt angered by it. She had done nothing to Zephra, but the woman acted like she was evil incarnate. Those at nearby tables cheered as well, though they knew not what they were cheering for. So it goes with group mentality.

The barmaid arrived and began taking orders, informing everyone that drinks were on the house, as they were seated at the table of the champion. The men ordered a second round of ale for each of them, and then Amparo gave her order. The barmaid looked at Lilly next, ready for her order, but before she could speak, Zephra beat her to it.

"Give her a Kilpa Firewater," she said, grinning. "I'm sure she would enjoy it very much." The rest of the table looked at her in disbelief.

"Really," said Amparo, her mood souring, "you should know better than to offer Kilpa Firewater to a human, let alone a newcomer."

"I'll have a Kilpa Firewater," Zephra countered, rolling her eyes at Amparo. A smug look crossed her face. She seemed to gain satisfaction that Lilly wouldn't order the drink. Lilly just smiled at her sweetly, and then turned her attention to the bewildered barmaid.

"I'll have a honey wheat pale ale, please," she told the barmaid, ordering the same drink she'd heard Amparo order moments before. The barmaid nodded and hustled back to the bar.

"They're really good," Amparo told her, smiling. She was impressed by the way Lilly was handling Zephra's not-so-discreet attempts to humiliate her.

The barmaid returned moments later with their drinks, and conversations flowed throughout the table as the night wore on. Opyre, after his fourth ale, jumped to his feet and bowed next to Lilly's chair.

"May I have this dance?" he asked regally. She smiled and accepted, slightly inebriated herself. Warrick followed suit and danced with Amparo, whose chime-like laughter melded with the music to create a melody of unparalleled beauty as she moved gracefully across the dance floor. Lilly was surprised how graceful Opyre was, considering the amount of ale he'd consumed already tonight. His mood was much more relaxed than when she'd first met him, but that suited her just fine. He was much more pleasant to be around now. They finished the dance and Lilly laughed as Opyre swung her around as the song ended. The dancers applauded the minstrel and headed back to their table.

"So," Zephra chimed self-righteously when they returned, "where are you staying tonight? By now, there are no vacancies anywhere in town." The thought hadn't occurred to Lilly. She'd assumed that accommodations had already been arranged for her. She forgot to take into account that they had no idea of her exact arrival.

"I have a spare bed in my room," said Amparo, coming to Lilly's rescue again. "You are more than welcome to stay with me." Lilly smiled at Amparo, grateful for the unspoken camaraderie between them.

"Thank you," Lilly replied. "I accept."

Zephra's eyes glazed over with an orange haze and she settled back in her chair, crossing her arms. Lilly decided that she would no longer avoid Zephra's attempts at humiliation, but confront them wholeheartedly. She had an ally, which gave her the courage to stand up to this woman who seemed so intent on trying to intimidate her.

"So," she said in the same haughty tone, "you never did tell me how old you are." Zephra narrowed her eyes and stood, putting her hands on the table as she leaned toward Lilly. The orange hue in her eyes turned to blazing crimson and her pupils narrowed into thin slits, like the eyes of a cat.

"Not that it is any of *your* business," she growled in a low voice, "but I am older than anyone at this table, in this bar or in the entire town. I'm older than you can ever comprehend and you would be wise not to challenge me again." Lilly lowered her eyes. That was one answer she had not expected. The humiliation she felt now was of her own doing.

The table was overcome with an uncomfortable silence. Zephra sat down, keeping her burning eyes on Lilly. Opyre and Dorwynn kept their eyes on their drinks. They knew better than to anger Zephra. Warrick decided to change the subject, drawing the attention from Zephra's anger.

"Are you planning to enter any of the events tomorrow?" he asked Lilly. She looked shocked.

"I doubt it," she replied. "I don't have any kind of combat training. I wouldn't last two seconds in that arena."

"Your former master didn't train your in weaponry?" Opyre asked in disbelief. "What have you been doing for the past six months?"

"Training in basic magick and reading. That's about it. I'm not about to attempt a dagger fight unprepared. That would be a dismal ending, getting my head chopped off before my training even begins." The others laughed.

"That's not possible," Dorwynn said. "The entire arena is magickally protected. Anyone who carries a weapon into the arena will find their weapon blunted, unable to slice even bread. It hurts to be hit, but it does no serious injury. Even weapons carried by the spectators are useless within the walls of the arena."

"I still don't think I'm ready for it yet," Lilly admitted. "Perhaps in a future celebration I will enter."

"Like you would ever have the nerve to enter the arena," Zephra muttered. Amparo stood suddenly, knocking her chair backward to the floor. She'd finally had enough of Zephra's attitude.

"No one pretends for a moment to be as perfect as you," she shouted at Zephra. "Why can't you just cut her some slack? You're acting like a spoiled child! Someone as old as you are should know how to show a little respect." Zephra stood facing Amparo, her eyes blazing with the same venom she'd had when Lilly had angered her. Her hair began to blow, though there was no breeze. The men jumped up from the table.

"You know the rules," said Warrick, his voice desperate. "No fighting in here and absolutely no magick." Zephra turned toward him, her face shadowed by a deep violet undertone. She looked like a burning candle, her hair causing the fiery effect. Warrick wilted into his chair and Zephra focused again on Amparo, who showed no signs of fear. Before anything occurred, however, Zephra returned to her normal appearance and sat slowly. Lilly was bewildered by her sudden change until she noticed that Dorwynn had discreetly taken her hand. It was his touch that had calmed her.

"It's getting late," he said. "Let's have breakfast at Migfelá's early tomorrow. Is sunrise alright with everyone?" Opyre guzzled this remaining ale and stood, swaying.

"Goodnight, all," he said loudly as he stumbled toward the door.

"Come, Zephra," Dorwynn said, "let's make sure he arrives safely. Good night, ladies." He and Zephra followed Opyre out the door. Amparo looked at Lilly and raised her glass.

"To your first night in Arthidgen," she laughed. "May the rest be just as interesting." Lilly laughed with her and clinked her glass to Amparo's.

"To Gustave, whose fortitude brought us all together."

"Here, here!"

The two friends talked and drank for another hour before they retired to Amparo's room, their light-hearted conversation continuing until the wee hours of morning. For the first time since she had come to Buthania, Lilly felt like a normal girl, a girl who had sleepovers and bouts of gossip, instead of the prophesized Chosen One who would save two worlds. Their conversations drifted from such topics as Amparo's opinion of the other Masters in the group and her unfortunate situation of losing her parents as a child, to Lilly's limited experience in magick and her own absent parent. Despite their age difference of ninety-eight years, their personalities were so similar they could have been sisters. Lilly's heart suddenly panged for Beth and guilt washed over her for abandoning her family.

"Stop feeling guilty," Amparo said as she searched haphazardly through a bureau drawer. "I'm an empath," she explained when she saw Lilly's shocked expression. "I don't know what you are thinking, but I can feel whatever you are feeling and you are feeling guilty."

"I'm thinking about my family," she admitted, completely comfortable to open up to her new friend. "I always blamed myself for my mother leaving, because of her timing. I guess I feel bad because I had no time to give them an explanation of why I left them behind and I don't want to think that they might be blaming themselves, or each other."

"Well," said Amparo simply as she found her lost item, an elaborately adorned silver hairbrush, "it's okay to feel regret for hurting someone. It's good, in fact, but regret can lead to guilt, which is *not* good. Guilt is consuming and it opens doorways for other consuming attributes. Everything happens for a reason and when you regret a decision you've made, it means you regret the outcome, which has ultimately brought you to exactly where you are right now."

"And my mother leaving, abandoning the entire family?" Lilly asked her. "What would the reasons be for that?" Amparo was silent, a thoughtful expression on her face as she brushed her long hair.

"Perhaps," she said finally, "your mother's absence was the factor that determined your decision to come here. Had she stayed and built the functional family you so desired, do you honestly believe you would have left it behind to fulfill your destiny?"

Lilly considered this possibility. She'd never thought of it quite like that before. She watched as Amparo expertly braided her hair as far as she could by hand and then finished it with the aid of magick down the length of her back. With her hair pulled away from her face, Lilly noticed her ears, which came to a point at the tip. She was an elf!

"I thought you knew," Amparo responded to Lilly's unspoken surprise, "or I would have told you."

"I didn't want to be rude."

"Nonsense," she assured her. "Someday I'll tell you all about the Elvin race, but that must wait for a later time." She lay down in her bed and pulled the blankets up to her chest. "We're expected at Migfelá's in less than four hours. Try to get some sleep."

Lilly settled into her own bed and closed her eyes. Sleep came easily and the dreams that followed were beautiful. Though nothing she dreamed was specific, images of peaceful times flashed in her mind, images of people helping others less fortunate than themselves, free education for all who wanted it, humans and magickal creatures alike living in harmony. The streets were void of homeless souls and wrongdoing and money mattered not. It was a perfect society, where both nature and the deities were worshipped together and the world was in perfect balance.

The last image she remembered before waking was of a castle. She did nothing more than wander the great halls as a voice echoed in her ears, repeating the same thing over and over: *They will all bow to you.*

Amparo woke her at five-thirty. They both dressed as quickly as possible and walked to Migfelá's diner, their animated discussion drawing the attention of fellow early-risers. They were the first of the group to arrive, which left them to find a table large enough for their group. It wasn't an easy task, as small as the diner was, but they managed to push two tables together in a secluded area.

Though it was small, the diner was cozy. It reminded Lilly of a fifties diner, minus the "new aged" technology. The walls were a neutral tan, broken by soft blue patterns across a portion of the walls. Navy curtains decorated the huge windows and the floors were bright and clean. Overall, the entire place was warm and inviting.

Zephra arrived shortly after and sat at the table, careful not to meet Lilly's eyes. Opyre stumbled in behind her and slid into the chair next to Amparo, his face littered with the effects of his overindulgence the night before.

"Where's Dorwynn?" he muttered. "He decided on the hour and he's the last one here." As if on cue, Dorwynn walked through the door of the diner, looking more refreshed than the rest of the group.

"Ladies," he said, placing a tiny seed in each of their hands, "I hope your night was pleasant." He seated himself between Lilly and Zephra and whispered inaudibly. The seeds the women held began to grow rapidly, each one turning into a beautiful, full-bloomed flower that resembled an iris in shape, though orange and pink hues swirled through it like a sunset on a clear night.

"Show off," Opyre muttered under his breath, and Dorwynn chuckled.

They dined on everything from eggs and sausage to pancakes to something called revola, a strange fruit-filled pastry that Lilly enjoyed very much. The conversation was energetic after a few cups of dryka, which was similar to coffee in both taste and effect, and focused primarily on the events scheduled for the day. They consisted of an archery tournament and an obstacle course the town had dubbed "The Fool's Journey", for someone had yet to complete it. Entries would be accepted until noon and the games would begin at one o'clock.

When their meals were complete, the group headed toward the arena. Amparo entered the archery tournament and registered her weapon, which was the main rule for entry. The contestants were required to use their own tools or weapons for the events they entered. Dorwynn and Opyre signed themselves up for "The Fool's Journey", which was open to anyone who wanted to try it.

"You should take a run through," Dorwynn said to the three women.

"Not I," Amparo insisted. "I'm reserving my energy for the tournament. Lilly, you should give it a try." Lilly didn't answer, returning instead a look of panic. Zephra snickered.

"I figured you would be scared," she said. She walked toward the entry booth and took her place in the line to sign up. A surge of courage and anger flooded Lilly's senses and she followed Zephra, her head held high as she flashed her a grin and stood behind her in the line.

"Quite a spitfire, isn't she" Amparo commented, noticing Dorwynn's admiring gaze.

"That she is," he agreed, his eyes shining as he watched her. Amparo didn't need to be an empath to know what he was feeling, for she could see it on his face.

"She's only fifteen," she reminded him gently. He averted his eyes from Lilly to Amparo.

"I know," he admitted seriously, "but she won't be fifteen forever." He walked away toward a small group of people and positioned himself near Opyre, joining the conversation at hand. Amparo shook her head, thinking to years before when she had reminded Zephra of Dorwynn's age. Zephra had looked at him the same way.

The obstacle course was an elaborate series of challenges, each of which were pieced together to form a complete circle. The contestants entered the course in the order they signed up. When the event began, Lilly watched as one contestant after another was knocked from the course's platform. Opyre made it nearly three-quarters of the way through before he was finally knocked out by an extremely difficult trial. Dorwynn made it to the same challenge and was knocked out at the same place. The crowd roared nonetheless.

"No one has finished the course since the man who designed it," Amparo informed Lilly. "No one has made it past that challenge for quite some time. It takes out almost everyone."

What was I thinking? Lilly asked herself as people continued to fail. She had let Zephra get to her. She had never before let what others believed about her sway her decisions, but something about Zephra affected her to her core. Now she was committed to this crazy scheme, something she never would have done otherwise.

Zephra's run through the course sent the crowd into a frenzy. She danced her way easily through the first four challenges, which encumbered nearly half of the ten-challenge series. The fifth and sixth challenges came close to dropping her, but she managed to slide through still standing. The eighth challenge, which had taken down everyone who managed to reach it, had knocked Zephra to the side, but she managed to stay in the game. The crowd doubled in size instantly as their din carried through the town, growing louder as more and more people joined to cheer her on. She fell in the ninth challenge, but the crowd was ecstatic. She had made it farther than anyone else.

"You're next," said the man at the entrance of the course. Lilly's heart raced as she was suited in protective gear that would help diminish the blows she was sure she would be dealt. She took the starting position and waited for the bell to sound, watching the four log pendulums swinging side to side, seemingly with no pattern whatsoever. When the bell sounded, she stared, waiting until she saw the opening, and then she sprinted through, making it safely to the platform between the first and second trials.

The second challenge consisted of two huge rotating trunks with large logs bore through them. As they rotated, the logs swung over the area where Lilly had to cross. She ducked the one that swung near her head, then jumped over another and landed on the next platform. Without stopping, she dashed up the narrow bridge, made of nothing more than wooden planks and rope. It swayed and rocked in all directions, but she completed it easily.

The fourth challenge was a steep incline, with a person at the top tossing huge balls down at whoever tried to get past. Lilly found that though they were large, they were painless, so she pushed her way through the bombardment to the platform at the top. The only way down was the next trial, which was simply a net, its spacing wide. Lilly found it more difficult than it looked at first, but she held fast, nearly falling twice before reaching the next platform.

She stood for a moment, contemplating how she would get past the next challenge, which was constructed of two log pendulums, only they swung back and forth instead of side to side. She tried to remember how Zephra had managed to slip past it, but her memory failed her. Finally, she decided to just go for it. She'd made it far enough that she felt confident in her abilities, even if she didn't finish the course. As one pendulum swung toward her, the other swung away. She took a few steps, following the one moving away from her, then stepped to the side as the other swung in the direction she was moving and jumped onto the platform, barely missing the log barreling toward her from behind.

Trial number seven was nothing more than an unstable floor littered with hundreds of marble-sized pebbles. Lilly skated over them expertly. Then came number eight, where everyone but Zephra had fallen. It was a combination of the first two, with both the sweeping arms and the pendulums swinging side to side. It was very difficult and Lilly watched it for some time, trying to locate the split second when the opening was obvious. When she found it, she dashed through, succeeding despite the fact that one of the sweeping arms hit her in the shoulder. She knew she'd have a battle wound from the blow, for it knocked the wind out of her.

She waited for a moment to catch her breath and looked into the crowd. They were bubbling over with excitement at having not one, but two competitors make it so far. She caught a glimpse of her group. Except for Zephra, who was fuming, they were proudly cheering her on. She regained her composure and focused on the next trial.

It was similar to the second one, but the arms that jutted from the logs rolling to and fro were much smaller, and they were spiked. There was a space in each of the rollers, a small gap where one or two of the spiked branches were missing. She stared down the middle of her path as the rollers twirled around it. They crowd waited in silent suspense for her to make a move. Lilly closed her eyes, blocking out everything else around her, then opened them, focusing on the task at hand. The rollers had to have a pattern. She watched for so long, a few impatient audience members began shouting at her to continue, but she paid them no heed. After seven cycles of the rollers, the opening revealed itself. She put her arms together above her head and dove through the gap, praying the she wouldn't impale herself on the spikes.

The crowd roared with applause as she landed on the platform. She'd made it father than anyone ever had, except, of course, for the man who had built it. As she stood there, watching the final challenge, she wondered how anyone could get through it. It was nothing more than a huge gap, which she doubted any human could jump. High above the gap was a round wheel which spun around like a ceiling fan, with ropes dangling from its perimeter. Attached to each rope was a huge ball, similar to the ones thrown at her during the fourth challenge. She didn't think that it would hurt too badly to be hit by one, though she knew it would knock her out of the competition.

The ropes spun toward her over the gap and she watched them move, wondering how in the world she could get past them. After staring for quite some time, she figured it out. Its simplicity, in fact, was so obvious, she couldn't believe it had taken her so long to see it. She knew she could finish now, but a new thought occurred to her: *Should* she finish? Ashya had told her to keep a low profile and not attract too much attention to herself, yet here she was, already a champion in the eyes of the town. When she noticed Zephra's expression, she decided she *would* finish. She'd entered the course because of her, so she may as well gain the satisfaction of beating it.

She jumped into the center of the gap, grabbing onto the rope and boulder dangling in her path. It continued to revolve, bringing her right back to the platform she'd been standing on. She rode the boulder around the back side of the challenge until it completed its rotation, and then dropped herself on the final platform.

Lilly felt a rush of excitement as the nearby audience clamored to congratulate her. Opyre was stunned and stood rooted to his spot, his mouth agape, as people pushed past him toward their amazing new victor. Zephra and Dorwynn stood with him, sharing his disbelief, while Amparo ran toward her, hollering loudly how proud she was of Lilly's success.

"She did it," Opyre said, his voice ringing with admiration. "That is the most incredible thing I've ever seen."

"I know," Dorwynn agreed. "I told you she's amazing." The hurt was clear in Zephra's eyes as she listened to Dorwynn's praises. She glanced at Lilly and allowed the anger to rise up within her before she turned on her heel and fled the group, barely making it to the edge of the forest before her hair burst into flames.

Zephra walked until she could no longer hear the crowd cheering, then leaned against a tree and stared at nothing in particular. Since she had met Dorwynn, she'd never seen his eyes light up like they just had around anyone but her. She glanced through the trees, glaring at the entire town as though it represented Lilly. She willed herself to hate this new person who cramped her style so, but hate would not come. For reasons beyond her comprehension, she felt connected to Lilly in a way she'd never been with anyone other than Dorwynn. She resented feeling this way, but she was also intrigued by it. Whoever she was, the connection she felt meant that this girl must be special.

Zephra trusted Gustave's judgment and knew that his wisdom was unparalleled, so when he had instructed her to wait in Arthidgen for the new apprentice to arrive, she had done so without question, just as the other Masters had. Gustave had disappeared immediately after giving his command and had not returned or made contact since. His blatant disregard for her since then sent fresh waves of anger coursing through her blood. Gustave, and now Dorwynn, had found better things to focus their attention on besides her.

Feeling the heat rise within her again, she stalked deeper into the forest and unleashed a massive ball of fire from her hand toward a nearby creek. She continued to shoot fireballs at the water, releasing her anger until Dorwynn approached her. Now over her anger, she allowed the sadness of her long life to wash over her.

At least he's alone, she thought, thankful the rest of the group hadn't followed. She stopped her rampage as Dorwynn reached for her hand, though she jerked it away when she felt his touch. A wounded expression crossed his face and he let his arm fall to his side.

"What's wrong with you?" he asked, his tone defensive. "You've been acting strange since Lilly arrived."

"I'm not the only one," she retorted.

"You don't like her, do you?" His eyes bore into her, searching for the truth.

"It's odd," Zephra admitted, "I don't want to, but I do."

"Why don't you want to like her?" he asked. Zephra looked at him, incredulous. She couldn't believe he had to ask. She turned away from him.

"You know why," she whispered.

"No," he said, "I don't." She could tell from the tone of his voice that he was getting angry, which granted her a small sense of satisfaction. She wanted him to feel as bad as she did.

"Are you really so blind?" she asked him, redirecting her anger at his obliviousness. "I've seen the way you look at her."

"Damn it, Zephra," he shouted, "we've been over this more than once. You know we aren't meant to be together."

"No," she exploded, turning to face him "I don't know that. *You* believe it, but I don't and I never will."

"Why not?!"

"From the moment I met you, I knew you were the one. I feel it with everything in my soul and I just don't understand why you can't see it, too." Tears streamed down her face and she let them fall freely. He wiped a tear from her face and looked into her eyes, which were back to their normal violet hue.

"I've seen a glimpse into my future, Z," he said gently, "and you are not a part of it, not the way you want to be. I am meant to be with someone else."

"And you think she's the one?" Dorwynn didn't respond and Zephra nodded her head, defeated. "I'll assume your silence means that you do." He lowered his eyes.

"What do you want me to say?" he asked her. "I'm not going to lie to you. I do feel that she is the one I'm supposed to be with."

"And if she doesn't agree with you?"

"Then I must deal with it, just as you must. You are my friend, Z, my best friend, but I can't give what you're asking of me. You've got to accept the fact that we are not meant to be."

"And you've got to understand that I will never accept that. I'm still your friend, Dorwynn, and I always will be. I'd rather have you as a friend than to not have you in my life at all, but I will *never* stop believing that we belong together, whether you do or not." She lowered her eyes, wiping away the few remaining tears before meeting his eyes again. There was a sadness in them, a deep regret for causing her so much pain. He pulled her into his arms and held her in his embrace, wishing he could make her understand how he felt.

"We should get back," she said, pulling away from him violently.

"Zephra…"

"I'm sorry," she said, her voice shaking. "I just can't handle you touching me right now." She walked away from him and he followed at a distance, allowing her the space she needed.

As they approached the edge of town, they heard screams of terror coming from the arena. Their argument forgotten, they both sprinted toward the sounds of panic as a woman's voice rose high above the rest of the commotion.

"Harpies!"

Attack of the Harpies

"Protect the children," a man shouted, the two small children in his arms crying as he ran for safety. People were running chaotically in all directions, grabbing children and pulling them toward the nearest shelter. The screams floating through the air jerked Lilly out of her glory. Amparo jumped into action.

"You should hide," she told Lilly, reaching for the bow slung over her shoulder. She grabbed an arrow from her quiver and took aim. Lilly looked in the direction of the arrow she released and watched as it struck the heart of the hideous creature flying toward them. Amparo took aim at another of the creatures closing in. "Go!"

"What about you?" Lilly asked, hesitant to leave her friend behind.

"Don't worry about me," she cried. "Just go!" Lilly followed the terrified mob of people as they scattered hysterically through the streets of Arthidgen. She found a spot behind a pillar where she could watch Amparo expertly defend the town, her arrow hitting its target every time.

The creatures attacking the town were harpies. Lilly had read about them and knew that they were notorious for stealing children capable of magick so they could rob them of their magickal talents. Their bodies were those of women, though their arms were not arms at all. They had no hands, only wings of white and purple feathers. The feathers extended over their thighs, which were attached to long, skinny legs and taloned feet, much like an eagle or hawk. Purple and yellow tail feathers jutted out behind them and were the full length of their legs. Dark green hair hung over their disfigured faces, their mouths open as hideous screeches poured from them.

Lilly watched as the harpies dove toward the crowd, snapping at people with their razor-sharp talons. They began to cluster into a huge black cloud hovering over Amparo, who was now aided by Dorwynn and Zephra. Dorwynn wielded his sword, which seared their already-scarred bodies though the blade was far beyond their reach, and kept the harpies at bay long enough for Amparo to release her arrows. Zephra shot fire balls at them, a new one appearing in her hand the moment she released the one she was holding. Her hair flew around her wildly like an out-of-control fire and Lilly thought she could see real flames there as well. Though the harpies were slowed by the assault, it by no means stopped them from their rampage.

Opyre was in the air, luring harpies from the massive cluster and attacking them with his dagger. One harpy grabbed his wing and he howled, turning the weapon on his attacker. She screamed as the knife pierced her flesh and fell to the ground, writhing in agony. Opyre continued to fly through his pain, fighting to eliminate as much of the threat as he could.

The sound of crying distracted Lilly from the brutal assault. A little girl of no more than six or seven searched for her mother, wandering aimlessly down the deserted street. One of the harpies turned toward the sound, then swooped from the sky toward the girl, its talons outstretched. Without thinking, Lilly ran toward them and threw herself over the child.

She screamed in unison with the harpy's cry as she felt its talons close around her shoulders, ripping through her skin. A searing pain shot down her arms and across her back, throbbing with every beat of the harpy's wings as it lifted her off the ground. Two more harpies joined Lilly's assailant, grabbing at Lilly's arms to aid the one carrying her. Lilly fought to keep the others away, though the pain was becoming unbearable. Her head became light and she could feel the dizziness begin to wash over her, pulling her toward unconsciousness. She could hear the screams of the girl she'd tried to protect as a harpy snatched her from the ground with little effort, and lucidity swept over her as she felt her energy recover. Her months of training in the magickal defenses jumped into her memory and she took action. Lilly called the child to her. The little girl disappeared from the harpy's grasp and appeared in her arms.

"Hold on tight," she told the frightened child. The harpy that carried her faltered, unable to bear the added weight. Her piercing shriek called nearby harpies from all directions as they screeched at each other in their strange language. Lilly closed her eyes and mouthed the words to bring forth the magick she wanted.

"Lilly!" Opyre shouted as he fought his way through the flock of creatures surrounding her.

"Take the child," she commanded, her eyes popping open at the sound of his voice.

"But..."

"Take her!" Opyre didn't argue again. He flew beneath the harpy carrying Lilly, which was still fighting to recover her lost altitude. Lilly dropped the child into Opyre's arms. With the added weight gone, she and her assailant shot high into the air. Two harpies chased Opyre, trying to reclaim their treasure, while the rest followed Lilly.

The magick inside her was ready to be unleashed and she struggled to keep it at bay as long as possible, saving it until she knew she would inflict the most damage. As the other harpies drew near, she forced herself through the excruciating pain to twist her arms around the legs of the one that carried her, wrapping her fingers around the base of the legs where they met the rest of its body.

"*Kita sira,*" Lilly whispered. She felt the magick surge through her blood, felt her heart skip a beat. Wisps of translucent light extended from her hands, still clinging to the creature, and surrounded the harpy. It shrieked just seconds before the magick tore it apart, thousands of tiny particles exploding into the air like a firecracker. The magick continued to pour from her body, surrounding and destroying one harpy after another, their cries on the wind long after their bodies deteriorated.

I did it, Lilly thought wearily as she slipped into unconsciousness, the magick still shooting from her body as she fell toward her inevitable fate.

Amparo sat beside Lilly's bed, fighting to keep her eyes open. She'd been sitting there for hours, waiting for any sign that Lilly was okay. It had been two days since the harpy attack. Lilly had destroyed every one of them that day, but at what cost? She hadn't stirred or moved since Opyre had saved her from crashing into the ground, which would have killed her for sure. As it was, her life hung in the balance, teetering on the brink of death.

Dorwynn had sent for a healer at once, but the healer had done little to help. He had mended her wounds to the best of his abilities, but could give no reason why she had not woken. His best guess was that the magick she had used drained her of too much energy, yet every remedy he tried to bring her back had failed. Dorwynn had kept a constant vigil the first night, afraid to leave her alone for even a second.

The archery tournament was postponed for a day so the people of Arthidgen could repair the disarray caused by the attack. The celebration of Lilly's victory had also been put off, leaving the entire town wondering when, or if, she would recover. No one's heart was in the rest of the celebration after the events that had taken place, though the honorary rituals were still scheduled to take place that night.

Amparo had declined her place in the tournament, choosing instead to keep watch over Lilly for that time. Opyre had entered the dagger tournament and claimed that the only reason he had won at all was because he had imagined he was fighting with the harpies again. Dorwynn was in a constant state of worry, which rattled Amparo a great deal. Normally, he was very good at hiding his emotions from her, but this time he failed miserably. She'd chased him from the room on more than one occasion so she could have some solitude to focus on her own emotions.

Her eyelids were heavy and she was losing the battle to stay awake. No one in their circle had gotten much sleep, and at half past dawn, they were still waiting for word from Gustave, who had been summoned after the healer left the day before. She had relieved Opyre at sunset the night before, volunteering to take the night watch since Lilly was in her room. Dorwynn had insisted on taking her to the town's hospital, but he was outvoted by the others, who reassured him that they could do no more for her than what had already been done.

Amparo's eyes snapped open as someone entered the room. She scowled when she realized it was Zephra. She hadn't said more than two words to her since the attack and her anger still outweighed her forgiveness.

"How is she?" Zephra asked, pulling a chair next to Lilly's bed.

"What do you care?" Amparo spat, stinging Zephra with her words. Zephra hung her head. Dorwynn was still uncomfortable around her over their argument and had been avoiding her ever since, and both Opyre and Amparo had given her the cold shoulder as well, unwilling to forgive her behavior, not that she blamed them.

"I'm sorry."

"I'm not the one you should be apologizing to."

"Why don't you get some sleep," she offered. "I'll keep watch for a while."

"So you can smother her in her sleep? I don't think so."

"Do you really think that I would do that?" asked Zephra. "I may not have been very nice to her, but I didn't want *this* to happen. I never wished her any harm and I still don't." She looked at Lilly, her anger lost in the aftermath. She only wished now that the girl would rise from her comatose state. Amparo sat on the other bed and closed her eyes, allowing only a single tear to escape. "I promise I will wake you if she changes at all."

Amparo nodded, overcome by her fatigue, and leaned back in the bed without bothering to get under the blankets. Zephra sat quietly, losing herself in the silence. She studied Lilly's motionless body. The girl was beautiful. Her copper hair fell around her face, framing it against the white pillow behind her head. Her skin was flawless, except for the small teardrop mark just beneath her left eye. Zephra touched the mark gently.

"I'm so sorry," she whispered, wishing the girl could hear her. "I had no right to treat you like that. My anger was meant for someone else." Zephra had bottled up her anger with Dorwynn for so long that she had allowed it to consume her. Of course, it was her nature to be so jealous, and so fierce, but Lilly didn't deserve to be the outlet for her repressed emotions. She truly regretted treating her so badly.

She also hadn't felt right since the attack, and she had a feeling that her connection with this girl was the cause. Nothing seemed wrong with Lilly physically, yet she would not wake. Something was going on inside her head, something that was keeping her trapped there.

Zephra kept her vigil, contemplating during the quiet hours on whether or not to use her own magick to bring the girl back to them. It could work, but the possibility that it could worsen her condition wasn't worth the risk. She decided to wait for a while. If Lilly didn't wake before long, she would seek the opinion of the others before attempting anything that might cause her harm. If her connection with Lilly was this strong, there was no telling how Zephra's magick would affect her. She could end up killing both of them.

The hours passed and there was still no change. Dorwynn arrived to check on her and Zephra decided, for the time being, at least, that she would put away her anger and focus on saving Lilly. She proposed her solution to him, including the potential harm she could cause and the fact that it might not even work.

"I am leaving it to you to whether or not to include the others," Zephra told him, "though I would prefer you seek their opinions as well. They deserve the same respect."

"Now you're concerned about respect?" he asked.

"Don't start with me, Dorwynn." She looked him dead in the eye, calm and serious. "This is not the place or time to get into such a discussion. We *will* talk, have no doubt, for we have both left many things unsaid that we must resolve. For now, I'll leave you to your decision."

"Wake Amparo," he said without hesitation. "I'll fetch Opyre." He turned and left the room in a rush. Zephra gently shook Amparo's shoulder. The elf stirred and opened her eyes. She jumped up in a hurry.

"What's wrong?"

"Nothing," Zephra assured her. "Dorwynn and I want your opinion about something." Zephra explained her idea once more, leaving nothing out. She had just finished explaining when Dorwynn returned with Opyre.

"I told him on the way," Dorwynn said, gripping the wall as he bent over to catch his breath. He turned to Opyre, who was just as winded. "Well, what do you think?"

"I don't know," he said. "I think maybe we should let this continue to unfold, let things take place the way they should. This might be exactly what's supposed to happen." Disbelief swam through Dorwynn's eyes as Opyre shrugged an apology.

"I agree," said Amparo, yawning. "I want her to wake, too, and I am just as worried as you are, but you know as well as I that everything happens for a reason." She looked at him pointedly, daring him to contradict her.

"Fine," he submitted, "but I think we should at least set a deadline. Another four hours and we let Zephra try."

"Six hours," Amparo countered.

"Agreed," he conceded, his shoulders drooping in defeat.

Over the next three hours, they rotated between keeping watch over Lilly and going to the diner for some food. As the fourth hour began to pass, Opyre decided to take a walk to clear his head. He invited the others to come, but only Amparo accepted. When he was sure they were gone, Dorwynn charged Zephra.

"Do it now," he commanded.

"Do what?"

"Your magick," he said. "Do it now." Zephra shook her head.

"No. We voted *and* we made an agreement," she reminded him. Dorwynn jumped up and flung the covers from Lilly's bed.

"We took a second vote. They missed it. Now do it, Z." The desperation in his voice gave her pause. The frantic look in his eyes dissolved her doubt. She took a deep breath and nodded.

Zephra hesitated, and then slowly knelt beside Lilly. She held her arms over Lilly's chest and closed her eyes. Her hair began to flow around her head and her eyes changed to dark crimson as her lids flew open. Her hands glowed orange as she moved them toward Lilly's head, placing one on each of her temples.

"Hurry," Dorwynn whispered. "They'll be back soon."

"Quiet," she snapped. "I need to concentrate." She held her hands over Lilly's head, her fingers wiggling ever so slightly, as though she were playing a soft tune on an invisible piano. The orange glow spread to Lilly's head, giving her dark hair the same fiery effect as Zephra's.

"They're back," said Dorwynn. Outside, someone knocked on the door.

"Zephra?" called Amparo. "Dorwynn? The door is locked. Would you open it, please? Hello?" She banged louder, causing Zephra to work faster. She moved her hands down the length of Lilly's shoulders and arms, passing over the places where her wounds had been. Lilly suddenly spoke, though she did not wake.

"No!" she shouted. "I don't accept." Suddenly, she began to convulse, her entire body shaking. Zephra grabbed her by the wrist with one hand and placed the other on her forehead. The banging outside got louder as Zephra worked to settle Lilly.

"What's happening?" said Dorwynn, his desperate cry echoing throughout the room. "What's wrong with her? Z, what's wrong with her?!"

Lilly lay on a dirt floor wearing only rags, surrounded by dozens of other women and girls. They were all extremely skinny, wearing rags or naked, lying close to each other for warmth. Feces littered the ground, a terrible stench saturating the air. Nearby, someone was dead. They had yet to remove the body, which had begun decomposing, adding to the acrid smell. Lilly was so exhausted she could barely lift her head to answer the person speaking to her. They called her Hannah. She closed her eyes, returning to the comfort of the darkness.

When she woke again, she found herself in the midst of hundreds of dark-skinned people called Cherokee. They were being herded together by white men with guns, speaking a language she could not understand, forcing them to walk. She wanted to return to her home to retrieve the necklace her mother had made for her, but they would not let her. She walked until she could walk no more. She fell to the ground as she heard her brother call her name: Galilahi.

She heard voices, but could see nothing. Her head was covered by a black cloth. She stood on a stool, listening to taunts from a group of people, a rope around her neck.

"Marion of Essex," a male voice boomed, "you are charged with the crime of performing the rituals of a witch and consorting with the devil, a sentence punishable by death. What have you to say on your behalf?" She said nothing, but closed her eyes, waiting for the inevitable.

Lilly opened her eyes and was surrounded by many men, including members of the clergy. They called her Jeanne d'Arc. She spoke, though she could not hear her words. The members of the clergy held a crucifix before her and she prayed as they lit a fire beneath her. As the fire danced at her legs, she looked across the sky. He was called Gabriel then and sadness was all she saw in his face.

I'm sorry, she said with her mind, knowing he would hear her sorrow. A tear slid down his face and his image faded from her sight. She felt a wave of sadness wash over her with the heat of the fire and she cried, not for herself, but for humanity.

Her face was still wet with tears, though now she was in a boat with three other people. Two of them were women, both cloaked, as was she. The other was a man, her baby brother, struggling to hang onto life until they reached their destination. His sword, Excalibur, lay on his chest, his hand still clutching the handle.

"We are almost to Avalon," she whispered in his ear. She knew she was breaking the rules and that it would mean her expulsion from the sacred land, but she cared not. Arthur deserved to rest in Avalon. She was the only one who could open the doorway and release his soul on the other side.

"Not yet, Arthur," she said, catching sight of the island through the fog, "just a bit longer." Her voice faded on the wind.

She was suddenly in another unfamiliar place. Her hood was pulled over her head to hide herself from the injustice of the people performing this terrible deed. Voices in her head assured her that he would be alright, but how could she believe that when they were nailing him to a wooden cross? He didn't cry out, not once. He knew this was going to happen and accepted his fate willingly.

Darkness enveloped her again and she wondered where she would find herself next. She waited for the darkness to dissipate, but instead, she saw nothing, she heard nothing. She walked aimlessly through the darkness until she heard a voice she'd never heard before but recognized nonetheless.

"Lilly. Come to me, darling." She walked toward the voice and noticed someone coming into view through the void, a woman with shining eyes and a radiant smile.

"Mom?" asked Lilly in disbelief. "Is it really you?"

"Yes, honey," she said, holding her arms open. Lilly rushed into them, losing herself in the first embrace she'd ever shared with the woman who'd given her life, the woman who'd left her behind. She didn't want to let go, but her mother pulled away from her first.

"I don't have much time, honey, so I must hurry with my purpose. I'm from Buthania. I was born here and lived most of my life here. My destiny led me to Earth, and to your father."

"Why did you leave us?" interrupted Lilly.

"Your questions will be answered in time, but I cannot tell you now. It would alter your course."

"But you are here now, in Buthania?"

"Go to my home in Elikrede. The way to find me is there, in a small house between the waterfall's edge and the stone garden." She turned, her image beginning to fade.

"Wait," Lilly said, "I had a vision about you, but it wasn't accurate." Her mother smiled and put her hand on Lilly's face.

"Do not dwell on it," she said firmly. "That vision was nothing more than a memory, modified to keep evil from finding you before you were prepared to protect yourself. You chose wisely to keep the name you were given. It keeps you safe." She hugged Lilly and looked into her face, her own eyes brimming with fresh tears. "Your instincts serve you well. Trust them and trust in yourself. That is all the advice I have to give." Her image faded away slowly as her voice echoed in Lilly's ears: "I love you, my darling girl."

"Wait!" Lilly cried, sobs racking her body. "Don't go!" She sank to her knees and wept, allowing at last all the guilt and despair she felt from her mother's absence to flow from her body with her tears. She cried for what seemed an eternity, until another voice from her past broke the silence.

"It's alright. You're not alone." A hand touched Lilly's shoulder and she lifted her head to come face to face with Adrian. He looked exactly as he had the last time she had seen him three years ago.

"Adrian," she gasped, rushing into his arms. "What are you doing here?"

"Following my own destiny," he replied, "and when you find me, do not call me Adrian."

"Why?" she asked, confused.

"It is my true name, the name given to me by magick itself. You are the only one who knows it. If anyone finds out, it would endanger my life, and possibly yours as well. Please don't tell a soul."

"I won't," she promised, "but what should I call you?"

"Call me what everyone else calls me. You will know what to do when you find me." He smiled, his blue eyes dancing. Gradual changes had begun to take place, changes so slight that Lilly didn't noticed them immediately. He now looked older, fifteen instead of twelve, the way he would look today. He took her hand in his and led her through the darkness. Together they walked, side by side, each taking comfort in the simple fact that they were together again.

"Where are we going?" Lilly asked after a moment. He smiled.

"Of all the questions you want answered," he laughed, "I didn't expect you to ask that one first. I want to show you something." He waved his hand across the empty space and the darkness faded away to reveal the most beautiful place Lilly had ever seen. A clear waterfall rained down and formed a peaceful lake. Flowers of every variety grew throughout the lush green grass. Adrian led her toward a large boulder in the field, a stone similar to the one in her clearing. A large tree grew beside it, providing adequate shade over the otherwise empty space.

"I found this place by accident," he told her, climbing onto the rock before helping her up. "It's my favorite place in this whole world. I come here when I want to be alone, when I want time to think. I've spent countless hours here, staring at the waterfall, thinking about you."

"You've been here all this time?"

"Yes." He stared at the waterfall and Lilly followed his gaze. Where they were sitting, a rainbow could be seen over the lake where the water fell. A flock of swans flew over the falls and settled on the smooth lake, their long necks bobbing gracefully under the water in search of food. Lilly was unsure of what to say to him. She'd been angry at him for leaving, but things were so different now. She still felt betrayed, but all the questions she'd wanted to ask him had faded. She was content to just sit in his presence.

She expected him to say something about what had happened to him in the past three years, but he said nothing. It was unlike him; he usually offered information, sharing everything with her before she had to ask. Now, he was quiet. He asked nothing of her, no questions about what she'd been through or the life he left behind. Caught between her resentment at his leaving and her elation at being near him again, she picked her brain, trying to think of anything she could ask him that might be helpful.

"Am I dreaming?" she finally asked. She'd been tossed through one image after another, none of them making very much sense to her.

"Yes and no," he answered, not helping a bit. "I can't tell you much about what you are going through, but I can tell you that whatever you've seen and experienced in this bizarre situation is important. It's relevant to your destiny."

"But none of it makes any sense," she pointed out.

"Not yet, but it will. It's impossible to put together a puzzle with only a few pieces, but more pieces will come in time."

"How will I find you?"

"You already know the answer to that, and so much more. It's here," he pointed to her temple, "in your subconscious." Lilly was becoming annoyed at him for dodging her questions. She grew quiet, wondering how much longer she had before her subconscious tossed her into another strange scenario. They sat in silence, watching the suns descend over the cliff. Hues of violet, pink and orange flooded the sky, casting the same tones over the silky-smooth lake. He jumped down from the rock and helped her down.

"It's time for you to go," he said. "You can't stay here forever." He walked with her away from the peaceful place and back into the darkness. "I want you to know how much I've missed you. I'm so glad you are here." Lilly frowned. If he was so happy she was there, why didn't he give her more clues about how to find him? He took her hands in his and placed a small seed in them, then closed his hands around hers. A warmth radiated from them and as she opened her hand, the seed sprouted into a beautiful flower as he faded away. She stared at the flower, unaware that her surroundings had changed again. Something in her mind clicked, but before she had time to focus on it, she realized that she was in a large room.

Zephra was there with her, standing near a sophisticated fireplace, a fire blazing inside. She was turned away from Lilly. There was no sound in the room, not even the sounds of Lilly's steps on the marble floor as she walked toward Zephra, who was now staring out a large picture window framed by dark green tapestry-like curtains. She turned to face Lilly, sorrow painted on her face. Her mouth was moving, but Lilly could hear no words.

"I don't understand," Lilly said, her words loud and clear. Zephra's mouth moved again, trying to explain something. Lilly shook her head vehemently, afraid, though she did not know why.

"No!" she shouted. "I don't accept." Zephra smiled sadly, her eyes shining bright.

"I'm so sorry," she said, her words finally audible. She mouthed a few more silent words, and then grabbed Lilly's wrist as everything went dark.

In the darkness, she could hear people shouting. Someone was banging on a door, frantically trying to get in. She recognized one of the voices. It was Beth! No, not Beth. Amparo. She was locked out. But who was in the room with her?

"What's happening?" a desperate voice asked. "What's wrong with her? Z, what's wrong with her?!"

"Nothing," said another voice. That one she recognized immediately. Zephra. "She's fine." She didn't sound very confident. The sound of the door bursting open was followed by a gasp.

"What are you doing?" shrieked Amparo. "You're going to kill her."

"Look," said Opyre. "She's awake."

The darkness lifted as Lilly opened her eyes. Zephra was the first face she saw. She was sitting on the bed next to Lilly, her hand wrapped around Lilly's wrist. Lilly jerked her hand away protectively, the dream she'd just had of her fresh in her mind. She looked around slowly, letting the room come into focus. Amparo and Opyre were standing in front of the door they had just charged through, their expressions a mixture of fear and shock. Dorwynn was standing behind Zephra, his eyes brimming with tears of happiness. Dorwynn. Adrian. It all fit.

She rubbed her wrist where Zephra had grasped it and stood slowly. She felt a little dizzy, but she knew she had enough strength for what she was about to do. She took a few steps toward Dorwynn, looking him straight in the eyes. She reached for him, wanting to caress the face of her best friend, craving the familiar action. Then anger took hold, anger greater than she'd ever imagined. She felt the icy glare as it flashed in her eyes, and in a swift movement that stunned everyone, she slapped him hard, then stalked out the broken door.

Alone with Dorwynn

Lilly leaned against a tree near the forest's edge, listening to the celebration. The town had been notified of her recovery and everyone jumped into action, planning as many of the postponed events as possible into the last night of festivities, which would last until dawn. People clustered around a huge bonfire, laughing, dancing and drinking, their hope renewed. Children played, women gossiped and boisterous men roared at the jokes being told, whether they were funny or not. It was a time for joy, but Lilly felt anything but happy.

She'd spoken to no one since she had woken. They left her alone, though she knew they all had questions. Smells from the boar roasting over the spit wafted toward her, and although she had not eaten since the morning of the harpy attack, she felt no hunger. Anger and betrayal were all she could think about. Dorwynn had lied to her. He was Adrian, though she was still trying to figure out how he could be, since he was now years old than she was. She knew it was him, though. The flower he had given her in her dream, or whatever it was, was the same flower he had brought to each of the girls the morning of the attack, the same flower that grew in Adrian's special place. She had not seen that flower anywhere in this forest.

Her last vision gripped her soul, still constricting her heart. The anguish she felt when she rejected whatever Zephra was offering, the pain and fear that chilled her blood when Zephra grabbed her wrist…none of it compared to the betrayal she felt when she'd woken to find Zephra's hand wrapped around her wrist. She didn't know why she left betrayed, but it left her curious about Zephra's true intentions. Now more than ever, she would guard herself from the woman.

She felt like she had gained years of insight in a matter of hours, though what she had learned made no difference on her outlook. She no longer wanted to train with Dorwynn; his betrayal left a deep wound in her heart. She wanted to go to Elikrede to find her mother, who was somewhere in *this* world. She wanted to find out the secrets that plagued her soul and gain some knowledge about herself and her family.

She was so lost in her thoughts that she didn't hear the footsteps approaching her. A hand touched her shoulder and she whirled around, prepared to defend herself. She lowered her hands when she saw it was Amparo.

"Are you okay?" the elf asked gently. Lilly didn't answer her. She turned her back to the town and stared into the darkness of the forest. Somewhere far from this place were the answers she needed. Amparo didn't prod. She sat on the ground beside Lilly and waited for her to speak. Lilly didn't feel like talking to anyone, mostly because she had to hide so much of herself anyway and she didn't know who she could trust with what information. She lowered herself to the ground. Sitting beside Amparo, she felt a little better. She did trust her, but she knew she still couldn't tell her what she had been through, not without giving away information that she knew she shouldn't.

"I don't know," Lilly finally responded. "I'm angry and confused, but you already knew that." Amparo smiled, confirming Lilly's assumption.

"You really hurt Dorwynn," Amparo told her.

"I didn't smack him very hard," Lilly spat. "He deserved more than what I did to him."

"He doesn't understand why you slapped him. It broke his heart." She looked Lilly in the eye, her emerald eyes shining with tears that threatened to fall. "In fact, none of us understand what's going on. We were all really worried about you." Lilly could see the truth in her statement and felt better knowing that someone cared for her. "Why did you slap him?"

"I have my reasons," Lilly told her, giving the same vague answer she'd received so many times. "I will talk to him when I am ready and he *will* understand, but I can't tell you. It is between me and him."

"I understand," said Amparo, not the least bit upset with her ambiguous reply. "You are an enigma, Lilly. Life is definitely more interesting with you around." Lilly smiled at her, and then let her

PTERIPPUS: THE AWAKENING / 131

expression fall back into its disturbed gaze. Amparo took her hand. "You were amazing during the attack," she said. "Where did you learn to do that?"

"I don't know," Lilly replied, steering her mind to a new mystery. Ashya had never taught her the words she had spoken and she couldn't remember if she'd read them from one of the books, so she really didn't know exactly what she had accomplished. In fact, she could barely remember what words she had spoken. All she knew was what she heard from the rumors circulating through the town. Somehow, she had destroyed every harpy in Arthidgen, but the gossip didn't stop there. Someone had said that the harpies had attacked two other towns as well, one of which was Jesfinarea. It was all but obliterated in the attack. Lilly's heart grew heavy as she thought about the children she'd given the candy to, children who, if they had survived the attack, were now prisoners of the terrifying creatures she had fought.

"I couldn't believe you made it through the obstacle course," Amparo admitted, "but I never thought you would be able to wipe out an entire flock of harpies. It's a shame you had to suffer so much from it." Lilly nodded, not really agreeing with Amparo, but not disagreeing either. Her anger began to take hold of her again. The abuse she had endured from Zephra ate at her soul, and the fact that Dorwynn shared such a strong bond with her only fueled Lilly's rage.

Amparo continued to sit with her in comfortable silence as the night wore on, until their solitude was interrupted by footsteps drawing near. Lilly knew it was Dorwynn and she felt her anger rise. Amparo felt it as well, for she put her hand on Lilly's arm, trying to give her some comfort. He approached them cautiously as Amparo stood.

"You need to talk to him," she whispered to Lilly before disappearing into the forest. Dorwynn waited for Lilly to speak. When she didn't, he sighed and sat beside her.

"How are you feeling?" he asked, genuine concern in his voice. She turned her head in his direction and glared at him, but did not answer. He sighed again. It was bad enough having one woman mad at him, but now there were two and he had no idea why Lilly was so livid.

"I know who you are," she said in a low voice that radiated her anger. When he didn't answer, she moved close to his ear and whispered, "Adrian." A look of shock crossed his face.

"How did you find out?" he asked, his heart beating wildly with panic. He hadn't expected her to figure out his identity already. His absence of denial sent fresh waves of fury through her and she stood in a huff.

"It doesn't matter how I found out," she shouted, releasing the emotions that were bubbling beneath the surface. "How could you lie to me?"

"How did I lie to you?" he asked. She stared at him, her back rigid as she walked toward him. He took a few steps backward and she advanced without stopping until she had him backed against a tree.

"Do you honestly not know," she asked, her voice so calm that fear shot through his spine, "or do you have so many lies that you can't keep track of them?" He lowered his eyes to avoid the vehemence in her stare. If looks could kill, he would have been a goner. "What else are you hiding from me?" she insisted.

"Only what you are not ready to know," he answered, defensive. Lilly felt the fury rise within her, a rage she'd never felt before. On Earth, she'd always been able to retain her emotions, as a general rule. Only when she let the anger build over time did she let it loose, as she did in her last session with Dr. Hoffman. Here, however, she had less control over her emotions, at least since she had left Ashya's and arrived in Arthidgen, since she had met the others. That, mixed with the years of anger she'd pent up at Adrian already, took away the power she had over her own will. The months she'd spent with Ashya learning how to gain control over both her powers and her emotions were useless...forgotten. She felt the magick warming her blood and her vision took on a strange luminosity. She could actually hear his heart begin to beat faster.

"What are you doing?" he asked, his voice shaking with alarm. She didn't answer. Her hands glowed and she lifted her arms straight out at her sides. A massive explosion of light erupted from her hands. A circular wave shot from the explosion, spreading outward from its core. At that instant, everything stopped. The noises coming from the nearby celebration ceased. The flames of the bonfire were motionless and the people surrounding it were fixed in place, trapped in their dancing, bowing and feasting. Dorwynn looked at the frozen display, his eyes wide with fear and awe.

"Lilly," he shouted, "snap out of it!" She showed no signs that she had heard him speak. Her eyes seemed to look right through him. He put his hands on her shoulders and shook her vigorously. Her head suddenly snapped in his direction and he froze out of pure fright. He backed away slowly, never taking his eyes off her.

"Adrian," she said, her voice ringing in an ethereal tone. She lowered her arms and narrowed her eyes. He changed direction instantly and walked toward her, completely under her control. She held her still-glowing palms up to his temples and dove into his mind.

Lilly, he said in his mind, fighting her with what little strength he had, *please, listen to me. Don't do this.*

Ani murat vorta, she commanded. He struggled to keep her out, but she was already winding her way through his mind, riffling through his memories. Soon, she would find what she was looking for and if she did, all would be lost. He tried again.

I know who you are, too, he said, giving her something to focus on besides invading his mind. She stopped, waiting for him to continue, though she did not abandon her actions. *Why do you think they sent me to you?* he continued, hoping it would bring her out of this unnatural state. She stood there for an eternity, completely motionless, and then lowered her hands. Her eyes gradually returned to normal and the spell ended, releasing the town of their unknowing captivity.

"Lilly?" he asked, unsure if she was even aware of what had just occurred. She was still glaring at him. He had grown up with this girl, but he had never seen her so angry. He hoped he would never have to see it again.

"I think you should leave now," she told him. He didn't bother to argue. She'd set him free of her control over him and at that moment, he wanted to get as far away from her as possible. He fled without a word and she watched him go. She didn't know what had just happened, but she knew something had. She remembered how he had answered when she'd asked what he was hiding, but there was a moment where she had blacked out. The next thing she remembered was seeing his face. He looked terrified and she realized that magick had taken control of her.

Amparo walked out of the forest, approaching carefully. Somewhere close, someone was scared nearly to death, which put her on guard. The fear dissipated as she got closer to Lilly, and it was replaced by anger.

"Where's Dorwynn?" she asked. Lilly pointed toward the town without looking at it. She sat on the ground on crossed legs and folded her arms over her chest, a deep furrow in her brow. Amparo knelt beside her and leaned close to her ear.

"I understand you are angry with him," she said. "I don't know why you are, but I do know it is not a good idea to dwell on it. Come and join the celebration, avoid him for the evening. A night to cool down might be the best thing for everyone."

"I don't want to go with him," Lilly admitted.

"What do you mean?"

"I don't want to train with him," she clarified. "I want Gustave to find someone else to do it."

"There is no one else," Amparo said. "You don't have a choice." Her words echoed in Lilly's ears as she had a flash from her earlier unconscious state. She was in the room with Zephra, repeating her rejection.

"I'm so sorry," Zephra said, *her voice sad though she was smiling, "but you don't have a choice." Zephra grabbed her wrist and everything went dark.*

"Lilly!" Amparo shouted as Lilly fell backward. She pulled herself up on her elbows, her head throbbing. "Are you okay?"

"No," Lilly admitted. "I don't know what's happening to me."

"Come on," Amparo said, pulling Lilly off the ground, "let's get you out of this mood." They walked slowly toward town. Lilly caught sight of Opyre and Zephra near a group of festive townsfolk. Zephra turned her head toward Lilly as if she could feel her stare. They locked eyes for a moment, their intense look uninterrupted until Lilly finally walked out of Zephra's line of vision.

The townsfolk began coming up to Lilly, congratulating her on completing "The Fool's Journey" and thanking her for her courageous sacrifice during the harpy attack. She smiled silently, not really in the mood to talk. No one thought ill of her for her quiet demeanor, as they all knew it had been mere hours since the ordeal ended for her. Someone handed her a plate of food and she accepted it gratefully. She scanned her food for anything harmful, just as Ashya had taught her, though she made sure no one saw. She didn't want to offend anyone, but with everything going on around her and her lack of trust for just about everyone at the moment, she didn't want to take any chances.

After finishing her meal, she sat in silence, listening to the gayety around her and staring into the fire. Her thoughts were still on Dorwynn, who was really Adrian, the best friend she never thought she would see again. Zephra was another person she thought about. The vision she'd had before, one small piece of a large puzzle, had just gained another piece, interlocking perfectly. She still had no idea what it meant, but she knew how she felt; a great loss, apparently caused by Zephra. She made a silent vow that she would not give Zephra the chance to make that vision come true.

Her thoughts were interrupted by a small child, the girl she had saved from the harpies. She smiled as the little girl approached her. Without a word, she hugged Lilly, who held her in the embrace as long as the child allowed her to. She saw the girl's mother nearby, her eyes brimming with tears. She mouthed a silent "Thank you" to Lilly, who mouthed "You're welcome" in return. She released the girl and kissed her on the forehead, watching as the child took her mother's hand and walked away. Lilly's soul was suddenly at peace, realizing that, despite the aftermath, she would have done the same thing if given the choice.

"That's what it is all about," Dorwynn said, approaching her from behind. "May I?" She nodded and he sat on the ground beside her. "You don't remember what happened in the forest, do you?"

"No," she said. She wasn't sure she really wanted to know. Dorwynn nodded, reflecting on his thoughts.

"I know who you are, Lilly," he said, his voice quiet. She looked at him with one eyebrow raised. "I was sent to you for a reason, a reason that I would explain if I could, but I honestly don't know how to." He looked at the crowd of people bowing to the fire, honoring their deities. Lilly had no response, but her eyes followed his gaze. "They celebrate Ostara with this fire festival. It is a celebration of life. They bow in honor of the mother of all, the perfect soul, and the father of all, the creator of life." He looked at her pointedly, the most serious look on his face that Lilly had ever seen. "Someday, they will all bow to you." He got up and walked away, leaving her with his words. She closed her eyes, the echo of his words hovering over her subconscious like a bird circling its prey.

Lilly took her time packing her things. She was dreading her time alone with Dorwynn. Although she knew he was Adrian, she didn't know how to act around him. He was so different now, nothing like he was when they were kids. Amparo helped her gather her things, feeling her doubt as well. Unsure of what to say, she kept her silence. She dared not bring up the events of the past few days and every other topic seemed nonsensical in comparison.

"I think that's everything," said Lilly, scanning the room one last time. She looked at Amparo with a sad smile. "I'm going to miss you so much." Amparo hugged her tight, feeling the same way about her. She didn't know why, but she felt a deep bond to Lilly despite the fact they had only just met.

"We'll be together again soon," she assured Lilly. "When your training with Dorwynn is complete, you'll train with me."

"I can't wait," Lilly told her. The thought of spending time with Amparo excited her. She enjoyed Amparo's company and, at the moment, she was the only person Lilly felt she could trust. She hugged her friend again, hopeful that the time would pass quickly until they were reunited.

She carried her pack outside, where the others were waiting with Dorwynn. While he began saying his own goodbyes, Lilly secured her pack to the horse she'd bought in Jesfinarea. Adair had been well cared for during her days of unconsciousness. She nickered, delighted to see her new master again.

Opyre gave her a long embrace. When he wrapped his strong arms around her, it gave Lilly a sense of security she hadn't felt in a long time. She looked forward to training with him as well; he was smart, powerful and didn't put up with nonsense. She had a feeling her time with him would be quick and wasn't sure if that was a good thing or not. She felt strange around him, yet not necessarily out of the ordinary.

"Take care of yourself," he whispered in her ear.

"I will," she vowed, "and thank you for saving my life."

"No thanks are necessary." He released his hold on her and for a second, she was sorry he had. "I will see you soon," he promised. She nodded, smiling.

Warrick, jubilant as ever, gave her a strong hug and told her that she would always be welcome in Arthidgen. He praised her on the agility in the obstacle course and for her bravery during the harpy attack. She gave him a modest smile and thanked him for his kindness, assuring him that she would return.

Then came the time for her to bid farewell to Zephra. The situation was wrought with tension. Zephra repeated her apology to Lilly for the way she had treated her, but the apology only reminded Lilly of the vision and the turmoil she'd felt. She was cordial when they parted, but by no means was she sorry to be putting distance between herself and the mysterious magickal creature that affected her so much.

Dorwynn said his farewells and then he and Lilly mounted their horses and started down the road. Lilly was glad to be leaving that place behind, for although it seemed a decent enough town, far too many strange occurrences had taken place there. She kept her distance behind Dorwynn. She had not spoken to him yet about what had transpired between them, choosing instead to contemplate the events in silence. He kept his discussions limited to what her near future entailed. Her training would be quick with him, he had assured her, because there was only so much he could really teach her. She was far more powerful than he. He had his instructions from Gustave and planned on following them as precisely as he could, barring no other unexpected events diverted him from his tasks. His information relayed, he spoke of nothing else. After nearly two hours of utter silence, Lilly decided she'd had enough. They had to resolve these issues or her training would be futile.

"Are we ever going to talk about what happened?" she asked him.

"No," he said, clicking his tongue. His horse jumped into a trot.

"Why not?" she demanded.

"I don't want you getting angry again," he replied. Lilly frowned. He sounded so arrogant now. "You were supposed to have control over your powers before you came to Arthidgen, before we began your training. It's quite clear that you arrived too early." Lilly pursed her lips together. How dare he make that assumption? It wasn't for him to decide if she was ready or not. His job was to follow the instructions he'd been given.

"Maybe I just learned the truth a little too late," she muttered bitterly. He didn't answer, but he did slow his horse until she caught up to him.

"Look," he said, defeated, "I was going to tell you, but we never had any time alone. The others know nothing of my history before Gustave found me and trained me. I couldn't chance them finding out. It would put us both at risk."

They continued their trek in silence as the hours passed. Lilly tried to figure out the pieces of information she gained while she'd been unconscious, but gave up on it after the first hour. She just didn't have enough information yet. She hated not knowing what was going on around her and even more, the silence between her and Dorwynn was starting to get to her.

"We need to stop," she told Dorwynn. "The horses need to rest and we need to eat."

"There is a clearing just ahead," he replied. "We'll stop there." They led their horses to the clearing and dismounted. Dorwynn opened a sack containing bread and dried meat and handed Lilly a slice of each. She took them, unsure if she should be grateful for something to eat or disappointed that it was the best meal they had at the moment. They ate their rations in a silence interrupted only by the sounds of their chewing while the horses grazed nearby.

The scenery hadn't changed much, except for the absence of buildings. The grass was pushing its way though the ground, already a brilliant shade of green. In the distance, the forest's edge was visible. Despite the fact that winter had just passed, the trees were vibrant, as were the plants scattering the border of the forest. Beyond that, the sky was darkening, a storm building on the horizon, a looming menace much like the moods of the two travelers. Lilly hoped they would find adequate shelter before it reached them.

On more than one occasion, Lilly thought she saw a person walking through the trees. Dorwynn either didn't notice or he didn't care, and Lilly said nothing to him about it. It was his job to protect her, but she began to wonder how safe she really was with him. Things here were still so new to her and anything seemed possible. She sensed that he was afraid, though she didn't know why she could feel it. He either wanted her to feel it or, somehow, she had absorbed enough of Amparo's talent to feel it. Either way, she wished he would talk to her about it so they could overcome the tension between them and make some useful progress with her training. She had so much left to learn and every hour that passed was one hour closer to the impending discovery that the Chosen One had arrived.

She knew she would have to take more care not to be discovered. Ashya had told her to keep a low profile, and already, the tales of her successfully destroying a flock of harpies was spreading. Arthidgen was a large town and anyone who passed through the town was sure to hear about it, as well as her defeating the obstacle course that could not be beaten. *She* had made the decision to run it, *she* had decided to throw herself into the middle of the harpy attack and if her identity was discovered by the wrong person, she knew she could blame no one but herself for the consequences.

"Where are we going?" she asked Dorwynn, trying to find a topic he would be willing to talk about. The absence of noise was driving her insane. She wanted him to talk to her, the way he used to when they were kids. Irritated, she picked at the bread in her hand, tossing it to a bird hopping through a nearby patch of grass. The bird ate the crumbs, chirping its happy thanks as it sorted through its newest treasure.

"We're going to Elikrede," he responded. "We will train along the way so you are prepared when we arrive. It is a town of magick, a city really, and most everyone there has at least one strong talent. It is a good place for an apprentice to hide in plain sight, should any more transgressions take place."

Lilly's mood lifted with the news that they were going exactly where she wanted to be. The mysteries of her mother were there and she was more than ready to find out the truth. Her mother was there, waiting for her as though she had known all along that Lilly would follow the path that brought her to this world. She thought about Amparo's reasoning that her mother had left for a reason and she wondered exactly how much her mother knew. She had so many questions and she filed that one with the others, saving them for the only person who would be able to answer them.

"What transgressions?" she asked Dorwynn after she'd had a chance to think about the rest of his comment. Sure, she knew that her actions in Arthidgen with the harpies were unusual, and her unnatural state afterward had confused everyone, but she'd learned a lot during that time, even if it didn't make much sense yet. It had happened for a reason, yet Dorwynn acted like she'd committed some kind of crime.

He sighed, trying to think of anything he could say to appease her. How could he answer her question when even *he* didn't know what had happened in the forest? Somehow, she had lost control of her senses, but what both amazed and frightened him was that she seemed to have complete control over the magick she'd used at the time. She had displayed more power than anyone he'd ever seen and the only side effect she'd suffered was not remembering the event, something he was grateful for at the moment.

"Look," he finally said, "things have been happening that I cannot explain. I don't have the answers. I don't know why you survived the harpy attack or why using the magick you did put you into a coma for two days. And the forest..." His voice trailed off and he stopped talking, hoping she wouldn't ask about it.

"What happened in the forest, Dorwynn?"

He shook his head, indicating that he didn't plan on answering her question. He knew he'd have to eventually, but he needed some council before talking to her about true magick. He knew only the basics, as did most souls in Buthania, and he knew that he could lose his magickal status if he tried to teach her something he barely knew himself.

"We'll talk about it later," he said at last. "Just know that by the time your training is complete with the four of us, you will have the answers to all your questions. I promise."

"You promise," she quipped. "You expect me to believe your promises after all the lies you told me?" She was baiting him, taking the opportunity to bring up the issue he was avoiding. He sighed is defeat. He knew she wouldn't let go of this until they had talked about it.

"You know me, Lilly, better than anyone else."

"Even Zephra?" she interrupted. He scowled. He hadn't gotten the chance to work out his troubles with Zephra yet and that bothered him a great deal. Despite the fact that he didn't feel the way about her that she wanted, she was still his friend. Having to leave without resolving their issues ate at his soul. He wanted to settle things with her, but he had no idea where she was now. She never stayed long in one place and she knew the land better than anyone.

"Honestly, I don't know," he admitted. "I spent my entire childhood with you, but I've changed a lot in the past three years, and Zephra was here then."

"Speaking of that," Lilly said, "how old are you?"

"I'm twenty-two," he said. "I was born here, in Buthania. My father died before I was born. I lost my mother not long after. The Council of Magickal Affairs sent me to Earth for my protection, yes, but also because it was crucial for me to be a part of *your* life. I came to Earth an orphaned child, appearing close to your own age, so that they were sure we would meet."

"Did you know all this when we were kids?"

"I discovered many things about myself and my family after I returned with Gustave. Be prepared, for you'll learn a lot about your family, too, things that you don't know and have never imagined possible." He looked at the sky, noticing the storm brewing in the distance, and stood. He checked the baggage on the horses, secured a loose strap, and then mounted his white steed. "It's time to go."

Lilly followed suit and they continued their ride until sunset. Dorwynn removed two bedrolls from the horses and laid them out, then built a fire between them. He debated about setting a makeshift tent, but he decided against it. If the storm reached them, it would be a good excuse to keep moving. He took a dagger from his pack and walked toward the forest as Lilly settled herself by the fire.

"I'll be back" he told her, disappearing behind the tree line. Lilly lay on her bed, if it could be called a bed, and watched the sky. The overcast sky hid the stars, but the bright moon cast a wide glow across the clouds, brightening a small corner of the darkness. She could hear some movement among the trees and wondered if it was Dorwynn returning or if it was the mysterious figure that had been following them since they'd departed.

Twenty minutes after Dorwynn had left, he returned with a rabbit carcass and a long stick, one end sharpened to a fine point. He worked the carcass onto the stick and held it over the fire, turning it over the coals. They watched in silence as the meat turned a golden brown. Lilly's stomach rumbled as the smell of the meat wafted in her direction. She hadn't eaten much the morning before leaving Arthidgen and she had eaten nothing during the days prior. In fact, thinking back on it, her last real meal was the morning before the harpy attack. The three days since it had happened seemed so far away now, and her stomach growled its desire as Dorwynn removed their dinner from the fire.

The warm meal did wonders for their dispositions and they spent the rest of the evening talking the way they had when they were kids, or as close to it as possible considering their situation. He told her some of what he'd been through since he left. Gustave had come to him on Earth and explained the destiny he was meant for. He followed the old wizard to Buthania and began his training in Earth magick, the element he was born into. After nearly two years, Gustave declared him a Master of Earth magick. He pulled his shirt sleeve up to his elbow, showing Lilly a small symbol on the inside of his right wrist, proof of his status in the magickal community.

The symbol was small, a strangely rounded and narrow triangle, its width no larger than a dime and twice as long. It looked like a tattoo, a greenish tint to the inside of the shape, but for the image on the inside. In a nearly invisible outline Lilly could see the figure of a faerie, its wings beating at an even pace.

"What it that?" Lilly asked, amazed at the mark.

"The faerie?" asked Dorwynn. "It's a blessing from the Elemental Children. Not everyone who has a Master mark has the image inside. It is a separate honor than comes only when an Elemental Child bestows it upon you. With it, one can call upon them whenever the need arises. They are pretty rare."

"What did you do to receive it?" Lilly wondered aloud, still staring at the mystical design. He frowned at the memory, wondering if he told her what terrible deed he'd done to receive such an honor would change her view of him. He didn't answer and Lilly, seeing that something about it caused him pain, decided to change the subject.

Lilly told him about her life on Earth after he had disappeared. She included the many dreams she'd had, though she left out the details that pertained to him. She didn't want him knowing about that yet since she wasn't sure if it was just a subconscious fear surfacing or if, somehow, she'd had a vision of the future. She did include how she'd felt after he left, how angry she was that he had left without saying goodbye and how lonely she'd been having no one else around who really understood her. She considered asking him again about what she couldn't remember of the night before, but truth be told, she was afraid of what might have happened. The fact that she couldn't remember it only strengthened her fear. Though she would never admit it, she knew Dorwynn was right. She had lost control, something she vowed to never let happen again.

The moon was high overhead when they finally settled into their makeshift beds. Lilly fell asleep immediately, while Dorwynn lay awake, lost in his thoughts. He felt like himself again, at least as much as he had since he'd left Lilly behind. Most of his life, he had never been able to truly be himself except around her. They had grown up together, becoming who they had because of each other.

He had never told her that he was in love with her, that he had been since they were young. She knew he loved her, but her assumption was that it was a love of friendship, not of passion. It was much like his relationship with Zephra, two types of love causing conflict in what was a great friendship. Zephra's words haunted him, echoing in his mind as he thought of her. What if Lilly didn't believe that they were meant to be together? He felt his heart grow heavy as he imagined that possibility and hoped their shared childhood would bind their futures.

Watching her sleep, he couldn't believe she was actually here. His emotions intensified inside him. Reminding himself that she was only fifteen, he tried to push them aside. He knew, however, that they would always be just beneath the surface, waiting anxiously for the day he could tell her the truth, not just about his feelings for her, but also secrets he had yet to share. He wondered what she would do when she found out some of those private mysteries. So many secrets had been forced upon him in the past three years, things he knew were crucial to keep hidden, but he knew, too, that someday she would discover them. His only hope was that when she did find out, he wouldn't have to relive her anger. He didn't think he would be able to convince her to stop if it ever happened again.

Events of the previous night flashed though his mind and he recalled images of her releasing her power with such exceptional force. There was no doubt in his mind that she was the Chosen One. Her obvious display of supremacy scared him to no end. What bothered him even more was that she seemed to have no idea what she had done or what she was capable of. By the time her training with the four of them came to an end, she would be unstoppable. His only hope was that when the time came to choose sides, when the inevitable war finally began, she would have enough control to accomplish what she must. One false move and she could destroy the entire world.

He rolled onto his side and got comfortable, watching Lilly's even breathing until he fell asleep. He was completely unaware of the dark shadow moving through the nearby forest or the fact that it had been following them all day. Had he looked that direction, he would have noticed the two red eyes glowing among the trees, unblinking, that had been watching their every move.

Dagana's Lament

"Sybil!"

Dagana's voice echoed down the hall of the massive inn. She knew the old crone could hear her even though her quarters were separated by more than twelve rooms from the queen's, which was located in the center of the royally-designated floor. Dagana stormed toward the door furthest from hers, scowling. She despised the fact that her Arch Requiest demanded such distant sleeping arrangements. She claimed Kylenin's powers interfered with her own, so Dagana had no choice but to honor the old woman's wishes.

Sybil was her father's sister. She had been Dagana's visionary her entire life, having been raised by her upon her mother's untimely death by one of her own spells. Her father was a half-human, half-elf who had left his young daughter in the care of his older sister, unable to bear the loss of his wife. Sybil, twenty-seven years his senior, was a Master of Fire Magick and an Arch Requiest, born with the natural gift of foresight. She had fostered Dagana's magickal skills since then, helping her to master the abilities she'd inherited from her father and perfecting her flair for all fundamental magick. Dagana had been declared a Master of Air Magick and a Master of both spells and potions only months before her own daughter had been born. Sybil had even predicted Laurel's future, denying Dagana the details for reasons she claimed were of everyone's best interest.

Dagana's mother had been beautiful, though she was only human, and had passed her exquisite appearance to her daughter. Unfortunately, she had also bequeathed her with half of her natural life-span. Dagana knew she would not live as long as an elf, as would her father and Sybil, though, by anyone's standards, she looked amazing for her one-hundred and seven years. She had been using magickal potions and salves for years, which gave her the appearance of a woman in her thirtieth year, but lately, they seemed to be losing their effect, adding twenty years to her façade over the past six months. Gray hairs had started to emerge throughout her sandy blonde hair. Wrinkles followed, defacing the previously smooth skin around her eyes and lips. She deeply resented the fact that she had not inherited the elvish ability to control her appearance.

She arrived at Sybil's door and raised her hand to the knob. It swung open abruptly before she could touch its cool metal. Sybil moved around her round black altar, grabbing bits of dried herbs from various bowls and tossing them into the cauldron before her. She had not inherited control of her appearance either, nor the vanity elves typically harbored, so she wasted no time bothering to mix salves that would conceal the deep wrinkles that littered her skin or potions that would change the color of her silky white hair. Her dark brown eyes were small and shrewd beneath the flaws of her two hundred eighty-one years.

"The dragon eludes you," she said, keeping her focus on the potion she was mixing. Despite her age, she was extremely nimble, moving so quickly that Dagana couldn't tell what she was throwing into the mixture. The sleeves of her dark green robes dangled over the ingredients, threatening to spill their contents, though they never did.

"Yes," Dagana answered her, disgusted with Sybil's nonchalant remark. "Your visions are unreliable." Sybil had predicted months ago that she should seek a dragon if she wanted to put her grandson on the throne, a dragon with a very special gift unlike any other in its race. They had been traveling ever since, searching the land where the dragons dwelled, but they had found no trace of the one they sought. The crone snapped her head toward Dagana at the accusation, sending a chill through her bones. She moved toward her with a long, bony finger extended in her direction.

"His dreams interfere with my visions," she croaked. "That sleeping draught I gave him is the only way I can gain accuracy. The time is now; he is dreamless." She returned to her work as quickly as she had abandoned it. "Come."

Dagana approached the altar, her sense of smell overtaken with the familiar scent of Sybil's concoction. She was one of very few prophets who could use a potion to call forth a vision of unparalleled precision, having discovered the recipe herself after more than three decades of trials and failures. Many prophets had tried, but none had been as successful as she.

The cauldron smoked and sizzled as she added the final ingredients and stirred the brew gently with a silver spoon. She continued to circle the cauldron with the utensil in a slow but constant motion until the liquid changed from its mossy green color to a deep golden brown. The old sorceress poured the mixture into a chalice made of black gold and seated herself in her velvet-lined chair. She sipped the drink until the cup was drained, and then let it slip from her fingers and clatter to the floor. Her dark eyes glazed over with a silver hue, her pupils as small as the head of a pin.

"You have not taken heed of warranted advice," Sybil uttered in an eerie, high-pitched voice. "You begrudge him nothing, therefore he knows no restraint. He relies on you too greatly and must rely on himself now to learn his true capabilities. His instincts will lead him to the one he seeks. The dragon will find him only after he learns to trust himself. He will rise to power under the influence of the mighty beast and he will rule over a great kingdom. You must allow him to travel alone henceforth. Only without you will he find the courage and strength required for his destiny. Send him to Elikrede unaccompanied."

"I can't," Dagana protested. "His powers fail him."

"His power shall return when he allows them to return. He must trust himself. He will not earn that trust in your presence."

"And if I refuse?"

"His destiny will not come to pass." The hag went silent and wilted in her chair, closing her eyes. She sat motionless and Dagana knew she would not speak again until morning. She turned on her heel and left the room, returning to the solitude of the royal bedchambers, trying to ease her mind in the unfamiliarity of the bed.

She slept fitfully that night, contemplating her dilemma. She knew she had to obey Sybil's command, but with Kylenin's powers growing worse with each passing day, she feared the outcome. He had made little progress gaining the control he'd lost over his magick and only three days ago, he had lost them entirely, unable to lift even a fork with his mind. For the two days prior to losing his abilities, he had returned to normal, as if nothing had ever gone wrong, but the hope Dagana felt when it happened faded as instantly as his powers. It was as though some unexplained force was draining him of his magick.

When he had lost total control, he'd also begun having horrific dreams, worse than just his occasional nightmares. He refused to give her any details, allowing them to fester in his mind. It was then that Sybil had instructed Dagana to put a sleeping draught in his tea, forcing him into a dreamless state so she could better determine the next course of his path.

Despite her misgivings, Dagana knew she would follow Sybil's command. She lay in her bed for hours, waiting until she heard him wake, and then forced herself to go to his room. She knew the moment she opened his door that he had experienced another nightmare. Every item in his room floated against the ceiling, hovering precariously above their heads. Kylenin was in a corner, cowering, his whole body shaking. His arms covered his head to protect it from the objects that threatened to fall. Dagana waved her hands, sending them to their respective places around the room. Kylenin jerked his head toward her, his eyes wild.

"I can't stop it!" he cried.

Dagana sighed as the realization of Sybil's words found her. She was right. Kylenin relied too heavily on her council. Praying her predictions about his powers were correct as well, she approached him cautiously.

"What troubles you?" she asked, lowering herself to the floor beside Kylenin. He gave her a look of exasperation. He hated when she asked questions to which she already knew the answers. He knew she was prodding for more specific information, something that frustrated him almost as much as the mysterious dreams plaguing his sleep.

"I dreamed of her again," he replied, excluding the details she craved to hear. "She haunts my soul. I fear her greatly, and yet, when I see her in my dreams, I feel a strong desire to find her." He stared at Dagana with such intensity, she could actually feel his yearning. "I *must* find her. I will have no peace until I do."

Dagana nodded slowly, which threw Kylenin into utter shock. He had expected her to protest. She hated to travel anyway, and they were already searching for not one, but two people. Now he was adding a third, which would increase the time they were away from the castle. Her lack of contestation made him curious.

"I agree," she said at last. His eyebrows shot up at her unusual compliance. "You should follow your instincts."

"When do we leave?" he asked, his excitement building. He jumped from the floor, but his face fell when she shook her head.

"*We* aren't going anywhere," she told him. "You will travel alone from now on." He stared at her, his expression unchanging, unsure if he'd heard her correctly. Surely she wasn't sending him out there alone. She would never do that. He convinced himself that she must be under a spell. She rose from the floor and opened the bureau beside them, emptying its contents onto the bed. Kylenin didn't move as she started to load his pack with the necessities he would require on his journey. She was almost finished with her task when she glanced at him, and nearly laughed at his fixed expression of disbelief.

"I've done all I can for you," she explained. "You are nearly a man. It is time you learn the value of solitude, as well as many other things I cannot teach you. You must figure them out for yourself." She carried his pack to him and fitted it onto his shoulder. "Come. We will prepare a horse for you, unless you would prefer to walk."

"No," he said, snapping out of his trance. "I would prefer a horse." He followed her out the door, matching her steps down the long hallway and all the way to the stables managed by the innkeeper. Their carriage horses were in separate stalls, all four as black as a moonless night.

"Choose one," she told him. He studied the animals. They seemed the same to him, but he noticed that one studied him as equally as he did them. He reached his hand out and the horse lowered its head, submitting to its new master.

"This one," whispered Kylenin. Dagana opened the stall and led the animal out. She took the pack from his back and waved her hand to create a saddle for him before strapping the pack onto it. He watched her, suddenly fearful. She was giving him no instruction. It seemed so out of character for her.

"Are you under a spell?" he asked.

"No," she said. "Come now, it is time for you to go." He climbed onto his horse and looked down at her, wishing she would offer anything that would help him with his task. He had no idea where to go or what to do when he got there. Dagana seemed unwilling to satisfy his doubts.

"What about my powers," he asked.

"They will return soon."

"Where am I to go? How am I to find those I seek? When should I return?"

"All I can tell you is that you must ride to Elikrede alone. From there, every choice you make is your own, as well as the outcome of each. Now go. Your destiny awaits you." He clicked his tongue at the horse and it began walking through the stable doors. Kylenin wished that she would give him a hug or tell him that she loved him, but he knew she never would. She hated such curious displays of affection, so he just waved his farewell and looked down the long road, wondering what exactly lay before him.

Once he was out of sight, Dagana hustled her servants to prepare for the journey home. The carriage was prepared, as were the meals they would need. She sent her personal affects to the castle with the wave of her hand and left the inn. Her black carriage, trimmed in gold and red décor, bounced along the worn roads, moving quickly in the opposite direction Kylenin had gone. The rocking of the carriage began to lull her to sleep and she allowed it to come, smiling at herself in the mirror affixed to the carriage wall before closing her eyes. She looked ten years younger than she had when she woke that morning. Sleep settled over her like a warm blanket and the smile on her face remained so long after she had drifted off, content in the knowledge that her life-long dream of having an heir on the throne would come to pass. Sybil had confirmed it. It was his destiny to rule and it was going to come true.

The Pursuer

Lilly shivered as the rain poured from the sky. The storm had caught up to them before the morning light, sending the horses into a frenzy as the clouds exploded above them. She and Dorwynn collected the animals, and then decided to abandon their camp, as sleep would be impossible. Their bedrolls were soaked and the fire sizzled as drops of rain landed on what few coals remained, barring any chance at getting it started again even if they did manage to find some dry wood to burn.

They had been on their horses ever since, riding north between where the river and forest met. Lilly was tired, and the added weight of her drenched clothing didn't help one bit. Adair pressed on tirelessly despite the extra weight, but Lilly could feel the animal's strength diminishing as they continued. They covered a great distance by the time they stopped for their first meal, having ridden for more than seven hours straight through the torrent.

Dorwynn led them closer to the forest's edge, trying to take advantage of the canopy's shelter, though the strength of the storm managed to barrel through it nonetheless. The horses, thankful for the reprieve, pulled kilpas from a low tree and filled their stomachs. Lilly and Dorwynn ate their cold meal of dried pork and hard bread before continuing their trip. Lilly had wanted to check her maps, but Dorwynn left her little time to do much of anything other than eat. Their pace slowed as the storm raged over them, turning the packed dirt road into a shallow river of mud. Adair's hooves were caked to the middle of her legs and she grunted her disapproval, though she never faltered in her course.

"How much further until we get there?" Lilly asked as the rained trickled down her face. She shook her head vigorously, trying to dislodge some of the water she retained, though she knew it was a moot point. The storm showed no signs of slowing.

"We're almost to the crossroad," Dorwynn replied. "Another few hours, maybe. From there, Elikrede is about four days away."

"Four days!"

"At least."

Lilly sighed. The wind grew stronger, causing her to shiver uncontrollably. She closed her eyes, wishing she had some kind of protection from the rain. She debated whether or not to use magick to solve her problem, but decided against it. The risk of exposure was too great. When her fingers went numb an hour later, she changed her mind and held her hands above her head. A spark burst from her upturned palms and formed a circular barrier over them, diverting the downpour over the magickal umbrella. As they continued to walk, the cover followed, hovering over her.

"That won't attract any attention," muttered Dorwynn.

"There's no one around to see it," Lilly pointed out, ignoring his sarcasm. She clapped her hands together and drew them apart in a wide motion. The magick blanket grew, covering him as well. Though it didn't protect them from the wind, the absence of rain allowed them to start drying, easing their chill. The horses picked up their pace and soon they were moving twice as fast despite the muddy terrain.

"You're going to use all your energy before we get there," he replied.

"I'm stronger than you think I am. I'll be fine."

He said nothing else. His despondent attitude had returned and it was starting to grate on her nerves. She never expected the one person she always thought would be supportive of her would be so distant when they met again. His disheartening mood was spreading through her as well, though she tried hard not to let it affect her.

With the shelter overhead protecting her face from the rain, she was able to see further into the distance. The crossroad was ahead, marked by a stake with two signs posted on it, each shaped like an arrow. One sign pointed to the east and read *Hydrabaene*. The sign pointing to the west read *Elikrede*. Her heart skipped a beat as she wondered whether or not Rohan was still in Hydrabaene, but it didn't matter. They weren't going to Hydrabaene. They steered the horses to the west, following the road into the forest.

Lilly abandoned her umbrella as the forest grew thick. She felt its contentment, relishing the long-awaited nourishment. It breathed new life into her as she felt her mood lift. Dorwynn's mood, however, showed no signs of improvement. She wondered what he was thinking and thought briefly about entering his mind to find out, then scolded herself for even considering the idea. No matter his disposition, he deserved the intimacy of his own mind.

Had she read his mind, she would have understood why he was so agitated. He had been angry the day before when she'd asked about that night in the forest, and though he knew he should probably have told her what had happened, he couldn't. He never expected he would fear her so much, something else that weighed heavily on his mind. They'd had a pleasant enough evening discussing the past, but he couldn't shake the conflict of emotions raging within him.

He also knew that they were being followed. He'd felt another presence since they had left Arthidgen. At the time, he assumed it was just another traveler. Now, he had a feeling he knew exactly who it was, though he didn't know why she pursued them. She was discontent; he knew her so well he could feel her moods without the gifts of an empath. He dared not tell Lilly that they were being followed. The last thing he wanted was for her to have more to worry about. The emotional link between her powers and her control over them was far too turbulent. He would find a way to take care of the situation, though he wondered what would happen once he did. His heart was heavy and his mind was cluttered. He pressed on, knowing that once he delivered Lilly to Elikrede, he would visit his secret place first and foremost. He had to clear his mind before getting too deep into her training. They couldn't both be an emotional wreck.

When they stopped that evening, Dorwynn immediately set up the tent, tethering each corner to a different tree. Their bedrolls were still wet, so he tied a rope high above where he planned to build the fire, hanging the bedrolls over them in the hopes that the heat would dry them in enough time so they could sleep comfortably. After wringing the water from her jacket, Lilly tossed it over the makeshift clothesline, and then immediately started searching for kindling. She managed to find a few dry branches that had fallen, but she knew they were way too green to start a fire. Anything that was dead enough to get the fire started was saturated with water.

"I'll see what I can find while I'm hunting," Dorwynn told her as he walked away.

"A bow would probably be easier than that dagger," she pointed out. He smiled and left her to her own hunting without responding.

The rain had finally stopped, but the leaves on the canopy's crest were now relieving their waterlogged state, shedding the water they'd collected during the storm. Dorwynn doubted he would find anything useful to eat, but he hoped the storm had kept the animals in their shelters long enough to stir some hunger within their bellies. They would have to come out to eat, and if they did, then so could he.

He scouted the forest floor until he found signs of a rabbit nest, and then settled himself against a tree opposite from it, waiting for the right moment. He held perfectly still, not even blinking, and let his eyes go out of focus. The sounds of the forest reached his ears as he centered his attention on listening rather than seeing. He could hear the faint rustling from within the nest and he knew there were babies inside, very young babies. He could not take the life of their mother, for they would all die without her care, so he walked sideways around the large tree and listened again.

Two trees to the west, some squirrels were chattering loudly. Four paces to the north of that tree, a group of pheasants emerged from the shrubbery, pecking from the wet ground the many insects brought to the surface during the rainfall. He reached for the dagger at his waist, his slow and deliberate movements unnoticed by the flock. In one fluid motion, he removed the dagger from its sheath, whirled around the tree and flung it at the birds. With perfect precision, the dagger slid into the heart of the largest, a female with a strong heartbeat. It was her heartbeat that had drawn Dorwynn's aim.

The rest of the flock scattered when he struck, his kill lying still on the ground. It was a painless death, but a death nonetheless. Dorwynn gathered his dagger and rinsed it clean in a puddle before wiping it on the hem of his shirt and replacing it in the sheath. He knelt over the animal and bowed his head in respect.

"Divine Mother," he whispered, "thank you for providing this life. You have nourished her well and now, she will nourish us. She sustains us another day, so know her death is not in vain. Your gift does not go unnoticed, and is received with gratitude."

He stood, grabbing the pheasant by its legs, and started walking toward the place he had left Lilly. His hearing remained acute from his meditative state, and he knew she was near. He could hear *her* heartbeat. When he slowed his pace, he noticed that she did as well. He stopped walking and waited until he heard her stop.

"Give it up, Z," he said loud enough that she could hear him, but quiet enough that Lilly wouldn't. "I know you are there."

Zephra emerged from the forest and walked toward him. She didn't look at him, though. She was trying to figure out how to say what she wanted him to know without stirring up a hornet's nest. They had issues, but those would have to wait until they had some time to talk without being overheard or interrupted.

"Why are you following me?" Dorwynn asked her. His tone came out harsher than he intended, but her unexpected arrival combined with their unresolved issues had him on edge. Because of his harshness, she got defensive, glaring at him as the emotions drowned her senses.

"What makes you think for one second that I am following *you*?" She raised an eyebrow, challenging him. He just glared at her.

"You don't have any reasons to want to follow her," he retorted. "If you did, you would be where I left her instead of here with me."

"I thought talking to you first seemed the better course of action."

"It is," he said, "but that doesn't answer my question. Why are you following her?" Zephra lowered her eyes, trying to think of the best way to answer. She didn't know how to say it. He waited patiently through her quiet censure, though he knew he should be on his way back to the camp. He wondered if Lilly had managed to get a fire started yet. If not, he would have to do that, too.

"I cannot explain it," Zephra said finally. "From the moment I laid eyes on her, I had little command over myself. Every emotion I had was magnified, like I was under some sort of spell. My feelings for you, something I have dealt with considerably well for a long time, just rose to the surface like a spawn emerging from the ground, and the way you looked at her only added fuel to the fire.

"When the two of you departed, I thought I would feel like myself again, but instead, I felt like I lost something. I could feel the distance between us growing with every passing second and I felt more distant from everything else. That's why I followed you, why I followed her. I need to understand what is happening, and honestly, I think it has everything to do with her, not you. Despite everything that has happened between us so far, I've *never* felt such a connection with someone, and I've lived a long time."

Dorwynn listened with great interest. He hadn't expected Zephra to concede and share her true feelings, but what amazed him was what those feelings were. She felt the same way about Lilly that he did. He had known the moment she came to Buthania; he felt her presence immediately. The only reason he didn't feel that way now was due to witnessing her power. His fear overshadowed everything else.

"Well," he said, "I can say that I understand, but I have no idea why she has that effect on people."

"Don't you?" Zephra asked. She had a feeling Dorwynn knew more about the girl than he was letting on. He looked at her and shook his head, then shrugged his shoulders.

"Come on," he told her, walking toward the camp. "You can help us start a fire."

They walked in silence, arriving to find Lilly sitting beside a minute fire, blowing through a reed onto the few coals she'd managed to create. Zephra watched with interest as she continued without looking up. Finally, a flame jumped from the coals and engulfed the dry limbs and leaves she'd scrounged from beneath nearby shrubs. She sat back, taking pride in her accomplishment.

"The fire is ready," said Lilly brightly as she looked up at Dorwynn. Her face fell when she saw Zephra. "What are *you* doing here?"

Zephra looked at Dorwynn. He plopped on the ground beside the fire and picked up the reed Lilly had dropped, working the fire high enough to boil water. Lilly glared at Zephra, her anger building. They'd only just left her behind. Lilly hadn't even had enough time to think about the dream she'd had of Zephra, and now she was here.

Zephra seemed uncomfortable beneath her glare. She was unsure if she should sit down and help or if she should just return to the forest and leave them alone. Lilly was obviously upset that she was there and though she had apologized for her behavior, she knew the girl had every right to be angry at her.

"She's going to travel with us to Elikrede," Dorwynn told Lilly without looking up from his task.

"What?!" Lilly jumped up. "After everything we talked about, you agreed to bring her along without discussing it with me first?"

"She followed us because she thought she could be of use during your training," Dorwynn said. He looked up at her and saw the anger in her eyes. "She's right, Lilly, and you know it. Your powers are out of hand and if anyone knows how to overcome the emotional connection tied to your powers, it's Zephra. Whether you like it or not, she's one of your trainers. Get over it."

Lilly stared at him, her mouth agape. She tried to think of some clever quip that would prove him wrong, but deep down, she knew he was right. She couldn't argue with his logic, but that only made her angrier. She turned her gaze to Zephra, her emotions bubbling to the surface. Trainer or not, Lilly didn't trust her. She was beginning to doubt Dorwynn as well. She knew he was afraid of her, but he refused tell her why, and she knew he was keeping other secrets from her.

She turned on her heel and walked away from them, storming into the forest. She raised her hand over her head, calling her jacket to her. It flew from the line where it hung and sailed into her open hand, sweeping past both Dorwynn's and Zephra's faces. The two watched her go. Dorwynn shook his head and returned to his chore while Zephra just stared after Lilly.

"Should we go after her?" she asked. Dorwynn shook his head.

"Let her cool off," he said. He pulled a small kettle from his pack and stood. "I'll be right back. We need water. Do you mind?" Zephra smiled and aimed her hand toward the fire, the huge flames lighting his back as he walked away. Zephra pulled her legs into her chest, hugging her knees, and stared at the fire until he returned.

After he set up the spit to hold the kettle, he settled beside Zephra. They stared at the fire, waiting for the water to boil.

"I should have stayed out of sight," she said quietly.

"No," Dorwynn replied. "She'll calm down in a while. She's just angry." He looked his friend in the eye and smiled. "You know, the two of you are quite similar. You're both powerful. You both let your power get away from you when you're angry, and both of you walk away before you'll admit that someone else is right. I'm surprised you aren't the best of friends."

Lilly was deep enough into the forest that she could no longer see them. She found a fallen log and sat on it hard, crossing her arms. Her jacket wasn't dry, but it was no longer saturated with water and kept her warm enough. She sighed. The anger was still there and she knew she'd better get control over it before something else happened that she wouldn't be able to remember. She closed her eyes and listened to the peaceful sounds of the forest.

The insects had come out, filling the forest with their chirps and buzzes. Birds had followed, emerging from the trees to search for the food singing to them. Drops of water fell from branches overhead, occasionally landing on Lilly's jacket with a soft thump. She breathed in deeply as the calm started to envelope her, but the interruption that followed distracted her from her meditation.

She could hear Zephra and Dorwynn talking, just as she had heard them talking in Arthidgen, as though they were standing right in front of her. They were talking about her. Dorwynn just told Zephra that they were alike. Lilly crossed her arms in solitary disagreement. She wasn't like Zephra at all.

"Why didn't you tell her the truth?" Zephra asked. Lilly focused on listening, hoping that she would hear at least a little of what the truth entailed.

"She doesn't understand the significance of connections like we do," was Dorwynn's reply. "When you are ready, you can tell her the reason why you are here. It would be better if she heard it from you anyway. Besides, what I told her wasn't a lie. She needs all the training she can get and you will be an enormous help. She's really powerful, Z. You have no idea what she is capable of and neither does she."

"Why don't you tell her?"

Yeah, Lilly thought, *try a little honesty, Dorwynn. I'm not an idiot.*

"I can't," he answered after a moment of silence, "and if you knew what she did in Arthidgen, you would understand why I can't."

"So tell me."

Lilly frowned. If he told Zephra what had happened before he told her, she would never forgive him. Whether she could remember it or not, what had occurred was between them. No one else should get to know the truth before she did.

"She used true magick," he said. "She knows my true name, Z."

"What?" Shock radiated from Zephra's voice. "How does she know your true name? Did you tell her?"

"It's difficult to explain, but she tried to break into my mind. I managed to stop her, but barely. She doesn't even know she did it. She doesn't remember."

"Do you think she was under a spell, that someone else was using her to get to you?"

"No, I think she did it on her own, but at some subconscious level. That's not all. She spoke the language of magick."

"Are you sure?" Zephra didn't sound convinced. "You know how much strength that takes. No human would be strong enough to survive the aftereffects."

"I'm sure," he insisted, "and she didn't suffer *any* effects, even after she pulled it back."

"Dorwynn," Zephra began, "I don't think…"

"She spoke the language of magick, Z. I know it."

Lilly decided to go back to the camp. Her anger was gone, having been replaced by fear and confusion, the same that Dorwynn was feeling. How could she do what he claimed and not remember it? Even more confusing was how she could speak a language she'd never heard or spoken before, one that, until now, she didn't even know existed. She'd read a book about the old language while studying with Ashya, but it made no sense because the old language was Old English, the first language, according to whoever wrote the book. So what was the language of magick and how could she, of all people, speak it?

Zephra looked at Dorwynn, wanting to doubt his words, but his sincerity of the event was too genuine. He retrieved his game, then pushed it into the boiling water, leaving only its feet exposed. Zephra just stared into the fire. How could this be, unless Lilly was the Chosen One? She considered the possibility. Gustave would have trained the Chosen One himself, would he not? She hadn't understood why he wanted this girl trained in all four elements, but he was such a stoic person that she never bothered to ask. He probably wouldn't have told her even if she had.

Dorwynn pulled the bird from the kettle and sat down to pull out its feathers. Zephra grabbed the kettle from the spit so Dorwynn wouldn't have to go trough the trouble of finding something to protect his hand from the heat.

"Do you remember what she said?" Zephra asked him after returning to her seat. She knew much of the language, though she rarely attempted to use it in her magick. She was immortal and even she didn't dare cross that line except for extreme circumstances, but knowing what Lilly had said might be helpful in figuring out what was going on.

"She said *'Ani murat vorta'*. I don't know what it means."

"It means 'Remove your barriers'." Zephra tossed a small ball of flames from her hand into the fire, increasing its strength so their dinner would be cooked before dawn. She looked at Dorwynn, who was creating a cloud of feathers in the air around him.

"It makes sense, you know," she pointed out after a moment. "She knows your true name. She was commanding you to let her read your thoughts. If she's that much stronger than you are, I'm surprised you were able to prevent her from doing it. How did you do it?"

Lilly emerged from the forest and sat beside them before Dorwynn had a chance to respond. They both watched her in silence, waiting for her to speak. She looked at Dorwynn, who went back to plucking dinner.

"He appealed to my morality," Lilly answered for him. She'd listened to the rest of their conversation as she returned, having to stop as she relived a flashback from that night. The world was still. There was only fear in his eyes, only anger in hers. He'd said something after that, and though she didn't remember what he had said, she remembered how she felt when she came out of it.

Dorwynn's head snapped up in surprise, wondering how much she had heard of their conversation and why, suddenly, she remembered that night. Zephra stayed silent, a calm look on her face. No matter how powerful Lilly was, she didn't know her true name, so she wasn't worried about the same events happening to her. She would stop her if she had to, by any means necessary.

"You remember?" Dorwynn asked. He didn't know whether to be afraid that she remembered or grateful that he didn't have to try to explain what she had done.

"I could hear you talking about me," she informed them. "It brought back a few memories."

"You could hear us?" Zephra asked. They hadn't been talking loud enough for her to heard them if she'd been sitting across from them, so how, she wondered, could Lilly have heard them so far into the forest?

"What do you remember?" Dorwynn asked, unconcerned with how she had heard them. He wanted to know if she remembered anything he hadn't told Zephra.

"The world was still," she said, a cryptic edge to her voice. "There was only fear in your eyes, only anger in mine, and then you broke through."

"What about the *Doret Gaia*?" asked Zephra, testing Lilly to see how much of the language she really knew.

"I don't know what that means," Lilly replied honestly. She figured it was something spoken in the language that she didn't know she knew, but she apparently didn't know enough to understand it.

"*Doret Gaia* is the language of magick," Zephra said. "Where did you learn the words you spoke?" Lilly shrugged. "Humans don't speak that language. Only a handful of magickal creatures do and as far as I can remember, even fewer speak it while using magick. It is the purest language. The more pure something is, the stronger it is. Every creature who knows the language knows that using it with magick takes an amount of strength that is beyond comprehension."

"What does *kita sira* mean?" Lilly asked, recalling the words she'd spoken during the harpy attack. Zephra's eyes opened wide in surprise.

"Where did you hear those words?" she demanded, her temper flaring, not from anger, but from fear. Controlling someone by their true name was a form of true magic, but those words were from magick itself. It was more than just a command; it was a death sentence.

"I don't know. I said them during the harpy attack, right before I passed out."

"No wonder you were unconscious for so long," Zephra yelled. "It would have killed anyone else."

"Calm down, Z," Dorwynn said, turning the naked bird over the fire on a makeshift spit. He could feel her anger rising and the last thing he wanted to witness was Zephra and Lilly in a duel. Between the two of them, they would destroy the entire forest. He took her hand and she jerked it away, her eyebrows furrowed in contempt, but she calmed herself before she let her emotions get away from her. She now wished she'd never followed them.

"Tell me what it means," Lilly prompted. Zephra frowned, her lips pursed together. She didn't look at Lilly, afraid that if she did, she wouldn't be able to control herself. Lilly sat next to the fire and looked at Zephra intently. "Please?"

"It is a command," she blurted. "It means *be lifeless*. You commanded them to destroy themselves."

Silence followed, overshadowed only by the thick fog of tension that hung over them. The realization that Lilly had given such a command ate at her. How could she have known that those words would destroy them? Where had she heard them? They were certainly not a part of any language she'd ever heard before and she was suddenly very afraid. She was using magick she had learned from no one and she could barely remember using it. What would happen to those around her if it happened again?

She was so lost in her thoughts, she didn't realize how much time had passed until Dorwynn handed her a chunk of fully-cooked pheasant wrapped in a piece of cloth torn from an old shirt. She watched as he removed another large chunk and gave it to Zephra, who took it without needing the shirt for insulation. They ate in silence, each contemplating the tumultuous circumstances that had brought them together and the relationships that were swirling chaotically among them.

They spent the rest of the night watching the fire, each reflecting on the cruel twists fate had dropping them in. Though a bit melancholy, Zephra was more herself than Dorwynn had seen her in the past week, and he was thankful his friend had returned to normal. He was also glad for Zephra's company, taking comfort in the fact that he wasn't alone with Lilly. If she got angry again, Zephra could protect him.

He fell asleep thinking about what he had to accomplish in the coming months before he was to deliver Lilly to the faeries, which would happen when she was ready to be tested for her Master status. Her tests consisted of magickal tasks, difficult tasks, but he was sure she would accomplish them easily. There were many more things, though, that she needed to learn, things that would be more easily learned if she were to spend time with the creatures of each specific talent. It wasn't in his original plans, but it was a possibility worth considering. If he decided to do it, it would be just as much work on his part to make it happen correctly than if he taught her himself. Her training would go much faster as well, something he was unsure if he wanted or not. His last conscious thought before falling asleep was telling himself that his wants did not come before the needs of others.

Sleep had trouble finding Lilly. She tossed and turned on her bedroll, wild dreams fighting their way into her head. Images of battle destroyed her peace, though she didn't wake. Zephra watched her for some time, and then put her hand on Lilly's forehead. Lilly jerked suddenly, and then relaxed, allowing Zephra to consume the nightmarish scenes.

Zephra lay awake for some time after that, staring at the clouds as they separated and diminished the further threat of rain. The stars held her focus as she tried to overcome the terrible feeling of loss she still felt. She was near Lilly, but the connection remained distant. Lilly didn't trust her and obviously didn't feel the same bond that both she and Dorwynn felt. She wondered if everyone who encountered the girl felt the same way. She pondered the possibility so long, it was just hours before dawn when she decided to get some sleep, and sleep brought to her a dream she hadn't experienced since she was in the infancy of her first life cycle, an involuntary vision quest, the only one she could ever have. It showed her how she came to be, how the Goddess Divine, the creator of all life, placed her newborn soul into the body into which she was born, the same body she had now, the same she would always have.

The memory had always bothered her, for she could never figure out why the Goddess would give her a soul that could incarnate into the same body over and over again, but could never reincarnate into a new one. The other detail of the dream that had always confused her, though, was that when the creator did her divine work, she shed a tear for Zephra's newborn soul, a single tear. She never spoke any words and once the soul had been placed into its body, Zephra could no longer see the creator in her mind. It was the closest link she had to a past life, this lonely memory of her creation. Every memory from then on was of her life, this life, the only life she would ever have. Jerking Zephra from the sleep she'd managed to find, she remained lost in her thoughts until the blazing suns crested over the horizon.

Shortly after they woke, they moved quickly to roll the beds, take down the tent and pack the horses. They worked in silence, each questioning if the entire journey would be filled by the lack of communication. No one dared ask the question aloud. Lilly led them down the road, her head held high like a queen leading her procession. Dorwynn followed her, keeping pace as she sped her horse.

Zephra continued on foot, keeping excellent speed with the others. Despite how unsure she was about Zephra's unexpected appearance, Lilly had to marvel at her agility and strength. No matter how hard she rode her horse, Zephra never fell a step behind. As they traveled silently through the forest, they failed to notice a figure concealing itself among the trees, a figure that, had the trainers seen, would have been recognized immediately as a dragon in its human form.

A Future of Tests

"To become a Master of Earth magick," Dorwynn told Lilly the following day when they had stopped for their first meal, "you will have a series of tasks that you must complete correctly. Learning to manipulate the earth will be your first focus. It is the most difficult to achieve, but once you do, your other tasks will come easily."

"Why do you call it earth," asked Lilly, "when we are not on Earth?" Dorwynn stared at her blankly. She asked such irrelevant questions to which he never seemed to have the answers. Zephra smirked, enjoying his discomfort. It was a welcomed change from his normal demeanor and Lilly seemed to push every button he had.

"Before this world was created, the words existed," he answered finally. "For the sake of sparing confusion among those who come from Earth, it's easier not to change anything more than necessary. Can we stay on focus, please?"

Lilly laughed inwardly. She'd never seen him try to teach before and was taking great pleasure in his stumbling. He was trying to be so serious, and though she knew that her training was important, she also knew that she had to find the humor in things or she wouldn't get very far. She nodded and let him continue, but she was in a great mood and was determined to stay that way.

"There is other magick you must also learn," he continued, ignoring the playful gleam in her eyes. "It isn't necessary for becoming a Master, but it's crucial that you learn as much as possible. I think there are some things you would better learn from other creatures. I can teach you a few things, but I am not nearly as adept at the others."

"Like what?" Lilly interrupted.

"Like premonition or communication with less sentient beings. For those things, we will spend time with the creatures who have the natural talent to do it. We'll detour through the ogre territory for some, and the rest we will focus on after we get to Elikrede."

Lilly had read about ogres. There were many things in human history that said they should be feared, and though she knew some things were myths, she had to wonder where the myths originated from if they weren't true. Surely there couldn't be so much fiction in historical fact. She let her mind wander, trying to imagine what she would do if an ogre attacked. They were almost impossible to kill since their blood contained such a high level of healing properties.

"Are you listening?" Dorwynn stared at her, one eyebrow raised in frustration. She focused on his words again, but she was growing tired of his ceaseless rambling. She was ready to *do* something.

"As I was saying," he continued, "you will spend a great deal of time with two of the magickal humans in Elikrede. An Arch-level sorceress will teach you about the spells and charms used in fundamental magic, and an Arch-level apothecary will teach you about potions. It will take a while to learn these things, so you'll get started with them as soon as we arrive, and between your lessons with them you will train in elemental magick with me.

"You also need to learn to protect yourself, not just magickally, but physically. We'll wait until we get to Elikrede, and then I'll teach you how to handle a sword. Zephra will teach you how to fight using a dagger on the way."

"What?" Lilly looked at Zephra, cringing at her wide grin, then turned her surprised look back to Dorwynn. "You're kidding, right?"

"I'm not kidding. If anyone finds out who you are, your life after that would be in constant danger. You have to know how to protect yourself if you get caught alone with an enemy."

"So you're going to let the enemy train me?"

Dorwynn frowned. Zephra jumped from the rock she'd been perched on and walked away from them without a word. Dorwynn shook his head and walked toward Lilly. She stood defensively, returning his severe look with her own.

"She's not the enemy, Lilly," he chided, his face only inches from hers. "Who do you think pulled you from the coma you inflicted on yourself by using magick stronger than you were ready for? You were slipping away from us. Zephra brought you back. She saved your life."

Lilly frowned and crossed her arms. She didn't care that Zephra had pulled her from the coma when all she could think about was what she'd witnessed in the dream. She didn't trust Zephra and until she was given a reason to think otherwise, she wouldn't trust her. Dorwynn defended her, making it that much worse, and Lilly's good mood disappeared as quickly as Zephra had.

"It's time to let bygones be bygones," Dorwynn said, trying to reason with her. "Let it go."

"You're one to talk," she spat at him. "You tell me that you've changed so much in the past three years, but even when I met you in Arthidgen last week, you were almost yourself. I thought, even before I knew who you were, that you could be related to the friend I lost three years ago. You haven't changed in the past three years, Dorwynn. You've changed in the past three *days*. I made a mistake, okay? I'm sorry that you're so scared of me, but maybe you should follow your own advice and let it go, because you have a responsibility to me right now. If you don't want to be near me, then do your job so I can move on." Lilly spun away from him and walked in the same direction that Zephra had, leaving him with the horses and their supplies.

"Where are you going?" he called after her.

"I'm going to get Zephra!"

Lilly found her standing near a stream, shooting fireballs into it. She watched, intrigued, as Zephra formed a ball in her hand and threw it with perfect precision, hitting the same place in the water each time. When she realized Lilly was behind her, Zephra quickly tossed the ball away. It landed at the edge of the stream and sizzled as the water seeped over it.

"Sorry," she said. "It helps me think."

"It seems like a useful talent," Lilly said. She didn't know what to say, but she couldn't do what Dorwynn said and just let it go. Until she figured out exactly what her vision meant, she couldn't abandon her instincts, but she could still be civil. She hadn't liked some of her teachers in school, but she put up with them until their lessons were finished. She could do it again.

"You'll learn it when I train you."

"Would you teach me now?"

Zephra gave her a small smile and shook her head. She wished she could comply; maybe it would relieve the tension in their relationship. She knew, however, that there was an order to how Lilly needed to learn her magick.

"Not yet," she told her. "You have to learn to control a more stable element before fire. It's dangerous. It's unpredictable and destructive and if you lose control of it, it can get away from you very easily and destroy everything in its escape path."

They stood in silence, each wondering what to say next. Things between them had to be resolved or Lilly would never get through this series of tasks. Lilly finally decided to bring up the one topic she knew they had in common.

"Is he always so…secretive?"

"He hides many things. He refuses to talk about his past, his childhood, his family. He claims that the past isn't important, only the future. It's rubbish, in my opinion."

"Why do you think so?"

"Those who do not know the mistakes of history, and of their past, are doomed to repeat them. He above all others should know that." Zephra looked toward the road where she knew Dorwynn was waiting, and then turned her gaze to Lilly. She couldn't believe that Gustave had decided to train her so young. She knew the children here who had magickal abilities began training as early as possible, but those who came from Earth to learn their abilities never trained like this. Gustave was trying to condense a decade's worth of knowledge into less than three years. He should have brought Lilly to them much sooner than he did or waited until her adolescent years were behind her, and the first chance she had, she would ask him why he hadn't.

"I know you don't trust me," Zephra told her. "I don't expect you to trust me and I won't be foolish enough to think you would be willing to start over and put the past week behind us, but I'd like to offer a truce. Whether you believe it or not, we have your best interests at heart and neither of us would let any danger befall you."

Lilly thought carefully over her words. She didn't trust her, but Zephra seemed genuinely concerned about her safety. She felt her doubt constructing a wall within her. Dorwynn's intentions were as questionable as Zephra's. He was Adrian, however, and she knew beyond the shadow of a doubt that he would never intentionally hurt her. She held her hand out to Zephra.

"A truce, then," she said. Zephra took her hand, sealing the unspoken promise. A bright white light emanated from their joined palms and Lilly withdrew quickly, rubbing her hand as the glow faded, though a peculiar warmth remained.

"What was that?" she asked. Zephra was rubbing her hand as well, a confused expression on her usually stern face.

"I don't know."

Lilly wondered if she was telling the truth. Too many strange things had occurred since meeting Zephra for them to have no explanation. There had to be a reason.

As they walked toward the road, Zephra thought about what had just happened and her mysterious connection to Lilly. She considered telling Lilly why she'd followed them, but she was unsure if she would accept it or fear it because there was no reasonable explanation for the connection between them. Whatever the reason, Zephra knew one thing for certain…her hand never glowed unless she was using magick. It was as if magick itself was trying to tell her something, but she had no way of knowing what it was trying to say.

"Did you get everything worked out?" Dorwynn asked when they returned. He was sitting on the ground beside their supplies, having relieved the horses since he had no idea how long a resolution would take. He plucked at the new grass, sliding a broken strand between his fingers, his mind heavy with his many burdens.

"Well," said Lilly, determined to break the tension within the group, "we came to an agreement. Rather than take out our frustrations on each other, we're just going to take them out on you."

He looked up at her with a blank expression. Zephra tried to contain her smile, but she couldn't keep a straight face.

"Whatever it takes to keep the two of you getting along," he responded nonchalantly, glad to see that they were both smiling. His mood lifted in the wake of their newfound truce and he leapt to his feet, reenergized.

"What next, ladies? Shall we continue our journey, or would you like to rest until morning, seeing as how we are already unloaded?"

Lilly knew he was asking her what she wanted, but she didn't know how to answer. She hadn't slept well the night before, so an entire afternoon of rest sounded wonderful. She longed, however, to get to Elikrede as soon as possible so she could find her mother. She glanced at Zephra, who could see the conflict in her eyes. She made the decision for Lilly.

"I'd like to rest," she offered. "You can finish informing Lilly of her future tasks, and if we have enough time before dusk, I'll teach her how to defend herself from unwanted attacks."

Lilly's heart skipped a beat at the suggestion. She felt the sincerity of Zephra's words, reminding her that they had her best interests at heart, but something just didn't feel right. She couldn't shake the fear that something bad was going to happen.

"Aren't all attacks unwanted?" Dorwynn asked, the playful gleam returning to his eyes. Lilly laughed in spite of herself as Zephra stuck out her tongue at both of them.

With their issues pushed aside, they spent the following hours discussing Lilly's training, or rather, Dorwynn spoke while the women listened. Dorwynn's plan involved many things Lilly hadn't expected. Their detour through ogre territory was only the first in several encounters with other races, though most of those would occur after they'd arrived in Elikrede. She would spend time with the centaurs, minotaurs and pterippi, where she would gain knowledge of the magick required to make predictions and to transform herself, which was a difficult ability to master and took quite a bit of strength, according to Dorwynn.

She listened as he described how they would travel to Griffon Cove, where she would be trained on another of her tasks, how to form a cave in a mountain. It was an extension of manipulating earth, though apparently stone was much more intricate and complex. She was captivated by his description of the cove and she could feel her excitement growing at the prospect of seeing the glorious creatures that lived there.

The rest of her tasks she would learn from him. They seemed menial in comparison, but in actuality, they were quite the opposite. Growing a plant in her hand, for example, seemed simple. Dorwynn had done it easily that morning in Migfelá's three times in a row, but the magick it took to accomplish the task was rather complicated, taking more strength and focus than she'd originally thought.

Another task was to create a namun, which was a circle of stones used during a great magickal feat to contain the massive amounts of power required for such things. Namuns were raised most often for magickal duels to prevent the magick expelled from harming bystanders. Stonehenge had been a namun, Dorwynn explained, and he said nothing else on the topic except that he would tell her more when it was time for her to learn how to do it.

The task that intrigued her the most was the construction of her wand. It would be the first task she would attempt for two important reasons: crafting a wand required the same magick needed for the tasks she would learn and attempt later, only using much less power, and it would be a functional instrument for her future use of magick.

"Your wand," he told her as they relaxed under the late afternoon suns, "is an extension of you. It is a tool of magick, but the only magick it contains on its own, other than the natural magick of the materials from which it is made, is the magickal signature of the one who constructed it.

Some masters of Earth make and sell wands, but the wand forms a connection to the maker's signature during its creation. They are completely functional for any user, but having that connection with your wand makes it that much more effective."

Dorwynn removed his wand from his pack and handed it to Lilly. It was made of a dark wood, deep red in color, with tendrils of gold throughout the grain of the wood. It was sanded smooth, all thirteen inches perfectly straight, with a blunted end. A black stone handle, just as smooth as the rest, formed the base of the wand. There was one ridge near where the wand met the handle that formed a thumb rest. A symbol was carved into the bottom of the handle that looked like a three-petaled flower with a ring around it. At the tip of each petal, a white crystal was wedged into the stone.

"What is the symbol?" she asked, tracing her fingers slowly over its carved edges.

"It is a triquatra. It represents the balance of three."

"What is the balance of three?"

"It is different for everyone," he said vaguely. She frowned at him and he sighed. "At its core, it is a circle within a circle. It is three pieces of one circle, each an equal third, which are arranged tip to tip and crossing over each other, and in the center they merge to form one heart. Some believe the three points surrounded by the outer circle symbolizes ourselves; mind, body and soul surrounded by continual change. Some think it means time; the past, present and future bound by the ring of eternity. Others take it as a symbol of life; birth, life and death revolving in an endless loop over and over again. It all depends on your beliefs."

"Why did you choose it?"

"In magick, it symbolizes the land, the sea and the sky; earth, water and air. They bond to form the heart; fire. The four elements, embraced by the spirit of the Divine, the soul of magick itself. That's what it means to me anyway, but I chose it simply because I was drawn to it. It symbolizes three. Three is my magickal number."

"Wait," Lilly interrupted. "Your magickal number?" She was beginning to feel the onset of a headache with all the information being thrown at her. They'd gone from discussing the creation of her wand to numerology on a whole new level. She'd asked the questions, though, and she rubbed her temples, wishing she hadn't interrupted his lesson.

"It's a whole new twist on magickal numerology," Zephra joked. Lilly eyed her suspiciously, wondering if Zephra had read her mind. Zephra didn't notice the look and continued with her explanation. "There are certain numbers that are connected to magick, and to each other through magick; two, three, five, seven, nine, and thirteen. Except for thirteen, which is a representation for the number of moon cycles in the year, the numbers are all connected. They are numbers that occur naturally in nature or magick. Two genders, two soul mates, two choices; good and evil. Three, you already learned. Five represents connection, the spirit of a female soul and the phases she experiences during her life journey, the four elements intertwined with the Divine soul, or the four seasons bound in a continual revolution of change. Many call this the symbol of the Goddess. Then there is seven. It takes four weeks of seven days to complete a moon's cycle, a woman's cycle, and it dates back to when the Christians began writing the Bible: seven deadly sins, seven virtues of Heaven, seven levels of Hell, seven planes of existence, and many more too tedious to recount right now. And finally, the number nine. It is a product of two and seven, connecting humans to their beliefs in the matter of religion. It is also three multiplied by itself, forming a singular connection of the balance of three in time, life and magick, or whichever way you want to believe it."

"Wow," Lilly whispered, more to herself than the others. She had one more question on the topic, but she was afraid to ask out of fear that it would steer the conversation further from her tasks. She was ready to get up and do something, but she asked anyway, just to get it over with. "If there are four season and four elements, then why isn't four a magickal number?"

"On its own," Dorwynn replied, "it is two twos, two sets of halves. When it comes to the seasons or the elements, they exist only when connected by a fifth. The soul of magick must be present for them to stand together. In a sense, it is the fifth element, or the in-between periods of time when the seasons change from one to another. They must all have a connection to remain whole.

"Well, I think we've discussed enough of this for now. You won't have to worry about it until you make your wand, and even then, there may not be any symbol that appeals to you. If one does, however, it represents your magickal number and should be placed on your wand, but only if you find true meaning in it."

Dorwynn stood and looked toward the setting suns. He took the wand that Lilly was still holding and placed it carefully into his pack, then reached for the dagger at his hip. Lilly stood as well. She hadn't noticed the cool air that had settled over them and she began walking toward the forest to look for firewood.

"Leave it be," Dorwynn told her. "Zephra will handle the fire tonight." He looked at Zephra and a small smirk crossed his lips. "Why don't you start teaching her how to use a dagger while I'm hunting?" he asked. She nodded and reached for her own dagger.

It was made of the shiniest metal Lilly had even seen. The blade was curved into the shape of a flame, and though the handle was the perfect shape for her hand, the edges of the handle reached over itself and formed two more blades, each smaller than the center, that also curved up and around the center blade. When she held it, Lilly thought it looked like a silver fire was burning in Zephra's hand, and considering her talent for controlling fire, it suited her well.

"You have a dagger, correct?" asked Zephra as she twirled her own between her thin fingers. Lilly nodded and began searching through her pack for the blade that Ashya had given her before she left. She hadn't used it once since she'd left Ashya, and it had managed to sink beneath the rest of her things. Finally, her fingers touched to tip of the cool steel handle. She grabbed the sheath and pulled it out. Zephra held out her hand and Lilly laid it carefully in her empty palm.

Lilly hadn't studied its detail closely the day Ashya had given her the gift. Under the crimson suns, it seemed to glow with anticipation at the prospect of being used. The sunlight brought to life the intricate detail of the sheath and handle. Symbols were emblazoned into the metal, forming a unique twirling design that connected them all. The stones lit up as Zephra inspected it carefully, turning it back and forth in her hand.

"An athame," she stated. "It is a good weapon, but it is a great magickal tool for directing energy. Like the wand is a tool of Earth Magick, the athame is a tool of Fire Magick." She handed it back to Lilly. "It will get no good use at the bottom of your pack. Wear it on your hip. You never know when you will need your weapon. Now, arm yourself."

Zephra held her fire blade in front of her as she crouched into a fighting position. She shifted her weight from one foot to the other, moving in a fluid motion around Lilly, who stared at her with a dumbfounded look on her face.

"I've never done this before," she reminded Zephra. She removed the athame from the sheath and tossed the sheath onto her pack. The blade grew warm as she held it and, for a moment, she felt as though the athame had been made just for her. She held it in front of her, imitating Zephra's stance, and suddenly, Zephra lunged toward her. Lilly blocked the attack instinctively, but her mood shifted as fear gripped her heart.

"Don't just stand there," Zephra yelled at her. "Move your feet!" She lunged again and Lilly sidestepped her attack. "Good! Again!"

Lilly studied her movements. She moved constantly, like a snake trying to confuse a predator with sudden changes in direction. She danced lightly from one foot to another, waiting for an opening, and then lashed out at Lilly. The force of her blows nearly knocked Lilly to the ground, but after recovering her footing, her anger grew enough that she went for Zephra, taking aim at her chest. Zephra moved out of her path so fast, she managed to avoid Lilly's advance and circle behind her with her dagger at Lilly's throat.

"And now you are dead," she said, straightening herself. "Not bad for your first attempt, but I think it might be wise to do some training to enhance your speed. I'm going to come at you with all I've got and I want you to block only."

She waited for Lilly to ready herself, and then she went at her, her lunge fierce. Lilly blocked the first few blows, but as Zephra's speed and force increased, she began using her arms to block. Zephra's blade slid over her arm and cut a deep scratch into it. Lilly dropped her weapon and grabbed her wound with her other hand.

"Don't use your body to block an attack," Zephra instructed, ignoring the cold glare Lilly sent her way. She picked up Lilly's dagger and gave it back to her. "Your body is the target and you *never* put the target in the path of the enemy. Use your athame. Forget that you are holding it and imagine it is a part of you, the only part of your body that is impenetrable from attack. It is an extension of you and when it is in your hand, you are joined to it. That connection makes you one. Try again."

Lilly tried not to focus on her injury as she thwarted Zephra's attack once again. Though Zephra was restraining her true strength, Lilly had trouble keeping up with her. She felt herself tiring by the second, and though she knew this was just as important as anything else she would learn, she was ready to stop. They were supposed to be resting and instead, they were wearing themselves out even faster. She didn't want to tell Zephra this, though, so she fought through her rising fatigue as long as she could.

Zephra seemed to be enjoying the sparring session. Her eyes had taken on a look of excitement, as though she thrived on the combative situation. It was only after Zephra cut Lilly again that Lilly had finally had enough. She rushed toward Zephra angrily, her dagger in front of her as though it was leading the way into battle. She progressed quickly with the adrenaline that coursed through her veins and before long, they were engaged in a violent dance, their blades coming dangerously close to piercing flesh on several occasions.

Lilly didn't know how it happened. They had been moving as one, advancing and blocking each other when Lilly felt Zephra's blade pierce her shoulder. It went deep and she howled in pain. The surge of anger that rose from within her cleared her head. In battle, this opportunity would be used to make the kill. Before she knew it, she used the moment to cause her own damage. Her athame slid through Zephra's chest with surprisingly little resistance. Zephra stumbled backwards, a smile painted on her face, and then fell to the ground in a heap.

"And now I am dead," she whispered to Lilly, still smiling. Her eyes closed as she exhaled her final breath. Lilly rushed to her side and tried to heal her with the magick Ashya had taught her, but she hadn't enough strength left to do any good. She watched in horror as Zephra's entire body began to glow from the inside. A spark blazed from the wound Lilly had inflicted, and she jumped back as Zephra's entire body burst into flames.

The Path Less Traveled

The fire was still burning, having nearly consumed Zephra's body, when Dorwynn returned with his kill, a badger-like creature with a long snout and gray fur. Lilly was still bleeding, though she was much more concerned with the murder she'd just committed. Dorwynn noticed Zephra's absence first, and then he saw the pile of ashes at Lilly's feet.

"Great," he muttered. "Now we have to build the fire ourselves." Lilly gaped at him in utter shock.

"Is that all you care about?" she yelled at him. "Zephra's dead. I killed her."

Her nerves shot, she replaced her blood-tainted athame into its sheath. Her shoulder throbbed where Zephra had stuck her, but she didn't bother trying to heal it. She doubted she had enough energy to do anything magickal, and her emotions were reeling. True, she didn't trust Zephra, but by no means did she wish her harm.

He smiled and shook his head. He knew Zephra would play this little game with Lilly, though he wished she would have waited until they were settled in Elikrede first. He tossed his kill beside where he would now have to build the fire himself before trying to explain. He sat beside the dead animal and began skinning it with his own dagger. Lilly winced with each cut the blade made in the poor creature's flesh.

"She's not dead," he told her. "I mean, she is, but really, she's not." Lilly stared at him, so confused she couldn't ask him how that was even possible. "Take a closer look at her ashes."

Lilly peered at the pile of ashes that had once been Zephra's body. Where her heart had been, the ashes fluttered. She knelt closer and noticed that a small baby bird was working its way from the ashes. She watched in amazement as the bird freed itself from the binding ashes and shook them free. Before her eyes, it grew a downy coat of bright red. It had a long neck and a curved beak, and deep violet eyes. It spread its wings as far as it could and shook its tail. In an instant, violet feathers sprouted from its tail and grew until they were three times the length of the bird's body. The down disappeared and was replaced by blood red feathers. The bird doubled in size and took to the sky, flying over their heads tauntingly.

"She's a phoenix," Lilly gasped. She'd read descriptions of the mystical creature in one of Ashya's books, but the only picture it had contained was a drawing from someone claiming to see it. Even in this world, phoenixes were extremely rare. No one knew how to find them or even how many existed.

"Yeah," Dorwynn laughed. "I expected she would do this to you, though I never expected it would be so soon. You should feel honored. It's a great sign of trust when a phoenix allows you to see their magickal form."

"Well," Lilly sighed, "she didn't have much of a choice after I stabbed her in the heart." He smiled again.

"She let you win. She's been training and fighting for centuries and she's better than anyone else I've ever met in my life. If she wanted to kill you, she would have."

Lilly thought about this while she collected wood for a fire. If it was a sign of trust, why didn't Zephra just tell her the truth rather than having her find out like this? It certainly didn't make Lilly trust her any more than before. If anything, it made her trust Zephra even less. It was a terrible trick to pull on someone who wasn't expecting it, but Lilly supposed if she had the ability, she would try to have some fun with it, so she decided to let it go. She figured she would find it as funny as Dorwynn did when Zephra played the trick on someone else.

Night fell as they cooked their dinner. The moon hovered over them, drawing their gazes toward the sky. The stars were visible tonight, and Lilly stared at them wishing she could find at least one familiar constellation in the clusters. Gazing at the unfamiliar sky, she was struck with a true sense of how far from her home she really was.

They ate in comfortable silence. Lilly tore pieces of meat from her share and fed it to Zephra, who, Dorwynn explained, would remain in her phoenix form until she reached maturity, when she would be able to return into her human form. According to him, it would take nearly a day before that happened.

When their meal was over, Dorwynn walked into the forest long enough to gather a few branches, which he brought back to Lilly. He dropped them at her feet before rolling out their beds. When he finished, he sat beside her in front of the fire.

"Something to practice with," he told her, picking up one of the branches. He moved his hand over it, his skin never coming into contact with it. It began to bend with the motion of his hand, twisting and turning whichever way he moved. He continued manipulating the branch until it transformed into the symbol etched on his wand.

"Manipulating the Earth," he said as he gave her the newly-formed twig, "forming a cave in stone and creating your wand all take the same magick, only at much different levels of strength. It is much like bending someone to your will. You must lend the person, or object, in this case, a certain amount of your own energy for it to bend to you. Too much energy will break it, so take care in releasing too much power."

He wondered if she could control the amount of power she would have to use, but he knew he would soon have the answer. He pulled a branch from the pile and laid it in her hands.

"Just hold it," he instructed. "It is no longer a part of the tree that gave it life, but it still has energy flowing through it. Feel the energy. Let it come into you and when you feel it, give your own energy back to it. Let it come from deep within your soul. Once you've done this, the limb will bend to you and you will be able to form anything from it. See what you want it to become in your mind and then make it so. The potential is endless."

Lilly held the limb for the rest of the evening, but she was so tired, she had no energy to lend to it. She contemplated what she would create, but the stress of her long day weighed on her. She felt no energy coming from the lifeless object. She set it down long enough to heal her wounds and then picked it up again, hoping the use of magick would spark the feelings Dorwynn had described. It was useless, however. Her fatigue caught up with her and she fell asleep beside the fire, the limb still clutched in her hand.

The world around her was still. Even the insects flying through the air hung motionless, trapped in perpetual flight. He seemed easy enough to control, walking straight to her without so much as a command.

He's a liar, she thought, *but he will not lie to me.*

She held her hand out to him, prying through the first barrier in his mind. His childhood, memories of his father, memories of her. She moved past these things she already knew. She found some memories of his life over the past three years; training with Gustave, practicing combat with Zephra, spending time in his special place.

She could hear him speaking to her, but his words were unimportant. She tried to move deeper into his mind, but his defenses there were much stronger.

Ani murat vorta, she commanded him.

His will was strong, but she knew she was stronger. The truth was hidden deep in his mind, and she was determined to find it.

I know who you are, too, he said, his voice echoing in her mind. *Why do you think they sent me to you?* She froze, ceasing her assault.

He sees only anger in your eyes, another voice interceded, overshadowing his words. She didn't recognize who the voice belonged to, but it was eerily familiar. *He is your friend and he loves you, but there is no love for you in his eyes now. There is only fear.*

She looked into his eyes. The fear she saw in them made her stomach drop. A sickening feeling came over her as she realized her treachery. This was not her. She released her hold over him and as he ran away from her, the inert world sprang to motion.

You cannot trust yourself any more than you can trust others, the voice in her head taunted. *Your deeds are more insidious than the deeds he has committed. You dishonor your destiny.*

Lilly awoke from her dream as suddenly as if someone had dumped a bucket of water over her. The fire had diminished to mere embers, and after brushing the dirt from her face and hair, she stumbled into the darkness to find more fuel. The pile of branches Dorwynn had given her was enough to get it going again, so after coming across a few fallen chunks of wood, she dragged them back to camp and tossed them into the fire pit. She stoked the fire until it blazed and warmed her chilled bones. Sleeping on the ground was not the best idea.

The dream she'd just had was fresh in her mind, playing itself over and over in her head. She looked toward Dorwynn, who, unbothered by the chill in the air, was sprawled on his bedroll, snoring loudly. Lilly stared into the early morning darkness with the knowledge that she was far beyond sleep, but the fire was rejuvenated, casting a bright glow over their camp. She rummaged through her pack for her journal, and then dragged her bedroll closer to the fire. She wrote until the suns peeked over the horizon.

She was stiff and sore as they prepared to continue their trek to Elikrede. Dorwynn said little as they packed camp, and when they got back to the road, he rode hard and fast, leaving Lilly no choice but to follow suit. The scenery flew by so fast she barely had time to notice any detail in it, though she figured it was the same as the past few days. The suns shone bright upon them and by mid-afternoon, they were both drenched from the sweat that even the wind couldn't keep away. The humidity grew heavier in the air as the day wore on and Dorwynn slowed his horse to a walk to look for a place where they could stop to rest.

They had left Zephra sleeping in a tree near their camp the night before, nearly five times the size she was when she climbed out of her own ashes. Dorwynn explained to her when they stopped that Zephra would remain out of sight until she was able to take on her human form again. She didn't want anyone to discover that she was a phoenix because there was a rumor that Dagana had found a way to trap their immortal souls. Whether it was true or not, he was unsure, but Zephra had learned long ago to trust the possibility of truth in the gossip and she didn't want to take any chances.

Lilly was still in awe over the fact that she was such a rare creature. She had so many questions for her, but she would have to wait until Zephra caught up to them later that night. They held the same routine as the previous nights. Lilly searched for enough wood to last them until morning and Dorwynn went hunting for the only warm meal they would enjoy that day. Lilly began to miss the dinners that her father had cooked, due mostly to the lack of spices on the meat she ate every night, but she ate without complaint. Anything was better than bread and jerky.

It wasn't until their meal was over that Lilly decided to bring up the topic they were avoiding. Zephra had yet to arrive, and Dorwynn was quietly staring into the fire, lost in his own thoughts. Lilly watched it for a while, absently fiddling with a spare length of rope she'd found dangling from a nearby tree.

"Can we talk about what happened in Arthidgen?" she asked finally. He lowered his eyes and frowned, dreading the conversation that was coming. He felt his defenses go up automatically.

"You remember," he stated. It wasn't a question. He knew she would remember eventually…he'd just hoped it would be after he was done training her.

"Some of it," she admitted, "but that isn't all I want to talk about. I can understand that you think there are things I am not ready for, but I need you to understand that I can handle whatever you are hiding. You never used to keep secrets from me, and knowing that you have so many things you feel you can't share with me makes me wonder if all the trust I had in you was misplaced."

"How can you say that?" he asked her in disbelief. "You know me better than anyone."

"Then I feel sorry for you," she said, "because I don't feel like I know you at all anymore."

She could see the hurt in his eyes, but she wasn't going to hide how she felt. She was just being honest. He threw pieces of dry brush into the fire, glaring at the glowing embers jumping from the flames.

"I could say the same thing about you," he spat. "You used to be so sweet. You used to have nice things to say to me and when I made a mistake, you had the patience to hear me out no matter how mad you were. You don't have that now. You're as hot-tempered as Zephra and just as withdrawn from people as we both are, and that is something you will have to get used to. Your life is not the same. People change when things around them change. I can't sit here wishing my best friend will come back and neither can you, because it isn't going to happen." He glared at her, wrestling with his anger at her for what had happened and his longing to make her understand. "I know I'm not the only one with secrets, Lilly. I'm not naïve enough to believe that you've told me everything and I don't expect you to, but aren't I entitled to have my own? Don't I deserve the same privacy?"

"You do," she said quietly. "I apologize for what I did to you, Dorwynn. I'm sorry, and I'll do everything I can to make sure it never happens again, but I can't promise it won't. I don't even know why it happened. I don't understand what is going on with me or why I can do things I'm not supposed to be able to do. Don't you understand how frustrating that is? I've got everyone telling me what to do and I know that everyone expects things of me, but I have no choice in the matter and I don't even know what I'm supposed to be doing. I'm on the path to a destiny I'm not sure is even mine and I'm only here because everyone else believes it is right."

"I know you better than that, Lilly. If you didn't think it was right, you wouldn't have come. You made the choice." He stood and dropped the rest of the brush into the fire. "You know, when you forgive someone for their misdeeds, it heals the soul. Why are you clinging to my mistakes when you know in your heart that I would never let anything bad happen to you?"

He didn't wait for an answer. He stalked toward his bedroll and flopped on it hard, turning his back to her and the fire. She shook her head, disappointed. She'd wanted to make things better, but she'd only made them worse. Of course, they had both gotten to say what was on their minds, which was something.

"You should take your own advice, Dorwynn," she said at last. "I'm not the only one who needs to let go of things and move on."

He heard what she said, but he did not respond. She stayed by the fire, still playing with the rope, and thought about everything they'd discussed. She didn't even realize that was how she felt until she'd said it. It had always been that way. When she was upset about something, talking to him always helped her to sort out her feelings. After he'd left her behind, she'd had only Beth to confide in, and then Ashya and Amparo only recently, but they weren't here now. She had felt alone when he had left, but now that they were together, instead of feeling better, she felt more alone than ever.

"It's hard to choose a side when both sides are right," said Zephra as she emerged from the shadows. Dorwynn's snoring grew deep and loud, and Lilly didn't know whether to be annoyed that their disagreement had so little effect on him or grateful that she had a few hours of peace from his insufferable mood. Zephra sat down beside her and tossed a fireball into the already blazing flames. "Because I can," she replied to Lilly's quizzical look.

"I'm not meant for this," Lilly told her. She didn't really want to confide in Zephra, but at the moment, she was all she had.

"Yes, you are," Zephra said. "I knew the moment I laid eyes on you that you were meant for something great. I also knew that my life would never be the same after you came into it." Lilly was taken aback by Zephra's fierce faith, and noticing her reaction, Zephra decided to tell her the whole truth. "I wasn't following Dorwynn from Arthidgen. I was following you." She told Lilly everything she'd told Dorwynn about the connection she felt with her. Lilly listened, shocked that she felt this way, but still battling the doubt within her, warning her to beware of something terrible. No matter how hard she tried, she couldn't get that dream of Zephra out of her head.

"He's right," she said at last, "but so are you. I wasn't there to witness what happened, but I know it frightened him and I know that it takes a lot to do so. And I don't know how common it is for you to react like you did, but I know that since I met you, I haven't been myself and I'm still trying to figure out why."

"I didn't mean to," Lilly said, her heart pleading for someone to believe her. "I don't know why anything has happened, but I would never knowingly hurt him. You have to believe that."

"I do, and in time, he will get over his fear, but getting over a betrayal of trust is hard to do. It takes a lot of time to regain trust, and sometimes things are never the same. I doubt they ever will be, but I do know him, and I know that he will not let fear consume him. He's not the type to allow vices into his soul."

"Vices?"

"Fear is a vice; one of the big ones. If you let it consume you, then all the others have an easy path to follow."

"What are the other ones?" asked Lilly, relieved the conversation had shifted toward a safer topic.

"So," said Zephra, smiling, "you want to know about the nine vices of evil. You probably already know them, but I'll tell you anyway. Mind you, they are in no particular order. They are each equally wrong. You know the seven deadly sins, right?" Lilly nodded. "Lust, gluttony, greed, sloth, wrath, envy and pride. Well, the other two are fear and abolition."

"Abolition?"

"It means destruction, a vice that seems to stay with me no matter how hard I try to overcome it." She paused, recalling her own years of devastation, then sighed. "You see, everyone is born with the potential to take in the vices of evil or the virtues of goodness. They have one or the other, or are indifferent, which, in my opinion, should be a vice in itself, but I don't make the rules."

Zephra went on to tell explain what they meant in more detail. Most people believed lust meant sexuality, but it actually meant indulging extravagantly, in everything from sex to material objects. Gluttony was a simpler term for overindulgence or being wasteful. Sloth was clear; it meant idleness, or failing to reach your full potential for lack of trying. Fear, envy and pride were self-explanatory, while wrath meant anything from anger, hate, prejudice or discrimination, and abolition was everything involving death and destruction. Then there was greed, which Zephra explained for some time. Greed was avarice, treachery, selfishness. Greed was the one that started wars and the one besides fear that would most likely allow the others to consume.

Lilly listened as she continued talking about the virtues of goodness: piety, moderation, hospitality, perseverance, wisdom, vision, integrity, courage and fertility. They were the nine virtues that Pagan followers strived for, each one an opposite of the vices she'd just explained. Lilly understood most of them, but a few she asked for more clarification, so Zephra ran down the list quickly.

"Piety simply means purity of the soul, or the simplification of life. Lust is its opposite. Moderation is gluttony's opposite. Hospitality means charitable or liberal. Perseverance is pretty obvious, and so is courage. Just like its counterpart, it leads the other virtues on the path toward your soul. Wisdom is deeper, meaning patience of other as well as the ability to forgive. Vision is simply kindness or admiration, though admiration of the wrong qualities can lead down the wrong path. Integrity, the other side of pride, means that you have learned humility, which I think you have after all that has happened, and fertility is a fancy word for creation.

"As I said, everyone is born with these qualities, based on their chemistry, or they learn them through their environment. The whole point of having free will is so that we can choose what we do, so we can learn right and wrong. If you choose not to overcome the vices you are born with, then you open the door to allow more to consume your soul. It is the coward's way out. It is the path toward evil, but even those who are evil have virtues. Do you know why?" Lilly shook her head, captivated. "It is a matter of balance. Evil people have virtues because good people have vices. No one is perfect."

They continued talking until the suns rose. It was the second sunrise Lilly had seen in two days, and she watched it, taking in the beautiful painting it thrust across the sky. Despite the tension between her and Dorwynn, she felt better than she had in a long while. Zephra's wisdom was beyond contestation. She'd been alive long enough to witness the truth in her words, and yet she could still admit she had her own faults. The thing she'd said that had the most impact, however, was something that made Lilly realize one of her own flaws: impatience.

"Everything I told you tonight is important," she said, "just as everything Dorwynn told you is important. You will be learning a lot of things during your training that may not seem important to you, but everything has relevance. Remember it, and when someone offers you knowledge, accept it, even if you don't think it's necessary. In time, you will find that it may be."

Though she still had her doubts about Zephra, she found herself admiring her. She had a way of speaking that kept you interested, and made you really think about what she was saying. Lilly realized suddenly that she enjoyed having her here, especially during her difficulties with Dorwynn. Zephra knew him well, not the same person she knew, but the older Dorwynn, the man he had become since he'd left Earth. If anyone could help her get through to him, she felt Zephra could.

Despite the fact she'd barely slept in the past two days, Lilly felt wonderful, as vibrant as the new day that greeted them. When Dorwynn woke, he grumbled a greeting to the girls, and then stumbled toward a stream that wasn't far from the road. Lilly had already packed her things on Adair, so while he was gathering his things, she went for a walk.

The forest was alive with the springtime. Birds were hopping vicariously across the forest floor, yanking on earthworms and caterpillars. Squirrels skittered up and down trees, chattering at their neighbors as they foraged for their breakfast. In the distance, Lilly heard a strange sound. She walked toward the disruption, and as she drew near, she saw the oddest magickal creature she'd seen since she'd arrived in Buthania. A bull was moving boulders from a worn path that forked away from the road they were traveling. What was odd about him, however, was the fact that he stood upright, walking around on two legs like any human would.

She watched him silently, and then decided to go back to camp, but when she turned to leave, she snapped a twig, shattering the otherwise tranquil morning. His head jerked up and he stared at her, still holding an enormous boulder. His eyes narrowed at the sight of her and he snorted, sending shivers down her spine. Fear gripped her as she wondered what he would do to her, but he went back to his work, grunting as he heaved the stone from the path.

"If you're going to stay and watch," he said breathlessly, "you could lend a hand."

"Oh," said Lilly to the creature's unexpected request, "of course, but I don't know how much use I will be."

She jumped down the bank she was standing upon and landed in the middle of the worn path. The creature grabbed another large boulder from the pile blocking the path and heaved it out of the way like he was tossing a bag of sand rather than a giant rock. Lilly tried to pick up one of them, but it didn't budge. The creature smiled and continued his work while Lilly leaned against her obstacle. The stone was cold, but as she rested against it, she felt the warmth of magick spread through it. She closed her eyes and imagined herself lifting the massive stone. In her mind, it lifted higher and higher until it no longer blocked the path. She imagined moving it to where he had tossed the others and when she opened her eyes, the boulder dropped from the sky and landed on the pile with a loud *BOOM!*

"Impressive," said the creature. "You must be an apprentice."

"How did you know?"

"You closed your eyes," he responded as he heaved another boulder from the rubble. "As you develop your powers, you'll stop doing that."

They worked in silence, their progress overshadowed by the sheer depth of their obstacle. It looked like a rockslide had collapsed, burying the path, but she couldn't figure out where the stones had come from. There were only trees above them, the brightening sky beyond that. Lilly's eyes snapped toward the creature as he grunted, and she realized what a spectacular being he was. He wasn't much taller than she was, but he was stronger nonetheless. His body was pure muscle, every one rippling as he continued his tedious work. He really didn't look much like a human, except for his arms and chest. His head had a more structured jaw line than a normal bull, and his eyes were a cross between the soft bovine eyes of a bull shaped like human eyes. The large ears jutting out from the sides of his head lay flat, burdened, no doubt, by the several hoops decorating each of them, thick rings of silver and gold. Two large horns protruded from behind his ears, nearly the length of his arms and completely smooth up to the points. His legs were massive, adorned from above with a tail that hung halfway to the ground. She watched as he walked, amazed at how his knees bent, much like a human's at the first joint, with a second set of joints below his knees that bent in the opposite direction. His feet were hooves, and silky blonde hair flowed over them from his ankles, though the rest of his body was covered in dark brown fur.

Lilly was elated that she had finally met a magickal creature whose introduction hadn't been arranged by Gustave, and one that she recognized at that! She'd been traveling for a while with very few encounters with other races, and she'd begun to wonder if they even existed. Seeing the minotaur before her was proof enough that they were here, existing among all the others.

She worked beside him, moving the stones with her magick while he heaved them aside, creating a small mountain along the edge of the path. She felt herself improving with each stone, and after the comment the minotaur had made, she tried to move the stones without closing her eyes. She knew she could do it with them closed, so imagining them move was no longer necessary. As she worked, it started to become second nature to her, as though her magick was nothing more than an invisible backhoe she was controlling. The stone blockade grew smaller, and by the time Dorwynn and Zephra found her, they were nearly finished.

Dorwynn watched as Lilly helped to finish what she'd started, paying close attention to her magickal prowess. She was moving the huge boulders as though they were weightless, lifting and tossing them with little effort. Moving objects was much easier than manipulating them, he knew, but it used similar magick. With just a little instruction and focus, she would master her tasks quickly.

"Hello, Dorwynn," the minotaur grunted as he tossed the final boulder onto the pile with the others.

"Voruum," replied Dorwynn. He jumped from the ledge of the bank and landed beside them. Zephra followed, her landing much more graceful.

"Is this your apprentice?" asked Voruum, wiping the sweat from his sloped forehead.

"Aye, she is."

"She's quite talented." Voruum put his hand on Lilly's shoulder. "Thank you for making my task so much easier. It is much appreciated."

"You're welcome," said Lilly, still breathless from the strain of moving so much. Though she'd used magick, her body screamed in pain as though she'd actually been lifting the massive stones herself. She sat to catch her breath, gratefully taking the water skein Dorwynn was holding out to her. She drank without stopping until her lungs demanded air, and then offered the skein to Voruum.

"How fare things in Ambala?" Dorwynn asked the minotaur when he'd emptied the skein.

"Very well," he gasped. He handed the empty container to Dorwynn. "The storm brought this mess to our road days ago, but the unexpected work slowed the progress of getting it moved. Many are busy planting now, so I volunteered."

A rustling sound further down the road caught their attention. Voruum stood when he realized it was his young daughter toddling toward them in search of her father. She watched them, her large eyes opened wide at the strange creatures surrounding her father, but she showed no fear as she passed them and found her father's arms. She looked just like him, the same dark coat and blond hair. She had no horns, and Lilly wondered if the females even had horns. Her eyes were deep brown, almost black, but they were soft and full of questioning wonder.

"My daughter," said Voruum proudly as he lifted her into his arms, "born this winter past. She is called Savara." She smiled when he said her name and wriggled in his arms, wrapping her own around his thick neck. He held her balanced securely in one arm while he lowered himself to sit and rest. "What brings you along our path?"

"We are going to Elikrede," replied Dorwynn. "My young apprentice has a good deal of training yet before her Master trials. We will be there for quite some time, I fear."

"Fear?" Voruum laughed and lowered his squirming daughter to the ground, who, having become comfortable with the strangers surrounding her, decided it was time to investigate. "Elikrede is a wonderful place to live. And," he added, his dark eyes twinkling as he looked at Lilly, "if it become less than pleasant, you are always welcome in Ambala."

"She will spend time there soon enough," Dorwynn told him. "I believe spending time among other races may be more beneficial for her than spending all of her time with me."

Voruum nodded and the group grew silent, watching Savara stumble about before them. She tripped, landing with a thud on the ground, and then looked around to see who was watching. Having all eyes upon her, she began to wail and Lilly rushed forward and scooped her into her arms, or so she intended. When she tried to pick up the child, she was stunned by her weight, for although she was a small being, she was surprisingly heavy. She was pure muscle, just like her father, and Lilly struggled until she finally lifted the child and stood her on her feet. Savara, who had grown quiet during Lilly's futile attempts, grinned as she toddled toward her father again.

"Did you notice?" he asked the others, smiling. "She checked to see that we were watching her before she cried out." He beamed as she scrutinized a sparkling rock lying in the dirt. "There is nothing more perfect than the innocence of a child before the world around her strips it away slowly, one piece at a time."

Voruum's words echoed in Lilly's mind. She closed her eyes and slipped into a memory quest, one of her own, of the time when she had eavesdropped on her father talking to Dr. Hoffman. She had crouched behind the half wall in his home as they talked about her and at the time, she had not understood what their conversation had meant. Of course, she had only been seven years old.

"Lilly portrays some very unique qualities," said Dr. Hoffman, seated in his most comfortable chair. Andrew paced the floor in front of him. "She's an indigo child, Andy. I might be wise for you to consider finding someone else for her, someone who can help to develop these qualities."

"No!" Andrew spouted. Dr. Hoffman watched him with interest. Andrew's comment had not fazed him in the least. "I understand your point, Eric, I really do, but I just want her to have as normal of a childhood as she can. Someday, she will discover what she will do with her life, and herself, and she can make the decision about her abilities. For now, let's just leave her be." Andrew lowered himself into a chair beside the doctor's. "There is nothing more perfect than the innocence of a child before the world manages to strip it away from her a piece at a time. Let her be innocent, just a little while longer."

Lilly opened her eyes and noticed the others staring at her in wonder. Concern littered Dorwynn's eyes, though he said nothing. He knew what had just happened. Lilly grinned, very proud of herself. She'd accomplished a memory quest on her own, only this time, she felt no side effects.

"I'd have to say that I agree with you, Voruum," Lilly commented when nobody spoke. Voruum smiled and nodded at her, then cleared his throat.

"Come, Savara," he said, and she tottered toward him. "We have many chores before nightfall." He picked her up with ease and slung her over his shoulder as she squealed in delight, clutching his neck with her tiny but sturdy arms. "It has been a pleasure," he said, his voice edged with a serene gentility. He looked at Lilly, his eyes as genuine as his voice. "You are welcome in Ambala, always." He bowed to her before he turned and walked away without looking back, but young Savara, with her innocent nature, whipped around one more time and let go of her father long enough to wave goodbye at them.

"What happened?" asked Dorwynn when they had disappeared from sight. Lilly looked at him with a secretive smile on her face and shrugged.

"A memory quest," she said, as though it were nothing.

"With no after effects?" He knew she was telling the truth, but he didn't want to believe it. She wasn't supposed to be doing it at all, but here she was, calling them easily with no effects…yet.

"I guess I'm getting stronger."

"Yeah," he sighed, wishing she understood the weight behind that revelation. "Try not to have them until you are *trained* how to do them, please. If you go too deep without the knowledge to help get you out of it, you'll end up in another coma, or permanently damage your mind."

"Sure," she said, not bothering to argue. She felt wonderful after the hard work she'd accomplished, and now she was ready to continue their journey. Three nights had passed since they had reached the crossroads, meaning they were roughly a day away from their destination, and Lilly felt her excitement growing beyond words thinking about their arrival. "Shall we return to the road?"

"No," Dorwynn replied, scanning the path they were still hovering around. After a moment, he began walking the opposite direction that Voruum and his daughter had gone. "This path leads to Elikrede. It takes us through the swamp, but the road beyond it is barely noticed. We can arrive unseen."

Lilly and Zephra followed. Lilly took notice of Zephra's unusual silence and wondered what she was thinking, but she dared not ask. Instead she followed her trainers quietly, taking in the changing scenery. The first difference she noticed were the trees, which began growing sparse as they progressed. The ground turned from damp to mushy to nearly liquid. Several times, they were forced to use rocks protruding from the ground as a bridge between the more saturated areas.

The air grew humid and no wind blew, soaking Lilly's shirt with sweat. She was glad she'd decided to bring her boots, for they were very functional at the moment, but she wished she had some shorts to wear. Her jeans clung to her legs, attaching themselves to her like a second skin.

An hour later, she felt better. They had crossed into a wetter region, but once more, there was a canopy over them, providing much-desired shade that proved worth the insects growing in both size and number. Lilly swatted at the pests and continued, trudging along behind the others. The grass was thick, as were the reeds surrounding the large pool of water next to the path they traveled. The path itself was barely visible against the ground, enough patches of weeds and grass to hide it well. Obviously, not many followed it as they were.

Moments later, Lilly realized why the path was obscure. A large creature, easily eight feet tall, was standing before the statue of a woman. It was very lifelike, more so than the creature itself, but for the fact that the creature moved and the statue did not. When the creature turned its head to look at her, she gasped at its grotesque form. She was unable to move her legs, afraid that a sudden movement would disturb the terrifying beast and send it into a rampage with them as its target.

"It's alright," Zephra whispered in her ear. "He will not harm us." She moved toward the creature and bowed. He nodded his acknowledgment and focused once again on the statue before him. He ran his massive hands over it as tendrils of light flowed from them. In a sudden burst of light, the statue sprung to life, a dark-haired woman dressed in blue where the lifeless gray monument had just been. The ogre nodded to the woman, and then turned away from her, meandering away from the humans that had wandered into his vicinity.

"What happened?" asked Lilly, her eyes wide. Dorwynn walked toward the disappearing creature, maintaining his silent treatment. Zephra looked at Lilly with a smile that sent shivers down her spine.

"Come," she said, her voice jubilant. "I'll introduce you." She proceeded after Dorwynn, a bounce in her step, leaving Lilly to lag behind cautiously, wondering exactly what she had gotten herself into.

The First Test

Orvak stared at the humans in his midst. Zephra, his friend for centuries, had introduced the strangers. The man was called Dorwynn. Though Orvak had no true knowledge of him, he recognized him from a few years before, when the mage Gustave had brought him through the swamp as they traveled to Elikrede. The girl, Lilly, he had never seen before.

She seemed wary of him, standing in the corner of the room and shifting her feet nervously as though the floor of his home was made of hot coals. Her behavior did not surprise him. Most humans who crossed his path had similar reactions.

Lilly observed Orvak as he listened to Dorwynn's explanation of where they were going and why. He watched Dorwynn as he spoke, glancing occasionally at Lilly throughout his description of her magickal education, including his plan to expose her to as many different races as possible. The ogre nodded his understanding, his small head bobbing up and down upon his rather large body.

He didn't look like the ogres she'd seen in storybooks or movies, of which most had green skin and were covered with rough, grotesque blemishes and long yellow fangs jutting from their bottom jaws. Instead, his skin was a sickly pallor, a mix of bluish-gray and brown. Not a single tooth protruded from his mouth, though his squared bottom jaw thrust forward from the rest of his face, the first of many distorted features.

He had no nose, but rather two nostrils in the center of his face. His eye sockets were sunk deep into his skull, the bones that formed his eyebrows jutting forward over them in the same disproportionate manner as his jaw. The two furry eyebrows moving like a pair of caterpillars involved in a strange dance were the only hair on his entire body other than the long lashes on his strange sunken eyes.

His bald head had a perfectly symmetrical shape, sloping from his forehead to his body, leaving no visible neck, and only holes where his ears should have been. His body was enormous, far too large in comparison to his head, which was centered between his broad square shoulders. His thick arms hung below his knees, resembling a gorilla though they did not reach the ground. His torso was large and long, and though his legs were massive, they seemed too short for the rest of him.

"You are asking me to teach her," said Orvak. His upper lips, which split between and just below his nostrils, fluttered when he spoke, while his bottom lip wrapped tightly around his jutting jaw. His mouth was very wide and his jaw moved not only up and down, but side to side. His deep voice was so gruff it snapped Lilly from her observations of the creature's appearance. She shuddered as she met his unnatural eyes, completely black with silver pupils that reflected her image perfectly in their metallic swirl.

"Not necessarily," replied Dorwynn, who showed no discomfort in the presence of the unusual creature. "Rather, I would like her to observe your efforts. She is a quick study. I think she merely needs some exposure to as much diversity in both the races and in their magickal abilities."

"I see." Orvak looked from Dorwynn to Zephra to Lilly. He rose slowly from his seated position. Already on guard, Lilly stiffened as the creature moved across the room. He went to a large ceramic jar perched on a shelf against the dirt-packed wall and removed it. His large hand barely fit through the opening, but he was able to remove a pinch of glimmering powder from the canister. Dropping the dust into a small pouch, he closed it and handed it to Zephra, who took it with a smile.

"The necessity will arise after the eve of Beltane," muttered Orvak. He returned to his previous location in the large wooden chair he'd been seated in before and looked at the humans again. "Leave us now," he instructed. "It is time for our first lesson."

Dorwynn nodded, dumbstruck, and left without a word. Zephra tucked the pouch into one of several pockets and bowed at the hideous being.

"Always a pleasure, Orvak," she said pleasantly, "and thank you. Your gift is appreciated." She glanced at Lilly before she left the house, taking a small amount of pleasure in the fear she saw in the girl's face. Lilly watched her trainers leave, overwhelmed by a feeling of abandonment.

Orvak pointed to the chair across from his own. Lilly walked toward it, each step slow and precise, wondering what the first lesson entailed. This creature seemed gentle, but all the myths she'd heard about ogres had to have come from somewhere. At that moment, alone with a beast such as that, she truly wished she had never chosen to step through that glowing doorway.

"You are afraid of me," he stated when she finally took the seat before him. His silver pupils narrowed as he studied her. She immediately began blocking her thoughts from him, though she felt it was useless. He seemed powerful enough to get through any obstacle in whatever path he chose to follow.

"You need not hide your thoughts," he replied. "I could not hear them if I tried. The type of mind communication of which ogres are capable is on a distinctly innate level."

"What does that mean?" she asked when she found the courage to speak. She perched on the edge of her chair, ready to bolt from the room if he made a move she didn't like.

"It means," he said as he reached for a platter that held some delicious looking pastries, "that if you are hungry, I can feel it. I cannot tell from your thoughts what you want, but I can feel your emotions, your needs and, depending on the being, your desires." He held the plate in front of her. "Take one. They are quite delectable."

Lilly took one of the flaky pastries, taking great caution in her gestures. She scanned the food, making sure there was nothing dangerous hidden within the folds of the crust, and then she took a bite. Orvak smiled at her wariness.

"It is a good habit," he said as he returned the plate on the table. "You never know the intentions of another."

He was silent as she finished the treat, noticing in her posture that she was beginning to relax. He turned in his chair, extending his massive arms toward another shelf, this one close enough that he did not need to rise to reach it. From it he withdrew a small stone, as black as his eyes and as shiny as the pupils. It seemed more like a hard metal, smoothed over until no blemishes could be seen. Barely larger than a marble, it was minute resting in his large hand. He held it out to her and dropped it into her hand.

"It is warm when you are in the presence of one who means no ill will," he said as she looked it over carefully. "When you encounter someone who means you harm, it will grow cold as ice. Keep it close at all times."

"Thank you," she said, surprised at the unexpected gift.

"It is time to go," he announced, standing.

"What about the lesson?" asked Lilly. He smiled and shook his head.

"It is over," he said. "Tell me, what have you learned?'

She shrugged, speechless. In the matter of a few minutes, there had been a hidden lesson and she had missed it. She thought hard and realized that the gift had been a test. She had scanned her food in front of him, but she had taken a gift without a thought as to what accepting it may entail.

"I suppose," she said finally, "that you were trying to teach me that I was wrong to be afraid of you."

"Fear is not a vice unless you allow it to keep you from moving forward in your life. Courage does not mean the absence of fear, but rather facing fear when it is necessary to do so. Your false perceptions of others, however, based on race or appearance, is a slight on your character. No matter what you know of a person or a situation, how you perceive it makes all the difference. Light can be found in the darkest of places. Good resides within evil and evil within good. Do not be so quick to judge. Remember that and your choices will be correct."

He spoke as though he could hear her thoughts, reaching to the core of her soul. She didn't know what he expected from her, but she understood the purpose of the lecture. She had judged him prematurely and he knew it. She nodded and stood, slipping the stone into her pocket.

"Your thoughts are cluttered with chaos. It clouds your mind. You must be comfortable with your new life before you are capable of living it. You will return to me when you are ready to be perceptive to the world around you. I will teach you many things, but I will expect much from you in return. Come."

He walked through the door. Lilly followed, stunned silent, amazed at his insight. Dorwynn paced the road that had brought them, looking a nervous wreck. Zephra was perched on a large rock, perfectly calm. She jumped to the mushy ground as Lilly and Orvak emerged from the house.

"That is all for now," he announced to Dorwynn, whose perplexed expression stayed plastered to his face. "Go to your destination. She will return later for the rest."

The ogre turned away from the group, meandering toward his house. He stopped at the door and turned to see all three still watching him. He smiled, his upper lip parting slightly.

"There is information locked in the depths of your mind. The answers lie buried within the confines of your own creation."

"Who?" asked Lilly. The ogre just smiled and turned his back on them, disappearing into his home. The three of them stared for what seemed a lifetime, and then Dorwynn looked through the swamp far past the house.

"The road awaits," he said, starting down the barely used path. Lilly followed, her hand wrapped around the black stone in her pocket. It was warm. Behind her, Zephra kept their pace, maintaining the silence she'd acquired since they happened upon Orvak.

They walked for nearly an hour, the scenery changing rapidly in the short amount of time. The swamp was butted against the edge of a mountain which was covered with a dense forest that hid it well. Lilly hadn't noticed it before, but the mountain was extremely high, towering over them like a sentinel. The road they had been following disappeared at its foot and Lilly looked up the hill.

"Now what?" she asked. Zephra smiled, but did not answer. Instead, she began climbing, grabbing at the trees and using them as a rock climber would use a safety line. Dorwynn followed, as unpleasant as ever. Lilly sighed and grabbed the lowest tree jutting from the edge of the mountain, wishing someone would speak and break the silence.

They ended their ascent at the mouth of a dark cave. The suns were now completely blocked by the mountain, though the sky was still bright enough to see the outline of the ground below. Lilly sat at the cave's entrance, breathing heavily from her strenuous climb. Zephra seemed unfazed by the effort, though Lilly could tell that Dorwynn was drained. He sat beside her until his breathing slowed, then bent forward and stuck his head inside the cave. He backed out, removed his pack and crawled inside.

"Come on," he called from within. "We're almost there."

Zephra followed him, then Lilly. When she made her way inside, she was surprised to find there was more than enough room for them to stand comfortably. She waited, letting her eyes adjust to the extreme darkness. A flash of light appeared, and Lilly saw Zephra's face, lit by the small flame she held in her hand. She couldn't see where Dorwynn was, but knew he was to her left when she heard him curse.

"A little brighter, Z," he said. The flame grew until Lilly could see Dorwynn rubbing a red mark on his head. He looked at the wall next to him where an edge of the stone wall protruded just above his eye level. He swore again and walked into the darkness. "Come on!"

"What did you think of Orvak?" she asked Lilly as they walked. Lilly shrugged.

"He's interesting," she said.

"To say the least," chuckled Zephra. "Do you want to know something very interesting about ogres?"

"Sure."

"When the war comes, you will find no ogres fighting against you. If they do fight, it will be for the side of good."

"How do you know?"

"Never in the history of the world has there been an evil ogre."

Lilly knew by her tone that she was serious. Thinking back on her behavior in the creature's home, she felt a pang of guilt for fearing him because of his appearance alone. That's what Orvak had meant in his final words to her. Did he think her character was slighted because she had been afraid of him, or had he been impressed that she had stayed with him despite her fear? She hoped for the latter, for she hated to believe that the creature might think so little of her.

Her mind was reeling with the overload of information from the past few days. She tried to focus on the fact that they were less than a day from Elikrede, less than a day from finding the house her mother had told her about in the vision, the house that held the clues to her mother's whereabouts. Her focus, however, drifted to Dorwynn. His mood was disheartening and the fact that he had barely spoken to her all day weighed on her mind more than anything else. Zephra was making conversation, but no matter how hard she tried to converse with her, Lilly could only hear the words she'd spoken in her visions.

I'm so sorry. You don't have a choice. Those words, and then pain, fear, darkness.

Dorwynn wouldn't speak to her and she didn't trust Zephra enough to share what she needed to share. She sensed Rohan was near, and more than anything she wished she could speak to him, though she dared not try. He was probably in disguise and if she contacted him, it could jeopardize whatever mission he was trying to accomplish. She longed for Ashya, whose conversations she missed terribly, and even for Amparo, whom she barely knew but trusted nonetheless.

After over three hours of silence, Lilly decided that she would travel by thought to see Ashya. Once they had settled into Elikrede, she would visit her mentor and vent her frustrations. Ashya would help her discover what had been happening to her, why she was able to do such magick with no training, magick she had witnessed from no one but was still able to do. Ashya would know.

By the time Dorwynn stopped, Lilly was so lost in her thoughts that she didn't realize he'd stopped. She ran into him, nearly knocking him into the rough wall of the cave. He shot her a nasty look and she just looked away, deciding he didn't deserve the apology dancing on her tongue. She threw her pack down in the center of the cavern he'd decided would be their camp.

"This is the halfway point," he said, dropping his own pack beside Lilly's. "Tomorrow we will be in Elikrede."

"How long will it take?" asked Lilly. He shrugged and plopped beside his pack.

"Four hours or so," he replied, not looking at her. "Give or take."

"Let's go," she prompted. "If it's only a few hours, we should keep going."

"We should rest," Zephra said before Dorwynn had a chance to protest. "It is nearly one in the morning now, and Gustave won't be there until sunrise anyway."

"Fine," she said, her tone a mixture of frustration and exhaustion that echoed throughout the cavern. She looked around the spacious room and realized that there were more than a dozen different tunnels leading from it in all directions. She couldn't even tell which doorway they had used to get there, making her wonder how she would ever find her way by herself later when she returned for her lessons with Orvak.

As her eyes adjusted to the darkness, she noticed a series of torches adorning the walls between each doorway. In the center of the room stood an ornate stone basin, polished and smooth and as black as coal. Intricate carvings were inlaid all around it in a series of patterns. The clear metallic liquid that the basin held ran within the carvings, forming a progressive trail of miniature rivers and pools within the deep crevices. Zephra, still holding the same ball of fire, sent it racing toward the top of the basin. The liquid caught fire instantly, winding its way along the curves of the basin where the liquid flowed.

It smelled like a combination of gasoline and cooking oil burning on an open flame. There was very little smoke, however, and the flames changed from a bright orange to a bluish color as the heat increased. She stared at the basin, captivated with the picturesque work of art the flames were creating.

"What keeps the flame burning?" asked Lilly. Dorwynn respond without looking at her as he stared at the dark tunnel doorways.

"Dragon bile."

"Dragon bile?"

"Yes," he muttered absently. "It burns for a long time and it is an easy enough fuel source to replenish."

"Are there dragons in here?"

"Probably," chimed Zephra, smiling. Lilly noticed the pleasure she was taking in her concern, just as she had right before she'd met Orvak, but Lilly didn't let her have the satisfaction this time.

"Good," she said as she plopped down beside her pack. "I haven't seen a dragon yet." Zephra chuckled.

"You haven't seen a lot of things yet," she said, seating herself at the edge of the flames.

They sat in silence around the beautiful basin and watched the ribbon of flames dance. Lilly couldn't stop thinking about how close they were to their destination. More than anything, she wanted to find her mother.

Go to my home in Elikrede. The way to find me is there…

Her mother's voice echoed in her mind. Her image was as clear as it had been since she first had the dream from the strange coma. Had it only been six days? It felt like it had happened ages ago, but Lilly guessed it was most likely because she was so anxious to get to Elikrede. They were so close she could feel it, and because she could think of nothing else, sleep evaded her yet again.

Zephra was the first to fall asleep, her even breathing lulling Lilly into a trance that was only interrupted when Dorwynn started snoring. Lilly plumped her pack, trying to make it more comfortable, and settled into it. The rhythmic sound of their even breathing created an odd symphony, finally bringing sleep to her, and with it, a calm that had evaded her since she'd left Ashya's.

The Struggle for Independence

Kylenin dismounted his horse, rubbing its neck as he looked around. The animal had ridden hard, bringing him to Elikrede almost a day ahead of schedule. It was still dark in the early hours of the morning and he debated over whether to find lodgings so late or just camp until morning light. He wanted his horse comfortable as well as himself, so he led the animal toward the large inn in the center of the main street, enclosed on one side by a restaurant and on the other side by a large stable, presumably belonging to the inn. After securing his horse to a post, Kylenin removed his pack and walked into the candlelit lobby.

A mousy boy sat behind the counter, very involved in the thick novel in his hands. Kylenin waited for the boy to acknowledge his presence, but the boy hadn't seemed to notice the arrival of a guest. Kylenin cleared his throat and still the boy didn't respond, his eyes moving rapidly over the page of his book. Finally, he peered over the wire-framed glasses that were perched on the end of his upturned nose. He methodically placed a ribbon in the crease and closed the book.

"May I help you?" asked the boy, his high-pitched voice a perfect match to how Kylenin imagined it would sound.

"I would like a room," Kylenin responded.

"Singles are four sarim a night," the boy said in a snobbish tone. "Meals are delivered to your room and are paid for when they are ordered. Stable boarding is two sarim a night, meals and groom service included."

"How much is a suite?"

The boy raised his eyebrows as if Kylenin had asked the stupidest question imaginable. He shook his head emphatically, his eyebrows still touching his hairline.

"The suites are taken."

"All of them?"

"The only empty suites," the boy said curtly, "are the royal suites. Are you *royalty?*"

Kylenin smirked at the haughty edge in the boy's words, imagining his face when he discovered he actually was royalty, but before he could enlighten the boy, he thought the better of it. This boy had no idea who he was, as well as most of the people he would encounter here. Dagana had kept him confined within the castle the majority of his early adolescent years, his last visit anywhere nearly three years ago. He could, at least for this short time away from her, be someone else.

"I have a horse tied up outside," he said. He flung his pack onto the counter and rummaged through it for the money pouch he knew Dagana had packed. It was full of shenti and laukti. He tossed a single laukti on the counter.

"Yessir!" The boy jumped into action, his hands flying immediately under the counter. He placed a pen and a small piece of paper in front of Kylenin. He scribbled in a blank space beneath the number scrolled neatly on the top.

"Write your name beside the room number," he pointed to the large number on the page, "and your horse's name beside the stall number beneath."

The boy walked out the front doors, leaving Kylenin the think about names, a pseudonym for him and a name for the horse he chosen as his own. After a moment, it came to him. When the boy returned, Kylenin handed him the pen and paper. The boy read it and smiled, sticking his hand out in front of him. A smirk played at Kylenin's lips as he shook the boy's hand.

"It's a pleasure to meet you, Wyatt. My name's Kiger. Ciarán has been taken to the stables." Kiger reached behind the counter and grabbed a key, then handed it to Kylenin. "Up the stairs. Go straight first, then turn right at the second hallway. Yours is the second door on the right. When you want a meal, leave your order in the mail slot." Having giving his instructions, the mousy boy returned to his seat behind the counter, picking up his book and removing the carefully placed ribbon to continue his adventure.

Kylenin flung his pack over his shoulder and trudged up the stairs, his feet getting heavier with every step. His room was farther away than Kiger's short description made it seem, but he finally found it. He pushed the small brass key into the keyhole and turned it, waiting for its familiar click before turning the knob.

The room was small and simply furnished, putting him instantly at ease. A single nightstand beside the small bed, a chair and a tiny desk-like table were all the room contained. He sighed with relief and flopped onto the bed, sinking into the blue quilt as though it were a tub of warm water. As tired as he was, it could have been.

Still, he had a hard time falling asleep. Now in the comfort of a warm shelter, no matter how small, he was truly alone. He'd barely slept on the journey, the prospect of being free of Dagana an overwhelming and exciting revelation. Glancing around the sparse room, he smiled, grateful to be rid of the clutter, the castle and all of Dagana's eccentricities. No statues in the corners, no paintings or heavy tapestries overtaking the walls. The window of his room was plain glass, not stained with a gruesome image. It eased his mind even more to know that if his powers failed him again, he had less to fear that he might drop something on himself.

Dagana had an infatuation with beautiful things and her taste in beauty was fickle, changing as often as her mood. Vases and sculptures, paintings and murals, even the knobs on the doors were ornate, so ornate that it was nauseating. When he had begun to lose control over his powers, the chaos of her muddle became increasingly irritating. One day, not long before they had begun their most recent journey, he had been staring at a particularly hideous tapestry, hating how it was so obvious on the wall, and it disappeared before his eyes. He didn't know where he had sent it, nor did he care. Needless to say, Dagana was not happy about her missing treasure. He still took a substantial amount of pleasure in that memory.

Everything in that castle was there because of her, and when she tired of it, she sent it away. For a moment, he wondered if that was why she had sent him away, but the feeling passed. He knew she did not love him, he doubted she knew what love was at all, but he knew she wanted him to come back, *needed* him to come back, in order for her dream to be fulfilled. It gave him a great sense of satisfaction to know this about her. Hell, it was the closest to love that she would ever come.

He sat up on the bed and began to remove his boots, hoping he could make himself comfortable enough to sleep. After ten minutes, he found his nightclothes and put them on. He plumped the pillows, rearranged the blankets twice and even tried lying on the floor, but sleep would not come. Exasperated, he rummaged through the pack until he found his wand and began playing with the candle out of boredom, first lighting it from across the room with his wand and then blowing it out with the wave of his hand.

He knew she was near, the girl from his dreams. He could feel her presence. He had come all this way to find her and now he would. New thoughts floated through his mind. What would he do when he found her? Would the duel he dreamed about actually take place? If so, who makes the challenge? Did he dream about the duel so that he would know how to be victorious, or so he could avoid it altogether?

He had no answers, only questions. Now, however, he had no one to ask those questions. It made him wonder again about Dagana's intentions. Surely she had not let him go because she knew he wanted it. She had never cared what he wanted. Nor was it because she trusted him. He knew that she trusted no one but Sybil, and he also knew she questioned her sometimes. His only guess was that Sybil had suggested it and had convinced Dagana it was something she must do.

Of course, it really didn't matter. She had already returned to the castle, *her* castle, or she was very close to returning, and he was here, in Elikrede, where his future awaited. He could feel the distance growing between them and a calmness he had never experienced washed over him. Yawning, he crawled into the bed again, sleep inviting him to submit.

He could see her sitting on a large stone, staring at a beautiful waterfall flowing over the edge of the cliff. Her hair blew in the breeze, the sunlight bringing out every shade of copper with a brilliant shine. He walked toward her, wondering if she knew he was there. She seemed so at peace, he didn't want to disturb her, and yet, he couldn't stop himself from approaching her.

"I know you are there," she said without looking at him. He froze, caught off guard, and waited for her to speak again. After a moment, she turned to face him. As before, her emerald eyes stunned him speechless. They shined as though they produced their own light and for a split second, he wondered if they did.

"I've dreamed of you before," she told him.

"And I of you," he said. Her posture relaxed a bit and she nodded in contemplation.

"What does it mean?" she asked finally.

"I don't know. I've been searching for you to find that answer."

"I don't have the answer. The only thing I know for sure is that we will have a duel."

"No," he said, shaking his head. "I won't take part in it."

"Why?" she asked. "Because you know you are going to lose?"

"Maybe."

"Seems foolish."

"It's not foolish!" he protested. "If you knew for a fact you were going to fail, would you still attempt something?"

"Of course," she said. "Everything happens for a reason. Perhaps there is a lesson you need to learn. If you never attempt anything because you are afraid you are going to fail, you will never get the chance to succeed. How can you appreciate success if you've never failed at anything?"

He had no response. She stared into his eyes and he suddenly felt uncomfortable, as though she was staring directly into his soul, his deepest fears on display for her to see. She turned away from him, her attention suddenly elsewhere. She gazed at the sky and it darkened, a mass of black clouds forming directly overhead.

"A storm is coming," she said, and then she turned her back on him and walked away.

"Wait," he shouted, not wanting to let her go. "What's your name?"

She turned around long enough to cast him a secretive smile. He smiled in return, not understanding his own actions. She walked toward him, coming so close he could feel her warmth, her eyes boring into his soul yet again. He found himself unable to speak, though he had no desire to end their conversation. She leaned close to his ear and he held his breath.

"I am Lilly," she whispered, and then she was gone.

His eyes flew open. Her voice still lingered in his ear, her breath still hot upon it. For a moment, he wondered if it had been real, but finding himself in the small bed reminded him of where he was. He stretched and smiled at the sunlight pouring through the window. It was a new day and now, he knew the name of the girl he sought.

Lilly awoke with a start, her newest dream fresh in her mind. She'd dreamt of the boy again, the elf with the long blonde hair and gray-blue eyes. He was looking for her. Though it was only a dream, she could feel that he was very close. She chastised herself for telling him her name without asking his in return, then reminded herself it was only a dream, though she doubted even that at the moment. The calmness she'd felt the night before was gone as she thought about the many mysteries of her new life.

She stood up and stretched, one last yawn escaping her lips. The stone lantern had long ago dimmed, though a single torch burned, casting light in the otherwise pitch black room. She couldn't see Zephra or Dorwynn and for a fleeting second, she wondered if they had left her behind. A moment later, however, she noticed one of the tunnel doorways glowing. Zephra emerged, carrying a torch which she placed on the other side of the doorway from which she'd just come.

"It's time to go," she said, her voice edged with a harsh bitterness.

"Where's Dorwynn?" asked Lilly as she picked up her pack, not daring to argue with the obviously irritated phoenix.

Zephra growled in frustration and sent a fire ball careening down one of the dark tunnels. Lilly, her eyes wide, was rooted to her spot. She waited in silence for Zephra to answer.

"I don't know," she said at last. "He left some time last night."

"He left?"

"It doesn't matter," sighed Zephra, though it was apparent to Lilly that it did matter. "He knows where we are going. I'm sure he'll meet us there."

She walked toward the same tunnel she'd come through only moments before and Lilly followed, wondering why Dorwynn had left without a word as to where he was going. Somewhere deep in the confines of her mind, she felt she knew the answer, but she couldn't quite grasp it.

The walk was silent for a while as they made their way through the dark tunnel, Zephra's fire ball their only light. It was only after she was calm that Lilly decided it was time for the two of them to talk. Though she knew Zephra was irritated at Dorwynn's disappearance, Lilly was grateful for it. She'd secretly been hoping for some time alone with her. Part of her was still afraid of what she might do, but Lilly refused to give into that fear. She wanted answers and she knew Zephra had them.

"So," said Lilly brightly, "how old are you?"

"Why?" asked Zephra.

"Just curious."

"Have you ever heard the expression 'Curiosity killed the cat'?"

"Have you ever heard the expression 'Satisfaction brought him back'?"

Zephra stopped walking and turned to face Lilly, a smile playing at her lips.

"That's a good one," she said. "Worthy of an answer, someday."

"Why not now?"

"Why do you ask so many questions?" Lilly caught the irritated edge in her voice, but she was determined to maintain a conversation this time. She couldn't handle the next four hours in silence.

"My mentor told me to learn as much as I can," responded Lilly simply, "and so did you." Zephra sighed, unable to argue.

"I'll tell you the story of my birth when you are my apprentice," said Zephra, conceding. "If you are truly ready to learn something right now, choose any other topic and we will discuss it."

"What do you know about the prophecy of the Chosen One?"

Zephra stared at Lilly for a moment, and then she continued leading the way through the dark tunnel. Lilly had asked her a question that no one but Gustave had ever bothered to ask her. Ironically enough, she was one of the few creatures who knew the prophecy word for word, since she had been there when it was first prophesized. It was long and complex, due mostly to the fact that it was about more than just the Chosen One, but Zephra decided to tell Lilly only of what she had asked. If she asked for more details, Zephra would tell her, but she hoped Lilly would ask no more. Amparo had a better way of explaining the finer details and Lilly would be able to understand it better then.

"She will restore balance between two worlds," said Zephra, repeating a small part of the prophecy pertaining only to the Chosen One. "She will return in human form, and of her own volition she will cross from Earth to save the world from annihilation. A war will follow her arrival and she will come to lead many races. She will fight beside them and when it is done, her reign will begin a Golden Age that will last eras."

"Wow," said Lilly, dumbfounded. Is this who Gustave though she was? If so, then it meant a war was coming. She wanted to voice her concern to Zephra, but Ashya had told her not to divulge the information to anyone. She would have to remember to ask Ashya about it when she visited her.

Silence ensued for most of the trek through the tunnel, but it did not bother either of them. Zephra was thankful that Lilly hadn't asked any more questions and Lilly's mind reeled with the small tidbit of information Zephra had given her. It was hard for her to believe that she was a chosen anything, let alone a savior, which is exactly what Zephra had described. She was suddenly aware of the fact that they were on their way to meet Gustave, who was really Rohan, and that he was the reason she was here. Why did he think she was the one? She would have to make sure he knew she had many more questions for him.

The sound of a waterfall brought Lilly from her thoughts. The sound grew louder and further down the tunnel, she noticed it was growing bright. Her excitement began to build as she realized they would soon be leaving the tunnel and arriving in Elikrede. When they got to the end of the tunnel, once again, it opened into a larger room, much like another cave, except that one wall was formed by the waterfall cascading in front of it. She could tell just by looking at the waterfall that it was a bright sunny day on the other side.

"Elikrede is on the other side," said Zephra, relieved that they had gotten this far with no serious trouble. "Come."

She led Lilly to a narrow path that extended from the hidden cave to the ledges behind the waterfall. There were many places to put her hands and feet, but she held tight, fearing the fall. Zephra moved with ease as though she had done it a hundred times. For all Lilly knew, she had.

As the end of their decent grew near, Lilly dared to look at the ground below. The grass was lush and green. A large boulder sat near the lake at the bottom of the waterfall, standing vigilant on the opposing shore, a single tree providing shade. The lake was not truly a lake, but a large pool of water with a small outlet further away from the falls. She smiled, recalling her dreams. She knew this place. She had been here in her dream the night before. She looked around, wondering if she would see the mysterious boy she'd met, but he was no where to be seen.

A small house was in the distance, a tiny shed behind it close to the lake's shore. Though it was bright, she realized the suns had risen recently, for they were low in the sky and shining directly at the waterfall. When her feet touched the ground, it took a moment for her legs to adjust to the solid ground before she could follow Zephra's fast pace toward the cottage. Running to keep up, she stopped short when she saw Gustave come around from the front of the house and smile, his long white hair whipping in the warm breeze. Zephra saw him, too, and she sprinted toward him, grinning ear to ear.

"Zephratia," said the old mage, extending his arms in welcome. Zephra threw her arms around him, which caught Lilly off guard, as she had never seen Zephra this happy and surely never expected such a reaction. He looked toward Lilly after she had released him and gave her a secretive smile. "Hello, Lilias."

"Gustave," acknowledged Lilly. "How are you?"

"Wonderful," he said, clearing his throat. "As you can imagine, I have been very busy preparing for your arrival. Come, let us go inside."

They followed him into the house. He went inside first, followed by Zephra, while Lilly lingered, staring at the house. From where she was standing, the lake was to the right of the house, the waterfall barely in sight further behind it. She looked to her left, expecting to see a stone garden, but the only thing she could see was remnants of last autumn. Heavy brambles and bushes in severe need of pruning covered the ground and created a barrier between the house and the forest lining it, some sprouting fresh buds in an attempt to stay alive. She wanted to explore, but she knew Gustave would have instructions for her. She entered the house, closing the creaking door behind her.

Dust covered everything. It was so thick Lilly was sure she could peel it off like a blanket. If Zephra noticed, she showed no sign that she did. It was apparent that Gustave either didn't notice or didn't care. His sleeves dragged over table edges, leaving clean streaks on the tables and spots of dust on his robes.

Heavy curtains hung over the windows, blocking the sunny day outside. Lilly jumped when Gustave slammed his staff on the hardwood floor with a loud *CRACK!* Sparks flew from the friction of the sudden contact and flew in every direction, coming to rest in lanterns and atop candles. In the dim glow, she noticed the same layer of dust on the curtains, which explained why Gustave had lit candles rather than opened the draperies.

"As you can see," he said in his gruff voice, "this house has been uninhabited for some time. A little work, however, will go a long way." He smiled pointedly at Lilly. "Your first task, I should think," he chuckled.

He paused, waiting for a reaction from the one of them. When he received none, he raised his furry eyebrows and shook his head. With a deep sigh, his demeanor changed to a more serious one.

"Where is Dorwynn?" he demanded. Zephra and Lilly glanced at each other. Neither spoke. Gustave shook his head again and continued. "No matter. Zephra, be sure to relay the message."

Zephra nodded. Gustave, satisfied with her response, settled carefully into a dust-covered chair and rested his staff against the wall easily within his reach. It quivered momentarily of its own volition, suddenly still with a single glance from its owner.

"Things are changing very rapidly," said the old mage, an ominous edge in his voice. "Dorwynn is to begin your elemental training immediately, for time is far shorter than expected. He is to deliver you to the faeries for your tests before the solstice, so be diligent in your education. There will be no time to rectify mistakes.

"Ryzale is Elikrede's Arch sorceress. She has agreed to educate you in the ways of Fundamental magick; spells and charms and such. Tsirama will teach you about potions and magickal concoctions, as well as magickal ingredients and how they work."

"The alchemist?" asked Zephra. "But she doesn't need these lessons to be declared a Master of Earth magick."

"Aye," agreed Gustave, "but she must know these ways of magick to ensure her safety in her future endeavors."

"But he's so...odd," spouted Zephra.

"Then be grateful I do not require *you* to train with him!" Gustave had grown irritated and Zephra said no more. "You will train with both Ryzale and Tsirama until Amparo comes for you, so be sure to continue your lessons with them after your Master declaration."

Lilly nodded, her mind filling with more questions than ever before. She kept her silence, however, and waited for whatever Gustave had planned. She was beginning to realize that no matter how much she fought it, she had no choice in the matter of her so-called destiny. Certainly arguing with him about it would do no good, so she resigned herself, for now at least, to his bidding.

"Has Dorwynn explained your tasks?"

"A bit," answered Lilly, "but he was a little vague. He said he'd explain more when my training began. But I would like to know more of it now."

"Ah!" Gustave straightened himself and leaned toward Lilly, a twinkle in his eyes that reflected the delight he took in her enthusiasm, or in his giving knowledgeable instruction. She imagined the real Gustave was a natural-born teacher. "I shall tell you more. Earth magick represents many things. It is the basis for Elemental Magick, a foundation for new beginnings. It also represents the order of things, for there is always an order to which things must progress. By no means is it simple magick, but it is by far the easiest Elemental magick to master, for as you will soon learn as you train in each element, it will only get harder. Earth is stable, firm and grounding. Air, in which you will train next, is more fickle, changing with the winds. After that, you will learn the dangers of the treacherous and turbulent Water, and finally, raging Fire, for which you will need the most control. All that, however, will come later.

"For your Earth magick, you will be tested with six tasks, all of which you must pass to receive you Master status, though, really, you will only be performing three different types of magickal ability at various levels of strength. Control is simply commanding the earth to your will, something you have already accomplished when you helped to clear the stones from the road." He chuckled at Lilly's surprised expression. "I see or hear of all things pertaining to my apprentices, dear one. Now then, manipulation is to change the form of the earth materials. Turning dirt into stone, for instance."

"Or turning limestone into emeralds," interrupted Zephra. Gustave shot her an impatient look and cleared his throat in response. Lilly smiled at her playful grin.

"Nourishment pertains to anything that grows within the earth, from which plants and many insects get their nutrients. Now I have explained to you the basics of Earth magick. Dorwynn will explain the details of your individual tasks as he trains you. Remember, though, as with anything else, the more you practice, the better you will be."

Lilly nodded and waited, as though he were about to say something else. Gustave waited as well, feeling as though there were something he had forgotten to tell the new pupil. He eyed her suspiciously as it came to him.

"Have you created you wand?" he asked.

"No."

"Has Dorwynn explained how to do it?"

"Yes." Lilly felt ashamed, though she knew she shouldn't. Even Dorwynn had told her that it had to wait until she was ready.

"You first task, then," he said sternly. "You cannot be tested without one, nor should you train without one. Zephra, you will remind Dorwynn."

Zephra, who had started to examine the dusty contents of the house, snapped to attention again.

"Oh, of course," she said.

"I suppose, then, that I have finished. Is there anything you wish to ask of me before I depart?"

Lilly laughed inwardly. If only he knew how many questions she wanted answered. She knew, however, there were few he would answer himself, so she pushed them to the back of her mind, save one.

"Do you know anything of a stone garden?" she asked. The look in his eye told her that he did, but there was something else, almost as if he knew *why* she had asked him that question.

"Only after you have finished righting the house," he said in a tone Lilly was unable to identify, "should you take a walk from the house in the direction opposite the waterfall." She nodded, another question playing at her lips. He noticed and prompted her to ask it.

"When you see Rohan, son of Ashya, would you ask him to visit here? It has been a while since I've had his company."

"I will relay your message," Gustave promised, a knowing twinkle in his eye.

"Thank you."

"Why did you wait so long to train her?" Zephra asked him. She had wanted to ask him while they were alone, but it seemed she would not get that opportunity during this visit. Gustave just shook his head.

"It was not within my control to change that fact. We'll just have to make do with what we've got. Now, if that is all," said the old wizard, "I will take my leave." He stood, extending his arms to Zephra. She smiled and hugged him, a broad grin painting her face.

"It is good to see you again," she said as she released him. "Take care of yourself, old man." Gustave chuckled and walked toward Lilly, offering her the same gesture of farewell. She hugged him quickly, feeling awkward in his embrace.

"Goodbye," he whispered in her ear before he let go of her. Though he was halfway across the room, he reached absently for his staff as though it were right beside him. It quivered in its resting place, clattering against the wall, and then it flew into with lightning speed into its master's waiting hand.

"Why the faeries?" asked Zephra out of the blue, the thought as sudden to her as the question was to Gustave. "Why aren't you going to test her?" Lilly and Gustave both looked at her questioningly, and then Lilly turned her gaze to him, awaiting his answer.

He lingered in place for some time in quiet contemplation, trying to decide whether or not to answer the sudden question. She stared at him quizzically, one eyebrow raised slightly higher than the other.

"You know how magickal signatures work," he burst out, causing Lilly to jump at the unexpected loudness of his voice. "It has been decided by the Council, against my better judgment, that she will be tested by the Elemental Children before she is truly declared Master. Their theory is that, if she is what they believe, her signature will change with each element in which she trains and that only the Elementals can keep her power hidden."

"It makes sense,' said Zephra slowly, her calculating mind drawing the most obvious conclusion between his insight and her own suspicions, "if they believe she is the Chosen One."

"Yes..."

"But you don't believe she is?"

"Now, I didn't say that..."

"Then why would the Council's decision be against your better judgment?"

Lilly watched their banter, her head going back and forth between them as they spoke. Gustave's face scrunched in frustration, a deep scowl unhidden by his wooly face. Zephra, whom he had known longer that anyone else, had always been the only one who ever dared to contradict him. He usually found humor in their combative banter. This however, was not the time to be anything but annoyed. She was undermining his authority in front of his newest apprentice. Her lack of respect for his high-standing position in the magickal community had always irritated him, but never as much as right now.

"Call it a hunch," he finally sighed.

"Your hunches have been wrong before," she pointed out. Although Gustave knew her observations were inaccurate, he didn't argue. Instead, he shrugged his shoulders and ran his free hand slowly over his long beard, smoothing it to a pearly shine.

"We shall see," was his vague reply. "Good day, ladies."

With a quick bow in their direction, he disappeared in a swirling flash of light, his voice a whispered echo that seemed to linger in the room like the cobwebs clinging to the walls: *There is someone at your door...*

Calm before the Storm

He was in Elikrede. Standing on the doorstep of an all-too-familiar house, he could hear the waterfall in the distance. From the position of the suns, he judged it was late morning. He promised himself that he would purchase a watch before training Lilly and reached for the doorknob, wondering how long he had been away.

"Dorwynn!" exclaimed Lilly as she flung open the door, leaving his hand grasping at nothing. "Where have you been?"

He shook his head and walked past her, not knowing how to respond. He looked around the house that had been waiting for them, searching for a clue to the duration of his lapse in time.

Though it was neatly organized, undisturbed dust still covered the majority of the house, and he sighed with relief. He hadn't been gone that long. He sat on the overstuffed sofa, which exhaled a small cloud of dust. Zephra, who stood beside Lilly with a knowing look on her face, walked into the kitchen and returned moments later with a glass of water. Dorwynn took the drink gratefully and guzzled the cool liquid while both girls waited patiently for him to say something.

"I don't know," he said finally. "How long have I been gone?"

"Since some time last night," responded Zephra. Dorwynn nodded and leaned back into the sofa. He laid his head against it and closed his eyes. Though he had no idea where he had gone during his blackout, he could tell that he had not slept.   Zephra covered him with a nearby blanket, gently shaking the dust from its folds beforehand.

Lilly scanned the room, finally taking the opportunity to take a good look around the house. It was the house her mother had told her about in her vision, the house between the waterfall and the stone garden. She hadn't seen the stone garden yet, but she was sure this was the house nonetheless, for though Gustave had been vague, his answer sparked her curiosity. She could hear the waterfall outside, the one from which they'd emerged only an hour ago. More than anything, she wanted to go find the stone garden. Then again, her mother had said the clues to her whereabouts were in the house. Somewhere among the cobwebs and beneath the blankets of dust were the secrets that would lead her to her mother.

"Come on," she said to Zephra, who followed as Lilly rummaged through cabinets and pantries, removing all the necessary tools for cleaning the house. Brooms and feather dusters, a bucket for water and rags for scrubbing, and an old rag mop were heaped into a pile in the middle of the kitchen floor.

"Where should we start?" she asked Zephra. "The dishes are covered in dust, so they'll all need to be washed, too."

"I'll do those, I guess," sighed Zephra as she walked toward the basin type sink. "What about the bedclothes and curtains?"

"I've been sleeping on the ground for almost a week," Lilly spouted. She smiled as she grabbed both dusters, arming herself against her current enemy. "I can handle sleeping in dusty blankets. If we don't get to those today, we can do them tomorrow."

Zephra nodded and began gathering the dusty dishes from the cabinets. Lilly dragged a chair through each room, using it to reach the corners where the cobwebs seemed the worst, working without stopping until every surface sparkled. By the time she had finished with the dusters, Zephra had washed all the dishes, wiped every surface in the kitchen, including the chairs, and had already swept the floor.

Together they scrubbed what the dusters couldn't finish, swept every floor in the house and found time to change the bedclothes on the beds in each of the two bedrooms. The curtains, Lilly decided, could stay where they were for a while. She and Zephra beat the dirt from the rugs they'd piled beside the back door and then, while Zephra went into the town for some food and supplies, Lilly replaced each rug in its rightful place and then wandered upstairs to take a long hot bath in the small bathroom that separated the two bedrooms.

Dorwynn woke with a start as the front door blew open. Zephra charged through carrying a large cloth bag cinched together with a thin rope in one hand and a dead chicken in the other, and walked past him into the kitchen where Lilly was boiling some water in the now shining tea kettle. She took the bag, eyeing the chicken as Zephra walked straight out the back door and began plucking the foul.

"Did I black out again?" he asked as he noticed the gleaming house. He heard Zephra chuckle from outside the door.

"No," Lilly told him with a smile. "We spent the day cleaning." She began removing the items Zephra had purchased: a bag of flour, a bag of sugar, a loaf of hot bread and a ball of butter, both wrapped neatly in cheesecloth, a small woven basket that seemed specifically designed to carry the eggs it contained, a pitcher of milk closed with a cork, a small paper sack full of green beans, and a small box that held twelve vials, each labeled with the name of a different spice.

They dined that night on roasted chicken, stuffing made from the bread Zephra had brought, and green beans seasoned with hickory salt. Dessert consisted of homemade cinnamon bread, which Lilly made from memory. It was her father's favorite dessert. *Quick, easy and delicious*, he'd told her when he first taught her to make it. He was right. Even with the few ingredients she'd had, it made the perfect end to their meal, and there was enough left for them to toast it for breakfast.

Dorwynn offered to clean the mess, knowing both girls must be tired after their long journey. He was now wide awake, having slept through the entire cleaning process, and he slowly began his work, taking time to enjoy the task, for it was in a warm place, a place where they would stay for the remainder of Lilly's training time with him. Part of him wanted to get it finished as quickly as possible, while the other part, the stronger part, wanted to prolong his time with her as long as he was able.

Lilly, after muttering a sleepy "Goodnight" to the others, went upstairs, and without thinking, entered the room to the right of the bathroom. Both rooms were the same size, but this room had a window that faced the waterfall, and though it was cold, Lilly opened the window a crack so she could hear it while she slept. A plush, green robe hung on the back of the door, and Lilly vowed to wash it the following morning, along with the dirty clothes in her pack leaning against the leg of the small table beside the bed.

As she was about to pull back the covers and crawl into the inviting bed with its fresh clothes, she heard voices carrying from the back of the house. She went to the window and peered out to see Dorwynn sitting on the step, Zephra leaning in the doorway behind him. Lilly listened to them, their voices as clear as if they were in the room with her, though low and whispered.

"When was your last one?" Zephra asked.

"I lost a few days right before Gustave sent me to Arthidgen," Dorwynn admitted, "maybe a week. The most I've lost at one time since I was a child, since before I came here."

Zephra waited for him to continue, hoping he would, for he had never spoken of his past to her before. After a moment, she decided he was waiting her for to continue their discussion, so she held onto the subject of his past in her next question.

"How long have you known her?"

"Forever," he answered, and then he said nothing. Zephra looked toward the waterfall, a longing look in her dark eyes, and then she ran suddenly toward it, so fast she was no more than a blur of flames. The beautiful form of the phoenix erupted from the moving fire, and they dissipated while she soared over the lake to fly in a zigzag through the falling water. From her upstairs window, Lilly watched in awe as the phoenix burst into a ball of fire and careened toward Dorwynn, who never so much as flinched, before Zephra emerged from the flames, clean and dry.

When she returned from her bath, Zephra began relaying the messages Gustave had given her for Dorwynn. Lilly grew disinterested, having already heard it from Gustave himself, and started looking around the room. The bed was centered against the wall, larger than the twin in her old room, but smaller than the full size her father used. A large, handmade quilt covered it to the floor on both sides. A round table sat in the corner opposite the door, along with two chairs, all made of a light cedar adorned with elaborate designs engraved within the wood and clawed feet carved into each of their legs. The wardrobe against the wall beside the door matched the chairs and table. Without knowing what drove her, she lifted the quilt to get a better look at the frame of the bed. It also matched, as well as the overly-stuffed bookshelf and nightstand on either side of the bed. Lilly wondered in amazement as she ran her fingers over the carved works of art who crafted such exquisite pieces.

She knelt in front of the bookshelf, moving her lips silently as she read the titles. One in particular caught her eye, a book that was so worn on the binding that she had to take it from the shelf to read the title. She opened the plain black hard cover of the book to the title page, taking care not to damage the spine further. What she found inside made her forget about what the book was called, for covering the title page were several sheets of paper, stacked and folded once and pressed thin.

She removed the pages carefully and opened them with trembling fingers. Her heart was pounding as she let her eyes run over the delicate paper. She immediately recognized the swirling penmanship of her mother's hand, a perfect match to the note in her baby book, the only thing her mother had ever left her...until now. She felt her heart in her throat, beating as fast as the wings of a trapped hummingbird, as she read the letter.

For my darling children,

I know that you will never understand my reasons for leaving you behind, but I want you to always remember that my love for you never faltered in my course. The only words of consolation I can offer are that everything happens for a reason...there is one for this as well. You may not know what that reason is, for I barely know myself. I am left to wonder if I have chosen the right course of action. I can only hope I have made my choices wisely and that, without my guidance, you are able to do the same.

I regret that I will not be there to watch you become who I've foreseen you will be, but I do not regret my choice, for I know the events that have brought me to where I am now are for the best. No matter what you hear of me as you continue your life journey, I want you remember that I did it all for you. Your safety is and always will be my first priority, even if I cannot be there with you. It is out of my love for you, my family, that I left you behind. I don't think I could ever fully explain what dangers would have befallen you if I had stayed. I hope that is enough to sustain your heart, for on that subject, I can say no more.

I have little legacy to leave you, but for the sake of my own contentment, I wish to leave you some advice, a sense of guidance from the mother who loves you so. First, I want you to be ever watchful, for whether times are peaceful or laden with the prospect of danger, YOU, above all, must be protected. Take care in whom you place your trust, but do not deny others your trust altogether, for what is the purpose of life without having at least one person you trust more than yourself? A very sad thing indeed, I should think. Be patient in your endeavors, for things that are supposed to happen will happen, but only in their own time. Remain steadfast in the loyalty you give to others and be generous when you have nothing left to give. If you look deep enough into yourself, you will find you always have more strength than you imagine.

Listen to the wisdom of those who have more of it than you, and listen, also, to the clues within your own pasts, for making an informed decision is always best. Your choices in life will take you to places you never imagined, whether they be right or wrong, so do not dwell on mistakes. A life of regrets is no life at all. Live and be happy while it lasts, for life is not about always being happy. It is about enjoying the happiness when you find it.

Finally, my darlings, I have one final request: Please make sure that your father knows my love for him is ever strong, and it will carry forth until we meet again, in a different time and place, as does my love for you, my strong little lord, my promise of hope, my light through the storm.

Do not forget to remember me...Mom

It took Lilly forever to read it through the tears clouding her vision. When she finished, she carefully folded the letter and returned it to its hiding place. She wondered why her mother had written it to both her and Beth. Had she thought Beth would also be there, or did she merely expect whichever of her children found it to pass it to the other? Her heart swelled with the love so obviously displayed by her mother, but the vagueness with which her mother had described her disappearance only left her wanting more information. It had no clues to her current whereabouts, and Lilly, now wide awake, was ready to look for more clues.

When she tried to rise from her position in front of the bookshelf, she found she could not move. Her legs were lead, pinning her to the floor. No matter how hard she pulled and twisted, it was for naught. She resisted a moment longer before her fatigue began to return, and then she relaxed, hoping that it would help to free her. Without warning, she felt herself thrust forward, as though someone had pushed her from her inert position on the floor. Nausea swelled in her throat and she felt herself put her hands out to catch the fall she could feel coming, despite the fact she was already on the floor.

She landed onto cool, damp earth, the wet grass curling through her fingers. The sky was eerily bright although it was night. Lilly rose and after brushing the dirt from her hands and knees, she walked toward the source of the strange light. Once again she was in awe of the peculiar magick that overtook her when she least expected it, but she was not afraid. She knew it was a quest, though how it happened intrigued her.

She arrived at a clearing and froze, for in the center stood a beautiful white unicorn, her golden hair falling in cascades around her shimmering body. A tear slid down her cheek, leaving a sparkling trail in its path. She stared, unblinking, at a swirling doorway, the same doorway through which Lilly had crossed with Gustave months before.

From the trees beyond the unicorn, an old wizard emerged carrying a uniquely familiar staff, his flowing white hair whipping around his face though there wasn't a breath of wind.

Gustave! Lilly recognized him at once and without knowing why, became defensive at the sight of him. Did he know about her mother? She kept her distance, for she felt it was what she ought to do, and watched the quest unfold before her eyes.

"I am sorry, Ashya," said Gustave to the crying unicorn. Knowing that this was Ashya only peaked Lilly's interest all the more.

I've lost him forever, she responded with her mind. Though she made no audible sound, Lilly could feel the despair in her thoughts.

"He shall return."

No, Ashya told him, tearing her gaze from the spinning void of light. *He will not find himself until it is too late, until I am gone from him.*

With that, she turned and sped away into the darkness of the dense forest surrounding them. Gustave watched her go, concern blazing in his eyes. After a moment, he turned toward the doorway and waved his hand across his view of it. His brow furrowed with confusion when nothing happened and he tried again.

Still nothing.

Suddenly, a burst of light erupted from the doorway, a flash so bright both Lilly and Gustave had to shield their eyes from its intensity. As the light began to dim, a woman appeared on the ground at Gustave's feet, a woman Lilly recognized immediately as her mother. Her dark hair was a tangled mess and she wore only a hospital gown, barely more than shreds.

"What happened?" shouted Gustave as he rushed toward her. His hand flew quickly past the doorway, closing it instantly, before he reached the woman's side. "Why have you returned?"

"To change the prophecy," she said breathlessly, "but I couldn't bring her with me."

"Who?"

"The Chosen One."

She collapsed from utter exhaustion. Gustave lifted his staff and banged it straight back down on the ground with a loud *CRACK!*

In an instant, they were all in the house in Elikrede. Lilly felt possessed to stand in a dark corner of the room as she watched Gustave carefully place her mother on the sofa. She looked exactly as she had in Lilly's first vision quest, though she now looked in much worse condition than when she fled the hospital. She stirred, her eyes fluttering sporadically before flying open. The scream of pain that followed was so frightening Gustave started, dropping his staff.

"I'll fetch a healer," he said, distressed. He grabbed his staff from the floor, but as he walked past her, she snatched the sleeve of his robe and pulled him close to her.

"No," she said, her voice strained and ragged. "Bring me paper and something to write with."

"You're going to die if I do not fetch the healer," he protested.

"I'm going to die anyway," she whispered. "Please, Gustave, the paper."

Gustave hesitated for a moment, and then he nodded and left the room to find what she wanted. Lilly watched as her mother leaned against the pillow, breathing slow and calm. She took a step closer to look at the woman she had never truly seen, the woman who gave her life and left it an instant later. Her mother lifted her head and looked toward her. She smiled as their eyes met, and for a moment, Lilly wondered if she could see her. She smiled in return and her mother raised one finger to her lips to gesture Lilly's silence. Lilly backed into the dark corner once again as Gustave returned with several sheets of paper and a feather-quill pen.

Her mother wrote fast, filling the pages Gustave had brought her as she struggled through obvious pain, stopping only when she was forced to wait for it to subside. When she finished, she folded the pages in half, save one, and handed them all to Gustave.

"Hide these well," she instructed. "Hide them where she will find them when she comes. This is for you." He took the unfolded page from her and scanned it quickly. "I'm leaving this house in your care until she arrives. Make sure she knows this was my home, as it will be hers."

Gustave nodded. He let go of the folded pages and they vanished into thin air. He did the same with the single sheet of paper before kneeling beside the woman.

"Promise me, no matter what happens, you will see to it that I am buried here, beside my father."

"Of course, my child."

Lilly could still hear his voice echoing in her ears as the scene faded from her vision, only to be replaced once again by the room she had left only moments ago. She wiped away the tears that were streaming down her face as the realization of her mother's whereabouts hit her. She was dead. She had been dead for Lilly's entire life, and she was now buried somewhere nearby – if, that is, Gustave had kept his promise to her. Tomorrow she would find out where.

Zephra, who was sitting at the table in the corner, cleared her throat to announce her presence. Lilly jumped and whirled around, stunned to find that she wasn't alone.

"What are you doing here?" asked Lilly, wiping the remaining tears from her face.

"Waiting for you," she replied, one eyebrow raised in curiosity. "Where have you been?"

"I didn't realize I'd gone anywhere."

Zephra looked her over, taking notice of the dirty patches on her knees and the smears across her face where Lilly had wiped away her tears with her unclean hand. Lilly noticed the dust covering her hands and the damp spots over each knee only a second before Zephra asked her, "Why are you so dirty?"

"She traveled through time!" Zephra paced the small living room floor at a frantic speed. Her eyes glowed a strange bright blood-red unlike any hue Lilly had seen them yet. By now she knew that Zephra's eyes were the key to reading her emotions. She wondered what this color meant.

"Calm down, Z," said Dorwynn, so nonchalantly that Zephra could only gape at him in shock. "She's been having erratic vision quests, so it was probably…"

"I saw her come back!" Zephra stormed toward Lilly and grabbed her wrist, pulling her toward Dorwynn. "Look at her. She came back covered in dirt. You can't bring dirt back from a vision quest, Dorwynn. She *went* somewhere!"

Zephra's grasp on her wrist tightened and Lilly shivered as the dream flooded her memory again, just as vivid as when she'd first had it. She yanked herself free of Zephra's clutch, shooting her an icy glare, but Zephra didn't notice. She was too focused on the fact that she had witnessed another event she could not explain, something she was not used to in the countless years of her life.

"What happened?" Dorwynn finally asked, looking to Lilly for the answer. She recounted her newest journey, omitting the personal details and sharing only what she felt was important to the event itself. She explained how she found the letter hidden within the book and how, after reading it, she was unable to move until she found herself within the quest. Dorwynn could tell she wasn't telling him everything, but he didn't prompt her for more answers. When she had finished, he told her to clean herself up and waited until she left the room before speaking.

"You *know* what this means," Zephra told him in a low voice after she had left the room.

"You need to calm down," said Dorwynn, trying not to show his own confusion and concern. "We don't know anything yet."

"She's traveling through time, Dorwynn! Where did she learn to travel through time?"

"Well, she's already been trained by a unicorn. Maybe she taught her."

"In preliminary study? A unicorn would know better."

"There's got to be a reasonable explanation."

"She can absorb powers *without* seeing them used. If she was trained by a unicorn who didn't use the power in front of her, that's the only explanation. We have got to train her now. She has no control over her powers. I don't have to tell you what will happen if she absorbs a power to great for her to contain."

He nodded, racking his brain for any other explanation. Absorbing powers was a rare enough talent, but he had never heard of anyone being able to absorb them unless they actually witnessed the power being used. He understood, too, why Zephra was so afraid. She was one of the rare few who had the ability to absorb powers, but even she couldn't do it without seeing it first. Zephra stared at him with her arms crossed, waiting for a response.

"I think you're overreacting," he said, and regretted it instantly.

"Well, I think you're underreacting!" Zephra no longer bothered to keep her voice low and her shout blazed throughout the house. Lilly felt her eardrums nearly explode, for she had been focusing so intently on their conversation that she received the shout at full volume. Her head now screaming with pain, Lilly tried to block the rest of their discussion, but found no matter how hard she tried not to hear them, Zephra's voice stayed with her.

"Zephra!" said Dorwynn, his sharp voice reaching Lilly's ears from the next room. She sighed, glad at least he was blocked from her mind.

"Don't, Dorwynn. I know what it can do to a person. I've lived it, but I can't absorb powers from every element and I have to *see* someone use a power before I can absorb it. It took me years to be able to block the ones I didn't want when I did see them, and I had much more focus and control than she does."

"I know!" Exasperated, Dorwynn stood and ran his fingers through his hair. He looked at a loss, his own fears bubbling to the surface, his attempts to stay quiet now forgotten. "I don't know what to do. Don't you think I'm scared, too? Hell, the only reason I let you come along when I found you following us was because I was scared to be alone with her!"

It was the second time that night he regretted his words. Zephra looked as though he'd slapped her. He exhaled, his body beginning to ache from the stress of the past week, and wondered what Gustave was thinking when he had asked him to train Lilly. He was only making everything worse. He took Zephra's hand and held it tight.

"I didn't mean that," he said softly. "I'm glad you came for that reason, but that's not the only reason. Your connection to her, what she was capable of in Arthidgen and now this...I'm afraid, Z. I'm afraid I'm not powerful enough to train her. I'm afraid Gustave is wrong about who she is, but I'm even more afraid that he's right. If something goes wrong, if I underestimate her at all, she could destroy everything and everyone, and the worst part of it is that I don't have anyone I can ask to help me sort out all of these problems."

Zephra nodded. She had never feared much of anything in her life, a luxury afforded to her only by her immortality, but she knew Gustave believed Lilly was the Chosen One. From the series of unexplainable events taking place around the girl, she believed it, too.

"Would it be easier for you to train her if I left?" she asked.

"No!" Panic flooded Dorwynn at the idea of having to deal with this alone. "Please, stay. We'll figure this out together, or at least get through her training more quickly. Then Amparo can deal with her."

Lilly, who had resorted to eavesdropping in the traditional way of hiding in the next room, chose that moment to step around the corner. Dorwynn could tell from the look on her face that she'd heard everything they had said, for aside from the anger strewn across her face, he also saw the look of pain a person only gets when they are truly betrayed. Fresh tears gathered in her eyes as both Dorwynn and Zephra struggled for something to say. Before either could utter a word, however, Lilly closed her eyes and disappeared into thin air, leaving them alone, together, with only their fears.

Lilly paced the floor of Ashya's home, so frustrated she thought she would explode if she stopped moving. Ashya watched her repeat her steps over and again, observing both the physical changes Lilly had undergone since she'd left only a week ago, and the changes in her magickal aura. The most noticeable change, however, was her lack of focus. Ashya waited, knowing she would soon hear what had turned Lilly from the balanced person she was the last day she'd seen her to the emotional mess before her now.

Lilly didn't know where to begin. So many things were not as she expected, and the turbulence in her relationships with Dorwynn and Zephra only fanned the flame of her aggravation. She'd hoped Rohan would be here, though somehow, she already knew that he wasn't. Glancing at Ashya, she tried to think of what to say. She didn't want to just start complaining, but she needed to talk to someone about her frustrations.

You've returned sooner than I expected, Ashya said inaudibly. Lilly nodded and plopped into her familiar chair. She closed her eyes and concentrated on her breathing until she relaxed enough to speak.

"Things aren't going the way I planned," she said aloud.

"They rarely do," Ashya replied. "Life has a way of interrupting plans. I expected nothing less."

"Well, I expected more," Lilly sighed. She twirled her finger around the necklace her father had given her, closing them around the small pendant as though it held the answers she sought.

"Why don't you start at the beginning?" offered Ashya. Lilly nodded slowly and began her story, omitting no details. When she spoke of the harpy attack and the words she had spoken, Ashya's eyebrows raised and her eyes were wide, though she said nothing. She told her of the dreams and Ashya nodded, knowing all too well the flood of quests that would inevitably come through while the girl was in a coma. She interrupted long enough to explain to Lilly that in such a state, the mind is completely closed to the rest of the world, which leaves it completely open to itself, with no disconnection between the subconscious and conscious mind.

Lilly talked for over an hour about the many things that were bothering her, like Dorwynn and his increasingly bad disposition, her conflict about whether or not she could trust Zephra, their discussion about her right before she had come, and how hurt she was about discovering her mother's death. She left the event in Arthidgen until the end of her rant, explaining how she couldn't remember the night at first, and then how images from that night came back to her, filling the gaps in her memory. Ashya listened, showing no reaction to Lilly's confessions until the girl stopped speaking. She contemplated how she should respond, and then stood.

"I'll make some tea," she said as she climbed the stairs to the kitchen, "and then we will talk."

Lilly closed her eyes and reached for the necklace again, though she had no idea why she was suddenly so aware of it. She let the solitude envelope her, feeling at home in the inviting atmosphere. She closed her eyes, the sweet smell of the lavender oil simmering over the candle on a corner table invading her senses with a soothing tranquility. By the time that Ashya returned with their tea, Lilly felt ready to listen.

"There are things happening right now that you cannot control," Ashya said after she'd settled in her chair. "There is one event, however, that is affecting your control of things over which you should have control, but don't. The betrayal of a trusted friend has caused you to lose trust, in him and in other things in your life, including yourself. Trust has never been something you gave easily, and this only proves your principle. You've let it affect your training and your control over your magick. You've let it consume your thoughts so deeply that there is little room for anything else."

"But I'm not learning anything else," Lilly said, throwing her arms in the air. "I'm doing everything I'm told, but I feel the only thing I am getting accomplished is waiting. I'm waiting to learn about my family. I'm waiting to find out why I am the Chosen One. I'm waiting for others to do what needs to be done. I'm waiting to learn something useful, not just irrelevant facts. I'm waiting, and the worst part of it is that I don't know what it is I'm waiting for, or why."

Ashya shook her head, a smile playing at her lips as she remembered the impatience of her own youth. She lifted her teacup to them, exhaling over the top to cool the steaming liquid, and then took a careful sip before responding.

"First," she said, "let me say that everything you learn is relevant. Whether you believe it or not, the facts you learn may be useful to you later. Remember what others tell you and whenever you have the opportunity, ask questions of others, for they have experience in the world that you do not, and experience is never learned easily.

"As far as waiting goes, all things will come in their own time. You've barely had time to get started, and with so many things happening around you, it will take more on your part to get through it a better person. Be patient with your trainer. While you may think he is procrastinating, he is merely taking the time to teach you what he feels you need to know. Give him time to teach, and give yourself time to learn. Knowledge is power of the highest magnitude. When the final battle comes, it will be the other's undoing."

Lilly wondered if what Ashya had said was based on one of her visions, but before she could ask, Ashya continued.

"I know young Dorwynn, and he has always known fear, at least since he has been in this world. He's dealing with a lot as well, and I must admit, your powers surprised me at first, which is not a feat easily accomplished. Except when he trained with Gustave, I doubt he's ever seen such power."

"That's another thing," interrupted Lilly. "How is it that I can do these things? You never showed me how to travel through time and I sure don't remember learning a language that no one speaks because they fear the magick behind it. I'm afraid, too."

Ashya sighed and finished the tea in her cup. She worried about telling her too much too soon, but it was obvious Lilly needed to hear a little of what was happening in the world. Ashya had seen a glimpse of what was to come, but her requiem quests weren't as reliable as most. She didn't want to make a mistake that would cause Lilly to take the wrong path in her destiny.

"The *Doret Gaia*," she began, "is a pure language. It is magick itself, existing in thought before the first word was ever spoken, before the first human appeared in the world. Every creature born into this world is born with the knowledge of this language, but over time, they are taught a spoken language and they forget the nature of the other, at least on a conscious level. It is still there, buried deep within us all, and while many can remember only a few words that retain importance in their own lives, the subconscious mind can release this knowledge in the moment of necessity."

"But I wasn't born here."

"That is true, but it is different with those born on Earth. While they, too, are born with the knowledge of the *Doret Gaia*, they are unable to access any of it from their subconscious. It is only after crossing from that world into this that it is possible to remember it at all, though it is rare that one does.

"You, my dear, are a rare soul. No doubt by now there are many who believe you are the Chosen One, myself included. The nature of your destiny, like the nature of magick, is a mystery. Since the first spoken word, the prophecy of the Chosen One has existed. Prophecies are just one more mysterious thing that magick has bestowed on us, completely different from the magick of requiem quests, which you will learn in time. While requiem quests are merely magickal glimpses into *possible* outcomes of future events, prophecies are accurate, delivered to a prophet by magick itself. They are vague and they may take hundreds of years before they come to be, but they are never wrong."

"Do you know the prophecy of the Chosen One?"

Ashya sighed. She knew the prophecy well, though how much of it she should tell Lilly, she knew not. It was long, and its meanings could have numerous interpretations, as it was translated from a language in which every word has more than one meaning. The most important reason, however, was the multitude of information about things Lilly had yet to learn, things she would need time to absorb and accept on her own before receiving such a directly unquestionable truth. If she discovered too much too soon, it could be detrimental to the course of her destiny.

"I do," said Ashya finally, "but I cannot tell you more than I feel you are prepared to accept. If you can deal with hearing part of it, I will tell you what I can."

"I guess I have no choice." Lilly was irritated that even Ashya felt she couldn't bear the weight of the entire answer she'd asked of her, but she knew better than to argue. She trusted Ashya more than anyone else in this world, including herself, so she forgot her irritation and accepted anything she could get.

"It is said," began Ashya, "that the Chosen One will be born of Earth on the eve of the Sabbat, though which one was not specified. She will choose her destiny of her own will. She will arrive to existing turbulence and unleash the fury of the building storm. Many will be drawn to her without explanation. At her side, so too shall come their absolution. Her blood..." Ashya stopped short. She cleared her throat and shook her head, and Lilly knew she would speak no more on the subject. She didn't mind, for she somehow knew the building storm Ashya had mentioned referred to the war for which she was being trained and she was ready to ask questions.

"So I brought the war to Buthania?"

"The war was already here," Ashya assured her. "It was building before you arrived and it would have been unleashed whether you had chosen to step through that doorway or not. If you are the Chosen One, your choice will make the prophecy true, not your coming."

"But if it was going to happen anyway, why does the prophecy say my coming will unleash the fury of the building storm? Why does it have anything to do with me at all? I mean, if I hadn't come here, the fury wouldn't have been unleashed, right?"

"Don't fret over that, dear one," said Ashya. "It isn't so simple. Do you think wars just spontaneously begin?"

"Don't they?"

"Your country is at war right now. How did it start?"

"Nine-eleven. Our country was attacked and..."

"And that's when it started for you," interrupted Ashya. "Do you think the enemy just woke up that morning and decided to hijack some airplanes and use them as weapons against their owners? They planned that attack, but for them, that war had already started. They were expecting it. Tell me, how long do you think Japan planned the attack on Pearl Harbor before they struck?" Lilly shrugged. "They studied their enemy for a long time, and when they hit, they knew where to hit the hardest, where it would cause the most damage. The best weapon in any war is the element of surprise."

"So, my crossing through the doorway did what, exactly, to cause this chain of events?"

"I don't know." Ashya sighed. "I wish I did, but true prophecies are never specific."

"What do you mean, 'true prophecy'?"

"Anyone can visit a prophet and get insight into their own future, their own destined events and certain outcomes. A true prophecy is so much more complicated than that. It is meant for everyone, along with all their events and choices. Every time a choice is changed, it forks toward different paths, different events. A personal reading is a pretzel, twisting and turning and sometimes even coming back around on itself. A true prophecy is the center of a spider web. The choices made regarding it affect everything attached to it, all the way through to the outermost strand. The war is just a point somewhere in between.

"To answer your question, there is no way to find out what your crossing did, but I do know that it did something to change Dagana's actions, and I'm certain she is now preparing for a war. She will try to surprise us, but if we are prepared, we may gain the advantage. That's why your training is so important. Dagana will never see you as a threat because you are human and she believes all humans to be weaker than her, but by the time your training is over, you will be more powerful than anyone else."

"What if I'm not?" asked Lilly, staring at her shoes.

"You already are," said Ashya, smiling. "Of that I am certain. You just don't know how to use all of your power yet. There is one more part of the prophecy I want you to hear. It says 'She will be powerful, but only when she is balanced, so too shall our worlds become'."

"What does that mean?"

"It means you have many things to figure out on your own and even more things to learn before you can know what it means."

Lilly nodded. It was just one more vague answer to suspend her curiosity and try her patience. They sat in silence while Lilly sorted through this new information. She knew she should go back to Elikrede and face the two people responsible for her well-being, the same two people she didn't trust, especially after their undeniable honesty. Still, there was one more question Ashya had yet to answer: how did she travel through time?

"Magick," replied Ashya before Lilly voiced the question, "though it was not your doing. For reasons only she knows, your mother put a remnant spell on the letter she left behind."

"A remnant spell?"

"It is a spell left on an object for another. It can be any object and it can be for anyone, or for only one. It depends on the intent of the spell caster, though I'm sure she left it for you alone."

"But it read, 'For my darling children'."

"Perhaps she left it for any of her children. The spell would require one with her blood to activate the magick." Lilly caught a flash of concern cross Ashya's eyes, gone as fast as it came, but was too thrilled at having some questions answered to add another. Ashya would tell her if it was really important.

"So I can't travel through time?" Lilly was relieved that, at least this time, she was not responsible for the latest unorthodox event.

"I'm sure you can," Ashya told her, a small smile on her face, "but not until you *learn* how to do it, and the only way for you to learn is to return to your trainers."

"I know," she sighed.

"Do not be so eager for things to happen. Before you know it, things will hit you harder than you expect and you will not have the chance to rest. Enjoy the slow times when they happen, for they will get fewer and father between sooner than you think."

Lilly nodded, knowing that Ashya's words were a warning to be heeded. She hugged her tight, relishing the embrace.

"Thank you for everything," she said. "I feel better. I'm sorry I came so unexpectedly."

"Do not apologize, my dear. Your visit wasn't as unexpected as you may think, and you are always welcome here, whenever you need or want to come. Would you do one thing for me, though?"

"Anything."

"Tell my son I need to speak with him when he is able to return, and to please come soon. It is of a very important matter I wish to speak."

"I will tell him," Lilly promised. Ashya smiled as Lilly closed her hand around her necklace and, with the wave of her other hand, disappeared before her eyes. Ashya closed her eyes, saying a silent prayer to the Great Father that her son would arrive in a timely manner, before it was too late.

One Step Forward

The house was still when Lilly returned. The only light came from the glow of coals smoldering in the fireplace, its pops and crackles the only sounds. In the near darkness, Lilly failed to notice the figure resting in the chair farthest from the hearth, quietly awaiting her return, so when his voice shattered the silence, Lilly nearly jumped from her skin.

"Traveling by thought," Dorwynn said. It wasn't a question. "You went to see the unicorn." Lilly nodded, unable to speak. Dorwynn nodded also, staring at her intently. "And before? Did you really travel through time?"

"I did," she admitted, and noticing his concerned expression, rushed the explanation. "It wasn't my fault. It was a remnant spell."

For a moment, he considered the possibility, and then he abandoned his chair to put another log on the fire. Lilly watched the process in silence as he went out the back door, returning a moment later with four logs and proceeded to place two of them carefully atop the bed of glowing embers. After a few minutes, the wood caught and the fire wrapped itself around them, feasting on its replenished fuel source with unending hunger.

They both remained silent, unsure of what they could say to lessen the tension between them. Lilly was still upset by what he had said, but her time with Ashya, no matter how brief, had erased her anger. Only hurt feelings remained.

"I'm sorry about what I said," Dorwynn muttered. "I didn't mean it the way it sounded. I've been a little off track lately."

"Why didn't you tell me you still had the blackouts?" asked Lilly as she sank into the soft sofa. Dorwynn sat beside her, painfully aware of how close they were, and shrugged his shoulders.

"When?" he asked. "Between the harpies and the coma and…after, there was never a good time to talk."

"What about right now?"

He looked into her sparkling green eyes and gave her a small smile. Despite his feelings over her frightening outburst, he felt his tension easing.

"I haven't had them for a long time," he admitted. "In fact, the last one I had before last night was about six months ago."

"And Gustave hasn't been able to figure them out?"

"Gustave doesn't know. Only Zephra knows, and you."

"I'll keep it to myself," promised Lilly. He smiled again, and she realized how nice it was to witness it. For a moment, it was as though he had never left her behind, except for the fact that he was years older than he should have been. It still affected her, though she was finally starting to get used to it.

"How is my father?" he asked. Lilly's smile put him at ease and he listened, content, as she described her last meeting with Dr. Hoffman. Dorwynn laughed when she explained her anger at his nonchalant behavior over his disappearance. When she recounted his loving words, his eyes filled with tears.

"I understand now," she said, "why he seemed so undaunted. Do you think he knows about all of this?"

"I don't know," Dorwynn told her. His father had never given any indication of knowing about this world, but it wouldn't have surprised him if he did know. He had always been very understanding of his son's unique abilities and with his decision to leave at so young an age.

"Do you think my father understands?" she asked.

He could hear the guilt in her words and understood it all too well. He reached for her hand and finding it, he squeezed it gently.

"I think if he doesn't, he will."

"I hope so." She reached for her necklace, weaving her fingers absently through the chain. The words her father spoke of its origin echoed in her mind: *It's been in my family for a long time, longer than even I could tell you, longer than anyone in the family can even remember. Promise me that you will keep it safe.*

"I haven't thought about them since I first arrived," she said as a lump began to grow in her throat. "Half a year has passed and I haven't thought about them. What kind of person does that make me?" She broke down, allowing her tears to fall. He put his arms around her, trying to soothe her guilt, but he knew he could not. It was something only she could do.

"It makes you," he said as he placed his hand on her face and wiped a tear from her cheek with his thumb, "the kind of person who has her own path to follow. It doesn't mean you don't love them."

She looked into his eyes and saw traces of her friend returning. Any lingering bits of anger vanished, and though she knew he was keeping secrets from her, she could feel her trust in him building.

"How long did you forget about me?" she asked, regaining her composure.

"I thought about you every day."

"Liar," she said, a smile playing at her lips.

"I did," he insisted, "but I also knew you were coming."

"How did you know I would choose to come?"

Dorwynn laughed out loud, but recovered himself quickly so he wouldn't wake Zephra, who was asleep in the extra room upstairs.

"You were always the adventurous one," he said. "Climbing the bluffs. Diving into the lake at Hyde Park so you could get a closer look at the ducks. Jumping Tern Gully on Ol' Man Jacob's horse…"

"That wasn't my fault!" Lilly protested, though she was grinning at the memory. "Besides, who was right beside me for all of those things?"

"Well, I may have followed you into the lake, but my horse followed you across the gully."

"Your horse took off first."

"It did not."

"Yes, it did."

Their eyes locked, both of them smiling, daring the other to protest. Lilly raised one eyebrow, a gesture she had always used to challenge him, and she saw the playful gleam in his eyes return, making their blue hue even brighter.

"Well," he said with playful arrogance, "I guess there's only one way to find out the truth."

"Memory quest?" asked Lilly, her excitement building.

"Memory quest," he echoed.

Dorwynn took her hands in his and held them tight, a hint of worry coursing through him as though he was making a mistake, but the feeling passed as quickly as it came. He shut his eyes as he felt the world around him change. The warmth of the fireplace was replaced with the cool breeze of spring as the darkness gave way to bright sunlight, evident even through his closed eyes. Images flashed through his mind, a recall of events leading backward to the memory he was trying to relive. Finally, the sensation passed and he opened his eyes.

Lilly was beside him, her eyes bright with elation as she absorbed the new scenery. She and Adrian, both nine years old, were sitting atop two horses walking a slow pace in unison. She remembered that their fathers were here also, somewhere with Ol' Man Jacobs, helping him to repair some broken fences on his property.

"...and then he said I looked like a girl," said Adrian. Lilly shook her head.

"So what did you do?" she asked, her eyes wide. The boy on the horse smiled, his eyes gleaming mischievously.

"I told him it was better to look like one than to act like one," he laughed. "And then he punched me. What could I do? I hit him back, so we both got in trouble and Dad came to the principal's office, and so did Brian's dad, and he told Dad that he should make me get a haircut and you know what Dad told him?"

"What?"

"Dad told him that if he would let his son be himself that maybe he wouldn't be so quick to judge other people. The guy's face turned so red I thought he was going to explode. Then Dad brought me home."

"Lucky," Lilly said sullenly. "You got in a fight and got the rest of the day off school. They probably suspended you, too, so you'll get more time off."

"Nope. Dad told Mr. Fuller that I shouldn't get suspended for defending myself because the other boy hit me first."

"Good," said Lilly, brightening. "I hate it when you're not at school. And a haircut wouldn't hurt, you know. You do kinda look like a girl."

Adrian stuck out his tongue at her and she grinned, leading her horse into the nearby forest, Adrian one step behind her.

"You did look like a girl," said the grown Lilly. Dorwynn shook his head and blushed.

Within the forest, the younger Lilly slowed her horse as they approached the fence surrounding the farmer's property. The horse bent its head toward the ground, trying to reach the slightly greener grass along the bottom edge of the fence. Lilly stared at the horizon beyond the fence, her mind wandering. Adrian looked at her, then turned his gaze to see what had captivated her into silence.

"What are you thinking?" he asked, a question he asked her often.

"I was thinking about how cool it would be to live in a forest like this, hidden from everything wrong with the world. Do you think there's anyplace in the world like that where we could go, just us, and live forever?"

"Maybe not in this world," he said. She gave him a strange look, but didn't respond.

Dorwynn watched the memory intently, waiting for their horses to run, but Lilly was focused on Adrian's comment. Had he known, even then, that their destinies would unfold the way they had? Once, he had been the only important thing in her world besides her family, and all she could remember of their childhood conversations was a blur of details strung together and held in place by his presence. Other than those years he had left her behind, she had no memories of him not being with her.

"Look," whispered Dorwynn, pointing to a figure emerging from some nearby bushes. Lilly redirected her attention, pushing her thoughts aside, and watched as a young girl snuck closer to the grazing horses, unseen by their riders.

"It's Beth," she gasped, and she watched in disbelief as her eleven-year-old sister slapped both horses on the haunches simultaneously. The horses darted forward at top speed, with Lilly and Adrian clinging to the reins, and ran toward an opening in the worn fence, both clearing it with room to spare. Beth, horrified, ran toward the house where she knew their father would be, while the scenery flew through the minds of the two observers, the trees whirring past as the gully grew closer.

Lilly's horse jumped the gully, barely landing a safe distance from the edge, Adrian's horse directly on her heels. Both children were terrified as the horses stopped, voicing their discontent with nervous whinnies. Adrian looked at Lilly and they both laughed.

"That was awesome!" shouted Adrian, his laugher rolling from his throat. "It was like we were flying!"

"Yeah," said Lilly, her heart racing with excitement, "but how are we going to get back?"

The scene of the children faded as Lilly realized their quest was over. She felt the familiar pull of the magick as the connection was broken and a moment later, they were sitting on the sofa in the little house in Elikrede, still holding hands, both enjoying the lingering sensation of excitement from their childhood adventure.

"That little sneak!" said Lilly, shaking her head in astonishment. "She could have killed us."

"A bit of jealousy, I'd wager." Lilly met Dorwynn's eyes, remembering the many times Beth had whined whenever her father suggested they visit the Hoffmans, always begging to go visit someone else instead. That day, all of her friends had been busy, so she'd had no choice but to go with them.

"Yeah, she always felt like a third wheel when we were all together."

"Not to mention, she was definitely *not* the adventurous type."
Dorwynn stared at Lilly, taking in her refreshing presence. Her eyes
glowed with delight, small flecks of yellow blazing through them like
fire, like Zephra's eyes....

"What?" asked Lilly, self-conscious under his intent gaze. He averted
his eyes, his heart screaming at him to tell her everything he knew he
shouldn't, his mind overriding that desire.

"You have an adventurous spirit," he said softly, careful not to let his
voice betray his emotions. "I think that's why you and Amparo get along
so well." He put his arms around her, holding her as long as he dared,
and then his kissed her forehead before letting go of her. She tried not to
show her surprise at this odd shift in his behavior, but she couldn't hide
the fact she was happy about it.

"That was fun," she said, and then added, "Adrian."

"Get some rest," he instructed as he stretched out on the sofa, his
heart racing at the sound of his true name being spoken, or perhaps,
because Lilly was the one who had said it. He closed his eyes, focusing
on his pounding heart, trying to relax enough to sleep, not knowing what
unforeseen events might occur in the days to follow.

Lilly went to her room, leaving Dorwynn alone with his thoughts.
Once there, she began to rummage through her bag, digging deep until
she found what she sought: the business card Dr. Hoffman had given her
at their last meeting. He had told her then that she could call anytime,
but she'd left that night. There were no phones here, and even if there
were, they certainly wouldn't connect to an entirely different world.

A thought struck her then, and after quickly changing into some
pajamas and crawling into bed, she tucked the card under her pillow,
clutching it as though her life depended on it, and slowly drifted to sleep.

Pain shot through his big toe as he stumbled through the pitch black
house in search of his ringing phone. He usually kept it at his bedside,
but for some reason he couldn't recall at that moment, he had left it on
the coffee table downstairs. He cursed the brightness of the sixty watt
light bulb that blinded him when he flipped the switch, and then he
rushed to his screaming cell phone before he missed the call.

"This is Dr. Hoffman," he said, trying not to sound like he had been
asleep only one minute ago. He groaned inwardly as he noticed the time:
1:37 am.

"Dr. Hoffman," said the voice on the other end of the line. The
connection was jumbled, making the voice seem small and very far

away, though when it spoke again, he knew instantly what caused the terrible reception. "Dr. Hoffman, this is Lilly."

"Lilly," he said, now completely awake, "where are you?"

"You wouldn't believe me if I told you," she said. Although he was straining to hear her, there was no mistaking the irony in her voice.

"Try me." She didn't answer for so long, he though he had lost the call, but he thought he could still hear her breathing, so he said the words he'd been waiting to say for many years. "Are you in Buthania?"

"How did you know?" exclaimed Lilly, astonished.

"I knew it!" he said, his excitement building. He'd been harboring the knowledge of another world, a secret world, for so many years, waiting until the time was right to let it all out. Finally, that time had arrived. He was overcome with giddiness, like a child on Christmas morning. "There really is another world, isn't there? A magickal world? What's it like? Wait...they have telephones there?"

"Not exactly. It's hard to explain. How do you know about Buthania?"

He sighed, reminding himself that although his suspicions were correct and his many years of wondering were confirmed, Lilly was still his patient above all else. He walked into his kitchen and, holding the phone with his shoulder, he made a pot of coffee as he started his story.

"When Adrian was young, he had blackouts. You know that. He was still having them when you first met him. What you probably don't know is that he came to me as a patient first. He was orphaned at birth and was in foster care when he began doing things that seemed...well, miraculous, for lack of a better term. He learned to speak before six months of age and by the time he reached nine months old, his vocabulary was that of an average two-year-old. At ten months, he was reading. His foster parents believed he was a child prodigy, so they decided to bring him to me to discuss how they should handle his gifts. The appointment was scheduled. At the time, it seemed like a normal case of child psychology.

"The day of the appointment arrived. When I walked into my office, Adrian, barely a year old and days away from being officially adopted, sat in the chair facing my desk. His foster parents both stood and they were downright afraid. They handed me a check for five times my normal session fee and told me they had decided not to adopt him. Then they left my office and never came back."

"How awful," whispered Lilly. "Why did they just leave him like that?" She felt the familiar ache in her heart, the despair of abandonment rattling her core as she remembered the years of her life filled with the constant void of her mother's presence, and she wondered if Adrian remembered the day his foster parents left him behind. Did he also live with the feeling of emptiness, pushing it deeper into himself when it surfaced as he tried to forget what he never could?

"I asked Adrian why he thought they would leave him. His simple reply was that they were afraid, and then he told me why, or rather, he showed me. In his hand was a tiny seed, one his foster mother gave him the day before when she had been working in her garden. Before my eyes, it grew at a phenomenal rate, without dirt, without water, without sunlight.

"I was speechless, but also very intrigued. By the end of his first session, which revolved mostly around his emotional state of being abandoned, he had informed me that it was meant to be this way and that *I* was supposed to be his father. I applied to be a foster parent and the state awarded me temporary custody until the adoption was final. I took him home that night.

"Over the next four years, the blackouts became obvious, so I focused mainly on trying to figure them out. We had many session of hypnosis, and though I never learned the underlying cause of the blackouts, I learned much more than I ever expected, things that seemed impossible and that, at that time, I discarded as nothing more than the strong imagination of a child seeping into his subconscious.

"He told me he came from another world, a magickal world he called Buthania. He said he lost his parents and that something called the Council decided to send him to Earth for his safety and to follow his destiny. He was reborn on Earth as a baby, but subconsciously retained many memories of his first seven years. Volumes of information poured from his mouth during those years, though he would never tell me the names of anyone from his memories and there were some questions that, even under hypnosis, he wouldn't answer. When I asked, he always said the same thing: 'I cannot say. It might upset the balance.' Every session he said that, and something else I could never figure out. As he was coming out of the hypnotic state, every time he would say, 'I'm not the only one.'

"As far fetched as it all sounded, everything began to make sense to me over time. I found myself believing in faeries and unicorns. I would listen to the tapes of his hypnosis sessions as though they were my own bedtime stories, dreaming at night of the Jermar Ocean where the merpeople could be found, and hoping that as I reviewed them, the tapes would reveal the piece of information I was lacking. I still couldn't find the reason *why* he was having so many lapses in time. It continued this way for some time, until the day he mentioned your name."

"My name?" asked Lilly. The doctor's many years of listening to people talk allowed him to hear the subtle change in her voice, a sense of awareness most people would have mistaken for disbelief. "But he didn't know me when we met."

"No," agreed Dr. Hoffman, "he said your name under hypnosis. At first, I didn't even realize it was you he spoke of. You see, I lost touch with your father after you were born. He was dealing with raising you and Beth alone, and when Adrian came into my life, all my spare time was spent with him. It wasn't until your father called me about your own behavior that I made the connection. I hadn't been accepting new patients at the time, but I made an exception for you. So many of the things you told me were just like Adrian's hypnosis sessions, except that you were saying these things while you were awake, fully conscious of it. That's when I realized it was your name he spoke and when, for the first time, I truly believed everything he had told me as undeniable truth.

"How could I not believe what two children were telling me? You had never met at that point, but you each gave specific details of this world, using the same strange names and terminology. After discussing it with your father at great length, we decided to introduce the two of you and from the moment we did, you were inseparable."

"I remember," said Lilly, a sad wistfulness in her voice.

"I wonder, though, if you realize that within months of your introduction, Adrian's blackouts nearly ceased. With the exception of a few times a year rather than several times a week, they stopped altogether, as did the visits from your imaginary friend. It was as though you were supposed to find each other. I thought it was a very odd coincidence, but I was so grateful for the improvement between both of you that I didn't care why you had improved or that I had never figured out what caused your strange behaviors. Perhaps that was a mistake on my part."

"I wouldn't call it a mistake," said Lilly after contemplating this new information. She remembered telling Rohan about Adrian and how she'd forgotten about him, and how, after Adrian had left, he'd returned and everything she'd forgotten about Buthania that she apparently knew as a child came flooding back in her dreams. "I think everything happened the way it was supposed to."

"So you've accepted his abandoning you?"

"I'm starting to realize that there is a lot more to the events in my life than I ever dreamed. I've accepted it and I've forgiven him for it."

"How is he?" asked the doctor, his excitement building. The memory of his son's departure echoed clearly through his mind. He recalled how wise he seemed for a twelve-year-old and how, despite the criticism he would receive from so many other parents, he had willing wished his son the best and allowed him to leave. At last, the time to find out if it had been the right thing to do had arrived.

"Well," said Lilly, hesitating as she contemplated what information to give him first, "he's twenty-two. I guess coming back changed him to what he would have been if he never left. He's still having some blackouts, but overall, he is well."

"What is he doing? When he left, he told me he had things to do to follow his path. I'm just curious about what that entails."

"He trained with a great wizard and became a Master of Earth magick. Right now, he's training me to do the same."

"A wizard." Dr. Hoffman's voice was a sigh of wonder and disbelief, though Lilly knew that he believed every word coming out of her mouth. "Is he a good teacher?"

"He's trying to be, but it's been a learning process for both of us. Neither of us has much patience with the other right now."

"Why not?"

"I don't know," admitted Lilly, not wanting to relive the details of the strange events happening around them for a second time that night. "I guess we both expected things would be like they always were between us, but that was a long time ago. People change a lot in three years."

"Yes, they do."

"How is my family? Is my father alright?"

"Your father is fine," said the doctor through a yawn. "He seems to understand even more than I do about all this, though he stays pretty vague about it. Beth took your disappearance hard, though. She's changed quite a bit since you left."

"I understand. Being abandoned changes a person." Lilly's heart tightened as she thought about her sister, guilt overthrowing her that she reanimated the sense of betrayal in Beth by leaving without explanation.

"Do not worry," said Dr. Hoffman. "I will tell your father you are safe."

"Tell him I love him."

"He knows. A father always knows, but I will tell him you said so."

"Thank you, Dr. Hoffman. I should let you get back to bed, I suppose, and get some rest myself."

"Would you answer one question for me first?"

"Of course."

"Is Buthania as beautiful as he described it?"

"It is the most beautiful place I have ever seen, even in my dreams."

"I thought so," he whispered, his eyes welling with tears. Before he told her goodnight and hung up the phone, he was sure he heard the distant sound of a waterfall on the other end of the line. When he returned to the comfort of his bed, he slept better than he had in a long while, and he dreamed of a magickal place with a purple waterfall cascading over a purple mountain and a black winged horse soaring over it, calling out his name.

Elikrede

The morning air was chilly as the suns peeked timidly over the horizon. Kylenin hugged his cape tighter over his thin shoulders, trying to stop his body heat from escaping. His sullen mood was clear by his meandering gait, his feet dragging the ground as he made his way along the cobblestone streets of Elikrede.

Yesterday had been uneventful. He had ridden Ciarán through the town, his eyes scrutinizing every person who passed him in search of the mysterious girl who plagued his dreams. He'd only eaten a small breakfast before setting out on his mission, and though he had not stopped all day, he had not found a trace of her anywhere. By the time the suns had set, he was tired, hungry and frustrated.

Today, he'd decided to leave his horse at the inn and explore the town on foot. He noticed many things he hadn't the previous day, taking the time now to focus on details he'd overlooked before. The main street, which was laid in cobblestone, wound a huge, open circle around an enormous fountain in its center. This served as the town square, though it was the only circular town epicenter Kylenin had ever seen. The ones he was used to were actually square, with corners formed of buildings erected upon intersecting streets. The buildings constructed around this circle were close together, though they didn't quite touch the other buildings surrounding them, and they varied in both size and in what type of materials had been used to build them. The taller buildings were made of brick or stone, while many of the single-story buildings were log or formed lumber, creating among the heart of the town a never-ending quagmire of change.

Five roads, equidistance apart, connected to the main street, running between some buildings, while between others were grassy yards, well-tended gardens or untouched plots of earth. Each road led toward a different area of Elikrede, whether residential, business or the older parts of the town that consisted of the amphitheater, sporting arenas and the judicial buildings. Kylenin had traveled all five of these roads, as well as many of the smaller roads connecting them. Though he hadn't seen a map of the town, he imagined it looked like a twisted spider web that had been haphazardly reconstructed after prey had escaped. He refused to waste his time today searching this oddly constructed town and decided, instead, to stick to the main circle. She was here, somewhere, and he knew she would eventually find her way to the center, for almost every building there was a shop of some kind and she was sure to go shopping sooner or later.

After visiting the restaurant located on the ground floor of a two-story brick building, the upper floor serving as living quarters for the town's butcher, Kylenin ate outside, studying the ornate details of the huge round fountain. A cement bench surrounded it in its entirety, where one could sit to enjoy the grandeur of the massive monument. The sphere that rose from its center was surrounded by five statues which, Kylenin realized, faced each of the five conjoining roads. From where he stood, he faced a mermaid, forever emerging from the pool of water in the fountain's basin. To her right was the statue of a dragon and to the left, a faerie, neither of which were accurate size. The faerie statue was as large as the mermaid statue, which *was* of correct size, that of a human woman but for the tail. The dragon, he knew, was close to the same size as the other statues, but he knew that a real dragon was nearly ten times as large as the monument depicted.

The Elemental Children, thought Kylenin as he walked counterclockwise around the fountain. As he suspected, a rearing unicorn was set in stone. Between it and the faerie was the statue of a woman, life-sized, holding her arms out to her sides as if offering an everlasting embrace. This last statue struck Kylenin as very strange, for nowhere in the history of the world was it written that any human deserved the prestige of the Elemental Children, and he stared at her face while he contemplated why she was there.

She had long hair that flowed around her like the robes she wore. Her expression was sad, every detail so exquisite he could almost see longing in her stone eyes. He noticed the subtle difference of the corner of one eye and realized it was a tear. The icy shiver it sent down his spine made him back away from her and he closed his eyes, shaking his head to empty her forlorn image from his mind.

Only when he backed away from the fountain did he realize there was another sphere above the first. It was crystal clear and was held in place only by the force of the water shooting upward from the sphere below. As the water rushed toward it, combined with the light of the full morning suns, it created an illusion within the sphere, a tiny spark of energy existing only for itself. Kylenin could only stare in awe, captivated by the wondrous beauty of the shrine, his mission momentarily forgotten under the statue's poignant gaze.

In an open field nearly a mile from the edge of town, Dorwynn and Lilly were beginning their first official day of training. They were so far from the house that it couldn't be seen, and Lilly could barely hear the waterfall, though the soothing sounds of the water trickled past them as it followed the river toward Elikrede. Though spring had just begun, the grassy field was already a lush green and Lilly had to extinguish the desire to remove her shoes and run through the soft new blades of grass.

"We're going to focus on manipulation first," said Dorwynn, his voice snapping her from her daydreaming. She watched as he focused on a flat area of the field and held out his hand, his fingers spread wide, his palm toward the sky. Slowly he lifted his hand, his arm shaking slightly as though it bore an unseen weight. The area he focused his magick on began to glow before it rose from the ground and formed a small hill.

"You can already move things with your mind," he said as he lowered his hand, the new formation losing its glow, "even very large, heavy objects, like the boulders you moved with Voruum, but manipulating the Earth is more than just moving it. It is reshaping something stable, completely changing its structure or shape to form something different, yet equally stable. Bending the branch, which I've noticed you've abandoned, is one example. Forming a hill on flat land or a cave within a mountain are some others.

"As I told you before, you must connect with the natural energy of what you are trying to change. You must feel its energy as your own and lend your power to it. It will lend you its own power, making you one until you relinquish the connection. Are you ready to try?"

"Okay," said Lilly, her voice shaking with excitement and uncertainty. She focused on a flat area of the field, just as Dorwynn had done, and extended her hand in a similar manner. As she concentrated, she felt the familiar warmth of magick flowing through her hand. The ground began to glow, quivering in rhythm to her unsteady hand.

Dorwynn grinned at her progress and Lilly noticed his reaction, her heart beating faster with anticipation. Suddenly, the glowing mound of grassy earth began to quake violently. Panicked, Lilly tried to break the connection, but she found it was not so easily relinquished. The ground burst open as she withdrew her hand, clumps of glowing dirt scattering haphazardly in all directions. The ground where they landed seemed to absorb their energy, not yet detached from Lilly's, and they caused sharp stalagmite-shaped stones to emerge.

Dorwynn jumped as one of the glowing clumps landed at his feet, barely dodging the piercing tip of the rising stone. Lilly felt the sporadic energy of the magick as the connection finally broke, and looked at Dorwynn apologetically. He picked himself up from where he had fallen and dusted the dirt from his clothes.

"I am so sorry," said Lilly, cupping her hands over her mouth, her expression a mixture of amusement and surprise. "What happened?"

"Well," said Dorwynn exasperated, "it takes a lot to contain and direct your power. Before we continue, you need to make your wand. It will help you to localize where you direct your power, not to mention the connection is easier to break with a tool separating the magick."

"Okay, so how do I make my wand?"

"We go to town."

When they arrived at the house, Dorwynn trudged up the stairs to awaken Zephra, who was still despondent from last night's incident. Lilly was in such a good mood, however, that Zephra's attitude didn't bother her. Albeit during a forced dream, she had communicated across the doorway with a non-magickal human. It had been easier than she had expected. She'd simply dreamed of a telephone and there it had been, ready to be dialed.

She dared not tell Dorwynn about it yet. For one thing, he was in a great mood despite the mishap this morning, and for another, she knew the information she'd learned was personal. She'd wait until they were alone. If he wanted Zephra to know, he could tell her himself.

So after they had all eaten, they began the two-mile walk to town. On the way, they discussed Lilly's magick and the explanation of the previous night's events, which eased Zephra's worried mind and alleviated her temper. With things settled between them, Dorwynn planned how their time in town would be spent, assigning tasks to everyone.

"Lilly's going to the wand crafter's shop to buy items to *make* a wand." He looked at her pointedly. "Don't get one that's already crafted. You have to make your own to become a Master."

"You already told me that," Lilly pointed out.

"Right," he said. "Well, while you are shopping, Zephra and I will call upon your other teachers."

"I'll visit Ryzale!" exclaimed Zephra quickly. "You can visit the crazy man."

"He's not crazy," argued Dorwynn, "he's just…strange."

"He's more than strange," countered Zephra. "He's the most curious human I've ever encountered, and I've been around a long time."

"Fine," he sighed.

The rest of their conversation revolved around what the trainers would be discussing with the Arch Sorceress and apothecary who would take part in Lilly's magickal education. Lilly listened for a while to the vague banter about spells and potions, but as the city came into view, her attention shifted to absorb the rustic details of the quaint community through which they were walking. The road changed as they traveled it, from packed dirt to neatly spaced cobblestone, with several other stone roads converging with it along the way.

Zephra slowed her pace, paying closer attention to the houses as they passed. She stopped before a wrought-iron gate wrapped around a disheveled patch of land, a small cottage in the center that was nearly hidden by the unattended ivy climbing up the outer walls. The stone walkway was overgrown with the brown weeds of the previous year, its uneven stones clashing with the tidy street as it wound a path toward the recessed doorway of the house, sheltered only by a tiny awning.

"Have fun," sang Zephra as she opened the gate and walked through, letting it slam shut behind her with a loud CLANG!

"Is he really that bad?" asked Lilly as they continued down the road toward town. Dorwynn shrugged.

"Zephra doesn't bode well with anyone stranger than she, especially if they're human." Lilly noticed the twinkle in his eyes and smiled.

"I'll show you where the wand shop is," he said, "and then I'm off to see Tsirama. Do you think you can make your way home when you are finished? It's hard to predict how long I'll be. Tsirama is easily distracted. A ten minute conversation might take two hours."

"I'm sure I'll manage," she replied.

"And you have money?"

"If I say no, are you going to give me some?"

He smiled and shook his head, pleased their relationship was improving. They walked in silence down the narrow street toward the center of town. It ended on the circular main street and Lilly stopped, staring in awe at the huge fountain before her and the statue of a beautiful woman forever awaiting an embrace.

"The wand shop is there," said Dorwynn, pointing to a small building directly across from and between the woman and the faerie statues. "Are you sure you'll be alright alone?"

"I'll be fine," she said as she walked toward the shop, her eyes lingering on the fountain. "Good luck with the crazy potion guy."

She left him standing by the fountain and approached the shop, the butterflies in her stomach fluttering violently with every step she took as the reality of her fate settled into her mind. Very soon, she would have a wand. Very soon, she would be training in dangerous magick, not only with her trainers, but others as well. Very soon, her fate and the fate of the world would collide with a force so great that the entire world would turn to her for a savior. As she opened the door to the shop, she felt the weight of her destiny, knowing that once she stepped inside, her life would change forever.

She entered the shop and her senses were immediately bombarded by its strange ambience. As the door swung shut, the breeze it created swept through a pan flute mounted on the ceiling, alerting the shop keeper to a customer's arrival. The walls and floors were made of a light ashy wood, as were the tables and shelves lining the shop. The lighting cast a soft gray glow around the room like a shadow caused from a wispy cloud that had decided to block the suns. An acrid mixture of patchouli and anise wafted toward her nostrils, so thick she could almost taste black licorice, a candy she'd always despised.

The shelf nearest the doorway held a variety of finished wands, some highly ornate, others quite simple, while most were an assortment between the two. Most of the wands were of a similar pattern; smooth wooden wand shafts and marble handles inlaid with a gem or two. The simpler wands were made completely of wood, though the shafts and handles were made of different types, while the most ornate wand she found was made completely of stone. She picked it up. It was heavy, the flawlessly smooth shaft being formed of black stone, while the handle was made of what seemed to be white marble and was littered with many colored gems.

"May I help you?" asked a voice. Lilly whipped around, the wand still in her hand, to face the shop keeper. She quickly abandoned the wand, replacing it to its rightful place of the shelf.

"I need to make a wand," she blurted.

"I see," said the shop keeper. "You must be training to become a Master."

"Yes."

"All of the materials you should need can be found at the back of the store. I assume you know what materials you seek?"

"Not exactly."

The shop keeper, who was a tall, thin man with soft eyes and a gentle voice, reached past Lilly with his long arm and picked up the wand she'd been holding moments ago, turning it carefully in his hand.

"A wand is an extension of the one who uses it," he said. "Every detail, no matter how large or small, reflects not only the user, but the one by whose hand it was created. I make wands for many. They are functional tools which serve their purposes well, but when one creates their own wand, it retains not only the energy of the one by whom it was made, but also the creator's unique magickal signature. When finished, it is specific only to you. Others may use your wand, but only you will be a part of it, and that alone makes it all the more powerful.

"I made this wand many years ago," he said, staring at it lovingly. "It's quite ostentatious, wouldn't you agree? It was a custom order by a woman, who, oddly enough, never returned to claim it, although she paid a steep price for its creation." He returned the gaudy wand to the shelf. "Many choose finished wands by finding the one that suits them. It speaks to them, and so they know it is theirs. It is the same for those who decide to create their own. As you search the materials you require, wait for those which speak to you. They will become the wand that reflects you."

"Thanks," said Lilly, unsure how useful his advice would be.

The shop keeper turned away and began to rearrange the finished wands. Lilly walked past him toward the back wall of the shop. Long round canisters held a variety of sticks, separated by the type of wood from which they were derived and by their various lengths and girths. Gems of every shape, size and color were organized accordingly in neatly arranged bowls upon the shelves. Rough, unpolished stones were separated into piles on the table that lined the wall, ranging from different types of marble to glossy volcanic rock. There were even small pieces of metal, some no larger than slivers, divided and neatly organized in a single box with many tiny compartments.

Lilly lingered around the materials, waiting for something to *speak* to her as the shop keeper had instructed, but she heard nothing. She lifted her hand to the stones on the table, running her fingers lightly over their unfinished surfaces. At first, she felt nothing but cool, rough stone, but as her fingers found the pile of black marble, the warmth of magick spread through them.

This is it! she thought, picking through the pile until she found the one radiating heat. Though it had a few jagged edges, it was relatively smooth compared to many of the other stones. It was almost completely black, with only a tendril or two of gray twisting through it.

She continued her search for the rest of her wand materials, touching each set of items until she felt the same warmth, the sign that something was meant to be a part of her creation. A stick barely six inches long and no larger around than a dime she found next. Derived from what was called a Deshila tree, it was almost pure white, the grain barely darker than the wood itself. A description written below the canister containing the Deshila sticks explained that it was extremely strong and that, over time, it grew stronger by means of petrification. Lilly wondered how hard it would be to form and considered returning it, but the pull she felt from it was too strong, so she kept it and continued with her search.

Among the gems, Lilly chose only one; a clear crystal yet to be shaped. It was small, and though she searched through the many other beautiful gems that caught her eye, to her dismay, it was the only one she felt she needed. She stood admiring the atmosphere of the shop, which, she noticed, began to make her feel more relaxed and focused the longer she stayed within its walls.

With a sigh, she approached the shop keeper to pay for her findings, when something gave her pause. Though she had already walked halfway across the store, she sensed the familiar warmth calling to her. She returned, searching carefully for the item she'd missed. After what seemed an eternity, she finally found it: a tiny piece of silver no larger than her thumbnail radiated more heat than anything she'd already found.

A shiver of excitement traced its way down her spine and she knew, without a doubt, she was ready to form her wand. She waited for the shop keeper to finish convincing the customer who had entered the store behind her that the wand he was considering was hand-crafted with the utmost detail and that, should he buy that wand, it would serve him as if he had crafted it himself. As the customer took his time scrutinizing the Terrabok wand, holding its red marble handle firmly in his chubby hand, Lilly's impatience coursed through her. Finally, the chubby man fished his coins from the depths of his oversized pockets, dropped them into the shop keeper's palm and flashed them both a grin, minus one front tooth.

Lilly waited for the shop keeper to calculate her purchase, and at last left the store, the weight of her purchases replacing the thirty kerim from her much lighter money pouch. Lilly rushed to the house, and finding it was empty, she took advantage of the solitude to attempt her first task. After she carefully inspected the materials she'd purchased, their warm energy radiating through her hands, she held the stick with her left hand

and ran the fingers of her right hand over its smooth surface, trying to change its shape.

Nothing happened.

She sorted through the rest of her materials, arranging them in order for creation and sighed as she stared at them. Unsatisfied, she rearranged them three more times before frustration overcame her and she abandoned her efforts.

She looked around the kitchen, searching for the solution. Outside the window, the suns' warm rays filtered through the waterfall, a very faint prism flashing in the spray like a strobe light. Her materials in tow, she walked out the back door and into the huge yard that extended to the massive trees nestled at the base of the mountain. Several solitary trees were scattered between the house and the tree line wrapping around the yard, nearly concealing it from passersby. On the other side of the house, a waterwheel turned by the motion of the flowing river, and Lilly realized that it provided both the running water and what little electricity they used to the house. It never occurred to Lilly before how these small luxuries were afforded.

She walked past a garden plot overgrown with weeds and a sheltered gazebo-like structure, the floor paved with broad stones smoothed over with decades of wear, past a seemingly abandoned beehive and a large oak tree with a rope dangling lazily from a thick branch that hung over the water, before she finally saw what she knew was there. Across the river, a single tree sheltering a large boulder stood in the center of a distant meadow. Adrian has taken her there in her dream, and she had been there again in the dream she'd had the night she stayed in the cave.

She walked toward the waterfall to the spot where she and Zephra had descended from the cave, and after securing her possessions, she began to climb. Her muscles, still sore from climbing down only yesterday, screamed their protest. When she reached the top, she flopped onto her back to catch her breath, and then slowly got up and followed the rocky ledge behind the waterfall. She passed the cave, edging her way carefully along the ledge as it narrowed and then widened again into a rocky path that led into the meadow.

She hurried toward the boulder, climbing onto it with a deep sense of satisfaction. Though she had never actually been there before, the place was familiar...home. She gazed at the waterfall to find a brilliant rainbow could be seen from that angle, as full and as vibrant as the shining suns that created it. Immediately at ease, she once again sorted through the items she'd bought to create her wand and cleared her mind to focus on her task.

For nearly half an hour she toiled with her attempts at crafting her wand, but the only thing she managed to accomplish was levitating the block of marble before flinging it against the shade tree. She retrieved it, wondering why she was failing so miserably, when out of nowhere, Orvak entered her mind. Her senses clouded and the memory of her lesson with him flooded her thoughts.

What lesson have you learned today? her mind asked from some deeply buried level. She thought about her day, back to her morning lesson with Dorwynn. He'd told her that she needed a wand to direct her magick, but the longer she pondered it, the more she realized the problem: she was trying too hard.

She climbed onto the boulder again, the block of cold marble in her hand, and crossed her legs. After getting comfortable, she closed her eyes and focused, not on the marble, but on the peaceful serenity of her environment…the rush of the waterfall, the occasional chirping of birds, the slight rustling of the new leaves as the breeze blew through.

The block of marble in her hand began to radiate warmth, slowing working its way through her hands, and then her arms. In her mind, she began to see her finished wand, a white shaft twisted into a spiral much like a unicorn horn, with a thin strand of silver sunken into its groove, melded into a black marble handle formed to fit her hand perfectly. The single crystal entombed in its center was positioned to rest comfortably in her palm.

She opened her eyes, the image fresh in her memory, and reached for the gem, but a new realization gave her pause. The block of marble in her hand was now longer and thinner than before, enveloped precisely in her clenched right hand. The gem, quivering impatiently where it rested, flew suddenly into her outstretched hand. Lilly's surprise was replaced with determination, for she quite obviously had the power to manipulate these objects, and now, she knew what her wand would look like.

The blood in her hands pulsed with the energy of the objects she held. She closed her eyes again, imagining the crystal taking shape and sinking into the marble handle. Though her eyes were closed, she could sense the bursts of light exploding from the two very different stones as they became one. An image flashed in her mind, fleeting an instant later, though it seared itself in her memory. A star, its five points connected by a perfect circle, the symbol of the Goddess Divine, was the symbol Lilly embedded on the side of the handle opposite the crystal.

She thought reshaping the wood would be easier than the crystal and marble, but it proved to be much stronger than the other components. She managed uniting the stick with the handle simply by manipulating the marble to encase the lower inch of the twig. She held the warm chip of silver in one hand, the wand in the other, and concentrated.

Lilly could not see the magick surging from her hands, twisting around the wood as it slowly began changing into a long, spiral shaft. Nor could she see the small piece of silver melt in the air to form a thin ribbon that wound its way around the spiral and settled into its groove from base to tip. So absorbed in creating her wand, she failed to notice the subtle noises of the young man who had wandered toward her and was now leaning against the tree, watching her with the utmost interest.

The girl seemed surprised at her magick as she inspected her creation, as though she was only just coming into her powers. He could not recall having ever felt surprised by his magick. To him, it came as naturally as breathing, but he knew most children with magickal abilities began coming into their powers between the ages of three and five, and by seven, were under the tutelage of a Master. If they excelled, they often became an apprentice at fifteen and remained so until they completed their required tasks for their Master status. But an apprentice would be well-adjusted to magick by now, so the sight of her closing her eyes to do magick and being surprised at its results made her that much more of a mystery to him.

He wanted to speak to her, but he was afraid he would startle her, so he watched as she waved her new tool around, already trying to get used to it as an extension of her hand. When he could stand it no longer, he opened his mouth, but before he could utter a word, her voice floated to his ears.

"I know you are there," she said without looking at him. He froze, caught off guard, and waited for her to speak again. That same moment flooded his memory, for it was the dream he'd had of her, and as he suspected, she turned to face him. As before, her emerald eyes stunned him speechless, blazing with such light it was as though they created their own light. Once again, he wondered if they did.

"I'm not dreaming again, am I?" he asked after a moment. "You are real, aren't you?"

"Yes," she answered, jumping down from the boulder. "I'm real."

A wave of dizziness washed over her when her feet touched the ground. Kylenin noticed and immediately rushed toward her, helping her to sit on the ground. He reached into his pack and removed from it a small parcel containing two pastries. He offered one to her.

"Eat this," he said, handing it to her. "You've exhausted your strength. It will help."

Lilly took the food and are it quickly while Kylenin watched, amused. When she finished, he produced a water skein and held it out to her. She drank gratefully before she realized her mistake. Ashya had trained her to always scan her food and drink for danger, and she had not.

"Thank you," she said breathlessly as she handed it back to him. She waited a moment to see if she felt any effects of possible poison, but she relaxed as he gulped from the skein before returning it to his pack.

"I've had dreams about you," he admitted, his eyes almost silver in the bright sunlight.

"So have I. The duel, our meeting here, and others. Do you know what it means?"

"I have no idea," he laughed. "I just knew I had to find you."

She smiled, and they stood in silence, staring at each other, both struggling to keep the conversation going, but neither knowing exactly what to say. He observed how the sunlight bounced off her hair, weaving through it like spun copper. He noticed the small, teardrop birthmark beneath her eye and as a sudden shiver ran down his spine, he remembered the strange statue from the fountain in town.

"That's a nice wand," spouted Kylenin finally, shaking the image of the woman from his mind. "Your Master will be proud."

"I hope so," she sighed, confirming his suspicions that she was indeed an apprentice. "I hope it works. My powers are a bit beyond my control."

"Well, a wand will definitely help with that. Control has always been an obstacle with me, but all it takes is a little focus and a good tool."

"May I see your wand?"

He kept his wand in his belt, close at hand should he require it in a pinch. He whipped it out and handed it to her. She was surprised to find it was very similar to hers in shape, though its black spiraled shaft was nearly three inches longer, with a white marble handle and black gem where hers was clear. Instead of the pentacle she had formed on hers, the symbol on his was the triquatra, the same three-pointed symbol which Dorwynn had marked upon his own wand. It amazed her how similar they were, as though his was the photographic negative of her own, but even more than that, she was amazed that his was in the same spiral shape as hers, for she had seen none shaped like it in any of the finished wands in the shop. She handed it back to him.

"You made it yourself?" she asked.

"Eight years ago," he answered, "when my grandmother decided I should train magickally, mostly so I could learn control. Everything else always came pretty easily."

"What about your parents?"

"My mother died giving birth to me," he said, unsure why he was telling a complete stranger such personal information. "I never knew my father. I don't know who he is, but I have a feeling my grandmother does and she just won't tell me. What about you?"

"I never knew my mother," Lilly admitted, and Kylenin's interest was peaked at this similarity between them. "She abandoned us after I was born. My father raised me and my sister until I left to be trained."

Lilly didn't elaborate, for she didn't want to give more information than absolutely possible, but she felt a sense of familiarity with this young man who seemed so much like her. She was relieved that he didn't pry for more, choosing instead to discuss their impending duel.

"What of this duel we're supposed to have?" he asked. "Do you think it will happen?"

"I think so," she told him. "Why would we both dream of such a thing if it was not to happen? Unless, of course, you decide not to participate."

He wondered if she was thinking about the conversation they'd had in their dream, and her secretive smile confirmed it. He smiled and nodded. Satisfied, she nodded also.

"I suppose we'll settle on a date later?"

"I'm just beginning my training," she told him, "so I don't know when I will be available or prepared."

"Maybe I should challenge you now, before you become prepared. Then, perhaps, I will win."

"Are you worried?"

"A little, but if I must lose, I'm glad it will be your victory and not someone less worthy."

Lilly blushed at the compliment and Kylenin blushed as well, uncertain what would cause him to be so forward. He plucked at the grass beside them, both leaning against the boulder, until Lilly finally stood.

"Are you feeling better?" asked Kylenin as he also stood, concerned her use of magick had drained too much of her strength.

"Yes, thank you."

He knew he wasn't ready to leave, and neither did she seem to be, but he could think of no more to discuss at the moment. She looked toward the small cottage beyond the opposite shore of the lake, and finding no activity, she turned her gaze to the waterfall. He followed her glances, wondering after her thoughts, but he inquired about none of them. Instead, he waited for her to speak, hoping she would want to continue their first meeting by proposing the next topic of discussion.

"Do you live near here?" she finally asked.

"No. Do you?"

"In that house," she said, pointing to the cottage she'd previously looked upon. "For now, at least."

Silence enveloped them again. Kylenin felt his wand, warm against his skin, and an idea crossed his mind, though had he been in the presence of anyone else, he never would have considered speaking it. For reasons he did not know, he felt comfortable in her presence, more so than he'd ever felt in his life with any other, and he didn't want to let it go.

"Would you like me to teach you to use that thing?" he asked, motioning to the wand still resting in her hands. She looked at him, so surprised by the offer she was at a loss for words. "Have you learned defensive magick yet?"

"A little."

"Come. I will show you."

Lilly stood rooted to her spot, hesitant to use any magick outside the presence of her trainers. She knew nothing of this young man, but she doubted he could manage to escape her power should any mishaps occur. She shook her head, hoping he would change his mind, but he just stared at her with a small smile of his face, waiting for her to join him.

"I don't think it's a good idea," she said. "I'm new to my powers and I still have so much to learn, and truth be told, I have very little control over them."

"Then you have nothing to fear," he laughed, "for I am *not* new to mine and, on occasion, I still have a hard time with control. Trust me, it is a lifelong lesson." He noticed she was still hesitant, so he added, "I promise I won't let anything bad befall you."

"It's not myself I am worried about," she muttered. He laughed again.

"We'll start slowly," he assured her, "but, first…" He shook his wand toward the wide open space in the field and the ground rumbled as five long, smooth, narrow stones, each roughly seven feet tall, rose from it and formed a circle with enough space in the center for the two of them to move comfortably. "…a namun, to contain whatever does go beyond our control."

Lilly smiled at him, awe and admiration reflected in her bright eyes. Her confidence restored, she walked toward the monument and stood at its center. The rush of energy uplifted her as its warmth made her pulse quicken, and the wand she just made was quivering as though it was excited at the prospect of being used. She touched one of the stones and found it warm and alive, the magick flowing through it so great that she was sure she heard a low hum echoing within the confines of the namun.

Kylenin entered the circle also, unable to tear his eyes away from her. He couldn't shake the feeling that he had met her before, and while he was content to blame the feeling on his many dreams of her, deep inside his mind he knew there was more to it than could ever be explained by something as simple as dreams. Perhaps they had known each other in a past life, perhaps it *was* just because of the dreams. Whatever the reason, he cared not, for he had found her.

"Have you learned any offensive magick yet?" he asked, and her thoughts immediately flew to the harpy attack, though she dared not tell him about that. She felt comfortable around him, as though they had known each other forever, but he was still a stranger and trust was not something she gave easily.

"Not really," she admitted. "I've only just begun my training beyond the basics. This morning was my first lesson."

"Really?" Kylenin didn't try to hide his surprise, for he had seen her use her powers to form her wand, so he knew she knew how to use magick, but it did explain her surprise when she had finished and why she closed her eyes during the process. "How was it?"

"It was terrible. I almost killed my trainer because I was trying too hard."

Kylenin laughed. "What did he do?" he asked.

"He told me I needed a wand," she replied matter-of-factly. He laughed again.

"Well, you now have a wand. Would you like to use it?"

"If you insist, but you've been warned."

Kylenin laughed again, and he realized how good it felt to find humor in something, anything. Humor and laughter had never been on Dagana's list of priorities. Thinking of his grandmother made him dread the thought of having to return to her, but for now, he was going to enjoy every minute until that time, so he pushed her from his thoughts and took out his wand.

"So what, exactly, are you being taught?" he asked, twisting his wand between his thumbs and forefingers.

"Earth Magick," she replied. "I'm training to be a Master, so I have to learn how to accomplish all of the tasks that come with it."

"Have you done any of them yet?"

"Only my wand, so far."

"Then I will show you how to manipulate earth. It's the basis for the magick you'll use for most of your tasks."

He aimed his wand at the ground, and as Lilly watched the wispy swirls of light flow from his wand toward her feet, the ground beneath them rose slowly, lifting her with it. She grinned at him, her eyes bright.

"Now, you try," he said as he disconnected from the magick. She still seemed hesitant, but she aimed her wand toward an unoccupied piece of ground and closed her eyes, to which Kylenin shouted, "No!" Her eyes flew open. "Keep your eyes open. That's part of your problem. You see it in your mind, which is fine, but when you open your eyes, your power flows too strong for you to contain it."

Lilly sighed and aimed her wand again, willing the earth to submit to her. When nothing happened, she lowered her arm and turned toward Kylenin.

"That's why I close my eyes," she said, frustrated. "I can't seem to call the magick forward unless I do, but afterwards, it blows up in my face."

"So, control isn't so much an issue as focus," he said. He came up behind her, close enough that he could whisper in her ear, and spoke in a low, soothing voice. "Magick is everywhere. It is in each stone, each blade of grass, each grain of sand. You are able to call the magick and use it, or you wouldn't have been able to form your wand. When you closed your eyes, you were able to focus on it, but that was stone in your hand. The ground which you are trying to manipulate is attached to that which you are not trying to change. When you close your eyes, you are feeling all of its magick, and you are using all of it, but you are trying to contain what wants to be used, so it escapes your control.

"Keep your eyes open. Look at your target and determine what you want to change and what you want to remain left alone. Use the magick of the parts you want to remain unchanged to keep it there. Its own magick will help to naturally contain that which you use, and because the natural magick is dispersed more evenly, whatever magick you direct will be more focused."

Lilly listened to his words, his slow, patient description of magick sinking into her mind as Ashya's instruction had, for she felt almost as comfortable with him…almost. She pushed thoughts from her head and stared at the ground, narrowing her focus only on the piece of earth she wanted to move and drawing an imaginary circle around it with her mind as a barrier to keep the surrounding ground firmly in place. She raised her wand, aimed it toward the center of her imaginary circle and slowly released the magick building inside her.

The ground quivered as tendrils of silvery light left her wand and flowed into it, lifting it slowly at first, and then faster as her heart pounded with excitement. She felt herself growing cold, the only warmth left in her body centered in her chest and down her right arm to her hand, which held her wand. She pulled away from the magick easily, though slowly, and her chilled body grew warm again. When she had finished, a hill no more than three feet high replaced the flat piece of ground where she had envisioned the circle.

"You see?" cried Kylenin enthusiastically. "A little more practice and it will begin to come naturally. In time, you and your wand will become so connected that it will seem to know what you are thinking and the magick you are casting will become instantaneous and exact."

"How often do you practice?" asked Lilly, still glowing with the excitement if her achievement.

"Every day," he replied. Her surprised expression prompted him to explain further. "I have used my wand at least once every day since I formed it. It creates such a bond that it cannot be easily broken, if at all. Should my enemy ever take it from my grasp in an attempt of harm against me, it would only backfire. Besides, diligence is one thing my grandmother demanded from me. She says that practicing magick daily keeps your feet swift, your hand steady and your mind sharp."

"She sounds like a wise woman."

"I wouldn't say that. She pushed me so hard I lost complete control over my powers for six months."

"When did you get control back?"

"I've been in town for two days now."

Lilly laughed, and as she looked at him, his gray-blue eyes bright with amusement, she was overwhelmed again by a sense of familiarity so great she wondered if they had met before. Of course, she was sure if she'd met an elf in the past, she would have remembered it. Still, there was something in his presence that made her feel as if they had known each other forever. *Who knows,* she thought, *maybe we have.*

Lilly was about to give voice to her thoughts when she heard Dorwynn and Zephra having a conversation in her head. They were walking toward the house from town, discussing how Lilly's schedule would work between her two new teachers.

"Well," she sighed, "I hear my trainers coming home. I'd better go. It was a pleasure, um…what is your name?"

Kylenin wanted, more than anything, to tell her the truth, but he was afraid she would find out who he was and he would lose her company, something he couldn't bear to imagine.

"The name's Wyatt," he said, holding out his hand in an official introduction, "and you are Lilly, right?"

"Yes, I am."

Smiling, she extended her hand, and as her skin touched his, a bright light flashed behind her eyes and sent a searing pain through her head. She quickly dropped his hand, allowing the strange symptoms to abate before studying his face for signs that he had experienced them as well, but it seemed he had not.

"If you would like, I can help you some more, even if only to practice."

The incident she just had seemed to escape his notice, and she was torn by his offer. It had to mean something. Then again, Ashya had told her to take advice whenever it was offered. The pleading look in his eyes convinced her that he posed no threat.

"I would like that," she said honestly, "but I don't know when I will be available between all of my lessons."

"Well," he said, ecstatic she had agreed to meet him again, "you can leave a message for me at the large inn in town, the only one with stables."

"I'll do that," she promised, "but can I ask you not to mention it to my trainers? I wouldn't want to offend them."

"It'll be our little secret," he said, winking at her. She smiled. "Goodbye, Lilly."

"Goodbye, Wyatt," she echoed, and as she made her way back to the house, she felt the resonance of his touch as clear as she could feel the rush of the waterfall cool against her skin, and was puzzled by what it meant.

The Curse of Broken Allegiance

Lord Rimetak fastened the last of his armor, and tugging at the joints to ensure everything was secure, he studied his appearance in the round mirror of his wife's vanity. The last time he'd been in his suit was nearly sixteen years ago, and though he had gained a few extra pounds since then, it still fit him quite well.

He'd been in the service of the queen then, her strategic advisor and the commander of her vast army. During the seven years prior to his discharge, his time was spent recruiting warriors, studying their fighting skills and training them to perfect their natural advantages. The queen supplied her army with weapons forged in the depths of Castle Ridaska by a group of renegade dwarves who had sworn their loyalty to her. The weapons were unlike any that mere humans could create, much stronger and made with metals that humans had yet to discover, let alone attempt to manipulate. Only the most powerful were able to work the metals as dwarves could, which made their weapons a valuable commodity. The queen, upon bestowing such a gift, required each of her warriors to swear loyalty to her alone by speaking a rite of allegiance which could not be broken without dire consequence.

Lord Rimetak had also sworn his allegiance to Dagana, the oath that bound him forever as her servant. At the time, his plans for the future were to fight for her and most likely die in battle. In fact, he had been in the middle of preparing soldiers for storming Nurzia, a suicide mission, by all rights, when Dagana had changed her plans, postponing any action until further notice. She had granted him a lordship on the spot and then sent him away until such time as she wished to proceed.

Yesterday, that time arrived. She had summoned him magickally, the notice arriving just as he sat to enjoy breakfast with his wife, Sarah, and their two children, Oliver, barely eleven years old, and Charlotte, only seven. The syrup he poured from the crystal decanter his wife had fashioned during her years of magickal training had yet to reach his pancakes when a letter bearing the Dagana's seal materialized in midair, hovering ominously over the breakfast sausage.

"What is it?" asked Sarah, her eyes bright with worry.

Lord Rimetak plucked the scroll from the air, broke the seal and read it, his curious expression melting into one of frustration and anger. With a sigh, he read the letter to his family.

"Lord Rimetak, your services are required at Castle Ridaska. The queen requests you arrive by sunset tomorrow, bearing arms."

"What are you going to do, Oliver?" asked Sarah.

"What else can I do?" was his disheartened reply. "I have no choice. I must go."

"Of course you have a choice!" yelled Sarah when they were alone in their quarters. He began to dig in the large closet in search of his armor, which had been buried beneath thirteen years of accumulated refuse. "You don't have to go, Oliver. It's been sixteen years. You have a life here now."

"A life afforded me by the queen," he pointed out. "A life that will not exist if I do not keep my oath."

"And what of your family?"

He sighed as he pulled the last of his armor from the closet and dropped it in the pile with the rest. He looked at his wife, her dark eyes as solemn as ever against her tanned skin and equally dark hair, and he was struck by her beauty as much at that moment as the first time he ever saw her.

"My allegiance was sworn to the queen before we were married. It takes precedence above all else. You know it must."

Sarah pursed her lips tightly and crossed her arms in defiance, her stubborn nature bubbling beneath her socially proper exterior.

"Well, she is not *my* queen. I've sworn no such oath to her."

Lord Rimetak was across the room in a flash. He grabbed his wife by her upper arms with such a firm grip, she winced in pain.

"Don't talk like that," he said in a low voice, his eyes blazing. *"Never* speak ill of her. Do you understand me?" Sarah nodded, fear swimming in her beautiful eyes. He released his grip, ashamed of himself for causing her such fright. "If she knew the way you speak, the way you feel, she would kill you without hesitation. The children, too. I could not bear that loss. Promise me you will never speak ill of the queen, no matter how evil she may be."

"If she is so evil," whispered Sarah as she drew close to his ear, "why do you still serve her? Break your fealty to her and give it to your family. Stay here with us."

"It is for the safety of my family that prevents me from doing just that. An oath to the queen is magickally binding. You, above all others, understand the mystery of magick, but you have no idea how far her powers reach and how much force is behind them."

"And if you die doing her bidding?" she shouted, pulling away from him. "What then?" Lord Rimetak pulled his frustrated wife into his arms and gently brushed a strand of her dark hair from her face, his hazel eyes locking with hers.

"Then I shall die knowing you and the children are safe and well. A man cannot hope for a more honorable death than that."

Sarah nodded as angry tears streamed down her face. She wiped them away with the sleeve of her dress, and after casting a disparaging look toward the pile of armor, she walked silently toward the closet and pulled his helmet from the corner of a high shelf.

"You'll need this," she said bitterly, shoving it into his hands.

"Sarah," he said as she walked toward the door. She stopped, her hand on the knob, and turned to face him.

"Don't!" she snapped. "I love you, Oliver, with all of my heart, but I refuse to applaud this undertaking you so obstinately pursue. How can you expect me to approve of you leaving us? What kind of a mother would that make me?"

She left him standing in the center of the room, slamming the door hard behind her to show she would discuss it no further. The rest of her morning was spent in search of things to not only occupy her time, but that provided a reasonable excuse to placate the children so they would not suspect she was purposely avoiding their father. Lord Rimetak knew, but rather that upsetting his family by arguing, he left his wife with her thoughts and occupied his children by allowing them to help polish his armor.

"Will you be going into battle, father?" asked his son with wide eyes. He had his mother's dark brown eyes; deep, liquid eyes full of curiosity and wonder.

"I don't know, Oli," said Lord Rimetak as he buffed his breastplate to a mirror shine.

The whole of the armor was as black as a night with no moon, adorned only with a red dragon centered upon the breastplate, the mark of Dagana's seal.   His helmet was magnificent, fashioned with two spiraled horns just above his ears.   A sterling black sword added the final touch, a single ruby resting within the cross-section of the hilt.   As he continued polishing the pieces, he recalled how menacing he had once looked wearing it, mounted on a steed fashioned in matching pieces across the chest and over the haunches, and a helmet uniquely designed to both protect and fight, for a spiral horn twisted from the forehead to a long, fine point.

He was not planning to take the horse's armor, afraid its added weight would overwhelm his steed on the journey to the castle, and he answered such when little Charlotte inquired about it.

"You must take it, Daddy," she said, her voice filled with concern.

"My horse will tire fast, love, if I take it," he explained gently.   "If there is a need for it, the queen is sure to provide proper battle armor."

"No!" she shouted, her small voice so loud that Rimetak jumped. "You must take *that* armor."

She looked into his eyes, a perfect match to her own in every way save one: hers blazed with her mother's fiery determination and stubborn nature.   The little girl leaned close to her father and whispered in his ear.

"It will save you, Daddy.   You have to take it with you."

She looked at him with such fierceness and pleading that he made the promise to his daughter, his mind swimming as he tried to figure any reasonable explanation for his daughter's eerie request.   It stayed with him the entire day as the horse's armor was sought, found and polished, and through their evening supper, which was kept in near silence by Sarah's refusal to acknowledge her husband.

That night, he dismissed the children's nanny and stayed with them, reading their favorite storybooks to them until they fell asleep. Afterward, he retired to his room and crawled into bed, wrapping his arms around his sleeping wife, where he slept without moving until morning broke.

He rose silently and dressed, the thought of leaving his family an unwelcome and unavoidable intrusion to the dreams he'd just had. Sarah's even breathing told him she was asleep, but as he kissed her forehead, she opened her eyes.

"Good morning, beautiful," he whispered, and she smiled as she always did when he addressed her in such a way, though tears formed in her eyes.

"I love you," was all she said, and it was all that was needed to be said. As he echoed the sentiment, it was all he could do to keep from shedding his own tears.

Moments later, he was racing toward Castle Ridaska. With his horse fitted in the heavy armor, the day-long journey was arduous. Had he been able to spare the time to change the armor, he would have changed horses, but then, without the armor his horse would have fared much better. If he only thought he regretted the armor during the trip, when he arrived at the castle, he was certain of his regret. The queen was pacing before the castle gates, a scowl marking her disapproval over being made to wait for him to arrive. The scowl changed at further inspection of his appearance to a look of utter satisfaction.

Yes, of his regret, he was certain.

"Lord Rimetak," said Dagana regally, "you never fail to surpass my expectations. The war has yet to commence and here you are, ready to charge into battle."

"Yet, Your Majesty?" he asked as he dismounted. Dagana waved her hand toward an old, pale stable hand.

"Groom!" she shouted. "Relieve this animal at once." She turned toward Lord Rimetak. "Really, Oliver, I would have thought you knew why I sent for you. After all, you are the most strategic person I've ever met."

"Thank you, Your Majesty."

"There is something different about you," she said, studying his manner. "Tell me, what has life brought you these years we've been apart?"

"A wife, Majesty, and two children."

"Ah, yes...children." She uttered the word with disapproval. "Children have a tendency to make a person soft, and yet, you came without question. Why?"

"I swore my loyalty to you first, my queen. I am a man of honor."

"Indeed." They walked toward the castle, Rimetak keeping an even pace with the queen as she walked. "If you want to return to you family, you need only say the word."

Had her offer been genuine, he would have been surprised, but he knew this woman well enough to know that she was testing the words he had spoken only moments ago.

"I live to serve you, my queen," he spouted, bowing to her. "The children have their mother to attend to them, plus a fine nanny to assist. I will serve you until such time as you choose to relieve me."

"As I said, you never fail to surpass my expectations." She stopped walking and looked him in the eye, her own eyes gleaming with an emotion he didn't recognize. Her lips curled into a frightening smirk, sending a chill down his spine. "Come," she purred. "We have much to discuss."

He found as he listened to her speak that he could easily slip back into the routine of her warfare council, not necessarily because he wanted to, but because strategy was something he had always been good at. Chess was his favorite game and he had won against every person who had ever challenged him. The one person who even came close to making him fall, oddly enough, was little Charlotte.

"What say you of my reputation?" asked Dagana, snapping his mind away from his family.

"I believe your idleness these many years has raised more fear and question than any of your previous activity."

"Yes," she agreed, "which is why, for now, our activity shall remain minimal. Until the need for certain actions arrive, all our effort will focus on strategy and preparation. Come, I want to show you something."

She led him through the castle, her footsteps echoing throughout the massive halls, to the doorway and up the winding staircase into the circular tower which sheltered her altar room. It was designed to her particular tastes, with elaborate fixtures on the walls, each of which held a long, black candle, and a large tapestry depicting an elfin queen on her throne, surrounded by her bowing subjects. The table before it was large enough to support the many magickal items she commonly used: decanters of potions for removing the effects of aging, a cauldron surrounded by bottles of magickal ingredients for those potions, a marble mortar and pestle, a wooden stand that held her wand on the occasion she decided not to carry it, and a crystal ball mounted on a sterling silver pedestal, the three legs of which were formed in the shape of dragon feet.

Beside the table, on a book stand nearly four feet tall, rested a large book containing maps of Buthania. It stretched almost seven feet wide when it was open, as it was now, the pages reflecting a map that included the entire mass of land that was Buthania. Rimetak was surprised at the sheer size of the book, and he wondered where she had found such a treasure. She answered his question before he had the chance to ask.

"I spent much of my time collecting over the years," Dagana stated, the wave of her hand flipping the pages from across the room. It stopped on a detailed cartograph of Elikrede, and Rimetak noticed the very distinct symbol at its center, for five common roads converged there to form the points of a pentacle. It was the symbol of the Goddess, and though he had never been there, he knew it was among the oldest of towns ever established, and one of the few that had avoided falling victim to the expanding blight of a metropolis.

"The past few years," the queen continued, "were spent scribing the maps I collected into this book."

"You made this, my queen?" asked Rimetak without bothering to hide his surprise. He regretted it instantly, hoping the queen would not take offense to his tone, but she did not notice as she stared lovingly at her creation.

"I did," she said in a voice so gentle it unnerved him. When she continued, however, her icy tone returned. "'Tis the only way the magick would bind to the map."

"What magick?" asked Rimetak.

Dagana's eyes gleamed as she told him what she had discovered. He listened, half in terror, half in awe, as she described the process of creating the book, scribing each map carefully with a concoction of ink and blood. Her blood, she told him, bound the magick of the book to her, but it was her grandson's blood that gave the maps their unique power: the power to see and track magickal signatures. He was dumbfounded by her declaration about her grandson, but even more so by the words she spoke next.

"He has the ability to see magick. Of course, you understand how rare a gift that is." Rimetak nodded, absorbing her words. "It still has its limits, mind you. I haven't been able to magickally obtain the identity of a signature that catches my attention, but none so important have attracted me thus far. Should one require further investigation, I shall accept the undertaking personally. Also, if one with the ability to see magick should look upon the book, they, too, would have the ability to see the magickal signatures, but to all others, it is merely a large book of maps. All in all, it is quite a unique object, wouldn't you agree?"

"Yes, Your Majesty. Your grandson must be very talented."

"He is," she agreed, a smile playing at her lips as her eyes danced with another piece of information, "and there is more. He is heir to the Elfin throne, and quite possibly the Chosen One."

"From the prophecy?!" Rimetak couldn't hide his shock at this bit of information. Dagana was all but grinning. "Are you sure?"

"Well, I did say 'possibly'," she pointed out. "My fool of a daughter ran off with Prince Alberic. She returned years later, alone, dying and about to give birth. The child would have died had I not saved him."

"But the prophecy. Why would you believe...?"

"When Laurel disappeared with Alberic," she interrupted, "I searched the land for them. They could not be found. I assume they went to Earth, for it would have taken more magick than either could have mustered to hide themselves from me for so long. Alberic is still missing, which makes me believe he is no longer in this world. Why else would he have abdicated his throne, unless he is dead, which is something else I have considered. Besides, does the prophecy not predict 'blood from two royal lines'?"

"I believe so, Your Majesty."

She gave a curt nod, as though his compliance confirmed her suspicions as truth, and closed the large book from across the room.

"May I inquire of your plans, Your Majesty?"

She smiled at him, her eyes so luminous that he almost regretted not listening to Sarah and declining to return to the queen. Deep in his bones he felt that she would be his end. He expected she had many new desires since he had last been in her presence, so he didn't expect her response.

"I want him on the Elfin throne." Rimetak was stunned into silence. "Come, let us get you more comfortable, and I shall reveal the new course of action we will take to make that dream our new reality."

She whirled away from him and out the door, and he trudged behind her, a fresh wave of dread nearly drowning him. She still wanted Nurzia. Ruling the humans wasn't enough for her; she had to have the Elfin throne as well. He sighed as he followed her to his chambers.

As he expected, her plans were to gather allies and build an army, so that, should her "agreeable" manner of obtaining the throne fail, she would have them at her disposal to take it by force. His job was to continue where it had stopped; recruit and train, although she had more for him than he ever imagined.

"I want you at my right hand," she said as she finished detailing her plans. "Now that you are here, I shall send word to allies already loyal, as well as those so far undecided. We shall hold our own council. I want your expertise to convince them to rally to our side."

"What makes you think I can convince them, Your Majesty?"

"This time," she said pointedly, "we shall prepare slowly, take our time to plan ahead, calculate each move before we execute. When the time for war is at hand, we shall come down on our enemies with such force, they'll be dead before they know that war has come."

She spoke with such passion, Rimetak believed victory was possible. Satisfied she had convinced him, she poured two glasses of blood red wine, and after handing one to him, she raised her glass.

"To victory," she said.

"To victory," echoed Rimetak, draining his glass as if to wash away the doubt of his precarious situation. She left him alone after that, the wine bottle next to his bed, and he drank the rest before collapsing into a dead sleep.

Ryzale

Lilly sat on her bed and stared at the blank pages of her journal. Between accomplishing her first task that day and the news that tomorrow she would meet the first of her two teachers, her nerves were frazzled, preventing her from falling asleep. After pacing her floor for an hour, and then skimming through a book or two, she'd finally settled on writing in her journal to help her relax, but even that was an impossible task. Pride and anticipation battled for her attention.

She felt like taking a walk, but it was pitch black outside; clouds had rolled in that evening, blocking the moon and stars. She wouldn't be able to make her way to town to visit her new friend, Wyatt, and she didn't dare attempt to try crossing the narrow ledge behind the waterfall in complete darkness. She couldn't even go downstairs for fear she would wake Dorwynn. She would have welcomed the company had he been awake, but he'd had a rough few days as well and really needed some rest.

Her only option, therefore, was to stay in her room until she could fall asleep. She closed her journal and set it across the top of the books on the shelf beside her bed, and then she stretched out on the bed to contemplate, once again, what so desperately clung in her mind.

After her impromptu lesson with Wyatt, she had returned to the house, her new wand in her hand. Dorwynn had inspected it carefully, and seeming both pleased and impressed, he returned it to her with his congratulations for the completion of her first task.

"Training will be much easier now," he had said. Lilly hadn't missed the relief that washed over him as he said it.

Over dinner, Dorwynn and Zephra had relayed the details of her education. Lilly would train with the sorceress Ryzale, the apothecary Tsirama and Dorwynn for five hours a day, each for two days a week. When her lessons ended each day, Zephra would spend an hour training her in combat. The remaining hours of the day, plus one day a week, were hers to do with what she wished.

She thought immediately of Wyatt and his offer to help her with her training to fill some of that spare time, and for a moment, she'd considered telling Dorwynn and Zephra about him, but something had stopped her. Even now, thinking about telling them of Wyatt gave her a strange feeling. Maybe it was because she was afraid they wouldn't let her train outside of their plans, maybe it was something more. Whatever it was, she decided to keep him a secret, at least for a little while.

She sighed and rolled off the bed, her mind no less cluttered, her excitement no more diminished. Unable to stand the confinement of the room any longer, she flung the door open and as quietly as possible, she wandered through the house. The single candle she carried was her only light, casting elongated shadows that crept along the walls as she moved down the stairs.

Dorwynn was sprawled on the sofa, snoring softly, one arm dangling over the edge. As Lilly reached the bottom step, he stirred and rolled onto his side. She froze, her hand between him and the candle's flame to block him from the light. Deciding she was foolish to risk waking him, she turned to go back to her room, but when the flame was blown out by the breeze of her sudden turn, she saw it: In the complete darkness of the house, a faint green glow floated just above her head.

She moved carefully up the stairs toward the barely-visible line of light. She realized when she reached the top step that it seemed to be on the floor, hovering mysteriously, and yet it was so dim, it illuminated nothing. Feeling her way through the darkness, Lilly approached it until her fingers felt the wall above it, which was no wall at all, but a door...her door. Her hand shook as she found the knob, and she held her breath as she turned it slowly, wondering what she would find.

There was nothing in her room but the same line of green light on the floor behind her table. She set the unlit candle on the table as she found her way around it. She reached for the light, but her fingers only found the place where the wall and the floor intersected. There didn't seem to be enough space through which any light could pass, yet it was there, waiting for Lilly to unlock its secrets.

Lilly rose and found the bed. She slid her hand under her pillow to retrieve her wand and returned to the strange glow that seemed to be calling her to it like a lighthouse guiding a ship home from sea. Her wand pointed at the mystifying object, she closed her eyes and tried to imagine it doing something, anything, but she knew before she even opened her eyes that it hadn't changed.

She spent the next hour trying to force a change in the snake-like glow, but no matter what she tried, it remained a constant fixture along the bottom of the wall, a teasing reminder that she wasn't nearly as powerful as she thought. Fatigue finally found her and giving up, she crawled into the bed and fell asleep at once, her wand still in her hand.

"Lilly!"

Kylenin was sitting on the boulder where he had first met her, thinking about the time they'd spent together earlier that day, and out of nowhere, she appeared beside the lone tree.

"Wyatt," she said, surprised, "what are you doing here?"

"Thinking of you, as a matter of fact." He grinned and jumped to the ground with ease. "What are *you* doing here?"

"I don't know," she replied quietly. "Are we really here? The last thing I remember is getting into bed."

"Another dream," he stated. "You must be thinking of me, too."

"Not before I fell asleep, but I guess I am now." She smiled, shaking her head. "I'm so confused."

"Why?"

"Everything. A year ago, I didn't even know magick existed. Now, I have powers beyond anything I ever thought possible, I see odd things that make no sense to me, though they seem familiar, and this. How can we be having a conversation in a dream and we can both remember it? I mean, you knew my name because I told it to you in a dream, but we haven't met before today. It was just a dream."

"Was it?" His gray-blue eyes bore into her emerald ones. "After all, we *are* communicating. Maybe it's some sort of subconscious telepathy."

"Are you telepathic?"

"Among other things," he said as he sat beneath the tree. She wondered about the amused tone of his voice, but before she could ask about it, he inquired, "So, what odd things have you seen?"

She sat on the ground in front of him and told him about the strange green light that had occupied her time before falling asleep, how it seemed to come from nowhere and how she only noticed it when the entire house was dark. He listened patiently to her detailed explanation, nodding as if he knew exactly what she was describing.

"It's probably a tasil," he told her. "It's a magickal entrance to a hidden area. They can be as small as a box, so as to hide a single item, or large enough to conceal an entire room. It is rather strange, though, that you can see it. Usually, they can only be seen by the one who created it."

"So why can I see it, and how do I open it?"

He shrugged. He was used to the unexplainable when it came to magick, but even he had never heard of someone being able to see a tasil unless the creator had left it open.

"I see you fell asleep holding your wand," he said, changing the subject. She glanced at her hand, only just realizing she held her wand. After studying it for a moment, she set it on the ground beside her. It instantly disappeared and Kylenin couldn't help but laugh at her shocked expression before explaining to her that it was only with her in the dream because her mind knew she was holding onto it.

"I'm sure when you wake, you'll find it lying beside you on the bed," he told her, still chuckling.

"Dreams are so strange," she said. "All dreams aren't like this, though. I've had other dreams of you, dreams I wasn't a part of. Are those real, too? And the dream of our duel. That hasn't happened yet. What makes this dream so different?"

"I'm not sure, but I had dreams like that, too, and each time I did, I woke up with the desire to find you, to discover who you are and *why* I kept dreaming of you. Perhaps that desire formed the connection between us?"

"But what's the connection, and why would we dream of each other before the connection was formed?"

Kylenin plucked at the grass on which he sat, wishing he knew the answers. When he lifted his eyes, Lilly was staring at him, her eyes hungry for the answers he couldn't provide.

"I don't know," he admitted, "but there's a significance to the way people are connected that stretches far beyond anything I can explain. As far as the other dreams, they are probably nothing more than dreams. Why, I had one of you not long ago where you were in a forest and you stopped time completely, and then you took control over someone with magick...true magick. Don't get me wrong, but a person with your limited magickal experience wouldn't have that strength to use that kind of magick, let alone survive the aftereffects. It just goes to show that sometimes dreams are nothing more than dreams."

Lilly wasn't convinced by his argument, nor his nonchalant attitude, for her heart was now racing wildly. He had just described that terrible night in Arthidgen, so she knew his dream had significance, but nothing would make her correct his view that it was a mere dream. She couldn't tell him that it had actually happened. She was now certain that all dreams, no matter how trivial they seemed at the time, were significant in some way, and the dream she'd had of him calling demons from the ground jumped into her mind.

"What's wrong?" asked Kylenin. Her heart skipped a beat, suddenly afraid he would somehow figure out the horrifying truth she didn't want him to know.

"Nothing," she replied hastily. "I was wondering if you might be wrong. Don't you think dreams might be future predictions, that maybe you are seeing something that hasn't happened yet?"

"It's possible, I suppose, but as it hasn't happened yet, there is no guarantee that it will."

"How can you say that?" she cried. "Even you believe we'll have a duel, simply because you dreamed it."

"Yes," he said slowly, thinking back to the dream, his torn ear, her healing touch, "but if one of us decides not to participate in a duel against the other, then the dream isn't a prediction. It may be a *possible* future event, but never certain. As soon as someone has knowledge of the future, they have the ability to change it. Once changed, the prediction once again becomes only a dream; the vision, only an imagined possibility. Does that make sense?"

Lilly nodded as she recalled Ashya's similar explanation of seeing the future. It did make sense, but her mind was overflowing with more questions. Why did he dream of that night in Arthidgen when she took control of Dorwynn? He couldn't change it now, for it had already happened. Why had she dreamed of him releasing those evil creatures from below? Had it already happened, or was it something she dreamed so that she could stop it from happening? Most of all, why were they dreaming together, as they were right now, with the ability to interact and remember everything? She had communicated with Dorwynn's dad on Earth, but she had tried to do that, and she had communicated with Beth shortly after arriving, but Beth was her sister, so she knew what that bond was. What was her connection to him?

"Do you think," she asked after a moment of quiet contemplation, "that we are able to communicate telepathically while we're awake?"

"I'm sure we can. After all, if we can do this while we're asleep, it would make sense that we could easily communicate with our minds while we're awake. Would you like to try it sometime?"

"After my lesson tomorrow," she said quickly, jumping at the chance to practice this magick. "I should be done by mid-afternoon. Since you are more experienced, I think you should contact me."

"Okay," said Kylenin, chuckling. "Tomorrow, then."

"Tomorrow."

She smiled as his image faded from her mind and was replaced with darkness, where a warm bubble of protection surrounded her, suspending her weightlessly in space. She could see nothing in the absence of light, having no clue to where they were, but she could feel him nearby, his presence as familiar to her as her own heartbeat.

As the first rays of morning spilled through the window and across her face, she woke and stretched lazily, knocking her wand from her bed where she'd abandoned it in her sleep. In the dim light of morning, she could no longer see the green light that had puzzled her the night before, but she decided, for now at least, its secrets could wait. She had more than enough new discoveries waiting for her…new lessons to learn, new questions to be answered, new magick to attempt.

The anticipation that had kept her from sleeping the night before flooded her once again, and refreshed, she jumped excitedly from the bed, dressed quickly and snatched her wand from the floor before flying down the stairs to begin the new day.

"Are you paying attention?"

The sorceress Ryzale had asked that question six times since Lilly had arrived only an hour ago. It wasn't that she was purposely letting her mind wander, but Lilly's excitement had quickly turned to boredom as Ryzale began lecturing in great detail on the different types of magick, something Lilly had already learned and was starting to understand more and more with each passing day from her own unorthodox experiences.

Lilly had tried explaining this to Ryzale, but the woman's stern eyes reinforced her strict tone as she snapped, "Don't interrupt!"

She tried to pay attention, but her thoughts soon drifted to the tasil. Wyatt hadn't told her it was a word from the *Doret Gaia*, but Lilly was certain it was. She wondered if a command from the language would open it and, wishing she could remember the language, she tried to clear her mind, hoping the solution would present itself and the words would just jump into her head.

Ani se...

"Are you paying attention?"

"Yes, Madam Ryzale," Lilly answered automatically. With a skeptical glance, Ryzale continued her lecture, gesturing with her hands, or rather, slapping her wand into her palm firmly to demonstrate the significance of her point.

Lilly's right hand began to tingle as the familiar warmth of magick crept slowly toward the wand she held. It, too, seemed bored with the present set of circumstances. Occasionally, she felt her hand twitch, as though the magick within herself or the wand was trying to escape, and she gripped the wand tighter, restraining the urge to use it.

"Are you paying attention?"

"Yes, Madam Ryzale."

Lilly focused on her teacher, determined to make it through this first lesson, but when Ryzale began discussing the dangers of using true magick, another lesson Lilly had already learned, she became distracted by the woman's appearance. She wore a bright purple velvet robe trimmed in emerald green satin and silver buttons. Her reddish-brown hair was littered with threads of gray and was pulled into a messy bun which sat lopsided on the back of her head, from which several strands threatened to fall. She wore thick, wide-framed glasses that teetered on the tip of her nose, and below them, her lips seemed perpetually pursed, whether she was talking or not.

"Are you paying attention?!"

"Yes, Madam Ryzale."

Ryzale sighed loudly to make her frustrations apparent and continued talking about the factors of fundamental magick. The wrinkles between her eyebrows were so deep, Lilly wondered if she ever stopped scowling, though she would know the answer to that question if she continued to ignore her lecture. Still, no matter how hard she tried, she couldn't stop her mind from wandering...

Wyatt was planning to contact her later with his mind. She was anxious to try using that magick from a greater distance, for if she could, she might be able to eventually contact Rohan, wherever he was. She hoped Wyatt wouldn't forget...

"Are you paying attention?!"

Ryzale's house was too organized. The many baubles she'd gathered over the years were positioned carefully upon shelves suspended on the walls. Her bookshelves were arranged perfectly according to size first, and then alphabetically. Everything down to the ornate rugs was arranged with precision on the hardwood floors. Though her teacher was dressed rather oddly, her house seemed more like a museum, each tapestry and decoration considered carefully before it was acquired and placed within the cottage.

"That's it!" snapped Ryzale, exasperated. "How can you expect to learn anything if you don't pay attention?!"

"I'm sorry," said Lilly. "I'm trying to pay attention, but I already know this stuff. I'm ready to learn more than this."

"Oh," said the sorceress in a mocking tone. "I was under the impression that you were here to learn fundamental magick, but since you already know everything, I guess you don't need me."

"That's not what I meant," protested Lilly, getting frustrated. "I know they told you that I'm new to my powers, but I'm not *that* new to them. I don't need to learn basic magick. I can do more then you'll ever be able to do, *naturally*, I just don't know how to do it yet."

"Yes," said Ryzale in stern compliance, "and it is my duty to teach you how to do it. Zephra told me of your abilities. Other than a few ubiquitous talents the Divine bestowed upon me, the magick I use comes only from hard work and patience, something which *you* currently lack. There is much more to magick than just power. The personality of the magician, for example, has a great effect on the outcome of his actions. Perhaps you are here to not only learn magick, but to learn patience, gain a little insight of the world around you. There is more to magick than you'll ever be able to learn in a thousand lifetimes. Even Zephra has unanswered questions, and she knows more than most."

Lilly stared at Ryzale, her eyes wide. She was stunned into silence. Ryzale's words, though delivered in a calm, all-knowing tone, had a harsh sting to them that only words of truth could carry. How could she ever learn enough in so little time to make such a difference as the one Rohan and Ashya expected of her? She felt herself flush, ashamed that she had been so rude.

"You might be surprised at how much I can do, you know," said Ryzale in response to Lilly's silence. She placed her wand on a narrow table that was butted against the wall behind her and picked up a small crystal that was the width of her thumb and twice as long. Whirling around, she muttered a word under her breath that Lilly couldn't hear and a whirlwind spun from the crystal's pointed tip, spinning violently as it grew larger. Paintings flew from the walls, figurines jumped from their homes on the shelves, vials of herbs and potions sailed through the air as all were sucked into the wild vortex of the magickal cyclone.

In an instant, it stopped. Ryzale returned the crystal to the table as every misplaced item returned to its rightful place. Lilly, her eyes wide with awe, started at the teacher she'd given so little credit. She was indeed a powerful sorceress.

"I may not have the natural ability that you have, but I have ability nonetheless. Your talents are useless without the foundation of an education. The most intelligent person in the world is nothing more than the village idiot without the know-how to use that intellect."

Lilly felt the sting of the insult, her confidence rising. Yes, Ryzale had talent, but she was treating Lilly as though she had none. Deciding it was worth the risk of whatever effects she might suffer, Lilly decided to show Ryzale that she was not the only sorceress in the room. She called the crystal on the table to her and, as it flew into her hand, Lilly was already willing forth the same magick Ryzale had just performed with it. The vortex spun from the tip once again as its suction began moving the already once-disturbed items. After a moment, Lilly righted the room and returned the crystal to the table, having never left her chair. Though she knew she shouldn't have done it, the shocked expression on Ryzale's face gave Lilly a feeling of great satisfaction.

"I'm a quick study," said Lilly.

"This I can see," replied Ryzale.

"I'm not trying to be disrespectful, but I already know what you are lecturing. I'm ready to learn what I came here to learn."

Ryzale was silent, studying the room, and more importantly, her new student. She had underestimated Zephra's description of her talent. This girl was more than just another apprentice. She was special. This realization Ryzale regarded with both wonder and concern. On one hand, she would be easy to train in magick, yet it would be more difficult to teach her the other equally-significant lessons she would require before leaving her tutelage. After a long moment of silence, she sighed and sat across from Lilly.

"We will skip the lecturing of basic magick," she said finally, "only if you can answer correctly the questions I ask you. A test, if you will. If I think you know what you must, we will begin with basic spell casting today. If not, we continue lessons my way. Agreed?"

"Agreed."

So began the test. Lilly correctly explained the three main factors of fundamental magick - timing, intent and phases of the moon - and she explained what each meant. Timing revolved around the strength of the days on which the spells were cast, as well as what times of day were stronger than others. Sabbats were the most powerful days, so spells requiring more power were often saved for such times. The moments of dawn, dusk and midday, when the suns were at their highest points in the sky, were also times of great power. The phases of the moon played a similar role to timing, though more in depth, for each phase lent a different type of strength to spells. The full moon held the most power, lending its strength to increase the power of almost any type of spell.

Intent was by far the most important factor, not only in fundamental magick, but all magick. Ryzale lectured briefly on this topic, for she wanted to be sure Lilly understood the repercussions of misdirected intent, and Lilly listened, her attention now undivided. She explained that a person must know *exactly* what they wish to accomplish with their magick before using it, for the slightest doubt would affect the outcome of the spell. A spell cast from emotion would push the intended outcome beyond the desired effect, which could severely injure both the target of the spell and the one who cast it.

"Intent," said Ryzale, "goes hand in hand with control. If you cannot control your emotions, you cannot control the outcome of your actions. That is something you must never forget."

Ryzale added to Lilly's explanation of timing, describing how timing not only applied to when the spell was cast, but also to the creation of tools and the collecting of objects used for the spells. Ingredients used in spells and potions were greatly affected by the time they were harvested, as Lilly remembered from the books she'd read in Ashya's library. A mushroom commonly used to heal magickal ailments was most potent when picked at daybreak, and though it still had an effect if picked at any other time of day, it usually required twice as much to have the same effect. Picking it at night would diminish all potency, leaving just a plain, non-effective mushroom.

Ryzale quizzed Lilly on the use of tools, on the nature of rare ingredients and in which element certain creatures were categorized. She was impressed that Lilly knew all thirteen months of the year and every Sabbat, as well as the basics of what each represented. Lilly recited what Ryzale had been preaching earlier about the different types of magick; that fundamental magick was centered around tools and ingredients, while elemental and true magick were centered in the body, that elemental magick was the most common form of natural magick and how it was not only the natural magick of plants and gems and such, but that it was based on the elemental sign under which a person was born. She recited the factors for natural magick: strength, knowledge and natural ability, though knowledge was required much more for true magick, for one wrong word from the *Doret Gaia* could have terrible results. After Lilly correctly recited the different level classifications of magickal skill - Arch Mage, Master Mage, Apprentice Mage - and that each level required education from a higher level mage and, for humans, a certain number of powers or Master status awards were needed to ascend to the next level, Ryzale conceded that Lilly was ready to begin casting spells.

"*Darenvar* is the word used to move objects," said Ryzale, her all-knowing tone returning now that she was once again the only one speaking. "It is used whether moving it toward you, away from you, or side to side, for once the connection is made with the object, your intent will direct it until you break the connection."

Ryzale aimed her wand at the broom cupboard in the corner of the room and said, *"Darenvar!"* The door of the cupboard jumped open and the broom popped out, sweeping its way across the floor. Lilly grinned as it swept the entire room under Ryzale's gaze and waving wand. Rugs and chairs lifted as the broom passed beneath them on its way toward the front door, which opened as the broom arrived to sweep the dust outside, and then everything returned to its proper place.

"Something you must always remember about magick is that it requires strength, no matter how simple the task. The easier the task, the more your energy is wasted. It took more out of me to do that than if I had swept the room myself. Magick takes more strength than what most humans have, which is why most humans have little or no magickal power. Those born with magickal talents are often much stronger than the average human, whether physically, mentally or both. It is that strength that makes the difference between having a talent and having a gift. Now, open the front door."

Lilly looked at the front door and it flung open.

"No! Use the word and your wand to close it this time."

Lilly sighed and did as she was instructed.

"Good," said Ryzale, satisfied. "Now, something larger."

"I mean no disrespect," interrupted Lilly, "but I can do this naturally. I moved boulders as large as this room. Can we skip to something new?"

"Very well," said Ryzale. "I'm thirsty. Would you like a drink, too?"

Lilly nodded as Ryzale left the room. It surprised Lilly that she had agreed, but she was so excited to learn something new that she didn't dwell on why her teacher had conceded so easily. Ryzale returned a moment later, and after handling Lilly one of the two glasses of iced tea, she sat in the chair directly across from her, watching her curiously.

When they finished their break, Ryzale asked Lilly to retrieve her crystal from the table. Lilly called to it, but it didn't budge. She tried again, focusing harder, but it remained motionless. She looked at Ryzale, who watched with a smirk on her face, her arms crossed. Finally, Lilly aimed her wand at the crystal and repeated the word for the spell that she'd used to close the door. The crystal floated across the room and landed gently in her hand.

"Very good," said her teacher in an overly patronizing tone.

"What did you do to me," asked Lilly breathlessly. She couldn't believe she was so tired after moving the small crystal, especially since she had moved it earlier with barely any effort.

"*Lompal,*" said Ryzale. "It is a potion that temporarily strips a person of their powers."

"What?! Why would you do that?"

"To teach you, as that is what I am here to do. You must understand the basics of magic, whether you have natural abilities or not, which includes more than one way of accomplishing what you must. Knowing how to accomplish something magickally without your powers will keep you from being completely defenseless should your powers ever fail you, as they have now."

"Because you poisoned me!"

"It has come to my attention," said Ryzale, ignoring Lilly's protests, "that you have the ability to absorb powers. Do you know what that means?"

"That I can see someone use magick and I can do it."

"Oh, it is so much more than that." Ryzale leaned forward in her chair toward Lilly. "Although that talent alone is rare, absorbing magick does not have to be witnessed to be used. If you are near a requiest, you will find yourself having visions of the future. If you are near an empath, you will feel the emotions of others when you are near them. If you get close to someone who can heal magickally, you will also be able to do it, whether you see them use the power of not. You literally absorb those powers, and their reversals."

"Reversals?"

"Everything in magick has an opposite. If you have a natural ability to do something, you have the ability to do its opposite. Someone who can easily communicate with the mind has the ability to overtake the mind of anyone they desire. One who can naturally heal with magick can also drain someone's strength with the same magick, provided they have enough of their own strength to overcome the other person. It's all in how you choose to use your powers."

"I can heal magickally," said Lilly quietly as she grasped this new information. The reality of her potential was becoming more real with every passing moment.

"Now, aren't you glad you know what its reversal is?" asked Ryzale.

"Not really," admitted Lilly. All the magickal mishaps that had occurred so far were frightening enough without knowing that she had the potential to go further than she already had. "Maybe you shouldn't fix my powers. There might be more dangerous things I can do that I don't know of yet."

"Nonsense. As powerful as you already are, I'm sure there is more that you can do, but that is no reason to turn your back on your destiny. You must learn all that you can do so you can learn how to control it, so you can use it to the best of your abilities for the good of others. As I said, there are not many humans who can use magick. Those who can are a great gift to the entire race, for those who aren't magickal tend to rely on magick to help with things they cannot do themselves, like healing. That is where humans like you and I are welcomed, even revered. Besides, as powerful as you are, the weak potion I gave you will wear off within the hour. I just gave it to you to make a point."

"Well, your point was made, loud and clear," Lilly assured her. "So, you are saying that if I was around a creature that can transform, then I should be able to do it, too?"

"No," said Ryzale, shaking her head. "It may be possible while in their presence, but you only retain those powers which you would have already been able to do once you learned how to do it. What have you learned simply by observing magick that you have retained?"

"Mind communication. Magickal quests."

"Then those are things that come naturally to you, something that you could already do, you just didn't know that you could. Be very grateful that you cannot consume powers. It is the rarest form of that type of magick, so rare in fact that I can count on one hand how many creatures over the past thousand years have been born with that gift, and none of those were humans."

"What's the difference between absorbing and consuming powers?"

"The powers you absorb from others stays with them, even if you retain the ability. If something consumes your powers, then they are gone forever." Ryzale dwelled over the thought of such an ability, and when she continued, her voice had taken on a cryptic tone. "There is a creature that exists, so powerful it can consume the very force of life from whatever it touches, so strong that no one can find a way to destroy it, but only contain it. It took the magick of five very powerful creatures to build the barrier that holds it now. To my knowledge, it is the only creature alive today that can consume powers."

"That's good to know."

"As are many other things," piped Ryzale. "We have much to do."

The rest of the lesson that day went rather smoothly. Lilly was humbled by Ryzale's lessons, and she put forth the effort Ryzale expected from her. Their remaining time passed quickly, and by the time she left Ryzale's cottage, Lilly was exhausted. Ryzale had more than proven her point about the hard work necessary for fundamental magick, for once the potion lost its effectiveness and Lilly's strength returned, she realized how demanding it really was. Spells were by far the easiest of fundamental magick, requiring only the correct words, the focused intent and the right amount of strength from the caster to achieve the proper results. Charms were spells that required all that a spell entailed, but also the use of the proper tool, or a chant, or particular objects and ingredients combined with the proper element, like burning sage to consecrate an altar. Potions were even more involved, and everything from the proper ingredients planted and harvested under the right conditions, the perfect temperature, even the direction the potion was stirred and for how long affected the potency and effectiveness of the concoction, which is why she would be learning potions from an Arch Apothecary.

Lilly walked toward the house with a new respect for the work of the Arch Sorceress. The effort and ability required even for fundamental magick was a precision that would take years to perfect. Luckily, she wouldn't have to learn everything this way. Ryzale was only going to teach her some of the most commonly-used spells, both offensive and defensive, and some lessons in charms, and then Lilly would stop training with her. Though she was tired, Lilly smiled as she trudged toward the house. However rough the lesson had started, all in all, it had turned out very well. Maybe Ryzale wouldn't be such a terrible teacher after all.

The Apothecary

"On guard!"

Zephra pounced from the tree and landed so close to Lilly, she almost landed on her. Lilly jumped backward, landing hard on her backside as Zephra grinned, waving her dagger menacingly before her. She knew she was supposed to train with Zephra for an hour after each lesson, but she'd expected the training to take place at the house, not on the way there. She reached for her own athame, which hung on her belt next to her wand, and took the defensive stance Zephra had already taught her.

Their weapons clanged against each other rapidly as Lilly blocked every blow Zephra delivered while trying to deliver a few of her own. She felt her strength waning quickly as Zephra overpowered her, and after a few more feeble attempts at a strike, she relinquished her weapon.

"Is that it?" laughed Zephra. "We're only warming up." She tossed the athame back to Lilly, who held it at her side, shaking her head.

"I'm too tired for this right now," she said. "I need to rest."

Zephra charged her, forcing Lilly to protect herself. She felt her adrenaline rush through her body as her anger grew, and before long, she equaled Zephra's movements.

"Good," shouted Zephra, pushing Lilly even further. Lilly tried to avoid her, but as fast as she was, blocking her was easier than moving out of her way.

"Did you hear me?" protested Lilly. "I'm tired."

"Your enemies will not wait until you are rested," said Zephra breathlessly, charging her again. Their battle continued until Zephra nicked Lilly's wrist with her blade, and when she paused to examine the damage, it cost her the battle. Lilly plunged her dagger into Zephra's heart and watched as she burst into flames. She sat to observe the birthing process of the phoenix, the rest of her lesson spent watching Zephra rise gracefully from her ashes, pausing only long enough to scowl at Lilly before flying away toward the house.

"Same time tomorrow, then," laughed Lilly as the bird flew away. It would be a day before Zephra was back in her human form anyway.

When she finally arrived at the house, exhausted from her first intense day of training with Ryzale, battling Zephra and the long walk home, she wanted to go straight to her room and collapse on her bed, but Dorwynn was waiting in the doorway, his arms crossed in disapproval.

"What happened to Zephra?" he asked.

"Ask her," replied Lilly.

"I can't. No one can communicate with her in her phoenix form. *Why* is she in her phoenix form?"

"She lost." Dorwynn's eyebrows shot into his hairline, and his jaw dropped, but he let Lilly walk past him and up the stairs.

Her bed looked so inviting, and she was about to flop onto it and stay there for the rest of the night when a familiar voice echoed in her mind.

Lilly, said Wyatt, *can you hear me?*

Yes, she replied, her fatigue growing stronger every second.

I can barely hear you. Are you okay?

I'm tired. Today took more out of me than I thought it would.

Oh, he said. *How did it go?*

Great, she replied, yawning. *I learned some spells today that I want to try soon, but I'm ready to learn more than what my teacher is teaching. I know I need to learn it, but there's no reason why I can't learn it quickly, right?*

Right, he replied, *and I'm the one to help you learn it. I know they are telling you that you need to learn the basics, but you really don't need to learn that much. You have natural ability.*

I tried to tell her that. She ended up stripping my powers.

You're kidding.

Nope. Lilly yawned again, her eyelids drooping as she swayed where she sat on the bed. *Listen, I really need to rest. I haven't had much sleep lately. Can we talk more tomorrow?*

No problem, he said. *Next time, you try to contact me.*

Okay. Good night, Wyatt.

Good night, Lilly.

She fell onto the bed, landing on her stomach, and stretched her arms wide. That is how Dorwynn found her when he fetched her for dinner. He tried to wake her, but she was out to the world, so he pulled a spare blanket from the closet and covered her with it, brushing the hair that had fallen around her face behind her ear and kissing her forehead before leaving her for the night.

She was in the same position the next morning when he woke her for her first lesson with Tsirama. She bathed, changed her clothes and ate as quickly as possible, and then she ran toward town so she wouldn't be late to the lesson.

If Ryzale had an opposite, Tsirama was it. While her house was organized in an all-too-neatly ordered way, his house was the reverse. Vials and cork stoppers were scattered over every flat surface of the house, save one large table with shelves attached to it from above, much like a vanity, only there were compartmentalized shelves where the mirror should be. Each shelf held a different ingredient or herb, and on the table were the essentials for potion work: a cauldron, a mortar and pestle, a silver spoon, a book of basic potions, and an object unlike any Lilly had seen, though it resembled the bottom half of an oil lantern.

"It is a firebath," explained Tsirama, who had emerged from a doorway hidden by mountains of books piled against a wall. He was barely taller than Lilly, with large, liquid brown eyes that appeared larger behind the wire spectacles that sat on his narrow, hook-like nose without the aid of ear pieces. His ears were large, his mouth small, and with the candlelight licking across his bald head, he seemed a little out of proportion.

"What's a firebath?" she asked, turning her gaze to the instrument.

"Holds fuel in bottom," he said, squinting his eyes to get a better look at her. "Little knob on side regulates amount of fuel expended at any given time, so one can correctly control temperature of cauldron."

"I see," said Lilly, trying not to focus on his strange accent as she examined the contents of the table.

"Well," said the apothecary, "let us begin. Open book to page one-seventeen. Follow directions exact. Make potion. You have one hour."

"Wait," said Lilly. "I've never made a potion before."

Tsirama waved his hand absently in the air as he walked away from her, dismissing her words. He rummaged through a stack of books, found what he was searching for, and then began hunting for a quill, never once responding.

Her hands shaking, she opened the book and found the recipe for *Lompal*, the same potion Ryzale had used on her the day before. After reading over the ingredients, she collected the necessary items from the shelves and brought them to the table, grateful that although the rest of his house was in complete disarray, at least his ingredients were neatly labeled and organized.

She followed the directions precisely, adding a pinch of this and a sprig of that, and then stirring for exactly seven minutes in a clockwise motion. As the directions stated it would, the potion turned from a murky orange color to a hazy clear concoction, indicating that it was finished.

"Forty-four minutes," said Tsirama from behind her. He had busied himself merely to allow Lilly the opportunity to succeed or fail, either result being of her own doing, and had observed her progress from afar. "You have gift at potions."

"How do you know it's right?" she asked.

"I know," he said, his eyes twinkling. He bottled the concoction, corked it, labeled it and placed it on the shelf with other vials labeled *Lompal*. "I must think."

He sat in a chair near the table, squashing the scrolls of paper that were lying in the seat. Tapping his long, skinny fingers of the wooden arm of the chair, he gazed around the room absently. Lilly watched him in silence, agreeing with Zephra that this man was very odd indeed. Finally, he stood and walked to the pile of books he'd searched earlier. He went right to the one he wanted and pulled it out, then walked with quick steps toward Lilly.

"Since you have no need for propaedeutic..."

"No need for *what*?"

"Means you have no need to learn preliminary basics of potions. You already know them."

"Then why didn't you just say that?"

"I did," said the little man, a serious look on his face. "Twice." Her confused expression almost made him laugh, but he knew it was not the thing to do as an educator. "Potions are easy, so long as you understand how they work."

He handed her the book he had retrieved, flipping it open to the correct page with the wave of his hand, and began to tidy the table where she had made the potion. Though the rest of his house did not show it, he was very particular when it came to the cleanliness of his work area.

"Keep it," he said as he washed the cauldron in a basin of water that had appeared out of nowhere. "That book has things you do not yet know, to explain rules of experimenting. When you make potion, you must always follow directions. Small deviation has big effect on outcome. Even if stirred wrong direction, potion will be wrong, though many interesting things come from mistakes." He chuckled as he replaced the cauldron and spoon on the table. "Went through open sacred doorway once...was trying to see through it. Too much reshnok."

"Wow," said Lilly as she skimmed through the pages of the book. There was an entire chapter on experimenting, which broke down a list of ingredients and how a minor deviation would change the potion, and how stirring the opposite direction or changing how long you stir might very well make the potion do the opposite of what you want. As she read, Tsirama's long fingers closed over the top of the pages from behind it and he pulled the book down from her face. He leaned toward her, his eyes filled with concern.

"This means not that you can do this," he said seriously. "I want you read this to know how things go wrong. Side effects are devastating and hard to fix unless you are knowing what was done to make it wrong. More reshnok, and lost forever I could have been. If you are not knowing what was done to make it wrong, antidote is nearly impossible. All instruction, all ingredients have purpose. Deviation from instruction has only minor changes. Deviation of ingredients has more, but all ingredients have antidote, though some very rare. Never do without first knowing how to do. Knowledge," he said, tapping the temple of his bald head, "is most important ingredient."

Lilly nodded, her eyes wide. He opened the potion book that was lying on the table and flipped through it, his eyes scanning the pages so quickly, Lilly wondered how he had time to read any of them. He stopped and looked up at her.

"Come," he said. "You do another potion, more difficult."

She sighed and went to the table. The potion described on the page was called *Eganer*, a concoction that enabled the one who consumed it to see the true form of someone hidden in magickal disguise, as well as anyone nearby who was invisible. Lilly read the entire potion before beginning, and in the description of the potion's effects stated that it only lasted about two hours, but by adding twice as much sepaga and a pinch of sespir, that time could be doubled.

Lilly worked the potion, which was supposed to take almost two hours to complete, this time with Tsirama hovering near the table as he watched her progress. He nodded as she expertly measured the proper ingredients, stirred in the appropriate direction and for the correct amount of time, added more ingredients and then lit the firebath, adjusting it to the right temperature. When the potion was bubbling over the flame, as called for in the directions, he grinned at her, his small mouth stretched wide over his teeth.

"Good, good," he said happily. "Must boil for twenty-two minutes. In meantime, read rules of experimentation. We begin experimenting soon."

The thought of being able to experiment with magick excited Lilly. Tsirama, odd though he was, was already her favorite trainer. She tried to read, but the potion boiling over the flame distracted her. Afraid she would forget to remove it from the heat when it was ready, she watched the clock until the time was up, and then she turned off the firebath and began to clean up her mess, respecting Tsirama's work space.

He was pleased with his new student, for she had done everything with perfect precision. Dorwynn had not told him of her aptitude, though Tsirama thought he might not have known of her abilities. She was a quick study, which also pleased him, for when he did his work, he worked with great speed and efficiency. His days were normally spent making potions for the townsfolk, taking their orders and making his living from their desires. He was always careful with the potions he made and used great discretion for whom he made them, often making them a bit weaker than called for so the humans wouldn't be injured if, perhaps, they were a bit overzealous.

After the potion cooled, it was bottled, labeled and stored in the cabinet. Although they still had almost an hour of lessons, Tsirama dismissed Lilly for the day.

"You need keep grimoire," he said before sending her on her way.

"What's a grimoire?" she asked, wondering where she would have to go to find some strange new magickal item.

"A book," he replied. "Some call book of shadows, some call grimoire, some call journal of magick. Is to keep thoughts, dreams, spells, potions...things of magick you want to keep for own personal use. Ryzale will want you to have, too, but she is slow in her directions." Lilly smiled at his observation of Ryzale. "Bring with you next lesson. You can copy potions done today."

"Thank you," said Lilly, surprised that he would let her have such magickal information without supervision.

"We are done," he said. "Read rules of experimentation for next lesson." With that, he turned and disappeared into a room hidden behind the piles of books in the main room of the house. She smiled and stepped outside, and since she wasn't nearly as exhausted as the day before and Zephra wouldn't be in her human form for at least another hour, she traveled by magick to her room in the house, retrieved the black journal Beth had given her and wrote as much as she could about everything she had already experienced. She wrote of her dreams, of her communication with Wyatt, of her lessons so far, and finally, as much as she could remember of the night in Arthidgen when true magick had controlled her.

Before closing the book, she turned to the back, and in the last few pages, she began a list of all the words of the *Doret Gaia* she already knew, leaving plenty of space for whatever else of the language she would learn. She closed the book and smiled, satisfied with her progress, and returned it to its place on the bookshelf before going to find Zephra for their lesson. Had she stayed a moment longer, she would have noticed as the book slowly started to glow, its cover becoming etched with a faint symbol, the symbol she'd placed on her wand, the symbol that would soon become a permanent fixture in her life.

The night after her lesson with Dorwynn, Lilly contacted Wyatt with her mind. She apologized for not trying the day before, and proceeded to explain why she hadn't. Zephra had pushed her hard during their lesson, and afterward had given her a lecture about how rude it was to kill her just because she was immortal, not to mention how dangerous it was to Zephra if the wrong person discovered her immortality. She didn't give Wyatt the details of the situation, wanting to respect Zephra's need for privacy, so she only told him of the brutal lesson and her exhaustion afterward.

Today's lesson went really well, she told him. *Dorwynn was impressed with how much control I had when I moved earth, but he thinks it's because of the wand. I didn't correct him, but I feel bad about not telling him about you. There's just something telling me to keep you a secret for a while.*

Do what you feel you must, he said. *When you don't know what to do, following your instincts is a pretty safe bet. Besides, everyone has secrets. It's part of what makes us who we are.*

I guess so.

You'll know when the time is right to tell him. If not, he'll find out on his own. There's no reason to feel guilty. If he asks you a direct question about it, be honest. Anyone asking a direct question is probably prepared for any answer, but that doesn't mean you have to offer the information. You aren't obligated to tell him every part of your life, are you?

I guess I'm not, she said after thinking about it for a moment. *I never really thought about it like that.*

That's what I'm here for...offering insight to apprentices everywhere.

Lilly laughed and sighed as she lay on her bed, the walls of the small room becoming an all-too-familiar atmosphere. Once again, she fought the desire to go for a walk, but it was a fight easily won, for she kept telling herself that tomorrow was her day. No lessons, no training...she only had to do what she wanted to do. Of course, she wanted to learn more, but it was a welcome feeling to know she had the choice of whom would be teaching her.

Her conversation with Wyatt lasted another hour, discussing magick and the mysterious connection that bound them together. Neither had an explanation for it, but they both knew that it was strong. Before saying their goodbyes, they agreed to meet the following morning by the rock for some more magickal "advice", which thrilled Lilly, for she wanted to visit Orvak as well, and she would have time to regain her strength after climbing the cliff to the waterfall and working with Wyatt before traveling there by magick. It was the only way to visit him, she reasoned, where she would have enough time to make her visit worthwhile.

Lessons with Wyatt were a breeze. He spoke with confidence about magick, but he did not carry the same condescending tone she heard so often in Dorwynn's voice. He seemed a natural teacher, taking pleasure in helping her learn. By the time they finished almost two hours later, Lilly had manipulated a stone to take the form of a pterippus, complete with golden highlights, having followed Wyatt's advice and forming what she felt in her heart. She was thinking more and more of Rohan, wondering when he would return, though she kept that to herself.

"This is wonderful," said Wyatt as he admired the miniature statue. "A fine beginning to a beautiful chess set." He handed it to Lilly, who turned it in her hands, Rohan still on her mind.

"Thanks," she said modestly. "A chess set might be a bit of a stretch, though. It would take a while to make all the pieces."

"You might be surprised. When my grandmother would drag me to the far corners of Buthania, I spent my time making pieces like this to pass the long hours in the carriage. It's a good way to keep focus and stay in practice when there's nothing else to do."

"I'll keep that in mind," she said as she tucked her creation into her pocket, "though I doubt I'll have much free time for a while."

"Yeah," he said. "Training will keep you busy, but I'll bet you are a Master before you know it."

"I still have a long way to go," she admitted, "which reminds me, I have somewhere else to be."

"You'd better go, then," he said, his hand out to bid her farewell. She took it with a sense of hesitation, and as she expected, a bright light flashed behind her eyes, blinding her until she let go of his hand. Again, he seemed not to notice the strange event, so she pushed it to the back of her mind and focused on the swamp, her next destination.

She appeared on his doorstep as a slight wave of dizziness washed over her, passing as quickly as it had arrived. She raised her hand to knock on the door, but paused, wondering if Orvak would think her rude since she had not planned this visit in advance. She finally knocked, deciding that it was the thing to do since she was already there. If she was interrupting him, then she would just apologize and leave, but not before planning the next visit.

Orvak opened the door, his silver eyes shining so bright Lilly once again saw her reflection in them, and then he opened the door wider, allowing her entry. Without speaking, he moved with rumbling steps toward the back of the house and returned with a large, rather fluffy chair, setting it before the only other chair in the room, which was three times larger than any chair Lilly had ever seen.

"Welcome," he said in a deep but gentle voice. "What brings you to my door?"

"Well," said Lilly, suddenly nervous, for she really had no particular reason to be there, "I thought I would come to visit."

"Then you are ready to perceive the world around you?" he asked. She nodded as she remembered his words from their first meeting. He rose from his chair and mumbled, "Come."

She followed him outside, staying close to him as he led her over the solid earth that supported his home and across a long wooden bridge pieced together with bundles of twigs rather than logs, making Lilly wonder how it supported his weight without snapping in two. The swamp beneath the bridge, blanketed by moss and lily pads very close to blooming, was a thick ruddy brown, not at all like the transparent water of the lake beside her house. Dragonflies the size of squirrels danced on the water as the sunlight rippled an iridescent rainbow along their pearly wings. One of them zoomed toward Lilly, who ducked as it swept past her. It hovered in her path, staring at her with giant bug eyes.

"She is merely curious," said Orvak, who was now standing on the bank across the bridge, staring at her with an expression on his face Lilly couldn't quite read. She edged her way to the end of the bridge, her eyes never breaking contact with the huge insect as it turned its still-hovering body in midair, just as determined to keep its eyes on her.

Orvak chuckled as Lilly reached his side, her wide eyes turning toward him, and then he turned away from her and continued walking. She followed, looking around for any more surprises like that one, but they were on solid ground again, walking a worn path toward a small island of trees in the otherwise empty meadow they just entered. They reached the dense patch of trees, which created a canopy overhead, and walked until they reached the center.

There were no trees at the center of the small forest, but rather an open circle lined with stones along the circular tree line. It was as though someone had placed the large stones for the purpose of keeping the trees from crossing into the circle. Within the large circle, there were five stones, each one very different and arranged in a circle equidistance apart. The space between those stones was large enough to hold two of Orvak, or maybe five humans.

"What is this place?" asked Lilly, her eyes darting between the center of the smaller stones and the edge of the forest. The light grazing through the canopy fell within the stones, casting a soft light in the otherwise dusky woods. Looking up, Lilly saw a break in the canopy and wondered if the absence of cover was created with purpose.

"This place," said Orvak, his quiet voice both gruff and gentle, "is where I talk to Nature. This is where Nature talks to me."

"Nature talks to you?"

Without responding, Orvak ambled toward the sunny center of the circle and sat on the ground, his short, thick legs stretched before him. Lilly followed and sat facing him, crossing her legs, her back rigid. He smiled at her, his silver pupils no larger than pinpricks as the sunlight poured over his face, and then closed his eyes. Lilly did the same.

They sat for a while in silence, Lilly wondering all the while what was going to happen. Growing restless, but not daring to break the silence, she let her mind wander, first to Rohan, who had been fresh in her mind upon her arrival, and then to her first meeting with Orvak. She lingered on these thoughts without knowing why, but soon she recalled how he had hidden the lesson in plain sight, and she knew the lesson had already begun. Breathing slow, deep breaths, Lilly tried to clear her mind, but unlike her lessons with Ryzale where she tried to focus on her words, she instead focused on nothing in particular, allowing only the sounds of the forest to enter her mind.

A slight breeze rustled the leaves of the canopy above them. A bird chirped, its song carrying triumphantly through the grove surrounding them. Flowers were in bloom nearby, for their sweet scent drifted toward her, filling her once again with a sense of renewal as spring settled into the glade. Everything that had been bothering her since she crossed through that doorway was forgotten, vanishing in the serenity of the moment as though time did not exist.

A deep, steady thumping began to pulsate in her ears, growing more defined with every beat, with softer and more rapid beats littering the background. Before she could wonder what these new sounds were, she heard the loud fluttering of wings as a flock of small birds fled their perch, chattering angrily at whatever had caused their fear. As they disappeared, the rhythmic beats began again, occasionally interrupted by the sounds of an animal moving through the forest.

And then she heard it: a song more beautiful that anything she had ever heard in her entire life rang in her ears, soft and caressing like a mother's touch, soothing like a lullaby. Entranced, Lilly listened to the celestial melody as the unearthly voice rose to crescendo before slowly fading away. As it faded, the other sounds dissipated with it, until Lilly could hear nothing at all. Whatever the reason, she didn't open eyes, although it was now so silent it seemed that sound, too, no longer existed. The only thing she could hear was the beating of her own heart, slow and steady, lulling her deeper into her trance.

She felt like she was floating, like she had fallen off the earth and was now hovering above it, far away from the clutter and the chaos. Her head was light, swimming lazily through her thoughts but never touching them, until she could think of only one thing:

Go to my home in Elikrede. The way to find me is there, in a small house between the waterfall's edge and the stone garden.

Her mother's voice echoed in the darkness, repeating the same words over and over for what seemed like an eternity. Suddenly, flashes of white light strobed behind her eyes, followed by a brilliant green glow swirling among it like a rope being pulled into a whirlpool. Her heart began to beat faster, and with each beat an image flashed in her mind and disappeared instantly. A chair and a wand in an unfamiliar room...the waterfall...her mother's house...a gravestone...a small room that glowed green...a thick book, also glowing green...a bright castle surrounded by hundreds of people...her father...Amparo...Wyatt...her own reflection in a mirror, Zephra standing behind her...the doorway. The images stopped flashing here as the silvery swirling doorway drew closer with each beat, growing brighter as it came closer...and closer...and closer...

Then there was nothing but darkness. No light, no sound, no smells...nothing at all, and she knew it was time to open her eyes.

At once, the normal sounds of the forest returned, although crickets now contributed to the choir. Orvak was seated before her, his eyes bright and inquisitive. He was smiling, a peaceful look on his grotesque face.

"Tell me," was all he said, but Lilly knew what he was asking. She told him everything she heard, everything she felt, everything she saw in her mind. He listened until she finished, never interrupting, but merely studying everything she said.

"What do the images mean?" she asked when she had finished describing her experience.

"Perception," he said, "is not something that can be obtained magickally, nor is it a magickal gift. It must be learned, though unfortunately, as people grow from child to adult, they tend to lose it, so it must be relearned, something which you started doing today. As time passes, you will be able to focus on particular sounds to pinpoint exactly how far from you it is, and from what direction it comes."

"But what does that have to do with what I saw in my mind?"

"Patience, vula," the ogre said gently. "The answers will come in time. Where was I? Ah, yes! When you closed your eyes, that sense was obstructed, leaving you able only to listen, smell and feel the world around you. You allowed yourself to abandon the thoughts that clutter your mind, therefore opening yourself to use those senses to hear and feel things that are always there, but so often overlooked. The beating you heard was your own heartbeat, and mine, as were the other beats the hearts of nearby forest creatures, only intensified at much greater volume because your ear was more focused to hear them.

"The images in your mind are things that, too, have always been there, but that you have overlooked until now, when you were able to perceive them within yourself. Alone, they may mean very little, but together, their meaning may become clear. You are searching for the answers to many questions, but one among all others left unanswered gives you a sense of loss."

"I want to find my mother," she admitted, although she felt an emptiness in the pit of her stomach at the thought of finding her.

"She spoke to you. She told you where to start looking."

"Yes, but I have searched that house and I have found nothing to suggest where she is."

"Nothing?" asked Orvak, a twinkle in his black eyes that had nothing to do with his silver pupils.

"Well," she said, "I did find something strange...a tasil. I don't know why I can see it, though, or how to get into it."

"Hmmm. A room hidden by magick would be a good place to hide things you wanted no one else to see, though I have never heard of one who could see the tasil of another unless it was left open. What if your mother made it possible for only you to see it?"

"Could she do that?" asked Lilly in awe.

"It is blood magick," said Orvak quietly. "She would have used your blood for the spell, or her own, in which case only those of her blood, her children, would have access."

"So how do I get inside?" Lilly could feel her heart beating faster as her excitement grew.

"Blood magick, if that's what was used, would require blood. A drop or two should suffice," he added when he noticed the look of panic on Lilly's face. "So, the green light, the waterfall, the house, the gravestone, the glowing room and probably the book all seem to fit this situation, whether you have seen these things or not. What about the rest of the images?"

"Well," said Lilly, wrenching her thoughts away from the tasil, "there was a castle, and then my father, then Amparo, a friend of mine, and then my sister, then myself, then another friend, Wyatt, and finally, the doorway I entered when I came here."

"What is the next question plaguing your mind, the most significant after locating your mother?"

"Finding out as much as I can about my family, her family. I know she came from here, so it makes sense that her family is also here."

"It does. You must figure out, then, how each of these images fit together to answer that question."

"How? It doesn't make any sense that friends would be mixed in with my family, unless they represent people who I feel are like family, but what about the castle, or the doorway?"

"Do either of those things have a connection to this question?"

"Well, I walked through that doorway and left my family behind."

"That may be all it means. I shall leave it to you, for you are the only one who knows the answer, even if you haven't found it yet." He stood, stretching his massive arms high into the air. Lilly stood, taking it as a sign that their lesson for today was at an end. "I have enjoyed our lesson, vula," he said with a smile. "Will you be returning?"

"Oh, yes," said Lilly, already excited at the prospect of another lesson with Orvak. "In four days, if that is alright."

"I'm always here somewhere," he said. "You may come at any time, but since you have decided to return, I would like you to practice your powers of perception until you can focus your hearing without closing your eyes. Once you can do this, we will begin to hone your other senses, including self-perception. Perhaps next time, your images will flow better and allow you to discover their meaning, hidden in the depths of your mind." He began walking away from her as he said, "Until next time, vula."

"What does vula mean?" shouted Lilly at his disappearing form. He turned, giving her a smile so wide his two upper lips split to show his top teeth, before turning again and disappearing into the trees. She watched him until he was gone, then focused on the house. After a dizzy moment, she found herself on the doorstep. Running through the front door and past a very curious Dorwynn, she could smell dinner cooking as she sprinted to her room. Once there, she placed the miniature pterippus on the table in her room, allowing her eyes to flicker to the corner where the tasil had been the last time she saw it. It wasn't there, but she smiled, for she knew the next time it appeared, she would enter the room hidden behind it, and flew back down the stairs in hopes that dinner was ready.

The Stone Garden

Her next lesson with Ryzale was nearly as boring as the first, for all the woman did was give her a long list of spells to memorize and practice, and afterward, Lilly walked the path toward home, knowing she would have to once again fight with Zephra. As expected, Zephra was waiting for her, though much closer to the house than usual. Lilly drew her blade at lightning speed as her trainer advanced.

They sparred like no two ever had, twisting and writhing beneath each other to avoid being struck. After Lilly's previous win, Zephra had become more ferocious, and soon, Lilly's face and arms were scratched and bleeding, though she began to move much faster than ever before. By the end of their hour, both women breathless and panting collapsed on the grass, struggling to regain their composure.

"You're getting faster," admitted Zephra. "Stronger, too, though I expected as much."

"You did?" asked Lilly, sitting up to look at her. Zephra nodded.

"The more you exercise, the stronger you get, right? Well, the more you use magick, the stronger you get, too. Keep it up and you'll be *almost* as fast as I am."

"Oh, good," said Lilly. "I'll have someone to live up to." She meant it as a joke, but whether Zephra noticed or not, she didn't know. A movement near the house caught her eye. She saw nothing remotely close to the house, just a slight rustling of the trees and brush on the side opposite the waterfall. A brilliant flash of purple and yellow appeared for a split second behind the trees, and then it was gone.

"What is it?" asked Zephra, following Lilly's intense gaze with her own.

"I thought I saw something."

"Where?"

"In the trees beside the house."

"It was probably someone going to the cemetery."

"What cemetery?" asked Lilly, her voice so high-pitched Zephra was taken aback.

"There's a small cemetery there, beside the house."

"Why didn't anyone tell me that?" shouted Lilly, jumping up at lightning speed and running toward the tree line without giving Zephra time to respond. It hit her at once how daft she had been. The house was between the waterfall and the stone garden, which is exactly what her mother had told her. The stone garden, she now realized, was no garden at all, but rather a graveyard. Why didn't she think of that before, and why hadn't it occurred to her to try to find it?

Because the way to find her is in the house, she told herself defiantly, but she knew that was no excuse. She needed to find the stone garden, something she had known since she first heard her mother's words, but she had carelessly abandoned the task in light of the many other things happening. Her heart swelled with excitement as she reached the trees, and walking a slow pace through them, the cemetery came into view.

A path comprised of flat white stones, pieced together with nothing but the grass surrounding it, wound its way along the gravestones, through their center and around the outside. Flowers grew at most of the headstones, though not many had bloomed yet, and in the center of all the headstones, a large monument was constructed, surrounded by a black iron gate. Though the rest of the cemetery was well maintained, the ground inside the gate was unkempt, as though the person for whom this shrine was built had no living soul who cared enough to keep it looking nice.

The brilliant flash of purple she had seen earlier caught her eye, and at once she recognized the creature to which the colors belonged. A single harpy was stooped over a rather new headstone, her head bent low, as though in prayer. Lilly hesitated, her mind returning to the harpy attack that had almost killed her. She waited for the creature to turn, to fly at her and attack, her hand already clutching her dagger, but the creature seemed not to notice her presence at all.

Lilly moved toward the obelisk as she pretended to study the other headstones in the cemetery, keeping the harpy in sight out of the corner of her eye. Meaningless names and dates floated across her eyes as she moved toward the center of the graveyard, and as she stepped into the gated area containing the obelisk, which was made of white marble, she noticed another shine, an exact replica of the one within the gate, though not nearly as old, standing directly behind it.

She studied the shrine, searching for anything that would identify who was within the tomb below, but there were no marks to be found anywhere. No name, no date, nothing but a small teardrop on the top edge of the monument, so worn that Lilly wondered if the shape was her imagination. She studied the other one, which wasn't nearly as worn, but there was nothing to suggest there had ever been anything etched on the stone. She ran her fingers over the cool stone, knowing without knowing how that this was where her mother's body rested.

It came as suddenly as the others, a vision quest so strong she felt as though she had been wrenched from the very fabric of time. It was the same as before, her mother writing the letters and giving them to Gustave, him hiding them and her request to be buried beside her father. Instead of vanishing, as it had when she inadvertently traveled back in time, this vision continued as her mother rose from the sofa and, in her dying state, disappeared from sight. Gustave had a strange, sad look on his face, but rather than follow her, he made his way up the stairs and to the room Lilly now used as her own.

Lilly followed, stopping short when she noticed the small, closet-sized room glowing green in the corner of the bedroom. She watched as Gustave entered the room, opened a book sitting upon a wooden pedestal and wrote on the first page with a hurried hand. When he finished, he closed the book and left, the magickal room closing itself behind him. She tailed him as he walked quickly from the house and into the stone garden, right to the place where she had been standing when the quest began. Her mind reeled as she watched him create a white marble obelisk, forming it behind the one inside the gate. He raised his arms high, and in a loud, clear voice, uttered words Lilly knew were the *Doret Gaia*: *Delave vesti birem seva sira!*

She was thrown from the memory as quickly as she was thrust into it, her head swimming as her knees failed to support her weight. She slammed into the ground, her eyes darting around the graveyard in panic as she remembered there was a harpy nearby and she was now in a vulnerable state. The harpy, however, was gone, but even that didn't make her feel better. All she could think about now was that Gustave knew much more than she ever imagined, and if he knew, then Rohan also knew, for was he not also Gustave?

ROHAN! she shouted with her mind, not knowing whether or not he could even hear her and not caring at that point if it gave him away. She waited for a response, and when one didn't come, she tried again, focusing all the energy she could muster to reaching him, but her attempts were in vain. If he had heard her, he surely would have responded by now.

Her legs like jelly beneath her, she rose slowly, using the obelisk she now knew was her grandfather's for support. She managed to get to the house, falling to the floor the moment she was through the door.

"What happened?" asked Dorwynn, rushing to her side.

"Another vision quest," she muttered, trying to fight the draining sensation daring to overcome her. "I need to talk to Gustave."

"He's busy," said Zephra, who was standing in the doorway to the kitchen. "He comes when he is able, not whenever you want him."

"I don't want to talk to him," Lilly said through gritted teeth, her anger rising beyond measure. "I *need* to talk to him, now!"

"Calm down," urged Dorwynn. He helped Lilly to her feet and led her to the sofa, pushing her into a sitting position before she could protest. "He is away now, but when he returns, he is supposed to be giving me some new instructions. I'll make sure to tell him you need to talk to him, okay?"

"What new instructions?" demanded Zephra. Dorwynn shrugged as he disappeared around the corner and returned with a glass of juice.

"Drink this," he said as he pushed it into Lilly's hands. Turning to Zephra, he replied in somewhat of a defeated tone, "You know Gustave. He likes his secrets, but you know as well as I do that he has more planned for me after this task is complete. Besides, did it ever occur to you that he may want to check on Lilly's progress? He won't stay gone for long."

Lilly drank her juice and kept her silence. She could feel Rohan was close, closer than she had felt him since they had first arrived, and she knew he would be coming soon. Dorwynn and Zephra retreated to the kitchen, and she could hear them discussing her. Zephra, in a very decided tone, was demanding that Dorwynn start teaching her to block the quests until she could learn them properly, and Dorwynn argued that there was no point, since the same magick that was used to block the quests could bring them on stronger than ever.

"Do you want her trying to have them?" he asked Zephra, cutting her off mid-sentence. "If she knew how to do it, I have no doubt she would."

"But.."

"No, Z. Besides, you know I'm not allowed to teach her something I cannot do myself."

"Come off it, Dorwynn! I know you can do..."

"Memory quests, yes" he interrupted again, "but not vision quests. That's Air magick, and I'm not that powerful. We'll have to wait until Amparo takes over her training."

They said no more, and since she would hear nothing of importance from either of them tonight, Lilly climbed the stairs to her room, her eyes instinctively going to where the hidden room had been in her quest and her spirits falling when she saw nothing there. She snatched her journal from the bookshelf and opened it to the back, recording the words Gustave had said in the vision quest so she could try to figure out what they meant. She also wrote the details of the quest, continuing them right after the entry of her trip through time. When she finally finished, she closed the book and replaced it on the shelf.

Wyatt, she called desperately with her mind. *I need you.*

It took him a moment to respond, but when he did, she heard the concern in his voice and felt better at once.

What's wrong? he asked. *You sound upset.*

Can you meet me? I need to talk to someone.

Of course. Where?

The place we first met.

She was there in an instant, her thoughts so muddled she barely noticed her weakening state. Wyatt appeared a moment later, and although she knew she would be blinded by light she always saw when she touched him, she threw her arms around him.

"Thank you for coming," she said as she released him and sat on the ground, leaning against the tree for support.

"Lilly, what's wrong?" he asked, concern blazing on his face.

Before she knew it, she was telling him everything that had happened in the graveyard. If he was surprised that she was having vision quests, he did not show it in his voice, but he was unable to offer her an explanation as to why it was happening beyond her control. He thought he knew more than most when it came to magick, but since he met Lilly, he was discovering more mysteries than he thought existed. He stayed silent while she ranted about the wizard who had decided to train her, who knew things about her, but which he failed to tell her.

"I'm just so angry!" she shouted. "I'm getting all these visions of my mother right before her death, but I don't know how she died, or where. I just wish these vision quests would actually answer some questions."

"Well, they have, haven't they?" he reasoned. "I mean, you know the wizard knows something, so now you can ask him, though I have to believe there is more to them than what you are allowing yourself to see. Otherwise, you wouldn't be having them at all."

Lilly pondered his answer, her anger starting to subside, but the next words he spoke ignited it all over again.

"Maybe it's better that you don't know."

"What?! Why would you say that?"

"I don't know," he said, casting his eyes toward the ground. "When I ask my grandmother about my family, about my father's identity and about my mother's past, that's what she tells me."

"And you're okay with that? Don't you want to know?"

"Of course I do," he said, "but that doesn't mean she's wrong to think it would be better if I didn't."

"Well," Lilly huffed, "I'm not like you. I have to know why I grew up without a mother."

"You aren't the only one, you know," whispered Wyatt.

"I know," replied Lilly, trying to keep her voice calmer then she felt, "but your mother didn't abandon you the moment you were born."

"No," he said through gritted teeth, lifting his eyes to her, "she died the moment I was born."

"Right, she died. She didn't choose to leave you. It's a completely different feeling when you grow up knowing that your mother left by choice, even if she claims to have a good excuse. At least you know *how* your mother died."

"Do you think that makes it easier?" he shouted, jumping up suddenly. "Do you think I like knowing that I caused her death? Believe me, if I could give back one piece of knowledge, that would be it!"

Turning away from her, he crossed his arms, and Lilly felt ashamed that she had made such a fuss over her own situation. His wasn't worse, but it wasn't any better, either. She let him stew for a moment, then stood and reached for his hand.

"I'm sorry, Wyatt," she said, trying to ignore the blinding light in her head as she clasped his hand. "You're right, and I'm so sorry I caused you pain."

Wyatt relaxed, and letting go of her hand, he wiped his face to hide his tears before looking at her. Tears were shining in her eyes, threatening to spill but never doing so. They sat awhile for no other reason than to be in each other's presence, and neither uttered another word until they finally said goodbye, both lost in their own thoughts.

Lilly walked back to the house, her exhaustion so great she couldn't have used magick if she wanted to. She failed to notice Dorwynn demanding her whereabouts as she walked straight to her room without so much as casting a glance in his direction.

"What was that about?" he asked Zephra, who was sitting at the kitchen table, staring at nothing. Noticing her dazed state, he said gently, "Zephra, are you alright?"

Zephra didn't hear him, frantically searched the depths of her mind, recalling the words of her father, the man for whom she had hatched thousands of years ago: *You will find yourself inexplicably drawn to a woman of great strength, having a connection with her so strong that you will be able to do things you could never before do, a connection you will come to understand over a great period of time. She will rise to power beyond all others. She will become a queen, and you will give your life to her.*

It was his prophecy that had always stuck with her, the same prophecy the oracle had repeated to her on more than one occasion. She had never fully believed it before now, but she had never before been able to hear a conversation between two people from nearly a mile away, and she was sure that Lilly was the reason for it. She wondered what Lilly would think if she knew she had heard her conversation with Wyatt, and though she wondered who he was, she knew she would not tell Lilly about hearing them speak, at least not right away. All Zephra knew for certain was that for the first time in her very long life, she was completely confident that she was on the right path, the path to her own destiny.

How she survived her first two weeks of training, Lilly would never know. She had expected it to be demanding, but having only one day of rest a week, and in turn using that day to train as well, she found herself utterly exhausted, both physically and mentally. The first few boring nights she spent enclosed in her room were forgotten as she soon came to appreciate the time she got alone at the end of each day, for it was the only time she could not only recover from the physical strain of her lessons, all of which were becoming more challenging by the day, but also contemplate the massive amounts of information flooding her mind. The stone garden, the hidden room, even Rohan's eternal absence were lost, pushed to the far corners of her mind during those first weeks as each of her trainers pushed her to her limits.

Tsirama was, by far, the easiest on her. The majority of their time together was spent wandering the nearby forest in search of magickal ingredients, though when something was found, it was only observed and recorded until the timing was right to gather it. The walks were slow, almost leisurely, but it was the conversation more than anything else that tired Lilly. Odd though he was, Tsirama was very intelligent, and as he answered every question Lilly asked with such great detail, she often pondered things long after they parted.

Her second lesson with him was this way. They scoured the forest floor for mushrooms, since, he pointed out before they began, the short rain the night before and the morning heat were the perfect conditions for them to pop, and during their trek, he quizzed her on the rules of experimenting while making potions. The entire lesson was spent reciting potential problems if instructions were improperly followed or ingredients were used that had not been collected properly. Their third lesson was spent in a different part of the forest discussing ingredients, and how the amount of strength a human has greatly affects his resistance to those ingredients. He admitted to her, after she swore not to tell a soul, that for the average, non-magickal human, he often diluted potions so there would be no serious side effects, but he always kept a supply of universal antidotes on hand should he ever need them.

"Kilpa juice is quick fix for minor problem," he informed her as he dug a stick in the ground to uproot a seemingly unidentifiable plant. "Kilpa root or powder for more serious problem, unless was used in potion and is causing problem. Then kilpa would only make worse. Pull."

"So what do you use," grunted Lilly as she tugged on the stubborn plant he was digging around, "when you can't use kilpa?"

"Can you think of nothing?"

Lilly thought for a moment, the plant gripping the ground harder the more she pulled at it. She loosened her pull and removed her wand from her pocket, then aimed it at the ground around the plant. At once, the loose dirt fell away from the roots. She picked the plant up carefully and handed it to her elated teacher.

"Ogre's blood?" she said.

"Good girl!" said Tsirama, clapping his narrow hands. "Oh," he sighed, staring lovingly at the plant, "this is wonderful. Come, I will show you how to extract serum from reshnok. Oooh, yes, serum is much more accurate than dry reshnok."

In her most recent lesson, the serum she had successfully extracted she got the pleasure to use, for only reshnok serum could be used for *Segvatele*, a potion to induce memory and vision quests. Lilly completed the potion, and for the first time, Tsirama offered to let her test it.

"I don't think that's a very good idea," said Lilly. "I have vision quests spontaneously without *Segvatele*."

"Do you?" asked Tsirama, his attention now fully on his student. "Can you have by your own will?"

Lilly told him of the night she communicated with Dr. Hoffman, how she had used his business card to force a dream. Tsirama listened, his dark eyes shining as she spoke. She included details of the dream to prove that she had actually spoken to him, for he told her things she never knew before then, like him hypnotizing his son.

"Ha!" exploded Tsirama, and Lilly jumped at the sudden interruption. "Hypnotism is blehya vision quest."

"Blehya?"

"Is magick word. Means non-magick. What you doing?"

Lilly didn't answer. She pulled out her journal and flipped to the back, where she wrote the newest word of the *Doret Gaia* and its meaning. She quickly flipped the book closed, but not before Tsirama saw what she had written.

"You trying to learn *Doret Gaia*," he stated, an air of disapproval in his voice.

"Yes."

"Don't!" he said forcefully as he poked his long finger into her chest. "That dangerous magick." His manner changed as quickly as the subject, for in a normal tone of voice he next said, "You were in restful state, good to harness enough power for vision quest and so far a distance. I see you have great power. You no need me teach you potions. You can do potions. Next, I will teach you control of quests. Sound to me like you need that more."

As with his previous lessons, Lilly left deep in thought, her mind racing over what she was learning and what she still had to learn. And it wasn't only his lessons that kept her preoccupied. Once she had memorized spells requiring only her wand and the proper word, which Ryzale dubbed wandspells, the sorceress made her try each and every one, whether she could do the task naturally or not. Lilly, it seemed, could do many things with her wand that she didn't think she could do naturally, but what she could do on her own accord was much more difficult to do Ryzale's way, often leaving her more drained that if she had done it her own way. Much worse was the endless barrage of questions Ryzale felt the need to ask while Lilly was casting the spells.

She quizzed Lilly on proper spell procedure, repetitively drilling her on the information at the beginning of each lesson. After practicing the wandspells each morning of their lessons, it was time for a more complicated spell, always accompanied with a series of questions about timing, intent, the moon phases, the holidays, the proper correspondences of candles, jewels and other items used in such spells, or whatever else Ryzale though she need to know that suited the situation at the time.

Ryzale pushed her hard, but Lilly pushed right back, answering every question correctly and completing every spell with perfect precision. When she required Lilly to start keeping a record of her magickal knowledge, Lilly produced the journal she'd been keeping since her first lesson with Tsirama, and returned it to her bag with smug satisfaction after seeing the surprised look on Ryzale's face.

"Very good, then," said Ryzale that day, clearing her throat to cover her shock. "When you return, we will begin working with charms. You will learn how to contain magick within an item and expel it, so bring something with you for the next lesson."

"Like what?"

"A trinket, a stone, anything really. Even your necklace could be used, though I wouldn't recommend it. One small slip could destroy it." Lilly wrote a reminder to herself so she would not forget to bring something. There was no way she was going to be forced to practice on the necklace her father had asked her to keep safe. It was the only thing he had given her that she had thought to bring.

Each day ended with Zephra, whose lessons were merely practice of what Lilly already knew. By the end of the first week, Lilly could almost defeat Zephra at hand to hand combat with a dagger, so Zephra made the lessons more challenging by increasing the distance between them and throwing balls of fire for Lilly to hit from a distance. It was a daunting task at first, for Lilly could hardly touch the flame with her blade, let alone hit its center. After her next visit with Orvak, with whom she spent her entire free day in light of her recent argument with Wyatt and her desire to let him get over it, she hit the center of her target over half the time, and by the end of the week, she barely missed a single target, for Orvak had stayed true to his word and helped her to hone her perception skills where her vision was concerned.   She practiced daily, concentrating first on sound while blocking her other senses, and then blocking out the sound to focus her eyes. It was a strange sensation, like using a pair of binoculars without having binoculars, but she advanced so quickly that Orvak's next lesson would enable her to focus on both sight and sound at the same time.

Of all her trainers, however, Dorwynn was the most ruthless. He had started pushing her harder than ever, and though Wyatt had helped her with Earth magick, it seemed the more progress she made in Dorwynn's presence, the harder he pushed for more. She created another miniature statue from stone, a wizard that closely resembled Gustave, and she accomplished it so quickly, he immediately took her to the waterfall, where he demanded she try to reshape the stone ascending to the cave.

It was a daunting task, draining her so much that she actually collapsed on her third attempt, but Dorwynn was relentless when he told her that they would train no further until she could manage it. She managed to accomplish it by the middle of their third lesson, and afterward, Dorwynn dragged her to the area of the yard that once held a garden.

"We're going to train here for a few days," he told her, waving his hand over the compacted earth. "First, we'll get the ground ready for a garden, and then, I'll teach you how to grow a plant from a seed. You'll have to be able to grow it in your hands to pass your test, but we'll start by practicing with them in the ground."

He worked with her, both of them moving and churning the dirt using magick, aerating it so it would be ready for planting what would later become her garden. Producing shovels, rakes and hoes, Dorwynn began scooping foul smelling pellets into the freshly turned dirt from a pile near where they were working, and only when Dorwynn began working it into the dirt did Lilly realize it was fertilizer.

"Where did you get that?" she asked, helping him lift and churn it into the dirt with her wand.

"Halfway between here and town," he said breathlessly. "The man with the farm raises rabbits. Chickens and pigs, too. He offered to sell you a few if you want to raise your own."

"I don't know how to do all that."

Dorwynn wiped his hand across his brow to stop the sweat from reaching his eyes, leaving a trail of dirt on his forehead. "Don't worry," he said, chucking the shovel deep into the pile and scooping it into the garden. "You will."

It was one of their better lessons, and exhausted though she was, she found herself looking forward to the sowing of the seeds, which continued during their next training session. For a change, he was very complacent while teaching her how to grow a full plant from a seed.

"This is a different type of magick," he began, his voice soothing as though the plant required it. "Rather than manipulating earth, you are lending your own energy to the seed, nourishing it, in a sense, giving it life. The suns and earth and water do all these things, but you have the ability to do the same, and at a much quicker rate. You must feel the energy it requires to grow, and then give just the right amount to coax it from its shell."

He held out his hand, a tiny seed in his palm. It quivered as he stared at it, and as his hand began to glow, a sprout emerged from the seed and began growing at a phenomenal rate. When it grew to be about four inches, Dorwynn tore his eyes from it and looked at Lilly, grinning.

"It's now ready to plant," he said, handing her the small spade shovel and motioning toward the garden. "Plant them without magick. I guarantee you will appreciate it more. A few months and you'll have more tomatoes than you can stand."

Lilly planted the first plant while Dorwynn dug two rows of holes for the remaining seeds, and then he sat with her while she attempted to make one grow. She concentrated hard, but the most she could manage was making the seed quiver on the dirt before it exploded.

"Just practice," said Dorwynn gently, "and try not to give it so much energy. That's why it keeps bursting."

Lilly kept trying, forcing herself to restrain the magick that seemed to be forcing its way out of her. She was concentrating so hard, in fact, that when Dorwynn disappeared into the house and seemed to be talking to himself, she noticed his absence nearly half an hour later, when she finally accomplished her task.

"I did it," she said, exhilarated. "Dorwynn?"

Without waiting for his return, she grabbed another seed and sprouted it in her hand, then another, and another. She planted what she had grown, and then she grew enough seeds to finish filling the holes already dug. Dorwynn still hadn't returned by the time she finished, and she returned to the house to find him ranting to Zephra.

"What does he want you to do?" Zephra asked.

"I can't tell you," pouted Dorwynn as he threw clothes into a knapsack, "but I can tell you that it's pointless. I have a job to do, and he can't even wait until I finish it before he's pushing me into another one. I should be here, not gallivanting across half the land to..." He stopped short, aware he had almost said more than he should, and pounded the rest of his clothes into the sack before packing some bread and salt pork and shoving them in as well.

"He's having someone deliver the horses we left before the swamp," he said, sounding a bit guilty. "I guess I should have retrieved them by now."

Lilly felt guilty, too. She hadn't given Adair a second thought after they had left her behind. With so much going on around her, she didn't realize how much time had passed since then until Zephra spouted, "Yeah, they've been there for weeks."

"It hasn't been weeks," protested Lilly. She had only just begun her training, hadn't she?

"This is the end of your second week of training," Zephra pointed out. "We spent a few nights more than that traveling here and getting things prepared for your training. Yes, it has been weeks."

While Lilly considered how much time had actually passed, Dorwynn glanced out the kitchen window before stalking into the living room to rummage through the closet. He emerged with his water skein, his traveling cloak and a large-brimmed hat Lilly had never seen before. She tried to control the fit of giggles rising in her throat as he perched the hat on his head.

"I shouldn't be gone more than a week," he said in a resigned voice. "The garden looks great, Lilly. I want you to use our training time to practice what you've learned so far, and we'll finish with your tasks when I return."

He paused, as though he wanted to bid them a better farewell, but he turned away from them without a word, slamming the door behind him.

"What was that about?" asked Lilly, who had missed the majority of the conversation. Zephra shook her head.

"Gustave won't be coming for a while," was all she said before darting into the kitchen. "Come on," she called. "We'll skip our session tonight."

That night, all Lilly could think about was that Gustave had contacted Dorwynn and sent him away, but he didn't have the courtesy to talk to her at all when she had so much to ask him. She fell asleep feeling angry and confused by Gustave's lack of communication, sad that Wyatt had not tried to contact her since their argument, which she now realized had been over a week ago, and frustrated that she had let so much time pass unnoticed without solving any of the mysteries plaguing her mind. So involved she was in her own turmoil, she didn't notice the faint green light seeping from the floor in the corner of the room, growing brighter as the light of the setting suns faded into darkness.

New Developments

The next few days passed without incident. In fact, other than when they were training together, Zephra barely spoke to Lilly at all. After an informative lesson with Ryzale, Lilly had successfully contained magick in the miniature pterippus she had created with Wyatt, a spell that could create brilliant light by uttering a single word while holding the object. Tsirama restructured their lessons, armed with *Segvatele* and its antidote, to begin teaching her to control her vision quests, and while it made for an interesting lesson, it didn't seem to help much, for she had no control over what she saw or how long she saw it.

She contacted Wyatt, who seemed thrilled to see her again, and they trained together during the time she would have been training with Dorwynn. She could feel herself getting stronger each day, achieving more than even she expected in such a short amount of time.

"You'll be ready to test in no time," he told her, grinning from ear to ear as he returned the namun she had just successfully raised. "What else do you still need to know?"

She was going to tell him that she still needed to learn how to change earth from one form to another, a task she was more than willing to begin, but she was distracted by a feeling so great, so familiar, that everything else faded from her mind. Rohan was near, and he was approaching.

"Um," she said quickly, "I'm sorry, but I have to go now. Can we continue this later?"

"Sure," he said, slightly disappointed. He had planned to spend the entire day with her in the absence of her trainer. "I'll see you later, I guess."

She disappeared instantly, arriving moments later on the doorstep in time to see Rohan riding Adair toward the house, leading Dorwynn's horse behind him. Not even the dark clouds rolling toward them could spoil the moment she saw him, his blonde hair blazing in what little sunlight the clouds allowed to pass, his dark eyes scanning the house for her presence. Lilly broke into a grin when their eyes met, and she sprinted toward him as he jumped from the horse and held out his arms in time for her to jump into them.

"I missed you so much," she said, restraining the happy sob that threatened to burst from her.

"I missed you, too," he whispered, holding her tight. "How have you been?"

"Going insane," she spouted.

"That well, huh?" he chuckled. "Come, you can tell me all about it."

They left the horses to graze in the field and walked to the house, Lilly clutching Rohan's hand as though if she let go of it, he would disappear. Inside, Lilly fixed them both something to drink and they sat at the kitchen table, each wondering where to begin. After an uncomfortable silence, Rohan decided to go first.

"Before you tell me all about your training," he said, sipping his tea, "I have a word of warning for you and your trainers. There is a dragon in Elikrede. She walks in human form."

"Okay," replied Lilly, uncertain why this was important.

"Well, dragons don't usually take human form. They can, but they rarely do. They feel it is beneath them, so when one is sighted in human form, it is very significant. A dragon in human form always carries importance for people doing important things, like you and your training. Just promise me you'll stay on your guard."

"I will," Lilly promised, "but how will I know when I see her if she is in human form?"

"Trust me, you will know when you see her. You can always tell when a dragon is..."

"A dragon?" interrupted Zephra, who appeared at the back door. She looked inquisitively at Rohan, who was taken aback at the sight of her.

"Y-yes," he stammered, unable to understand the sudden tightening compressing his chest, "in Elikrede."

"You'd think we'd have noticed a dragon arriving," she said casually. "It's not like they're hard to see."

"Not if she is in human form."

The look of shock on Zephra face was priceless to Lilly, who was annoyed that they were so rudely interrupted. Zephra lowered herself into the chair nearest her without taking her eyes from Rohan.

"Human form?" she gasped. "What is it doing here? Who is it looking for?"

"What makes you so sure she's looking for anyone?' asked Lilly, who apparently hadn't grasped the full weight of the situation. Rohan and Zephra both looked at her incredulously. "What?"

"A dragon who walks around in human form is unusual," Zephra told her. "There is no reason for it unless she is looking for someone, and if she's looking for you, she's either an ally or an enemy. There is no in-between."

While Lilly digested Zephra's words, Rohan struggled to breathe, an invisible weight crushing his lungs. Zephra watched him, curiosity reflected in her eyes. He looked familiar to her, but she couldn't place where she'd seen him before.

"I'm Zephra," she announced, jutting her hand toward him. "And you are...?"

"Rohan," he coughed.

"Rohan," she echoed. "Are you alright?"

"I will be," he said, rising slowly from his chair. "If you will excuse me, I think I need some air."

He walked out the door through which Zephra had just entered, stumbling as he went. Lilly glared at Zephra, wondering why she had chosen that moment to return to the house and thus, interrupt what Lilly knew was very limited time with Rohan. Zephra still seemed focused on the news of the dragon, but when she noticed the darts Lilly was shooting at her with her eyes, she decided to open the lines of communication.

"He's nice," she said, and though Lilly tensed, she pretended not to notice. "Who is he?"

"He's my imaginary friend," stated Lilly. Her mood lightened as confusion crossed Zephra's face, and she realized how good it felt to be the one with the knowledge for a change. "He's my protector," she continued, her voice now serious. "He's been watching me my entire life, waiting until I was ready to come here. It was his mother who first trained me."

"Oh," said Zephra, finally making the connection. He was Ashya's son. "You know, it surprises me that Gustave allowed her to keep you for so long. You could already be training in Air magick by now. I wonder why he waited six months before he decided you were ready to train with us."

"It seemed to me," Lilly said, restraining the anger building inside her, "that it was in his plans from the start. Perhaps he was waiting for someone else to be ready."

"Maybe."

Silence poisoned the air between them, and while Lilly knew her reasons for her anger, Zephra had no clue, and reasoned that they had spent too much of their time together doing nothing but fighting, even if it was all for training. Her own discomfort was that she could actually feel Lilly's anger, and she wasn't the only one noticed. The tension between them was so thick that Rohan could feel a difference in the room when he returned.

"Ladies," he said warily, "is everything okay?"

For a moment, no one spoke. Then Zephra, in an overly cheery voice, announced, "It's fine. I'm going to town for a while. I want to see if I can find out anything about this dragon." She stood so fast her chair flipped backward. She waited for a reaction, and receiving none, she added, "I'll bring food for dinner," and then left without bothering to right the chair.

"What's going on?" he asked when Zephra had gone.

"Nothing," Lilly assured him, though she could tell he wasn't convinced. She took out her wand, pointed it at the chair without looking at it and flicked her wrist. The chair snapped forward, landing perfectly at the table. "We've never had a very easy relationship."

"Why not?" Rohan returned to his own chair, his doubtful expression now one of awe. He had been watching her here and there, always invisible, of course, but he had somehow not been watching enough, for her powers had obviously far surpassed his expectations.

"It's a long story," she sighed, unsure of how much she really wanted him to know.

"Lilly," he said, and she lifted her eyes to meet his, "I haven't been watching you so often now that I have returned. Now that Gustave has returned..." He paused, shook his head and continued. "I've missed much. When I left Mother's, I had a long task ahead of me, one I thought I would have finished before you left her. Unfortunately, circumstances beyond my control prevented that until now. I want to hear it all; the good, the bad...everything. I will think no less of you, no matter what has happened in my absence."

She closed her eyes to prevent the tears from pouring down her face, but one escaped, trailing its way down her cheek. Rohan wiped it away gently, then took her hand and tugged it, smiling.

"Come on. Let's go for a walk."

As they walked around the back yard, the fresh air helped Lilly relax, and she began her story on the day she left Ashya's. She told him about everything that happened in Arthidgen, from meeting her trainers to the terrible night before they left, and every event in between, including a very detailed account of the aftereffects of using true magick.

"That's where the tension lies between Zephra and me," she informed him, pausing to lean against the tree at the water's edge and staring across the lake. "I can't get that dream of her out of my mind. I don't know what she was saying, but when she grabbed my wrist, something happened. I can't even describe it, but I have never felt such a terrible sense of loss in my life. It was like she was literally killing me, draining me of life, and when I woke up, she was holding my wrist in exactly the same place as she was in the dream."

"And then what?" asked Rohan. She shrugged and started walking again.

"And then I lost control in the forest. The next day we set out for Elikrede. Dorwynn and Zephra brought me here. Well, Dorwynn brought me and Zephra followed. She claims she has some unexplainable connection to me, but I don't feel that with her."

"Don't you?" asked Rohan. She stopped and stared at him, confused. "Well, you say you heard her talking with Dorwynn in your mind on more than one occasion. Did it ever occur to you that it is because of this connection she feels toward you? You are interpreting the connection, even if you don't think you feel it."

"I don't know," said Lilly. "She was horrible to me from the moment we met, and that dream was too real. Besides, it only makes sense that I have a connection with Dorwynn considering our past."

"Lilly, I have known you for your whole life, yes?" She nodded, and he grabbed her shoulders, leaning toward her to make his point. "You have become rather close-minded in the process of expanding your mind. That dream was one small piece of a very large puzzle. Do you think for one second that Gustave," he lowered his voice to a whisper, "that *I*, would put you directly in harm's way? She has her issues, as we all do, but Gustave trusts her beyond all others and his destiny is to prepare the Chosen One for her destiny."

"You are Gustave," she whispered forcefully, her face inches from his, "but how well do you really know her?"

"That's not how it works," he said, and Lilly crossed her arms in defiance.

"Well, you need to explain to me how it works, because just as much has happened to me since we got here, and I discovered some things about Gustave that I need to discuss with him."

"Finish telling me what happened..."

"No. I want some answers."

"Fine," he sighed, leading her closer to the waterfall. "I am not the real Gustave. There is no Gustave, not since the wizard himself died. He was more powerful than any other human of his time, so powerful, in fact, rumor has it he lived for hundreds of years. Many thought he was immortal, so on his deathbed he chose his favorite apprentice to continue his legacy. When the young apprentice accepted the task, the wizard performed a spell, encasing as much of himself as he could within the only magickal tool he ever used...his staff. His identity, his memories, his experiences and all of his knowledge of magick were contained within it, to be passed from one wizard to another over time.

"I don't know how many wizards have assumed the position, nor for how many years the legacy has continued. I do know, however, that while the staff can collect the memories and knowledge of each wizard who uses it, it can only obtain those things while the wizard is using Gustave's identity."

"Can you access those memories," Lilly asked, excitement replacing her annoyance, "even if you didn't experience them?"

"Only when I am Gustave," he said. "Why?"

Lilly continued with the multitude of revelations over the past few weeks, filling him in on her relationship with Dorwynn since the night in Arthidgen, her trip through time, her visit to his mother, her strange dreams, the vision quest of Gustave and the tasil, the flashes she saw while with Orvak, and her new friendship in Wyatt. When she finished, she watched him for a reaction, but aside from his stunned expression, he was otherwise unaffected.

"Wow," he said finally. "No wonder you're so riled up. If I had that much information shoved into my head, I'd explode."

"Thank you!" she cried, exasperated. "But that doesn't even include my training. I don't know what any of it means. I can't get a straight answer out of anyone, and if I don't find out soon, I'm afraid I'll lose sight of what I have to do. I feel like I already am."

"So find out what it means, Lilly! You have people all around you who are willing to tell you everything you need to know if you would simply ask them. What they tell you may not be the answer to your question, but it may very well lead you to finding the answer yourself. You are not helpless. You are the most competent person I know, and if you really wanted to figure things out, you would stop waiting for everyone else to take action and just do it yourself."

Lilly stared at him, dumbstruck. Overhead, thunder crashed, and the storm clouds burst with such force they were drenched before the thunder's echo faded. She just stared at him, unable to believe what he just said.

"What about staying safe and not drawing extra attention to myself?"

"I'm not telling you to defy every rule," he said, ducking under the nearest tree, "but sometimes, it doesn't hurt to bend one now and again." He wrung the water from his hair and shook his head. It was still sopping, and it clung to his neck and back as though it was painted on him.

"I can't, Rohan," she said in disdain. "There's too much at stake."

"What's wrong with you?" he asked incredulously. She opened her mouth to protest, but he continued before she could say a word. "When you were younger, you weren't afraid of anything. You were daring and reckless, and willing to take risks. I know things changed after Dorwynn left, but you were never the same after that, and now, you're letting him and everyone else make you feel inadequate, like you aren't meant for this, when I know for a fact that you are."

"What?" she retorted. "Even you thought your mother was going too fast, that I wasn't ready for what she was teaching me."

"So I was wrong! I admit it. I mean, look at everything you've already done, all the things you are still learning to do. You used true magick without even being taught to use it, and not only did you survive it, you didn't suffer anything for it."

"That was an accident," Lilly snapped. "I didn't mean to do it."

"You meant to kill the harpies."

"Yeah, but that almost killed me."

"But it didn't," he said pointedly. "How can you have done these things and still not believe you are meant for this? How can you allow what everyone else thinks to keep you from doing what you feel is right?"

He was staring at her, a determined expression fixed upon his face as he waited for her to answer. She shook her head, and looking at her feet, she whispered, "I don't know."

"It's time you figured it out," he scolded. "What about this Wyatt fellow? He seems to think you have potential."

"He doesn't know about all the stuff I've done."

"And you don't want to tell him?"

"No," she admitted, wiping her face as rain streamed over her. She was grateful for the rain; it hid the fact she was crying again. "I'd like at least one person here to appreciate me for who I am, not for my *destiny*." Her words were harsh, and although she didn't mean to hurt Rohan, she could tell he took them to heart. "I'm sorry," she said. "I didn't mean you, but you are never here, and I need a friend. Dorwynn hasn't been a friend since he became my trainer."

"Tell me of this Wyatt," said Rohan, sitting on the ground and leaning against the tree.

Lilly sighed, suddenly tired of talking, but she sat beside him and related everything about her relationship with Wyatt; how they met, their intertwining dreams and the strange connection between them, and of the strange light behind her eyes whenever she touched him. She explained her dreams of him before they met, and how he had also dreamed of her, saving the shared dream of their duel until the end.

"What do you think I should do?" she asked when she had finished. Rohan looked thoughtful, and stared at the raindrops breaking the surface of the water for so long, Lilly wondered if he had heard her. Finally, he stretched his legs and turned toward her, his eyes shining and an odd smile on his face.

"I think you should do what you feel is right, when you feel it is right, not only with this duel, but with everything you are going through right now. The ogre told you how to open the tasil, so open it. The apothecary wants to teach you how to control your quests, so let him teach you. I don't know about the light you keep seeing when you touch Wyatt, but it seems significant, so keep trying to discover what it, and everything else, means. You can do it, Lilly. I know you can. You are more capable than you think you are."

"What if something goes wrong?"

"Things have already been going wrong." He leaned forward, looking into her emerald eyes, still bright with tears, and ignoring the crushing sensation in his chest that suddenly reappeared, he added, "Just once, wouldn't you like to be responsible for what goes wrong, make it happen instead of having it happen to you?"

"It's not the simple," she muttered, "when someone else is making all the decisions."

"Who's that?"

"Gustave. You."

"No, Lilly," he said, shaking his head, and she looked at him, a mixture of defiance and confusion on her face. "I am not the one making all the decisions. You are. I showed you the path; you chose to walk it. I directed you toward capable hands, and while I hope you choose to heed their advice and learn from them, only you can choose to do that, just as they each chose to accept the challenge of getting you further down the path and closer to your destiny. You say you want to be appreciated for yourself and not your destiny, but it is only your destiny because you chose it to be so. You are who you are because of the choices you make. So you must ask yourself, Lilly...who are you?"

"Hey!" came a shout from the house, their solitude shattered. They looked up to see Zephra standing in the doorway, as soaked as they were. "What are you guys doing out there in the rain?"

"Getting wet!" Rohan shouted back. Lilly smiled through her tears, and she could feel something stirring deep inside her, as if Rohan's words had been the spark she needed to light the fire in her soul.

"Come inside!" shouted Zephra. "You won't believe what happened in town."

The Pterippus and the Chameleon

"Feel better?" Zephra asked Lilly as she returned from her room wearing dry clothes. Lilly nodded, rubbing a towel vigorously over her drenched head. Zephra, completely dry with the aid of her own magickal abilities, was now preparing a stew, which was already boiling over the stove. She had refused to tell them anything until they changed into something dry. Since Rohan had left his pack on Adair and all of his belongings were soaked, Zephra dug out a shirt and a pair of trousers Dorwynn had left behind, tossing them to Rohan to wear while his things dried.

He appeared in the kitchen moments later, water still dripping from his long hair. Lilly tossed him the towel she used to dry her own hair, resisting the urge to laugh, for the shirt sleeves came halfway between Rohan's wrists and elbows, and the trousers were several inches too short.

"Dorwynn is not a tall guy, is he?" asked Rohan with a grin, wringing water from his hair with the towel.

"I think those are left over from when he first arrived," chuckled Zephra. "He was just a boy then."

He stared at her, losing himself for an instant in her violet eyes. The tight feeling in his chest made it difficult for him to breathe, but he couldn't seem to look away from her, as though she had put a spell on him. She held his gaze for a moment, then turned away sharply and began chopping vegetables.

"The dragon is most definitely searching for someone," she said, throwing onions and carrots into the stew pot. "She's inquiring all over town about any new arrivals, and..."

She stopped talking, chopping potatoes fiercely and tossing them into the pot carelessly, and refused to look at them. Lilly was sitting at the table, Rohan directly across from her, and she was in a much better mood than before Zephra had left. Rohan's words, no matter how harshly they had been delivered, were exactly what she needed to hear to boost the confidence she had so long ago lost. She waited for Zephra to continue, but Lilly could tell there was something she didn't want to say.

"And what, Zephra?" she asked, prompting her. Zephra slammed the knife on the wooden cutting board with a loud BANG! Both Rohan and Lilly jumped at the sound, and neither said a word, both watching her.

"Well," she said hesitantly as she turned to face them, "don't get angry, but when we were traveling from Arthidgen, I thought someone was following us. After we went through the cave, I didn't feel anyone anymore, so I just assumed it was someone else traveling through the woods. It was the dragon, I'm sure of it, and I think she was following you. I think she's looking for you now."

"Oh well," said Lilly after a moment. Zephra gaped at her. That was one reaction she had not expected. "If she's looking for me," Lilly continued, "let her find me. If not, then we have nothing to worry about, do we?"

"What if..."

"I'm tired of 'what ifs', Zephra. What if I get struck by lightning when I'm walking in the rain? What if I fall off my horse and break my neck? At least I'll get to feel the rain on my face or the wind in my hair before I die. I'm tired of worrying so much."

"Wow," said Zephra. "Get you away from Dorwynn and you're a whole new person."

"Yeah," agreed Lilly, "or maybe I'm tired of trying to be something I'm not." She looked across the table at Rohan, returning his smile.

"And what's that?" asked Zephra as she put a lid on the stew and joined them at the table.

"A child."

Lilly seemed to come alive as she told Zephra how she had been feeling lately, and Zephra accepted everything Lilly told her with a calm manner. Their communication issues, it seemed, were coming to an end, but Lilly still couldn't get past the dream enough to believe any sort of connection existed between them but that of student and master.

Rohan watched the banter between the women with a great deal of interest, though his own mind was reeling out of control. The pains in his chest were something he had not felt in a while, since he had left Lilly with his mother months ago, and he had never hurt this badly before. He expected to feel it again in her presence, for he believed she was his leyartha, but he had never experienced anything like *this* in his whole life. The pull was stronger, so strong he had a hard time focusing on much of anything, which he could not understand.

It had never confused him before now, either, for though he'd felt a pull toward Zephra in the past, it had always occurred while he was disguised as Gustave. He'd always assumed it was a remnant of the old wizard's identity, and everlasting love for an immortal creature that somehow enabled a piece of his soul to remain with the physical identity imprinted within the staff. Now, in the presence of both Lilly and Zephra, and as himself, he realized what a ridiculous notion it seemed. How could he have ever believed a soul could be split? He knew even everlasting love carried forth into the next life, so there would be no reason to split a soul, even if it could be done. If he'd have remembered the translation of the word leyartha before now, his foolish assumptions would have been contradicted, for the word literally meant "light of the soul".

It wouldn't be such a problem if he would have realized this error before, for he could have prepared himself for such a situation, but now he wondered what he should do. His entire life, he felt Lilly was his soul mate, always ignoring the pull toward Zephra until now, when he finally met her as himself. Now, he was clueless, for he had never known anyone who had felt the pull of leyartha for more than one person.

Lilly filled his thoughts wherever he went, a constant vision always in his mind. He spent many nights invisible, watching her as she slept, for night was the only time he had to spare, but he could never tell her he was there. Too much was at stake for him to sacrifice it all for his feelings. He had to repeatedly remind himself that he was meant to serve her, to protect her, and to guide her to her destiny, which is not something she could do if he declared his feelings for her, so he restrained himself as he knew he should.

He looked across the table at the two women. Zephra was now arguing with Lilly that she still needed to follow the advice of her trainers, as they knew what was best for her. Her eyes turned brighter, small flecks of orange appearing within the violet hue. Lilly, who was holding her own in the argument, had also changed in appearance while he was lost in his thoughts. He could see tiny flecks of yellow-orange in her eyes as well, as though they were reflecting Zephra's. At once, an image of Lilly crying while Zephra held fast to her wrist flashed through his mind. He felt the terrible sadness she had described, the feeling that she was dying a painful death, and his throat constricted. Gasping for breath, his heart racing, he jumped to his feet and fled the room.

"Rohan?" asked Lilly, concerned. She followed him from the room.

It can't be, he told himself, trying to even his breathing. *Don't tell her what you saw. She won't understand it. It will ruin everything. She can't know. Don't tell her!*

"Don't tell me what?" she asked, and he cursed the fact she had learned to read minds.

"Have you considered the possibility that the strange connections you have with others is because you are so good at that? You spent too much time with my mother."

Lilly perched herself on the arm of the sofa facing Rohan, who was now standing between her and the front door. He tried to compose himself, hoping the conversation would steer away from what he had just witnessed. He couldn't tell her what he had seen, what he had felt, as real as if it had happened to him. How could she ever understand what was happening, what it could mean? He wasn't sure if he even understood it, but he couldn't blame Lilly for what she felt toward Zephra, for it indeed felt at that moment as though he was dying.

"You know, you aren't the first person today who's told me that," she told him, and he sighed, relieved that she hadn't pushed him to tell her what he knew he never could.

"Yeah?" he gasped, still trying to catch his breath.

"I think you're wrong, though. I don't hear their thoughts. I can hear them speaking to each other as if they were sitting right next to me, but only when they talk to each other. It's never happened when either of them talk to anyone else, at least not yet."

"Do you hear all of their conversations?"

"I doubt it."

"So you were probably fairly close to them when it happened?"

"Well, yes, and..." A sudden realization struck Lilly. "...and each time I heard them, they were talking about me."

"That might have something to do with it," said Rohan, hoping his voice wouldn't betray the pain he was feeling, "but I doubt that the subject of the conversation has anything to do with the connection. If you only hear them when they are speaking to each other, then you have a connection with one of them, or both of them. Either way, keep in mind that magickal connections go both ways."

"Meaning?"

"Meaning if the connection lies with between you and Zephra," he whispered, struggling to get the words out, struggling against the weight pressing against his lungs, "and you can hear her conversations because of it, then she can probably hear yours. Whatever the connection, it always works both ways."

"I'll...are you okay?" Rohan was doubled over, gripping his stomach, no longer able to hide his obvious pain. Lilly, noticing his condition, jumped off the edge of the sofa and walked toward him, but he jerked away from her before she could touch him.

His face was a ghostly white, his entire body trembling, burning, as though he'd been tossed into Zephra's boiling pot of stew, and he could feel the bile rising in his throat, despite how constricted it seemed to be. He had to get out of the house, away from them until he could control whatever was happening to him.

"I don't know," he stammered, stumbling as he made his way closer to the door. "I need some fresh air. I'll...eat later." He almost choked on his last words as he fell out the front door. Lilly heard him retch as the door slammed, and deciding to leave him alone for a while, she returned to the kitchen. Zephra was stirring the stew, and she joined Lilly at the table with a knowing smile on her face.

"What?" asked Lilly, baffled by Rohan's sudden bout of illness and appalled that Zephra was smiling about it.

"I was wondering how you heard us talking that night in the forest," she said simply. Lilly's jaw dropped.

"You could hear us talking?" she whispered. "Just now?"

"Well, you weren't exactly talking quietly, now, were you?"

"Oh," said Lilly, relief flooding her voice, "I guess not."

"You thought I heard you two the way you heard me and Dorwynn." Zephra said this in such a matter-of-fact tone, Lilly wondered once again if Zephra could read her mind. She nodded. "No," said Zephra. "I was just eavesdropping."

"Have you ever heard me talking to someone in your mind?"

Zephra didn't answer immediately. She had only recently heard the conversation between Lilly and Wyatt, but she wasn't sure she should tell Lilly the about it. She'd overheard what Rohan said about the connection going both ways, and it confirmed in her mind what she already knew: her connection to Lilly was significant, whether Lilly was ready to believe it or not.

"Have you?" Lilly prompted, eyeing her suspiciously.

"Who's Wyatt?" she finally asked, unwilling to lie to the girl, but knowing she couldn't avoid answering the question. Lilly's eyebrows shot so high on her forehead, Zephra almost laughed, but she knew that would only anger Lilly, so she quickly added, "It only happened once. You were having an argument with him."

Lilly was silent, unable to speak. She hadn't wanted her trainers to know of Wyatt, and now, there was no way she could avoid telling Zephra, at least, about his role in her life. She stood, fetching herself a glass of water, and gulped the entire glass in one shot, trying to clear her head enough to talk about him. She'd already told the story once today, and she really didn't feel like talking about him to Zephra of all people, but with a sigh, she returned to the table and began the story again.

Outside, Rohan was finally feeling better, though he was now soaked again from the relentless rain. He decided to unload the horses, removing the saddles and the rest of his sopping traveling items before running a grooming brush over their coats, removing burrs and twigs from their manes and tails, while his mind raced the entire time.

What's wrong with me? he wondered. *I feel like I'm losing my mind.* His thoughts swarmed around Lilly and all the feelings he had for her that he knew he shouldn't feel. He didn't know why he had the sudden flash of her dream of Zephra, but what he thought it meant couldn't be possible, could it? *No,* he told himself forcefully, but he knew Zephra would never hurt her like that without having a good reason, and though he'd never heard of it happening before, deep down he knew it was a possibility. He also knew he could never tell Lilly, because if she knew what it could mean, she might try to stop it, and if she stopped it from happening, the consequences could be devastating. This event, and all the others she witnessed during her magickally-induced coma, were for Lilly to solve alone.

His thoughts turned toward Zephra, and he found himself wondering about her motives. She was immortal. She would survive no matter what happened in the future, but when that fateful moment arrived, and he had no doubt that it would, would she turn on Lilly, or would she make the ultimate sacrifice to save her? He felt sick again at the thought of Lilly being in danger, or was it the thought that this other woman might very well be the cause of it that bothered him so? And why did he feel this way in her presence, when he had been around both her and Lilly countless times before and, aside from a slight stir in his heart with each of them, he'd never felt like this?

Perhaps it's because they are together, he thought, reasoning that if one of them was indeed his soul mate, his leyartha, then it could be the reason for his current condition. But why would it affect him so, and which one was the light of his soul?

The only solution he could figure was to spend time alone with each of them, more than anything to see which of the two women had a greater effect over him. The rain fell harder as he let go of Adair's reins and removed the bridle, and he lifted his eyes toward the sky, where the shadows of thunderbirds flying through the thick clouds distracted him enough to forget for the moment the series of doubts flooding his core.

Rohan stayed in the rain, sitting beneath the farthest tree from the house, and stared at the sky as the thunderbirds roared slowly over the lands surrounding Elikrede. He'd always wanted to fly with a thunderbird, just once, to feel the sensation of being in control of a storm cloud. He had flown through one once, but without the presence of the thunderbirds, it had been a cold, wet, dull experience. The storm tonight was relatively calm despite the amount of rain falling, but as it drifted to the north, an outburst of thunder echoed, followed by a series of lightning bolts that shot through the clouds, never touching the ground, and he knew at least one of the massive birds soaring among the dark clouds had been angered.

His stomach growled, and he realized that he hadn't eaten all day, although in his previous condition, he was thankful he hadn't. Now, however, he was starving, and he debated whether he should attempt entering the house for dinner and risk a relapse or wait until he knew one of the women had gone to bed. He finally decided that he would wait until the rain stopped, and when it finally ceased and the clouds began to part, the suns were gone, leaving a clear, star-filled sky above him.

It was a glorious sight, watching the clouds fade into nothing, leaving a perfect view of the bejeweled sky. He forgot his hunger as he lost himself in the night, and it wasn't until he caught the wonderful scent of stew that his stomach reminded him.

"I thought you might be hungry by now," said Lilly as she appeared behind him with a bowl of stew. He accepted it gratefully, and nearly inhaled the first half of the bowl before pausing to breathe.

"Thank you," he said, his mouth full.

"No problem," she said as she sat beside him, unaware of the wet earth beneath her. "Are you feeling better?"

"Much."

"What happened?"

"Too much traveling, I suspect," he lied, guilt gripping his soul like a fist around his heart.

"Oh," was all she said, faithfully accepting his explanation, and Rohan could barely swallow the next bite.

They sat in silence for some time, Rohan finishing his meal while Lilly gazed at the stars. She searched the sky for constellations, something she used to do quite often, but she found nothing familiar, and it reminded her of how far from home she really was.

"Beautiful, aren't they?" asked Rohan softly, setting his empty bowl on the ground. Lilly glanced at the bowl, and without bothering to use her wand, sent it into the house with the wave of her hand. Rohan smiled, shaking his head. "You're pretty good at that."

"I guess," she said, pulling her knees into her chest and wrapping her arms around her legs. She rested her head against them, looking at Rohan, and in that moment, he realized that she was no longer the child he'd spent his life observing. Her eyes had always carried an air of wisdom, but now, they seemed alive with knowledge and filled with a sense of dread he'd never seen.

"What's wrong?" he asked, and when she replied with a shrug, he said, "Come on, Lilly. I know you. Tell me what's bothering you."

"Homesick, I guess. Everything is so different here."

"You knew it would be."

"I know," she sighed, staring up at the stars again. "Even the sky is different, though. Foreign, like someone took all the stars from it and just threw them back in no particular order. I miss being able to look around and see something familiar."

"Do you want me to show you something familiar?" asked Rohan. "Granted, it isn't exactly the same, but it might make you feel a little better."

"Okay."

He stood, turning circles as he scoured the sky. "There!" he exclaimed, pointing. "Do you see that bright star and the dim one beside it?" Lilly stood, and leaning close to him, her eyes followed the direction of his outstretched arm until she saw them. "The star below the dim one is in the Pegasus constellation on Earth. Earth's sun is directly on the other side of that star, almost the same distance away as our suns here."

"Does it belong to a constellation here?" she asked quietly, captivated.

"Well," he said, looking for the rest of the stars, "the bright star there makes the eye and the dim one slightly below and off to the right is the shoulder. The two stars extending upward form the wing. The star Earth's sun is behind is the extended hoof, the dim star above and to the left is the tip of the nose, and the three stars scattered below all of those are the rest of the hooves. It's an interesting correlation, but the constellation here honors the same soul as the constellation there. On Earth, he was known as Pegasus, the first pterippus. Here, he is known as Verasant, but they are one and the same. Would you like to hear the story?"

"Yes, I would."

"He was the first of my kind, born when man was still new to the Earth. In those days, magickal creatures still flourished there, as did magick, and the few humans who were gifted with magick, along with many magickal creatures, were revered as gods and goddesses. Poseidon, ruler of the merfolk and himself a merman, was believed to be the god of the ocean, and in a sense he was, for he had the power to control the tides, a trident his tool of choice. The entire ocean was at his command and he ruled them well, albeit with a firm hand.

"Like many creatures of the water, King Poseidon was more logical than emotional, though he eventually grew discontent with the absence of change. He had an eye for beautiful women and the power to attain all that he wanted, and because he had a fickle nature, he had many women, whether by their choice or not, for he often used magick to take them against their wishes. There was one woman, however, who caught his eye, which in itself was a great feat, for she was not a woman at all, but a Gorgon, a creature of great magick and unbelievable beauty. Her name was Medusa, and he seduced her. Many wonder how he could view her, for looking upon the face of a gorgon would turn one to stone, but the rumor is that his heart was already hardened from the cold ocean, and that alone saved him.

"Now, all this happened during a time when humans were trying to make a place for themselves among the so-called gods. Heroic men went in search of dragons and other creatures of terror to slay. One hero, a man who was known as Perseus, decided to slay Medusa, for stories had erupted that she was an evil creature. Well, humans will believe anything told to them that they cannot themselves explain, so he hunted her, and when he found her standing on a cliff overlooking the ocean, he decapitated her without question.

"Now, when different magickal creatures breed, especially those of differing elements, new magickal creatures are born, usually rare creatures with exceptionally rare powers. Medusa's union with Poseidon resulted in the birth of two new creatures, born from Medusa's blood during her decapitation. The first, a boy, already half-grown, armed by magick with a golden sword. The second, a white horse, also half-grown, with wings so wide he lifted himself immediately toward the sky.

"He was a gift, you see, to the young hero, for the gorgon Medusa had, in fact, turned to the ways of dark magick, her heart broken by Poseidon's rejection after he had seduced her, for she had fallen in love with him. Once very beautiful, her adoption of the ways of evil became reflected in her appearance, for gorgons, at the time, were some of the most powerful creatures there were. Snakes replaced her silky hair, and her smooth, supple skin became leathered and a sickly pallor. Others of the magickal community had been trying to defeat her for some time, to prevent her evil ways from spreading, so when the young human achieved what they could not, her winged foal became his reward. He was called Pegasus, the first of my kind, and he served the humans well, leading heroes to their glorious victories and producing new springs across their lands. He also aided the magickal community, for he had the unique ability to control thunderbirds, something no other creature could do. He spent his entire life serving others, and as a reward, when he died, the humans honored him in their eternal sky, and we honored him in ours."

"Wow," whispered Lilly in awe. "So, what happened to the boy?"

"The boy, Chrysaor, was not a boy at all, but a rare magickal creature called a chameleon. He took the form of a boy at the instant of his birth, for he saw Perseus and mimicked his appearance. There is not much record of his life, for he was as changing as his father, and being a chameleon made it possible for him to literally disappear. You see, a chameleon can change into anything, and it's not like transforming or transfiguring yourself, where you have to still take the form of living things. A chameleon can become a rock, a tree, a door, anything. They hide in plain sight, blending perfectly within any environment, and since they can become anything, they are extremely difficult to identify."

"That's kind of scary," said Lilly, thinking aloud. "Are chameleons good or evil?"

"Either," Rohan told her. "Like most creatures, they are what they choose to be."

"Can they be defeated?"

"Every creature has its weaknesses, and they die like any other creature dies, but if you only want to capture one, it becomes a challenge. A chameleon's weakness is its own reflection, a reflection of its true form, but catching one in its true form is difficult because they rarely take their true form. If you are lucky cross one in true form, a mirror will captivate it so that it will never look away. It would be trapped forever."

Lilly's mind ran over the wealth of information Rohan had just supplied, storing it in her memory. She felt better after hearing the story of Pegasus, the first pterippus. She found a sense of relief in the fact that their worlds were more intertwined than they seemed, like she wasn't as far from home as she felt. She smiled at Rohan, whose heart jumped a little, and with an eerie sense of melancholy, she remembered the message Ashya had given her to deliver to him.

"You need to go see your mother," she said quietly. "I think it's important. She asked me to send you to her as soon as possible."

"I was planning to visit her next," Rohan replied.

"How soon will you leave?"

"Tomorrow." Her face fell, and though he hated seeing her sad, his heart leapt at the thought that she wanted him to stay. "I have more to do, and you have more to learn. But I'll be back before you know it and I promise it won't be as long between my next visit."

"Good," said Lilly. She put her arms around him and hugged him tight, then whispered "Good night," and disappeared into the house.

Rohan watched her go, his heart beating wildly, and wondered for the first time in his life if he was doing the right thing. There was so much she didn't know, so many things she had the right to know, and he contemplated the conflict in his mind. If he told her now, told her everything he was trying so hard to keep from her, things would be different, better. She would know it all someday anyway, so what was wrong with telling her the truth?

Do you even know the truth, said a menacing voice in the back of his head, *or do you just think you know it?* He spent the rest of that night lying on the ground and staring at the stars while he pondered this thought. He fell asleep telling himself over and over that he knew the truth, but not really believing it.

Ashya's Secret

How could he make such a mistake?

Rohan flew at lightning speed toward his mother's hidden cottage, cursing himself. He hadn't meant to say it; it had just...slipped out. Of course, she was all but asleep when he'd said it, so she probably wouldn't remember, but still, how could he be so stupid? He replayed the night in his head, wondering what exactly had happened..

He'd been nearly asleep after his long night of internal struggles when he heard her screaming, and not just a scream, but a cry of pure terror. He'd flown up the stairs in an instant and burst through the door expecting to find some terrible creature attacking her, but she was asleep.

"Lilly," he'd said, trying to ease her awake, "what's wrong? Lilly, honey, wake up."

She'd awoken then, throwing her arms around him so tight he'd winced in pain. She had done nothing but hold him, shaking violently. Zephra had come in, and upon noticing the scene had asked what was happening.

"Just a nightmare," he'd told her. "I've got it under control."

"Are you sure?" she'd asked, and he'd heard the concern in her voice.

"Yes, I'm sure. Go back to bed."

When Zephra was gone, Rohan was finally able to get Lilly to speak, but she had just repeated the same two words over and over again: *Shattered mirror.*

It had taken almost an hour to calm her enough to talk to him, but by then, she could hardly remember the dream, or so she had claimed, for she'd been perfectly content to stay in his arms. She'd finally started to doze, and he'd woken her long enough to tell her he was going to get an early start on his trip.

"Goodbye," she'd said, already slipping into unconsciousness. "I'll see you soon."

"Bye," he'd whispered, and as he leaned down to kiss her forehead, it had escaped his lips without warning. "I love you."

The instant the words were said, he'd held his breath, hoping she was too asleep to realize what had just happened. She was still, her breathing deep and even, so he'd relaxed, but too soon.

I know, had come her words to his mind, and she'd said nothing more.

He was never so glad to leave her behind before that moment. Now, he only hoped his ridiculous declaration wouldn't upset his master plan. If he screwed up now, everything he'd done over the last fifteen years would be for nothing. How could he be so *stupid?!*

He flew for an eternity without stopping, the wind beneath his huge wings forcing him forward in strong thrusts. He could fly faster, he knew, but he kept a constant speed, hoping to calm himself before he reached his mother. She'd be able to read it in his thoughts, and he didn't think he wanted her help in this particular situation. Besides, Lilly was asleep, so perhaps he was making a bigger deal out of it than necessary.

Dawn was breaking when he finally reached the cottage. He landed gracefully in the front yard and before he could change into human form, the front door opened and Ashya smiled at him, not a bit surprised he was there.

"You knew I was coming," he said, now human. It wasn't a question.

"I hoped," she said, her voice melodic, as though she was amused about something. "Welcome home, son."

"Mother," he said, giving her a quick hug. "You needed to see me?"

"I wanted to see you," she corrected him. "I need to speak with you. It is important."

"Well, here I am."

"Once again in disguise, I see."

He looked at her, confused. Whenever he changed into human form, this was always what he looked like. Her amused expression was replaced by one of sadness.

"Has it been so long that you have forgotten your true form?"

"I don't understand what you mean, Mother," he said, feeling a bit defensive. He waited for her reply, but she only shook her head and breathed, "You will" before disappearing into the house. He followed, more confused than ever.

When he entered the house, he was taken aback by the changes in the library. Every flat surface was covered with scrolls and open books, more than he'd seen out at one time. One book, in particular, caught his eye. He couldn't recall having ever seen it before, but somehow, it was familiar. Lying open, its pages seemed to be made of satin-thin layers of gold. The elegant writing was a deep blood red which was reflected off the facing page, creating the illusion of flames spreading across them. He drew closer to read the writing, but before he could make out one word, the book slammed shut with a loud *thump!* and vanished.

The rest of the chaos began to react, one organized step at a time. Scrolls rolled themselves in a flash, books slammed shut, emitting clouds of dust and disappearing in the wake. Wide-eyed, Rohan turned to his mother for an explanation. She tucked her wand into her flowing sleeve and sat without her customary tea service, and Rohan knew instantly that this wasn't a social visit at all. Only after he sat as well did she begin.

"Later, my son," she said in a tired voice, and he wondered how long she'd been pouring over the mess in her library. "We have much more pressing matters to discuss. I've got new information regarding Dagana."

"What kind of information?" he asked, now worried.

"All kinds, some more accurate than others." Rohan knew she meant that some were still bound to change. Some of her visions were clearer than others, which meant they were less likely to change over time, so this is what he thought she meant. He was shocked, however, by the confession that followed. "I've got a source from within the castle. This person is feigning loyalty to the queen and reports only to me."

"Who is it?" he wondered aloud, trying to think why anyone would be willing to put himself in harm's way like that.

"Obviously I cannot answer that question. The fewer people who know, the safer this person is, and right now, I am the only one. You know as well as I that there are few who can protect their thoughts from the queen."

"I protect them from you," he said pointedly. She smiled.

"Sometimes."

"And Lilly."

"Yes, but has Lilly ever tried to invade your mind?"

"Not really."

"This person's identity is not important," said Ashya in a tone that ended the subject. "What is important is what has been discovered." She leaned closer to him, her blue eyes solemn and laced with fear.

Rohan shivered. He'd never seen her so afraid before. She stood suddenly and began to pace the long floor of the library.

"Dagana has recalled all of her former allies. Once she is sure of their loyalty, she will begin searching for those who have not yet chosen a side to persuade them to her cause, and you know her persuasion techniques."

"We knew this would happen," interrupted Rohan. "Why is this news?"

"Because she is no longer trying to recruit numbers," said Ashya. "She is tracking magickal signatures, searching only for power."

"She's tracking? How?" Rohan's breath caught in his throat, his thoughts on Lilly. She was powerful, and instead of being the responsible advisor he should have been, he'd told her to do whatever she had to do, no matter the consequences. What was wrong with him?

"No one knows how she's doing it, but there is no doubt that she is tracking, and she has been for a while. This house is safe, of course, but you will need to tell Lilly to use keep her magick to a minimum. Strictly training."

"Of course," whispered Rohan, cringing.

"There are rumors that are also very disturbing, though they have yet to be confirmed."

Rohan shifted in his chair, his body tense as he waited for her to continue. He gave an involuntary jerk as her thoughts grazed his mind, and he lifted his eyes to hers slowly, fear creeping through his veins.

"Why are you thinking about mirrors?" he asked, his voice unsteady. Caught off guard, Ashya's eyes widened in surprise at the difference in his voice, not wondering this time, but accusing.

"It is rumored that Dagana has discovered how to trap not only souls, but bodies, too, containing them within a realm accessible through mirrors. It sounds farfetched, I know, but my thoughts keep coming back to it. That was what I was researching when you arrived, to find out if it was even possible."

"Not as farfetched as you think. Lilly had a nightmare only hours ago about shattered mirrors. That's all she would say, 'shattered mirror', but she was terrified. I've never seen her like that before."

Still pacing, Ashya's mind worked rapidly to piece together this information with the rest of what she knew. Why would a shattered mirror be terrifying, unless someone was physically trapped inside it and it was the only way to escape?

A terrifying thought, wouldn't you agree? responded Rohan to her escaping thoughts. She smiled.

"One thing is certain," she continued aloud. "Taking into account my own visions, and now Lilly's dream, we must assume this rumor to be true. If it is true, once Lilly has her attention, she will want her. And if other things I've seen are true as well, Lilly may be in danger very soon."

"What else have you seen?"

"You know how inaccurate my visions are, son, so don't..."

"Mother," he barked, "what else have you seen?"

She hesitated and Rohan groaned inwardly. He'd heard stories of her many accurate predictions and had yet to hear even one that wasn't, so he couldn't understand why she had so little faith in her visions. He saw her flinch and wondered for a moment if she'd read his thoughts, but she showed no reaction if she had.

"There is one vision that has been bothering me. I've had it many times, each time more precise, clearer than the one before, and it is like nothing I would ever dreamed possible, which is why it's so frightening." She held her breath, afraid to drop the bomb, while Rohan sat on the edge of his seat. After taking a deep breath, she cleared her throat and said, "Dagana will form an alliance with a dragon."

"What?!"

"A dragon, Rohan, and if enough of the others follow, the giants will be close behind them. Their alliance with the dragons will not be broken."

"They wouldn't, though. The dragons, I mean. They'll each decide for themselves."

"Can you be so sure? Dragons are logical creatures. If they find logic in the reasons for the first alliance with Dagana, or if they see in logic in following, they will decide to follow."

"What can we do about it? How do we stop the first alliance?"

"It is too late for that," sighed Ashya. "The decision to form the alliance had been made. It is only a matter of time until it happens. Whether or not the rest will follow will only be clear after they choose their course of action."

Ashya finally returned to her chair, her hands folded in her lap, her mind on her many thoughts. They sat in silence for a while, until Rohan noticed the change in her eyes first, the intense, sorrowful look he'd seen so many times during his childhood. When he'd noticed it then, he'd tried to hear her thoughts, but she'd always kept them guarded, and when he'd asked her what was wrong, she'd always replied, "Nothing, son. Just missing your father."

He was certain she was thinking of him again, but he still couldn't help asking her what was wrong. She surprised him when she didn't reply, choosing instead to stare at the empty table where the mysterious magickal book had been. He waited, unsure of what to say to snap her out of her trance. She finally turned her eyes toward him, tears threatening to spill.

"There are many things I want to tell you," she began, casting her eyes downward toward her folded hands, "about your father. I have my reasons for not discussing it with you in the past, but I fear if I do not tell you now, I'll never have another chance."

"What do you mean?"

"I mean that we are both busy. A war is approaching in which we are both heavily involved in our own ways, and this may be the only time I have to tell you what I know before it is too late for you to do your part. I can only tell you what I know, which is still more than any other, but there is more to be discovered that only you can find."

"Why?"

"Because that is what your father wanted, and I made him a promise that I would I would do exactly as he asked if he ever disappeared."

"If he died, you mean," interrupted Rohan.

She didn't answer. Instead, she waved her arm across her view of the empty table and the same, mystical book reappeared. Another wave of her hand brought the book floating gracefully into her lap. She ran her fingers slowly over the violet and yellow design, tracing its chaotic pattern across the bright red binding. In the center was a large, round violet ring, a smaller black circle within its center, like the eye of a giant. Closed, it looked enormous. He'd never seen a book so thick, other then Gustave's, of course.

"This book belonged to your father," said Ashya, and Rohan could hear the strain in her voice as she spoke of him. "He kept every part of his life here, and all that can be read, I have read. There is much more in here that is only for you. It is a unique spell, but you are the only soul who can lift the protection he placed on it."

Rohan reached for the book, but Ashya returned it to its invisible state once more and shook her head.

"Not yet, son," she told him. "You have more to do before you can begin your quest, one of which includes protecting Lilly. I will tell you what I know for now and you can have the book when you accompany her to Nurzia."

"Why..."

"I've already spoken to Belmoré and he thinks it is wise to have the Chosen One under extra security while in their kingdom. I believe Amparo has sent word that she plans to remain there with Lilly until after the celebration on Yule. After that, you may begin your search."

Rohan sighed. He was already pushing the timing of his plans, without having to include staying with Lilly until Yule. Then again, he would get to spend some time with her, and the elves were very hospitable. He would be there for their Yule celebration, too, which was the envy of celebrations across Buthania. He considered what he still had to accomplish before Yule, and decided some things could be put off until after the celebration.

"What makes you so sure I'll be searching for anything?" he asked. "If everything about him is in the book, what else is there?'

Ashya closed her eyes and took a deep breath, exhaling slowly. When she opened them, they glistened with fresh tears. She cast him a sad smile.

"There is much more," she whispered. "Your father is not what you think he is. I've always allowed you to believe he was a pterippus because it is what we led everyone to believe. Keeping his identity a secret was key to his survival."

"If he wasn't a pterippus," said Rohan, nearly choking on his words, "then what was he?"

She hesitated, her eyes full of guilt and sadness, his eyes pleading for an answer. Exhaling the breath she'd been holding, she uttered the last words he ever expected her to speak.

"He was a phoenix, son."

Rohan couldn't breathe. Logic crumbled around him as his mind raced over the volumes of information within his mind, thoughts bombarding one another so fast he couldn't focus on any single one, scouring the possibility, the *impossibility*. He was waiting for his mother to laugh, to tell him she was joking, but her serious face never changed. Impossible! His father couldn't be a phoenix. Immortal creatures cannot breed, yet his mother just told him that his father was one. Immortal creatures cannot die, but his father was dead, wasn't he?

"... I made him a promise that I would I would do exactly as he asked if he ever disappeared."

"If he's a phoenix," he said, his mind snapping to attention, "then he's still alive, right? I mean, immortal creatures can't die, can they?"

"It's more complicated than that," Ashya sighed. "It is explained more thoroughly in the book, but the truth is, I don't know what happened to him. He never discussed with me any plans he had to leave. He was thrilled at the idea of becoming a father, especially since he never thought he would, but he disappeared. No goodbyes, no information, nothing. I can only guess he had a good reason to leave, probably involving the safety of his child."

"Am I his child?" he asked. "I mean, I thought it was against the laws of nature for an immortal creature to procreate."

"The laws of nature change. It's called evolution, and yes, you are his child."

"Then what does that make me?"

"You, my son, are a pterippus," she said firmly, "but you are unique. You have always known that. Never in history has a pterippus been born with a horn, but you have one. Never has a pterippus been able to take human form, yet here you are, a contradiction to history."

"But you're a unicorn," argued Rohan, still unable to fully believe what she'd told him. "It makes sense that I have a horn and can take human form. I get it from you."

"Even though every other child with a unicorn and a pterippus parent is born one or the other, but never both?"

Rohan opened his mouth to speak, but no words came. She was right and he knew it, but everything in his soul told him to reject this as the truth. He couldn't accept the possibility that everything he believed about his father was wrong. It didn't matter that he'd never met him. His father's legacy was the only concrete thing in his life, and if that changed, if everything he believed was false, what was real?

Your strength, his mother's thoughts interceded. *Your purpose. Your kind heart. These things have not changed, Rohan. Trust that.*

"How can I trust anything," he spat, frustrated, "when I can't even trust my own feelings? I don't even..."

And suddenly, the rest of his problems came together. The strange way he felt is Zephra's presence began to make sense. She was a phoenix. It hadn't been latent feelings left behind by Gustave that had urged those feelings forth, but his father's phoenix blood, *his* blood, that forced that attraction. It was nothing more than a natural bond that formed between similar magickal creatures who shared the same kind of blood, immortal blood, pulling them together like opposite ends of two magnets. This realization eased his mind, for it meant that even if everything else was falling apart, he could once again have faith that his feelings for Lilly had never faltered.

He was so lost in his thoughts, he didn't noticed when Ashya had slipped silently from the room, so when she returned carrying two mugs filled to the brim, Rohan started, which caused Ashya to jump as well, nearly spilling the contents of the mugs.

"I didn't mean to startle you," she apologized as she handed him a mug. "I thought we could both use something to drink."

"Thanks," he muttered, unaware of anything but the questions burning in his mind. The more he thought about it, the more some things made sense, while others became more confusing. He sipped his drink as he pondered his next question, afraid to ask it, but even more afraid not to.

Ashya waited patiently for him to speak, and when he didn't, she stole a glimpse into his mind, pushing just beyond the surface.

He was afraid to ask any questions about his father, yet he was desperate for answers just the same. His mind also revolved around Lilly, about some bit of knowledge only he knew, but when she tried to delve deeper, she felt the harsh push to get her out of his head.

"I'm sorry," she said quickly. "I shouldn't have pried."

"No," he said, his voice hard, "you shouldn't have. You could have asked."

"Alright. What else do you want to know?"

"I don't know if I want to know anything else," he shouted, jumping from his chair to pace the floor. "This is all too much. I mean, all these years, I believed my father was dead because that is what *you* would have me believe, and now you tell me that he's an immortal! He's alive, somewhere out there, and has never chosen to return. You say he was thrilled to become a father, but isn't he at all interested in his child? What has him so afraid that he hasn't once come back to see you, the love of his life? And where is he now?"

"I do not know what his reasons are, but he never would have left if he didn't think he had any other options."

"Stop defending him! He chose to leave, right? Isn't it you who told me we always have a choice, even if you contradicted yourself when you sent me away by not giving *me* the choice?"

Ashya cringed and Rohan knew he had hurt her, but his anger was far more real than any other emotion right now and he didn't care. All he could think about was that both of his parents had abandoned him. First, his father had left without leaving any kind of explanation as to why, and then his mother had sent him away against his will. Now, fifteen years later, she expected him to be okay with all of it.

"I know how hard it was," she said, trying to speak without letting her tears fall, "and I know that you will never forgive me until you see the results for yourself, but I do not regret my choices. It was necessary…"

"I know!" he roared, "and you are right. I'll never get over you sending me away. Never."

"Never is a long time, son."

"How long?"

"What?"

"How long? I mean, if my father is immortal, am I? Will I just have the average life span of a pterippus, since that's what I am, or a unicorn…what is it, five hundred years…or will it be longer?"

"I don't know," she replied, her eyes laced with concern. "It is something I have considered, but it isn't a very easy theory to test."

"No, I guess not," he sighed, his anger subsiding to exhaustion. "And there's nothing in his book to indicate where he might be?"

"If there is, I cannot read it."

"May I look now?"

"No. You have other things to do first. If you read it now, you won't want to stop until you have all the answers to your questions, and it is important for you to protect Lilly in Nurzia. Dagana is planning something. I don't know what it is or when, but Lilly cannot be there when it happens. You have to be there to make sure she stays safe."

"Fine," he muttered, crossing his arms and plopping in the chair. "Can I ask just one more thing?"

"You can ask anything you want."

"If he is immortal, why would he be so afraid? I mean, he can't die, and if someone were coming to harm us, he could protect us better than anyone else, right?"

"Can you imagine what it was like for us then? Dagana was at the height of her power and everyone lived in fear. Some of the most powerful creatures disappeared without a trace. Rumors flew of her abilities, one of which included the power to trap souls, which, quite obviously, is becoming more of a probability every day. Many believed, many still do, that she was stealing powerful souls to gain their powers. Now, I ask you, if you were extremely powerful and had an immortal soul, and you were faced with the prospect of being trapped for all of eternity without even death as an escape, would that stir enough fear in you to take extreme action? Can you imagine a worse fate?"

"Could she have trapped him?" asked Rohan.

"I don't know that, either. That is something you will have to find out when it is time, after Lilly leaves Nurzia. Never forget that she is your top priority."

Rohan nodded, losing himself once again in his thoughts. He hadn't expected a visit to his mother to be so troubling. His father was a phoenix. He was alive, immortal, and out there somewhere, in hiding to escape the threat of a terrible fate, unless...

What if Dagana *had* found him? What if he was trapped for eternity? How long could he last before she finally broke him, before she forced him to relinquish his immortal soul to her? He shuddered at the thought of Dagana being immortal, a thought that could potentially become a reality, and he decided right then what course of action he would take as soon as his tasks were complete. He would go to Castle Ridaska and search for his father, if, of course, the book held no clues to his whereabouts.

"I've been invited to Nurzia for Samhain," said Ashya as she stood, interrupting his thoughts. "I'll bring the book with me so you can begin reading it, as long as you promise me you will stay with Lilly until she leaves the kingdom."

"I promise," whispered Rohan. Ashya nodded and left him with his thoughts, which alternated between Lilly and the connection between his father and the evil queen. He sat without moving until the final rays of the suns disappeared behind the trees, casting a shadow of darkness throughout the room. Without bothering to say goodbye to his mother, he fled her cottage, flying into the moonless night and away from the haunting feeling he felt he would never escape.

I love you, my son, she whispered, though he heard it clearly in his mind. *Be safe.*

And I love you, he said, and though he was already miles away, he knew she was crying.

A Rising Evil

Rimetak let his eyes roam around the table where more than fifty magickal creatures were seated, all waiting for the queen to enter. Some looked interested, while others seemed annoyed and a few, indifferent. One of the three dwarf kings grunted about punctuality, but Rimetak chose to ignore it, hoping Dagana hadn't heard. He knew the extent of her wrath when someone spoke ill of her and he did not wish to witness it again.

The queen entered regally, her long red robes billowing behind her. The entire table stood, dipping their heads in a respectful bow. Dagana walked toward the throne, which Rimetak held out for her, and after she was seated, the rest of the occupants of the room followed her lead. Rimetak remained in his standing position to the right of her throne, knowing she would tell him when she wanted him to sit.

"Welcome," she said, scanning the room. "It is a pleasure to see such a large turnout. I had not expected so many to remain faithful these many years."

The same dwarf king who had commented on her lack of punctuality stood, though he was barely an inch higher than when he was seated. His hair was thick around his worn face. He slammed a weathered hand upon the table, a gesture dwarves used to demand attention, and turned toward the queen.

"Several of us," he said gruffly, "have only returned out of utter curiosity. Fifteen years is a very long time, and you have been idle. It is a great cause for concern, especially after our last battle."

Dagana did not falter. In fact, a smile spread slowly over her face. The dwarf's gaze remained fixed, but Rimetak noticed a slight change in his stance. The inch he'd gained by standing was gone, diminished by the queen's smile.

"I understand your concern completely," said Dagana, "but you are only half right. Fifteen years is a long time, but during that time, I have been anything but idle, which is why I have chosen to assemble you all here today. Please, Klysair, be seated." The dwarf climbed into the chair with some difficulty as she continued. "As you all know, my Arch Requiest is more accurate than any prophet in this land. It was on her urging that I *postponed* my plans so long ago. Since then, not only have I obtained the ability to track magickal signatures..." She paused to absorb the shocked looks on the faces of the throng surrounding her, and with a smile, she dropped an even bigger surprise, "...but the very powerful child I've nurtured these many years, my grandson, is currently obtaining an alliance with a creature who will turn the tides in our favor."

"What creature!" squeaked a grotesque gnome, his thin lips curled over his pointed teeth.

"A dragon."

Every creature seated around the massive table began talking at once, shouting over each other in an attempt to be heard. Dagana looked at Rimetak, who bellowed for them to stop shouting, but no one heard him over the chaos. Dagana looked at the shouting crowd, and amused, she simply raised a hand. The room was instantly quiet.

"According to my requiest, who has had the same vision many times, I am assured this alliance will be forged, giving us more of an advantage than we already have."

"And what advantage is that?" a deep voice boomed.

"During my 'idle' spell, as Krysair so eloquently stated, our enemies have become unaware of my plans. They are surely expecting me to rise to power again, for the Council remains steadfast, but they have no reason to expect when it will happen. Many have grown less fearful that a return to power will even happen, no longer fearing me as a threat, and *that* will be their downfall! When we do attack, it will come as a surprise and they will fall in greater numbers, thus minimizing the threat against us when the war begins."

"Their numbers are much greater than ours," argued the same deep voice. Dagana and Rimetak tried to distinguish who was speaking, but neither was able to do so.

"Indeed," agreed Dagana, pursing her lips in frustration. "However, I no longer have a desire for a vast army, but rather a powerful one, which brings me to another point. You have been most loyal to me over the years, despite my lack of communication, but anyone who wishes to break your oath of loyalty may do so right now without consequence. I must warn you, though, that if you are no longer my ally, I shall consider you my enemy when the war is at hand. The same is true for those of you who have yet to swear your loyalty to me. I ask you to decide quickly, for this meeting will proceed no further until the disloyal parties have gone. Secrecy is our greatest asset at this point."

Murmurs flew around the room. Each dwarf king spoke to his own subjects, the Cyclops to his advisor, who shook his head vehemently at whatever his Chief suggested, and the gnomes snarled arguments among themselves. The rest of the creatures had sent only one of their kind, their respective leaders, to make decisions on their behalf. A veiled gorgon stroked the head on each end of the long, venomous snake wrapped around her neck and shoulder. She seemed content with the happenings of the meeting, and it pleased Dagana that she had their support. They were priceless allies.

While the chattering continued, Dagana felt her chagrin grow, for she had expected to find among the group at least one vampire or werewolf in attendance, but none were present. The giants, of course, would have nothing to do with her without the support of a worthy dragon, but that matter could wait until she had the dragon. The harpies were useless to her, their bouts of rage and disorganization during battle quickly diminishing their numbers. That much was obvious from their recent attack in Arthidgen. An entire fleet had been destroyed. They were a dying breed and Dagana had little desire to bother with them.

She knew very few Earth creatures would come to her side, though she was sure some outcasts' support could be gained. Maybe she should find the banished faeries and recruit them, though what could she possible offer them that would bring them to her cause? They were Elemental Children and could manage their every goal without help, and an alliance with a dragon...who could ask for more than that? One strong Elemental Child on her side would be enough to secure victory. Then again, if she could find a way to gain loyalty from the merfolk as well...Her mind held that thought until she noticed the room was quiet and absent no one.

"What of our reward for our continued loyalty?" asked a lamia, coiling her snakelike tail closer to herself and lifting herself high above the others, her arms crossed over her chest.

"You each will be awarded a region to rule as your own, without interference from me…assuming, of course, you remain loyal."

The lamia lowered herself, coming level with the rest of the nodding group.

"What is your plan, my queen?" came the unidentified booming voice, though even he now seemed interested.

"Lord Rimetak," commanded the queen, and he stepped forward.

"We will spend the immediate future training in combat," he said, his voice made more formidable by his unique battle helm. "Once I have observed your armies strengths, I shall determine where to send them. Some of you will recruit the undecided to join us, some will scout the lands so that we may drive the battles to where we have the advantage when the war commences, and some shall lead attacks on the towns to ignite fear among the humans. Our queen will then offer them protection from their assailants in exchange for their oaths of loyalty."

"Not that I need the added armies," she interrupted, "but it will ensure they cannot be recruited by our enemies."

"Once they accept, the queen's regiments will camp in their towns, thus exponentially expanding our range. Our loyal armies will be stationed carefully throughout the land like pieces on a chessboard, ready for the strike."

"Then," said Dagana, her eyes glowing, "I shall ride to Nurzia with my grandson to claim the throne. If it is not relinquished by right, I shall have just cause to declare war and it will begin."

"What makes you think the elves would ever consider allowing you to claim the throne?" asked the gorgon in a whisper, her veil fluttering around her chin as she spoke.

"Because, Dawfain, my grandson is the rightful heir to the throne, and the elves have no idea of his bloodlines."

"They will require proof," Dawfain's soft voice floated across the room. "Do you have it?"

"Not yet," said Dagana, clenching her jaw, "but I will. Once the alliance with the dragon is forged, I shall begin my search, and I have a good idea of where to start. Besides, even with proof, they may decline. King Belmoré holds fast to his throne. War is certainly imminent."

The rest of the room nodded, and all seemed more than ready to begin the fighting immediately, but Dagana was subdued. She looked at Rimetak, who drew near and bent so she could whisper in his ear, and after nodding twice, he straightened himself.

"By the law of the oath of loyalty," he boomed, "what was spoken in this room may not be repeated to anyone outside its walls. You are to return to your armies and prepare them for their arrival to Castle

Ridaska. Do not march until you receive word. We do not want to draw attention to our cause by appearing organized. That is all."

The room cleared quickly, though Dawfain, with her intriguing pet amphisbaena, lingered.

"It pleases me," she said softly, "to see that you have also acquired patience during your idle time. It is an admirable virtue. Good day, Your Majesty."

The gorgon left in one graceful sweep across the room. Dagana frowned and looked at Rimetak, who removed his helmet and wiped the sweat from his brow.

"Was I so impatient?" Dagana asked him. He shrugged.

"Yes," he replied, "but not overly, and you are more patient than you once were."

"Indeed," she said distastefully. "Raising so powerful a child forced me to become so, unfortunately."

"On the contrary, your Majesty, your patience has made you a more formidable opponent. A snake will wait forever for the perfect time to strike, but his aim is true. His victory comes from his patience, and so too shall yours."

"Thank you, Rimetak," sighed the queen. "You may retire for the day. You have done well."

"As you wish," he said as he turned, "and thank you, Your Majesty."

Once he was gone, Dagana immediately took to Sybil's chambers, her brisk footsteps echoing down the long corridors to her room.

"The dragon is in Elikrede," Sybil said the moment Dagana entered. "She bides her time in observation, but she will return with him."

"You are sure?" asked Dagana, unable to believe her good fortune. Her followers had remained true and seemed anxious for action. Many were more loyal than ever before, and the plan seemed infallible. The day couldn't get much better.

"Of course I'm sure," snapped Sybil, her wrinkles deepening from irritation, "but before you count your blessings, I've also seen something very disturbing."

"What?"

"I had a vision today of your fall from power, as well as my own."

Dagana, her mouth agape, her eyes wide, was stunned speechless, and could only stare stupidly at the crone. Sybil shook her head, rolling her eyes, and began cleaning the clutter of her latest requiem quest from her altar.

"Calm yourself," she said sternly. Dagana closed her mouth, but her wide eyes remained. "It isn't in the near future." She stopped her busy hands and raised her eyes to Dagana, a tiny smile stretching her puckered lips. "Well, mine isn't so much a fall from power as a slow draining. A stronger requiest is born and is beginning to come into his powers. As his studies come to include magick, they will grow, and as his powers grow stronger, mine shall weaken. It is the natural order of things. Rare powers are rare because so few have them. It was only a matter of time before my powers faded."

"And what of my downfall?" demanded Dagana.

"A fire rages, consuming all. If you place yourself in its path, and you will," Sybil sighed, shaking her head, "then it will consume you."

"What does the fire represent?" asked Dagana.

"That I do not know," said the seer, "but if it consumes you, it will lead to your downfall, and eventually your demise."

"When will you know?!" shrieked the queen, her blood boiling

"In time, but I warn you now, be wary. You will face many strong enemies, any one of which could lead to your undoing. You must recruit the unique, those with rare powers, for if many with rare abilities stand against you, a victory will fall from your grasp."

"What of Kylenin's future?"

"Your blood will rule Nurzia. That has not wavered..."

"Good."

"...yet." emphasized Sybil, scowling at the interruption. "Consider a plan to begin gathering support for your grandson. The possibility of a rival for the throne looms on the horizon."

Dagana stalked from the room without a word, pounding her heels into the hard floors as she stormed toward her chambers. At least Kylenin would take Nurzia. That, if nothing else, was certain. She had to ensure he would take the throne before the impending war, which was certain to come whether or not he became king, but who was this other threat? What was the fire raging toward her and what events would bring her within its path? If she only knew, she could change something, stop her downfall before it was too late. She was no longer thinking of the wonderful plan that a short time ago seemed so certain to be a success. She swept through the door of her room and sank into her huge bed, drawing the curtains tightly around it as if they might protect her from the unknown threat headed her way.

A Series of Nightmarish Events

Lilly woke with a start, her heart pounding against her chest, her lungs ready to burst from her shallow, rapid breathing. She took a deep breath, exhaling slowly, and ran her shaking hands over her face. Her fingers were wet when she pulled them away, and she realized that she'd been crying in her sleep. She fumbled through the darkness for the nightstand drawer that now housed her two most precious items: her Grimoire and her wand.

With her wand, she lit the lamp on her table, with her newest spell, *Enyarten*. Somewhere in that word was the magick word for fire. Fire...one talent that did not come naturally to her, nor easily, for that matter, as she had recently discovered during lessons with Ryzale when she'd struggled harder than she ever had. Ryzale had looked especially smug for the rest of that lesson.

Her room now aglow, her nostrils still adjusting to the burn of the dragon bile fueling the lamp, she dug ferociously for a pen, her whole body still shaking. This was the strangest one yet, worse than all the others in both mystery and terror. Flipping past the few pages of her first seven months here, the numerous pages of spells, potions, dreams, instructions for charming and decharming objects, and other things she'd learned over the past two weeks since Rohan left, she finally found the next available page and began writing.

I had the same dream again, worse than ever before.

She paused, her words almost illegible, like the scribbles of a small child. She flipped through the pages again, slowly this time, to count how many of her dream entries began with that same phrase.

Six.

She checked the dates. Each entry was two days apart. She'd been having the same dream every other night since Rohan left; the first occurring the very night of their conversation under the stars. Including that first one and the one she had just now, that made eight times, eight nights of confusion and terror. Turning to that entry, she noticed the same shaky writing there, becoming less so the more she had written.

There was really no reason to write it down. She remembered that first dream as if she just dreamed it, but Rohan had been there to comfort her, to reassure her that it was just a dream. She'd awoken in his arms, so scared she had actually hyperventilated while she was asleep. She had been so distressed that she had trouble recovering her breath, and she'd barely noticed when Zephra came in or when Rohan sent her back out, assuring her he had everything under control. Trying to block the violence of the nightmare, she'd squeezed her eyes shut, but all it did was allow the images to become that much clearer, and when Rohan had asked her what she had seen, all she could say was, "Shattered mirror."

But it wasn't the mirror that had frightened her. It was the fact that it had shattered, that after the frightening crash of glass, a bloodcurdling scream echoed down the mysterious dark hallway she found herself in. Just thinking about the terror and panic of that scream sent chills down her spine even now.

She'd relived that same scene eight times, each time exactly the same, although the mirror was really nothing compared to the rest of the dreams that followed it, dreams that became more clear and continued only a little more than the previous one before her subconscious forced her awake. Nothing really made much sense, but what she felt in the hazy emptiness was enough to fling her into immediate consciousness.

The dark, cold hallway lined with mirrors of various shapes and sizes, each coming into view and out again as the light seemed to travel the hallway with her, was endless. Her reflection appeared in only one mirror, and behind her reflection, Zephra stood over her, also gazing into the mirror, though Zephra was not behind her in the hallway. Then the mirror shattered...the agonizing scream echoed, and Lilly felt nothing but pain. Excruciating pain unlike anything she'd ever felt before or could even describe, as though she was the broken mirror, never to be repaired.

Wyatt came next, enticing her from the hallway, gesturing her to follow him. He never spoke to her, not even with his mind, but she followed him as he walked away from her. The longer she followed him, the more disturbed she became, as though she knew he was leading her to danger, but she could not catch up to him, nor could she stop herself from following him, no matter how unwilling she was.

The surroundings in each dream with him were different, each place unfamiliar, and she grew more wary as he led her across the unknown. Darkness crept slowly over them, and she followed him through it, her hand outstretched to touch him, as though that was the only goal of her dream, to touch him again, just to see what happened. He always managed to stay just out of her reach, running ahead to increase the distance between them, then waiting while she stumbled over harsh terrain, struggling to keep up. When she reached him, he darted off again, and her mind screamed at her to keep going, to touch him...that was the most important thing now...forcing her to keep following him through the pitch of night, a terrible sense of dread overwhelming her.

Whether or not she caught him, she didn't know. That part of the dream had never progressed beyond the screaming in her head before it ended, though the sense of warning was still present, and it was replaced by an even more unusual scene. It wasn't terrifying, but for the fact that, once again, a mirror was involved. She and Amparo were preparing for some kind of event, a rather formal event by how they were dressed, and when Lilly went to the mirror to inspect her reflection, Amparo at her side, her father's image appeared in the mirror, observing her from the other side.

She could not hear him, but there was something in his eyes, something that made her wonder if he was the one in danger. She tried to ask him what was wrong, why he was so worried, but he shook his head, a clear gesture that he could not hear what she was saying. He raised his hand to the glass and she mimicked his gestures, feeling only cold glass beneath his hand, as though a window separated them rather than a mirror. He gave her a sad smile, and then faded away, and all she could feel was the terrible sorrow that she had lost her father all over again. She could almost feel her heart breaking by the crushing sadness.

Amparo, however, pulled her out of the sorrow and led her blindly toward huge white doors that opened into a massive cathedral, where a throng of excited spectators waited, stuffed in the great, wide room and spilling out through the open front doors, where thousands more stood waiting, trying impatiently and with little success to see inside the doors. The dream stopped there, the sorrow still overshadowing the darkness that followed. She never got to see what they were waiting for.

The green glow was next, and this, perhaps, was the most terrifying of all, not for what content the dream contained, but again, for what she felt when it ended. It started with the green glowing line that she still hadn't unlocked, though in her dream, the doorway was revealed and she walked into the room hidden behind it. The entire room was glowing green, or rather a thick book was glowing, lying complacently on a pedestal overhanging a table covered in magickal items. Not the type of items she was used to, either. Candles, yes, but she had never seen some of the things on the table before, things that seemed more like they would belong to an evil wizard than a good one.

Still, something drew her to the book and she opened it. A swarm of glowing, spinning green balls spiraled from the open pages and raced out the door. She followed, the book forgotten as they raced out the front door and flew toward the graveyard she'd found, the stone garden. They stopped over the white marble obelisk surrounded by the black gate, hovering precariously until she caught up, and then they dove beneath the earth, a spiraling vortex of green being sucked into the tomb like a violent tornado. She didn't know what to do then, standing beneath the starless sky as the trail of magick continued endlessly toward oblivion beneath the surface.

Suddenly, the ground exploded, and Lilly was thrown toward the edge of the cemetery. She cracked her head on the headstone furthest from the explosion, and when she saw a ghostly figure shrouded in a shimmering gold cloak, she thought she was seeing things. The figure, a man she did not recognize, walked toward her, his mouth moving as though he was speaking to her. She didn't understand what he was saying, for his words were all spoken in the *Doret Gaia*, but she felt awe, peace, exhilaration, and then pure terror as the figure attacked her.

Until tonight, she thought that was the most frightening part of her dream, but the most recent installment brought even more terror, more pain, more sorrow, all at the same time. Like the rest of these dreams, there was no sound, no voices besides the one in her head, but it didn't matter that she couldn't hear...she could *feel*. Tonight, she felt it all.

She sighed, her breathing almost normal again, and raised her now steady hand to the blank page of her journal, pausing briefly before continuing her first sentence, and then she hunched over the book as the words flew from the pen.

I had the same dream again, worse than ever before. Most was the same, though there was more in the dream with Amparo. I never noticed before how many people were waiting in that room. I still don't know what they are waiting for; maybe I never will, but there were thousands of them, like every human in the world gathered at that one place. I also never noticed the bottles on the table in the green room, full of thick, brown liquid. I don't know why I noticed them now, in the split second before I chased the balls of light, but I did, so it must be relevant. No, tonight there was another piece, the final piece, I think. It would seem so, since I was being tortured to death, right?

I was in a room in a castle...that much is clear. It might have even been a dungeon, but it didn't have the dungeon feel, so I can't be sure. What I am sure about is that I was in Dagana's castle, in a small, dark, circular room, sitting in a chair in the middle of the room. She was talking to me, but as always, I couldn't hear what was being said. Her eyes glowed bright red, gleaming like fresh blood.

Lilly shivered again at the thought, wondering if the evil queen she'd never seen had blonde hair and blood-red eyes.

She tortured me with her wand. It was the only other object in the dream besides the chair, which I almost broke as she inflicted excruciating pain on me. I remember trying hard to keep her out of my head, suffering through it all, but that only angered her, which made her try harder to get in. When she stopped, she said something to me that nearly made my heart explode. I wish I could remember what it was, but all I remember after that is crying gallons of tears and the look of satisfaction on her face when I told her everything she wanted to hear. I don't know if the terror of her words or the shame of my confession has me more upset over this dream, but with all of them together...

Lilly stopped writing, a new thought occurring to her. Together...this recurring nightmare was always the same, always a series of dreams occurring in the same order, the same feelings, the same people. But what was the connection? She could feel she was close to the answer, so close her fingers began to tingle with the prospect of figuring it out. In a flash, it came to her and she flipped through the pages until she found the entry of her first lesson with Orvak, where he had introduced the theory of perceptions to her. She looked over it again.

It was all there...the chair and the wand, the waterfall, the house, the graveyard, the book, the room, a castle, her father, Amparo, Wyatt and then herself...all images that had flashed through her mind like a strobe light, here and gone in an instant. She hadn't known then what any of it had meant, but now it seemed that it was all connected, much more than she'd thought.

...everything, everyone from that day with Orvak is here in this endlessly repetitively dream, but what is the connection? What does it all mean, mixed up together in one endless nightmare? Maybe I should visit Orvak. He'll help me see what I've missed. Maybe if I figure it out, I'll quit dreaming it so often. I hope so. I don't think I can handle having this nightmare every other night for the rest of my life. Insanity would be better than that, and that's exactly where I'll end up if I don't figure it out soon. Orvak will know how to handle this.

She had lessons with Tsirama tomorrow, but she would put those off for now. He was explaining quests again, educating her so they could begin exploring them together. That would just have to wait. She didn't think she could handle any more clues from her past that led to nowhere, not now, when there was so much more information crammed into her head, struggling to be released.

The realization that these dreams began when Rohan left made her thoughts shift in an entirely new direction. The first night, he had comforted her through the ridiculous terror of the shattered mirrors, but then he had left, intending to visit Ashya after promising her that he wouldn't be gone so long this time. His departure left a strange, unexplained void within her greater than she imagined it would. She felt different, and while she didn't know if it was their conversation the night before he left or the actual act of leaving that affected her so greatly, she knew for sure that he was responsible for the change. Throughout everything that had happened to her since she left Ashya's, she had always felt he was near, even though she knew he wasn't. Now, she couldn't feel him at all, and worse than that, Dorwynn still hadn't returned from his mysterious task, so she was left only with Zephra for company.

Zephra's demeanor over the past two weeks could only be described as subdued, for she spent a great deal of time merely watching Lilly's lessons with her different teachers. Lilly found this irritating, especially when she was trying to get time alone with Wyatt, who had taken over Dorwynn's duty of training her on her tasks. She snuck off at first, but Zephra had soon found a way to track her and had figured out what she was doing.

"Who is he, really?" she asked Lilly yesterday while they were tending the garden she'd started before Dorwynn left.

"Just a friend," quipped Lilly. She really hadn't wanted to discuss this with her before, and she definitely didn't want to share the details of their time together. It wasn't Zephra's business.

"A powerful friend."

"Yeah."

Zephra paused then, looking up from her tedious weed-pulling. She'd given Lilly a small smile and continued her work. "Well, since Dorwynn seems to have disappeared altogether, someone else should be training you. It may as well be him."

Lilly hadn't known whether she was upset with Dorwynn or Wyatt, for she had heard the animosity in her voice, but Zephra had said nothing more on the issue. Lilly didn't bother offering any extra information about him, either. What would Zephra do if she found out about the one thing she hadn't told her about him, about the duel they were supposed to have? Would she stop her? Would she help her prepare?

Not that she would need help. Wyatt had been training her well, as had Tsirama and Ryzale, and Lilly was sure she was about ready to be tested, though she knew she couldn't until her actual trainer delivered her for the test, and since he had not returned, nor even contacted them since he left, she had no idea when that would happen. Not that it really mattered to her. She enjoyed spending time with Wyatt. He explained so much more to her than Dorwynn ever had, not only about Earth Magick, but other things as well, like how her journal changed as she wrote new things in it because, magickally, it was becoming a part of her. Every spell or potion, every dream and lesson she wrote made subtle differences to its appearance.

It was just one more thing she never imagined possible in the world of magick, but, then again, did she ever imagine she was a powerful sorceress destined to save the world? Nope.

Wyatt seemed to enjoy training her, too. He'd recovered quickly from their argument and jumped at the chance to spend more time with her. Since their reconciliation, he'd helped her perfect her tasks. She could now raise a namun with ease, petrify wood with just her hands, change coal into a diamond with her wand and manipulate grown plants. He'd tried to teach her how to form a cave into the stone side of the cliff behind the waterfall, but it was a bit much for her, and after he'd spent half an hour righting her mistake, he'd decided to let Dorwynn take over that particular task. Besides that, all that remained to be learned was to call upon the element itself, something they would start on during their next lesson.

"Using the element to aid in your magick," he informed her during their most recent lesson, "will help you to manage the task of the cave."

With a sigh, Lilly closed her journal and stuck it in the drawer. Her mind reeled as she poured over the possible connection between the series of dreams invading her sleep, but there wasn't enough sense in it to make it fit. She yawned and sank into her pillow, concentrating on Orvak. Clever, wise, brilliant Orvak...the one soul who would know how to find the answers still buried deep within the recesses of her overstimulated mind.

"You are quiet today, vula," said Orvak.

His statement of the obvious made Lilly smile. They were sitting in the glade of stones, where they had been meeting each time since Lilly's first visit. Today, Lilly was quietly sorting through her thoughts. Normally, she was the first to speak during their time together, so her unusual silence intrigued the ogre.

"It is not your usual day for a visit," he said when she didn't speak. "What troubles you?"

Lilly wasted no time explaining everything about her recurring dream. Every detail, no matter how insignificant it might seem, was relayed with perfect accuracy. She spoke for an eternity, but Orvak held true to his patient nature and listened without interruption, though on more than one occasion she noticed his caterpillar eyebrows raise questioningly.

"Well," she said breathlessly when she finished, "what do you think?"

Orvak was quiet, as he always was when pondering something, and Lilly was accustomed to sitting in silence for some time while he thought, for he never spoke on any subject until he'd considered it thoroughly. It was one of his many personality traits Lilly found comforting. Her previous visits were spent not only learning everything he would teach her, but also studying his keen wit, his calm nature and his amazing sense of the world around him. He was quickly becoming one of Lilly's favorite people. While she waited for his reply, her mind wandered to the last entry of him in her journal:

Orvak, I think, has taught me more about humanity than any of the humans training me now. He always seems to know exactly what I need to hear and he never fails to shed light on my human flaws, but always in a way that makes me want to better myself. His logic is unquestionable, his emotion absolute, and yet, for a nearly immortal creature, he regards me as his equal, even with his unfathomable experience. Lessons with him aren't like lessons at all, but rather good conversations with a wise friend, more like advice than a lecture, and when I leave his company, I find myself always in a state of contentment, and awe.

Lilly considered the words she had written and the truth they held. These were the reasons, after all, why she brought this particular problem to him. Despite his grotesque appearance, he had a gentle way about him, and as far as she was concerned, he was the smartest being she'd ever met and probably the smartest she was likely to ever meet. She believed with all her heart that he would help her solve her mystery, but she knew she would have to wait until he had scrutinized every fact.

She was focusing on a butterfly sipping nectar from the blooming trees just beyond the tree line. He flew to another flower, and she listened to the air rushing beneath his wings and the soft whistle they made when they came together. A second butterfly, much larger, flew near the first in a rush, and the little one was lifted from the tree into the updraft, beating his wings desperately to regain control.

"Vula," said Orvak, and the second Lilly heard his voice, the butterflies were forgotten, "do you know what requiem quests are?"

"Sort of," she replied, searching her memory. "Aren't they visions of the future?"

Orvak chuckled, his silver eyes sparkling in the sunlight.

"You are partially correct," he said. "Requiem quests are as much visions of the future as memory quests and vision quests are visions of the past. They use the same magick, each requiring different amounts of strength. In this, you have experience, with the vision quest involving your mother and the wizard, and with the memory quest of your father when you were young, in this life. That one, you controlled well, but the others drained you terribly. Requiem quests require not only a great deal of strength, but also great concentration. When you are asleep, your mind is clear and focused on nothing in particular. You are also resting, your body replenishing your lost energy. It makes sense to me that if you cannot control the onset of the other quests, requiem quests would also be uncontrollable, wouldn't you agree?"

"So, I'm viewing the future in my sleep? Wait, will all these things actually *happen*?" Lilly's voice rose higher with every word, as did her panic.

"No, vula. Viewing the past and the future are very different. The past has already happened. The future has yet to happen. Visions of the future are only what is likely to happen. Whether or not it happens depends on the choices made by those involved. If these dreams are requiem quests, they are merely glimpses of predestined events and the likely outcomes of those eventsbased on what choices those involved are apt to make at this moment in time.

"If you continue to have these quests, expect that they will change over time, for it only takes a small thing to change someone's mind, and these events may not occur for months or years. People, like the seasons, change with the passing of time. When they change, their choices are bound to change as well. No vision of the future is absolute."

Lilly nodded, closing her eyes in relief. The warm rays of the suns spilled through the canopy and onto her face, and she basked under it for a moment until her mind was clear once again. Orvak, ever patient, smiled at her, his upper lips stretched over his teeth, parted like a hanging curtain. She couldn't help but smile as well. As used to his appearance as she was, she still found herself wondering how such a hideous creature could be so understanding, so kind, so soft-natured. Of course, his appearance was becoming so regular to her that she barely noticed his misshapen features anymore, but rather the beauty in his oddities. His eyes, though rather eerie because they were so unusual, were also amazing…deep, bright silver disks floating in darkness like a full moon in a dark night.

She stared at them for a while, and he stared back. She wondered what he was thinking, and though she was curious, she was also content to sit with him in complete silence. He was a great comfort to her, and she was grateful to have a friend in him. With a sigh, she broke the silence, knowing that she had come to him for help and if she were to receive any, she first had to ask the questions.

"What do you think the connection is between these visions and the flashes I had on my first visit to this place?"

"Your internal perceptions," he said slowly, "began that day. Those images may have unlocked the doorway to the answers. Do you remember what you told me that day, what your one question was?"

"Finding my mother."

"Yes." He was silent for a moment, and his tone changed as he cleared his throat. "Vula, you do know where you mother is, don't you? You have figured that out by now?"

"In the stone garden," she said. "The graveyard. I know that, but finding her means finding out who she was before she came to Earth, who her family is…who *my* family is."

"Ah ha! That is the connection."

"What do you mean? I don't see it."

"These dreams, these visions, are somehow connected to who you your family is, not necessarily who is involved, but the events. Perhaps these events, though not the outcomes, must occur so you can find the answers you seek"

"Is it going to take that long?" she asked, disappointed.

"Finding the answer to a question usually leads to more questions. You are looking for more than your family. You are searching for yourself, which happens to include your family. A quest to find oneself is a long road indeed. The way the dreams are divided, though, may mean something. Perhaps a new discovery with each event, perhaps something else. Should we try to focus on only one piece of the puzzle at a time? Maybe we can put them together with less difficulty."

"Alright," she said, perking up. "Which one?"

"I suggest you start with the one which includes things involved in your life right now."

"The green room and the book inside it. And the graveyard."

"Very good. When you find that room, something contained within the book will lead you to the graveyard. Perhaps that is where you should start."

"What about the other dreams? I mean, visions."

"They will finish when you allow them to finish. Only when you can accept that they are not absolute will your mind let go of its fear. Push your fear aside, vula, and let your dreams conclude."

Lilly nodded and looked down at her hands. She hated to leave his company, but she still had plenty of time to get started on her search. Rohan had told her to go for it, and now Orvak was telling her it was time to try. She hadn't seen the tasil since she first discovered how to possibly open it, but maybe, just maybe, she didn't have to wait until it appeared. She knew where it was located, in the corner behind the table in her room.

She lifted her eyes to look at Orvak. He was smiling, an amused look on his face and a sparkle in his eyes.

"What does vula mean?" she asked playfully. She asked him that question every time they parted, though he never told her the answer.

"Go," he chuckled. "Find your answers." Lilly grinned, jumped off her stone seat and kissed his cheek.

"Thank you," she said. "Thank you so much. I'll be back soon."

He was still chuckling when she disappeared from sight. She was the most delightful human he'd ever encountered, and so willing to learn. She was powerful, yet kind and compassionate. He didn't put much faith in the prophecy of the Chosen One, especially since prophets often mistranslated the *Doret Gaia*, but Lilly was making him a believer. She was one in whom he could have faith. His vula...she was destined for great things indeed.

In Plain Sight

Zephra was no where to be found when Lilly returned. She never followed Lilly when she went to visit Orvak, probably because Lilly traveled magickally to get there. Lilly had no idea what Zephra did when she was gone, but she really didn't care. She raced up the stairs to her room and wrote the events of the day in Her Grimoire. When she finished, she closed it and ran her finger over the outline of the symbol appearing on the front. It seemed to have a slightly green tint. Instinctively, she looked toward the corner of the room. It took only a moment to decide. She reached for her athame, relished in the scraping sound the metal made when it was removed from its sheath, and after holding it carefully in both hands, she ran her finger along its sharp edge.

It was a small cut, no larger than a paper cut really, but it bled a lot. Lilly kneeled in the corner behind the table, the blood threatening to drip on the floor. She caught the drip with her thumb, and rubbing her thumb and cut finger together, she spread it over the entire tip of her finger. She reached for the place where she had last seen the tasil, the minute crevice where the light had shown through, and pressed her bloody finger into it.

At first, nothing happened, and she thought it hadn't worked, but suddenly, the green glow appeared on the floor. It rose slowly, the green light now pouring from the hole being created in the wall. It didn't stop growing until it was the size of every other doorway in the house. She stood slowly, unable to peel her eyes from the sight of the room.

The inside of the room resembled the images in her dream. It was a small, square room with walls that looked like they were made from stone, though Lilly knew better. She raised her hand to feel them, and they even felt like stone, cool and smooth. The table in the center of the room was wooden and was cluttered with many magickal items such as crystals, scrolls, a quill and ink bottle and candles galore, but there were a few things Lilly was unsure should be there: vials, a few of which looked like they contained blood, a skull with a melted candle atop his brow, and a wooden pedestal with the face of an old, warped wizard carved into its base. Sitting on the pedestal under a dried puddle of wax from the candle beside it was a closed book, green light glowing from between the pages.

It was covered in dust and looked like it hadn't been opened in a hundred years, though Lilly guessed it had only been about fifteen. She reached for the book, lifting the melted candle from it carefully. The wax came off the book easily, still attached to the rest of the candle. She wiped away the blanket of dust and studied it. The outside of the book looked as though it had been made from smooth tree bark, and a ribbon of what seemed like roots of a plant formed a design between the corners, each of which were tipped with bronze. It looked like roots were holding its binding on the outside of the cover, and at the center was the same design that was appearing on her own grimoire, a pentacle.

She opened the book carefully and scanned the first page. The dark green writing was small and neat and very elegant. She leaned closer and read the only sentence on the page.

The end is the beginning is the end...show the book what I am to get in.

A riddle. Lilly rolled her eyes and traced a circle over the page with her finger. Suddenly, the green glow exploded from the book, so bright she threw her hands over her eyes to block the light. It dimmed, revealing writing on the page that wasn't there before.

This Grimoire is a collaborative effort of the Arch Mage Gustave of Elikrede and his apprentice, Master Sorceress Laurel of Elikrede, created as a legacy for the future...

Lilly stared at the two signatures beneath those words, reaching toward the swirling scrawl of her mother's hand. Her mother had been Gustave's apprentice, too. This was her grimoire, her altar room, and Gustave helped her create the book. This struck Lilly as odd, for she knew a teacher wouldn't do the work for a student, so why would he participate in adding to it?

She shook her head and started flipping through the pages, looking for the clue that would lead her to the stone garden. Most of the pages were blank, or had just a title and nothing else, so she almost skipped the page she was searching for. In the center of the page, there was a single line written in the same elegant hand:

A coffin is just a box; it is defined by what's inside ...

Could it be that easy? thought Lilly as she traced a rectangle with her finger. When nothing happened, she looked curiously at the page, then her finger. The blood had stopped. She squeezed it hard and a small drip bubbled to the surface, but it was enough. She rubbed it with her thumb, then drew the shape again.

The blood on the page glowed green at first, and then faded into gold, along with the center of the entire shape. It rose from the page, or so it seemed at first, until Lilly realized it was a box rising from the page. It really was a coffin, only buried within a single page of the book, and only her blood could resurrect it. When the glowing subsided, Lilly reached for the golden box, which was etched on all sides with strange symbols Lilly had never seen, something of a cross between Chinese writing and ancient runes. She opened the box slowly.

A silver ring rested on a green velvet pillow, as bright and unblemished as the box which contained it. The band looked like a tiny piece of rope made of silver, which twisted at the top to form a triquatra. She turned it in the light and the colors of red, blue, green and yellow danced their rainbow over its surface. Subconsciously, she reached for her necklace. She stared at the ring sitting in the box, and realized there was a small scroll of paper tucked into the lid. Prying it loose carefully, she removed the scroll and opened it to read the very tiny writing on it:

within the buried walls I lie
adorned beneath the stone
it bears no mark, save for the sign
Salvation bears alone
the Power of our fickle souls
so great and yet so weak

keeps magick secrets hidden well
before the eyes that seek
one armed with Knowledge, strong and pure
can find the only key
and organized, the right words said
reveal the prophecy
only blood of royal lines
can bear the sacred crest
to unlock Truths kept hidden by
my eternal rest

Lilly read the scroll over and over until she had the words memorized, then replaced it in the lid. She didn't dare remove any items from this room. It was obviously well protected, as was everything else in it, so it would be safer here than with her.

She closed the box and set it on glowing rectangle on the page of the book. It sank slowly beneath the surface of the page. She closed the book, and after a curious glance at the skull on the table beneath it, she left the room. The doorway disappeared as she stepped through it, but she knew how to find it now. She ran out the front door toward the graveyard. The stone garden...did her mother always use riddles?

She went straight to the obelisk monument inside the iron gate. She ran her fingers over the worn stone, searching for the mark. Close to the top, she finally found it; a small etching of a teardrop along one edge. A teardrop was the mark of salvation? She touched the birthmark on her cheek, and a feeling unlike anything she'd experienced before washed over her. She felt a sense of herself, as though a lost piece of her soul was returned, and she knew then that she was really meant to help people, to save them.

She sat on her knees before the towering stone and stared at it while the light rain that had snuck into the sky fell lightly around her. This was the gravestone from the poem, she knew it. What she didn't know was what the rest of the poem meant. If the secrets were hidden before the eyes that seek, it was hidden in plain sight. Then again, both the tasil and the box containing the ring were hidden in plain sight, too. She sighed. After the dream she'd had, there was no way she was going to attempt a resurrection in a graveyard, at least, not until she knew she could do it the right way.

I'll wait until after I'm declared Master, she told herself, and then added, *unless Wyatt wants to help.*

She stood, her knees wet from sitting on them, and looked around the graveyard. Her heart caught when she realized the harpy was hovering around the same headstone as before, though she was staring at Lilly intensely. Lilly froze in fear, but the harpy simply nodded at her, then turned away and began walking the path that led from the stone garden. Only when her back was turned did Lilly realize why this harpy looked so different. Her bright feathers were so thick she looked more like a beautiful bird walking upright than the harpies she'd fought.

"Wait!" called Lilly, running to catch up. The harpy stopped. "May I ask you something?" The creature nodded. "Who are you visiting so often?" The harpy looked sadly toward the headstone.

"My mother," she squawked, her voice very much like a parrot's. Confused, Lilly looked at the headstone again. The harpy continued. "The human who raised me."

"I'm sorry," said Lilly. "How long ago did she die?"

"A few months. She became ill over the winter and lasted only until the first day of spring. The following day, she closed her eyes and did not open them." The harpy brushed a long feathered finger under her eye, presumably to wipe away a tear, though Lilly couldn't see one. "It was for the best, I suppose. If she had been alive, the shock of the attack that day would have killed her."

"What attack?" asked Lilly, though she had a pretty good idea.

"My brother, her son, lives in Jesfinarea with his two children. On the day of Ostara, a large group of harpies attacked the village. My nephew was taken. I received the news the day we buried her."

"No!" gasped Lilly. She'd heard some children were taken from the town and at that moment, she wished she'd stayed there instead, though there would have been no one to save her if she had.

"Well," the harpy squawked, "that is my sad story. What is yours?"

Lilly hesitated, wondering how much she should say, but Rohan had told her to do what she felt was right. Everything in her soul was telling her to trust this creature, so she began her story. She told her of her mother leaving her when she was born and that she was buried here, along with another mysterious member of her family. When she pointed out the headstone, the harpy made a chirping noise.

"I know who's buried there! His name was Finerin and he used to live in the house just beyond the trees." She pointed to Lilly's house. "But that was long ago. He married and a few years later, he died. The house stood empty for many years, until the day his child came to claim it. She lived there for a time with an old wizard, and then she just disappeared. Rumors spread over time that she died as well, though no witness could be found. Some say the wizard declared her dead to gain access to the house, which she left to him upon her death, but I don't believe that. The old wizard only stays there from time to time, and now, I guess, so do you."

"Finerin," said Lilly slowly, "must have been my grandfather. How do you know that story?"

"Everyone in Elikrede knows that story. Finerin was the first person buried in this graveyard."

"Really?"

"Until he was buried, which he demanded in a written instruction to be carried out upon his death, everyone who died was burned. No one knows why he chose to be buried, but they followed his orders and built the obelisk and the iron gate. After a time, others began to choose burial, though many still prefer cremation."

"He chose to be buried because his tomb hides a secret," said Lilly, thinking aloud.

"What secret?"

"I don't know, yet, but I'll figure it out someday."

Lilly walked toward her grandfather's grave and stared at it. No matter what secrets were hidden with him, she knew they would lead her closer to her magickal family. That reason alone was enough motivation to figure out the poem.

"My name is Tiryn," said the harpy. "It means 'rise above'. My mother thought it would remind me to be good."

"It must have worked," said Lilly. "You seem good to me."

"Thanks," said Tiryn with a whistle, "but I give her the credit for that. She was the kindest woman I've even known. See, her husband died during a battle with a fierce flock of harpies, leaving her alone to raise their infant son. After the battle was over and the harpies gone, she went in search of her husband's body. She found my egg a few feet away from where he was slaughtered. In the confusion of the fight, one of the harpies had lost her egg. My mother buried her husband and took me home, where she hatched me and raised me as her child. I think she wanted to prove to herself that creatures aren't naturally evil, that they are raised that way. I think that both are possible, but I also think she was the reason for my person. I wouldn't be who I am without her."

"Why would a harpy bring her egg into battle?" Lilly asked curiously. "Didn't she know that was dangerous?"

"Harpies are vicious creatures. They fight amongst themselves, which is why most of them are bald. They'll fly past another and yank out a talon full of feathers for no reason. They also break each other's eggs when they are left alone, which is why my harpy mother brought her egg, I suppose. It was just as dangerous to leave it behind."

"Wow."

"I know. That's why it kills me to know my nephew is with them."

"Do you believe he is still alive?"

"Yes," said Tiryn fiercely. "He's a strong boy. They stole several children that night, but they only steal magickal children. Joss is more powerful than most. He'll withstand them for a while, but they will get the best of him eventually, and they've had him for so long. You have no idea how hard it is to face my brother knowing that I share blood with those nasty creatures." She ducked her head under her arm-wing and made soft sobbing noises.

"What else can you tell me about harpies?" asked Lilly, her mind working rapidly. Tiryn looked up at her warily.

"Why?"

"If I know my enemy, I can better defeat them."

"You can't defeat them," insisted the frightened harpy. "They will fight to the death and, well, look how sharp these are!" She lifted her foot to prove her point. Her long talons came to a sharp point.

"Look," said Lilly in a serious tone, her mind calculating a plan. "I think I can rescue the children, if you are willing to help me. I'm strong, much stronger than anyone believes, and if we can find a way to get into their lair undetected, we could save those kids."

"How do we get in there undetected?"

"Let me think." An idea formed in Lilly's mind, her confidence rising as she remembered Rohan's words. "We don't," she said, hoping the harpy wouldn't think she was insane for what she was about to propose. "I mean, not exactly undetected, but if we had a reason to be there...you know, like hiding in plain sight."

"How do we do that?"

"Well, if you captured me, you would have to deliver me to the lair, where the other children are being kept. Do you think you could do that, you know, act like a harpy?"

"Considering I am one? I think so. Let's see...I know they prefer to attack smaller towns. It gives them a better chance to escape with children. And they are notorious for attacking on Sabbat celebrations. People are always having a good time and let down their guard."

"When is the next Sabbat?"

"Beltane? About two weeks."

"Alright. We go that night. If they have an attack planned, the lair will be virtually empty."

"What if it's not?"

"It will still work," Lilly assured her, her adrenaline spiking from an equal mixture of fear and excitement at the prospect of doing something daring. "We can do this. I can be ready in two weeks."

"Are you sure you want to do this?" asked Tiryn. "What if something goes wrong?"

"Then we gave it our best shot." Lilly looked toward the house, certain Zephra was back by now. "I have to go. Meet me here in three days. I'll have all the details worked out by then."

Lilly ran toward the house, leaving the bewildered harpy staring after her. She was shaking with excitement when she reached the house. Finally, she was taking steps to make something happen, and if she succeeded, she would save the lives of countless children in the process.

Maybe, she admitted to herself, *I really am a savior. I guess there's only one way to find out.*

Lilly was still thinking about her plans to rescue the children from the harpies as she walked toward Ryzale's cottage two days later. Tsirama had been unable to switch days for her to go see Orvak, so he allowed her skip a lesson yesterday, having no problem with it since she was the best student he'd ever had. Wyatt was also unavailable yesterday, though he was very mysterious as to why, so she'd spent the day doing some much-needed housework and tending to the garden, pulling weeds from around her thriving plants.

When she arrived at the cottage, Ryzale was sitting in her living room on a wooden stool, her back rigid and a paintbrush in her hand. Her spectacles were perched on the end of her nose as she stared at the canvas before her.

"Good morning," she said to Lilly without looking up from her work.

"Good morning," repeated Lilly. She sat in her usual chair for her morning quiz, watching Ryzale curiously, as she waited for her lesson.

"True masterpieces can rarely be recreated," said Ryzale as she swept the paintbrush across the canvas, "because the art is in the imperfections, a special beauty that you never knew existed." Ryzale continued to paint, and after a few moments of silence, Lilly began to wonder why she hadn't stopped. Finally, Ryzale looked away from the canvas and focused on Lilly. "What do you enjoy?"

"What?" asked Lilly, taken aback.

"What do you enjoy?" repeated Ryzale. "What do you like to do in your free time?"

"In my free time, I train. Well, yesterday I cleaned the house, tended to the garden..."

"That isn't what I meant. How long has it been since you've done something you've wanted to do?"

"Honestly, I don't know."

"I don't either, and today, I want to paint." She studied her canvas again, and choosing her color, she touched the brush to the palette. "I'll see you at our next lesson. I expect you to do something today that you want to do. Have some fun."

Lilly's jaw dropped. Of all her trainers, Ryzale was the last one she expected to give her a day off for no reason. Once the shock of the announcement wore off, she tore through the front door and ran toward the house. Suddenly, she stopped. She had the entire day to do whatever she wanted. Her teacher had demanded it, and her mind suddenly went blank. What did she want to do?

She closed her eyes, concentrating on the house, and a moment later she was standing on the front step. Inside, Zephra was curled up on the sofa, immersed in a book. Her head snapped up when Lilly walked through the door.

"Why aren't you at Ryzale's?" she asked.

"She told me to take the day off," quipped Lilly. Zephra eyebrows lifted in response, but she made no remarks. Lilly flopped sideways into the chair across from Zephra, flinging her legs over one arm and resting her head on the other. "She told me to do something I want to do."

"What do you want to do?"

"I want to know more about the *Doret Gaia* and true magick. I think it's time I understand it."

"I don't think that's a good idea," Zephra said. "True magick is dangerous. If you try to use it and something goes wrong..."

"Why is everyone so afraid of me knowing this?" demanded Lilly. "I'm already using the magick. Wouldn't it be better if I actually knew what I was doing? Maybe it would help me gain control."

"No." She returned to her book and muttered under her breath, "Can't you just take a day off?"

"Please, Z," begged Lilly, pretending she didn't hear Zephra's remark. "I need to know this."

"It's not a good idea," insisted Zephra. "True magick is dangerous. It's unpredictable and extremely volatile. One small slip could destroy you. One mistake, Lilly. That's all it would take."

"Well," huffed Lilly sarcastically, "learning about it won't help me control it at *all*, I suppose." Lilly sat up and leaned toward Zephra, her eyes serious. "I don't want to use true magick, Zephra. I just want to be able to control it when it uses me."

Zephra was silent, considering Lilly's argument. She couldn't deny the girl made a good point. Besides, she probably new more about true magick than anyone else, anywhere else. If she said no, Lilly would just find someone much less qualified to tell her, and that would be a much bigger problem. With a sigh, Zephra closed her book and nodded slowly. "What do you want to know?"

"Everything," breathed Lilly, her eyes eager. She shifted in her chair, curling her legs beneath her, and leaned forward in anticipation. She'd gone over this scenario in her head more than once, practicing every possible retort in preparation. Even so, she never expected it to be quite this easy.

"That may take a while." Zephra wasn't nearly as enthused about the conversation. She sank into the sofa, staring at nothing as she thought. After a moment, her eyes focused on Lilly, their violet hue deeper than normal.

"Before I tell you anything," she began, and Lilly sat a little straighter, "you need to understand something about true magick. No one knows everything about it. I doubt anyone ever will. One of the most wondrous mysteries of the *Doret Gaia* is that it protects itself, and in essence, the entire world, so there is no need to waste your energy trying to block it if someone enters your mind. It does that on its own.

"However, if you know it, you can tell someone else, but don't! There aren't many who know more than a few words of the language, let alone the specifics I know. I'm not going to tell you everything now. I can't. There's far too much involved, but what I tell you, repeat to no one. If this knowledge wound up in the wrong mind...well, I can't even imagine the horrors the world could face."

Zephra glanced at Lilly, whose eyes were wide. Assured that Lilly would heed her warning, she continued.

"The *Doret Gaia* was the first spoken language..."

"Wait a minute," interrupted Lilly, already frustrated with the impromptu lesson. "I thought Latin was the first language, then I read in a history book here that Old English was the first language, which still confuses me, and now you're telling me that the *Doret Gaia* is the first language. Which one is it?"

"No one *knows* which was the first spoken language," Zephra stressed, scowling at the interruption. "Much in history had been lost or destroyed over thousands of years, and much more was never recorded, so there is no proof either way as to which came first, though speculation is always abundant. Most humans here are speaking the language of their ancestors, and while they came from many divided lands, Old English was the most common spoken language at that time. That language evolved into what it is today...another form of English, which is very convenient for you, I might add. Imagine having to learn an entirely new language before ever beginning your training."

"But so many English words derive from other languages, like French or Latin. It doesn't make any sense for English to be the first language."

"The further back in history you go, the more inaccurate it becomes. Records were lost, burned, even rewritten. A series of events wiped out hundreds of years of fact, leaving us to fill in the gaps now."

"Like what?" interjected Lilly. "Give me an example."

"Okay." Zephra pursed her lips together in thought, and Lilly couldn't tell if she was trying to think of one example, or if she was sorting through several. After a moment, a smirk crossed her face.

"Around 590 A.D., a pope named Gregory I declared an edict banning the education of common people to learn Latin, which he considered the language of the holy. Only servants of the church were educated. Commoners weren't allowed to learn to read or write, or learn proper grammar. Society was cast into illiteracy for a thousand years."

"Wow."

"To say the least. A lot of information can be misconstrued in a thousand years, whether on purpose or by mistake. How is anyone to know the correct origin of every word in every language with only a fraction of the population keeping records? It's not possible. The only thing that is certain is that the *Doret Gaia* existed long before man spoke his first words. It was the language of telepathy, when words were first created for everything that existed, giving them identity, a significance among the formerly overlooked. So pure was the language that when water was needed, the mere thought of the word brought rain. The thought of bountiful trees made the forests thrive."

"But if man wasn't speaking yet," Lilly wondered aloud, "who was speaking the language to give it a voice? I mean, thoughts don't need words if you are communicating with the mind."

"True," acceded Zephra, "but whoever said man was the first creature to *speak*? It was the Elemental Children who first spoke the language of magick, thousands of years before the cavemen even drew on the walls. Since not all magickal creatures were telepathic, they had to communicate somehow."

Zephra leaned toward Lilly, her violet eyes flashing hints of fiery orange, a warning.

"I want this to stay between us," she said in a quiet, but firm voice. "No one is to know where you are learning this. If someone asks, we treat it like every other unexplained thing you can do, as a mystery. Tell anyone and we stop talking about true magick...forever".

Lilly nodded, her eyes wide.

"Okay," exhaled Zephra, satisfied.   She leaned back, getting comfortable again. "I'm not going to start throwing information at you like all your training lessons now.   Since you won't be using true magick," she lifted an eyebrow at Lilly, "there is no rush. Therefore, you can learn at the right pace, and since you are studying fundamental magick, that's where we are going to begin."

Lilly rolled her eyes, and felt instantly guilty. It was Ryzale, after all, who was kind enough to force a free day on her. Zephra eyed her, then jumped out of the chair. Lilly stared after her in shock. A moment later, she returned carrying the large candle from the kitchen table. Her eyes danced as she walked past Lilly and out the front door.

"Are you coming?" she called as she disappeared. Lilly flew from the chair, sprinting after her.

Zephra walked toward the open meadow near the edge of the river, carrying the candle in front of her like it was a cake. She set it beside the bank and backed away from it, looking at Lilly.

"Light it," she commanded.

Lilly, still confused, shook her head and grabbed her wand. She aimed at the candle and whispered, "*Enyarten*." The five wicks on the candle lit at once, their little flames dancing in the breeze.

"Good. Do you know what that word means?"

"No. I know it lights when I think of a flame and say the word."

"*Yarten* means fire, quite literally. It controls fire the way a true name controls anything else magickally." She held up her palm, and a small fire ball whirled above it, spinning ferociously, a tail of flames trailing behind it as it spun. In an instant, it froze, the flames barely waving, as though they were in slow motion. Lilly could see the heat ripple the unchanged wind as it passed through the flame. Then it was gone, disappearing into itself with only a small wisp of smoke as evidence it was even there.

"*Enyarten* is the spell," she continued. "Any noun in the *Doret Gaia*, when preceded with *en-*, is the spell to control the...the noun. The same is true of verbs preceded with *da-,* turning them into a command, in a sense. Can you push the wind toward the candle to blow them out?"

"No."

"The human spell is *envonet*."

"*Envonet*," whispered Lilly, aiming her wand at the candle. A gust of wind changed direction as it crossed the path of her aim, whooshing toward the flames so fast it took the lingering smoke from the wicks. The flames seemed to vanish rather than be extinguished. She grinned.

"So, *vonet* means wind?"

"It means air," Zephra corrected. "That's part of why this is so dangerous. When you use true magick, it covers a broad spectrum of meanings. Almost every word in the language has more than one meaning, though the meanings are usually similar. This is why your intent has to be perfect, and I mean *perfect*, when you use it. Accidentally, of course."

"Of course," said Lilly, taming her enthusiasm. "So, what is a word that has more than one meaning?"

"Well," said Zephra, pondering, "*murat*, for example, means barrier, but it also means defend."

"Hmm," muttered Lilly. She sort of knew that one already. It was one of the words she'd said to Dorwynn that night in Arthidgen. Zephra seemed to notice Lilly's desire to change the subject, so she positioned herself halfway between Lilly and the candle.

"Try to light them without your wand," she instructed. "Just be careful. A little bit goes a long way."

"What?!" Lilly's mouth hung open in equal shares of shock and fear.

"It's just to illustrate a point," soothed Zephra. "It's nothing too dangerous, I swear."

"I'm starting on *fire*! Are you crazy?!"

"Rather sane, actually. I'm starting you on the element I can control if something goes wrong. Now, say the word and focus on lighting the wicks."

Panicked, Lilly stared at the candle, using the perception skills Orvak taught her to hone in on her target and block the senses that didn't matter. No longer able to hear the echo of the waterfall in the back of the house or the previously cawing blue jay in the nearby tree, she whispered the word for fire: *Yarten.*

A flame burst from her right hand, forcing her to drop her wand, and streamed toward the candle. One second, the wicks were lit, and the next, the entire candle was on fire, a smoldering, bubbling puddle of wax. Zephra's hand was up in an instant, the stream of fire soaring smoothly into her palm.

They stood for a moment, the trail of fire flowing out of Lilly's hand and into Zephra's. Suddenly, a blinding sting coursed over Lilly's hand, and with it, the sound of the waterfall reached her ears and the smell of burning flesh touched her nostrils.

"Break the connection!" yelled Zephra, straining to absorb the flame.

"How?"

"Your wand," she stressed, gesturing toward the ground at Lilly's feet. "*Enonatas*. Point it at the water."

Lilly grabbed her wand, her blazing palm aimed at Zephra, and pointed it at the water, all but shouting the word as she felt the blisters rising under her skin. A great wave of water jumped from the river and landed directly on her. Zephra caught the remaining trail of fire, and then burst out laughing at Lilly's now drenched form.

"I'm sorry," she giggled. "It's not funny."

"No," agreed Lilly, less than amused. "It's not."

"Are you alright?"

"No." Lilly held her scorched hand out to Zephra. The burn was bad, the skin gone, a handful of blisters in its place. Zephra gasped.

"I'm so sorry," she whispered, taking Lilly's hand from the underside. Even there, Lilly could feel how tender the skin was, though her palm was worse by far. Zephra placed her free hand over Lilly's, sandwiching it between them without touching her burnt flesh.

"What are you doing?" asked Lilly, trying not to wince. Zephra's hands began to glow then and Lilly felt an immense relief, though the painful stinging was still there.

"I'm drawing out the heat," she explained. "I can't fix it, but I can stop it from getting worse."

"I can fix it," stammered Lilly, swaying from side to side, suddenly exhausted. Shaking her head to wake herself, she pulled her hand from Zephra's. "I can do the rest." Lilly placed her good hand over the burnt one and, with every ounce of energy she had left, slowly healed the damage. Zephra watched in amazement as Lilly's hand healed to near perfection. Only trace amounts of evidence from their lesson were present. Slight swelling and red spots, but no blisters.

"Why did you stop?" asked Zephra, intrigued.

"I have to rest for a minute. That took a lot out of me."

"I can imagine."

Lilly's knees caved then, and she sank to the ground. Zephra sat beside her.

"I'm sorry," she repeated. "I've never had to worry about that part. I've been doing this so long now, I forgot about the protection factor."

"The protection factor?" echoed Lilly.

"I forgot that you have to be able to protect yourself from a weapon before you can use it. Sorry."

"It's okay."

"Didn't you notice the pain, I mean, right at first?"

"No."

"Why not? What were you doing? I've never seen someone that focused before."

"Orvak taught me how to..."

"I should have known," groaned Zephra. "You can't exclude your senses when you are using true magick. You couldn't feel the fire. I'm sure you couldn't smell it either, right?"

"Not until I lost my focus," admitted Lilly. "Sorry."

Zephra threw her head back, laughing. Lilly eyed her in confusion.

"What's so funny?" she demanded.

"Just a couple of sorry fools, aren't we? I mean, we're going behind everyone's back to practice nearly prohibited magick and we're apologizing to each other for things we're doing wrong during our tryst. Ironic, really."

"I guess so," said Lilly, her strength slowly returning.

"Come on." Zephra jumped up and pulled Lilly from the ground. "Let's rest a bit, and then I'll show you how to deflect magick. It will help you to protect yourself, should you ever decide to do that again."

"Not anytime soon," mumbled Lilly, and Zephra chuckled again.

Blood Magick

"I have a question," announced Lilly as she sipped her third glass of water. The first two she gulped without breathing, her body dehydrated from their lesson.

"Just one?" laughed Zephra. "That's a first."

"Probably not," retorted Lilly, trying to glare at her, but failing miserably. Their rocky relationship had recently taken a turn for the better, and sometime during that change, Lilly realized she was beginning to trust the mysterious woman, maybe even like her. "You remember Dorwynn telling you about that night in Arthidgen, right?"

"Yes." Zephra's now serious expression confirmed her affirmation.

"Well," hesitated Lilly, unsure of how to begin, "that night, everything went wrong. I still don't know how it happened, but I remember some things about that night that don't make any sense now."

"Like what?"

"Like, how did I freeze time?" Lilly words flowed now, her curiosity drowning her hesitation. "And how did I do it without saying anything?"

"What were you thinking at the time?" asked Zephra in such a smooth, even tone that Lilly was suddenly reminded of Dr. Hoffman.

"I don't remember," sighed Lilly, rubbing the dull ache beginning at her temples with her nearly healed hand. "I know I was furious, more than I have ever been in my whole life. I wanted to be able to yell at him without anyone hearing me."

"That's it?"

"That's it. The next thing I remember, everything was still and he looked so..." Lilly hesitated, trying to find the right word, then shook her head. "...afraid. Then, somehow, I let go, and everything was normal again, everything except us."

Zephra cast her eyes downward, her brows furrowed. Two separate thoughts raced through her head at once. The first was an aching desire to know what Lilly meant by 'us'. The second was Lilly's original question. How *did* she stop time without speaking? Pushing aside her personal thoughts, she focused on the magick. It was, after all, her first duty.

"How many other times have you used true magick?" she asked.

"None, that I know."

"At least one other time," corrected Zephra. "The harpies."

"Oh, yeah."

"And you said the words *kita sera*. Become lifeless. You were under attack and you said those words intending for them to die as a means to save yourself. But, *kita* also means inert, and when you wanted the world to be still, it became still."

"But I didn't say the words," Lilly reminded her. Zephra's eyes stared into the distance, a new idea forming. She turned to Lilly with a mixed expression: her mouth was set in a straight line, but awe danced in her eyes.

"It may not matter," she whispered. "You said them once. In rare cases, once is all it takes. After that, thought and intent trigger it."

"Meaning?"

"You can use true magick by thought alone." When Zephra spoke this time, Lilly could hear the awe in her voice, and then a strange smile crossed Zephra's face, her eyes glowing.

"How rare is it?" asked Lilly, wary.

"I only know of two, maybe three who can do it, though I'm sure there are a few more out there somewhere. It's not something you want to advertise."

"Why not?"

"Many reasons, the most important of which is that you don't want an enemy who also has that gift to find out just how powerful you are."

"Okay," breathed Lilly. "So, who else can do it?"

"Your friend Rohan is one of them," commented Zephra. Lilly felt her jaw drop. Zephra also noticed, and explained. "I didn't recognize him when he first arrived. You see, he had the talent at infancy. Gustave brought me to consult with Ashya about it. He was only months old, and already walking, talking and flying. He could transform between his human and pterippus forms with ease, or just sport his wings. Under Gustave's supervision, he could manipulate any form of earth by the end of his first year, and before he was three, he successfully performed every task required for Master of Earth Magick."

"All because of true magick?" wondered Lilly aloud. Zephra nodded.

"He was too young to understand what it meant or that he was even doing it. It came naturally to him, as did Fire Magick. That was something for which no one was prepared. Magickal creatures born under a specific element don't usually do that. I trained him myself. By the time he was six, he was Master of Fire and officially an Arch Mage. Of course, the following year he went to Earth and there he stayed for fifteen years. He probably doesn't remember he can do that. It's probably good that he doesn't. The other person who can do it is someone else you will recognize."

"Who?" Lilly was dangling on the edge of her seat, her curiosity about to knock her right off of it.

"Dagana."

Lilly almost choked. Yes, she recognized the name all too well.

"Dagana?" she repeated in a shocked whisper. "But, isn't she...?"

"...the evil queen hell-bent on destroying everything good in the world? Yep, that's her!" Zephra's sarcastic gaiety sent shivers down Lilly's spine. "She's powerful, Lilly. Why do you think everyone is so afraid of her, even if she hasn't done much in the past decade or so? They all know what she can do and how powerful she really is. She flaunted her power to earn that fear and there was never anyone powerful enough to stop her. Until now, anyway."

Lilly looked into Zephra's glowing eyes and saw the same awe flooding them. She wanted to speak, but the words stuck in her dry throat. She reached for the water in front of her, drained the glass, and then slammed it on the table. She opened her mouth, but still, no words came. Her mind was racing too fast to speak a thought before a new one took its place.

"What if," she began, her words coming slowly as she tried to focus on one question at a time, "I'm not the Chosen One? What if Gustave is wrong and this isn't *my* destiny?"

"After all you have seen and all you've discovered you can do, how can you doubt it?" demanded Zephra, one eyebrow raised in disbelief.

"I don't know. It feels like all of this should be happening to someone else."

"Let me ask you something. If it had been someone else who had been given the choice to come here, do you think they would have come? Would anyone else have made the choice so unquestioningly while so ill-informed? Whether you realize it or not, you've had faith in your decision from the beginning. Shouldn't that count for something, even if Gustave is wrong?"

"But if he is wrong," argued Lilly, "if I'm not the Chosen One, then what am I doing here?"

"*If* that is the case, then maybe you are meant to inspire hope in the true Chosen One." Zephra leaned forward, her eyes serious. "Just so you know, I believe you are."

"Why?" Lilly doubt wasn't hidden by her quiet whisper.

"A memory, something that is mine alone. You'll know someday, but I'm not ready to share it yet. It's...something from my childhood."

"You were a child?" blurted Lilly, and Zephra laughed.

"Is it so impossible to believe? I lived the normal life of a human child until my early adult years. Once grown, I just stopped aging."

"Oh." Lilly was silent for a moment, her thoughts still spinning through her muddled brain. Was she the Chosen One, or was she just supposed to inspire hope in her? Of course, no one could answer that question for her, but if she wasn't the Chosen One, were Gustave and his apprentices wasting time training her when they should be searching for someone else?

"Dorwynn believes you are, too, you know." Zephra's announcement shattered Lilly's train of thought. For the first time, she was grateful to be interrupted.

"Why?"

"I don't know. I asked him what he thought and he told me. He never gave a reason."

"What about Amparo and Opyre?"

"Opyre doesn't have much faith in anything. He's a bit of a pessimist, if you hadn't noticed. He wants to believe, but he fears the letdown. Amparo...is difficult to read. She believes in what she can see or has seen. If there is irrefutable proof, she'll believe it, but until she has that proof, she's a perpetual skeptic." Noticing Lilly's crestfallen look, Zephra continued. "Don't worry, though. They'll still do what needs to be done, and they will do it faithfully. They just think as many others do. They cannot have faith in what they haven't seen. It's just one more obstacle to overcome."

"As if I don't have enough," scoffed Lilly. "Can we please change the subject?"

"Sure," said Zephra. "Do you have any more questions about true magick?"

"Too many, probably, but I was wondering one thing. How does the true name thing work?"

"Leave it to you to ask one of the most in-depth questions about true magick."

"Sorry."

"I'm kidding," said Zephra, shifting in her chair. "It's part of the language I forgot to tell you. Here's the easiest way I can explain it. In any other language, the name of a thing is not the thing itself. It is merely a label used so someone will know to what you are referring. True names, the entire *Doret Gaia* itself, ignores this logic. The pure language is absolute. Remember how I told you it gave the formerly overlooked an identity? Well, your true name is your true identity, to magick anyway. Since the beginning of time, since magick first named your soul so it could identify you, your true name has been the same throughout every life. It will remain so until the end of time."

"Dorwynn told me that someone knowing your true name is dangerous," said Lilly. Zephra didn't miss the very slight pause before she continued. "How is it dangerous?"

Zephra sighed, exhaling slowly, and said, "True magick is based on the *Doret Gaia*. You now know the words for fire and air, so you can manipulate them to your complete will, assuming, of course, that you have the strength to control them. You saw how easy it was to lose control today."

"All too well."

"If someone knew your true name, and if they were stronger than you are, they could manipulate you the same way. They could turn you against your family, your friends. They could get into your mind to learn your most guarded secrets, or they could suggest the most horrible act, and you would be compelled to comply."

The thought of someone else having that kind of power over her made Lilly shudder. Imagine what Dagana would do with her if she ever learned her true name! Zephra already told her that Dagana could use true magick, and Lilly was sure she was the stronger of them. Lilly would be the queen's puppet, doubling her power in an instant. An image flashed before Lilly's eyes; the queen standing over her, her eyes glowing red...

"How do I find out what my true name is?" she asked, trying to keep her voice calm.

"It will come to you when you are ready to know it."

"What does that mean?"

"It means I can't tell you."

"What if someone else finds out my name before I do?"

"That's impossible. The only way someone else will learn your true name is if you tell them, and you won't know it for a while."

"Why not?"

"Some questions must wait for answers." Zephra shrugged her shoulders apologetically, and when Lilly didn't speak, she took the opportunity to ask a question of her own, something that had been bothering her since Lilly mentioned him. "What is your relationship with Dorwynn?"

"What?" asked Lilly, taken aback. "Nothing!"

"I didn't mean romantically," assured Zephra, though she was thrilled with Lilly's almost appalled reaction. "I mean, you said earlier that 'everything was normal again, except for *us*'."

"Oh, that," said Lilly, relaxing. "We grew up together since we were five years old. When we were little, we couldn't be separated. Every spare moment, we spent with each other. He was my best friend and no matter how difficult things got, I could always go to him and feel better. It was like I wasn't complete when he was away from me. Then, when we were twelve, he just vanished. He left, came here I found out later, but from the moment he left, I was lost. It was like I was a zombie. I was so bad, my dad put me in therapy again, but that really didn't help much since my psychologist was his fath... well, the man who raised him on Earth.

"The moment I stepped through that doorway, everything inside me changed. I didn't feel incomplete anymore, until that night I lost control. He changed that night, and so did I. I feel like I lost my best friend all over again, and the worst part of it is that he's so different now, I don't think I'll ever get that friend back."

Zephra nodded. She wanted to tell Lilly not to worry, but she couldn't. She knew Dorwynn's behavior had nothing to do with Lilly's episode in the forest. He was in love with her, probably since before he came to Buthania, but Zephra knew it wasn't her place to tell Lilly that piece of information, just like she knew it wasn't her place to tell him that her own theory was correct. Lilly didn't feel the same way he did.

The two women sat in silence for hours after that, each lost in their own thoughts as they watched the light give way to darkness. Zephra mind had drifted to the fact that Dorwynn had still not returned from Gustave's task, while Lilly's had led her from Dorwynn, to her first months in Buthania, to her dreams, and finally, to her impending duel and her newest friend who was also an absent figure in her recent days.

She fell asleep that night with Wyatt on her mind. When she woke the next morning, she was still thinking of him, but for a very different reason. In her dreams, she had seen him being carried away from her on the back of a large red dragon.

"Do you really think this will work?" asked Tiryn...again. "What if something goes wrong?"

"It will work," Lilly assured her for the fourth time, though she was beginning to have her doubts, not in their plan, but in Tiryn's lack of confidence. "Are you sure you can do this? The hardest part of this plan will be making them believe you belong there. If you can't do that, then it's pointless to worry about anything else."

"How are we going to do that, by the way? I am *not* pulling out all of my feathers."

"You won't have to." Lilly opened her grimoire, flipping through the pages for the potion she was sure she copied into it. She smiled when she found it, thinking how ironic it was that she was resorting to using fundamental magick for her first proactive incident when she'd started her training believing she didn't need to learn it at all. "This potion will transform your appearance, but you won't be able to take it until we're almost there. It only lasts two hours."

"Oh, good," sighed Tiryn.

Halfway through reading the ingredient list, Lilly realized they had overlooked a very important detail, something crucial to their success.

"Do you think two hours will be enough time?" she asked. "We have no idea how big the lair is or where the children are being held."

Tiryn hung her head for a moment, and shame flickered across her eyes. She had not shared this part of her life with any human, and the memory was a weight on her shoulders, one she could never forget.

"When my brother got married," she began, "I decided it was time to find my real mother. It was hard to grow up being so different, especially with the violent reputation of other harpies, and he was my only friend. I didn't feel like I belonged here anymore after he was gone, so I went to the lair, to my kind." Lilly had no trouble detecting the bitterness in her voice. "I lived with them for a time, but the longer I stayed, the more I saw what kind of creatures they are. It made me realize I belonged in Elikrede with my real family. I returned to my mother scarred, and most of my feathers were missing, but she welcomed me home like I had only been gone a few days."

"How long did you stay with them?"

"Over six months. It was long enough to know I could never be like them. They attacked me more than the others because I wouldn't hunt with them. They despise each other, in all truth, but their self-preservation dictates the power-in-numbers theory. The bigger the flock, the better chance for victory. I had nowhere near the strength they had, either, because I refused to feed on the powers of the children they took. I don't know why I stayed with them for so long, too long, while they attacked me, drained me of strength. I wasn't strong enough to fight them or protect myself, but I was strong enough to leave them. When I did, I never looked back."

"You stayed with them so long," said Lilly, "so this plan would work. I have the magickal strength, you have the inside knowledge. That's why this will work."

Lilly, where are you?

Wyatt's voice ringing in her head was a relief, and she couldn't help but smile. With a quick slam of her book, she was instantly on her feet.

"I have to go," said Lilly, "I'll work on the potion, but I think we should test it before we stake our lives on it, just to make sure it works."

"Okay," agreed Tiryn. "When?"

"I have lessons with my potions Master in two days. We can test it the day after."

"I'll see you in three days," said the harpy. She walked toward her mother's headstone as Lilly darted toward her house.

Where are you? she asked Wyatt as she ran.

Our place, came his response. *Can you come here? We need to talk.*

I'm almost to my house. Why don't you meet me there? We can have lunch and I'll introduce you to Zephra.

Is that okay?

Sure. Walk the stone ridge behind the waterfall. It's easy to climb down the other side. Walk toward the house. I'll be standing by the back door.

I'll be right there.

Lilly sprinted through the front door, across the living room and kitchen, and straight out the back door. She could barely see Wyatt's form emerging from the curtain of water, but she was so absorbed, she didn't realize Zephra was standing behind her.

"What are you staring at?" she whispered in her ear. Lilly jumped a mile, her heart pounding in her throat.

"You scared the hell out of me, Z!"

"Sorry. What's going on?"

"I have a guest. He wants to meet you."

They watched Wyatt run across the yard toward them in long, graceful strides. He leapt over the garden in one smooth motion and landed so close to the house, he bowed to Zephra and Lilly before walking any further.

"Ladies."

Zephra held out her hand, one eyebrow arched higher than the other. "I'm Zephra."

"Wyatt. A pleasure."

"There is some pulled pork on the stove and bread in the cupboard," said Zephra. "You are welcome to stay for lunch, Wyatt, but I'm afraid I have an errand I must attend. Stay as long as you like. Lilly, a word?"

"I'll be right back," said Lilly, pointing out the bread cupboard as she followed Zephra out the front door.

"I've got to find Dorwynn," she said the second Lilly was in her sight. "He's been gone a long time. I'm going to try to contact Gustave so he can find out where he is, and I think he should know about the dragon."

"Oh, the dragon's not here for me. She was looking for Wyatt."

"How do you know that?"

"I dreamed it. Last night."

"Find out for sure," she said, glancing toward the house, a wary look in her eyes, "and be careful. I'll be back as soon as I can."

"Good luck." Lilly waited until Zephra was out of sight, then closed the door and returned to kitchen where she found two plates on the table and Wyatt, already sitting and looking thoroughly proud of himself.

"Hungry?" he asked.

"Starving."

They took their time eating, for they both had so much to say to the other, they couldn't wait until the end of the meal to talk. Wyatt planned to bring up the duel first; he was anxious to get the date set, for Lilly didn't know it yet, but a dragon was waiting for him. He wanted to tell her, but before he had the chance, she figured it out.

"You're leaving, aren't you?" she asked, but it wasn't really a question. He nodded anyway. "With the dragon?"

"How did you know?"

"I dreamed it. So, when are you leaving?"

"I convinced her to stay until Beltane," he said, relieved that she wasn't upset over this turn of events. "I figure that would be a good day for a duel. We'll leave right after."

"I can't duel on Beltane. I...have plans. What about the day before?"

"Okay," he said, and then he removed his wand from his belt. "I guess it's time to make this official." He aimed his wand at Lilly and stood, his voice loud and regal. "Lilly of Elikrede, I challenge you to a duel to be held one day before Beltane. As the challenger, I declare that offensive spells must be only of fundamental magick. Defensive spells may be from any type of magick. The winner shall be declared after three effective strikes. Do you accept these terms?"

Lilly stared at him, dumbfounded. He smiled, then motioned to the wand on her hip.

"Aim your wand at mine and say 'I accept these terms'."

Lilly took out her wand, aimed it at Wyatt's and repeated the words. A spark flashed between their wands, a small but fierce burst of energy, and vanished half a second later.

"It is done," said Wyatt, lowering his wand. "We are officially committed to this now. Do you want to practice?"

"No. I had something else in mind." Her emerald eyes twinkled as she glanced at him, and he was sure it was excitement he saw there. The small smile that crossed her lips intrigued him, and he leaned toward her in anticipation.

"The tasil. I got inside," she whispered.

"Really?" he breathed, his own excitement building at the prospect of an adventure. "What's in it?"

"My mother's altar room." Lilly paused, a small twinge in the back of her mind warning her not to continue, but she overrode that feeling as another took its place: the need to share a bit of herself with her friend. She looked into his eager face and smiled as she continued. "It was different than I expected. Her grimoire was there, obviously, but there are so many other strange things in there, things I've never seen or read about in any of my training so far."

"Like what?" His rapt attention and genuine interest in the tasil prompted Lilly to do something she never thought she would do.

"Would you like to see it?" she asked.

"Do you always leave it open like that?" he asked the moment they were in her room.

"No," she replied, wondering about his disproving tone. "I did this morning because I planned to work in there later. I'm surprised you can see it, though. No one else can." She tried to remember whether it had been obvious when Rohan was in her room, but other than the dream, the events of that night are a blur, so she couldn't be sure. Still, neither Zephra nor Dorwynn had made a single comment about seeing a strange green light, so she was sure they'd never noticed it.

"Well," admitted Kylenin in a bored tone, "I can see magick, so concealment charms are easy for me to see through."

"Oh," muttered Lilly, a new thought suddenly occurring to her. She had never asked anyone about seeing magick. She could see it, and she had naturally assumed that everyone could see it, or at least everyone magickal, but what if she had assumed wrong? "Um, how rare of a gift is it to see magick?"

"Pretty rare," he explained. "Even my grandmother can't see it, and she's one of the most powerful people I've ever known. Why, can *you* see it?"

Lie! shouted a voice in her head. *Don't tell him you can see it. Don't tell him...*

"I don't think so," she muttered, unable to outright lie to him. He accepted her answer, though, making his own assumptions.

"Trust me, you would know it if you could."

She felt guilty about her deception, but she had a feeling she was right to do it. Never had she heard a voice so easily in her head, as though whoever was speaking to her was right behind her. She hoped he wasn't able to feel her emotions, for he would ask why she was feeling guilty and she would surely tell him the truth. He didn't notice her, however. His eyes were roving over the collection of strange objects on the table in the green-glowing room.

"What kind of a person was your mother?" he asked warily as his eyes scanned the unusual items. They stopped on the skull resting atop the table, inches away from the carved wizard who was part of the table itself. "Is that real?"

His inquiry came out as a whisper that sent shivers down Lilly's spine. Suddenly, she regretted sharing this room with him.

"I suppose it is," she murmured. "Why would anyone put a fake skull in a place so...sacred?"

"Decoration, maybe," he answered, but he shook his head and shrugged. "If it is real, then she's the kind of person who would use blood magick."

"Of course." Lilly's nonchalant reply threw him and he stared at her in shock, so she explained her reaction. "That's how I got inside. I used my blood to open the door."

Kylenin exhaled, his eyes wide. Instantly, terror fixed Lilly to her spot. She'd never seen a face so full of fearful surprise.

"What is it?" she asked unsteadily.

"Well..." Kylenin inhaled and shook his head, then tried again. "It's just that if your mother was using blood magick, she must have been powerful. Blood magick is very powerful, so she would have to have been as well, but..." His voice trailed off as he thought of how to reveal to Lilly a part of her past she might not be prepared to learn. She waited as patiently as possible for him to continue, and when he didn't, she prompted him further.

"What?" she encouraged, though she dreaded his answer, and with due cause, for the next words out of his mouth sent chills along her spine and a sinking feeling in the pit of her stomach.

"Either she was really evil," he said, his voice clear and ominous, "or she was trying to protect herself from someone really evil. There is no other reason for blood magick."

The reality of his words hit Lilly hard enough to knock the air from her lungs, and her thoughts turned to the evil queen she had yet to meet. Could she be the reason her mother ran away, why she returned here to die? If so, then the protection spell would have been rendered useless, unless...unless it was meant to protect someone besides her mother. Her mother knew that her children, or at least one of them, would return to her house someday. Did that strange skull still hold the power to protect? A shudder tingled down her spine, and she realized Kylenin was staring at her, waiting for a reaction.

Clearing her throat, she finally spoke. "I guess I'll find out soon enough." He looked at her questioningly, but she didn't respond to his expression this time. Her mind was calculating the long list of questions about her mother, her unknown family here. Tsirama...he'd told her when she was ready, he would take her further into her quests, and she planned to hold him to it. First, the harpies, but after, she would finally do something proactive, something she would instigate, and she vowed to start finding the answers she sought.

Over the course of the next few days, she'd gotten a confirmation from more than one other person about the uses of blood magick and the blasphemy it seemed to invoke. Ryzale had, of course, confirmed the dangers of it, and told her about how much strength a person had to have to create such magick.

"Even for protection, it takes extreme power," she explained, her voice a pitch higher than normal. "Obviously, the skull is not hers, which is something else to wonder about, but a spell powerful enough to protect against a strong evil would probably kill most. Perhaps her death was even a premeditated ingredient, so to speak."

As if Ryzale's words weren't bad enough, Tsirama continued with the gravity of the situation by adding, "Blood magick hard to undo. A spell cast so desperate is impossible to betray, but motivations are great. Death, after so serious a reaction, is all one could hope to have delivered."

From that moment forward, Lilly wondered if her mother had indeed committed the ultimate sacrifice and poured herself into magick that would protect her daughter...a daughter who could do nothing but question her mother's motives. A nagging though in the back of her mind asked, *What if she was evil? What does that make me?*

"Come," said Tsirama. "This potion you desire needs time. We begin now."

So far, so good, thought Lilly as Tsirama hovered over her. She carefully measured and added the right mixture, grateful for her good luck. Tsirama had all of the ingredients she needed, and there were many rare ones that she'd never heard of that the potion required. She was also glad that as of yet, Tsirama hadn't asked her why she wanted it. When the potion began to simmer, Lilly looked at the clock, noting the time so she could remove the cauldron after exactly four hours.

"We have much time to wait," said Tsirama. "Let us return to your own memory now. The better you control easy quests, the best you will control visions."

Lilly threw herself into her self-induced memory quests with the aid of *Segvatele,* grateful for the potion. She had more strength, which enabled her to easily control the direction of the quests, and she didn't feel so drained after they were over. Most were simple memories, with nothing relatively significant to her life besides just the memory, so she never took the time to write them all down. Her quest today wasn't one of those.

Lilly sat on the floor of her home, leaning against the back of the sofa, the area she had made for herself that no one else entered. She was only five years old, her hair pulled into pigtail braids that curled upward. Beth used to play dress-up with her, often forming her hair into weird shapes...that one had been her Pippi Longstocking style, and every time Beth styled her hair like that, she had called her Pippi. Sitting across from her, his legs crossed, was a boy of thirteen, and Lilly grinned as she remembered who he was.

"Pippi," sang her almost seven-year-old sister from the sofa where she was sprawled watching cartoons. "What are you doing back there?"

"I'm talking to my friend," the tiny Lilly said firmly, possibly even angrily. "Tell me again," she sang, clapping her hands.

"Lilly, honey," her father interrupted before Rohan could comply, "we've talked about this. Rowen is imaginary."

"He is not," argued the child, her lower lip jutting forward in a pout.

"He is. No one can see him or hear him but you. If he's real, we should all meet him."

"He would see me if he still believed in magick," said Rohan to her small self.

"I know," she giggled. "He doesn't believe. Tell me again about the spells." She leaned her pigtailed head toward him.

"Spells are one of my favorite types of magick," he said. "Some you can do with just a wand, and some need different things to work, like stones or ingredients."

"When can I have a magick wand?"

"You have to make your own."

"Well," said the child, "what's the powerfulest spell you can do without a wand?"

"Spells where you have to make a potion to use it, and you have to put drops of blood to make the strongest potions."

"I want to make a potion spell with my blood." Her excitement was shattered by her father's sharp voice.

"Lilias Hope!" He rushed toward her and grabbed her upper arms, shaking her lightly to make his point. "First of all, you never, *ever*, put blood in potions," he growled, his voice a rough whisper, and her eyes popped open in shock. "Blood magick is wrong, very wrong. Second, I don't know who exactly to whom you are speaking, but it must stop. You are not ready yet, and you can tell him for me that I said so, unless you want to tell me who it is, and I'll address him myself."

And then, the quest ended abruptly, the shock of new knowledge prying the quest from her control. Lilly was shocked for a number of reasons, but mostly over the fact that her father had spoken of magick as though he not only believed in it, but actually knew all about it. What could it mean, and if it was true, if he knew, then what had possessed him to put her into therapy?

"What did you learn?" asked the apothecary.

"I don't understand," said Lilly. "He knows about magick. How does he know about magick?"

Tsirama stared at Lilly, a blank look of his face. She ranted, detailing her life on Earth, of her sessions with Dr. Hoffman and her issues after Adrian left, and then she described the quest. Tsirama listened, nodding now and then as though everything she said was perfectly normal.

"What did you learn?" he repeated when she finished.

"I learned that my father's been lying to me my entire life!"

"Not lying. Protecting. Think again of his words."

Lilly stared at him in shock. He raised an eyebrow, waiting for her to follow his instructions, so she moved her anger aside to remember.

Blood magick is wrong, very wrong... You are not ready yet...

"He knew I would come here," she stated, the truth overwhelming her. Tsirama nodded, his face bright. "Why wouldn't he tell me?"

"You were not ready. You should not know anything until you are ready. A father knows this. Raises new questions for you, does it not?"

"Too many."

"Do not fear," chuckled Tsirama. "Questions make life interesting. Without them, you are bored, and boring. Come, let us quest once more. Perhaps some answers will be found."

"Or more questions," she muttered, but she took the *Segvatele* again. In an instant, she was sitting across from her father at the kitchen table, her hair still in the Pippi style. She realized then that she had never seen her father look so concerned, not even when she withdrew from everyone after Adrian left.

"Lilly," he said, his voice solemn, "I need you to tell me about Rowen. Who is he?"

"He's my friend," said the little girl.

"I know that," sighed her father, "but who is he? Where is he from? What..." Her father seemed to have trouble speaking the words, but he finally choked them out. "What manner of creature is he?"

"He's a pterippus, Daddy. A black one, with big wings and a long horn made of gold dust. He came here to keep me safe."

As her young self jabbered on about Rohan, Lilly watched her father's face grow more and more concerned, but he showed no hint of disbelief. When she stopped talking, her father nodded. He folded his hands together and held them in front of his mouth, his brows furrowed. He closed his eyes and released a heavy sigh.

"Okay, honey," he said, defeat lacing his words. "Go play."

"He believes," gasped Lilly, snapping from the quest. "I told him about Rohan and he believed it."

"Indeed," said Tsirama, glancing at the clock. "It is time to bottle potion. Come."

Lilly took the cauldron from the flame, and while it was still steaming, she separated the potion into seven bottles, Tsirama corking each one after it was filled. He eyed the bottles, then turned to Lilly, no longer able to contain his curiosity.

"What plans have you for this?" he asked, swinging one of the corked vials like a pendulum between his thumb and index finger. Lilly cringed. She should have known it wouldn't be so easy. She shoved three of the vials into her pockets and handed the rest to him. He took them to his shelves, arranging them on an empty shelf labeled *Segdasevam*. "I no intend to stop you, but perhaps others should be aware?" He turned his huge eyes toward her. "Ignorance begets error."

"The fewer people who know, the better," said Lilly. She began cleaning the cauldron, but Tsirama's silence distracted her. He was only silent when he expected more from her. Sure enough, when she lifted her gaze to him, he raised an eyebrow at her as if to say, *Is that all?* She sighed and scrubbed harder. "It's not dangerous. I just need a disguise for something. As long as it works, I won't be in any danger."

"It will work," he assured her, seemingly satisfied with her reply. "May hurt little bit."

"How much?"

"Depends. How much to change?"

"Not much."

"Then not much hurt." He took the cauldron from her hands, startling her. "I shall finish. Go now."

"Bye," said Lilly as she gathered her books, and though she had just put them there, she checked her pockets for the potions, curling her fingers around them as she walked out the door.

That night, Lilly had no problem filling the pages of her journal, including every detail about her curious memory quest. She noted that she would have to convince Rohan to accompany her on it next time. Perhaps together, they could discover the mystery of her father's knowledge. She wrote about blood magick, having already started a separate section for information about that branch of power, and concluded her entries with every question that plagued her thoughts. The list was long.

Was the evidence of blood magick from her mother's hand enough to prove she was evil, or was she hiding from evil? How much of this world did her father really know? Did he know about her mother's involvement in magick? Did he care? Had he always known she would be leaving him? And if he knew, if he was part of this deception, why in the world did send her to a psychologist?

It really didn't mean much in the grand scheme of things, she guessed, but somehow, she felt herself desiring the answers nonetheless. If her father was somehow a part of this life, if he could *stay* a part of this life, she could hang onto the missing part of her family. When the war ended, they could be together again, forever. Would her destiny allow that? Could her father possibly be more than her past, but perhaps, her future as well? Could fate be that kind?

"I don't know what any of it means," explained Kylenin the following day, leaning against their boulder. "I've never had the talent for quests, to be honest. I know nothing of my former lives, and the only memories of my youth that I can recall are the ones I remember without magick. I'm sorry...I wish I could help you more."

Frustrated, Lilly shot balls of lightning into the waterfall. They sizzled like frying bacon when they touched the wall of water, though the smell wasn't nearly as pleasant. During one particular attempt, Lilly lost control of the little ball of energy, and it sailed haphazardly toward Kylenin, who somehow failed to notice.

"Wyatt," shouted Lilly, trying to steer it away from him, "look out!"

He ducked in time; the ball sailed past his head and exploded on the boulder behind him.

"Sorry," apologized Lilly, her brows furrowed in concentration.

"You're so upset," he commented. "You're usually so cool and calm. It's an interesting twist. Something I've always noticed about my magick is that when I'm upset, when I don't have control over my emotions, I have little control over my powers, too. Emotions and magick go hand in hand."

"Yeah, I've noticed that, too," sighed Lilly. "I guess I should try to keep my emotions in check. I'm just so frustrated with everything. I'm ready to test for my Master status, but my trainer, who was only supposed to be gone for a week hasn't returned yet, and he left almost three weeks ago. I'm trapped here with the one person I trust the least, and as soon as our duel is over, you're leaving, too. Now, on top of that, I find out my father knows more about things than I think, and I can't communicate with him to ask him about it, which just makes me angrier than ever."

"Hey," soothed Kylenin, recognizing the symptoms of losing control, "I know it's hard, but you have to keep moving. It wouldn't be worth the journey if it wasn't a little difficult, right?"

"I guess not," agreed Lilly, and then she grimaced. "Why is it so much harder than it should be?"

"Maybe you have a better reward waiting at the end."

She smiled, wishing that were true. The duel loomed closer each day, and each day took closer to the time they would part. It saddened Lilly to be losing the great friend she had found in him, but his parting words to her eased her sadness.

"If you ever need anything," he offered, "you know how to find me." He'd tapped his temple with a smile, and she nodded.

She returned to her room that night in better spirits, and slept peacefully for the first time in a very long time. It wasn't a dreamless sleep, which would have been more restful than the one she had, but she didn't care. It was a happy dream, full of the wonder and beauty of Earth. Her father walked through the woods surrounding their home, Lilly holding his right hand, Beth holding his left. Nothing significant happened in the dream, though it served as a reminder of their time spent together, and for the first time since she'd come to this world, her guilt over leaving them behind faded. Only love remained.

The Dragon and the Duel

"You *what?!*"

"Wyatt challenged me to a duel and I accepted."

"How...why...what would possess you to do such a thing?! I leave you alone for one night and..." Zephra threw her hands in the air, then glared at Lilly. "Dorwynn was right. You are reckless."

Lilly frowned. She woke that morning refreshed, her confidence restored. The date for the duel was set, the dragon was no longer an issue and her plan to infiltrate the harpy lair was running smooth. She'd expected to receive support from Zephra, but Zephra seemed pretty upset about the duel. In fact, she was downright livid.

"As if we don't have enough problems," she cried, "now you're involved in a duel." She turned toward Lilly, her hair beginning to flow from the heat of her anger. "It's a good thing Dorwynn isn't here, because he would probably murder you for this."

"What's the big deal?"

"The big deal," said Zephra through gritted teeth, "is that this will cause us unwanted exposure. Magickal duels attract spectators. The whole town will come to watch, not to mention every magickal creature who hears of it!"

"So what?!" Lilly slammed her hands on the table and stood so fast her chair toppled backward. "I'm tired of hiding and training and waiting for things to happen to me. They happen whether I try to avoid them or not, and they attract attention, so why shouldn't I have a say in what happens? Just once, why can't I be responsible for what goes on around me? I can't just sit back and wait for the next incident. If I don't take action myself, if I don't *choose* to experience things, then I won't be prepared for what's coming, and believe me, I know it's coming!"

They stared at each other, neither willing to surrender the argument, until Zephra noticed the faint flecks of yellow in Lilly's eyes, flickering like tiny flames, just as her own eyes did when she was angry. She drew in a quick breath, and then, with a heavy sigh, she closed her eyes.

"Fine," she surrendered, "but I want to know why he wants this duel. Someone with so much experience shouldn't be dueling an apprentice."

Lilly confessed to Zephra her dream of Wyatt, and how, in the dream she was the victor. She tried not to share too much information, but Zephra's doubt was written all over her face. Against her own judgment, Lilly told her everything about her connection to Wyatt. Zephra's face turned to shock when Lilly told her the rest of the dreams, to suspicion when she described their first meeting because of the dreams, to anger when she detailed the intense depth of their training, and finally, to confusion and concern when Lilly described the strange feeling she had whenever they touched.

"Like the light between us in the forest?" asked Zephra.

"No," said Lilly. "This light is behind my eyes, and it hurts. I don't think he notices when it happens."

Zephra didn't respond. She stared out the window for an eternity, pouring over the wealth of information Lilly had unleashed upon her, trying to decide how to handle it all. Lilly waited in silence, though she was impatient for Zephra's response. When she was just beginning to regret sharing so much, Zephra finally spoke.

"What are the terms of the duel?"

"What?" It was the last question Lilly expected.

"The terms. As the challenger, he should have set terms."

"Offensive magick can only be fundamental. Defensive can be any type. A winner is declared after three effective strikes."

Zephra nodded. She sat in silence, staring out the window again, then rose and began pacing, stopping only long enough to look at Lilly and shake her head before pacing again. It was like this for half an hour, until Zephra plopped into her chair and folded her hands together, leaning toward Lilly.

"We should focus on your defenses," she said. "How much has Ryzale taught you?"

"Well," said Lilly, unsure how to answer. She had learned a lot from Ryzale, but how much was there left to learn?

"Come on," sighed Zephra. "We have a lot to do if you actually think you have a chance of winning."

"Where are we going?" she asked, following her out the door.

"To see Ryzale."

The time between their last visit and the day of the duel passed rather quickly for both Lilly and Kylenin. Lilly, her mind on many other things besides the duel, was left to Ryzale's mercy. The sorceress drilled her over every spell she had learned since her first day, focusing especially on the ones involving offensive magick, demanding an instant response to each question.

"Lightning," said Ryzale.

"Enlaris," said Lilly in a bored voice.

"Don't tell me," Ryzale shouted. "Show me."

"Enlaris," she repeated, aiming her wand at the nearest window. A lightning bolt shot from her wand, shattering the glass. Before Ryzale could utter a protest, Lilly repaired the damage. Ryzale cleared her throat, shooting Lilly an exasperated look.

"Cause blindness."

"Datome."

"Cause total sensory deprivation."

"Darende."

"Good," sighed Ryzale when Lilly returned her sight. "Very good. I think our training is done."

"What?" asked Lilly, unsure she heard her right.

"I'll be present at the duel, so I will be able to see how effective your training with me has been. It shall serve as a great examination, don't you think?"

"You're testing me at the duel?"

"Yes. Your performance will determine whether or not you qualify for status in fundamental magick. You may go. I'll see you at the duel."

Lilly left Ryzale's house in shock. She hadn't expected today to be their final lesson. Gustave had told her she would still be training with her long after her Master trials. When she found Zephra waiting for her by the tree where she frequently attacked her for combat lessons, she told her the news. Zephra was just as stunned.

"I can't believe she isn't going to test you over defensive magick," she exclaimed as they walked home together. "Is she reviewing any defenses at all?"

"No. She knows I can defend myself with more than fundamental magick, and since I can use any type for my defenses, she thinks our time is better spent learning all I can about offensive magick."

"Well, I think you should at least know how to protect yourself from an attack," suggested Zephra. "I can teach you that, if nothing else, though, if you want to practice more true magick than that..."

"Protection will be enough." Lilly stopped her from suggesting any more lessons. She had more than enough on her mind. The duel was only days away, Beltane and the harpies the day after that, and Dorwynn still had not returned, which further postponed her Master trials. She might be worried about him if Zephra hadn't told her how common it was becoming for him to disappear for days at a time, so instead, she became increasingly angry at him.

She used that anger during Zephra's lesson with a strong spell, albeit still human, that would deflect an attack, much like a shield. *Adamurat*...protect oneself. Lilly practiced with Zephra for hours on end until the day before the duel, making the shield stronger, more impenetrable, until she was sure that even if she didn't get in a good strike, she would at least be safe from whatever he threw her way. She didn't know why, but she felt a twinge of fear, and she fell asleep that night thinking of creatures rising from the ground at Wyatt's command.

News of the upcoming duel spread throughout Elikrede like a raging wildfire. The whole town was buzzing about the mysterious young elf who challenged the old wizard's new apprentice, not only because of the duel, but also because of the fact that the dragon that had been wandering through town in human form was now always at his side.

Tangaia could see the curiosity in the human's eyes. She could feel their stares whenever their gazes fell upon her walking arm in arm with Kylenin. She paid them no mind. She was sure many of them believed in the concept of soul mates, and that many of the believers would claim to have found theirs, but she doubted that any human in the town had ever felt the pure magick of uniting with their leyartha. The majority of human minds weren't magickal enough to recognize it. Their hearts weren't strong enough to see it through, let alone survive it.

She made no secret of the fact that she thought humans were the lowest of the magickal community, and while Kylenin did not protest her remarks, he rarely agreed with her. His reply was always the same: "Just wait until you meet Lilly." He spoke of her often, and though

Tangaia knew he now belonged with her forever, she still felt a pang of envy whenever he mentioned the girl's name.

It was on the day of the duel that Tangaia met the mysterious girl, and the meeting came as a shock. She was the same girl Tangaia had been following through the forest, the girl who had, for some strange reason, led her to Elikrede, and to Kylenin. When she had lost her trail in the forest, Tangaia continued toward Elikrede, having overheard their final destination. She hadn't understood at the time why she felt so drawn to the girl, the attraction as strong as metal to a magnet, but when she arrived in the town, she felt a different pull, much stronger, like opposite ends of two magnets. She followed it to Kylenin and knew without a doubt that he was the reason she came to Elikrede.

The girl was nothing extraordinary - she was human, after all - but Tangaia felt the same attraction to her as she had when she first started following her. She held a certain beauty beyond a normal human, but it was her magickal aura that Tangaia found most intriguing. Most humans had very dull auras, hazy, like trying to see a rainbow through a thick fog. This girl, however, had a bright green aura, as vibrant as her eyes, and it radiated from her like light from the suns.

She cannot be a mere human, thought Tangaia. *She must have the ancestry of some magickal creature.* She stared at the girl severely, as though if she stared long enough, she the human girl's parentage would be revealed.

Lilly stared at the dragon with equal severity. She now understood what Rohan and Zephra meant about how easy it was to recognize a dragon in human form. The creature was captivating. Her hair was blood red, just long enough to brush the glistening scales covering her shoulders, which shined like rubies under the suns. They covered every part of her body that wasn't clothed by her leathery pants and top, which were also a deep red, and though her body was the shape of a human, her face was more like a cross between a human and a lizard. Her features were in the right places, but her nose was very narrow, just two slits for nostrils, her mouth wide like the hinged jaw of a snake, and her eyes were like a cat's with the same elongated pupils.

Wyatt was beside himself with contentment. Complete strangers began to approach him on the street, wishing him good luck in the duel. He smiled at the irony of their words. A few weeks ago he'd been needing luck, and seemingly had none. Now that fate had bestowed it upon him, he was receiving wishes for it at a constant rate. He wasn't concerned about the duel anyway. He knew he would lose...he still remembered what Lilly had told him in that first dream they shared. There was a reason for everything. He believed that now, even if he still wasn't sure what it was, but he no longer feared losing. More than anything, he was ready to have it behind him, for now that he found the dragon, he wanted to take her back to the castle, back to Dagana, who would finally be happy with him.

Tangaia left him with Lilly in the middle of the arena at the edge of town and went to the risers surrounding it. The whole town was gathered there for the first duel in over three years, and there were many magickal creatures present who, Tangaia was sure, did not live in Elikrede. Whispers and rumors flew through the crowd, bets were placed on who would be the victor, and shouts of good wishes were extended to both participants. Tangaia shook her head in disgust.

Humans, she thought as she found a seat. *So easily entertained, so easily distracted. No wonder the queen has such power over them.*

Tangaia rarely allowed herself to be impressed by any creature, let alone a half-human, but this particular human-breed had earned her respect. She had been observing the queen for many years and knew beyond doubt that she was brilliant. No other human-breed had the power and potential with magick that Queen Dagana possessed, and using that power with such magnitude was what caught Tangaia's eye. She knew, just as Tangaia did, that the humans could not be left to their own devices. They needed a ruler to govern them, to protect them from themselves. The queen's ability to recognize this fact alone was enough to earn the dragon's respect, but her capacity for gaining support through her power was what held that respect. With a sigh, the dragon resigned herself to the spectacle about to take place, hoping it would soon end so she could meet the woman she so admired.

"She's beautiful," said Lilly when they were alone. Kylenin grinned.

"Yes," he agreed. "She is." He looked at Tangaia, now seated with the rest of the town, and Lilly let her gaze follow his. Among everyone gathered to watch, one person, in particular, caught Lilly's eye. She was exquisite, her white-blond hair reflecting the red of her dress. She shimmered from head to toe, a halo of light surrounding her. Lilly wondered who she was, but before she became too distracted by her thoughts, Wyatt interrupted. "Shall we begin?"

Lilly nodded, her eyes roving over the crowd once more. Ryzale, her severe eyes already scrutinizing every action taking place, was sitting beside Zephra, who was grinning, much to Lilly's surprise. Tsirama was several risers above them, his bug eyes gleaming with excitement, and behind him, the exquisite woman in red was watching her with unwavering attention.

A hush fell over the crowd as the duelists took their places within the sanctioned circle of stones. Kylenin removed his wand and waved it with gentle ease, and a ghostly swirl of light swarmed around the stones, creating a hazy mist that shrouded the circle like a bubble. It glittered as a beam of light rippled over the interior. A low hum began to emanate throughout the circle, a steady pulse that reminded Lilly of the chanting of a choir of monks, a soft, slow, regular beat. Everything else was silent, too far away to be significant. She could no longer hear the cawing of the nearby jays or the rush of the river. It was as though the world, for that moment, existed only within the stones, and they were the only beings in it.

Can you hear that? asked Kylenin, his thoughts as soft as the hum.

It's beautiful, Lilly replied. *It's like the Earth in singing.*

It's the magick centering around the stones. No matter how out of control things may get... - Lilly detected the smile in his thoughts before it spread across his face - *... the barrier will not let the magick escape.* He crouched into a defensive position, his arm curved so far in front of his face that his wand was pointed behind him.

She was caught for a moment in the gleam of his gray-blue eyes. She could see him challenging her there, and combined with his stance and the wide grin on his face, he looked menacing, almost evil. A shudder racked down her spine, sending a chill over her whole body, and the distant memory of a dream jumped to the forefront of her mind. He had the same look on his face in the dream.

I know you're supposed to win, his thoughts whispered, *but I'm going to make you work for it.*

An instant later, she was on the ground, all the air knocked out of her. The crowd burst with muted applause. It took her a moment to overcome the shock of his strike, but when she did, the spell was already on her lips, her wand aimed at his feet.

Enlaris.

The ball of lightning bowled him over, and before he could recover, she sent another at him that struck his chest, slamming him to the ground again. Seconds later, they were both standing, their wands staring into the tip of the other.

You caught me off guard, he said, rubbing his chest.

You're one to talk, she retorted.

Her spell hit his halfway across the vast space between them, creating a miniature fireworks display of green and yellow, and then, she couldn't breathe. An invisible hand tightened its grip around her neck, while Kylenin's raised hand was empty. She gasped, struggling to break the hold, trying not to panic.

Darende, she mouthed, raising her wand toward his face. All expression left his face as the spell hit him, but she knew this would not be considered an offensive strike. It merely allowed her to escape his. She gulped the air, composing herself to make a strike, when she saw a ribbon of red light streaking toward her. *Adamurat,* she breathed, hoping the protective spell she'd practiced for so long would work. She felt her strength diminish like air deflating from a balloon, but the red light that would have hit her face hit an invisible barrier in front of her and sent it sailing toward the one who cast it.

It was over. The applause was no longer muted, now a roar in her ears as the stones stopped humming and the magickal barrier around them dissolved. Lilly sank to the ground, weaker than she'd ever been practicing that spell with Zephra, which told her how powerful his spell must have been. Across the field, Kylenin was holding his ear. Even as far as she was from him, Lilly could see the blood dripping from between his fingers, and though she felt another shiver down her back at the thought that if his attack had hit her she would be injured far worse, she got up and walked across the circle to where he sat.

Move your hand, she said. He obliged, and she healed the huge gash that had nearly removed the tip of his ear. It was a slow process, due to her lack of strength, but a hush fell over the crowd once again as they watched her, and then murmurs droned an even tone before she was interrupted by something louder in her head, and far more annoying.

So much for keeping her a secret now, Zephra's voice echoed, laced with sarcasm and laughter. Lilly looked toward the place where Zephra was sitting, knowing before she saw him that Dorwynn had returned.

Dorwynn knew there was a duel taking place in Elikrede before he could see the village through the trees. The applause announced the event as thunder proclaims the storm. He broke into a sprint, hoping to catch some of it before it was over, but when he crested the hill to the arena, he felt sick. Lilly was taking her first steps into the circle to face the elf that was her opponent. He scoured the crowd until he saw the wave of fire, then rushed toward it.

"What's happening, Z?' he asked.

"Where the hell have you been?"

"What? I was exactly where I was supposed would be. Why is Lilly in a duel?"

"Well, she was challenged to a duel, and since her trainer, the one responsible for guiding her, wasn't here to do that, she accepted."

"Dammit, Zephra," he shouted, "I though you were going to keep an eye on her. I leave for ten days and all hell breaks loose!"

"Ten days? You've been gone almost a month, Dorwynn."

"I have not. I..."

"Yes," insisted Zephra, interrupting him. "Tomorrow is Beltane."

Confusion crossed his face as he thought over the past week and a half. It had taken him three days to get to Ingvenal, and though it was difficult, he had managed within four days to convince the dwarf king that he should allow himself to obtain an audience with Gustave's newest apprentice. The three days it took to travel back to Elikrede made an even ten days, and as far as he knew, he hadn't had a blackout, but if it really was Beltane, what had happened during his missing time? How long had it been since his trip, or did his blackout occur before he ever arrived? He frowned. He would never know. He certainly couldn't go back to the king and ask him. How would that look after having finally convinced him to see Lilly, something he'd lost confidence in already and was initially the whole reason for the trip?

"Beltane?" he whispered. "It can't be. I..." He looked at Zephra's face, the obvious frustration confirming his fears. "I can't be losing more time."

"Face it, Dorwynn," she spouted. "You are losing time, and if you can't keep yourself under control, I'm going to have to take this to Gustave. I know you don't want me to do that, but this can't continue. You aren't going to be any good to us if you disappear for weeks on end, especially if you can't remember why."

"Don't tell him, Z," said Dorwynn. "Please. She's almost ready for her tests..."

"She is ready," corrected Zephra.

"Okay," he conceded. "She's ready to be tested, and then Amparo will be here to take my place. Just don't tell Gustave. He'll assign someone else to visit the others."

"Maybe he should."

"No! If someone else tries to recruit the giants, they'll fail. You *know* that. We can't have them joining the other side. It would throw away any chance we have of winning. Do you want to lose that chance?"

"Fine," she sighed in frustration. "I won't tell him, but I think you should. What if you black out for longer next time during something really important? What if someone needs you and no one knows how to find you?"

"You know."

"I'm not responsible for you, Dorwynn!" she exploded. "I'm responsible for her, and myself, and that's all."

"Well, it's not like you were doing your job here. She's in a duel!" He pointed toward the arena at the exact moment Lilly was thrown to the ground by a spell. He cringed, and then, as he watched Lilly's rebuke strike her opponent in two successive shots, his eyes widened in shock. He turned toward Zephra, seething. "Don't you know who that is?"

"His name is Wyatt, I think."

"That," he said, as quietly as he could through his clenched teeth, "is Kylenin, the queen's grandson." Without fail, several nearby spectators gasped and disappeared before he could blink, returning seconds later with several others in tow. The word spread through the audience, which grew to three times its normal size in a matter of seconds. "Why is she dueling him? What are you thinking? It's been hard enough to keep her a secret from the queen without Lilly dueling her grandson. What do you think will happen if she wins? Do you think the queen will just understand? She's going to force the queen's hand, Z."

"I doubt that. Besides, he challenged her, remember?"

"Yeah, and why do you think he did that?"

Zephra didn't answer. Lilly had told her about the dreams and their connection, but the girl had only recently started to trust her and she certainly wasn't going to betray that trust by telling him anything. She just shrugged and turned to watch as Lilly hovered in the air, gasping for breath. Ryzale nodded beside her as Lilly used the sensory deprivation spell, and Zephra sighed in relief when she used the protection spell that they'd rehearsed so many times.

It was that spell that ended the duel. Kylenin's spell reflected off Lilly's and shot directly back at him, striking his ear. The audience roared in applause, raving about the unexpected turn of events, and then, a moment later, a hush fell over them. Lilly, in the presence of the entire town and many other spectators, was healing her opponent's ear with magick. Dorwynn's face was just as shocked as the rest of the crowd's, his mouth hanging open stupidly. Zephra grinned.

"So much for keeping her a secret now," she laughed. Dorwynn glared at her, his eyes piercing as he continued to watch his pupil. She offered her fallen opponent her hand, helped him to his feet, and then bowed to the murmuring crowd. Kylenin bowed also, a grin on his face, and the dumbstruck audience, after a hesitant moment of shock, exploded into another round of applause. Dorwynn clenched his fists so hard he could feel the blood leaving them, and said in a whisper he was sure no one else could hear, "I'm going to kill her."

"I think Kiera wishes to speak with you," said Zephra, looking beyond his head. He turned to see a beautiful woman beckoning him to join her. "Go," prompted Zephra. "You need a few minutes to calm yourself anyway." She pushed him gently toward the woman.

"I'll be right back," he warned, but Zephra just smiled and turned her back on him as he walked away.

"Where's Dorwynn?" asked Lilly when she finally made her way through the throng of spectators, the queen's grandson and the human dragon on her heels. "I want Wyatt to meet him."

"He'll be right back," she said, over-smiling at the trio. "Wyatt?" She stared at him expectantly.

"Yes?" he asked with a confused smile. She held her expectant smile a moment longer, then turned her eyes to the dragon. "You've made a new friend, I see."

"Yes," he said in a rush. "Zephra, may I present Tangaia."

"A pleasure," said Zephra, and to everyone's surprise, she bowed. Lilly's jaw dropped, but Tangaia was instantly impressed with the respect Zephra showed her. She bowed her head in return, the corners of her wide mouth turning upward.

"Indeed."

"I'm happy to see you have found what you've been seeking."

The dragon's smile disappeared. She stared hard at the woman before her, who returned her stare with equal scrutiny, and a hint of sarcasm, but Tangaia wasn't shaken. She flashed Zephra what Lilly could only guess was her own overacted smile.

"As am I," she said, taking Kylenin's hand. Zephra frowned at the glance they exchanged, but returned the smile to her face before the dragon could detect any change.

The conversation faded from Lilly's ears as a new one took place in her mind. She looked past Wyatt and his dragon, past Ryzale engaging in an animated discussion with Tsirama, past the several rows of excited humans and creatures chattering about the results of the duel...beyond them all, she found him. He was talking to the woman in the red dress. Closer to her now, Lilly could see how the dress seemed to be a part of the woman, the laces up her back fading into the iridescent skin of her lower back.

When will you bring her? asked the woman, her voice like the tinkle of wind chimes.

A week from now, replied Dorwynn.

So long?

I was away for a time, he explained, and despite the distance, Lilly noticed him lower his eyes. *I must ensure she is ready.*

She is ready, young Master, the woman said, *but keep her the week if you wish. Her next training begins not until after the final harvest. Time is of plenty, for now.*

Dorwynn nodded to the lady, who turned suddenly to look at her. Lilly turned her eyes back to Tangaia as though she had heard nothing. From the corner of her eye, she saw Dorwynn bow as the woman, in a great burst of light, became a tiny red blur hovering before him before disappearing altogether.

"We leave tonight," said Tangaia, snapping Lilly back into the conversation.

"You aren't staying for the celebration tomorrow?" she asked.

"I've been away too long already," said Kylenin, "and the trip is lengthy. We should be on our way as quickly as possible." He tugged Lilly from the others, his voice low. "I convinced her to stay long enough for the duel to take place, but she's anxious to meet my grandmother."

"I have no doubt," Dorwynn said behind them. Lilly jumped at the sound of his voice, then spun around to scold him for his rude tone. She stopped short when she saw the furious look on his face.

"Wyatt, this is my Master trainer, Dorwynn," she mumbled. "Dorwynn, my friend Wyatt." Dorwynn stared at the boy's extended hand, then crossed his arms over his chest, watching with satisfaction as he lowered his arm to his side, clearly wounded.

"What is your problem, Dorwynn?" asked Lilly.

"She doesn't know, does she?" he asked, ignoring her.

"Know what?" she asked, looking back and forth between the men. They glared at each other in silence. "Someone say something!"

"His name is not Wyatt," Dorwynn finally answered. "It's Kylenin Wyatt, Queen Dagana's grandson. You just fought the heir apparent to the throne, an offense punishable by death."

"Is it true?" asked Lilly, crossing her arms, but she knew the answer. His eyes were glued to his feet - a sign of guilt. "Wyatt! Is. It. True!"

"It's true," Dorwynn said with a smirk. "He won't even look at you."

"Dorwynn, leave," she commanded, her eyes glued to Kylenin's face.

"I'm not leaving you alone with him! He's..."

The look in her eyes when she turned to him cut him short. Yellow flames burned in her green eyes, edged with other hues. Her eyes had looked like that right before she lost control in the forest. "This has nothing to do with you," she said, her voice eerily calm, just like before. "Leave." Without a word, Dorwynn left them alone, no longer fearing for her safety and certainly not caring about his.

"Wyatt?" she said softly. He didn't move. "Kylenin!" she barked, and his head jerked up. "Why did you lie to me?"

"It wasn't only you," he began, watching her reactions as he spoke. "No one knew. I..." He heaved a sigh, struggling for the right words to answer her question. How could he explain this to her where it made any kind of sense? "My entire life, if I was seen in public, it was only at my grandmother's side. Everyone knew who I was. You have no idea how frustrating it is, everyone bowing all the time, afraid to speak for fear of offending me, or worse, offending her. This is the first time I've ever been away from the castle without her. I didn't tell anyone who I really was because, well, I guess I just wanted to be someone else for a while, someone normal."

"So you became Wyatt?"

"My middle name," he confessed, nodding. "Still me, just a different part of me."

She nodded, another serious question burning on the tip of her tongue, but would he tell her the truth? She could ask Dorwynn, but how accurate would his side of the story be with his very evident grudge? She watched the boy for a moment, gauging his expression. He seemed sincere enough.

"Have you met Dorwynn before today?" she blurted, and was shocked when he nodded.

"I never knew his name. It's been so long, I didn't even recognize him until he said my full name. It was about three years ago, when the royal entourage passed through a small town called Omsael. Do you know it?" Lilly shook her head. "The queen is fond of shopping and the variety of wares in the town intrigued her, so the six carriages and two dozen guards stopped. She went into the shop alone, and as usual, I was angry at her for something. I can't even remember why now, but I was mad, so I waited until the guards were preoccupied and I ran off. I didn't know where I was or where I was going; I just ran until I was far away from the royal party.

"When I stopped running, I found myself at the gate of a small, secluded cottage, and inside, a boy barely older than myself was practicing magick. He didn't notice me at first, but when he did, he asked if I knew magick. To make a long story short, boys can be very competitive and he ended up challenging me to a duel. I was about to accept when the queen found me. She...she was furious, and trust me, you don't ever want her angry at you. She hit him with a powerful spell - it wouldn't surprise me if he still had the scar - and she threatened him with death for attempting to duel the heir to the throne. The surprise on his face after learning my identity was what saved his life that day, though she left her impression on him. 'This is Kylenin Wyatt,' she told him, 'your future king. You now know his face. Never forget it.' Apparently, he never did."

"Apparently," echoed Lilly, calculating the facts in her mind. His story seemed true enough, and Dorwynn would certainly hold a grudge against him for that, but she couldn't shake the fear gripping her soul. He looked so evil during the duel that she was afraid even before she knew who he was, and now, she just couldn't be sure. "Why were your spells so intense?" she asked, her words laced with hurt. "You almost did some very serious damage." His shoulders drooped another fraction.

"I know you have something planned tomorrow," he all but whispered. "I don't know exactly what it is, but I know that whatever you are about to face will not be easy on you. I figured you need to know what 'almost' feels like. That hint of fear you feel when you realize that what you do is dangerous might just save your life."

Lilly was thoughtful for a moment, considering his words and the emotion behind them, but it was the sincerity she saw in his eyes that convinced her. No matter what his behavior before, right now he was genuinely concerned for her. Yes, he'd lied to her, but only about something as simple as his identity. She had briefly considered hiding her own identity when she'd first arrived. If she had, would he have seen the justification of her deceit?

"You're right," she said with a bright smile that eased Kylenin's mind. His posture straightened as she continued. "I may be biting off more than I can chew, but I have to do it, and now that I've won our duel and I know that you weren't letting me win, I feel that much better about my decision. Thank you, Wyatt."

"My name is Kylenin," he reminded her. She smiled at him again, tears brimming in her eyes, and she stepped toward to give him a hug. The blinding light intensified, so much brighter than before that it was painful, but she held him for a moment through it all.

"You'll always be Wyatt to me," she whispered into his ear where a very thin scar, so thin she could barely see it even that close, glowed with silver light. His arms tightened around her and the light burned, her eyes stinging with more than tears. She released him then, and the instant they broke contact she could see.

"I'll try to contact you tomorrow night," he said. "We'll see if we can still communicate over so far a distance."

"If I survive," she quipped, keeping her voice as calm as possible.

"You will. The strength of your protection spells is impressive, and I don't impress easily." He flashed her a smile before he walked away, and when she could no longer see him, she sank to the ground and cried, a delayed reaction to the worst pain she never imagined she could feel.

Dorwynn was watching from a distance, waiting for Kylenin to leave and grateful the dragon was anxious to depart Elikrede, for he would be far away from Lilly. He watched her hug him and started walking closer to her, slowly, to allow Kylenin to be gone, but when she sank to her knees, sobs racking her body, he broke into a dead sprint.

"What happened?" he asked. "Did he hurt you?"

"I'm fine," she muttered, inhaling a deep breath to recover herself. She met Dorwynn's eyes, glaring at him. "Must you always think the worst of everyone?" she spat at him, then stood, turning on her heel, and walked toward Zephra before giving him the chance to answer.

"So you've joined together against me, is that it?" Dorwynn paced the hardwood floor of the living room, stomping hard enough that the sound echoed throughout the bottom floor of the house. Lilly looked at Zephra, who was sitting next to her on the sofa, and crossed her arms, trying to resist the urge to throw something at him to stop the *CLACK! CLACK! CLACK!* of his heels on the floor. A painful throb had begun to ravage her head and every *CLACK!* made it worse.

"I thought we were all on the same team," she muttered as she leaned forward and started to massage her temples in a circular motion. The clacking of his heels stopped as he paused long enough to cross his arms and glare at her.

"Oh, Dorwynn," chided Zephra, "don't be so dramatic. If you were related to Dagana, would you want everyone to know?"

"I wouldn't trap someone into breaking a law punishable by death," he retorted, turning his glare on her.

"Enough!" shouted Lilly, wincing at the pain caused by her own volume. "No one else would have known who he was if you'd have kept your mouth shut, Dorwynn. He didn't even remember you until after what you said to him. Everyone in town knew him as Wyatt until you showed up, and now everyone in town knows that I was in a duel with royalty. You're blaming me for putting myself in danger and Zephra for not preventing it, but your inability to control your temper and think before you act is what put me in danger this time."

"You don't know, Lilly!" he exploded, and her head nearly burst. "I was almost killed because of him."

"The duel challenge three years ago," she said, and his jaw dropped. "What was it, about six months after you arrived? Any of this sound familiar?"

Zephra stared between the two, her eyebrows raised in interest.

"How do you know about that?"

"He told me, and I also know he was a kid. So were you, for that matter, so just back off! He wasn't happy with what Dagana did that day...he was embarrassed. Why do you think he hid his identity from everyone? He's her grandson and he can barely tolerate her. He understands why you're acting this way and he doesn't judge you for it, but you judge him because of who he's related to, so you tell me, Dorwynn, who is the one leaning closer to the evil tendencies?"

"I don't trust him," Dorwynn said quietly.

"You don't have to trust him," countered Lilly, crossing her arms again. "That's my decision."

He was about to rebuke her argument, but he closed his mouth before sound escaped. She was adamant, her jaw set, one eyebrow raised, daring him to cross her. He knew if he continued, she would only defend Kylenin more. Dorwynn would consider any contact Lilly had with him dangerous, but he was gone now, on his way back to his evil guardian, so Dorwynn conceded.

"You're right."

"What?" Lilly didn't think she'd heard him right.

"You're right," he repeated. "I don't trust him, but I trust you, and if you think he's worthy of your trust, that's good enough for me." It was a lie. He did trust her, but he would never trust a boy raised by someone as evil as Dagana...never.

"Good," said Lilly, eyeing him suspiciously for a moment before announcing, "I'm going to bed."

She was halfway up the stairs when Zephra called, "Good night, Master Sorceress Lilly of Elikrede." Lilly paused as the reality of those words hit her. She was officially a Master of fundamental magick. She had earned status among the magickal community. Smiling, she went to her room, hoping she could suffer through her headache long enough to record the day's events, though she doubted she could forget today even if she wanted to.

Downstairs, Zephra busied herself with dusting and straightening the tables and their contents, while Dorwynn stared at her in disbelief.

"Where were you?" she asked, wiping the three-tiered candelabra that really needed more of a good polishing. "You should have been here."

"Don't put this off on me," he hissed. "I left *you* in charge of her."

"Well, maybe if you were here, where you should have been, you would have recognized him sooner and then none of this would have happened. What the hell, Dorwynn?" she snapped as he grabbed her wiping cloth, whipping it from her hands. She spun around, eyes on fire.

"Don't," she said as he opened his mouth to speak. "You can't just come back here and start yelling at everyone, especially when you were gone weeks longer than you were supposed to be. Where were you?"

"I don't know, okay?" he snapped.

"That doesn't excuse your absence," she snapped back, snatching her cleaning cloth from his hand. "Who do you think trained her in your stead? I certainly couldn't do it. You're just lucky there was someone here who knew Earth magick."

"Who?" he asked incredulously. "Not Kylenin."

"There was no one else, and before you get into another rant over it, I think Wyatt did a spectacular job."

"His name is Kylenin," said Dorwynn, fuming. Zephra shrugged.

"Not to her," she said. "Whatever his name, he trained her well. She's ready to be tested."

"I'm her trainer. I'll decide when she's ready."

"The faeries believe she's ready, too, or the queen herself would not have come to you."

"Kiera came to see the duel," he said, but he knew Zephra was right. The queen took human form so Lilly would notice her presence, he was sure of it.

"Did you notice the way the dragon looked at him?" asked Zephra, changing the subject. It had been bothering her all day. Dorwynn shook his head, but she could see her fears written all over his face. "If they unite, this is going to get much worse. Dagana will rise faster with a dragon at her side."

"That's why Gustave brought her here early, to help with our already slim timeline."

"How would Gustave know Dagana would recruit a dragon, or that a dragon would even entertain the idea?"

"I've had dreams of their union," admitted Dorwynn, "and of her return to power. Gustave believes they are quests."

"You can't do quest magick."

"I know, but the dreams stopped when Lilly got here. Besides, their union is really the least of our problems. Once Dagana hears how powerful Lilly is, she's going to watch her. We have to be more careful than ever."

"I know," said Zephra, not hiding the concern from her voice. "Let us hope he believes in their friendship as much as she does and Dagana never learns of her power.

"The dragon will tell her."

"Perhaps not. She thought everyone was pretty insignificant."

"I doubt she thought Lilly was insignificant. I don't think anyone would believe that." He sighed and sank into the sofa. "I still don't trust him. I'll never be able to trust him. Just don't tell Lilly. I don't want to make her mad."

Zephra didn't answer. She finished wiping the top of the mantle, then tossed her rag into the basket of laundry beside the back door. She agreed not to say anything to Lilly, though she was quite certain she had heard every word they had said.

The whole town, it seemed, was still buzzing about the amazing duel that, albeit short, turned exciting results. The townsfolk chattered about it nonstop throughout the course of the next day, the voices of two ladies rising over the rest.

"...and she's not even a Master yet. She's still an apprentice!"

"I heard the duel served as her test and she was declared Sorceress at its end."

"She bought her wand supplies in my shop," boasted the wand maker louder than the ladies, and it was followed by the "oohs" and "ahs" of nearby patrons, several of whom began searching through his display.

Despite that it was a well-known fact, however, no one spoke of the identity of her opponent, something for which Dorwynn was grateful. Everyone seemed to know the taboo of dueling royalty, as well as the fact that endangering their life even by accepting a challenge was an offense punishable by death, and no one wanted to lose the new mysterious apprentice in their midst. Their candor over the situation, combined with the first good night of sleep he'd had since he left, was all Dorwynn needed to relax and enjoy the upcoming celebration.

As he strolled through the center of town with Lilly, still listening for Kylenin's name among the masses, he noticed she was preoccupied. It was different though; she was nervous, even fidgety, as her eyes scoured the grounds for nothing in particular.

"If you're looking for Zephra," he said, "she'll be along later. She's helping Tsirama set up for tonight's celebration."

"I'm not," replied Lilly, still looking around at everything but him. He waited for her to say more, but he may as well have not been there.

"The faeries want me to bring you to them in a week," he said, trying to spark her into conversation. "I though we would spend a day or two practicing for your tests before we set out for Saurabean."

"Okay," was her vague reply.

"It will take about a day and a half, so I thought we would spend a night in Ambala. You can visit Voruum and Savara."

"Sure."

"And then, if we have enough time, we'll dive from the cliffs of Griffon Cove."

"Mm-hmm."

"Lilly!" he snapped. She finally looked at him.

"What?"

"You aren't listening to me. This is important."

"Sorry."

"What's wrong?" he asked, stopping in the middle of a mass of people milling through the fairgrounds. "I'm sorry if I upset you yesterday, okay? I overreacted."

"I'm not upset," she assured him, but he wasn't convinced.

"Aren't you? You've hardly looked at me all day, let alone said one word to me."

"I'm sorry," she repeated, and she sounded like she really meant it. "I've just got a lot on my mind."

"Don't be nervous about your tests," he said, and a mixture of guilt and relief washed over her. She hated to deceive him, but there was no way she was going to tell him the real reason she was worried. To her misfortune, his mind was ahead of hers, already on the events of that night. "You're going to love tonight," he rambled now that he had her attention. "That's when the best of the celebration begins. The fires are lit at sunset and burn until dawn."

"Fires? There's more than one?"

"The fires are symbolic of purity," he explained, pointing to two nearby hilltops where there stood large piles of wood for burning. "After they are lit, the farmers will drive their cattle through the pass between the two fires in hopes of improving fertility among the herd. Next, married couples will pass between them, if they so choose, to improve and revitalize their relationships, and to enhance the possibility of offspring. Then, courting couples will take their turns to strengthen their upcoming vows, and finally, singles in hopes of finding a partner will stroll between them. All of this takes place before the reenactment of the Great Rite, which is the finale of the evening."

"The Great Rite?" asked Lilly, forgetting for a moment her stress and its cause. She remembered reading about the rites of Beltane, but it was called something different. "You mean the Great Marriage?"

"Some know it as the Great Marriage, some, the Great Rite. The Rite is usually a reenactment of the more traditional Marriage ceremony. Not many communities host the traditional rites. It's a deeply spiritual rite, and when it is held, it must be accurate."

"What's the difference between the rituals?"

"Well, the ritual we'll see tonight is more like a modern wedding, only performed with the spoken rites of the Great marriage. The bride and groom, and the rest of the town, for that matter, reenact the traditional ceremony rather than follow through with the actions. They speak the words, and in the end they are married, but other than the words and passing between the fires on the way to the altar, nothing is really the same."

"Well, tell me about it. Something that is different."

Dorwynn sighed. "It's hard to explain without knowing the ritual. I'll tell you about it when we witness the rites tonight."

"Okay," said Lilly, disappointed that she would miss it.

"I can say that it is a great honor to be the couple chosen to wed during that celebration. We'll see more than one wedding today, but the couple that weds during the Great Rite has the greatest chance to conceive that night. They say a child conceived on Beltane is destined to do great things in life. They are leaders, or they are invoked with great magickal power."

"Wow," was all she said. Dorwynn chanced looking in her eyes, hoping to read the emotion in them. She was staring at him, her eyes their bright emerald color. He was caught for a moment in her stare, and then, embarrassed, he cleared his throat, averting his eyes to the nearby food court.

"Shall we eat?" he said, offering his arm to her. With a vague nod, she linked her arm in his, and together they went toward the food vendors, browsing the tents along the way, which sold everything from inexpensive trinkets and charms to fine jewelry made of precious stones and metals, easily concealed daggers to large swords and shields, various capes, cloaks and robes, not to mention every size of footwear, and finally...food.

Every type of food imaginable was being sold from more than twenty tents, and the smells of spiced pastries and fresh bread were the first to draw Lilly's attention. Her stomach, though unsettled by her nerves, growled nonetheless. Since she hadn't eaten yet today, and since she would need some energy for later, she settled on a meal that she figured would be light on her stomach. It tasted wonderful, but the vegetable barley soup didn't settle well, and the honey wheat roll, though fresh and moist, stuck in her throat.

Her mind returned to her situation. As irritated as she had been at Dorwynn's absence, she was equally irritated over the ill-timing of his homecoming. She had already been nervous about raiding the harpy lair when she realized that she had the added task of figuring out how to ditch Dorwynn, who didn't seem likely to leave her side willingly. She was still stewing over her newest problem when Zephra pranced toward them, her face brighter than Lilly had ever seen it.

"What are you so happy about?" asked Dorwynn. Her unorthodox behavior stumped him as well.

"I can't wait until tonight," she exclaimed. "Gustave's magick show is like nothing you've ever seen, and every year he does something grander. You'll love it!"

"Settle down," laughed Dorwynn. "You're putting Amparo to shame."

Lilly's stomach dropped. Gustave would be in Elikrede tonight. Did he figure out that she was up to something? She convinced herself that there was no way he could know or he would have tried to stop her already, but even if he didn't know, he might want to see her before his show, and no matter what, he would notice her absence.

"Lilly!" shouted Zephra.

"What?" she snapped.

"Why are you mad at me?"

"Why are you shouting?"

"Because you didn't hear me the first three times I said it."

"She's been doing that all day," said Dorwynn. "Irritating, isn't it?"

"I don't know," said Zephra, studying Lilly's appearance. "She looks pale, don't you think?"

"Stop talking about me like I'm not here!" said Lilly.

"And she's irritable."

"I'm going home." Lilly turned on her heel and started pushing her way through the growing crowd. Zephra burst with laughter.

"Wait, Lilly," she said, serious again. "I'm sorry. I couldn't resist. Really, though, are you okay? You don't look well."

"I don't feel well," she admitted. It was the truth, after all.

"Maybe you should go rest for a while," suggested Dorwynn. "Some sleep would probably help, and you'll be rested for the celebration tonight. You don't want to miss it."

"No, I don't," she said, and added silently, *but I have to.* She walked away from them slowly, as if she wasn't feeling well, but she actually felt much better. Zephra had unknowingly provided Lilly with the perfect excuse for both dodging Dorwynn and missing Gustave's performance. Her only issue now was getting out of the house before anyone came looking for her.

Once out of their sight, she magicked herself to the house and immediately set to work preparing for tonight. Two of the three potions remained. They'd used the other to test its effects on Tiryn. Two hours and twelve minutes later, her feathers returned and she quit complaining about how it had gone wrong. Lilly, who'd been reading the book about experimenting in making potions, had learned the properties of sespir root, which, when added to most potions in the correct measurement, doubled its duration. The potion was perfect. That news had eased some of her tension over their mission, but each minute brought her closer to it, closer to the potential that anything could go wrong.

You needed to know what almost feels like, Wyatt's voice echoed in her head. Well, she knew, and the fear of it rang true with each beat of her heart.

Their plan was to leave about an hour before sunset so they would arrive within an hour after, keeping the same schedule as the harpies, most of which would be leaving during that time and be gone by the time the last rays of sunlight struck the horizon. She still had a few hours before they would leave, so securing the potions, she stuffed them in her pocket. She was taking nothing else, since the harpies would take her possessions before throwing her in with the children. It bothered her that she wouldn't have her wand, but she couldn't risk losing it. With a sigh, she stretched out on her bed and fell asleep.

Savior in the Making

She awoke with a start, listening. She had heard a noise, and it had woken her. She waited a full minute, but the only thing she could hear was the rush of the waterfall and the crickets singing their twilight song.

Twilight! She jumped out of bed and bolted for the door. It was time to meet Tiryn and begin their journey. She felt for the potions as she ran down the stairs, stopping short when she noticed Dorwynn sitting on the sofa, waiting for her.

"Feel better?" he asked, his arms crossed.

"Yes."

"Good," he said, standing. "I'll walk you to the celebration. They're about to start the fires." Lilly's heart sank. She had to tell him and she had very little time for a confrontation. "What's wrong?" he asked when she didn't react.

"I can't go," she blurted. "I have something else to do."

"What?"

"It's my business, Dorwynn," she said, ducking past him through the front door.

"It's my business, too, Lilly," he shouted, right on her heels. "I'm your trainer, and as such, I'm in charge of your safety as well as your education. I need to know where you are at all times."

"You didn't know where I was when you were gone," retorted Lilly, still walking.

"No, but Zephra did, and she was in charge then."

"Fine," sighed Lilly, stopping so quickly that Dorwynn nearly slammed into her. "I'm going to rescue some children, okay?"

"From where?"

"The harpies." She stormed off again, but he caught her arm, grasping it tight.

"You can't do this, Lilly," said Dorwynn. "I won't let you do this."

Lilly tried to free her hand from his, and when she couldn't, she glared at him, her stare icy.

"You don't have a choice," she said, jerking harder and wrenching herself free. "I'm going, Dorwynn."

"What are you going to do?" he asked, following her as she walked off again. "Huh? How do you think you will survive an entire fleet of harpies? There will be hundreds of them there. You can't do what you did last time. It'll kill you. You need help."

"I have help."

"Who?"

Lilly hesitated. Did he know her, or did he only know of her? She dreaded his reaction either way. "Tiryn."

"The harpy?!" he said incredulously. "You honestly trust her with your life? She's one of them!"

"She was raised by a human," spat Lilly, "a good human, and who are you to judge someone on their race?" Dorwynn stuttered, but couldn't respond. She was right. "I don't trust *anyone* with my life, Dorwynn, but I do trust that she loves her family enough to save her nephew."

"And the rest of them? There could be more than twenty children being held prisoner there. How do you expect to save them all?"

"I don't know yet, but I will find a way."

"I'm coming with you."

"No, you aren't," said Lilly. "You only get us caught. Just turn around and go back to the celebration."

"No."

"Don't make me force you to stay."

"You promised you wouldn't do that." She stopped, turning slowly to face him, and took his hand, sending shivers down his spine.

"I did," she said in a soft tone, "and you promised to trust me."

"I know," he sighed, "but I don't think..."

"I can do this, Dorwynn. I know I can. I need you to trust me enough to know I am right." She waited for his answer, her eyes pleading, her hand still in his.

"Fine," he said, defeated. "I trust you, but I still don't like it. Just promise you won't use any true magick."

"I'll do my best," she promised. She squeezed his hand before letting go, and then sprinted through the trees into the cemetery.

He knew he shouldn't have let her go, but he couldn't turn down her request for his trust. It was a touchy subject anyway, and it struck his heart when she said she didn't trust anyone with her life. As much as he hated it, he had to let her go, and the stress of the situation caused his head to pound. It was tolerable for a while, and then Gustave's voice boomed in his head, the barrage of words he shouted causing the throb in his head to resonate throughout every nerve in his body.

What have you done? How could you let her go, you foolish boy? If she survives this, deliver her to the faeries at once. It's obvious you have no longer have control over her.

I never did, he thought as he walked into the house, no longer interested in the celebration or the wonderful show his mentor had in store. He sat on the sofa feeling as though his energy was being drained and fell into a dreamless sleep before he realized he'd closed his eyes.

"We're almost there," whispered Tiryn, hopping to the top of a large boulder. "I can see the entrance."

"Good," said Lilly, leaning against a nearby tree. Their trek had taken more out of her than she expected it would. "Come down. You can't shift up there." Tiryn hopped to the ground and walked toward Lilly, who stood straight to remove the potions from her pocket. "We need to find a place to hide one. If we take too long inside, we'll need one ready out here."

"Right," said Tiryn, searching the tiny clearing. Her keen eyes found a crack in the boulder just large enough for the bottle to fit. "Here," she said. "Put it here." Lilly slid the bottle carefully into the hole. It scraped against the edges of the rock, but the bottle just fit.

"Okay," she said, a fresh wave of adrenaline coursing through her veins, "this one is yours." She pulled the stopper from the bottle and handed it to the beautiful bird-woman. Tiryn drank quickly, and the potion's effect was instant. At once, her feathers disappeared in erratic clumps. Scars that looked years old appeared over some of the bald spots, and her eyes lost their vibrant gleam.

"Are you alright?" whispered Lilly, as she had during their test. Tiryn nodded. "Are you ready to do this?" Tiryn nodded again. "Okay," said Lilly, holding her arms out at her sides. "Let's go."

Tiryn took as much care as possible as she picked Lilly up, but she had to grasp hard enough to carry her to the entrance, which was located toward the top of the small mountain that sheltered the lair. She felt Lilly wince and loosened her grip.

"It's okay," Lilly told her. "I can handle the pain. Just don't drop me." She looked to the ground below and Tiryn tightened her grip again. It was painful, but not terrible, and it was much better than falling to a sudden death, for the ground, aided by the darkness of night, disappeared quickly from her sight. She could feel they were getting close to the entrance, but she had one more thing to tell Tiryn before they were there, something she was saving for the last minute. "If they force you to feed on me, do it."

"No!" protested Tiryn, nearly losing her grip.

"You have to," she whispered. "They may test you and you have to be able to do it. Just enough to make it look real. I'll be able to resist you if you don't overdo it."

"Are you sure?"

"Yes. Promise me."

"I promise," agreed Tiryn, "but only if you promise not to be angry with anything I do."

"Of course not, so long as you don't kill me."

They were silent after that, knowing from that point on that they both had a role to play. Everything important was covered, and as they drew near enough to hear the harpies that had stayed within the lair, Tiryn's sudden call to them pierced the quiet night, causing Lilly's heart to jump into her throat. She was reminded of the attack in Arthidgen, and suddenly, she was no longer acting afraid...she *was* afraid.

The inside of the lair was a gaping hole within the mountain, adorned with narrow ledges and tiny caves Lilly could only assume were individual roosts. There were a few harpies perched on the ledges, and as Tiryn descended to the floor of the lair, Lilly could see a larger group of the creatures gathered on a flat platform at its center. The largest of them cocked her head to one side as Tiryn tossed Lilly toward the edge of the circle. Her shoulder stuck the hard stone edge, sending fresh pain over her limbs before she'd had time to regain feeling in them.

"What is this?" she screeched in delight. The others milled together for a closer look. One of them got a little too close, and Tiryn snapped her sharp beak at the intruder.

"Mine," she hissed. The other harpy hissed in return, but she stepped away from Lilly.

"If you didn't plan on sharing," cawed the large leader, "why did you bring it here?"

"I will share," said Tiryn in a firm voice, "when my place here is established. She is part of the negotiations."

"I see." The large harpy drew closer to Lilly, and she could see the scars that covered every visible inch of her skin, so many more than Tiryn. She shrank away from the vile creature, covering her face with her hands, while the harpy drew closer, examining the newest addition to their food supplies. "She is powerful. You have done well. Feed, and then we shall negotiate your return."

Lilly prepared for the draining feeling she knew was coming, but though she expected it, the force of the assault struck her powerless for a moment. She clenched her jaw, trapping the scream rising in her throat as her body thrashed on the floor. When the pain started to subside, she was first aware of the mess on the floor, a cluster of feces and torn feathers. She threw up, then sank back to the floor.

Upon the platform, Tiryn's beak was clenched over the right wing of the same harpy who had wandered too close before. Screeching in pain, she yanked her wing free and flew to the topmost ledge of the inner wall, hissing in protest.

"No sharing until we are done negotiating," she hissed. The leader of the harpies seemed unconcerned with their exchange, looking bored, as if this was common. Lilly was sure it was.

"Take her to the prison," said the leader to another of the creatures at her side. "Come, let us discuss the terms of your arrival."

Tiryn took one last glance at Lilly as they dragged her toward the tunnel she knew led to the prisons, and then she followed the leader through another tunnel that led to a private room. She knew she had overdone it, though she'd tried not to, but the strength behind the potion enhanced her own strength, and by the time she realized it, it was too late to stop. Of course, the greedy harpy who'd joined her in the feed didn't help matters. She closed her eyes, hoping that Lilly was still strong enough to carry out their plan.

Lilly lay on the floor of the prison, surrounded by seven children who stared at her with wide eyes. The room was small, leaving barely enough room for her to be stretched across the floor. She sat up, ignoring the pain as she moved, and leaned against the rock wall.

"Are you alright?" asked a boy of eleven or so. Lilly nodded.

"Are you alright?" she asked him. He nodded, as did the other six children. As she looked over them, she realized the rest of the children were girls. "Are you Joss?"

Sadness crossed over the boy's eyes as he shook his head. "I'm Quinn," he said, his voice so quiet that she could barely hear him. "They just took Joss and Evelyn."

"When?"

"Right before they brought you."

"Where did they take them?"

"To the feeding room."

"The feeding room," echoed Lilly, her mind conjuring a terrible image in which two small children lay on the floor of a room, writhing in pain and surrounded by harpies. "How long will they keep them?"

Quinn shrugged his small shoulders and sank to the ground beside her. He moved his hand to where hers rested and slid his fingers into hers. She gave his hand a gentle squeeze as she looked over the room, trying to figure out how to get out of it. There was a solid iron door beside the wall where she sat, though she saw no handles or locks. Other than iron, there was only a very small, narrow opening she assumed was meant to serve as a window to check the prisoners. Her hand might fit through it, but she doubted that would do any good.

"You're here to rescue us, aren't you?" whispered Quinn, staring up at her, his eyes bright with hope.

"How did you know?" she asked, smiling at him.

"I dreamed you would come."

"You dreamed of me?" Lilly was surprised that the boy had been dreaming of her. She hadn't dreamed about this particular journey.

"Yes," he said, nodding. "Every night for two weeks."

Two weeks, thought Lilly. *I decided to rescue them two weeks ago.*

"Tell me about your dream," she said, hoping it might hold the answer to their escape.

"In my dream, you just appeared here with us. You told us you were going to take us away from this, and then you opened the door and we ran through tunnels, lots of tunnels, 'til we were outside."

"Do you remember how I opened the door?" Lilly asked.

"No, you just opened it."

"What about Joss and Evelyn? Were they with us?"

"No."

"Did we find them before we got outside?"

"No," he repeated, his voice not so quiet now. The girls watched him, listening intently to his words. "It was just us. We got outside and kept running 'til we got to a big rock in the forest. We stopped there, but one of them followed us and..."

"And what?"

"I woke up," he whispered, hanging his head. "I was scared, so I woke up." Lilly put her arm around him and he buried his head in her shoulder, grateful to have someone to comfort him.

"I do that, too," she said in a soothing tone.

"Really?"

"All the time."

Lilly looked at the iron door again, trying to work out in her head how it was locked. There was no visible sign from this side, but something was keeping the door shut. She stood, trying to peek out the poor excuse for a window, but the only thing she could see was the stone walls of the tunnel outside the door. She closed her eyes, willing herself to imagine the door opening, the lock, whatever it was, unlocking so the door would open. She didn't expect it to work since she had no idea what kind of mechanism held it shut, but it was worth a try.

"If I could see the lock," she said, more to herself than the others, "I'd know which way to move it."

"Here," said the smallest girl in the room from behind her. Lilly turned to face the child, a blonde girl that could be no more than six or seven. In her tiny hands was a shard of glass from a broken mirror. "I found it in a hole when we got here. I keep it safe there. You can use it if you want to."

"Thank you," she said, taking the mirror shard. With great care, she worked her hand through the small opening on the door and tilted the mirror until she could see the locking mechanism. A long, flat metal bar slid through a latch attached to the wall. It was attached to the wall on the other side by a ball hinge, so it could only be slid out of the latch so far and then had be lifted from a latch on the center of the door.

She was still weak from the feeding Tiryn and the other harpy put her through, and the bar was heavy iron like the door, so sliding it from the first latch was a slow process. She managed to slide it as far as it would go, but it wasn't enough to come free of the latch on the door, so Lilly, with every ouch of strength she could muster, tried to lift it. The weight was too much for her, and after struggling with it as long as she could, and achieving nothing, she collapsed.

"It's too heavy," she gasped. The girls cowered together, crestfallen, but Quinn stepped toward her.

"Let me help you," he said, offering his hand. "I can give you strength."

"How?"

"A gift," he said. "I can lend you energy. It's how I kept the others alive so long, but..."

"But what?"

"I couldn't save them all." She heard the sadness and guilt in his voice.

"No," she whispered. "You can't save everyone, but you saved some, didn't you? Why don't you show me how you do it?"

She took Quinn's hand, and still holding the mirror shard, she pushed her strength again as hard as she could. A warmth shot through her body, starting with the hand Quinn held and rushing through her everywhere. She dared a glance at the boy, who seemed unaffected by the transfer of energy. She focused on the mirror again, aiming it toward the iron bar that held them captive. As she focused on moving it, it rattled against the door, sending loud echoes down the dark corridors of the tunnels, and with a final *CLANG!*, the bar jerked upward, freeing itself from the latch and releasing the door.

"Thank you, Quinn," she said, inhaling a deep breath. "You have an amazing gift." She turned to the girls, all of whom were staring at her in awe, and handed the mirror shard back to the smallest. "Put this where you found it," she told her. "Someone else might need it someday." The girl nodded. "Everyone else hold hands. We don't want to lose anyone." Lilly squeezed Quinn's hand and smiled. "Ready to get out of here?" He grinned, nodding.

Lilly pushed the door open slowly, taking care not to make any more noise than necessary, and then ushered the kids, linked together like a train, down the dark tunnel. It was pitch black, but with one hand holding Quinn's and the other stretched in front of her, trailing along the walls, she led them through the darkness to a well-lit hallway.

"Which way?" she asked Quinn, hoping he remembered enough details of his dream to get them out.

"Left," he answered without thinking about it. "If we go right, we'll end up in the center of the lair."

"Left it is," said Lilly, leading their train. She moved fast, tugging the children behind her. There were no doors or caves in this tunnel, just walls of solid rock. They ran through it, taking each turn and twist with care and speed. Some were difficult, as the tunnel wound and twisted at odd angles and inclines. Lilly lost track of their direction with all the changes. Sometimes she thought they were even going uphill, but then the floor would change and suddenly, they were going downhill again.

The tunnel began to narrow as they ran, getting smaller and smaller the further they went, and after another twenty minutes of snaking through the shrinking corridor, hunched and stumbling through the utter darkness, they were forced to start crawling. Lilly could feel the warm blood trickling from her palms as the jagged edges of stone sliced through them. She could feel the cuts forming on her knees as she dragged them over the same stones, and she knew her jeans were shredded there.

"What's your name?" asked Quinn from behind her.

"Lilly."

"Another flower," he muttered.

"What?"

"All of the girls but two are named after flowers. Daisy, Rose, Acacia, Violet and Willow."

"Willow is a tree, not a flower," said Lilly, jerking her hand to the side as another sharp stone sliced through it.

"Still a plant," he mumbled.

"And the other girl? What's her name?"

"Elizabeth," piped a small voice behind Quinn, "but I have a sister named Ivy."

"See what I mean?" sighed Quinn, exasperated. "Flowers."

"Ivy is a plant, too," said Lilly.

"There's nothing wrong with being named after a flower or plant," came another voice close to the end of their little train. "My mother says plants are powerful."

"They are," said Lilly, "and names are important. They mean something."

"Yeah," said Quinn, "that's why I wanted to know yours. My dad was a language teacher. Name meanings were his favorite part, before…"

"Before what?"

"He died trying to save me from the attack."

"I'm sorry," said Lilly, and hoping to change the subject, she answered his question. "My full name is Lilias Hope. Do you know what it means?"

"Is that really your name?" asked Quinn in disbelief.

"Yes. What does it mean?"

"It means 'the hope of the Divine promise'."

"Oh." Lilly turned the phrase over in her head. The hope of the Divine promise. Another thought jumped into her mind, a piece of information buried deep within. "What does Sophia Elli mean?"

"Um, it means 'truth in the Divine word'. Why?"

"Just wondering."

"How is Elli spelled?" he asked, a new curiosity in his voice. Lilly told him. It took a minute for his response, but he finally said, "That's interesting."

"What is?" asked Lilly.

"That name and your name use all the same letters, and they almost mean the same thing. Weird, huh?"

"Very," said Lilly. *Too weird,* she thought, *to be a coincidence.* She knew at once that her mother had planned it that way, so that no matter which name she had chosen, it would still be her identity. She was the hope, the truth…the Chosen One. For the first time since she arrived, she felt the power of that possibility.

Silence surrounded them as they continued through the tunnel with no end in sight. Lilly's mind was turning not only with what Quinn told her, but also with the words of the little girl who wasn't named after a plant: *Elizabeth...I have a sister.* She wondered what her own sister, her Beth, was doing, but there was no way to know, so there was no point dwelling on it. She pushed the thought from her mind and focused on the infinite darkness surrounding them.

Tiryn followed the Alpha through the tunnels leading to the Sacred Room, a place reserved only for the Alpha and her guests. This was not the same Alpha who was in charge when Tiryn was here before, but she was grateful for that. She had yet to be recognized, and if luck was with her, she would make it out of the lair before she was.

The Alpha's second was waiting for her. She eyed Tiryn suspiciously, then turned to the Alpha. "Two wait in the feeding room."

"You are dismissed," said the Alpha. The harpy bowed and left the room, and she turned toward Tiryn. "Tell me, what do you want in exchange for the girl?"

"The girl is mine," demanded Tiryn. "She is very powerful and I will not relinquish her, but I will share her." Tiryn drew out the last words, hoping the Alpha would be tempted to continue the negotiations. Lilly needed time to get to the prison and get the kids out without being seen. So far, Tiryn had heard no alarms, but for all she knew, Lilly hadn't made it there yet.

"I expect nothing less," said the Alpha, "but I am curious how such a powerful child failed to escape a single harpy."

"The element of surprise. I discovered her mourning in a cemetery and I snatched her before she could react. She was quite easy to control after the first feeding."

"They always are." The Alpha circled Tiryn with slow, deliberate steps, scratching her talons on the smooth stone floor with each one. She stopped in front of Tiryn after one complete circle. "What do you want for *sharing* the girl?"

"Respect among the fleet," said Tiryn, lifting her head in arrogance, though she felt anything but, "and should you name me your second, you would always be the first with whom I share."

"My second!" squawked the Alpha, ruffling the thin layer of feathers over her wings. "I will not second a stranger. That honor must be earned! You are dismissed."

"Of course," said Tiryn, trying to contain her fear. She knew the Alpha was angry, and she also knew that she was completely alone should it come to a fight. The only thing that kept her strong was the fact that she looked menacing. Lilly's potion gave her the appearance of a gnarled harpy who looked like she'd seen some tough fights, but every second that passed brought her closer to the end of that magick. "Bring me my girl and I will go."

The Alpha glared at her before turning a broad circle and leading Tiryn out the door and back through the tunnels. They were halfway through the tunnel to the prison when great screeching and cawing echoed toward them. The Alpha ran toward the noise, Tiryn close behind her, and found three harpies shouting and flapping their wings.

"Silence!" roared the Alpha, and the din stopped. "What is it?"

"The prisoners have escaped!" squawked one, hopping nervously.

The look that crossed the Alpha's face frightened them all. The three harpies bowed at her and then fled, leaving her alone with Tiryn. It made Tiryn feel better knowing she was evenly matched, for she was sure a fight would come. Playing the part of the tough creature she was pretending to be, she glared at the Alpha.

"You let my catch escape," she said

"What!" shrieked the Alpha. "Your girl helped my entire catch escape."

"Perhaps if your cells were better built, this would not have happened," said Tiryn. "How do you plan to repay me?"

"Repay you?"

"I came here with a prize," said Tiryn, ruffling her feathers in defense. "I will not leave without one. Do you have nothing to offer, or shall you name me your second?" She knew the queen would never accept, but Lilly had gotten the kids out of the prison cell. There were still some in the feeding rooms.

"You will never be my second." The Alpha paced for a moment, then walked through the tunnels toward her chamber. "Come with me. We will see what I have left. It matters not," she twittered as she walked, more to convince herself than her guest, Tiryn was sure. "The fleet will bring a fresh, strong population tonight. These were becoming useless anyway."

"I do not want useless captives," Tiryn announced in a louder voice, reminding the Alpha she was right behind her. The Alpha gave her a blank look.

"Of course they are not useless," she said in a seductive voice. "I am just mourning the loss of the rest of them, and your loss, as well. I am certain you will be pleased with what I gave give you, and I will be restocked this night, so we shall come to an agreement and both be content with the results."

Tiryn nodded once to acknowledge the Alpha. They reached the feeding room, which was not even a room, but a shallow cavern within the stone wall at the end of the tunnel. Two children huddled against the darkest part of the cavern wall.

"Two of them," said the Alpha in satisfaction. "That should replace one girl."

Tiryn stared at the children in silence, though her head was screaming, *Joss! It's Joss!* She wanted to run to him, to console him and tell him that it was alright, but instead, she turned to the Alpha, her face twisted. "This is all you have to offer? They are pathetic!"

"You may take the two and leave now," said the Alpha, her voice more powerful, "or you may wait until the fleet returns and have your choice of one. There is no guarantee, however, that they will be successful."

Tiryn knew they would be successful. They always were, even if they only brought a few, but that didn't matter. Making sure the Alpha believed her would keep them safe, and keeping Joss safe, getting him home and healthy, was all she cared about.

"I'll take these," said Tiryn. "I've spent all the time here I care to waste."

"I couldn't agree more," said the Alpha. "No one will cross you. They will be searching for our missing prisoners. Do not return to this place." She spun away from Tiryn, her talons scraping the floor before lifting off the ground and soaring to main entrance where Tiryn knew she would give the command to have every available harpy begin the search.

"Joss," whispered Tiryn. "Come, Joss, we have to go." The dirty little boy dared to lift his eyes to the creature speaking to him, and Tiryn felt a pang of pity. "It's me, honey. Tiryn. I'm in disguise. Come, we have to go now."

"Tiryn?" he asked.

"Yes. I'm getting you out of here."

"We're never getting out of here," wailed one of the girls. Her voice rang in the darkness, echoing off the stone walls and reverberating so loudly in Lilly's ears that she could feel the vibration in her teeth.

"Ssh!" she whispered. "Yes, we will." *We have to,* she added silently. Their tunnel had turned into a narrow wormhole barely large enough for Lilly, but she inched her way through, pushing the stone walls with her magick just enough to keep them moving forward.

"I think we're going deeper into the mountain," piped Quinn. "We should be out by now."

"Oh!" cried a girl, and a few of the others groaned in response.

"We're going the right way," Lilly assured them, but Quinn, with his quick wit, thwarted her again.

"But there's only stone in front of you. The hole is gone."

"No, it's n..." Lilly paused when she felt the stone wall in front of her. Sure enough, it was smooth. The hole had gotten smaller, but she hadn't noticed when it disappeared altogether. How long had she been digging them through the mountain? She closed her eyes, which changed nothing in the utter blackness, and heaved a sigh, trying to think of how to get them out of this situation. There had to be a way out.

"I smell water," piped a tiny voice. It was the same small voice that had given her the mirror, the way out of their last situation. Lilly took another deep breath, inhaling through her nose, and she could smell the fresh scent of incoming rain. She inhaled again, trying to find where the scent was the strongest, where the stone was thinnest and the scent could get through. Searching the surface of the stone with her fingertips, she found a miniscule crack. She placed her hand over the crack, feeling the energy of the stone, and with a small internal push, she unleashed the magick within herself.

The stone split with a deafening *CRACK!* Jagged pieces of the huge stone tumbled down on them, but the soft glow of the moonlight and the cool rush of air that struck them when they emerged from the darkness renewed their senses. They ran toward the cover of the forest without stopping until they couldn't see the sky through the canopy.

"Wait," breathed Lilly the moment the sky was out of view. "I have to rest."

Quinn and the six girls hovered around her like a brood of baby ducks swarming their mother, staring up as though there was no shelter. After a few moments, Lilly was recovered enough to lead them to the boulder where she and Tiryn planned to meet after their escape. Despite what it took to get them out of the mountain, her side of the plan couldn't have been any better. The only downfall was that she hadn't been able to save Evelyn and Joss.

"Joss!" shouted Quinn, running toward the boulder where two children were waiting. The boy ran toward Quinn and the two nearly collided in their embrace. "How did you get out?"

"My aunt rescued us," said the boy, pointing to the harpy hiding behind the boulder. Quinn jumped in fear when he saw her and walked backward toward Lilly, trying to drag Joss with him. "It's okay," said Joss, smiling, "she's not one of them."

"She looks like one of them," said Quinn, feeling for Lilly's hand, his eyes never leaving Tiryn.

"It's alright," said Lilly, squeezing his hand. "It's a disguise, which reminds me..." She found the crevice where the potion was hidden and stuffed it into her pocket. Tiryn pulled Lilly away from the children, her head bent close to her ear.

"We can't leave here," Tiryn told Lilly while the children chattered with each other, Quinn still eyeing the harpy, "but we can't stay here, either. They're looking for you and the others, and when they don't find you from the sky, they'll start searching the ground."

"I figured they would," said Lilly, keeping her voice low so the kids, especially Quinn, couldn't hear their conversation. "We'll just have to be as careful as we can."

"That's not all. They'll have a new group of kids trapped in the prison before morning. That's the only reason the Alpha let me take these two."

"We have to destroy the lair," Lilly told her. Tiryn looked appalled, even through the gruesome disguise already twisting her face.

"How do we do that?"

"With this." Lilly pulled the potion from the boulder and shook it in front of Tiryn's face. "Two ingredients will turn this into a completely different potion, and they're both fairly easy to find in the forest."

"What does it do?"

"Help me find the ingredients and you'll find out. We need the stamen of a stirkpa flower and a blue moonrush mushroom."

"Come on," burst Tiryn, making the children jump in surprise. "I know where there is a flower, and the kids can help find the mushroom."

Tiryn disappeared into the thick of the forest while Lilly tried to describe to the children what the moonrush mushroom looked like. The seven girls and Joss started scouring the floor of the forest for the mushroom, while Quinn lingered beside Lilly, worry written on his little face.

"She's in disguise?" he asked. Lilly nodded. "She's a harpy, though, a real harpy."

"Who was raised by a caring human who taught her how to be good," Lilly assured him. "I trust her. Joss trusts her. You should, too."

"Okay," he said, though he didn't stray far from Lilly's side. Together they walked through the forest in silence, their eyes on the ground, until Quinn quipped, "Moonrush mushrooms don't surface without moonlight, you know. Someone is going to have to go into the open to get one."

Of course, thought Lilly. *Why would any of this be easy?* She led Quinn to the edge of the tree line, where the canopy ended and the ground flowed in a wide open space. High overhead, she could see the fleet of harpies circling right above them, and she knew if she ran into the openness of the thick grassy meadow, they would see her at once.

"There!" said Quinn, pointing into the open meadow. "By the dead tree...there are two or three of them."

Lilly squinted, trying to see something, anything. She could barely make out the outline of the dead tree in the moonlight, let alone anything beside it. "Two or three of what?"

"Blue moonrushes," he said. "Look!"

Lilly narrowed her eyes, but could see nothing. She focused, blocking all the sounds to enhance her perception of sight, and a moment later, the soft blue glow of the moonrush mushroom came into her view.

"How did you see those?" she asked. He just shrugged and looked up at her, his face serious.

"How are you going to get them?" he asked. Lilly didn't answer him. She stared at the ingredient she needed, out and easy to see, *too* easy to see, taunting her. "Well?"

"I don't know, okay?" snapped Lilly. The boy squeezed her hand, pushing his power slowly into her. At first, she didn't feel it, but it warmed her hand, then her arm, and when it reached her chest, her heart felt like it would explode. "What are you doing?"

"Sorry," muttered Quinn, dropping her hand. "I don't mean to do it. It just comes out sometimes."

"What does?"

"Lending energy. It happens without me trying to do it."

"I know how you feel," murmured Lilly, thinking of the many things magick has done without her trying to do anything.

"I can drain energy, too," he whispered, looking around to make sure no one else could hear him. "I'll never do that on purpose, but when the harpies fed on us, I did it once and I felt stronger. If I didn't get rescued, that's what I was going to do to keep everyone alive."

Lilly didn't know what to say to him, so she put her hand on his shoulder, but when she looked down at him, her hand wasn't there. Her arm went to his back, but her hand, the part of it touching him, wasn't there. She lifted her hand from him and it appeared again. She lowered it to him once more, and once more, her hand disappeared.

"What's happening?" she asked him, intrigued.

"Sorry," he repeated. "Sometimes I lend too much and it throws some powers off course. I don't know why, but it seems to affect invisibility more than others."

"But I don't have the power of invisibility," she said, still staring at her hand.

"Yes, you do."

"I didn't before tonight."

"Are you sure?"

"Of course I'm sure. How could I just suddenly get a power out of the blue like that?"

"You can absorb powers," said Quinn. His very matter-of-fact tone left Lilly waiting for more.

"How do you know that?" she asked him when he didn't continue.

"I just know things like that about people," he said as if it was nothing special. "Just humans, mostly, but sometimes other creatures. It's kind of frustrating, sometimes, especially when you know someone bad has a really strong power. It's kind of scary. You're alright, though. You can do lots of things."

"I can become invisible?" she asked, staring at the faint blue glow across the field.

"You can do more than that," he said, his eyes bright. "You can see magick and move things with magick and conjure and..."

"We'll talk about this more later," she interrupted. "Right now, we need that mushroom." She let go of his shoulder, her hand appearing once again, and she rubbed it, smiling. "I'm going to try it. Tell me when you can't see me anymore." The little boy stared at Lilly, his eyes intense, as she tried to imagine her entire body disappearing like her hand just did. Quinn was silent as she felt herself struggle.

"Why don't you use it defensively." he suggested. "That seems to be more natural for you."

"How do you mean?" she asked. This boy was surprising her, and making her more curious, with every word he spoke.

"You're trying to use it in an offensive manner by getting the mushrooms without anything or anyone seeing you. That's too big. Try to become invisible because you *need* that mushroom and you *can't* let the harpies see you. Focusing on the danger you're hiding from is easier than just trying to become invisible."

Lilly smiled. "You're a pretty smart kid, you know that?"

"Thanks," he said, smiling in return. "You're invisible, by the way." Lilly looked down at her body and saw nothing. Her body, her clothes, even the potion bottle was gone. She could feel it, but she could see nothing. "Anything you touch will be invisible, too, but the more you try to hide, the more it will use your energy, so be careful. You don't want to appear out there where they can see you."

"Thank you, Quinn," said Lilly, trying not to sound sarcastic. He couldn't help it that he was so logical, nor that his honesty was so brutal. "I'll be right back. Why don't you go tell the others we found the mushrooms. Tell them to get ready, because when the potion is done, we'll won't have much time to run."

"Be careful," said Quinn. He watched her weave through the grass, her footsteps the only visible proof of her presence, and then he disappeared into the forest where the rest of their clan was still searching for the elusive blue mushrooms.

Lilly made it to the dead tree without being seen, though she felt exposed without the canopy of the trees. There were three small mushrooms, their bioluminescent glow as soft as it had been when she first spotted them from so far away. She chose the smallest of the three - the amount of potion she had only needed a tiny bit of it. When her invisible hand touched it, it disappeared. She ran back to the trees as fast as she could and started to turn toward the boulder where Tiryn had the flower she needed, but the sight of the stirkpa flower, it's long feathery stamen blowing in the breeze only inches from her face, stopped her in her tracks.

Lilly grabbed the plant, which disappeared at once, and with a sigh, she forced herself to wait, to meditate long enough to turn off the defensive feelings holding the invisibility in place. Finally, the plant, the mushroom, the potion and her hands which held them all appeared. She stripped the feathery plumes from the stamen and shoved them into the bottle. As they dissolved, neutralizing the reshnok to lower its potency, the potion turned a bright blood red. She shuddered as the memory of the vials of blood in her mother's altar room came to her. When every piece of the plant was dissolved, she pushed the button of the mushroom through the top and quickly pushed the cork into the bottle. It would take longer to dissolve, but the result was exactly what Lilly had planned for - the potion was already bubbling. She'd brought the extra potion in case their plan took too long, but she'd been hoping she wouldn't have to use it for another disguise, because she wanted to try this experiment, and now she had a reason to do it.

She held the potion for a few moments, focusing on each ingredient she'd used, the perfect symmetry of the bottle, the solid hollowness of the cork. The potion vibrated in the bottle as the bubbles came faster and faster, stirring the concoction, turning it dark purple. Deciding she'd focused long enough, she thought of the prison, of the wall she'd leaned against and the cold stone floor, and with every last bit of her energy, she conjured the potion to the prison.

Her head spun, but she ran anyway, getting as far away from the mountain as possible, racing toward the boulder and her companions. *The mushroom is the catalyst that starts the chain reaction...the cork expands, the pressure builds...*her thoughts failed her suddenly as she tried to remember if Tsirama's book of potion experiments had said anything about the *size* of the explosion...

"Lilly!"

She didn't realize her eyes were closed until she ran into Tiryn. Popping them open, she gasped, "We have to go now!" Quinn grabbed her hand and she felt a surge of heat streak through her veins. She gasped again as the shock of energy flooded her, and then they linked hands and ran as Lilly kept herself, Tiryn and the nine rescued children hidden from the angry creatures scouring the trees for them from above. The potion would be turning black by now, the bubbles building pressure, the mushroom adding their magick. Any minute, it would explode, and Lilly wanted to be as far away from it as possible.

She felt the earth shake before she saw the flame rising from the harpy lair. The harpies flying in the area were struck by a deluge of fiery tongues slipping through the tunnels and shooting out the side of the mountain from weak spots like the one she opened to escape. Others burst into flames from the heat of the volcanic explosion shooting out the top of the lair.

"Run," shouted Lilly, her adrenaline spiking her power as she dragged them faster though the dense forest. The children let go of her hand as they noticed the explosion, each appearing as they did so. Quinn was the only one who didn't appear until Lilly finally lifted the invisibility.

"What was that?" asked Tiryn in awe.

"That's what happens when you add those two ingredients to that potion," she sighed, squeezing Quinn's hand, and together they all rested, watching the harpy lair burn like a candle in the night.

The Fire Spinner's Omen

The Beltane celebration in Elikrede grew with every second of the sunset's fading light. The entire crowd gathered for the lighting of the fires and the witnessing of the Great Rite, which started the night's events. While everyone else in town observed the ceremony, Zephra was pacing behind the arena's stage waiting for Dorwynn and Lilly. She was secretly grateful that she had an excuse to miss the ceremony - she'd seen enough of them to last her a lifetime - but she was starting to get worried. Dorwynn had left to get Lilly hours ago and Zephra hadn't seen either of them since.

Her pacing intensified as the townsfolk started migrating to the arena, where Gustave's magickal extravaganza would soon take place. His shows were the envy of other towns, and while he didn't plan one for Elikrede every year, trying to entertain in a few other towns important to him, he held them more there than anywhere else. She smiled at what he had planned for that night, gloating to herself that she was the only other person who knew of it besides the wizard himself. Of course, that was only because he wanted her to help control things if it got out of hand, but it was more than anyone else knew.

The fact that neither Dorwynn nor Lilly had surfaced by the time the entire arena was packed ate at Zephra, but as she was in charge of helping to contain things for Gustave, there was no way she could try to find them now. If they missed it, then that was their loss, and they were running out of time. In less than five minutes, Gustave would be starting his show.

Those minutes passed without result, and the jabbering crowd fell silent as the first spectacle of the evening began. An explosion of red flames tore through the stage, followed by a sparkle of red lights in the shape of a massive dragon. The creature snapped its jaws, then belched a great roar to release another set of flames, this time bright yellow. The yellow outline of a unicorn sparkled next, prancing its way from the flames and streaking across the stage. The audience applauded as the unicorn shook her wild mane and the falling lights turned blue and took the form of drops of water. They spun in a vortex until all the lights were blue, then took the shape of a mermaid swimming through the night sky. When they separated, they fell like rain, and where each landed, the light turned green, blanketing the entire stage before a faerie emerged cloaked in green, large at first, then shrinking smaller and smaller until the lights vanished altogether.

The arena was black, barely lit only by the moonlight, though the audience erupted in a burst of loud clapping and whistling. Zephra could see Gustave stepping toward the center of the arena, though most could not, so when he lifted his staff, they did not see. They knew nothing of his presence there until his staff hit the ground with a deafening *CRACK!*, silencing the crowd, and flames burst from it, flying all directions to ignite the torches placed throughout the arena.

"Welcome," his voice boomed, loud enough to be heard on the grounds outside the arena where many more were crowded to catch a glimpse of the show. "It is good to be home at long last. As many of you know, my quest these many years past has been to travel between our twin worlds to seek special souls and train them in the ways of magick. One of my earliest apprentices is here tonight, a Master of Fire magick and one of the best. Should my old strength fail me, have faith she will save you!" A gentle roll of laughter swept through the crowd. "My newest apprentice, Lilly, has been living among you recently, training in preparation for her test on Earth Magick. I wanted to introduce her tonight, but it seems she cannot be found. Alas, she will miss the grand finale, but I promise it will still be grand, so grand, in fact, that even I do not know what will arise from the box!" The audience laughed louder, clapping their approval.

"Before the main show commences, I do have one very important matter to address." Gustave's voice grew more somber, and he cleared his throat before he continued. "Rumors abound of the recent harpy attacks of neighboring towns. It should be known that these rumors are true. While they are known to attack on Sabbats, their behavior has become erratic, unpredictable, and while I don't expect they would attack a town as strong as Elikrede, I do expect many of our neighbors will need our assistance in time. We must give it to them, whether it be food or lodging or just a shoulder to cry upon. Our willingness to sacrifice for the sake of others, our compassion for them, is what separates us from the beasts. It was good to see you all again, my dearest friends."

The roar from the audience was so loud she was sure Dorwynn and Lilly could hear it from the house, and she thought about flying there to get them, but Gustave was starting his show. She knew he really didn't need her, but he felt more comfortable having another strong person to control the fire if anything went wrong, so she stayed to enjoy the show from a view closer than anyone else.

The four human women dancing among the fountain of fireworks were dressed like faeries, though anyone who'd ever seen a faerie in human form could see the difference. The illusion was beautiful, but Zephra wasn't very impressed. Humans could never be as graceful as faeries, and there was no way to match how their wings looked forming their attire.

A jester was next, but there was rarely a trick one could do or a joke one could tell that she hadn't seen or heard before. She started pacing again, debating whether or not she should go find Dorwynn and Lilly, when Gustave was suddenly in her path.

"What's wrong?" he asked when she nearly ran into him, "and where is Dorwynn?"

"He went looking for Lilly," rushed Zephra, ready to get the telling over with. "She didn't feel well earlier and went to rest. He went to get her a while ago, but...I don't know where they are."

"Hmmm," said Gustave, looking toward the direction of the house though it was much too far away to see. "Dorwynn may be nursing a wounded ego. I gave him quite a tongue thrashing earlier."

"Because he was gone so long," assumed Zephra. "I was going to talk to you about that. He's been having blackouts..."

"No, my dear," he interrupted. "He let Lilly go on a rescue mission."

"What! After yelling at me for letting the duel happen, which was *not* my fault, he let her go alone?"

"Yes. He is to take her to the faeries at once. I'll not have him behaving so recklessly. It is his job to keep her from doing so. Besides, as his blackouts are becoming more frequent and longer in duration, I feel it's time to pass her to Amparo for training."

"You already know about the blackouts?" asked Zephra. She wasn't surprised, but the fact that he knew about this and didn't warn anyone was the part that shocked her the most.

"Of course I know," he replied, "and I know about the duel. I know things about my apprentices that even they do not know. Dorwynn knows of his problem, to be sure, but so do I. These lapses in time are not new to him. They have affected him since he was a small child."

"Well," said Zephra, irritated that Dorwynn's issues were common knowledge, "they *are* getting worse. That little adventure you sent him on kept him away from us longer than you planned and it's affecting Lilly's training."

"How so? She has accomplished the tasks she set forth to learn, has she not?"

"No thanks to Dorwynn. Someone else had to do all the work."

"Several someones, from what I hear, but I have my reasons for Dorwynn being her first trainer. I ask that you will not question them."

"Of course," she mumbled, and then lifting her head, she dared to ask them the one question she'd been waiting to ask when they were alone. "Do you really believe she is the Chosen One?"

"I do," he said with a nod, "and what do you believe, Zephratia? Do you think this *child* is the one to save us all?" By the way he stressed the word child, she knew he was referring to her first meeting with Lilly.

"I do," she said. The brutal honesty of her confession brought tears to her eyes as she struggled with her next question. "And Dorwynn? Is he Lilly's leyartha? Is he the Hero of the prophecy?"

"That remains to be answered," Gustave told her, "and not by me. You know that." She nodded, ashamed she had asked him such a question and embarrassed that he had seen her cry. She wiped the tears from her face as he continued, his old voice soft, "There are many who go through life never knowing the devotion that comes with finding your soul mate, nor the sacrifice in that devotion. Be grateful you get to love him, even if it is only as his friend."

He sat with her for a moment, both of them silent, as he thought back to his last visit as Rohan. He'd been so confused over his feelings then, but now he knew. His father's blood, and whatever part of his soul Gustave had entranced with his identity, was causing his slight pull to this girl. His heart pulled him toward Lilly. He knew this because his heartache matched Zephra's. He saw it in her face. Dorwynn did not want Zephra as she wanted him, but Lilly...even if she did want Rohan in return, he could not have her. He knew it, and it killed him to know that she would turn to Dorwynn in his absence.

"Come," he said gruffly after a moment. "The finale is almost afoot. I want to see his spectacle, and then I must depart."

They turned in time to see a human man take center stage. He waved to the front of the crowd, shouting for them to put out the torches.

Throughout the stadium, the torches were extinguished one by one. Then the man lit the end of a long chain and began his show. Zephra watched the show with intrigue as the fire spun in wide circles around his head and body, and then is small circles on his hands, so fast they looked like her fireballs. This human was playing with fire as she did, but without any magick.

"Have you not seen fire spinning in your many years?" asked Gustave, his eyes also on the showman.

"I've heard of it, but I never stopped long enough to watch before," she whispered.

"He is quite amazing. I cannot wait to see the end. He throws fire at a chest to create an image of the future, and the images, so far at least, are accurate. Once, the flames formed a Gorgon's head, and two days later a Gorgon swept through the town. Two people were turned to stone before they captured her, but I believe it would have been more if someone had not remembered the story and image from that night."

Zephra didn't respond. Her eyes were glued to the spinning fire, moving faster and faster. The man created many images with his flames in the darkness: a butterfly, a planet circling a star, a petaled flower, but none of them compared to the image that rose from the chest sitting on the stage as his last small flames soared into the box. When it exploded, sparks and flames shot straight up like an orange comet and its tail. When it reached the sky, it exploded again, and from the conflagration rose the shape of a huge bird, a bird with tail feathers the length of its body and fire in its heart.

"It's a phoenix," shouted someone from the crowd, followed by "ahh's" of admiration. Both Zephra's and Gustave's hearts froze at the sight, each harboring their own fear of what this could mean, as the bird soared over the amazed crowd, enchanting them with its captivating song. Fire dripped from the bird in the form of feathers, igniting small patches of grass in the center of the arena, before it soared to the ground, where it landed in the thick of the fire. Every flame jumped toward where the bird landed, burning higher until the bird disappeared, an image of its newborn form emerging a moment later. The bird continued to rise from the flames, fly around the arena and dive into them over and over again until the flames formed the images of the fire spinner's story.

"Thousands of years ago," he said, his voice drawing everyone's attention, "before magick was born into our world, it thrived on Earth. Over time, the humans there forgot the essence of magick, and the creatures of magick began to die. When the Elemental Children came forth to give their sacrifices for the creation of Buthania, the creatures followed, bringing their young with them to start life anew. The last of the dragons followed alone, leaving their eggs behind, for magick had not touched them. They were hollow, and bore no life.

"Hundreds of years passed, and the eggs were destroyed...all save two. They were found by humans, passed from family to family to be used as decoration upon a shelf or in a garden, until they came into the hands of the humans for whom they would hatch. The births of the phoenix pair, and their lives beyond that, remain a mystery. They are elusive creatures, so rare that many believe they no longer exist. It is said in legend that the phoenix will rise once again during a time of turmoil, arriving to lend its light through the darkness, but it must first walk its own path of sacrifice, so that it will be worthy when it calls for sacrifice from others. Times of darkness lie ahead. Have faith that there will be a light to lead you through it."

There was only silence in the darkness when the last flame died. It hung over the arena like a dark omen, but the audience, after absorbing the fire spinner's words, roared with cheers and applause. The torches were lit, and then the people abandoned their seats, dispersing in every direction for the remainder of their evening. Soon, groups of them would be milling around smaller fires, telling stories and conversing until dawn. Zephra looked at Gustave, her eyes wild. He knew she was concerned about the fire-spinner's words. He was just as concerned for reasons of his own.

"I didn't know about the phoenix," he whispered. "I'm sorry."

"What does it mean?" she whispered back.

"I don't know, but I swear to you that I will learn all I can."

"I decide to come here and then this...this...charlatan predicts this," she hissed. "I can't stay here now!"

"Relax," said Gustave, taking her by the shoulders and leading her outside the arena walls. "There is nothing to indicate this message was intended only for Elikrede, or when it will take place, or that it even pertains to you."

"Even though the other phoenix hasn't been seen for sixty years!"

"Enough, Zephra! Do you want to reveal yourself? The fact he hasn't been seen is reason enough to believe it is about him and not you. Calm yourself."

Zephra nodded, taking a deep breath and exhaling with a loud sigh. A light flickering on the horizon, one that had not been there before the show, caught her attention. Her eyes narrowed as she tried to figure out if it was a particle of light left over from the show, or something else. It looked like a candle burning in the night, very far away, but large enough to be seen.

"What is that?" asked Zephra. Gustave looked in the same direction and frowned.

"That is my newest apprentice exposing herself," he muttered. "Come. Let us meet her at the edge of town."

Gustave and Zephra waited for Lilly by the river, and when she burst from the trees with a full-feathered harpy and a group of ragged, dirty children, Gustave had to restrain the equal amounts of awe and fear seizing his soul from showing on his face. *She did it,* he thought, *but at what cost?*

"Gustave," she said brightly when she saw him. She was holding the hand of the tallest child with her, only one of two boys. The other clung to the harpy, a resident, he knew, of Elikrede. "You're still here."

"Yes," he said, trying to sound stern. "You missed the show."

"Sorry," she said, though she looked anything but sorry. Her face was alight with victory.

"I was due to leave as soon as the show ended, but I think, perhaps, that I shall speak a word with you before I depart. Zephra, take the children. Lilly, come with me." Quinn was reluctant to let go of her hand, but she nodded, assuring him that it was alright. She staggered when he let go, but she followed Gustave away from the others.

"Don't be mad," she said when they were alone. "You told me to do what I needed to do, so I did it."

"I know," he admitted, "but I was wrong. I should have warned you to be more careful not to expose yourself. We live in dangerous times, Lilly, and I was reckless to suggest what I did."

"But..."

"Look," he interrupted, "I know you did a wonderful thing tonight and I know what it must have taken for you to do it, but you have to promise me that you won't do anything like this again. Until you are no longer my apprentice, you must stay in the company of the trainer assigned to your care. Promise me."

"Fine. I promise." She said it in a dismissive way, and it made him wonder if she was taking him seriously. "I have a new power."

"What?"

"I have a new power," she repeated. "Invisibility. I know I didn't absorb it from you, or I would have been able to do it when I first got here. I didn't have it before I left tonight and now I do. I want to know how I got it."

"What happened tonight?"

"Before I tell you, I want you to promise you won't be mad."

"Fine. I promise."

Lilly told him everything, starting with meeting Tiryn and making the potion, and gave him very specific details of the harpy feeding on her and all the things Quinn had told her about her powers. When she told him how she created the bomb, she watched for his reaction, expecting him to be angry, but all she saw shock. She almost laughed at his expression, but she didn't want to make him angry, so she restrained herself and waited for him to process her story.

"To answer your question," he said finally, "since magickal protection already comes naturally to you, the protection spell you used did to the harpy what it did to your friend during the duel." Her eyes grew wide, but he just smiled and shook his head. "It reversed the spell onto the caster. Harpies can't absorb powers. They devour them. They take them from others. She was trying to steal your power, but she ended up giving you one instead."

"And everything else?" she prompted.

"Remember your promise," he said, his face serious. "Come, I must go soon, but I want to meet this Quinn. I have a feeling I'll have to keep my eye on him."

Dorwynn didn't know how long he'd been out of it, but it couldn't have been for very long, an hour, maybe two. He looked out the window at the fires burning in the distance and, seeing their sizes and the scatter of people around them, he realized he must have been more tired than he thought. He didn't even remember falling asleep, but he figured he needed it. He never felt rested anymore.

He stretched, twisting his neck to each side to work out the stiff spots, and noticed a dim flame burning on the horizon. He froze as it occurred to him that when Lilly left earlier that night, she'd gone in that direction. He squinted his eyes and was just able to make out the outline of the mountains in the soft glow of the fire. He wanted to believe as he ran to saddle a horse that it was nothing, just another Beltane celebration, but he knew there were no towns anywhere near where that fire burned. No one lived that close to a harpy lair.

He expected many people would still be out during the late hours, but when he arrived to the center of town, it was so crowded he was forced to dismount his horse and shove his way through a tight-packed, rather excited crowd. Knowing this crowd could only mean one thing: something unusual had happened. He pushed harder through the throng, but the closer he got to the fountain, the thicker the crowd seemed to be, making it harder to get through them and making him more anxious to find out what had happened.

His heart almost failed him when he saw her by the fountain. She was safe! She was covered in dirt from head to toe, as was the small boy clinging to her hand, but she was safe. He was so relieved he didn't know if he wanted to kiss her or kill her. Zephra was with her, and Lilly's back was to him as she talked to another young woman, both of them exchanging glances with the boy. The town magistrate was next to her, shouting to a few men who were preparing horses for three waiting coaches and the group of children standing before each one.

"We need more horses for that one," said the magistrate, walking to one of the carriage. "It's going to Vergof."

"So far north," whispered a man behind Dorwynn. "The harpies are broadening their hunting grounds. Someone should inform the Council."

"Ssh!" whispered another. "Don't talk about that in public."

Indeed, thought Dorwynn, though he knew the first man was right. The Council of Magick should know of the harpies' change of hunting behavior. If they were flying that far, working that much harder to find their prey, they might become a bigger threat. *My next task,* he thought, *after Lilly is finished with her training.*

He managed to get through the spectators just as Lilly kneeled to the boy's level. The boy looked afraid, his dark eyes wide as he glanced between Lilly and the woman. Dorwynn took a step backward to let Lilly finish whatever she was doing, though he couldn't help but overhear the end of her conversation.

"Daisy and Willow are going to Hydrabaene," she said, her voice soft and soothing. "Acacia and Evelyn are going to Vergof, and Violet, Rose and Elizabeth are going to Jesfinarea. Joss is going to stay here, with his aunt. His father wants him to stay here while he moves their things to Elikrede." Lilly looked up at the woman standing beside her. She stood as the woman kneeled to look him, though he still clung to her hand.

"Quinn," said the woman, smiling at him. "My name is Delilah. Lilly told me that you have no family?" Quinn nodded. "Well, I have a husband, and a little girl, but I don't have a little boy. Would you like to come and stay with us?" She held out her hand to him and he stared at it, then looked up at Lilly, who nodded.

"Thank you for saving us," he said to Lilly, his voice clear and bright. She squeezed his hand again before he let go, taking the hand of the kind Delilah. "Goodbye."

"I'll come to see you soon," Lilly called as he walked away.

Dorwynn was caught for a moment at the sight of her standing beneath the faerie statue covered in dirt, her eyes so bright they almost glowed. She and Zephra were both staring after Quinn, who could have been Moses parting the sea of people as he walked through them.

"Where's Dorwynn?" Lilly asked after Quinn had disappeared.

"At the house, pouting," said Zephra. "Gustave yelled at him for letting you leave."

"I wasn't pouting," said Dorwynn, and they both jumped. "I fell asleep."

"I didn't use true magick," said Lilly, "and I already promised Gustave I wouldn't do anything alone again. Next time..."

"Next time!" he hissed, grabbing her arm and pulling her away from the eyes of the crowd. "Next time, Lilly? There won't be a next time. There can't be. What you did tonight was reckless! I never should have let you go."

"Don't start, Dorwynn," said Lilly in a tired voice. "We managed to save all the children in the lair, and an entire flock of harpies is now gone. We survived."

"Barely," stressed Dorwynn, "and only by dumb luck. Things turned out alright this time, but you may not be so lucky next time. Haven't you learned by now that you can't just use massive amounts of magick without there being consequences? Dammit, Lilly, you don't understand how magick works."

"I'm learning quickly," she said. He bristled at the sarcasm in her tone, his anger exploding from him like a volcano erupting.

"Why must you make everything so difficult? I can't keep you safe if you are going to keep doing things like this. First the duel, and now this. Do you think Dagana won't hear of this? You may as well have walked up to the castle door and announced your presence in Buthania. Do you think it's easy to keep you hidden from her?"

"You think this is easy for me?" she hissed, only inches from his face. "I gave up everything - my family, my home, my entire *life* - to come here and follow a destiny I'm not even sure is mine. When I finally do something that offers a small amount of proof that I am the Chosen One, all you can do is tell me how wrong I am."

"As if challenging one of the most powerful people in our world to a duel and winning wasn't enough proof, let me walk into the lair of creatures I nearly died defeating last time I fought them. I thought you were smarter than that."

"I did a good thing tonight, Dorwynn. I rescued nine children, trapped for the past six weeks, from some very nasty creatures. Isn't that why I was brought here, to be a savior? Don't you dare criticize me for that."

"How can you save anyone if you are dead?" he asked, his eyes boring into her. It wasn't so much his words that shocked her, but the calm tone of voice in which they were delivered. "Don't go looking for trouble, Lilly. Soon enough, it will come looking for you."

Lilly stared after him as he stormed through the crowd of people, most of whom were returning to their respective homes or fire gatherings, chattering while staring and pointing at Lilly. She shook her head and sighed.

"Something I've noticed about people," said Zephra from behind her, "is that they spend too much time talking about their devotion and not nearly enough time showing it."

"What do you mean?" asked Lilly. Zephra nodded toward the townsfolk returning to their celebrating, slinging pints of ale about while telling tales and laughing a bit to loud at their own jokes.

"I've watched people through the years," continued Zephra, her eyes still on the crowds around the fires. "They celebrate their holidays, but they don't really respect what they are celebrating. Well, some do, but most people just come to the party for the sake of the party. They believe, but they rarely do anything worthy enough to show their devotion, unlike Delilah taking Quinn into her family. They don't honor the Gods in which they believe anymore."

"Some do," said Lilly, staring at a young woman holding a sleeping baby to her chest as staring into the fire, a serene look on her face.

"Some do," agreed Zephra, "but the point is that God, or Allah, or the Goddess, or whatever deity that's out there created all of this, all of us, with no thought of reward or praise. He, or she, doesn't want anything paid back - he wants it paid forward. He wants us to show our love for him by giving it to others. When it is done, he bestows his blessing, but he wants to know that it is deserved. Understand?"

"You think I earned his blessing tonight," said Lilly, nodding as though she answered her own question. Her face was still bright, her eyes a fiery green-yellow from her fierce joy that even Dorwynn couldn't weaken. A small smile crossed Zephra's lips, her deep violet eyes swimming with shadows.

"No," she said. "You are the blessing." Lilly looked at Zephra, disbelief replacing her expression at the unexpected compliment. "That is why it's so important to everyone to keep you safe. You did a great thing tonight, Lilly, and Dorwynn knows that, but he's right. You have got to be more careful. I've lived a long time and I've seen my share of good and evil, but I've never seen anyone who matches Dagana when she's at the height of her power. She is a snake, lying in wait for the perfect time to strike, and the people of this world are the mice, who, since she went into hibernation, have become less wary of their enemy. The most dangerous enemy to have is one who is patient. Don't be the mouse that attracts her attention. You aren't prepared for the strike."

Lilly didn't know what to say. She'd never heard Dagana described like that before, and though Zephra had told her she believed she was the Chosen One, Lilly never thought Zephra would describe her as a blessing. The veils of distrust were lifting as she wondered how an immortal creature like Zephra could feel that way about her, a mere human girl.

She had trouble falling asleep that night, even after a hot bath and a good meal. Her mind was reeling, not only over the fact that she had rescued the children and destroyed a harpy lair in the process, or her newfound trust for Zephra because she thought Lilly was a blessing, but also the vivid image of Dagana torturing her with Dorwynn's words echoing in the background: *How can you save anyone if you are dead?*

She wondered if Wyatt had made it home yet with his dragon. Part of her wanted to talk to him, her friend, while another part of her struggled with the strange light she saw whenever she touched him. It had been so intense, so painful that she had cried even after the pain ended. She felt guilty for doubting him, especially after defending him to Dorwynn as she had, but how could she not question his intentions when he was raised by such an evil person?

No, she thought. *I'll wait until he contacts me. He'll be dealing with enough when he gets home. I'll dream about him soon enough, anyway.* She shuddered despite the warm night and pulled the blankets tighter around her. Outside, the candle on the horizon burned still, while the mountain beneath it turned to ash.

The Spawn

"You've returned," said Dagana without looking up from the map that showed the winding path of the mysterious magical signature that bothered her so. It was still in Elikrede. Her head snapped up suddenly to face Kylenin. He had just been in Elikrede yesterday when she was watching the other one, his magickal signature still lingering there on her map. "How have you arrived so quickly from Elikrede?"

"You've been spying on me," he replied, glowering at her. He hated the fact that she never gave him his freedom, though he had to admit she'd played the part of letting him go quite well.

"I brought him," Tangaia said regally. She bowed to the queen and waited for an acknowledgment. Dagana stared in shock at the dragon before her, having just noticed she was there. Tangaia straightened her posture, unused to bowing as a general rule, and never for so long. "We decided to fly to spare some time. We have much to discuss."

"Indeed," said Dagana, lifting her chin. "Might I ask if you noticed a certain human there, a very powerful sorceress?"

"Lilly!" exclaimed Kylenin, and regretted it instantly. He knew Dagana would only be concerned about her if she were a threat or a possible ally. Lilly would never be an ally, and her fate as a threat would be short-lived. He hoped Dagana didn't try to find her. He didn't wish her any harm. She was his only connection to the world outside the castle, his only real friend, and the bond between them was so great he knew if something happened to her, he would feel it, too.

"You met her?" Dagana asked, a chilly edge to her voice.

"He lost a duel to her," Tangaia offered. Kylenin shot her a look of pure hate, feeling anything but devotion for the first time since he found her. She smirked.

"WHAT?!" Dagana's voice sounded throughout the entire castle.

"Calm yourself, my queen," said Tangaia, and the queen's eyebrows shot up in surprise, unaccustomed to being commanded to do anything. "It is not as terrible as you think. In fact, it may play to our advantage."

"And why, exactly, would you believe that?"

"He gained respect among the village of Elikrede," said the dragon, talking as though she was teaching a classroom of small children. "They all expect he will be king, and a king who admits his faults as eloquently as he gains support among the masses. Aside from that, many strong enemies already believe this girl is the Chosen One."

"Kylenin is the Chosen One," argued Dagana.

"No," Tangaia replied, "he is not, at least, not the one in the prophecy. He is, however, one of the four souls destined to live the Great Battle."

"The evil soul?" Dagana whispered. The dragon nodded. "And you know this because you are his counterpart?" Tangaia nodded again. Dagana sank into her chair, taking in this new information. Her plans would change immediately. She would have to find the Chosen One as quickly as possible, before the other side realized their mistake, if, in fact, they had made one. She suspiciously eyed the dragon in her midst.

"How do you know for sure this girl, or Kylenin, for that matter, is not the Chosen One?"

"I have seen her aura. It is green, not white." She turned her gaze to Kylenin. "His has no color, but is merely gray."

"She is still powerful."

"To be sure," said Tangaia, looking over the map of Elikrede, "but as she is not the Chosen One, might I suggest you leave her be for a time? The faith your adversaries have in her will detract attention from you until such time that you find the real Chosen One and kill her before she becomes a threat."

"They will train this girl. She will be a difficult enemy."

Tangaia laughed, almost hysterically, while both Dagana and Kylenin watched in shock. "She's not that powerful," said Tangaia. Dagana glanced at Kylenin, who was shooting an evil glare toward the dragon, thereby confirming her words. "Besides, she *is* human. I have no doubt you could sway her, if not magickally, then by appealing to her emotions. To keep someone close to her heart out of harm's way, she might be persuaded to submit. I shall take it upon myself to gather information in the meantime, with your permission, of course."

"Eventually," muttered Dagana. "I want you both here for now. In light of this new information, I have some arrangements to make. I will get someone to prepare quarters for you, and when I return, we shall talk." Tangaia bowed her head to the queen, who smiled at the courtesy as she left the room, and then turned toward Kylenin.

"Keeping the queen uninterested in this girl is my gift to you," she said to him. "I know she is dear to you, and I want you to have everything dear to you, but if she becomes a problem, I swear I shall be the first to take her away from you."

"Thank you," he said, and though he wanted to say more regarding the threat she just gave him, he held his tongue. He knew Lilly wouldn't be a problem - he'd warn her not to become one.

"Go to bed, Kylenin," rang Dagana's voice as she sailed through the doorway. "You need some rest. You have a new course of training that starts tomorrow."

"What else could I possibly learn about magick that I don't already know?" he asked. Dagana frowned.

"There is always more to learn about magick," she scolded, "but that is not what you will be learning. You are almost a man. It's time for physical combat training." He stared at her in disbelief, and she stared back, daring him to retaliate. "Goodnight, Kylenin." He exhaled through his nostrils like a bull, his jaw clenched, but rather than give her the retaliation she expected, he walked toward Tangaia, took her hand and kissed it before leaving the room in silence.

"That boy never ceases to surprise me," muttered Dagana when she was alone with Tangaia.

"I'm certain he'll surprise you more in the coming months," said Tangaia. "Tell me, my queen, what are your plans to secure his position on the throne?"

"Finding him a queen was the first step," she said, gliding to her precious map and stealing a glance of that signature...Lilly. It now had a name. With a smile, she looked at Tangaia and said, "And here you are. It now falls to you to make him *want* to be king. Inspire him as only his future queen can do. With you at his side, he is sure to succeed."

"I am at your side as well, my queen. Do you not desire success?"

"I would not dare to presume a creature of your magnitude would assist in my crusade." Dagana bowed her head to the dragon this time, a gesture of equality. After all, if she was going to be his queen, she deserved the respect due to one. "I would be honored to offer you any position you desire."

"I am particularly fond of strategy. Perhaps you are in need of an advisor?"

"You want to command the army?"

"You misunderstand me," said Tangaia, meandering with cat-like grace toward the queen. "I do not wish to command nor control any forces. Assisting to plan their actions would suffice, but someone else can command them. We have far too many other, more pressing matters to address."

"Indeed," said Dagana, staring at her map again. "You're sure this girl isn't the Chosen One?"

"Quite sure."

"Which means she is still out there somewhere."

"Yes, and most certainly unaware of her destiny. If she hasn't been found yet, she's probably still on Earth."

"Then we must go to Earth to find her." Dagana smiled at the thought. She'd never been to Earth, and she always wondered what it was like, what it had that appealed to so many. "Of course, that will take some time to plan."

"Time, we have. Everyone believes she is the Chosen One, and she is gifted enough to hold, or even gain, their faith."

"I don't like that she's so powerful," muttered Dagana, her eyes drifting to the vibrant signature the girl left on it. "I should dispose of her now, before she becomes more powerful."

"Have no fear, my queen," said Tangaia. "I will take it upon myself to ensure she does not become a problem, but we must forget her for now. Let your enemies have their pet, let them waste their precious time training her for a while. Then, if she will not join you, you can dispose of her. By then, we will have found the true Chosen One, and there will be nothing anyone can do to challenge you."

Dagana sighed. She was never one for allowing a problem to go unattended, but she dared not contradict a dragon. Their logic was irrefutable, and somehow, she was graced with the honor of having one as her royal strategist. Luck couldn't be more on her side than it was right now.

"A spawn has escaped!" Sybil's shrill cry broke the quiet reverie as she burst through the door. She stopped short when she saw Tangaia, her eyes wide and bright. "Oh, you've arrived! We've been expecting you for some time. We are honored. Forgive me if I do not bow. It would take a week to repair my ancient bones."

"Of course," said Tangaia, amused at once by this woman, "and the honor is mine."

"Indeed," said Sybil, and then, shuffling to the map, she flipped the pages until she found the mountain range outlining Orthix Zanbar. "A spawn," she said, pointing to the black trail weaving through the forest.

"There hasn't been a spawn sighting in ages," said Dagana, bending over the page, her eyes alight with new fire. "It seems to have emerged here. What is that?"

"Harpies," said Sybil, wrinkling her nose. "Apparently, their lair was destroyed this night. Whoever destroyed it was unaware they held a spawn captive."

"The harpies are more powerful that I thought," muttered Dagana. Tangaia bent over the map also, studying the jagged, erratic movements of the creature marked by a narrow black trail surrounded by a dark gray halo that seemed to spread outward from its wake. "Spawns are difficult to contain."

"And even more difficult to control," agreed Tangaia. "Perhaps recruiting the harpies should be something to consider. If they have the ability to control the spawn, and if they are loyal to you, you will have a very formidable weapon in your possession."

"Quite right," said Sybil. "Now that an entire fleet has been destroyed, they will come together under your command in exchange for safety from their new enemy."

"But who is the enemy?" asked Dagana, her nose almost touching the map. Already, the form of the mountain containing the harpy lair was changing shape on the page. "The spawn's signature consumes all magickal signatures it crosses. Do you think that girl is responsible?"

"I doubt it," said Tangaia, "but anything is possible. For all we know, the spawn could have been the cause of the explosion. We should prepare for that possibility if we are to contain him near the castle."

"No," said Dagana in a flat voice. "We'll let the harpies keep the spawn in their possession, but I want their allegiance. They'll not use that monster against me." She glowered for a moment, as though that's exactly what she thought the harpies were plotting, and then regained her focus. "You and I shall gather the harpy Alphas," she said to Tangaia. "Flying will save time. Sybil, continue to track the spawn. When we get the harpies' cooperation, we'll need to know where it is heading."

"That's a pointless task," mumbled Sybil, "erratic as spawns are."

"It's all we've got. Now, to convince Kylenin that it's in his best interest to stay here. He'll want to come with you, you know."

"I'll convince him," said Tangaia, her confidence impressing both Dagana and Sybil. "He begins physical combat training tomorrow, correct? Have you someone trustworthy to guide him?"

"I do, though he does not yet know it."

"Very well. You speak to your man, and I shall speak to the prince. We'll leave at dawn. It is a good time. The harpies will have their new prisoners. They'll be happy." Tangaia swept from the room, a regal air to her manner. Sybil turned to Dagana, her mouth set in a thin line.

"My visions are shifting," she said, cringing. "The spawn escaping has affected something."

"What?"

"It has yet to be determined. I continue to search for a clear vision, but the future is now uncertain. Events are changing."

"What about Kylenin? Does he still take the throne?"

"He does," said Sybil in a tired voice. She sighed and hobbled toward the door. "He does."

"We've just arrived, and you're leaving already?" Kylenin crossed his arms, his eyebrows pushed down in frustration.

"We talked about this," said Tangaia, her voice smooth and sweet. "You knew this would happen."

"Yes, but not so soon. I don't want you to leave, and I definitely don't want to start training for physical combat."

"If you already knew combative action, I would gladly contradict the queen about requiring you to stay here, but since you do not, and since you need to know it, you will do it, even if you don't want to do it."

"Because a king should know such things," he said with sarcasm, mocking Dagana. Tangaia smiled and shook her head.

"War looms on the horizon, my love," she said, moving closer to him. "You were born in a position that will place you in the center of it. Would you go unprepared?"

"My magick..."

"Magick can be thwarted! Did you learn nothing from your duel?"

Lilly's words flooded his mind then. *Perhaps there is a lesson you need to learn.* Tangaia was right. Magick was strange, unpredictable, and somehow, he had forgotten that. She saw the lesson at once, and as much as he hated to admit it to himself, he was going to have to start trusting her judgment, even if he didn't like it.

"I suppose not," he muttered.

"I just found you," she purred, her breath warm on his ear as she leaned toward him. "Don't make me wonder about your safety every time I have to leave. Train well, learn all you can, and when you finish, you will be twice as powerful."

He smiled and took her hand, captivated by her cat-like eyes. Right now, they looked like a sunflower, the pupils perfect circles. He wanted to give her everything she desired, but he wanted one very important thing from her as well.

"Promise me something," he said.

"Anything," she whispered.

"Don't be like her. Don't hide things from me."

"Of course not," said Tangaia. "Ask me anything, and I'll tell you all I know."

"Where are you going, and why is it so important to leave so soon?"

Tangaia leaned away from him, truly relaxing for the first time in months. She pulled her legs beneath her in her chair, getting comfortable as she had those first few days when they'd spent endless hours talking, so lost in their conversation that those days passed like hours. He got comfortable as well, knowing full well he would stay awake all night just to listen to the sound of her voice.

"Have you ever seen a spawn?" she began.

It is a creature so savage, said the velvet voice, *even our side cannot leave it to run free.* The voice seemed familiar, but Lilly couldn't quite place who was speaking. She could see nothing but darkness, but whoever was doing the talking was as clear as if she was in the same room. *Tonight, there was an explosion within the mountain where it was contained, and it escaped. We have to catch it, to imprison it again before everything is destroyed.*

How do you know it didn't cause the explosion? another voice asked. This one, she knew well. Wyatt...and the other voice must be the dragon.

We don't know, but I don't think even a spawn could cause so much damage at one time. Images exploded in Lilly's head, firing in rapid succession: the harpy lair, the glowing blue mushrooms, the potion changing, the explosion, the mountain burning, almost melting from the inside out, a bony black hand clawing through the ashes, and then, blackness again only one second later. *You see why time is of the utmost importance.*

Can you catch it? asked Wyatt, and Lilly could hear the concern in his voice for...what was her name? *Tangaia?* he pressed after her hesitation. That was it! Tangaia.

No. That's why we have to go to the creatures who kept it contained before tonight. The harpies will catch it again...

"Rise and shine!" a voice called from outside her door. "Get up. It's time to go." Lilly groaned, cursing Dorwynn for disturbing her enlightening dream, and rolled out of bed to begin their quest.

"You're going to love Ambala," he said as they rode the path from Elikrede. It made a wide arc around what Lilly discovered was actually a tiny mountain. The tunnels they'd taken snaked all through it, but Dorwynn told her it was better to arrive riding a horse, more respectful. "I'm sure Voruum will be pleased to see you again."

"I'd like to see him, too," she said, "but I wish we could have stayed a day or two. I hate leaving Quinn all alone."

"Quinn is not alone," said Dorwynn. "He's with his new family."

"He doesn't know them. We left him surrounded by strangers."

"Joss isn't a stranger."

"Yeah, but he's scared of Tiryn."

"With good cause!" laughed Dorwynn. "She's a harpy."

"She isn't one of them," muttered Lilly. "If it wasn't for her, I would never have thought to rescue them, and without her help, I wouldn't have been able to save them. I wouldn't have found Quinn."

"What is it with you and this boy?"

"Why?" she asked, smiling. "Jealous?"

"No. Curious. You never get this attached to anyone."

"Never?" Still smiling, she squeezed her legs together to prompt Adair to a trot and said, "I guess he reminds me of you at that age."

Dorwynn coaxed his horse forward, but didn't respond. There weren't words to describe how he felt at that moment, but he knew if he opened his mouth, he would say things he shouldn't. He used her age as an excuse, but she was almost of age - it was just a few months until her sixteenth birthday - and she was so mature for fifteen that he had a hard time remembering they weren't the same age anymore. The real reason he couldn't tell her how he felt about her came straight down to fear. What if she didn't feel the same way? He always believed she did, but that was a long time ago in a very different place. They were both different people now.

They rode in silence at an even trot, Lilly's mind on her dream the night before. Something about it bothered her, she just couldn't remember what it was. The details were faint, but her feelings when she woke were clear: guilt. Her actions last night changed something, and she felt like it was for the worse.

"I really screwed up last night, didn't I?" she asked, guilt ringing in her voice.

"Look," said Dorwynn, his own voice edged with a hint of guilt, "I shouldn't have been so hard on you. Things have been strange lately and I've been having a hard time with it."

"You were right, though. I just made things worse."

"Maybe, maybe not, but I'm not going to sugar coat it. There's a reason we don't meddle with magick. Sometimes the result is greater than we expect. Something this big usually changes things in one way or another. You have to think how your actions are going to affect others, and the bigger the action, the more it will affect. Before you do anything, you should ask yourself if your goal is worth the change. Is there one soul out there worth the lives of many?"

"I guess it depends on the soul," she said. Dorwynn's heart skipped a beat. She had *no* idea! "So, what happened to you? What strange things are bothering you?"

"The blackouts are getting worse," he said, and Lilly could see the frustration written on his face. "I'm losing weeks at a time now. I don't remember what I do or where I go, but I know I do things. I eat, and travel, but if I do more, I can't tell you. I just don't know."

"Is there a trigger that starts them?" asked Lilly. "Maybe if you could figure out what starts them, you could try to avoid it."

"That's the problem. I can't avoid it. There isn't really a trigger for the shorter ones. They just happen, and I can deal with that, but the long ones..." His voice trailed off. How would she handle *this* piece of information?

"What?" she pressed. "What's the trigger?"

"Gustave."

"Gustave?"

"Since I have returned, I've had a blackout at some time during almost every task he's assigned me. Usually, they're only a day or two, and he always gives me plenty of time to get it done, even with the blackouts, but since you've returned, even before you came to find me, they've been more frequent and much longer."

"I wonder why?"

"I don't know," he said, narrowing his eyes in frustration, "but I have an idea. I think Gustave is using me magickally to do things for him that he knows I wouldn't agree to do, even if he commanded it."

"What?" Lilly couldn't believe Rohan could be so deceptive; then again, he did say there were certain traits of the real Gustave embedded in his identity. Would the real Gustave have done something like that?

"He's using me for something, and when I'm done training you, I'm going to see if I can find out what it is."

Silence was their companion for the rest of the ride. Lilly spent her time watching the scenery change from the thick forest edging the mountains to a thinner, glade-like wood, and finally, a lush green meadow. She stopped her horse where the trees lined the meadow so she could stare.

It was more beautiful that she could have imagined. Unicorns stood in groups, sparkling as they grazed under the suns. Topaz, onyx, ruby, diamond...her mind could only fathom precious stones. Brown, black, red and white were too plain to describe them. A beige baby pterippus soared from the trees to her right, stumbling during his touchdown beside a full-grown pterippus strolling through the field. She fluttered her cream and chocolate wings when the colt landed, then folded them, whipping her lion-like tail behind her.

Looking closer, Lilly noticed structures built among the trees all around her, and milling about the structures were groups of centaurs and minotaurs, carrying baskets or working in nearby gardens. One centaur in particular caught Lilly's eye. She was lying beneath a tree, her four legs folded under her, while her human arms plucked flowers from the grass, weaving them into an intricate pattern. Her entire body was a deep gray, like pewter, all the way to the tips of her pointed ears, though the hair on her tail as well as her head was jet black. She looked up and smiled when she noticed Lilly staring at her, then motioned for Lilly to come closer. Lilly dismounted Adair and handed the reins to Dorwynn without a word. He just smiled and let her go.

"Do you like it?" asked the centaur when Lilly sat in front of her. Lilly looked closer at her creation. The flowers were put together to form a shawl, the bell-shaped white ones the background and the purple star-shaped ones creating the symbol she'd grown so used to seeing.

"A pentacle," whispered Lilly. "It's beautiful."

"Do you know what it represents?"

"It's the symbol of the Goddess Divine. Each point represents one of the elements."

"And what else?"

"The spirit?" said Lilly in an unsure voice.

"In other words, the soul. Just as important as the other four in sustaining life. It is in perfect balance, each point equal from the other and from the center." Lilly studied the shawl again. It indeed looked perfectly symmetrical.

"And the triquatra?" asked Lilly, thirsty for more information.

"What about it?"

"Doesn't it represent the elements for life, too? There are only four sections to represent the four elements. There's no place for a fifth."

The centaur smiled. "Well, that all depends on what you believe. Some believe, many in fact, that fire is the key element to the soul, the rage and passion and joy. You see, earth is a broad term. Literally, earth, or a solid structure, or body, which incidentally enough is made mostly of water, just like the planet. To have life, a body must also have air. We breathe air from our planet, just as it breathes air from us, only a different type, through the trees and plants."

The centaur used her front hoof to draw the beginnings of a triquatra in the dirt, her fingers still working over her creation and plucking small white flowers from the ground. "Now, these three elements represent the three points, with fire at its center, but there is one part of the symbol that has yet to be placed."

Lilly studied what she had drawn and realized what was missing. "The circle."

"Precisely. Three elements that together create a body, circled by fire as the suns circle us, which would make the center represent the spirit."

"But the circle on the pentacle..."

"The symbols are neither in opposition or similarity to the other. It is all in what you believe."

Lilly looked at the beauty around her, pushing her perception slightly. Nearby, birds chirped, insects buzzed, and a warm breeze blew through the trees, rustling their leaves to sound like murmuring voices.

"If a soul is required for life," she asked, "then how do you explain insects being alive, or trees? They don't have souls, do they?"

"Again, you are thinking too literally. A soul is more than just your emotions or your moral compass. It is everything you feel, from the wind in your hair, to the sting of a slap, to the pain that comes when your heart breaks. Insects feel it when you crush them beneath your feet. You are right - they have no emotions, as far as you know anyway - but they are simple forms of life, with nervous systems. As far as trees and plants go, they have no nervous systems and no more of a soul than a hair on your head, but that, in a sense, is what a tree is to the earth...a single hair, only it is alive. The earth, a living thing, is mother to us all, and I believe that just as our bodies sprang from the earth, so too our souls sprang from her soul."

Lilly stared at the two symbols, her gaze bouncing between the two.

"You are wondering about God," said the centaur.

"Curious."

"The circle on the pentacle, or the other point on a six-pointed star, or the space between the rest of the triquatra...any of those things could represent the God, the Goddess, or the pair as one. It depends of your faith, on your own beliefs, and none are wrong. Why, even a Christian cross has five points, if you include the point created where the lines intersect. Personally, I think one cannot have a mother without a father, or vice versa. A father cannot give birth and a mother must be impregnated to give birth, wouldn't you think?"

The centaur stopped working and looked at Lilly with a small smile, raising one eyebrow. She turned the human half of her body to the side, running her hand over the bulge in her abdomen between her four legs. Lilly realized then that she was pregnant. She blushed.

"It doesn't really matter, though," said the centaur, plucking another white flower, "what you believe, as long as you have faith in something you feel is infallible. If you don't have faith in something, you have faith in nothing, including yourself. Some believe in science, some believe in God, or more than one God, in a Goddess or in the God and Goddess as one, known as the Divine. Many here are putting their faith in you."

"Me? Why me?"

"Generations upon generations of men and creature alike have died believing the Chosen One would someday arrive, as it has been preached since the beginning of our world, and now, here you are."

"Who told you I was the Chosen One?" she whispered. No one was supposed to know that. She barely believed it herself.

"I speak too often of you, I suppose," boomed a voice from behind her. Lilly jumped up, coming face to face with Dorwynn and the minotaur at his side.

"Voruum!" she cried, grinning. "How are you?"

"I am well," he chuckled. "My lands, has it only been six weeks? Your hair is so long!"

"I haven't noticed," she said, consciously feeling for the end of it. It didn't seem much longer to her. "Who told you I was the Chosen One?"

Voruum smiled, leading his guests away from the centaur, who smiled and continued adding white flowers to the edges of her growing creation. She and Dorwynn followed him to a cabin not much bigger than the bottom half of her house. There were no rooms inside, just a cast-iron stove, a log table and three log chairs. The rest of the space was empty except for a pile of folded blankets stacked in one corner.

"My wife has a special gift," he said, sitting at the table. Lilly and Dorwynn took the other two chairs, which Lilly discovered were very uncomfortable. She shifted, trying to make the best of it, but her back was already starting to hurt. "She's one of the rare souls magick has chosen to speak for her."

"A prophet," whispered Dorwynn.

"In fact," continued Voruum, "she's very anxious to meet you. She's seen you coming for some time. Perhaps we should try to find her?"

"Yes, let's," said Lilly, jumping up from the torture of the chair. How could anyone sit there for long? Besides that, she was dying to talk to a prophet, not just someone who could see visions of the future like Ashya, but someone who received the information straight from magick. Maybe she could finally get some answers.

Voruum led them through the heart of Ambala. Herds of young centaurs, unicorns and pterippi bounded and flew over the vast meadow, while their many parents grazed on the fresh grasses or worked deep within the huge vegetable garden that looked like it would be able to feed the whole town when it reached maturity. Voruum scouted the children, looking around for a sign of his own child.

I wonder where she is," he said, looking back at his house and the trees behind it. "Maybe she took Savara to the river."

The wind changed direction then, wafting a familiar and frightening scent toward them. Before Lilly's mind could register the smell of smoke, a voice floated eerily on the acrid wind: *Birem elsera bora.* Voruum ran toward the river, his eyes wild. The herds in the fields began to run also, shouting for their children and gathering them as they fled. Beside her, Dorwynn grabbed her hand, tugging her as he started to run.

"We have to hide," he said, his voice desperate, as she caught a glimpse of the terror approaching them.

Until last night, she never would have believed such a terrible creature existed, but hearing it described and seeing only a tiny flash of its appearance was nothing compared to the horror of seeing it with her own eyes. Its black body was nothing but rubbery skin stretched over a skeleton, so tight the bones might have been individually wrapped in it. Its four feet were the same distance apart, and it seemed to slink forward, then shift sideways suddenly without pausing for the change, its joints bending in every direction as it moved. The empty holes surrounding its broad, flat head held a faint glow, and Lilly realized that each one was an eye - not empty, but just as black as the rest of it. Razor-sharp teeth lined its mouth, wrapping more than halfway around each side of its head, which was attached to a thick neck protruding from the center of its back. All this, however, was the least of the horror. Surrounding the creature and trailing along behind it was a dark mist that spread outward from its path, smoke that burned without fire.

"Lilly," shouted Dorwynn, yanking on her hand. "Come on!" He let go of her hand to pick up a young unicorn near him, and ran toward the forest, still shouting at her. Lilly just stared at the creature in shock, knowing there was no place safe from it.

"Spawn," she whispered, and the creature changed direction as though it had heard her, running straight toward her as flames began to appear along its trail.

"Lilly!" Dorwynn was beside her again, his arms empty as he tried to get her to move. "What are you doing? We have to hide."

"It's a spawn, Dorwynn," she said in a flat tone. "Where are we supposed to hide?"

"A spawn? How do you know it's...?" He stopped talking when he saw the look in her eyes. It wasn't fright, or even surprise. There was no mistaking that look of guilt.

"This is my fault," she stammered, her eyes welling with tears. "It's burning now. Everything is burning."

"We don't have time for this, Lilly. It doesn't matter. We have to get away from it...now! Come on!" He yanked her hand and she followed blindly, letting him lead her through the tears clouding her vision as the details of her dream rushed back to her. *An explosion within the mountain where it was contained...* "Quick! In here."

Dorwynn shoved her into a burrow in the ground, dug out much like a bomb shelter, its entrance hidden between two large trees. He crawled in behind her as she squeezed closer to the others hiding there. Most of them were children, cowering together as close as possible, shivering in fear. She huddled with them as the spawn spread its destruction over their fields. The flames trailing in the wake of its path ate everything they encountered, consuming the livelihood of these creatures like an insatiable cancer, the black mist lingering overhead. She heard the crackling of the fire as the creature scoured the ground above them, its pace slowing, and she knew it was looking for her. Fear ripped through her, drawn out like a blade slowly piercing her heart as she waited for it to find them.

Protect them, she repeated to herself, her eyes shut tight. *Protect them from this evil.* She opened her eyes to glance at the children with her, and at Dorwynn, his eyes wide with shock as he stared at her. She knew he was wondering how this was her fault, how she knew what the creature was, but she couldn't look at him. All she could do was think of Voruum, his wife that she wanted to meet, his baby daughter, the centaur who had welcomed her to Ambala...

"Where are you going?" whispered Dorwynn when she started crawling through the hole frantically.

"I have to help them!" she cried. "I can't just hide in here. I have to do something."

"There is nothing you can do," protested Dorwynn. "It will kill you."

"I have to try," she whispered. She looked at the children, then at him, her eyes serious. She lifted her hand, caressing his face, and said, "Protect them, Dorwynn. I know you can. Seal the door after I'm out."

"Lilly, no!" he said, but he was too late. She was gone. He sealed the doorway, manipulating the earth around it until he was sure they would not be found even if the creature saw her emerge, and waited, his heart threatening to explode as he heard the cries of terror above them.

The chaos was staggering. It took her a second to gather herself, but when Lilly saw the spawn ravaging its way through the life of Ambala, snapping its jaws at every creature in its path, destroying everything beautiful and magickal about this place, she could feel her blood begin to boil, her limbs getting warm.

Careful, she told herself, trying to push back the magick threatening to burst from the inside. *You don't want to make things worse again.* It was no use, though. The magick was stronger than she was. She had to let it go.

The spawn paused in its rampage, lifting its head like it was sniffing the air, though Lilly could see it had no nose. Whatever magick she released was floating slowly, almost lazily, toward the creature, and she could tell when it felt the magick strike. It roared, rushing toward her so fast she barely had time to become invisible before it reached her. She ran, appearing when she was far enough away that she could recover before turning invisible again, doing this over and over. It followed her each time as she led it farther and farther from Ambala, screeching its frustration. Magick surged in her again and she sent it toward the spawn, which twisted its head in a wide circle, all four of its three-fingered hands gripping the ground as it howled in fury.

A second later, everything was silent. She didn't feel the explosion, though it tossed her halfway across the meadow. She got to her feet, stumbling aimlessly toward the line of trees that only minutes before housed the residents of Ambala. The houses, the trees, the meadow – all were burning now. Her ears were ringing from the blast, and she could hear nothing more. She looked around for the spawn, but it was gone, the gray mist already starting to lift as the unharmed inhabitants began emerging from their hiding places to assess the damage.

"We need water!" someone cried, and a stampede of adult centaurs disappeared into the trees toward the river.

Onatas, thought Lilly, only half-comprehending the situation. She held her hand out as though she expected to catch a raindrop despite the lack of rain clouds. *"Onatas,"* she whispered, trying again. *"Onatas."* It didn't work. The only water she caught was the tear that rolled down her cheek and into her open hand.

Lilly walked through what was left of Ambala, the acrid smell of the still-burning land assaulting her senses. Most of the plain was scorched. Their food, their homes, their lives - all were destroyed by the evil that had swooped down upon them. Their existence was ripped apart at the seams, never to be the same. The children, most of whom had never seen any evil, let alone something so terrifying, cowered behind their parents or huddled in small groups, afraid of what else might happen. Many of the adults were searching for survivors, helping them from the rubble as the others returned with water to extinguish the raging fires. The rest wept their lament as they found a loved one who had not survived. The sadness in their eyes was so haunting, it bore deep into Lilly's soul, searing into her memory for years to come.

Lilly didn't feel her own injuries as she walked through the chaos, nor did she notice the blood trickling from her head. Above the cries of the victims, the screams of despair of those left behind, she heard a single voice shout her name, a deep voice she knew well. Afraid to turn toward him, she did anyway.

Voruum, his flesh torn and bleeding, ran toward her, his young daughter lifeless in his arms. She was badly injured, deep gashes seeping blood. Soot covered her body and much of her flesh was scorched off. It looked as though she was nearer to the explosion than Lilly had been.

"Help me," he cried. He gently put his child into Lilly's arms and whispered, "Please," before falling to his knees.

Lilly put her on the ground, her hands already warming as the magick flooded into them. She held them over the worst wounds first, and as her hands glowed, white tendrils of light moved across the burnt flesh, gently removing the damaged skin and healing the layers underneath. It took a while, but Lilly finally healed the child enough that she would survive the cuts, bruises and one broken arm that Lilly had left. It was daunting, much more so than healing her hand or Wyatt's ear. She couldn't heal her completely, but she had saved her life.

"She'll need to mend a bit more, but she's going to be fine. Now you," she said as she turned to Voruum.

"I'll live," he said breathlessly, already tying a cloth around his arm to stop the profuse bleeding. "Save your energy. There are more out there worse off than I."

"I can't save them all."

"No," he said, his voice laced with knowing despair as he looked around. "You can't save them all, but you can save some."

Already, the survivors were gathering those wounded. Among them, Lilly noticed another minotaur, a female with soft features and deep eyes, holding a wound on her chest. Blood trickled through her fingers and she staggered before dropping to the ground. Lilly went to her first.

"No," said the minotaur when Lilly started healing her. "My daughter. She's injured...with her father...Voruum."

"Savara will be fine," soothed Lilly, closing the hole in the creature's heart as the woman slipped into unconsciousness.

There were so many, too many, and Lilly could only heal them enough to save their lives. She did more for the injured children, but luckily, Dorwynn had protected them well. Savara seemed to be the worst of them, while most were more frightened than anything else. He didn't speak to her yet; there was nothing to be said. She could see the questions swimming in his eyes, but she knew he was waiting for the right time to ask them. She was grateful for that. He went with a group of centaurs to search for more who needed healing, and Lilly kept healing who she could, hoping her strength would outlast the wounded that kept arriving.

The fires had burned themselves out by the time night fell, and Lilly had healed everyone who was injured to the point they would survive. Her head hurt, her arms felt like they were on fire, and her entire body ached, no doubt from the amount of magick she'd used trying to lead the spawn away and then healing so many. She looked down at herself, noticing for the first time the gashes and burns on her arms. She looked and felt like she'd been wrestling a lion and the lion had won.

Despite her pain, and despite the knowledge that this was her fault, all the doubts over her destiny, all the worries about whether or not she was the Chosen One, and all the fear that she might have made a mistake in coming here vanished as she collapsed beside Voruum, who was cradling his now fully-awake baby in his arms.

"You did well," he said. She smiled and, in a final act to prove that, Chosen One or not, she was meant to be here, she touched his arm where the worst of his injuries still bled, healing it enough to close the wound.

"Lilly," said Dorwynn in relief, and then a look of horror crossed his face. "Are you alright?"

"Yeah," she said, though she was suddenly overwhelmed with exhaustion. "Why?"

"You're still bleeding," he said. "Here." He ripped a piece of his torn shirt loose and pressed it to her head. When the makeshift bandage made contact, her head all but exploded. She pushed his hand away, taking the cloth from him. It was already stained with a streak of crimson. "Come on. We need to get you healed."

"I can't do any more," she said, her voice barely audible. Her head spun, and suddenly, everything seemed surreal, as though she was watching a late-night horror film and just starting to nod off. She felt the darkness envelope her and tried to fight it, but the darkness won.

She was in the place between asleep and awake, and she knew she wasn't dreaming because she ached from head to toe. Something was different, though. Her head wasn't throbbing anymore, and her arms no longer felt like they were still burning.

"How long has she been like this?" a sweet voice murmured. It sounded like wind chimes.

"A few hours," came Dorwynn's voice. "She saved many lives tonight."

"As well as nine the night before, from what I have heard," said the chime-like voice with a hint of awe. "We have indeed found our savior, have we not?"

"I believe so, but I wonder what she believes. She said something tonight when the spawn attacked that I don't understand. She thinks this is all her fault."

"We will make her see otherwise, though I understand why she feels that way."

"Why?"

"The spawn was being held prisoner by the harpies she defeated. When the lair was destroyed, it survived and managed to escape."

"How did she know this?"

"I do not know, but I do know that it would have been released anyway. The harpies were striving to unite with Dagana, and the spawn was their bargaining chip. It is better that it happened now, while she was here to save so many."

It wasn't her fault! Lilly, still half-asleep, sighed with relief.

"She is waking," said the unfamiliar voice. "Stay with her. I will find you when we are done."

The woman who was speaking left before Lilly managed to open her eyes, but Dorwynn was there, hovering over her. He looked so worried, and a fresh pang of guilt swept over her, even if all this wasn't her fault.

"How are you feeling?" he asked.

"Better." She sat up and looked around. They were still in the field, though most of the inhabitants of Ambala were nowhere to be seen. "Where is everyone?"

"They've taken to the forest for the night. Tomorrow, they will begin to rebuild."

"Where will they build?" she asked. "Everything is destroyed. Their crops, the entire meadow..."

"Everything is not destroyed," interrupted Dorwynn. He ran his hand over the charred earth, stopping over the one blade of tattered grass left behind. His hand glowed as the magick swirled into the ground. Moments later, a patch of fresh grass the size of a dinner plate shot through the dirt. "The roots still live."

"You can't grow an entire meadow of grass, Dorwynn," she sighed. "You don't have the strength."

"I know that, but the faeries do. They arrived while you were sleeping."

"Faeries?" Lilly looked around the now empty field, but all she could see was a swarm of fireflies...colored fireflies. Miniscule streams of red, blue, purple and green filled the dark sky, darting to and fro so fast they could barely be seen. She looked at her arms, realizing for the first time that she her wounds were gone. "Is that who healed me?"

"Yes." He took her hand in both of his, holding it tight. "This wasn't your fault, you know."

"I know. I heard you talking to...someone about it. We should probably tell her that Dagana is going to the harpies. She wants the spawn."

"How do you know that," he asked, "and how did you know it even escaped?"

"A dream, as usual," she said, though she was starting to think it was less of a dream and more like overhearing the conversation.

"Well," said Dorwynn, a bitter edge to his voice, "Dagana would have had the spawn for sure if you hadn't let it escape, and everyone you saved tonight would have died, but now, she'll have to work to get it. Maybe we can get it contained before she finds it."

"Is that even possible?" He shrugged, then pulled himself to his feet and offered her his hand. She took it, unable to believe how tired she still was. Her legs felt like rubber, barely able to support her, and she sank back to the ground. "I can't yet."

"Well, we have to move. They're about to begin."

"Begin what?"

"You'll see." He slid one arm under her knees and the other around her back, then carefully lifted her off the ground and carried her to the edge of the forest. Lilly noticed there were several of the less injured creatures also in the trees, there to observe what was apparently a big event. Dorwynn set her down on an old tree stump that was overgrown with ivy, creating a nice cushion, and stood behind her, his hand resting protectively on her shoulder.

The gray mist had lifted while she was sleeping, and the night was clear and crisp. Lilly shivered, and a moment later, Dorwynn's jacket was covering her shoulders, his hand still resting there as if he was afraid to let go of her. She smiled and leaned against him, feeling the urge to sleep again, until a haunting melody of voices floated toward her. Over the damaged field, the faeries hovered as if waiting for a sign. A red light appeared in the center of the swarm, brighter than all the rest.

"That's Kiera," whispered Dorwynn. "She's the queen."

Kiera's voice carried over the vast field then, calling to the other faeries. There were no words, only an undecipherable chant, and the others began to gather, forming a wide circle around their queen. They joined the chant, the song swelling as the twisted and turned gracefully over the charred remains of Ambala, their dance slow and methodic as it formed a living, moving pentacle.

The wind sang as the chant grew louder, blowing through the trees to create a melody unlike any Lilly had heard before. She closed her eyes, letting the sweet song lull her into a peaceful trance, then opened them again, not wanting to miss the magick before her eyes.

It was as though the faeries, joined together in their dance, were one, a conduit for magick itself. Their formation complete, the pentacle glowed bright white, and a silver mist covered the remains of the broken land. At first, Lilly could see no change, but the magick was doing its work, repairing the burnt plants and reviving the roots still living beneath the ashes.

It was a slow process, but everyone who watched was captivated by each movement, each angelic note created by the faeries. They all joined the outer circle, flying together as one, their colors mingling as they gained speed to create the illusion of a rainbow spiraling to the ground.

Then it was over. The music faded as the faeries flew away in a single, straight line. Only two remained: Kiera and one other, a deep purple faerie barely bright enough to glow. Lilly could see the silver ribbons of magick surround them, and then the faeries were gone, two exquisite women in their places.

"Time will heal what remains," said Kiera to those among the trees. "Rest easy."

Even in the darkness, the newborn plants could be seen working their way through the earth, the magick still flowing through the meadow. It wasn't as lush as when Lilly had first arrived, but it was so much better than the blackened earth of a few hours ago. The harvest would be meager that fall, but there would be a harvest. Ambala would survive. That was all that mattered, and they retired, grateful for that much.

The woman standing before Lilly was the same woman she'd seen at the duel, her blond hair tinted a strange hue of red. She wore the same metallic red dress, with the same cape-like top that resembled her pearly wings, almost like they were made of the same material. She shimmered, even in the dull light of the moon, and the halo of light surrounding her was still there, as though she glowed from the inside out. The woman beside her could have been her reflection, though her dress was violet and her hair, a rich chocolate brown, had a violet tint.

While Lilly distracted by the faeries, Dorwynn and Kiera were talking in low voices. Kiera shook her head and put her hand on Dorwynn's shoulder, looking peaceful, though Dorwynn hung his head, shame clouding his eyes. Lilly concentrated, blocking her other senses to hear what was being said.

"Do not feel guilty, Master Dorwynn," whispered Kiera. "You could not have foreseen the outcome. You need not bear the burden of blame."

"What is she talking about?" asked Lilly when he returned to her side.

Dorwynn sighed. He didn't want to tell Lilly what he had done for the faeries, the favor that earned him their blessing. It was a gift he didn't feel he deserved anyway, but especially now that his concerns about doing it had been proven founded. More than anything, he feared Lilly's reaction, so much so that he couldn't bring himself to be the one to answer her question.

"Kiera can explain it better that I ever could," he said, lowering his eyes. "She has my permission to tell you everything." He lifted his eyes to meet the queen's and she nodded once, acknowledging his unspoken request. "Just remember that everything worth achieving requires great sacrifice. Try not to think less of me." Lilly nodded, confused, and reached for his hand.

"No matter what you've done," she said, "I know your intentions were good."

He smiled, relishing the warmth of her touch, and leaned toward her, planting a feather-light kiss on her forehead.

"Be safe," he whispered. "I'll be waiting for you at home."

"Bye," she whispered. She didn't know why, but her heart felt heavy with sorrow. Maybe it was the look in his eyes, or the fact that he didn't feel he could tell her his terrible secret, or perhaps the way he said he would be waiting for her...whatever it was, it gripped her heart, squeezing tighter and tighter with every step away from her he took.

"Come, child," said Kiera, extending her hand toward Lilly as Dorwynn's form disappeared in the darkness. "Your future awaits."

The Faerie Queendom

In the beginning, there was only a void. That void was the Creatrix, the womb for all life. The Creator, her equal in every sense, was the spark within her womb that grew, expanding the void to encumber the universe as a whole. In their union, they are the Divine.

And so the world was born of the spark, bursting energy forth, but it was hollow, without life. So the Divine set forth to provide the elements needed to sustain life. The Creatrix cried tears of joy for the birth of the world and thus came the Water. She spoke loving words to it and thus came the Air. She laid upon the world in an eternal embrace and thus came the Earth. Her heart sank to the core, and thus great Fire raged, coursing through its veins as blood courses through each living thing.

Then the Creator took from the great mass of energy four souls, giving one to each element, and life was born unto the world, emerging from the elements in massive bursts of evolution. Eventually, the age of humans arrived, taking all she had given, all she had to offer. She cried for them until she had no more tears. She spoke to them until her breath was gone, but they chose not to listen. Her heart broke until there was no passion, no fire left in her soul, and her body, the land upon which the humans lived, began to die.

In despair, the Divine called before them four of their children, each born of the first souls given to the elements by the Creator, and requested from them a great sacrifice for the welfare of all life. The Creatrix would give birth to a new world, the Creator to a new spark, to create a place for the worthy to begin anew, to continue their legacy. The Elemental Children were to breathe new life into the hollow, and in exchange for their great sacrifices, they would have endowed upon them the gift of prosperity eternal. Their prosperity would be bestowed with all the wisdom their element encumbered, all the magic their element contained and the singular ability to walk upon the new land in human form, should they so choose...

And thus, the new world was given everything it required to sustain life anew. Jermar, the turbulent merman, sacrificed his body to create the Water. Buthania, the stable faerie, gave her body to form the land. The passionate dragon, Coremdey, gave her body and heart to the depths, beating fire through the soul of the world. And I, the unicorn Niran, will sacrifice myself upon completion of this historical account to bring forth Air, therefore completing the balance required for life, leaving behind only this record as a burden of proof to the continuation of life, so that no incongruities shall plague humankind to their own existence. – passage from *The Creation of the World: as told by the Creators.*

Lilly waited patiently as Kiera delved into her mind, sorting through the information she had learned so far. She remembered things as the queen viewed them and was amazed at the precision Kiera had as she sorted through her mind.

"I see you have yet to learn how to call upon the Elements," said the queen. "Do not worry. It is not difficult. It seems you have mastered the rest of your tasks. I must admit, your learning processes are rather unorthodox."

"To say the least," said Lilly. She looked around the dense forest, unable to see much beyond the soft glow of the two human faeries at her side. Kiera smiled.

"Faeries," she said, her voice the soft tinkle of tiny wind chimes, "are children of Elemental Earth. Our existence maintains the balance of nature, as does the existence of each Elemental child. Our vocation is to assist nature in all her glory, bringing life to the unborn seeds, as well as many other obligations you shall learn about before you leave. You will help us to revive the forest, for the season of spring is at her peak. The trees will bear fruit soon." She spoke as though she was in awe, as though it was a miracle that fruit trees would soon bear fruit. "Of course, you will only be with us a few days, but it will amaze you how much you will learn in such a short time."

Kiera stopped walking and looked up at the huge tree before them. It was the largest tree Lilly had ever seen, and as she followed Kiera's gaze, she noticed it was swarming with lights of every color. Some flew in wide circles around the tree, while others darted from branch to branch, leaf to leaf.

"Give me your hand," said Kiera. "You will learn to transfigure at a later time. For now, I will transfigure you. With your permission, I will call forth your magick to help."

"You have it," Lilly told her, entranced by the woman's words. She felt a rush of excitement at the prospect of transfiguring, unconcerned with what she was about to become.

"Eklain," she said, and the violet faerie took Lilly's other hand. Warmth spread through her fingers, her hands, her arms, all the way through her core until she felt the heat in her heart. She could feel them drawing from her strength, and as the sensation became uncomfortable, she tried to distract herself by focusing on how the magick worked. She grew weak as the discomfort turned into pain. It wasn't unbearable, but it was enough to make her realize why someone would choose not to do it, even if they could. She wondered if Rohan felt this way every time he changed his identity.

The pain lasted until the change was complete, and then, she was weightless. To her left, a metallic red faerie, her pearly wings a blur that still reflected her vivid color as she hovered in midair. The blonde hair was gone, replace only with two long antennae that curled over at the tips. To her right was the violet faerie, her antennae shorter and straight. She looked around, letting her new eyes adjust to her surroundings. Every tree and flower had a glow around it, down to each individual leaf. The forest looked completely different from this point of view, and she wondered if this was how insects viewed the world. A leaf near her could very well be used as a blanket. She looked down and panicked. She couldn't even see the ground, they were so high up. She felt herself falling, her heart racing, and closed her eyes, knowing she wouldn't survive the fall. She opened them when she realized she was no longer falling. She was flying! The other faeries smiled. She waved at them, and then paused to stare at her arm. Her skin was a vibrant green, the same color as her eyes, and it had a metallic quality to it as it shimmered under its own light.

"Come," sang Kiera, motioning to Lilly. She and the other faerie flew toward a knot in the huge tree, which was so much larger now that Lilly couldn't see anything but the tree. High above a thick branch, the violet faerie landed on a small step barely large enough for one faerie to stand. Her skin changed like a chameleon, camouflaging to look like the bark to the tiniest grainy detail, until Lilly could barely see the outline of her body, and then she disappeared. Lilly flew toward the step and Kiera nodded, smiling. Lilly landed on it facing the knot and lowered her wings as she had seen the purple faerie do. The tree disappeared as she was thrust through the door and out the other side.

She stood on a narrow path, a normal-looking wooden door behind her where she had just entered, though it had no knobs or hinges. Kiera appeared as she entered through it and looked out at the wide space within the tree. There were rooms built inside the interior walls, as well as little caves that were actually walkways to other parts of the queendom. Faeries of every color darted throughout the open spaces between the walls. A single walkway spiraled along the inner wall of the tree, starting at the doorway they just came through and ending at an open floor far beneath them. The whole place, above and below, was lit up in a rainbow of colors, glowing like a jar full of fireflies.

"This is my queendom," Kiera told Lilly, her voice filled with warmth. "Welcome to Saurabean."

"Something has to be done soon, my queen," said an electric blue faerie next to Lilly. More than a dozen faeries sat at a round wooden table in Kiera's throne room, a plethora of metallic colors, and she had invited Lilly to sit in on the royal conference she said she could no longer postpone. "The faeries of Nuathlyn destroy more of the Orthix Zanbar each day. If they are not stopped..."

"We cannot deprive them of their own dwelling, Shira," said Kiera, raising her hand to stop the faerie's protests. "They are already banished, and we cannot bring them back to Saurabean. We must try to develop a compromise that suits all."

"Nuathlyn was the compromise," argued Shira, frowning, "and yet, they continue to spread death. Should we forsake half the forest for them?"

"Should we forsake them for half the forest? They are living creatures also."

"Creatures who feed on death!"

"Calm yourself, Shira." Kiera's tone made the blue faerie snap her jaw shut. She clenched it as if restraining a barrage of words threatening to escape. "This is an important matter, but one that cannot be resolved easily. Have faith I will address it very soon, but for now, I would like to introduce you all to Lilly of Elikrede, Arch Mage Gustave's most recent apprentice. We will be hosting her Master Trials."

The other faeries fluttered around her, their voices a melody of bells as they welcomed her. The only faerie who did not offer her words of welcome was Shira. She hovered in the corner of the room, her head bent in whispered conversation with the queen. Though Lilly couldn't hear what passed between them, she could tell Kiera was struggling to remain diplomatic with her council member. Her face was composed, but her eyes burned with frustration. The rest of the group flew from the room in two and threes as they chattered about the magickal apprentice in their midst, and as the room became silent, Lilly caught the tail end of Shira's words.

"...mistake to let another apprentice attempt to solve this problem only to fail. After what happened last time…"

"Enough, Shira," said Kiera, looking at Lilly. "I have heard your argument and I will take everything into consideration before making my decision. You are dismissed."

The blue faerie lowered her wings, dropping to the floor beneath her, and scowled at Lilly before zooming from the room.

"What is Nuathlyn?" Lilly asked Kiera after all but Eklain had left. As the queen's second in command, Lilly had discovered it was Eklain's duty to remain in the queen's presence unless the queen dismissed her, which was a rare occurrence.

"It is also a queendom," said Kiera, landing beside Lilly. "It is the reason Master Dorwynn chastises himself. You see, as sentient creatures, we are driven less by our instincts and more by our own wills. Therefore, we may choose to be good or evil. Faeries who choose the path of evil, those who commit evil acts, become banished from Saurabean. Until two years ago, those banished had no dwelling. They roamed without purpose, causing them to become feral, overly hostile, committing more heinous acts than those of which they were already capable. In an attempt to alleviate the situation, we decided to provide for them their own dwelling, though there were many here who resisted the idea. Young Dorwynn was still an apprentice then, but his unusually strong skill for growing plants provided me a way to create Nuathlyn without the assistance of the others who refused to participate. He had his own fears, but he accomplished the task as a personal favor to me."

"And earned your blessing," said Lilly, remembering the sacred mark.

"Yes. Over time, the home he grew for them, the only tree in existence that feeds on darkness instead of light, began to steal energy from the surrounding plant life. Death now spreads from it in all directions. I blame myself for this outcome, just as he blames himself."

"But, why?" asked Lilly. "You tried to do a good thing, and it's not his fault the tree is killing everything, is it?"

"I asked the favor of him," sighed Kiera, "because, as a faerie of light and life, I was unable to perform the magick necessary to grow a tree that could thrive on evil. Dorwynn has the singular ability to direct that magick, and it was necessary to keep Nuathlyn alive. No one, especially myself, could have foreseen such a result. My decree created this situation. The responsibility of resolving it now falls to me."

"How?"

"That is the riddle I must solve. I cannot deprive the banished faeries of their queendom, for their wild ways have abated since its creation, but I cannot allow such death to continue spreading. The tree thrives, growing stronger every day. If it isn't contained, it will spread throughout the forest, killing everything in its wake."

"I'm strong," said Lilly, jumping up so fast she hit the ceiling before she realized she was flying. "Ow." She rubbed her head, still trying to get over the fact she had antennae. "I could try to contain..."

"It is a tree of death," interrupted Eklain, her angelic voice ominous, "kept alive by the blood of the innocent. It consumes life, and if you get too close, it will consume yours. They say that a person who sees their reflection in its eye shall become overwhelmed with despair until it steals away their very essence."

"Its eye?" asked Lilly. "It has an eye?"

"It feeds on evil," chimed the faerie, her violet eyes wide. "It has become an abomination so vile that the blood of its victims courses within it. Only the pure of heart have a chance to survive, but the odds of survival decrease each day it grows stronger. You, above all others, cannot be put at risk."

Lilly asked no further questions. She didn't want to know any more about the faeries of Nuathlyn and their evil tree, and she prayed Eklain wouldn't continue. Kiera must have known what she was thinking.

"Eklain," she said, her voice bright, "would you be so kind as to prepare quarters for our guest?"

"Of course, Your Majesty," said the other, disappearing in a flash of violet light. Kiera waited until she was gone, then turned to Lilly, her eyes both stern and pleading.

"She is right," said the queen. "We cannot afford to risk your safety, but if you feel you are capable of containing this evil, I must request that you do so. Take great care in your actions, for you now know the result of unbridled magick, but I must ask this of you. I fear you may be our only hope. I do not have the support I need to rectify the situation."

"I'll do whatever I can to help," said Lilly, and suddenly, the prospect of facing the abominable tree wasn't so bad. Somehow, she felt she could do it, not only for Dorwynn's peace of mind, but also to make up for her own mistake of releasing the spawn. She shuddered as the thought of it still ravaging the land crossed her mind. *Yes,* she thought, *I'll repay this debt.*

"That is all I can hope for," said the queen. She looked toward the archway leading from the room and lifted herself from the ground, her wings whirring like a hummingbird's. "Come. By now, I'm sure they've gathered for your first night with us."

"What about sleep?" asked Lilly, unsure what time it was, but certain it was the early morning hours.

"Are you tired?"

"Actually, I'm not. How strange."

"Not as strange as you may think, young one. We faeries do not sleep, and as one of us, neither will you. You will feel no fatigue, no inclination to rest, and you will find your strength will not falter."

"Really?"

"Not until you are human again. Come now. The rest of the queendom awaits."

Lilly followed Kiera through the winding tunnels, vaguely reminded of the cavernous tunnels of the harpy lair. When they arrived at the center of the tree, it was already filled with faeries, most of whom were cluttering the floor. A few were perched atop bundles of branches woven throughout each other, crouching like little metallic frogs. Their eyes were even frog-like, wide and round, taking in every detail she had to offer. She wondered if her eyes were just as wide, staring in awe at the colorful crowd.

"Welcome," rang Kiera's crystal clear voice. "Tonight has brought a series of life-altering events. You all know of the destruction of the harpy lair, as well as the revelation of their rising power by the discovery of the spawn they held captive. It is a blessing in these dangerous times to have knowledge of such avarice, though the cost was the destruction of Ambala. We did not arrive to stop it. We did, however, manage to get there in time to save lives, as well as reestablish their livelihood. The balance is restored.

"For those of you who are not aware, the faerie beside me is Lilly of Elikrede, Arch Mage Gustave's most recent apprentice. She has the natural power to heal beings just as we have the power to heal plants. She saved many lives tonight. Due to the unique nature of her training, we will host her Master Trials in the coming days. Until that time, she will remain a guest of Saurabean to learn all she can of our purpose as Elemental Children. I know everyone will share with me the honor of her presence, and I'm certain she'll receive the respect she deserves."

Kiera's eyes rested on an electric blue faerie perched on the highest branch in the room. Lilly was sure it was Shira. The rest of the faeries dispersed, their movements marked by a whirlwind of tinkling bells and chime-like echoes, flitting and bounding among the tunnels. Only Shira remained on her perch, eyeing Lilly and the queen, a cloud of doubt shadowing her wide, exotic eyes.

Being a faerie was, so far, the easiest of her magickal training, not to mention the most enlightening. Her fears, her doubts, her unanswered questions...all had vanished from her thoughts as she absorbed the nuances of the world around her. Life was all that mattered now, and it thrived beyond anything Lilly could have imagined. Auras of glowing light surrounded every leaf and blossom on every tree, every individual petal on every flower, every blade of grass emerging from the rich earth.

She spent her first day with the faeries observing their rituals of assisting nature with the passing of spring, watching how their halos of light swirled around the blooming fruit trees and how insects like bees and butterflies swam through them to gather and carry pollen to other blossoms, thus continuing the process of the season. Blooms opened wider as the faeries cast their light toward the plants, nourishing them as though they radiated sunlight.

The insects captivated her the most. She'd never really noticed them, but now that she was nearly their size, it was evident how much she had overlooked. Most flitted from one place to another, their basic nutritional requirements driving them about their purposes, but some of the more cunning creatures, like the spiders, drew her rapt attention. It was a large spider, its black and yellow body nearly half her own length and the span of its legs more than double that, with a striped pattern cascading down its oblong body. The web in which she sat was a beautiful orb of perfection, built between two long reeds that blew together in the breeze. The insects that flew into the net-like web, or near enough to it to be caught, were left to struggle until their energy drained. The spider stayed patient, waiting for the least resistance before claiming her prize.

It's a battle everywhere, thought Lilly, perched upon a wide-capped mushroom as she watched the spider wrap her meal, saving it for later.

It is, another voice jumped into her mind. Already, she was used to this form of communication, so Lilly knew it was Kiera talking to her. *The battle for survival, however, is vastly different from the battle of good and evil.*

But in the end, isn't that what it's all about...survival?

Evil pursues to obtain as much as possible. The spider takes only what she needs to live, nothing more.

Surviving the battle is still the point. Fight or flee - either choice is one to survive.

As is everything in nature, said Kiera, *but you are basing your observations on creatures merely surviving, not living. They do not strive to reach their full potential when what they do is enough to survive. They do not wish for more than they need, nor do they try to obtain it.*

A lot of humans are like that, too.

Indeed. You will find many humans meander through their lives without purpose, though they all have a reason for being. Just as the moth in the web will feed the spider, so, too, the humans will feed the fire when the battle takes root.

How do you mean? asked Lilly, the spider no longer holding her interest. Her thoughts hadn't been about her future of unavoidable events, but faerie or not, she was inherently human and she wanted to know everything she could about what was to come.

What do you really know of Dagana? asked the queen, her eyes a vibrant red. Lilly shuddered as she recalled the same color of the queen's eyes in her dreams.

"Evil queen," said Lilly aloud. "That's about it." Kiera nodded.

"That she is, but do you know over what race she rules?" Lilly shook her head, her antennae bobbing side to side. "You have yet to understand the dynamics of a royal society, but most races here are governed under such a system...one ruler, or a pair at most, looking out for the best interest of the kingdom's subjects. Dagana rules the humans, Lilly. For decades she's ruled them, taking her powers to tyrannical proportions. Then she was idle for a time, after the death of her husband, and there was a bout of ease among the human race. When she returned, she was stronger than ever, and she had a new design. She wanted to rule over other races. She gathered an army and attacked, her main focus the kingdom of Nurzia, the elfin kingdom.

"She was not strong enough to defeat them, but her actions against the magickal community called forth the necessity of leaders and rulers of the different races to join together to create a commission, a unified group sworn to protect themselves and each other from Dagana's threat. The protection of humans is included within that decree. Dagana continued to recruit every ally she could, preparing a grand army for the war that would win her the world, when out of nowhere, she went idle again. Many years later we discovered she was raising a child, and though we continued to watch her, she remained inactive. She was still a stern ruler, but her tyranny had ceased."

"That's good, though," said Lilly, her eyes wide. "Isn't it?"

"If there is one thing we know of Dagana, it is that she returns from her idleness stronger than she was before. Last time, she was gone only four years, but her power more than doubled in that time. This time, it was fifteen years before she started showing any proactive action, which only began in the past year."

Since I arrived, thought Lilly. It was a random thought, not one she necessarily wanted to share with Kiera, and she hoped Kiera hadn't heard it. If she had, she showed no signs that she did. A yellow butterfly large enough for Lilly to ride was chirping among the flowers above her head. She watched it, caught for a moment in the glory of her surroundings, then turned back to Kiera and asked, "Do you think she'll be powerful enough to win this time?"

"We hope not," said Kiera, "but since there is such a division among so many races, it will be a difficult war to predict. The final battle between good and evil will force those divided to choose a side. They cannot fall away and take no part of it, for this war will affect the world."

"Why don't the other races join?"

"Many races wish to coexist simply by ignoring everything beyond the world they've created for themselves. They want no part of a war they believe has nothing to do with them." Kiera smiled then, stretching her wings and fluttering them, sending little flecks of prisms along the leaves and grass. *Have no fear, Lilly,* said Kiera, her thoughts gracing Lilly's mind like a warm breeze. *We of the Council are keeping a very close watch on Dagana.*

Kiera flew away in a flash of light, taking her rainbows with her. Lilly gazed for some time into the jungle around her, her thoughts a muddle of facts and emotions. She could feel everything around her - the plants, the insects, the other faeries - life breathing, an entity in itself, soothing her even as she considered Dagana and the war she knew was a result of her coming here. She reflected on everything she'd experienced with the faeries so far, committing every detail to memory. She fluttered her wings, casting her own rainbows along the plants, trying to decide what she liked best about this part of the world. She still wasn't used to the fact that faeries didn't sleep. She wasn't tired at all, though it was harder to keep track of the time without a sleep cycle.

Before she realized it, a series of storm clouds overtook the sky. Lilly flew toward the tree of Saurabean, taking shelter among the vast leaves from the huge raindrops tumbling from above. She left behind the prisms, the butterfly chirping among the blossoms, the spider and the moth, the glowing blades of grass and leaves on the trees, as a faint song was carried by the wind over the forest, soft and soothing like a lullaby, with the thunder keeping time, deep and menacing like a death march.

Each raindrop was lit from within, and when they struck an object, they burst into thousands of miniscule droplets, each one with its own tiny light inside. Lilly could feel plant life all around her rejuvenate with each drop of fresh rain as they drank it in. She was so absorbed, she didn't realize how close she was to Kiera and Shiva until their voices rose above the noise of the storm.

"I'll hear no more of it, Shira!" Kiera's voice, even in anger, was beautiful. "If you desire me to take your opinion seriously, do not force it upon me at every interval."

Lilly turned to the shouts in time to see a red streak of light and Shira, her wings beating at dangerous speeds, staring after her. Lilly turned around, pretending she didn't hear anything and hoping Shira wouldn't notice her there. A moment later, however, the blue faerie was standing over her, her arms crossed and a scowl on her face.

"She thinks you're strong enough to solve our problem with Nuathlyn," she said, staring down at Lilly. Lilly avoided her gaze. "She thought he was strong enough, but look where we are now. You know, if you're so strong, you should contain the spawn while you're at it."

Lilly lifted her head then, and with a serious look said, "I'm going to try or die trying. I can't promise you anything...except hope."

There was silence between them. For a while, only the thunder, the slight whistle as a raindrop fell and the splash when it struck could be heard. Shira sat on the branch beside Lilly, watching the sky grow darker as day gave way to night. Lilly could tell Shira wanted to talk but didn't want to be the first to speak, so she took the lead.

"What's you favorite part of nature?" she asked. The faerie looked shocked for a moment, then smiled, staring into the darkness.

"Mushrooms," she said. "They require just the right amounts of the four elements to exist, or they cannot come to be. Wind spreads their spores to multiply, but too much heat, not enough moisture, even a minute change in the earth's minerals, and nothing happens. Despite all that, there are more than ten thousand species of mushrooms, and each one requires a different amount of the elements. They're amazing."

"Amazing," echoed Lilly, and the two sat together in a more comfortable silence than before as Lilly thought, *I am the mushroom. Without the proper amount of magick from each element, I will not become the Chosen One.* This thought stayed with her as the night grew darker and she wished she could sleep, if just for a while. She almost missed her dreams...almost.

The Prophet Nadalice

"That is an unfair assessment, Nyeka," said Shira to a dark orange faerie with short, curly antennae. "You weren't there to know that's how it happened."

"Neither were the humans who wrote the damned thing," argued Nyeka. "When they wrote the Bible, they thought the world was flat! What else did they believe that was so far off course? How could they even presume to think they knew what they were scribing for all of history, and humanity? The Tree of Knowledge and the Tree of Life are one in the same, and yet humans still believe they are separate entities. No matter what we do to show them otherwise, they still put their faith into that abomination of a historical account."

"The message is the same, Nyeka," said Shira.

"That tree grew from magick itself as a gift for the new humans on Earth. It was *supposed* to bring them life and knowledge, and the men who wrote the Bible said it was wrong to eat from it! How can you defend that?"

"Must we continue this perpetual debate now?" said Eklain, her voice calm. "Our guest has come to say goodbye."

Lilly waited patiently while they argued their points, listening to each with unbiased attention. She had to admit to herself that they both had strong arguments, but why they were arguing, she didn't know. Kiera watched them banter with an amused look on her face, as though this was nothing out of the ordinary.

"I leave today," she said when the arguing ceased, "to take Lilly to Zalera, who will administer her Master Trials. When she passes, she will be returning to her home. Anyone wishing to bid her farewell must do so now, taking short time about it."

The rush of faeries coming toward her was overwhelming. They shook her hand, hugged her, whispered unintelligible advice and wished her luck, all of it happening so fast that it was over before Lilly could retain any of what they said. Shira remained after the others disappeared, holding her hand out to Lilly.

"Good luck," she said. "I hold to your promise of hope. Make sure you do the same."

"I will," said Lilly. She pulled the faerie into her arms, and when she broke the hug, she noticed the confusion on Kiera's face. She said nothing, and the queen asked her no questions. They left the sanctity of Saurabean, shooting like bullets into the sunlight of the afternoon.

Lilly flew with Kiera over the forest, the deep green canopy covering the underlying earth like a thick blanket. Earlier that day, just as the morning suns were cresting the horizon, Kiera had shown her how to call upon the element of Earth. It was easier than Lilly thought it would be, just a mediocre form of true magick, much like the spells of fundamental magick, which required her only to speak the words *kryet birem* before she attempted her earth tasks.

From below, Lilly was sure they were nothing more than two streaks of lights zooming through the sky as they flew toward Griffon Cove, the site where Lilly would attempt her Master Trials. The safe house was kept by a faerie named Zalera, the only faerie who remained in human form at all times.

"One child of each element," said Kiera earlier that day, "remains in human form to keep a safe house designed specifically for training purposes. Magickal signatures cannot be detected there, so there is no chance Dagana may discover the identities of any apprentices. Ashya's home is also a safe house." That made sense. Lilly always wondered why Ashya never took her unicorn form, something she very much wanted to see, but now realized might never happen. "When we arrive, I will teach you the nature of transfiguration. It is always easier when you are changing into something familiar, and since you are familiar with yourself, it shouldn't be a problem."

Right, thought Lilly, *as long as it doesn't hurt so much this time.*

"Transforming is uncomfortable," said Kiera, responding to Lilly's unspoken concern, "but transformation is simply changing your appearance. A magickal disguise, if you will. It doesn't hurt as much as transfiguration, or shapeshifting, as many call it, because there is no major change in size or anatomy. Shapeshifting is painful because it involves becoming a completely different creature. As you become accustomed to changing, you will find yourself becoming faster at it. The pain subsides faster, as well."

"Does everyone who can shapeshift feel pain?" she asked, wondering again about Rohan. Most of the time he was human, but when he changed into a pterippus, he was so big. Surely he didn't feel as much pain as she did when they changed her into a faerie.

"Those who are born with the ability become used to it, and those who learn it, if they change often enough, can become desensitized to the pain, but it is always there until the change is complete."

They were at Griffon Cove before she knew it, and when Kiera landed at the opening of a cave, she changed into her human form at once. Lilly hesitated. She already knew how the magick worked, but she feared the pain, and with good reason. Kiera's advice was to focus on her human form and release the magick when she was ready, but when she let go, when she allowed the magick to overtake her senses, she almost screamed from the pain. It hurt so much more than when they had changed her. She endured it, just as she endured the pain from her last embrace with Wyatt, and finally, she was human again.

"Very good," said Kiera. "Rest. I will find Zalera."

Kiera entered the cave while Lilly fell to her knees, trying to regain her composure. Her legs felt like rubber and her head pounded, and she felt heavy, like her whole body was made of lead. The absence of wings had more of an effect on her than anything else and she had a hard time believing she'd only been with the faeries for three days. She'd gotten so used to it that it seemed like much longer.

While she waited for Kiera to emerge from the cave with the human faerie, Lilly gazed at the cliffs around her. A line of mountains surrounded a beautiful paradise cove of water on three sides, and within the mountains were hundreds of caves, occupied with the most amazing creatures she had ever seen. Griffons soared among the caves, perching on the small rock ledges in front of their nests to observe her. One in particular was watching her with rapt attention from across the cove. It was female, for Lilly could see that she was close to giving birth, and she paced around her own nest ledge before settling in front of the door, her deep black eyes never leaving Lilly.

"Griffons," said a voice behind her. Lilly turned to face the faerie, who shimmered from head to toe like a giant diamond. Her skin sparkled and her hair looked like spun silver. Even her eyes were white, just a bare hint of silver flecks among her irises. "I've never seen one so interested in a human. You must be special."

"I am Lilly."

"Greetings, Lilly," said the faerie. "I am Zalera. Let us begin your trials."

The trials involving the plants were the easiest, especially after spending time as a faerie. She grew a tree from a seed in a matter of minutes, and then, as her next task was to manipulate an already grown plant, she moved the tree, roots and all, lower on the mountain along a ridge of bushes, where she planted it deep within the earth.

She raised a namun easily, though creating a cave within the mountain proved to be a more difficult task than she thought it would be, but since she was required to also show that she could call upon the element for support, she whispered the words *kryet birem* rather than focusing on the fact that she should have brought her wand. It took a while, and she could feel her strength dissipating as she finished the cave, but when she was done, there was a new nesting area for the creatures of Griffon Cove.

"I am informed that you created your own wand," said Zalera when she had performed her last task. "It seems there is but one thing to do. Kiera?"

Kiera stood before Lilly, her arms outstretched to take her hands. Lilly felt a warmth flow through her as she took the faerie's hands, different than the heat of magick, but just a wondrous. Kiera smiled, bowing her head first to Zalera and then to Lilly.

"Like the steady Earth," she said, her voice ringing with awe and inspiration, "your education in the ways of Earth Magick becomes the foundation for your future endeavors, solid and unmoving. It is up to you to use this knowledge for the good of all and to maintain the balance of all things greater or smaller than yourself. Wielding such power should be respected and honored. You have completed the tasks set forth to obtain the status of Master Sorceress of Earth Magick. Master Lilly of Elikrede, I congratulate you on your success. It has been an honor to be involved with your education."

"Thank you," said Lilly, her voice barely a whisper. Her sense of accomplishment at that moment was greater than anything she'd ever felt. She released Kiera's hand, and as she did, a swirl of green light surrounded her hand, searing a painless green crescent on the inside of her right wrist, the mark of her status among the magickal community.

"No, Lilly," said Kiera, "thank you for what you plan to do for us and for whatever you said to Shira to ease her mind. You are special, and you must always remember that you are. Come. We must get you to the safety of the forest floor."

Kiera transfigured into the small red faerie, but Lilly took a step back, looking down at the ground over the edge of the cliff.

"Um, I'll find my own way down," she said, trying to avoid having to transfigure again. Zalera smiled, and without a word, she motioned to the griffon across the cove who had been watching Lilly during the course of her trials. The creature stretched her broad wings, which were the same tawny color as the rest of her body, and flew toward them, landing in front of Zalera, who whispered into the creature's ear. The griffon bowed her head, then turned her back toward Lilly and lowered the wing nearest to her.

"She will take you to the edge of the forest near Ambala," said Zalera. "From there, you can find your way home."

"Are you sure?" asked Lilly, staring at the creature in awe. "She's pregnant. Should she be carrying me?"

"She is strong. I would not recommend turning down such an offer. It is a great honor to be offered service by a griffon, especially for a human. Declining may insult her."

"Thank you," Lilly whispered to the creature. She bowed her head, allowing Lilly to swing easily onto her back, then turned toward Zalera, who seemed like she was listening to a voice that wasn't there.

"Of course," said Zalera, nodding once to the griffon. "She wishes you to return to Griffon Cove after your first harvest."

"Yes, of course" said Lilly, delighted by the invitation.

The griffon peered over the edge of the cliff, then spread her wings and dove. Lilly gripped her own arms, which were wrapped around the creature's neck, and scolded herself for being afraid to transfigure. This ride was more terrifying than any pain she could endure, and she closed her eyes, holding tight until the vertigo passed. The griffon leveled as the canopy of the forest drew near, and she soared lazily above it, slowing her speed to a tolerable level for the human upon her back. Lilly relaxed, enjoying the rest of their journey until the griffon took a nosedive into a barely visible space between the trees, landing with feather-light steps on the ground below.

"Thank you," said Lilly as she slid from the creature's back. She ran her fingers over the silky feathers around her head and down the length of her smooth coat to her haunches, amazed at the beauty of the creature. "It was an honor." The griffon stared at her, and though Lilly could not understand how the creature communicated with Zalera, she felt by the look in her eyes that she, too, was honored by the ride.

She could have gone straight home. She'd magicked herself there so often over the past six weeks, it took little strength to do so anymore, even from Orvak's swamp, and Ambala wasn't much further from there. It would have been easy, but Lilly couldn't suppress the urge to check on the inhabitants of Ambala, especially Voruum and his family.

The walk through the forest was different. For the first time since she had arrived, she was completely alone, and as the last rays of the suns disappeared, giving way to the bright moon, she noticed how dismal the forest seemed. The canopy was so full it allowed very little moonlight to pass through the heavily intertwined branches. What little light that found its way through the sparser areas was just enough to cast an eerie glow, forming shadows upon shadows that all but concealed the worn path leading to Ambala.

As she walked, she dreamed of the paradise straight above her, just beyond the mountain ridge, where the gorgeous creatures there dove into the water only to emerge with a large fish, where they soared above the clouds and shined beneath the light of the bright suns, which reflected off the water in the cove, making the whole scene more dreamlike. She only caught a glimpse of how the cove narrowed where the mountains came together, then expanded into a calm ocean, so still it could have been a mirror lying on the ground, but she knew she could not dream of a more beautiful place. Rohan's description did not do it justice.

Alone, the dense forest seemed like the memories of a nightmare. Animals moved silently through the trees like spirits, stopping as she crossed their paths as though she was the spirit. She quickened her pace as the trees grew farther apart, and before long, she could see the newly built homes among the tree line. For a moment, she wondered if she was in the right place, for the meadow looked nothing like it had when she left it three days ago. Already, their gardens were growing again, and the growth was tremendous. New grass had emerged in the recently scorched meadow, and the smell of the damp earth brought with it the promise of growth and renewal. The faeries had performed a miracle. The creatures of Ambala would have their crops, and Lilly wanted to cry from the joy of knowing they would survive the brutal attack.

She wandered around the edge of the meadow, searching for the familiar face of her friend. Others were milling about, working even in the darkness to repair what damage remained. The centaur she had met when she first arrived was cradling an infant in her arms. Her arm was still badly burned and she was missing patches of hair and fur, but she looked content as she gazed at her newborn child.

"May I?" asked Lilly as she approached her, standing on her tiptoes. The centaur smiled and lowered the baby to her level. "He's beautiful."

"Yes," she crooned, stroking the sleeping child's face. Lilly touched the burn on her arm, healing it before the centaur could ask what she was doing. Since she didn't protest, Lilly continued to heal the rest of her wounds, which were minor in comparison to the many she'd healed days ago. "You have the natural power to heal," said the centaur.

"I know," said Lilly. "I didn't see you the night of the attack. I thought maybe you..." She couldn't finish her sentence.

"No," said the centaur. "He came that night while I was hiding in the woods. His father found us the next morning." She hugged the child to her chest, staring at Lilly all the while. "You will notice that people are drawn to you. They will feel compelled to be close to you, especially if they are lacking in some way, and they will be honored to be in your presence. It comes with the gift of healing."

Lilly didn't know how to respond to that, so she smiled and said, "I'm glad you and your son are safe. I must find Voruum, but would you tell me your name before I go, so that I may visit you again?"

"Chloe, and I named him Ramier."

"Goodbye, Chloe. Take care of him."

"Voruum's hut is the third one past the well. Goodbye, Lilly."

Lilly walked past the well, which still held proof of the attack on the charred stone, and found the small hut butted against the tree line. A soft orange glow filtered through the only window, light from a fire, no doubt, and Lilly shivered, wondering if she would ever be able to look at a fire again without images of the spawn flashing in her mind. She knocked gently on the door, and the sound of hooves on soft ground came from within before the door swung open. Voruum's wife, a brown and white minotaur who resembled her husband but for the horns and a few inches in height, smiled as she recognized the girl who had saved her life.

"Welcome, Master Lilly of Elikrede," she said, her voice deep, but soft. "Please, come inside."

"She's doing well," said Voruum's wife, looking at her daughter sleeping in a small bed of hay in the corner of the room, a single blanket draped over her. Lilly had learned her name was Nadalice, she and Voruum had been married for three years and they wanted a large family. Savara was their first child.

"I can heal her arm now, if you like," offered Lilly, looking at Savara and the makeshift cast on her arm.

"Thank you," said Nadalice, "but I think the natural order of things will do that quite well enough. We cannot shelter our children from every hardship, or they will not have the strength to deal with it later in life, when they might not have help." Lilly nodded, staring at the cup of creamy liquid before her. She still hadn't tasted it. "It's minotaur milk," said Nadalice, noticing Lilly's wary look. Lilly took a careful sip, not wanting to offend Nadalice. It was thicker then she expected it would be, and very sweet. It reminded her of eggnog.

"Will Voruum be back tonight?" asked Lilly, licking her top lip.

"Much later. He's with the others in the forest gathering supplies to continue our reconstruction."

"He said you wanted to meet me. May I ask why?"

"I knew you were going to save Savara's life. I saw it in her future."

"You can see the future?" asked Lilly, intrigued.

"Not in the sense you may think," said Nadalice. "There are many who have the talent who see it as though it is a dream, a continuous scene flowing through their subconsciousness. What I do is very different. I'm a prophet, not a requiest. Magick speaks to me directly, and what images I do see are quick, hazy flashes that often depict events, though not necessarily outcomes."

"So you receive prophecies like the prophecy of the Chosen One?" asked Lilly, and Nadalice chuckled.

"I'm not that in tune with my gift," she said. "The prophecies I receive come only when I am focusing on a specific person, touching them or something of their possession. I could read you, if you like."

"Yes, please," said Lilly, sitting straighter in her uncomfortable chair. Maybe Nadalice could help her figure out what so many of her own visions meant, if that's what her dreams actually were.

"Alright," said Nadalice, "but before we begin, there are a few things you should know. Reading the future, whether requiest or prophet, is an imperfect art. The future has yet to happen, and while certain events are destined to happen, outcomes can change. The events that occur around each of us, and the choices we make regarding those events, determine our destinies. This reading is based not only on the events destined to occur in your life, but also the choices you are apt to make at this time. Because we change with every event that occurs, and therefore our choices change, the outcomes change as well. Knowing the future is enough to change it, and in some cases, knowledge of a future event can bring it into being if you try too hard to avoid it. Reading the future is practiced only to provide insight of events or situations you will face, not to predict results, so let nothing I say to you alter your choices as of yet."

"Okay," said Lilly, entranced. Nadalice laid her hands on the table in front of Lilly, her palms up. Lilly put her hands in them.

"First, I will read you as an individual, and then we shall delve into your future." Nadalice wrapped her fingers around Lilly's, closing her eyes. Lilly felt the warmth of magick enveloping her as the minotaur's breathing slowed to a deep, meditative pace. Savara's gentle snores and the crackling of the low fire in the hearth were the only sounds in the room, and they formed a rhythmic beat that lulled Lilly into the same meditation.

"Your soul is torn," said Nadalice, her voice low and even, though ringing with a higher-pitched echo. "Never have you felt truly whole, and so your soul remains in perpetual turmoil. Though your heart is pure, your head is cluttered. Such over-complications often lead to poor decisions. Your distrust of others distracts you from your destined path. You follow willingly those charged with your care, but you are a born leader. Many will follow you just as readily, but many more will need persuasion. You will be the key to their salvation."

Nadalice paused, her body rigid as though she was listening to a voice far in the distance, her eyes moving under her lids, like she might have been dreaming. Lilly was shaken by the information she'd already given her and how accurate she was in that information. She waited, wondering if there was more, but afraid to say anything for fear it would break the prophet's concentration.

"A history of misunderstanding requires correction," she continued, never opening her eyes. "Your past is relevant to your future. A decision made in desperation for answers will bring enlightenment to complete the awakening. A blood bath, a willing spill. Powers that will grow beyond anyone's expectations. Take care not to allow them to turn you from the destiny you are *meant* to follow."

Blessed by the four elements, rang another voice, angelic and seductive in Lilly's ear. Nadalice continued her reading without stopping, oblivious to the voice interrupting her.

"Though your identity is hidden, do not deny it. Denial of who you are will lead to a great downfall. Acceptance begets success. You are bonded to those close to you by lifetimes of connections. They are significant to your destiny. An unlikely ally, an unexpected foe. A deadly evil contained. One will keep you on the right path; one will distract you from it. You will rescue him, he will rescue you. A declaration of love will destroy the heart of two, or the lives of many..."

...dark one made of light...

"Betrayal will come to you from two whom you trust, one by subconscious fault, one by selfish design. Use logic rather than emotion to issue judgment. An unforgiven trespass will lead to disaster. A pure heart will carry you from danger. In a fatal distraction, she will sacrifice her life for you, and it will weigh on your heart forever..."

...will die thinking only of you...

"A grave mistake will be made; a great price will be paid. A truth discovered will alter the course of your life and the lives of those who put their faith in you if you stray too far from your course. A significant gathering in a sacred place where only fools journey, the answer to an ancient question..."

...even nothing is something...

"The death of one shall be the life of both. A sacred gift lies dormant within. A great leap of faith is required to fulfill your destiny. Become lost in an invisible city to find the hidden path. Stoop to the level of your enemies to gain victory over them."

...they will all bow to you.

Lilly dropped Nadalice's hands and felt the connection with magick break as the final words of the haunting voice echoed in her mind. The prophet opened her eyes, and noticing the stricken look on Lilly's face, took her right hand again.

"Don't let it overwhelm you," she said, her eyes deep with understanding. "Remember what I told you before we began. The events may still occur, but your choices will determine the outcome."

"That's what scares me," whispered Lilly. She felt shaken to her core as the words of the prophet and those of the mysterious voice mingled in her mind. What frightened her most were the references to the deaths bound to happen in her future, of which both Nadalice and the voice spoke. Even worse, Lilly had no idea *who* was destined to die, but the fact that someone was going to sacrifice her life for her and die thinking only of her only made her feel less significant. Was she worth that kind of sacrifice?

"Hello, my love," said Nadalice with a smile, drawing Lilly from her thoughts. She turned around to find Voruum standing in the doorway behind her.

"Hello," he said. "Have I returned at a bad time?"

"No," said Nadalice, rising from her chair to kiss her husband. "We are finished." She turned to Lilly, who rose from her own chair, the discomfort of it long forgotten, and hugged her. "It was a pleasure, Lilly. You are welcome here anytime you want to come."

"Than you," she whispered, feeling self-conscious under Voruum's scrutinizing stare.

"I will retire so that you may have some time alone." Nadalice kissed Voruum's cheek and whispered, "Goodnight" in his ear, then began to clean the cups from the table.

"Come, Lilly," said Voruum, holding open the door. Lilly stepped through it into the darkness. By now, everyone who was milling about when she arrived had retired for the night, and the still of night had long since settled over Ambala. She walked with Voruum toward the vast meadow into its center, where he sat on the ground. She sat beside him.

"She read for you?" he asked. Lilly nodded. "I figured she would. She was hoping you would let her. Are you alright?" Lilly shrugged, too overwhelmed to speak about it. "Don't worry. I don't want to know what she told you. A reading is a very personal thing. You should take heed in what information you share with others, as well as in whom you confide. It's unwise to tell everything to any one soul. You never know how they might use the information."

Betrayal will come to you from two whom you trust...

"I'll remember that," she said quietly. They sat together in silence, Voruum's eyes lifted to the starry sky. Lilly looked up as well, searching for the familiar constellation Rohan had pointed out to her only weeks ago. She couldn't find it, but as late as it was, she figured it had settled beyond the horizon.

"War is inevitable," said Voruum, his declaration shocking Lilly. "It's written in the stars, in our histories. I have known for some time that I would see it in my lifetime."

"That doesn't mean you have to be involved in it," said Lilly. "You have a family who needs you. Your place is with them."

"They are the very reason I will fight," he said, looking at her. She could see the resolution in his eyes. "They deserve a better world than this, and I will do all I can to make sure they have it. When the war comes, I will be at your side. My loyalty lies with you and no other." He turned his eyes toward the sky again, though Lilly was staring at him in utter disbelief. "I speak on behalf of everyone in Ambala. We are yours to command."

A Riddle Solved

Lilly was never so glad to be back home. She was as quiet as possible, expecting everyone to be asleep, but Zephra was lying on the sofa, wide awake, when she entered the house.

"What are you doing up?" asked Lilly. "It's the middle of the night."

"I was waiting for you," said Zephra, sitting up to make room for Lilly, who plopped down beside her, exhaling a deep sigh. "Congratulations."

Lilly looked at the mark on her arm, brushing her finger over the green crescent. It shimmered in the light of the only candle in the room.

"Thanks," she said. "Where's Dorwynn?"

"I let him have my room. He's...dealing with some issues right now."

"Gustave?"

"He told you?"

"Yeah." Lilly leaned into the sofa, resting the top of her head against it and staring at the ceiling. There was a cobweb dangling from the corner over the door, reminding her of the daily maintenance she'd recently been too preoccupied to notice. There were probably cobwebs all over the house, and dust, but she couldn't make herself care. "Do you think Gustave is using him?"

"Dorwynn is convinced he's using their connection to make him do things he wouldn't normally do," said Zephra, choosing her words carefully, "but I think Gustave is better than that. He's just not capable of that kind of deception."

"Yeah," sighed Lilly, grateful Zephra agreed with her, "that's what I think, too." She closed her eyes, relaxing as the familiarity of home surrounded her. She knew she should go to bed, or at least record in her journal everything that had happened over the past few days, but all she wanted to do was sit, relax, breathe.

"Are you tired?" asked Zephra.

"Not really," said Lilly without opening her eyes. "I should be, but I've got too much on my mind."

"Tell me about it."

"I don't even know where to start."

"How did you know about the spawn?" Lilly opened her eyes and lifted her head, looking Zephra dead in the eye.

"He told you?"

"Of course," she said. "How could he not tell me? He said you healed a lot of people, too. Probably saved their lives."

"I had to. It was my fault the spawn was there."

"How do you know that?"

With a sigh, Lilly began her story. She told Zephra about the dream right before leaving for Ambala and gave her a very detailed account of the attack on Ambala, including how she lured it away and the explosion it caused before it disappeared. She skipped over her time with the faeries, and after a brief description of her Master trials and the griffon that delivered her to the forest, she repeated Voruum's words to her about the upcoming war.

"He swore his loyalty to you?" asked Zephra, incredulous. "They're such peaceful creatures. I can't believe he would commit his whole community to such a thing, especially since the war hasn't even started yet."

"This war is going to be bad, isn't it?" asked Lilly.

"Aren't they all?"

"Yeah, but...well, some are bigger than others."

Zephra nodded, amazed that Lilly had, for lack of a better term, recruited the first of her followers. She could see in Lilly's eyes that there was much more the girl wanted to divulge, so she went to the kitchen, returning with two glasses of tea and some cookies. Lilly took one from the plate, her eyebrows high in surprise.

"Yes," said Zephra, "I baked. I got bored."

"They're good," admitted Lilly, taking a bite.

"Thanks," she said, settling back into the sofa. "The war will come, and when it does, everyone will have to choose a side. I'm just surprised that people are already pledging themselves to you."

"I'm not. I saw a prophet while I was there." Surprise returned to Zephra's face, but she said nothing. "She told me there would be many who would follow me, but that more would have to be convinced."

"Well, it seems you have followers, and word of your feats is spreading. Before long, you'll have more."

"So much for keeping a low profile," muttered Lilly. Zephra smiled.

"Personally, I don't think it's such a bad thing. I mean, we'll have to work harder to keep you out of Dagana's reach, but people are hopeful. They're desperate for a savior, and they'll follow whoever they believe will be that savior."

"And if I'm not," asked Lilly, "what happens to all of them?"

"Why do you doubt it?"

"The prophet said I shouldn't let my great power distract me from the destiny I'm meant to follow."

"So?"

"I don't know," sighed Lilly, rubbing her temples. "The way she said it made it seem like I might be following the wrong one."

"What else did she say," asked Zephra, intrigued, and then she added, "if you don't mind my asking?"

Voruum's warning about sharing the information flashed through Lilly's mind, and she knew she wouldn't tell Zephra everything she had learned, but she needed to talk to someone about it, and who better than an immortal being with the experience to help her figure some of it out? She was silent as she sorted through everything in the reading, choosing what to tell her and what to keep only for herself. Zephra waited patiently until she was ready to speak.

"She said I was a born leader, though I don't see that, and she said that I would be the key to their salvation."

"Do you need any more proof of who you are, Lilly? Who else would be the key to the salvation of so many but the Chosen One?"

"She said so many odd things, though. It's like she was talking about someone else, but I know it was about me. Some things weren't even complete sentences, just phrases that made no sense."

"Well," said Zephra, "it's hard to decipher everything a prophet says. Magick speaks to them in ways no one else can comprehend, and they are responsible for translating it into words you can understand. It tends to make them speak in riddles."

It came out of nowhere. She hadn't thought about the riddle since she first read it from the scroll hidden inside the tasil in her room, buried within the pages of the grimoire itself. *Salvation...*one of the words capitalized in the poem...*and organized, the right words said reveals the prophecy...they are responsible for translating it...* Suddenly, everything clicked.

"Oh my gosh," she gasped, jumping from the sofa and racing up the stairs to her room, Zephra close on her heels.

"What's wrong?" asked Zephra as Lilly grabbed her dagger from her nightstand and then kneeled before the hidden doorway. "What are you doing?" Lilly ignored her as she sliced the end of her thumb, and she ignored the look of shock on Zephra's face as she wiped a drop of blood on the edge of the wall, opening the door to reveal the grimoire, the pedestal, and all the contents of blood magick it contained. Before Zephra could ask her anything else, she had the box in her hand, the ring and scroll inside.

"Come with me," said Lilly, rushing past her down the stairs and out the front door. She ran as fast as she could to the stone garden, stopping in front of the gravestone in her dream, the one where her grandfather was buried. "I figured it out," she said, gasping for breath as she handed the scroll to Zephra, who couldn't hide her astonishment. She read it as Lilly continued. "Don't you see? The right words said are the words in the poem that are capitalized, only they have to be spoken in the *Doret Gaia* and in the right order."

"And then what?" asked Zephra, too shocked by the turn of events to be cautious.

"Let's find out," said Lilly, exhilarated at the prospect of getting some answers bubbling through her voice. "Quick, translate the words."

"Salvation is *adiner*," said Zephra, looking at the scroll. "Power is *turmak*. Knowledge is *lamkile*. Truth is...um...*ozia*."

Lilly nodded, turning toward the gravestone, when a thought struck her. She looked at Zephra and asked, "What does vula mean?"

"Why would you ask me that?" whispered Zephra in a tone that made Lilly even more curious.

"That's what Orvak calls me."

"He calls you vula?"

"Yes. What does it mean?"

"I'll let him tell you," said Zephra, taunting Lilly with a smile. "Trust me, it will mean more coming from him." Lilly frowned, which made Zephra's smile broaden. "So, are you going to do this or not?"

Lilly circled the obelisk, searching for the worn carving of the teardrop. When she found it, she put her hand on it. It might not help to touch it, but it couldn't hurt. She repeated the words Zephra had translated and waited. Nothing happened.

"Maybe the words aren't in the right order," suggested Zephra. "Try them a different way."

"How?"

"I don't know. Say them in reverse. It makes sense. Truth is knowledge. Knowledge is power. Power is salvation."

"*Ozia lamkile turmak adiner,*" whispered Lilly. The teardrop on the stone began to glow green, and a low hum rumbled within the ground beneath it. Lilly took a step backward to stand beside Zephra, whose eyes were locked on the swarm of glowing, spinning balls of green that shot from the top of the obelisk, spiraling around it before they dove beneath the earth, a vortex of green light being sucked into the tomb. Lilly froze with fear as the memory of her dream rushed back to her.

"Get back," she said, tugging on Zephra's arm. "We're too close."

"Too close for what?" she asked, still watching the trail of green light burying itself beneath the stone.

Lilly ducked as the ground exploded, and though she wasn't thrown from the tomb, she scrambled further away from it, hiding behind a tall headstone to watch what she knew was coming. Zephra was close, hiding behind a headstone near her, her eyes glued to the obelisk. A ghostly figure appeared in the dying green light, shrouded in a shimmering gold cloak, a man Lilly did not recognize but from the dream she'd had of him. He walked toward her, floating over the damp earth. She stood as a feeling of awe settled over her.

He began to speak, his words spoken in the language she was just beginning to learn, and she could do nothing but stare at his mouth as it moved. Zephra was beside her again, and she spoke as he did, translating as much as she could so Lilly could understand.

"He was a member of the royal family," she said, trying to listen to him as she spoke, "murdered before his time. He saw visions of his demise, and in an attempt to protect his child, he chose to be buried rather than cremated so that she could use his blood, no...his bones, to remain hidden from evil."

"The skull is his," whispered Lilly, more to herself than Zephra.

"His blood is that of royalty, and his own prophecy said that his blood would be the key to salvation." Zephra gasped, turning her wide eyes to Lilly, who almost fainted when she heard those words. "Lilly..."

"He's still talking," she said in a rush.

"He instructed his daughter how to protect herself, and if that protection failed, she should enter the doorway to the beyond and find peace with a new life in the new world, but she should return before her death to open the path to her own children, so that his bloodline would continue here."

The figure drew closer to Lilly, and she stepped away from him, preparing for the attack in her dream. He wore a sad expression, one of longing and suffering, and he lifted his transparent hand to caress her face.

"He says there is no need to fear him. He can see in your eyes the purity in your soul. He thinks you look like your father. He wishes to tell you more, but..."

Zephra stopped talking. The man turned toward her, nodding, and Zephra shook her head in protest. He nodded again, pointing at Lilly, his face now stern. He said something to Zephra which Lilly did not understand, and Zephra answered him in the same language. They had their argument for a moment, and then Zephra turned to Lilly, closing her eyes and taking a deep breath before she spoke.

"He wishes to tell you more," she said, though it was clear in her voice she did not want Lilly to know whatever it was the spirit was saying, "but his daughter's prophecy must be told only by her. He says your mother was special, too, and more powerful than anyone thought she would be, but her power wasn't enough to save her life. She ran out of time before she could conceal her spirit as he did, so the spell you used to awaken him will not work on her tomb, but he knows you will find a way to discover what you must. Her past is important to who you are and what you must do for your own destiny." Zephra paused as the spirit once again caressed Lilly's face, now streaming with tears. He was gazing at her as he spoke his final words. "Your tears are the sign of this world's salvation. They are a gesture of your never-ending compassion. That is what this world has always needed from you, what it needs from you now. Always shed a tear for them, and they shall always be saved."

The figure smiled a sad smile, brushing his ghostly fingers over Lilly's cheek as though he was trying to catch a tear. He nodded to her once, almost a bow, and then he floated toward the obelisk that marked his tomb. He lifted his hand in a farewell gesture, and then he faded away as the first rays of the morning suns struck the stone above him.

"Lilly, stop!"

Lilly was walking toward the house, but for as fast as she was going, she may as well have been running. Zephra kept pace beside her, trying to calm her down and failing miserably.

"This is why I didn't want to tell you what he said. I knew you'd get upset."

"I'm not upset," said Lilly. "Really. I'm just ready to figure everything out."

"You will," said Zephra, "but you need to slow down. In the past week, you've fought in a duel, invaded and destroyed a harpy lair, went up against a spawn, and healed an entire town." She grabbed Lilly hand and jerked her to a stop. "You need to take a break."

"Zephra, I've been waiting to find out about my mother since I first arrived here. I had to train, so I waited. I had to master my trials first. I've done that, and I only have so much time before I have to start it all over again with Amparo. This might be the only opportunity I have."

They stared at each other, neither willing to relent. Lilly didn't push the issue; she didn't even try to pull her hand from Zephra's grasp. The desperate look on her face was all it took for Zephra to concede. She let go of Lilly's hand.

"You need to eat something," she said, crossing her arms, "and you need some sleep. Amparo isn't coming to get you until after the first harvest. We have plenty on time to focus on this."

"We?" asked Lilly, smiling. Zephra sighed, rolling her eyes.

"Come on," she said. "I'll make you some breakfast."

Breakfast, however, was already cooking. The smell of sausage hit them when they entered the house, and they could hear the sound of eggs being cracked and sizzling as they dropped into a skillet of hot grease. Dorwynn was at the stove, tossing empty eggshells at the garbage can halfway across the room.

"Where did you go?" he asked as he shook pepper over the eggs. "I thought it was your morning to cook."

"Something came up," said Zephra. She took three cups from the cupboard, poured dryka from the kettle on the stove into two of them, and filled the third with the fresh orange juice sitting on the countertop. Dorwynn noticed the third cup and whirled around, smiling when he saw Lilly sitting at the kitchen table.

"Lilly," he said. "You're home."

"She arrived early this morning," said Zephra, handing a cup of dryka to Dorwynn and the juice to Lilly.

"I see you passed your trials," he said, turning back to the stove. "Congratulations. Welcome to the wonderful world of magickal society."

"Thanks," she mumbled, sipping her juice. Now that she was sitting, and in a comfortable chair no less, fatigue washed over her. She yawned against her will.

"You see," said Zephra, "you need to sleep." Lilly rolled her eyes, but yawned again, and Zephra shot her an I-told-you-so look.

"Breakfast first," said Dorwynn, setting a prepared plate in front of each of them.

"You're in a good mood," said Zephra. "What's the occasion?"

"Can't a guy just be in a good mood?" He started humming as he walked away, while both girls stared at him, Zephra confused, Lilly amused. He returned to the table with his plate and forks for all of them.

"It looks great, Dorwynn," said Lilly. "Thank you."

"No problem," he said, biting into a sausage. "I saw Quinn yester..."

"How is he?" interrupted Lilly, perking up.

"He's adapting very well to family life. He's worried about you, though. He wanted me to ask you if you would visit him soon."

"I'll go today."

"Tomorrow," said Zephra. "You need to relax, and he can wait one more day to see you."

"Okay." Lilly was dying to see Quinn, to tell him about the faeries and Griffon Cove, but she was so tired, she didn't have the strength to argue the point. Zephra was right. She needed to rest. "I'm think I'm going to go to bed now."

"You've barely eaten anything," said Zephra. "Finish your breakfast first." Lilly rushed through the rest of her breakfast while Dorwynn watched, fascinated by their exchange. When she cleaned her plate, she drained her juice in one shot and carried her dishes to the sink. "I'll do the dishes. Goodnight, Lilly."

"Night."

"What's with you bossing her around like that," asked Dorwynn, "and with her listening, for that matter?"

"Nothing," said Zephra, finishing her meal. "She's so tired she's not really thinking clearly."

Dorwynn shook his head and carried his empty plate to the sink. He was about to sit back down when Lilly peeked around the corner and said, "Dorwynn, can I talk to you for a minute?"

"Sure." He followed her to the living room, standing near the front door and out of Zephra's earshot. "What's up?"

"Remember when I woke up from the coma after the harpy attack?"

"Vaguely," he said with a grin.

"I had a lot of dreams, or visions quests, I guess. One of them was about you. We had a conversation and you told me about not using your true name and, in the quest, you gave me a flower that you grew in your hand. That's how I figured out who you were."

"I always wondered how you knew it was me."

"That was you in the quest, right?"

"Yes," he answered cautiously.

"Why don't you remember that conversation? I mean, I asked you specific questions, which you answered. How come you didn't know how I figured it out?"

"Wow," he said, sighing. "Well, I don't really know. Quests aren't something I'm able to do, so I don't understand the form of magick behind them, but I used to dream about you all the time before you came, about how our first meeting would be when we found each other. I remember wanting to tell you about using my true name, or not using it. I remember dreaming about the flower, too. Quests and dreams are similar. I know that they take place in the same part of the mind, which is probably why you experienced the quests while in the coma. I guess maybe, somehow, you were able to tap into my dreams, or my subconsciousness."

"Oh," she said, a little disheartened. "Okay."

"Why do you want to know?"

"Just curious, I guess."

"Lilly..." he said in a tone that told her he knew there was more to it.

"I saw my mom in one of the quests," she admitted. "I talked to her, too. I just wondered how it worked, so maybe I could talk to her again."

"I see. Well, Amparo is the quest expert. If it can be done, she'll be able to tell you how to do it."

"Okay, thanks." She started up the stairs, stopping after one step and turning to look at him. She stared at him, noticing the difference in his appearance, studying his eyes, his smile, and for the first time since she was twelve years old, she saw her friend in him again. She stepped closer to him, put her arms around him and hugged him tight. "It's good to see you again, Adrian," she whispered in his ear. "I missed you." She let go of him, smiling at his bewildered expression. "Goodnight, Dorwynn," she said in a normal tone, and climbing the stairs, she sang, "Goodnight, Zephra!"

"What was that all about?" asked Dorwynn, returning to the kitchen.

"All of what?" asked Zephra, absorbed in her dishwashing.

"She's acting strange."

"I told you, she's tired. Four nights of no sleep is catching up to her."

"She was a faerie for three of those. Faeries don't sleep."

"I know, but creatures who require sleep are used to giving their minds a rest. She's been learning and doing and thinking for four straight days."

"Yeah," said Dorwynn, looking at the ceiling toward her room, "I guess you have a point, but there's more to it. Something happened while she was gone."

"What makes you say that?" asked Zephra, her hand suspended in midair over a plate, now absorbed in the conversation.

"All of a sudden, she's worried about talking to her mother. Has she said anything to you?" Zephra didn't respond. She started scrubbing the few remaining dishes violently, like she was shining a pair of shoes. Dorwynn stepped up right behind her, leaned close to her ear and said, "Zephra, what happened?"

"I can't tell you," she said, rinsing the last plate. She got out a dry towel and started wiping them, putting them into the cupboard. "It's not my story to tell, but I can say that the worst part of it was that it made her more determined to find out all she can about her mother. It wasn't bad at all."

"I don't think she needs to do anything else right now. Things are starting to move way too fast. She needs to take a break while she can."

"I know, but try telling her that."

Upstairs, Lilly was sprawled on her bed, too tired to get under the covers, but aware enough to have heard them, loud and clear, in her mind. That was the last thing she heard of their conversation before she fell into a deep sleep.

The book was different. It wasn't so ornate as when she found it, and it didn't glow green, but she could tell it was the same book. The pattern around the edges were starting to appear, the symbol on the center already rooted in place. It wasn't on the pedestal, either, but sitting on a plain wooden table against the stone wall of a large, rather empty room.

Then she saw her mother enter, no more that fifteen or sixteen herself. She walked to the book, carrying a small vial in one hand and a feather quill in the other. The young girl took her place in front of the book, opened it to a blank page, and, setting the vial on the table, pricked her finger with the quill, proceeding to squeeze the blood on her finger into the vial. A puff of purple smoke rose from the bottle. When it cleared, the girl began to write. Lilly couldn't see the words on the page appear, but she could hear every sweep and scratch made by the quill, every clink against the vial as her mother tapped away the excess ink. When she finished writing, the girl pricked her finger again, producing a fresh supply of blood. She collected it with the tip of the quill until she had enough, and then signed her name on the bottom of the page. She blew on the page until the ink was dry, and then she closed the book as everything went black.

Lilly woke with a start. She felt like she'd just fallen asleep, but the suns hanging low over the horizon told her she'd been asleep most of the day. With a yawn, she got out of bed and put on fresh clothes. She found the box with the ring and scroll in her pocket when she changed, and since she had to return them to the book anyway, she decided she would look through it again. It was clear to her now that the blank pages in the book were not blank at all.

It felt strange to look at the pedestal again, now that she knew it was her grandfather's skull perched upon it. Were the vials of blood his, or hers? She pushed the thought from her mind. It didn't matter. She knew they were all used for blood magick, and now she knew that her mother was not evil, but trying to protect herself from it.

She opened the book and replaced the box, then started flipping through the pages one at a time. She skipped the ones with titles on the top, studying the blank pages, but not really knowing what she was looking for. They all looked the same. She was beginning to wonder if she was going to have to bloody her finger for each page when she found it. The entire page was blank except for a signature, her mother's signature. She would know the handwriting anywhere. Without thinking, Lilly snatched the first sharp utensil she found and pricked her finger. It was sharper than she thought, and the blood welled up so fast that a drop landed on the page before she realized it. Suddenly, words appeared, glowing gold at first, then turning dark purple.

To strengthen quests - this works better than Segvatele.

A short list of ingredients materialized next, which Lilly recognized were all pretty rare, and then a spell:

With coursing of blood
And whispers of breath
To spirit and soul
From bone and flesh
Open the path
For soaring through time
Let mysteries past
Here intertwine

The instructions below read: *Drink the potion, say the spell, sit down fast. Lasts about two hours.*

Lilly flew to her nightstand, copying the contents of the page into her own book as fast as she could. She closed the tasil, and started for her door, then thought the better of it and closed her eyes. A moment later, she was standing in front of Tsirama's house. She knocked on the door impatiently, her hand shaking with excitement.

"Master Lilly," he said when he opened the door. "Ready for another quest, are you?"

"Yes," she said, walking past him into the house. "I brought my own spell this time."

"What spell?" he asked, more curious than cautious. She handed him her book, opening it to the page she just copied. He read over it, his eyes growing wide.

"No," he said, slamming the book closed and tossing it to her. "Destroy that. Too dangerous."

"I'm doing it with or without you," she said. "It will be less dangerous if you help me."

"Those ingredients," he said, still shaking his head. "How they will affect a human, I do not know."

"A human wrote the spell, and she survived it. I already know I'm stronger than she was. Please. I have to do this."

Tsirama paced his tiny house, looking up every so often at Lilly, his cabinet, his potion table. With a sigh, he went to his cabinet, gathering the few ingredients she would need and placing them on the table. He returned to his cabinet, standing on his toes to reach a small crystal ball on the top shelf. He placed it on a stand beside the cauldron, then looked at Lilly and said, "Come."

"Thank you," she breathed.

"Perfect this has to be," he warned. "These ingredients are strong. This one," he said, picking up a vial of burnt orange liquid, "innocuous in small quantities, but overdose is fatal." He stared at her, his large eyes more serious than she'd ever seen them. "Fatal."

"I understand," she said, easing the vial from his long fingers.

"If unsure about measurements, use less."

"Okay." Lilly lit the firebath beneath the cauldron and opened her book to the potion. She read over it three times, then began the process. Tsirama hovered over her, watching as she added the liquid, which was labeled piliphan extract, with a dropper. Two drops was all she needed. Satisfied she was on the right track, Tsirama collected his clutter of books and scrolls from his sofa, then placed a pillow at one end.

"I'm done," she said, staring into the cauldron at the small pool of liquid on the bottom. "There's not much in there."

"Not much needed," said Tsirama. "Come. Your rest place is prepared." Lilly found a clean dropper and collected the potion from the cauldron, then went to the sofa. Lying down, she looked up at Tsirama hovering over her. He smiled, his large eyes reminding her of the faeries, though he looked more like a bug than a frog. "Here I will stay, until you wake."

Lilly nodded. She got comfortable, settling into the fluffy pillow behind her, and put the dropper in her mouth. It tasted the way smoky air smells, and it was ice cold despite the fact she'd just removed it from the fire. With a sigh, she smiled and handed the dropper to Tsirama.

"With coursing of blood and whispers of breath, to spirit and soul from bone and flesh, open the path for soaring through time, let mysteries past here intertwine."

She fell asleep at once. Tsirama hovered over her a moment longer. Her breathing was deep and even. He felt her pulse, and content that all had gone well, he shook his head.

"Young people," he muttered. "No patience."

The Ultimate Quest

"What have you done?" shouted Dorwynn, bursting through the door. Tsirama looked up from his book, his face calm.

"Nothing, I have done," he said, jerked his head toward Lilly. "She, on other hand, very determined."

Dorwynn rushed to Lilly's side. She looked asleep, her chest rising and falling in even rhythm. He whirled toward Tsirama, his face painted with rage.

"How could you let her do this?" he demanded.

"Left me no choice," said Tsirama, turning a page. "Would have done it anyway, she said. Better here with me than alone, yes?" He looked up from his book again, his eyes curious. "How knew you that she was here?"

"A wild guess," he said, holding back his anger. Tsirama raised an eyebrow. "I know you've been helping her with quests. She mentioned something about them before she went to bed. When I found it empty, I figured she would come to you. I can't believe you let her take a potion for them. She has enough trouble without the added strength. What did you give her? *Segvatele*?"

"I gave her nothing. She made potion herself from her own book."

"What!"

"Stop with the yelling," said Tsirama. "Look, she smiles. All is well." Dorwynn looked at Lilly, who was indeed smiling in her sleep.

Whatever she was experiencing, it was good. He sighed, perching himself on the edge of the sofa beside her. Tsirama closed the book in his hands and approached them, staring down at his pupil. "She has much power, more strength than ever I have seen, but she has too much here..." He pointed to his temple. "...and not enough here." He put his hand over his heart. Dorwynn averted his eyes, staring at Lilly, whose smile was gone. He could feel Tsirama watching him. "Ah. You have affection for her, yes?"

"Yes," he admitted.

"But tell her, you will not."

"She's too young."

"Posh! Almost of age, she is. Fifteen, sixteen, thirty...irrelevant, age is. When love is found, is felt, months should matter not. Fear rejection, you do. Waste your life because of that fear. Hmm. Pity."

Dorwynn didn't respond. He knew the apothecary was right. He feared she would tell him she didn't love him like he loved her, but worse than that, he feared his declaration of love would drive her away from him, a fear so great it threatened his sanity. He couldn't imagine his life without her in it. He stole a glance at her still form, his attention only on her. She was completely still, too still, he suddenly realized. Tsirama noticed the problem at the same moment. He flew across the room at lightning speed, searching vigorously through his cabinet an instant later.

"What's wrong?" asked Dorwynn as he stood over her lifeless body, staring down at her.

"Something..." said Tsirama, his keen eyes scanning his vials.

"She's not breathing!" shouted Dorwynn. He climbed onto the sofa and straddled Lilly, leaning over her dying body and tilting back her head. Holding her nose closed, he put his lips to her mouth and began breathing for her. A moment later, he felt for a pulse. It was so faint, so slow, he couldn't be sure he felt one at all. He was trying to decide whether or not to begin chest compressions when Tsirama struck his shoulder gently.

"I am depleted," he said, waving an empty vial before Dorwynn's nose. "Must have ogre's blood."

"The nearest ogre is hours away! She'll be dead by the time he gets here." Dorwynn began breathing for her again, keeping her faint pulse from disappearing altogether.

"I have no rieja, either," mumbled the apothecary. He returned to his cabinet to find anything that might counteract her condition.

"Rieja," Dorwynn muttered to himself. Zephra had rieja. The ogre had given her some during their visit. He leaned over Lilly, his ear close to her mouth. Her breathing was erratic, but she was breathing. "Don't worry," he whispered in her ear. "I'll be right back." He brushed a strand of hair from her face, his heart pounding. "I will always come back for you." Then he flew toward the door, shouting at Tsirama, "Prepare the bath. I'll get the rieja."

Zephra! He stood at the end of the path leading to the house and pushed with his mind as hard as he could, hoping beyond hope that it would be enough to cover the distance.

Dorwynn? Relief washed over him when her voice grazed his mind. *What's wrong?*

Something happened to Lilly. Hurry. We need the rieja.

I'm on my way.

He raced back into the apothecary's house. Tsirama was filling a large basin with water, one bucket at a time, from the well outside his house. Dorwynn went to Lilly's side. Her chest heaved and shuddered, and then she stopped breathing again. Dorwynn felt her pulse, which was now racing faster than the wings of a hummingbird in flight. Without thinking, he resumed mouth-to-mouth resuscitation, praying Zephra would make it before her heart stopped as well.

Each time his lips made contact with hers, an image flashed in his mind: the first day they met in his own backyard...their horseback ride over the gorge...the day they decided, at the age of ten years old, that they would get married someday...the first time he saw her after she came to Buthania, looking perfect as she asked about him...the hug she gave him just this morning, a step closer to how they used to be...a vision of her in a white gown on her wedding day...and the images faded, becoming more faint with every breath he supplied to her.

"Breathe, Lilly!" he shouted, feeling her pulse again. It was still racing, faster than before, if that was even possible. "Breathe!" He was vaguely aware of Tsirama behind him, staring into a small crystal ball he held before the flame of a candle, as if it held all the answers. "You recorded it," he asked, incredulous, "and you didn't check it before she took the potion?"

"Kilpa powder," said Tsirama, shaking his head. "Single grain extra. Fell from under her fingernail. Hmm. Much more potent than extract."

"You think?!" Dorwynn continued his mission, exasperated with the man. What was the point of recording the potion being made if he didn't check it first? "Come on, Lilly," he whispered, desperation washing over him. "Don't leave me. Breathe!"

She was dreaming. She knew she was dreaming, aware of it even in sleep, for it was a dream she'd had many times before. She was a small child the first time her angel appeared to her, no more than seven or so. He was younger then, too; a pale young man with hair so blonde it was almost white and eyes the same color of the sky on a bright spring day.

"Hello, Jeanne," he said, his voice like a song so beautiful, it made her want to weep for joy.

"Who are you, sir?" she asked, curious about the remarkable man dressed all in white, though not afraid of him, nor shy, as she was with most strangers.

"I am Gabriel. I come to tell you of your destiny."

"My destiny?"

"Yes." His voice echoed in her ears, resounding like the voices of a choir of monks. "You will do great things, Jeanne. You are a savior."

"I am just a girl," she said, bowing her head. "Jesus Christ is a savior."

"Yes, he was."

"He *is*," she said, her head snapping upward to meet his eyes. "The Lord Christ is eternal."

"Christ died over fourteen hundred years ago. How can he save anyone if he is dead?"

"You speak blasphemy."

Gabriel began to glow then, the edges of his white gown turning gold with the light emanating from him, a light brighter than the sun high above them. It was so bright, she had to look away. When the light faded, he stepped forward, his white wings spread wide. She dropped to her knees, bowing to him.

"Jesus Christ was destined to become a savior," he said, his voice regal, "and so he became. You, child, have a similar destiny, and so, too, shall you become a savior."

She met him in secret for six years, and he spent that time telling her of the beautiful world from which he came. Angels such as he flew over the clouds, where rainbows could always be seen. Some had the power to heal, performing the miracles of life, restoring health, curing the ill. He was describing Heaven, and her heart swelled with love and joy whenever he spoke of it, whenever the memory of his words came back to her. Even now, in her sleep, she could feel the depths of that emotion coursing through her blood.

They had met in the forest the day his presence became known to another, as nature was his favorite place to be. She'd asked him that day why he preferred to meet outside rather than in a church.

"Were not the trees and grasses and flowers present before the churches were built?" had been his only reply, and from that moment forward, she never again questioned his wishes.   When she was questioned about with whom she was speaking, she confessed, and shortly thereafter, the others appeared: Catherine and Margaret, and Michael.   She honored them as she honored Gabriel, following their commands without question, even when they led her into war, to the prison that now contained her, and to her fate in the morning when she woke.   She didn't not blame them, however, for they were messengers of God in Heaven.   They were angels, saints, and if it was God's will that she die for their cause, she would accept it without question.   Her heart felt too much love to feel any other way.

The joy was still strong in her heart when they woke her.   It lasted as they led her through the angry crowd toward the stake in the center of the pavilion.   It only grew stronger as they tied her to the wood, and when she looked over the crowd and the men preparing to execute her, her heart swelled with emotion.

This is how He died, she thought.   *He sacrificed Himself so they would remember His message.   I willingly do the same.*

What message is that?   She could hear the anger in his voice, the pain in her angel's heart.

Faith.   They claim to have faith, but they have none.   They shall wander this lonely world until they do.   Sadness washed over her then. The only cause of her sorrow was her pity for them, those who ridiculed her, who threw their rotting food at her as the executioner read the charges against her and the sentence she would suffer, all because she would not renounce the truth of what she had spoken.   A single tear slid down her left cheek.

And until they do have faith, so too shall you *wander this Earth.   They do not deserve your tears.*

I shall always shed a tear for them, and when I am worthy of fulfilling my destiny as a savior, I shall be with you in Heaven.   I shall wander here only until you find me again.   I have faith that you will.

I will always come back for you.

Will you let me see you, just once more with these eyes?   Gabriel appeared to her then, his face bright in the sky.   Sadness was all she could see in his eyes, and he allowed his own tears to fall.   *Do not cry for me, Gabriel.   Cry for them.*   The fire was then lit at her feet, and she could feel his pain as he watched it dance at her feet.   *I'm sorry,* were her last words to him.   She remembered asking the people to pray for her, asking the clergy present to hold a crucifix for her to see until she died, but she couldn't not see if they did.   Only the image of Gabriel, her angel, burned in her mind, as the rest of her body burned from the growing fire.

Her legs, her clothes, her bound hands - all were scorching from the blaze. The pain was excruciating, but still more bearable than the sadness she felt for humanity. She allowed the tears to fall freely then, until the heat dried them before they could fall any longer. She held her breath as long as she could, resisting the acrid smoke swirling around her, the smell caused by her own body burning, but the heat forced her mouth open. If she screamed, she did not hear it, but the hot air rushing into her lungs burned her from the inside when she finally inhaled.

Then, it was over. Her body felt light, as if there wasn't a body at all, like she was floating toward Heaven, but Heaven was not where she arrived. The room was dark, but for the glow of the fire burning below the huge iron cauldron, and so hot that her clothes were drenched with sweat. When the door burst open, a cool breeze rushed past her.

"Shut the door," she hissed.

"He betrayed you," said young Jane, her apprentice for the past three years. "You must hide all this. They come as we speak."

"I shall not hide who I am," she said, "but you, child...leave here at once. They do not come for you."

"Marion, please," begged the girl, her voice a desperate whisper. "They'll sentence you to death."

She stared at the girl, her young face full of fear. Shaking her head, she tossed a sprig of dried lavender into the simmering cauldron.

"So be it," she said. "The Goddess will grant me mercy, even if the men do not." Her voice echoed as the darkness filled her eyes and her body again became weightless, a spirit in the smoke...

She was hiding in the bushes, listening to the meeting she was forbidden to attend. The elders were gathered around the fire, and she was close enough to hear everything they said, close enough to feel the heat of the fire as the wind blew it toward her. They were debating whether or not the tribe should be moved. Her father was among them.

"The white men herd us like they herd their cattle," he said. "We must leave this place before they come here." Many of the others nodded their agreement, their voices mingling together to create a single, undecipherable shout. It subsided only when the chief lifted his hand, his eyes roaming over the group. Her heart was pounding so hard, she feared they would hear it, but they, too, were waiting for him to speak.

"The Gods gave us this land," he said, his voice calm and low. "We will not be driven from it by the white devils. When they come, we will stand against them..."

"...and they say if we resist, they will kill us," whispered a woman's voice as the scenery changed again.

She was lying in front of the fireplace, wearing the nightgown her grandmother gave her for her last birthday. Her mother was trying to speak quietly enough that she could not hear, so she looked at her picture book, pretending she couldn't hear what her parents were saying, but listening closely to every word. It was scary. The German army was collecting everyone, taking them away from their homes, just because they were Jewish.

"Hannah," came her father's voice. She looked up at him, at the star of David sewn to his coat that glared back at her. "Move away from the fire, child. You are too close..."

"I brought some dry clothes, too," said Zephra as she burst through the door. She stopped short at the sight of Dorwynn on top of Lilly, breathing for her, his eyes flooded with tears. Tossing the bag of rieja to Tsirama, she went to Dorwynn's side. "Let me take over."

"No," he said, his voice shaking with the rest of his body. The images he had seen while breathing for her were gone now, and he was afraid if he left her side, she would cease to exist, destroying him in the process. "I'll do it."

Zephra touched Lilly's forehead, the heat radiating from her body so hot she actually recoiled from it like she'd been burned.

"Dorwynn, move," she said. "She's too hot." Dorwynn ignored her. The only thing in his world right now was Lilly...nothing else existed. "Dorwynn!" Zephra pulled him off of Lilly and he whirled around, coming nose to nose with her.

"I won't lose her," he said, choking on the words. Zephra's face softened. "I can't lose her."

"She's burning up," said Zephra, her voice soft. "If I don't get some of that heat out of her, you *will* lose her." Fear replaced the rage in his eyes, and he stepped to the side, allowing Zephra access to Lilly. She placed one hand on Lilly's forehead, the other on her chest, and began to draw the heat from her body. She handled fire like it was nothing more than a child's toy, but the heat coming from Lilly made her feel like her hands were ablaze, her fingertips sizzling. "Oh, sweetie," she whispered to the lifeless girl, "what did you do?"

Tsirama pushed himself through Dorwynn and Zephra, reaching for Lilly's hand. He pricked her finger and squeezed three drops of her blood into a saucer lined with the sparkling white powder. When the third drop fell, the powder swirled around it, forming in its path a shimmering red ball the size of a pea.

"Clothes off," he commanded. "Bare skin to touch as much water possible." Staring in awe at the red pea, he carried it to the basin of water he'd prepared in the center of the room and dropped it in the water, which bubbled, turning bright red. "Bring her, now."

Zephra quickly unbuttoned Lilly's jeans, yanking them off by the ankles, and then inhaled a sharp breath at the sight of her legs. The skin was blistered and bright red, almost the same color as the water in the tub, and some places were turning black. Dorwynn stared in shock at her charred skin, bile rising in his throat as he realized what was happening.

"She's burning alive," he whispered, swallowing the lump in his throat.

Zephra swept Lilly into her arms before Dorwynn could even move, drawing out as much heat as she could as she carried her across the room. Her arms burned as they did when she was in battle shooting streams of flames from them toward her enemies. No matter how hard she pulled the heat from Lilly's body, the girl grew hotter still, the skin on her legs blackening worse as each second passed. When Zephra lowered her into the tub of red liquid, Lilly shrieked, writhing and thrashing, her spine arched, her head thrown back. Unable to break Zephra's firm grasp, she went limp, and Zephra was able to get her into the water up to her neck, her own hands still absorbing the heat.

"Why is she burned like that?" asked Dorwynn, glaring at Tsirama.

"Extra kilpa powder makes potion stronger," he said, his eyes huge as he watched the process. "Her mind makes real what happens in quest."

"And if she dies in the quest?" asked Dorwynn. Tsirama's eyes were glued to Lilly. He didn't answer. There was no need.

"She's not dying," said Zephra, relief flooding her voice as she removed her hands from Lilly. "The blood bath is working. Her temperature is dropping. She's breathing on her own again." She stepped backward as both men rushed to the tub, Dorwynn hovering over Lilly as Tsirama timed her pulse. When both seemed satisfied of Lilly's recovery, Zephra pulled Dorwynn toward the door. "We need to talk."

"But..."

"She's healing, Dorwynn. Tsirama will watch her."

Tsirama nodded, waving his hand absentmindedly at them. Dorwynn tore his eyes from Lilly, lying in a pool of what now resembled blood in both color and thickness, and followed Zephra outside.

"What is happening?" she asked, running her hands through her hair and allowing the warm air to cool her neck. She couldn't remember ever feeling so hot, not even after her worst rage when her hair flamed from her anger. She exhaled a long, deep sigh, her eyes closed as she forced herself to relax, and then she turned to Dorwynn. "When she wakes up, you need to be careful."

"Why?" he asked, his voice high. "What did I do?"

"It's what you're going to do. You're letting your emotions get the better of you."

"I can't help it, Zephra," he said, getting defensive. "I love her."

"That's my point. She's fifteen, Dorwynn."

"Almost sixteen," he argued. "She'll be of age in a few months."

"Here, yes, but standards on Earth are different. You, of all people, know that."

"Look, I don't need a lecture from you..."

"Do you think she's your leyartha?" Her question caught Dorwynn off guard, his jaw dropping. He didn't answer; he couldn't. Zephra nodded. "I thought so," she said. "Don't be selfish, Dorwynn. She doesn't need to deal with anything else right now, especially after tonight. You need to pull yourself together before it affects her."

He thought about her words as he peeked through the window at Lilly. She was still unconscious, but her color was returning to normal. He sighed, the weight on his shoulders lifting. He didn't want to give her anything else to worry about, but he didn't know if he would be able to leave her when it was time without telling her how he felt. If something else happened while he was gone, she would never know the truth. Could he live with that?

"How did you know I wanted to tell her?" he asked without looking away from Lilly.

"I can see it in your eyes," whispered Zephra, taking care not to let her own emotions taint her words. "The desperation. You look at her like a man in love. I see the difference now. You never looked at me like that. It was never love with me, was it? It was lust." His shoulders dropped again, the invisible weight returning, but he said nothing. He felt guilty about his time with Zephra, not for what happened between them so long ago, but for how it mislead her about his feelings for her. "If you tell her that you think she's your soul mate," she said, her voice firm, "that you are in love with her, how do you think she's going to handle having to break your heart if she doesn't feel the same way, or having to watch you leave her behind if she does? You know you can't stay with her through all of her training. Sometimes, Dorwynn, ignorance really is bliss."

"You're right," he said as her point finally sunk in. He gazed through the window again, noticing the erratic movements of Lilly's chest as her breathing stabilized. His own chest tightened as he made his decision.

"My task here is complete. She's a Master now. The longer I stay, the harder it with be for everyone when I go. Once I know for sure that she's okay, I'm leaving."

"Where will you go?" asked Zephra.

"I need to know for certain if Gustave is responsible for my blackouts. I guess I'll investigate that for a while. Amparo isn't due to arrive until after the first harvest, but she can't be left alone, especially after this little stunt."

"I'm not going anywhere," Zephra assured him. He nodded, expecting nothing less.

"I'd better get back inside," he said. "She'll need to be removed from the bath soon. Are you coming?"

"No," said Zephra. "You don't need me anymore." The hard truth of her words slammed her into reality, and she knew she needed to be alone.

"Okay. I'll see you later, when I bring her home." Zephra nodded. "For what it's worth," he said as she turned away from him, "I am sorry." Her shoulders fell a fraction, but she didn't acknowledge his words. He watched her until she was out of his sight, then sighed and went back into the house.

A Connection Formed

He flew as fast as he could, but he wanted to be far enough away from the castle to transfigure without anyone noticing his presence. He had to be fast, though. The information he learned just moments ago could mean a dangerous twist to their cause. He hated this form, especially how he saw through its eyes. His view of everything was distorted, like he was looking through a glass sphere from the inside. He could see where he'd already been, too, something he could never get used to, no matter how many times he took this form. He tried to stop more than once to shift into something different, but he was so fearful of being noticed, he dared not change in front of any living creature, even small forest animals that might also be someone in disguise, and the forest was teeming with life. He was exhausted, a sign he needed to eat, but there was no way he would eat while in this form. He'd rather die of starvation.

Of course, being a fly enabled him to easily hide in plain sight while spying on the queen. He doubted anyone knew of his presence within the castle. Who would believe anyone could transfigure into something so small? To the best of his knowledge, he was the only being capable of it. He was an expert at transfiguration, not only able to become something as small as an insect, but also able to become something as large as a small dragon, and his accuracy was perfect. He loved spouting fire while roaring at whatever was close enough to him to frighten. Yes, being a dragon held much more prestige than being a nasty little fly.

Thinking about his abilities always brought him memories of his parents. They were shapeshifters, each only able to transfigure into a particular form, but he owed his unique talent to them. They were also the reason that he was the only member of the Council of Magick who was there to represent only himself, the reason he belonged to no particular race since he was literally one of a kind. The thought tied him in knots, and the only comfort he could bring himself was the knowledge that he would soon be with the closest thing he had to a mother, the woman who recruited him to her side and opened the door to him becoming a member of the Council.

He didn't feel a sense of relief until he saw the cottage ahead of him. Ashya was in her garden, tending to her outside plants. He landed on the front door, close to the opening, and waited until she entered the house, then flew into the enchantment room. It would be best to change there. Even if he had been followed, no one would see through the perimeters of her safe house. He started his transfiguration just as she walked into the room, growing from the tiny fly he had just been into a tall young man, ignoring the onslaught of pain that accompanied every change.

"Jax!" said Ashya when he appeared. "You startled me."

"Forgive me," he said, his voice urgent. "I have news from Ridaska."

"Sit," she said, conjuring two chairs for them. He sank into it, enjoying the first pause he'd had in three days. "What news?"

"The queen has allied herself with the dragon," he said, exhaling a breathless sigh. "Two days ago. She left yesterday with the dragon to begin recruiting harpies in an effort to obtain a spawn that recently escaped their hold. Before she left, she demoted her man at arms as her bodyguard, choosing the dragon over him for protection and strategies of war. He is still High Commander of the armies, but his main duty now is to train her young grandson in physical combat."

"Physical combat?" sighed Ashya. "Would she put him into battle?"

"She claims she wants him to be able to protect himself. That's not all." He took a deep breath, preparing to tell the worst news yet. "The identity of your protégé has been revealed. Right now, Dagana believes she is not important, but she will be watching her."

A look of horror crossed Ashya's face. She stared at the man before her, his turquoise eyes an ocean of discontent. He, too, knew how this event would change their plans.

"Tell me everything you can about this Rimetak situation," she said. "The visions I have of him conflict greatly. I must know if this event will lead to his alliance with us."

"You should not go to those creatures without protection, my queen," argued Rimetak. He was walking through the courtyard with Dagana, having just learned of her plans.

"I have a dragon to accompany me, Rimetak," said Dagana, her mouth turned up at the corners. "That should be more than adequate protection. Besides, I do not wish to relieve you of all your duties. You are still my High Commander. You will have the armies, and I still need you for protection, but for my grandson, not myself. He is a natural at magick and has long since surpassed even my abilities, but he has no knowledge of battle." She stopped and looked at him in the eyes. "He must be protected at all costs. He must be prepared to protect himself by never falling into the position to be taken. I trust you above all others to see to it is done."

"Of course, Your Majesty." Rimetak bowed to his queen, hiding the scowl on his face as she dismissed him.

That was how he came to be here, training the queen's grandson how to wield a sword. It was obvious he had natural talent, and obvious he hadn't had any formal training to develop that talent. He was quick to defend, but awkward while advancing, and Rimetak knew that if you had no offense, defense was pointless.

"Don't let fear stop you from taking a strike." Rimetak rushed Kylenin, swinging his sword and backing him into the stone wall of the elaborate arena. He knocked the boy's hand with the hilt of his blade, causing him to drop his own sword into Rimetak's waiting hand. He crossed the swords over Kylenin's collarbones, their sharp edges at his neck, their tips touching the wall behind him. Rimetak stared at the trapped boy, his silver eyes swimming with fear as angry tears began to well in them. The anger over his own demotion melted away at that instant. It wasn't this boy's fault the queen had replaced him with a dragon. If a dragon had come to him offering to assist with strategies of battle, not to mention protection, he would have rejected all others, even the queen herself.

He retracted the swords and offered his hand to Kylenin, who accepted with some hesitation. "Fear will disable you faster than your strongest enemy, but," he said with a gleam in his eyes as he handed the boy his sword, "if your enemies fear you, their fear will be their own undoing. Come, let us go again."

"He's forming a bond with the boy," said Ashya when Jax finished talking. She stood, pacing the floor as she thought over the best way to protect Lilly. "I want you out of Ridaska for a while," she said, stopping in front of him. "Let him foster the child. He will be better off with Rimetak than any other, and with both the queen and the dragon away for a time, the boy may yet rise to amaze us all. In the meantime, Lilly will soon return from the faeries, and my son will accompany her and her trainer to Nurzia. I want you to find them on their way. Go with them, and stay with them until I call for you." Jax nodded, accepting the orders like any good soldier would. Ashya nodded, too, and sank into her chair.

"In disguise, my lady?" he asked. She smiled at him and took his hand, gripping it with all the love of the mother he never had.

"No," she said. "I would rather you meet young Lilly as yourself. I see a great friendship in the making, and she would not take kindly to starting it under false pretenses. Besides, I don't think she'd be fond of a fly for a pet."

"Of course not," he said, a smile creeping over his lips. "A new friend would be a nice change of pace."

"You will like her immensely," said Ashya, conjuring two steaming mugs of tea and handing him one. "You are very similar creatures. She, too, has a gentle nature, a peaceful way about her. I worry sometimes that what she must face in the coming years will destroy that peacefulness in her, but I like to believe she is strong enough to overcome the hardships."

"What are her motives for joining the cause?" he asked, curious about this friend he had yet to meet.

"She has not experienced the struggles you have endured, but she, too, has issues of abandonment, problems trusting others, feelings that she belongs nowhere. That motive, more than the rest I believe, is the reason she has come."

"I know how she feels," said Jax, sipping his drink. His parents, after being banished by their respective races, committed the ultimate act of selfishness. Together, they took a potion that ended their lives, though not before trying to coax him into the same plan. Even as a small child he knew enough to refuse, but they took their own lives knowing he would be left alone to deal with what he was - a half-breed with neither race willing to accept him. "I've never really belonged anywhere."

"You belong here," said Ashya, and he returned her warm smile. "You are welcome to stay until it is time to meet with the others. My son's room is unoccupied. Come. I will prepare us some dinner and we can move to a discussion of happier things."

"Thank you, Ashya," he said, standing when she did. "You've always been the closest thing I've had to a mother, and I will always be grateful for your presence in my life."

"It is an honor, Jax," she said, leading him from the room, "and it is my honor to be that for Lilly, as well. One more thing you have in common."

Jax smiled. He'd heard much about the girl from Ashya, but he never imagined she'd be so similar to him, even if she wasn't an odd mixture of magickal creatures. Now, more than ever, he couldn't wait to meet her, and his greatest hope was that when she found out what he was, she would be able to look past it to see him for *who* he was.

"Have you ever had ale before?" asked Lord Rimetak, setting a large mug in front of Kylenin. He grinned.

"Are you kidding?" he laughed, picking up the mug. "You're forgetting who my grandmother is. She'd flog you if she knew you even brought me inside a pub."

"Right," said Rimetak, sitting at the tiny round table across from the boy. "Why don't we keep this our little secret?"

"My lips are sealed." Kylenin took a huge gulp from the cup, coughing as the liquid scorched his throat. Rimetak laughed, handing him a napkin.

"I should have warned you," he chuckled, taking a swig of his own drink. "Sorry."

"No, it's fine." Kylenin coughed again, then took a smaller sip, which went down smoother. He smiled as he stared around the room. The pub was small, with only seven tables and one long bar wrapped halfway around the interior walls. It was nearly empty, too, with one drunken patron slumped over his drink at the bar and one couple at a table, leaning close together over it, oblivious to the rest of the world. "I never had a father, you know."

"Everyone has a father," said Rimetak.

"I never met my father," Kylenin amended, "or my mother. She died when I was born."

"I heard something of that." Rimetak stared at his cup, wondering where the boy was going with this train of thought.

"This is nice. It's something I imagine my father and I would have done together, had I been fortunate enough to know him."

"Have you considered looking for him?"

"I've thought about it, but I doubt I will. I don't know where he is, or who he is. I don't even think he knows I exist."

"Why do you think that?"

"The way my grandmother acts, keeping me so close to her all the time. I feel like she's trying to keep me hidden from someone." He took another drink, becoming more comfortable with the way the ale went down his throat. "I just don't get her. Was she always like this?"

"Oh, no," said Rimetak. "She was much worse."

"Worse? Is that even possible?"

"It's possible. Compared to how she was at the height of her power, she's a kitten." Kylenin spit his ale across the table, spraying Rimetak. "Are you alright?" he laughed, wiping his face.

"Sorry," said Kylenin. "I never thought I'd hear anyone describe her as a kitten. She's so...she just..." Kylenin sighed, taking another drink as he tried to gather his thoughts. "She acts like she gives me everything, you know, but in reality, she's given me nothing."

"That can't be true."

"Can't it? Sure, she feeds me and clothes me. I have a roof over my head, but she's never shown me real love, and she hides me away from the world, claiming it's for my protection, but I know better. She means for me to be king and she'll stop at nothing, and I mean *nothing*, to obtain it. This trip to Elikrede was my first trip alone, anywhere."

Rimetak nodded, knowing all too well the ways the queen's mind worked. His own experiences at her bidding still made him shudder. If this boy knew what she'd done in the past, how cruel and ruthless she really could be, he would be grateful for the way she was now.

"Tell me," he said, leaning closer Kylenin, "in your opinion, what is her worst quality?"

"The way she uses others to get what she wants," he answered without having to think about it. Rimetak nodded again.

"And her most admirable?" he asked. Kylenin had to think about that one for a while, puzzling over it as he drank his first adult beverage.

"Her diligence, I suppose. When she's determined, she'll do whatever it takes to get what she wants."

"There's a fine line between the best and worst, isn't there?" Rimetak stared at Kylenin, his gray-blue eyes reminding him so much of another young person who once felt the same way about the queen. "She's not all bad, son," he said, trying to convince himself as much as the boy before him. "She just has misguided priorities."

"Why does she want so badly for me to be king?" asked Kylenin, talking to his cup. He lifted his eyes to Rimetak's, guilt washing over him. "I'm not even sure I want to be king."

"Why not?"

"I'm not much of a leader."

"That is only because you've lacked the opportunity."

"I've lacked many opportunities," said Kylenin, rolling his eyes. "How can she expect me to do anything when I've never done anything? The only thing I can do well is magick. I'm Arch-level already. Did you know that?" Rimetak shook his head. "I'm more powerful than she is, too, or I will be, but she doesn't know I know that. I let her believe I'm ignorant of that fact. I don't know why, but even as powerful as I am, I don't think I'll ever be able to stand against her."

"I wouldn't recommend it," said Rimetak, "and magick isn't the only thing you do well. You have a talent, a natural grace with the sword unlike anything I've ever seen, but it is worthless without proper discipline. You must develop it as you have your powers, practice until it is perfect. When I have finished training you, you will be the best swordsman who ever lived, other than myself, of course."

"Of course," said Kylenin, smiling at the man before him. He was the perfect example of what a father should be: firm, yet supportive, and with a genuine concern for his child. Though he wasn't his father, Kylenin was beginning to trust the man in a way he could trust no one else. Could he trust him enough to tell him...?

They finished their drinks in silence, Kylenin dwelling on thoughts of Lilly. What was it that drew him to her, even now, after he had found his leyartha? Why did he feel such concern for her? He wanted to see her again already, but he knew that he would not be able to see her for some time, if he ever saw her again. That thought dampened his mood, and he couldn't help but think of the last dream he'd had of her, the night Tangaia left the castle with his grandmother. She was walking through a burning land, blood running down her face.

Rimetak was quiet, too, thinking of the last time he was in this position, helping to ease the heart of an unhappy young girl desperate to escape the queen. He wondered who Kylenin's father was, for his face didn't resemble hers at all, but his eyes...he had his mother's eyes. They were the same light color, the same shape, and they held the same look of desperation, though he knew the reasons for it were very different. She had needed to escape. She had been more like her father, a kind man who would give everything he could to help another in need. She had been powerful, too, though nowhere close to Dagana's. She had come to him for help to escape, and though his oath of loyalty to the queen had prevented him from it, she did not hold it against him. He knew if that oath had not been given, they would have disappeared together to live their lives in bliss. Instead, they met in secret, their affair short-lived.

She had found a way to escape shortly thereafter, and she had taken it. As much as he loved her, he couldn't begrudge her that.

"Why so quiet?" asked Kylenin, studying Rimetak's face.

"No reason," said Rimetak, clearing his throat. "I was thinking of your mother, actually."

"You knew her well?"

"I did, though your grandmother never knew. I...um..." The words stuck in his throat. He coughed, clearing it again, and continued. "We were in love, but our respective circumstances could not allow us to be together. She was the queen's daughter, and I...I would not have been worthy enough in Dagana's eyes to be her husband. She had her own plans for your mother."

"What happened to her?" asked Kylenin.

"She fled. To where, no one knows. She returned to the castle, gave birth to you, and died. That is all I know of her after she left." He stared at the boy, wishing he had more to tell him. "You remind me of her. You have her eyes."

"I met a girl," blurted Kylenin. "When I went to Elikrede."

"A girl, eh," said Rimetak, grateful for the change of subject. "Attractive?"

"Beautiful, but it's more than that. There is something about her, like I've known her my entire life. I never felt truly connected to anyone until I met her. I can't explain it, but I can't stop thinking about her, hoping she's okay. I have a terrible feeling she's in danger. I fear for her safety, but I know there is nothing I can do for her. I hate being afraid. You see! That's why I'll not make a good king. I have no courage."

"The absence of fear is not courage, son," said Rimetak. "It is faith. Courage is admitting your fears and facing them despite being afraid. Can you think of this girl, fearing for her well-being and knowing you can do nothing to keep her safe?"

"I don't know," he admitted. "It kills me to sit here, even now, when I feel like she needs my help. I wish I could talk to her, just to know that she's alright."

Rimetak said nothing, but nodded his understanding. He once felt that way, just as helpless, and though he loved his wife and his children, it still ate at his soul when he thought of his first love, how she had appealed to him for help and how, despite his wishes, there was nothing he could do for her. He couldn't help at that moment regretting his past actions. If he had helped her, if they had been able to stay together, the boy before him now might very well have been his own son.

Kylenin sighed. He'd been trying to contact Lilly since his return, but neither their connection nor their combined power was enough to cover the distance between them. Once again, he was forced to be content with only dreams of her. If the dreams weren't so frightening, he *would* be content, but how could he be when he could feel she was in terrible danger? He vowed to himself he would find a way to contact her, no matter what he had to do. His mother had fled. He could do the same, just long enough to make sure Lilly was well. A second later, he changed his mind, sighing in relief as her voice touched his mind, soft and faint, but clear as day.

Wyatt?

The Awakening

She was herself again, or so she thought. This body felt more familiar than the others, but she could see nothing. Vast darkness stretched out infinitely before her. She heard voices, muffled and yet amplified, as though she was underwater, trying to hear someone above the surface. Was she underwater? Could she be a mermaid now? Wherever she was, she knew she was not alone. She could feel him near, just as she could in every life before...

The logical side of Lilly's brain took note of that piece of information. Had she been able to feel his presence in her other lives? She thought she felt him in at least one other, and certainly this one, but all of them? She concentrated on the darkness, forcing the quest to work itself out. Already she could tell she had better control of them, and then suddenly, everything snapped into focus. He was close...close enough to feel his heartbeat, close enough to talk, but he wasn't talking now. Was he underwater with her, or was he on the surface with the others, and why in the world couldn't she see?

She reached through the darkness of the sea, trying to find him, her arms not responding to her like they should. She tried harder, listening to the rush of liquid around her as she moved, and then, suddenly, she *really* felt his presence. The flashing light behind the utter darkness of her eyes strobed in time with her rapid heartbeat.

Wyatt? she called with her mind, but he did not answer her. Irritated, she decided to leave this strange quest and travel to the next, for if he was so close and would not answer, he did not know this as his name. The next quest, however, did not come. The darkness stayed, as did the feeling of being wet, though the sensation of being underwater subsided.

She was different. She could tell at once that things had changed, though how, she would never be able to explain. Even as the sounds of the room met her ears and she received confirmation that her thoughts were valid, she couldn't describe, even to herself, what had been altered. She only knew something was different...*she* was different.

Tsirama's voice was the first she heard. It was muted, as though he was very far away from her, and she struggled to cling to the familiarity of his accent, straining to hear his words.

"Yes," he said, obviously talking to someone else. "Different, she will be."

"How so?" came another voice. Dorwynn. She was sure of it, but even his voice didn't sound right, like he was speaking through someone else's vocal chords.

"That, I know not," replied Tsirama. She wished she could open her eyes to see the exchange taking place between them, but she had no strength to lift her heavy lids. "Kilpa powder overdose does strange things. One grain makes huge difference. Lucky to be alive, she is."

How does he know what went wrong? she thought, wondering why he didn't stop her from drinking the potion if she'd gotten it wrong. Dorwynn answered the question for her.

"Next time, check your records *before* you let her drink anything." His voice was harsh, a clear command. "We can't risk any more than we already have."

"True," breathed Tsirama, not the least bit put off by Dorwynn's harsh demand.

They were silent then, and Lilly was able to focus on other things, like the fact that she could feel someone else in the room, someone unfamiliar. Someone was watching her, for she could feel the intensity of being observed rolling over her in waves. She could feel Tsirama and Dorwynn as well, though she couldn't justify to herself how or why. Tsirama was distracted, concentrating hard on something. Dorwynn was a nervous wreck, his mind seared by a vast onslaught of emotions all at once. Fear, panic, love, hate, anger, anticipation...hope.

"Do you have any ideas?" he asked, resuming the conversation.

"Any possibility," said her potions teacher, now sounding like he was absorbed in something entirely different than their conversation.

"Unleashing of latent powers, maybe. Diminishing of active powers. Who knows? Is very unpredictable. We know nothing until she wakes."

"How long will that be?" muttered Dorwynn, low enough that Tsirama probably didn't hear him. And why was his voice ringing like that? It had an edge to it that she'd never heard before. A stranger would find it pleasant, but it irritated her. It didn't sound like him at all.

Suddenly, a new voice interrupted her thoughts. It wasn't even a voice, for she heard no reaction from either of the men in the room with her, but rather an echo in her mind, clear and haunting, unmistakably someone's thought, she was sure of it.

Wake, it told her, slow and melodic like a siren's song. She had never heard a voice so beautiful, and yet so poignant at the same time.

I can't, she thought.

You are stronger now, the voice chimed in her ear, and she couldn't help but believe what it said. *Open your eyes. The world waits for you...*

Lilly struggled against the weight of her eyelids, her breath coming in quick gasps, but her body wasn't responding to her like it should...just like the quest right before she was here. She pushed harder, but it was a challenge. Though her eyes were still closed, she could hear Dorwynn and Tsirama rushing to her side...a chair scraping across the hardwood floor...their footsteps as they approached her...two hearts beating, one calm, one nervous.

"Lilly?" said Dorwynn, his voice edged with desperation. "Lilly, honey, wake up." *You have to wake up. I can't go on without you. I have so much to tell you. Crap, I can't. Zephra's right, Dorwynn. Get it under control before she wakes up...*

Lilly listened to his words, which didn't sound like him, and the stream of thoughts that *did* sound like his voice...normal. She relaxed, focusing on what he said. He called her 'honey'. That was new, and the rest...what couldn't he tell her? She was so tired of people thinking she shouldn't know things. If they would just tell her, she wouldn't have to take such extremes to find things out for herself.

Open your eyes! the voice commanded, and her eyes flew open against her will. It took a moment for her vision to focus. Dorwynn's blurry form hovered over her until he was shoved aside by Tsirama, whose long, cold fingers were around her wrist, checking her pulse. Darting her eyes back and forth as her vision improved, she scanned the room in search of the other person speaking to her, but there was no one else present. In fact, nothing was out of place except for two shiny orbs floating high over her, lingering near the ceiling, slowly fading from sight.

"What is that?" she inquired, surprised at the sound of her own voice. It, too, sounded like it belonged to someone else.

"What?" asked Dorwynn. There was no anxiety in his voice, but she could feel it in his heart.

"Never mind," she sighed, trying to lift her leaden body into a sitting position. It posed a difficult challenge.

"No." Dorwynn placed his hand on her chest just below her collarbones, exuding slight pressure that was more than enough to stop her. "You need more rest. You don't have your strength back yet."

"Let me up!" she cried, smacking his hand away as a surge of anger overwhelmed her. His hand recoiled as if a bee had just stung him.

"Different," warned Tsirama in a whisper, though Lilly heard it loud and clear. Dorwynn nodded and backed away from her slowly.

"I'm fine," she said.

"Are you sure?" asked Dorwynn. His hurricane of emotions had mellowed, diminished to his concern for her, aching disappointment and...what was it...longing?

"Just give me a minute, okay?"

Dorwynn nodded, returning to his chair, his eyes never leaving her. She rubbed her temples. She didn't have a headache, but her head felt odd, like her mind wasn't working right. How could it be when she was hearing strange voices and feeling Dorwynn's emotions? Tsirama held a candle close to her face, and she squinted from the bright rainbows flashing in her eyes...just like that last quest. The lights flashed whenever she touched him...why? Tsirama pulled her eyelids open to look at her pupils.

"Find answers, did you?" he asked.

"Not the ones I was looking for," she said. "I went back too far."

"I told you potion was dangerous. Such ingredients too strong for humans. Your maker of potions was more than human. Half-breed, perhaps."

Lilly froze. Was her mother a half-breed? Her grandfather was human, so her grandmother must have been...what? Elf, maybe, or angel? She ran down the list of magickal creatures who could procreate within other respective races. Any of the elemental children could, since they could take human form, so mermaid, faerie, unicorn or dragon, plus vampire, werewolf, valkeyre...

"Who wrote the potion, Lilly?" asked Dorwynn, interrupting her thoughts. He wasn't defensive or demanding, just curious, but she bristled protectively, feeling the emotion surging through him.

"What's wrong with you?" she asked, her eyes meeting his.

"What do you mean?" He looked wounded, but apprehension was now his primary emotion, a sudden surge of concern that released just enough adrenaline to increase his heart rate a fraction of second. Lilly frowned, her mind working at new speeds. She noticed his change in heart rate, his sudden shifts of emotion that changed so fast they were difficult to distinguish...*she* noticed, but he wouldn't be able to detect things like that.

"Never mind," she said. "Can we go home? I'd like to get a good night's rest in my own bed."

"Sure," said Dorwynn, now burning with curiosity. *Why does she think something is wrong with me? She's the one acting strange. Stupid potion! Where did she get it? Who would be foolish enough to give her something like that?* "Let's go."

Lilly expected to feel lightheaded when she stood, especially considering how her head already felt. Instead, she found herself strong, alert. She gazed around the room, taking in the finer details she'd never noticed before...the delicate pattern carved around the table's edge like lace around the hem of a skirt...the gold inlay swirled within the silver hands of the clock...the faint hint of lavender hanging in the air around the sofa. Lavender...a magickal herb...she'd used it before...

"Lilly," said Dorwynn, snapping her from her drifting thoughts, "are you sure you're okay?"

"Yes," she assured him. "Just thinking. Goodbye, Tsirama."

"Goodbye," said the little man, preoccupied. He was rummaging through his cabinet, collecting empty vials and setting them on the table beside dozens that were full of dark red liquid...blood. He let her pass him, but before she could reach the door, he caught her arm. "Take nothing else with kilpa powder," he warned, his voice firm. "No extract, no root. Once in your blood, some always stays. Rest takes long time to leave. Promise me."

"I promise," she said. He let go of her arm, returning to his work. Dorwynn, ever the gentleman, held the door for her as they left. Outside, the warm air carried with it the scent of fresh berries and honeysuckle blooms. Lilly inhaled, enjoying the new sensations. She could feel that her perception skills were stronger...she didn't even have to try to hear the waterfall, though they were far away from it.

"Let's magick there," she suggested.

"Let's walk," he said, grabbing her hand and holding it like he did when they were kids. "I need to talk to you." *Besides, you'd probably magick us to your dad's house.* Lilly ignored that, doing her best to block his thoughts, but it was hard to do. "You're a Master now, so my job of training you is done. Amparo will be here to take over soon."

"Will you stay until she arrives?"

"I would love to..." *more than you will ever know*... "but I have my own mysteries to solve. I need to find out what Gustave is up to. It may not be what I think it is, but there is more to that old man than anyone wants to believe."

"When are you leaving?" she asked.

"Tonight."

"What?" she exclaimed, pulling him to a stop. "You just got back."

"I know..."

"You just started acting like you again. What is with you?"

If you only knew, he thought. *If I could only tell you...* His thoughts shifted from words to sporadic memories flashing through his mind: how she looked during the quests, him trying to save her life, her lying in the pool of blood as she healed, an argument... *I can't help it, Zephra! I love her.*

She let go of his hand, trying to break the connection between herself and his emotions, for they told her more than the words still echoing in her head. He didn't just love her, he was *in love* with her. It wasn't something she was prepared to face. Romance was the last thing on her mind with everything else happening right now, and Dorwynn...did she feel that way about him? She did once, a long time ago, but they had been kids then. Things were different now, weren't they?

"Sorry," she said, resenting the way her mind suddenly grasped everything now.

"Please, don't be upset," he said, taking her hand again. "I'm trying to do the right thing this time."

"What's that?"

"Say goodbye to you before I leave, maybe spend some quality friend time with you first."

She nodded, forcing a smile. They walked the road home in silence. It was a nice night, and Lilly took the time to notice the halos of light surrounding the larger stars in the sky, the fireflies beaconing to one another throughout the field, the faint sound of thunder echoing somewhere on the other side of the mountain. Focusing on little things made it easier to block Dorwynn's thoughts, though his emotions still found a way through.

"Take care of yourself," he said to her when they were standing at the front door. "I won't be gone too long."

"Are you going to say goodbye to Zephra?" she asked, her hand on the doorknob.

"Yeah," he said, sitting on the step. "She knows I'm leaving, so she'll be out here soon. You go to bed. She's going to stay with you until Amparo arrives, and when she gets here, do me a favor: Listen to her."

"Bye, Dorwynn," she whispered, smiling. She went to her room, taking the time to pull back the blankets and put on pajamas. She crawled into bed, snuggling into the blankets despite the warmth of the night and waited, knowing if she stayed awake long enough, she would hear their conversation. Sure enough, a few moments later, she heard the front door open.

"Did you tell her?" asked Zephra. Dorwynn didn't answer, but he must have shaken his head, because Zephra continued. "It's for the best, Dorwynn. She doesn't need anything else to distract her."

"She already suspects something," he said. "She's...that potion...it did something to her. She's different, Z."

"I know. I can feel it."

"Just be careful."

"I will."

"About earlier..."

"Don't, Dorwynn," said Zephra, interrupting him and leaving Lilly to wonder what had happened between them. "I've lived long enough to know how it works. Don't worry. I'm not going anywhere. I promise."

Lilly missed the rest, for the sweet sensation of sleep overwhelmed her, forcing her to relinquish control over herself. Dorwynn was leaving. Zephra was staying. Amparo was coming. She fell into a deep slumber, comforted by the knowledge that though she attempted so much on her own, these people, those closest to her, would always be there for her. For the first time in her life, she trusted that much, but like always, it was her dreams that broke her faith.

She was standing in the middle of a great battle, creatures charging each other all around her. A black minotaur drove a stake into the heart of a harpy, who released a screech with her dying breath. A hideous woman with the lower body of a snake shrank to the size of a real snake as a spell hit her. Others were dropping at her feet, instantly paralyzed as they, too, were hit with spells. A bolt of lightning struck the ground inches from her feet, and she knew that was a spell, too, for there was not a single cloud in the sky to make the lightning.

In the sky high above her, winged creatures of every kind were participating in the same battle. Some carried passengers, like the hippogriff that screeched as its front talons gripped the first of three necks of the enemy it was after...a chimera. A reptilian head dropped to the ground and the hippogriff reached for another head, one that looked like a lion, but was struck by the chimera's huge lion paws before it could inflict more damage. It momentarily lost its balance, but recovered, screaming its displeasure, as did the evil-looking woman riding it.

Angels, pterippi and dragons swarmed the skies, fighting against their enemies, some of which were of their own races. The ground was littered with the bodies of dying beasts, blood saturating the ground beneath them. Lilly stared in shock, remembering this dream with vivid detail. She looked toward the mountains in the distance, knowing she would see the bright red dragon hovering over them. The only proof of the green dragon was the stream of fire shooting upward from between the mountains.

I don't need to go there, she thought, thinking of what was about to happen. She dodged the centaur that raced by her, oblivious to her presence, then ran as fast as she could, looking toward the sky, waiting for the inevitable. She couldn't see which creature he was riding, but she knew he would soon fall from the sky and land at her feet.

"Lilly!" She turned toward the sound of her name being called, recognizing the familiar voice. Voruum ran toward her, a war axe in his hand. "Look out!" She ducked as he swung his axe over her head, hitting the armored enemy that was rushing her from behind. "Get out of here!" shouted her friend, running toward the center of the commotion. Without thinking, she grabbed her dagger from her boot and charged after him, striking a man about to spear a centaur she recognized from Ambala.

The chaos was staggering as the army of men, all wearing black armor clad with a red dragon, drew their weapons upon the masses of creatures already fighting their fellow soldiers. The sheer quantity of soldiers was enough to overtake those still fighting on her side, so she lifted her right hand, barely noticing the three crescents now emblazoned on her wrist, and aimed it toward the army. They parted straight down the center of their regimented line, tumbling like dominoes as her magick shot through them.

She continued to fight, causing as much damage to the enemy as she could, but the sensation of loss overwhelmed her. She turned toward the direction of the source, and suddenly, her world caved in. He was there, only yards away from her, lying on the ground with a spear in his chest. She was at his side in an instant, pulling him out of the line of fire. She couldn't look at the battle now. She knew the devastation being caused, the creatures who were dead or dying, those fighting to the death with torn flesh and protruding bones. She'd seen it all before.

"Stay with me, Dorwynn," she said, gazing down at his face. Blood poured from his chest and he tried to speak, but the spear had gone through his lung. All he could do was gasp and produce gurgling sounds when he opened his mouth. She jumped into action, yanking the spear from his chest and placing her hands over his wound. "Hang on," she said, her hands already working their magick. His eyes grew wide as the hole in his lung was repaired, and then everything went black.

She was in another familiar place when she woke...bound to a chair in the middle of the round room. Her head ached, and she knew at once that someone had delivered her a blow that knocked her out. She didn't know if she'd saved him, but it didn't matter now. She was a captive, and Dagana was standing over her, wand in hand.

"Why am I here?" she asked, staring into the queen's blood-red eyes. "I'm not the one you want."

"Ah," said the queen, aiming her wand at Lilly, "but you are..."

She woke with a start, the queen's voice still echoing in her mind. The sky outside her window was dark. She couldn't have been asleep very long, but she felt fully rested, better than she had in a long time. She got dressed, feeling alert and vibrant, but she wondered what to do. Zephra was probably sleeping, along with the rest of the world, and though she thought about Wyatt, she decided to leave him be. He would be sleeping now, too.

Write it down, said a voice like the one she'd heard when she awakened from her quests. It wasn't exactly the same, but it had a similar haunting edge. *Write everything.*

She snatched her book from her nightstand, lit her lamp, and began to write. She started with her quests, amazed that she remembered the fine details, like the smell of her skin burning, or the way her pajamas felt as she read before the fire. She wrote until her hand hurt, filling page after page with the smallest details...anything she could remember. She didn't realize it until after writing about the dark underwater quest, but except for that one, every quest had two things in common: they all involved fire, and they all pertained to being captured, whether discussing it or already being a prisoner. Even this last dream showed her captured by the queen.

She read through previous pages until she found what she had written after the harpy attack, when she'd gone through the same quests. She was already captured in those, moments from death in each of them that she'd experienced tonight. They had also occurred in reverse, ending with one she had not experienced this time. She shook her head, unable to believe she had been Joan of Arc in one of her past lives. That was the key, she was sure. Why else would her quests have started there? It was important, for both times she had relived that life longer and received more details than any of the others, but why was it important? Closing her book, she vowed to put that on her list of unsolved mysteries.

Hungry, she decided to raid the kitchen, leaving the rest of the unknown for later. Her mind was loaded with more than ever, but was still amazingly clear. She moved through the hall and down the stairs without making a sound, trying to respect that Zephra was resting. There was no light, but she was still able to see through the darkness as she made her way to the kitchen.

"Hello," said Zephra, sitting at the table in the dark. Lilly jumped.

"Zephra!" she gasped. "You scared me."

"Sorry," she said. "Why are you awake? I figured you'd be tired after last night."

"I slept."

"For three hours."

"Why are you awake?"

"I slept for a while. Besides, phoenixes don't have to sleep. We *can* sleep, but we don't require it. When I decide I need to give my mind a rest, I choose to go to sleep, to escape for a while, you know?"

"I do," said Lilly, sitting at the table with her. "When I was a faerie, I remember thinking how nice it would be to escape from reality." She reached for a strand of hair brushing against her neck and pulled it all into a ponytail. "You think I'm different, don't you?"

"You heard us," said Zephra, already knowing the answer. Lilly nodded, and Zephra sighed, straightening in her chair. "Yes, I can sense something different about you, something I don't think I can explain."

"Try."

"Remember when I told you about our connection? That's different now. I could tell when you woke up from...whatever was happening to you. I knew when you were awake upstairs. I can feel your consciousness now, not just your presence, but your awareness. Your mind is clearer, and your powers are stronger, if that's even possible."

"I know what Dorwynn wanted to tell me," admitted Lilly. Zephra raised an eyebrow, waiting for her to continue before giving away anything. "I could hear his thoughts, feel his emotions. I couldn't do that before."

"Can you feel mine?" asked Zephra.

"I don't know. I can't hear what you are thinking." Lilly glanced out the window, noticing the subtle changes in the black sky. She wouldn't have noticed so soon before, but she could tell that dawn was approaching. "Other things are different, too."

"Like what?"

"I notice the tiniest changes in things," she said, her words flowing fast. "Scents are more noticeable, sounds are clearer, colors more vivid. Everyone's voice sounds different, but still like themselves. I only slept for three hours, but I feel so alert."

"Rieja will do that."

"What is rieja?"

"Rieja is the skin cells that ogres shed when they sleep." Lilly's eyes widened. That was a new one. "Ogre's blood can cure almost anything that goes wrong magickally. Rieja has the same qualities, but unlike ogre's blood, it can be saved and stored for long periods of time. A few drops of your blood was all it took to make it work. The main side effect of rieja treatment is enhanced perception, which explains some of your issues, but your strength improving, the fact that you require less sleep, your powers and mental capacity increasing...all these things are probably caused by the overdose of kilpa powder."

"How bad was it?" asked Lilly, guilt swimming in her eyes.

"It was pretty bad," said Zephra. Lilly felt a sudden surge of concern race through the phoenix.

"As bad as after the harpy attack?"

"Worse. I've never seen anyone so deep in a quest and actually come back out of it."

Lilly was silent, watching the sky out the window grow lighter. Her mind wandered to that day, to the way she felt when she woke to find Zephra clutching her wrist. She hadn't trusted her after that dream, but now, she trusted the woman more than she ever thought she would, enough to tell her about the quest that stuck out most in her mind.

"In my quest," she said, staring at her hands as she traced the wood grain in the table with her finger, "I was being executed, burned at the stake. I felt everything. The smell of my skin burning, the flames climbing up my legs, my whole body cooking. It seemed so real."

"It *was* real," said Zephra, a hard edge to her voice. Lilly looked up, noticing the fire behind her eyes. She couldn't speak. "You were so hot when I got there, I could barely stand to touch you, and I can hold fire in my hands! Your legs were so charred, they were black. I don't know how you lived through it. If I'd have been any longer getting there, you wouldn't have." Feeling the heat of her own emotions building, Zephra took a deep breath, trying to relax. "You stopped breathing."

"I was holding my breath," said Lilly, casting her eyes toward the table again. "The smoke was choking me."

"In the quest?" asked Zephra. Lilly nodded. "Dorwynn kept you alive through that. He was breathing for you when I got there." She paused, waiting for a response from Lilly, but Lilly said nothing, so she led the conversation in a new direction. "What do you think?"

"About what?"

"About what Dorwynn wanted to tell you?"

"I think I don't want to think about it," said Lilly, groaning inwardly. "I have too many other things to worry about right now."

"That's what I told him," said Zephra, frowning. She tried to read more from Lilly's face, but Lilly turned away, staring out the window.

"I still can't hear your thoughts," she said, not looking at her, "but I can feel your emotions. What else do you want to know?"

"I don't want to know," said Zephra, following Lilly's gaze out the window. "It doesn't matter anyway."

Lilly felt the pain in Zephra's heart and how hard she had to force herself into quiet submission. *She's in love with him,* she thought, *but he's in love with me, and I'm...what am I?* She dwelled on that question as she watched the sky turn a lighter shade of blue, with several shades of pink coating the layers of wispy clouds hanging on the horizon. One cloud was moving, not the way a cloud moves in the wind, but more like a serpent slithering through the air. It seemed closer than the others, like it was right outside the window, and as it twisted and rolled, Lilly caught sight of two black orbs shining at the tip of what resembled a head. They were eyes, which meant the cloud wasn't a cloud at all, but a creature.

"What is that?" asked Lilly, squinting her eyes. The cloud creature stared at her with its huge, beady, black eyes.

"What?" asked Zephra, sitting forward to look out the window. "I don't see anything."

"You don't see that?" asked Lilly, her eyes never leaving the creature. Zephra walked to the window, almost sticking her head out of it to see what Lilly was seeing. The creature turned its head toward Zephra, cocking it to one side, and then focused once more on Lilly.

"There's nothing out there," said Zephra, coming away from the window. "What do you see?"

"A creature," she said, "right in front of the window. You almost put your head through it." Lilly felt Zephra's concern spike. Seeing creatures that weren't there must be something she didn't expect.

"This is beyond me," said Zephra. "Maybe you should see Orvak."

"Maybe you're right."

"A strange side effect," said Orvak. "Rare. Not one I've ever known to happen."

"What side effect?" asked Lilly. She'd spent most of the day relaying everything that had happened to her since the last time they'd met, starting with her duel with Wyatt and ending with the description of the creature she saw this morning out the window. She felt ashamed telling him about the spawn and her potion mishap, but he never so much as cast her a disappointed look during her speech.

"Seeing stryders," he said. "Ogre's blood causes enhanced perception in some, in yourself as well, you say. Kilpa powder increases the strength of other ingredients. Perhaps the combination enhanced your perception enough to enable you to see them. Interesting."

"What are they?"

"Come with me," he said, his smile parting his two upper lips. "I want to show you something." She followed him outside, over the bridge through the swamp and into the meadow behind it. He stopped there to watch her reaction. Her eyes grew wide as a pair of beady black eyes approached her, attached to a six-legged creature that resembled a giant walking stick, though the sticks were branches and it was covered in leaves. The creature watched her as well, sending shivers down her spine. "It's alright," said Orvak. "She's just curious about you." He held his hand out to the creature, which went to him after a few more seconds of staring at her.

"You can see them," said Lilly, looking across the meadow. There were two more pairs of the same eyes staring at her, though the creatures to whom they belonged were very different. One looked like a pile of molten lava with four legs, and four toes on each foot that looked to have joints in them, holding it even higher off the ground, with spikes of solid flames along its spine. The other looked very much like a spider, but white and beige, and its legs were feathered, walking through the field on air instead of the ground.

"I've always seen them from time to time," said Orvak, "but they are a constant presence since you first came to my door. They are unusually drawn to you. It wouldn't surprise me if they've been following you since you arrived in Buthania, but as no one else can see them, and you only recently, I guess we'll never know."

"No one?" she asked, staring at them in awe. "What are they?"

"They are magickal creatures. The ability to see them is more than rare, it is unique, as are they. In a sense, they are souls, entities that choose a form specific to their element. They lend strength in elemental magick, when they choose."

"Are they good or evil?"

"They are neither. They simply are. They are untamed, as wild as magick itself, but they tend to be drawn to those who are good. Most ogres can see them."

"Can you speak to them?" she wondered aloud. Orvak smiled, pleased at her interest in them.

"They speak when they choose, but only in the *Doret Gaia.*"

"One spoke to me when I was waking up from my quests. I spoke to it, too. If they only speak the *Doret Gaia,* how did I talk to it?"

"You were speaking their language. It is the only way."

"How?" she asked. "I barely know the language."

"Magick works in mysterious ways, vula. Stryders are just the beginning of the wonders of magick."

"What other secrets does magick have?"

"There are always questions to be asked," he said, sitting on the ground, "always mysteries to be pondered. We are each of us born with curiosity. Like a baby bird emerging from his nest for the first time because he wonders where his mother has gone, or a puppy who follows an unusual scent because he wonders what created it, every creature is curious of the world around it."

"But if all creatures, sentient or not, are curious, what defines being sentient?"

Orvak chuckled and patted the ground beside him. Lilly sat, settling in for the lengthy conversation to come.

"That very question, vula, makes all the difference. The puppy, when his curiosity is satisfied, does not look beyond his own world and wonder what is beyond it. He will be curious only as far as his world takes him. He will never leave the world he knows unless necessity forces him to do so or his instincts tell him he should.

"Sentient creatures, like you and I, look at the world into which we are born and we wonder what is beyond it. We do not need to explore it, but our curiosity, and the feeling of wonder we experience when it is satisfied, gives us the desire to experience it again. We want to know more, to feel more, to see more, but we cannot let curiosity deter us from our needs. There are some mysteries that should remain mysteries."

"Like what? Shouldn't we try to learn as much as we can?"

Orvak sighed, staring silently into the now setting suns as he pondered how to properly explain the answer to her question. There was a delicate line between not enough knowledge, and too much.

"Do you know," he asked in his quiet way, "what causes the colors in the sky when the suns set?"

"The light from the suns refracts as they gets closer to the horizon, bending the wavelengths differently, so we see it differently."

"Does knowing what causes it make it more beautiful, more awe-inspiring?"

"No."

"Does it make it less awe-inspiring?"

"Not really."

"Do you not think you would stare longer at the beauty of the sunsets if you wondered what caused it, if you were still curious about why it is there?"

Lilly stared at the bright pink balls on the horizon, the fluffy clouds of violet, pink and orange absorbing the colors like a canvas absorbs paint. A deep violet-blue sky was that canvas, a momentarily infinite work of art suspended for all to admire. She didn't answer Orvak's question - there was no need. He had made his point.

"You are right," said the ogre softly, their eyes still glued to the setting suns, "that we should always learn, but the answers to your questions will not always improve your life. Some have the potential to destroy it." He looked at her pointedly, his left eyebrow raised high on his bald head. His strange eyes were kind, but stern, and she knew he was referring to her potion mishap. She nodded her understanding. "Learn, both often and plenty, for when we stop learning, we stop living, but remember two very important things: Knowledge has the ability to diminish your sense of wonder if you let it, and the pursuit for answers may lead to dire consequences rather than satisfied curiosity. You must learn to be content with the possibility that you will not know everything you want to know. There are certain questions that should remain unanswered. That is where faith enters, but that conversation we shall save for another time."

Orvak turned his gaze back to the sunsets, and together they watched in peaceful silence until the last rays of light disappeared over the horizon, casting them into the complete darkness of the moonless night. Even after the suns were gone, after the stryders had long since left the sanctity of the meadow, Lilly wasn't ready to leave, but she knew she must. With a sigh, she turned to her mentor, her friend, and gave him a playful smile.

"Are you ever going to tell me what vula means?" she asked.

"Yes, vula" he teased, smiling his parted smile, "but not today."

A Secret Revealed

The following three days passed without incident, though Lilly was having a difficult time adjusting to her new condition. She only slept for three or four hours a night, always waking refreshed and alert, and always dreaming the same dream before she woke, though the details changed. Sometimes she was captured by Dagana. Sometimes Dorwynn died. Last night, she managed to heal him and escape the queen, only to find herself afterward at the end of a long black sword. The man who caught her was dressed in the most ornate armor she had seen, sleek and black, and emblazoned with the same red dragon as the others, but made with fancy horns. His horse had matching armor, a spiral horn jutting from the head of it. He didn't strike as she expected he would, sitting instead atop his horse and staring at her as though he was having an internal debate about what he should do to her. She woke up before she knew what he decided.

Her short sleep cycle was only the beginning of her issues. She and Zephra spent the first day in the garden pulling the overgrown weeds from between their tiny crop, and though Lilly knew they had to be pulled for the survival of their vegetables, she felt the life within the weeds diminish as she yanked them from the ground. It bothered her more than she wanted to admit. Her only comfort was the relief rushing through the tomato plants after the parasitic plants had been removed.

The second day was much harder for her. She went to town to visit Quinn, but when she arrived at his house and knocked on the door, the nosy woman next door who was spying on her from behind the curtains told her everything she needed to know without saying a word. Her thoughts were enough to inform Lilly that the family had taken a trip to Hydrabaene so Quinn could meet his new grandparents who lived there. They would return in a few weeks.

Disappointed, she wandered through Elikrede, taking in the old nuances. She was drawn to the center of town, to the fountain with the elemental children and the crying woman. The water shooting out the top created thousands of miniature rainbows, one for each drop of water, and she lost herself in the vivid colors. She could have stared at it all day and would have, but the thoughts of passers-by raided her mind, making it hard to concentrate on anything. Several of them recognized her, shifting from some insignificant thought to their memory of the duel or her return from rescuing the children from the harpies. The term Chosen One was considered often, which only reminded her of how the prophet had said, "...the destiny you are *meant* to follow." Unable to block the errant thoughts of everyone who passed her, she fled to the sanctity of her house, grateful she couldn't hear what Zephra was thinking.

The rest of her time was spent practicing her magick, as she wanted to keep herself prepared for whatever future events might occur that would require its use. She was amazed at how easy it was now, how little effort she had to expend to accomplish her goal. Her aim was dead perfect, and she had better control over even the most difficult magick she dared use. She wanted to practice true magick again, now that she had such control, but a firm 'No!' from Zephra put an end to that desire. She didn't bother trying to argue with her. Deep down, she knew it wasn't a good idea anyway.

After watching Lilly practice for a while, Zephra decided they should continue with their physical combat lessons. Since she was already adept with her dagger, Zephra thought Lilly should learn to wield a sword. She expected to feel clumsy, expected the sword to be awkward and heavy, but she found herself easily matching Zephra's skill with the weapon. She blocked her advances and even managed to get in a good blow before she dropped the sword.

"Where did you learn to handle a sword like that?" asked Zephra, handing the fallen weapon back to Lilly. "You could barely hold a dagger when I met you."

"Too many dreams of war, I guess," said Lilly, swinging the weapon before her eyes, watching the gleaming rays of light whisk down its perfect shape. "Again?"

Zephra grinned, and Lilly rushed her, noticing that, as with her magick, she had to expend little effort to do what she wanted. She was quicker, stronger, and more agile than ever, and she noticed that her once soft arms and legs, though always lean, were now firm and toned. It made her realize that she had started changing long before she even took that potion, she just hadn't noticed.

"Who's winning?" came a voice from behind her.

"I am," said Zephra, knocking the sword from Lilly's hand during the second of distraction, flinging it into the air. As Lilly whirled around to see who was behind her, Zephra caught the sword with her free hand, grinning.

"Nice," chuckled Rohan, tossing his pack on the ground beside him as Lilly flew into his arms.

"What are you doing here?" she asked, holding him tight.

"I told you I wouldn't be gone so long this time, didn't I?"

She released him and stepped back to get a better look at him. His hair was tied back at the nape of his neck, the blonde highlights swirling through it like spun gold, and Lilly was sure she could she faint hints of gold shimmering throughout his skin, a trait she'd never noticed about him but that he surely inherited from his mother. She couldn't tell what he was thinking, which surprised her, for she'd always been able to catch pieces of his thoughts before, and assumed it would be easier now that she could hear everyone else's. His blue eyes were bright like the morning sky, and as she tried to distinguish what else was different about him, she felt what he was feeling.

He's happy, she thought. *Relaxed. I've never seen him like this.*

"How long are you staying?" she asked before he could wonder why she was scrutinizing him.

"A long time," he said, his smile so big it didn't look like it belonged to him. "My only task for the next six months is to stay with you, to keep you safe, and out of trouble, until after your stay in Nurzia."

"Elf kingdom," said Zephra before Lilly could ask. She'd been doing that a lot the past few days, answering questions before she'd asked them and finishing her sentences, as if she could somehow hear what Lilly was thinking, or feel her emotions.

"Right," said Rohan, glancing briefly at the woman still holding both swords. "My mother thinks it would be wise for you to have some additional protection while you're there. Except for a few little things that might arise, I'm all yours until after Yule."

"I'll let you two catch up," said Zephra, grabbing Rohan's pack as she walked past them into the house. Rohan watched her go, his emotions under complete control now that he knew the reason for them. He was glad to have so much time with both of them, as he had many questions for Zephra, the only other creature in existence like his father, the only creature who shared blood similar to his own. Maybe she would be able to help him in his search for answers.

"It seems your trust issues have subsided," he said to Lilly when Zephra was gone. "Things are better?"

"Much," said Lilly, wiping the sweat from her brow. "She saved my life...again. How can I not trust her?"

"I see you took my advice to heart."

"What do you mean?" she asked.

"You are responsible for what has been happening to you now, are you not?"

"Oh," she said, her smile fading. "I suppose so."

"Come on," said Rohan, chuckling. "Let's talk."

Lilly did most of the talking as they walked through the back yard, reliving the events as she told him about the past two weeks. He knew of the duel and the harpy lair, but the other things hit him hard. She told him how she knew about the spawn, how she lured it away from Ambala, and how she saved as many as she could that night.

"I had to," she said, leaning against the tree under which they'd had their last conversation. She picked at the dirt under her fingernails, a reason to keep from looking at him. "It was my fault for letting it out."

"I think it was for the best," Rohan told her, pulling her chin up so she would meet his eyes. "Imagine what would have happened if they released it later, when you weren't near enough to help."

"I know," she said, "but I can't help feeling guilty about it. I need to figure out how to trap it so I can put it back, someplace where no one can release it again."

"That may not be the best idea. You saw what it can do. Do you really think you can do something like that all by yourself?"

"Maybe not, but have to try." She turned away from his discouraging gaze. "Don't worry. I've learned my lesson when it comes to magick. I'm not going to just run off on some foolhardy mission, but when the opportunity presents itself, and I know it will, I'm going to do everything within my power to fix it."

"Then I will say nothing more on the issue," he promised. He leaned against the tree, closing the distance between them to a mere foot of space. "Tell me about the potion. Where did you find it?"

"In my mother's grimoire," she said. He was the only person she trusted with that information. "I dreamed about her writing it and when I woke up, I found it. I thought maybe it would help me figure out more about her, what kind of person she was, but all it did was take me back to my own past lives. You were in one of them."

"Was I?"

"You were an angel...Gabriel. You found me then, just like you found me now."

"Jeanne d'Arc," he mumbled, and her jaw dropped.

"How...?" she began, too surprised to continued.

"I've spent a lot of time taking quests into my own past lives. I had to find out what I did wrong, so that I wouldn't make the same mistake with you in this life. I don't think I could watch you die again."

"It wasn't your fault," she whispered. "They didn't believe."

"I should have come to you long before your religious beliefs were so firm. That's why I came to you this time right after your birth. You accepted me as a part of your life before you even learned to speak."

"Even though I forgot about you and the stories you used to tell me?"

"You're here, aren't you?" He waited for her to respond, but she stared across the river, a thought jumping to the front of all others. "What's wrong?"

"I took a memory quest to when I was really young, four, maybe five years old. We were inside my house and you were telling me about blood magick, and then my father snapped. He started yelling at me, telling me that blood magick was wrong. He knows about magick, Rohan. He knew then."

"I remember that day."

"I just don't understand," she said, confusion and sorrow washing over her. "Why put my in therapy? Why wouldn't he want me to believe in something he knew was true?"

Rohan was silent, his thoughts revolving around one of his own memories of Lilly's father, one Lilly knew nothing about, that held answers to that particular question. He knew he should wait to tell her, especially after everything she'd recently been through. It would only raise more questions she might not be ready to face, but would there ever be a right moment? He was here now, and if he told her, he would be here to help her through the worst of her emotions.

"You know, don't you?" she asked. "I can see it in your eyes."

Rohan sighed. Right moment or not, he knew he couldn't deny her what she wanted so desperately to know. He held his hand out to her, ignoring the fire that shot through him when she put her own hand in it. His feelings for Zephra might be under control, since they weren't really his, but his feelings for her were a different story. They would never change, nor could he ever share them with her.

"Before we do this," he said, recovering himself, "I want you to know that you are about to learn things you may not be ready to handle. Just remember that I'm here for you, as I have always been, and know that I wasn't trying to keep anything from you. I figured you would be ready to hear this when you asked about it. I just hope I'm right."

"I'll be fine, Rohan," she said, squeezing his hand, but he felt the pressure only around his heart. "Trust me...I've been through worse." He nodded, and after taking a deep breath, he closed his eyes, meditating on the memory. It was as clear to him as if it had happened yesterday...

Lilly recognized her surroundings at once. They were in the wooded area behind her father's house, the sun dancing just above the western tree line as twilight dawned. Her father, as young as he was in her last quest of him, was alone, staring into the trees, his hands on his hips.

"Come out," he demanded, his voice full of the parental authority she'd heard so often over the years. "I know you're there." Andrew crossed his arms, his frustration written on his face. He waited in silence, his eyes glued to the movement in the trees from where a beautiful black winged unicorn emerged. *Not Rowen,* he thought. *Rohan.* They both heard the recognition in his thoughts and in his voice when he spoke. "Rohan?"

I am, thought the creature. Lilly heard him, which she expected, but was surprised that her father did. His response shocked her even more.

"Ashya would be proud to see you," said her father. "Mylhan, too, though I'm sure he would appreciate my request for you to speak to me man to man."

You knew my parents? asked Rohan. Andrew didn't respond, and Lilly knew he was waiting for his request to be fulfilled. Rohan took the hint as well. He began to glow, the gold flecks in his skin and hair acting as conduit for the magickal light shining within him. Lilly stared in awe, fascinated by the mystical cyclone of light that swirled around him as his skin grew lighter and his wings grew smaller and smaller, disappearing from sight. His body cracked as it twisted and turned, his joints reshaping themselves as he stood erect, his long face shrinking. Her mind caught every painful detail of his transformation, as though she was watching it in slow motion. It was both frightening and miraculous, and when it was over, there was not a man standing in his place, but a boy of twelve. The only thing about him that resembled a man were his eyes, which glowed bright with curiosity. "You knew my parents?"

"Your mother is Ashya the unicorn," said Andrew, his voice softer now, "High Mistress of the Council. Your father was Mylhan, who disappeared three days before your birth. You were born on the eve of spring under a new moon at the stroke of midnight. Three moments of power converged as one when you entered the world."

"How do you know that?" whispered Rohan. Lilly could feel the desperation in his heart, the need to have as much information as he could. She recognized it all too well.

"I was with your mother the night you were born, as were many other members of the Council. We had just decided to send a search party to find your father when Ashya had a vision that changed our plans. You were born only hours later."

"You were on the Council of Magick?" asked the boy. Andrew smiled at the skeptical look on his face. "What was the vision?"

"I don't know." Lilly took that moment to search her father's eyes, knowing that if he was being dishonest she would find it there, but he was telling the truth. "I can only assume she saw that he was dead, or she saw that we would not find him." Andrew put his hand on Rohan's shoulder. "You don't know how sorry I am, son. I wanted to find him, too. Your father was my dearest friend."

Neither spoke for a moment, each lost in his own thoughts. Rohan was trying to hide the tears in his eyes, wiping his face furiously. Andrew was simply watching the boy, waiting for the right moment to ask his own questions.

"You've come for Lilly, haven't you?" he asked when the boy had regained his composure.

"I am to protect her," he said, his voice taking on an air of duty, "for now." Andrew nodded, thoughtful.

"When will you take her?"

"When she is ready to make the choice for herself, and when she is old enough to understand what comes with that choice." Her father nodded again.

"I must ask, then, that you leave her be until that time comes. She cannot have a normal life on Earth when she sees magick every day. She should be allowed that normalcy." Rohan nodded this time, and Andrew, his face saddened by the weight of his request, glanced toward his house. "Will you tell me before you take her?"

"Of course," said Rohan.

"Should you ever need anything," said her father, clearing his throat, "you need only ask. I will do all I can to help you."

"Thank you, sir, but I'll be alright."

The quest faded into a similar scene, though the trees were fuller and the sun was high in the sky. Andrew was much older, looking more like he did the last time Lilly saw him in person, right before she left him forever. He looked worried, his hands cupped around his mouth as he called Rohan's name. Relief flooded his face when Rohan emerged from the trees, already in his human form, a full grown man.

"What's wrong?" asked Rohan. "Is Lilly alright?"

"She ready," said Andrew. Lilly heard the sorrow in his voice and could tell that he knew he was going to lose her soon.

"Are you sure?" asked Rohan. "I thought we were going to wait until she was eighteen."

"Plans change," said Andrew, his voice hard to hide his emotion. "Since Adrian left, she's been lost. She's so depressed, I don't think she even realizes that time is passing. She just wanders through each day without purpose. Some days, she doesn't talk to anyone at all. I've considered putting her back in therapy so she'll talk to someone, which I hate having to do, but I see no other way around it unless you are willing to take her early."

"If you think she is ready," said Rohan, "I will take her." Andrew nodded, running his hands through his graying hair.

"Her fifteenth birthday is next month," he said, sighing. "I will do my best to prepare her, but I cannot allow her to know of my history before she leaves with you. I don't know how much I'll be able to do. It will be up to you to contact her again. Remind her of when she was young, when she believed in you."

"Do you think she'll choose to come with me?"

"I think she will," said her father. "She has nothing here but myself and her sister. She will find purpose in Buthania."

"Will you ever return?"

Andrew sighed again. Lilly could see how that question troubled him, as if he had many more secrets he couldn't spill. He shook his head, gazing toward his home, the life he'd built on Earth.

"My other daughter needs me here," he said. "Lilly is strong enough to go on without me."

"But..."

"Consider the rules, son. My return would mean my final crossing, and I'm not prepared to commit to that yet. Perhaps, in time, things will be different, but for now, this is how it must be..."

"Are you alright?" asked Rohan.

Lilly sat on the ground, pulling her knees into her chest and wrapping her arms around them. She rested her chin on her left shoulder, her head turned as far away from him as possible, staring at nothing though her eyes reflected all the pain she'd experienced over the past few months.

She shrugged in response to his question and heaved a sigh before closing her eyes.

Rohan said nothing else, allowing her time to process her thoughts, but he ached to know those thoughts. Was she hurt that he hadn't told her sooner? Should he have waited until later to tell her, when things had settled down more? Would she try to do something dangerous again to get more answers? What if knowing this information changed the course of her destiny? His own thoughts grew more intense with every second she let pass without making a sound, so much so that he wanted to speak so she would, but he could think of nothing to say.

"What did he mean by 'the rules'?" she asked after twenty minutes of silence. Rohan sighed, relieved she was speaking, though it surprised him that this was her first question.

"When someone from Buthania goes to Earth," he explained, "that is their first crossing. They are only allowed to cross one more time. If they choose to return, they can never cross again. There are exceptions, of course, like Gustave, but this rule keeps the balance between our worlds in check. It is the same for someone who comes from Earth."

"My father's from Buthania," she said. "All this time, I was searching for my mother's family, *her* past and *her* reasons for leaving, and my father..." Her voice faded as she pieced together the culmination of what she'd already known and what she just learned. "Your identity is hidden, but do not deny who you are."

"What?"

"That's what the prophet told me," she said, lifting her head and finally meeting his eyes. "I thought it meant that I was hiding my identity, but now I know...it was hidden from me."

"And the part about denying who you are?"

"I don't know," she said. "Maybe when I find out who my parents really are I'll want to deny it."

"Or maybe," said Rohan, brushing a strand of hair from her eyes, "you shouldn't forget who you are when you do find out."

"That's just it," she said, tears welling in her eyes. "My whole life, I've defined myself by the people in my life: You, Adrian, my trainers and teachers, and now my destiny. I know, I know. It's my destiny because I chose it, but what if I don't know why I chose it? What if I just followed you through that doorway because I had no idea who I was, and I thought maybe you did?"

"Do you need me to tell you?" he asked, cupping her face in his hands. A tear fell from her eye, landing directly on her birthmark of the same shape. He wiped it away with his thumb. "You are someone who does for others without a thought for her own safety, someone who sneaks into a harpy lair to save the life of one child, and not only saves nine lives, but destroys the entire harpy fleet in the process. You care more for everyone else than you do for yourself, which is why you define your life by those in it. You are kind, generous, selfless to fault, and there is no one better in either of our worlds I'd rather put my faith in than you...not even myself. This is the part of who you are that you should not deny. It doesn't matter what your parents may have done or who they are. Their choices made you who *you* are...the glorious person standing before me now."

"I still want to know so much," she sighed, leaning her head against his shoulder.

"I have no doubt," he said, putting his arm around her. He understood all too well the desire to know about your parents, especially the ones you never got the chance to know. He hated having to wait for that information himself, but he was glad that since he was forced wait, he would be spending the time in between with Lilly. "A long journey lies before us," he said, staring at the pink suns disappearing over the horizon, "but we'll get there. We've already made it this far."

"Doesn't seem very far in the grand scheme of things, does it?" she asked, the suns in her vision wearing bright pink halos. She closed her eyes, taking comfort in his presence.

"Maybe not," he said, holding her close, "but it's further than we've ever gotten. That's good enough for me."

She was here, she was trained, and she was on the right path toward her destiny as the Chosen One. Whether she believed or not, he knew in his heart that she was the one who would save them all, even at the expense of her own life. He just hoped she would never have to make that choice, praying with everything inside him that his own vision of the future was wrong, that she wouldn't have to sacrifice herself to be their savior. He would sacrifice himself instead, if it meant she would live. Now that this world had felt her presence, it wouldn't be able to exist if she did not.

"What are you thinking?" she asked, still staring at the setting suns.

"You can't tell?"

"The potion changed some things. I can hear almost everyone's thoughts now, but I can't hear yours anymore. Strange, huh?"

"Very strange," he said, though he was secretly relieved. It was hard enough not being able to tell her how he felt, but having to be on guard, blocking his thoughts all the time when he was in her presence, was overwhelming. Being able to relax around her would be a welcomed change. "I was thinking of the future, wondering how many more mysteries will arise that we'll have to solve, how many more secrets will be revealed that we'll have to face."

"Too many," she sighed. "There are always questions to be asked, always mysteries to be pondered."

"Who told you that?"

"Orvak."

He looked down at her, amused at her lightheartedness. She met his eyes, smiling, then returned to the wonder of the sunsets and the bright pink hue cast on the waterfall cascading over the cliff, a new and beautiful work of art provided by nature that would soon disappear. She snuggled into his chest, and it was all he could do not to keep himself from bursting. "I'm glad you're here. It feels right. Things just aren't the same when you're gone."

"I know what you mean," he said, hoping his voice wouldn't betray his feelings. "Our paths may lead to the same place, but sometimes we have to take different roads to get there. Don't worry, though, if I have to leave you now and then. I'll always come back for you."

"I know," she said.

War loomed on the horizon, and those on the other side of that war were hungry for her blood. Danger crept closer with every passing minute, and the only thing she had besides her unpredictable powers and the secrets of her parents were the trainers assigned to educate her and Rohan, her real-life imaginary friend. No matter what lay ahead, he was the constant that would see her through it, her shelter in the storm. She was safe with him, and despite her doubts over everything else, she would never lose her faith in that.

When the war is declared,

every race will have to choose a side...

    Lilly's first year in Buthania was nothing less than extraordinary, but when Amparo arrives to take her to the Elfin Kingdom, she soon discovers how vast Buthania really is. New friends are made, new magick is learned, and secrets are revealed that will test Lilly's faith in others, and in herself. Her magickal education, however, is only half the battle. Dagana has resumed her position as the ruler of humanity, and her edict to register all magickal humans puts Lilly's fate at risk and puts her cunning to the test. It will take all her knowledge and resourcefulness to dodge the queen's watch while facing her greatest challenge yet...recruiting those who wish to remain neutral in the impending war.

    Don't miss the next exciting installment in the Buthania Chronicles...

Pterippus
The Quickening

COMING SOON!

SPECIAL THANKS

I have so many people to thank, I must apologize in advance if I leave anyone out…

First, to Kenny, Savvy and KC, for putting up with my overabundant use of the phrase "I'll just be a minute." Your patience and understanding mean the world to me, and I am blessed to have your love.

To Mom…I'm everything I am because you loved me.

To JR…getting to witness your excitement reading the first book is priceless. Thanks, buddy.

To Deb, for your unwavering support throughout this entire process. I couldn't have done it without you, sis.

To Jessica…your genius in the art of web design is a gift, but your love as a sister is priceless.

To Bridget…your refusal to read this until its completion was the best motivation I could have for finishing it. I hope you love it, sis.

To Stephanie… for lending your own creativity to ignite mine. Your artwork has not only brought to life the images of my imagination, it has sparked ideas within me that moved the story in a new and wonderful direction. This book would not be what it is today without your eager participation, nor would I be who I am now without your amazing presence in my life. Your light shines bright. You are and always will be…my vula.

To Martin…for sharing your talent to give vision to the fans. I am in awe, sir.

To Allen, for all the wonderful criticism. Never be afraid to tell me what you think. I appreciate the feedback and accept it with open arms.

To Monique…knowing you are always there means more to me than any words can express. I couldn't ask for a better friend.

Mr. Epley…Steve…how do I express in words the foundation of learning you contribute every day? You are a mentor to most, a hero to some and an educator to many, but I am just thankful I can call you *friend*.

To Mindy Gilman, for prophesizing my future long before even I could see it. I guess you were right.

To Jim Brickman, A Perfect Circle, Dave Matthews, Dream Theater, Switchfoot, Nickelback, Shinedown and One Republic, not to mention the many other talented musicians whose creativity sparked my imagination. I can't thank you enough.

Finally, to Stephen King, for writing *On Writing: Memoirs of the Craft*. Your insight helped in a way that no other could, and though I murdered a few of my darlings, I now know that it was okay to do so. Also, thank you for writing *Dreamcatcher*…I'll tell you the reason why someday, if we ever meet, for that information is only for you to know.

About the Author

Kristl Thompson was born and raised in the heart of the Midwest. She spent her days wandering the woods surrounding her home, absorbing the scenery which would eventually become the background of Buthania. Her love of the written word grew from a young age, writing poetry, short stories and sequels of her favorite books, and continues to this day, reading novels of every genre and writing the first of many novels to come. She currently resides in the Midwest with her husband and two children. *Pterippus: The Awakening* is her first published novel.

www.ingramcontent.com/pod-product-compliance
Lightning Source LLC
Chambersburg PA
CBHW071332020726
47502CB00001B/75